TESS OF THE D'URBERVILLES

AN AUTHORITATIVE TEXT
HARDY AND THE NOVEL
CRITICISM

→》》《《←

SECOND EDITION

➤➤ A NORTON CRITICAL EDITION ◄◄

THOMAS HARDY

TESS OF THE D'URBERVILLES

AN AUTHORITATIVE TEXT
HARDY AND THE NOVEL
CRITICISM

➤➤◄◄

SECOND EDITION

➤➤◄◄

Edited by

SCOTT ELLEDGE
CORNELL UNIVERSITY

W · W · NORTON & COMPANY

New York · London

Lord David Cecil: from *Hardy the Novelist* (London, 1943, and Mamaroneck, N.Y., 1972), pp. 34–39, 147–53. Reprinted by permission of David Higham Associates, Ltd., and Paul P. Appel.

Donald Davidson: from *Still Rebels, Still Yankees*, pp. 43–61. Copyright © 1957 by Louisiana State University Press. Reprinted by permission.

Albert J. Guerard: from *Thomas Hardy: The Novels and Stories* (Cambridge, Mass.: Harvard University Press, 1949), pp. 2–6, 82–85. Copyright © 1949 by the President and Fellows of Harvard College; copyright © renewed 1977 by Albert J. Guerard. Reprinted by permission of the author and publishers.

Ian Gregor and Brian Nichols: from the *Moral and the Story* by Ian Gregor and Brian Nichols (London, 1962), pp. 132–35. Reprinted by permission of Faber and Faber.

Irving Howe: from "Let the Day Perish" in *Thomas Hardy* (Masters of World Literature Series). Copyright © 1966 by Irving Howe. Copyright © 1967 by Macmillan Publishing Co., Inc. Reprinted by Macmillan Publishing Co., Inc., and Weidenfield and Nicolson Ltd.

Hugh Kenner: a review of J. Hillis Miller, "Thomas Hardy: Distance and Desire," from *Nineteenth Century Fiction*, vol. 26, no. 2, pp. 230–34. Copyright © 1971 by The Regents of the University of California. Reprinted by permission of The Regents and the author.

J. T. Laird: from *The Shaping of "Tess of the D'Urbervilles,"* pp. 158–60, 162–63, 165–66, 169–71, 175–77. Copyright © 1975 by Oxford University Press. Reprinted by permission of Oxford University Press.

Dan H. Laurence: "Henry James and Stevenson Discuss 'Vile' *Tess*," in *Colby Library Quarterly*, III (May 1953), pp. 164–68. Reprinted by permission of the editor and *Colby Library Quarterly*.

D. H. Lawrence: from "A Study of Thomas Hardy," in *Phoenix: The Posthumous Papers of D. H. Lawrence*, pp. 482–88. Copyright © 1936 by Frieda Lawrence; © renewed 1964 by the estate of the late Frieda Lawrence Ravagli. Reprinted by permission of the Viking Press, Laurence Pollinger Ltd., and the estate of the late Frieda Lawrence.

J. Hillis Miller: "Howe on Hardy's Art," in *Novel*, II (1969), pp. 272–77. Reprinted by permission of *Novel*.

Richard Purdy: from *Thomas Hardy: A Bibliographical Study* (1954), pp. 69–77, 286. Reprinted by permission of the Oxford University Press.

Dorothy Van Ghent: from "On *Tess of the D'Urbervilles*" in *The English Novel: Form and Function*. Copyright © 1953 by Dorothy Van Ghent. Reprinted by permission of Holt, Rinehart and Winston.

Virginia Woolf: from "The Novels of Thomas Hardy," in *The Common Reader*, vol. 2. Reprinted by permission of the Author's Literary Estate, The Hogarth Press, and Harcourt Brace Jovanovich, Inc.

W. W. Norton & Company, Inc., 500 Fifth Avenue, New York, N.Y. 10110

W. W. Norton & Company Ltd., 37 Great Russell Street, London WC1B 3NU

Copyright © 1979, 1965 by W. W. Norton & Company, Inc.

Library of Congress Cataloging in Publication Data

Hardy, Thomas, 1840–1928.
   Tess of the d'Urbervilles.
   (A Norton critical edition)
   1. Hardy, Thomas, 1840–1898. Tess of the d'Urbervilles.   I. Elledge, Scott.   II. Title.
PZ3.H222Te   1979 [PR4748]   823'.8   78-16891

ISBN 0-393-09044-2 Paper
ISBN 0-393-04507-2 Cloth

2 3 4 5 6 7 8 9 0

Contents

Essays in Criticism

Selected Bibliography

Preface to the Second Edition

Sixteen years after finishing his last novel, Hardy prepared the Wessex Edition of his collected works, published by Macmillan in 1912. In the General Preface to this handsome edition he classified his fourteen novels under three headings. The first of these classes, "Novels of Character and Environment," contained, as it happened, all the novels that he and his readers, then and now, have judged to be his finest: *Far from the Madding Crowd* (1874), *The Return of the Native* (1878), *The Mayor of Casterbridge* (1886), *Tess of the d'Urbervilles* (1891), and *Jude the Obscure* (1895). Of these Hardy chose *Tess*, probably the most widely read of all his novels, for Volume I of the new edition. It had been given a mixed reception by the reviewers in 1892 (one pronounced it Hardy's greatest novel while another was damning it as "an unpleasant story told in a very unpleasant way"), but it was an immediate success with the public. Within a few years it had gone through many editions in England and America, and had been translated into German, French, Russian, Dutch, Italian, and other languages.

In spite of the popular success of the work, however, Hardy had been deeply discouraged by two experiences connected with its publication. He was forced, as a concession to Victorian prudery, to delete or alter several episodes before any magazine would publish it serially, and Hardy resented such censorship because he thought it violated the integrity of any novel that sought to be true to life, and because, as he insisted, it obstructed the channel between the writer and the public. But of greater consequence than this irritation, later allayed by his restoring the novel to almost its original form when it was published as a book, was Hardy's resentment of what he considered the "muddle-mindedness" of those critics who accused him of preaching a "pessimistic," un-Christian philosophy. His aim, he said, had been that of an artist, to give "impressions not arguments," and he could not understand why he should have been blamed for writing a novel that embodied "the views of life prevalent at the end of the nineteenth century, and not those of an earlier and simpler generation." After *Tess* he wrote one more novel, *Jude the Obscure*, a kind of complement to *Tess*, but he claimed in later life that it was these experiences with *Tess* that led him to the decision to stop writing novels. It may be argued, though, that Hardy had simply grown tired of fiction and that he was pleased to be financially secure enough by that time to be able to devote the last thirty-three years of his life to his first and true love, the writing of poetry.

In his poems, Hardy once said, he was able to express his "ideas and emotions . . . more fully than in prose," and for that reason his poems are a valuable commentary on his novels. Another useful source of information about the ideas and feelings expressed in Hardy's works is a biography that, except for the last few chapters, he himself wrote (though it was posthumously published as the work of his widow). In the critical apparatus at the back of this edition of *Tess*, under the heading "Hardy and the Novel," I have, therefore, included poems that illuminate the novel, and selections from the autobiography that help explain its genesis.

I have been able in this Second Edition to include excerpts from J. T. Laird's *The Shaping of "Tess of the d'Urbervilles"* (1975), a definitive account of the history of the novel from its first draft to its final revision in the 1920 reprint of the Wessex Edition. These excerpts, together with selections from the work of Richard Purdy and of Ian Gregor and Brian Nicholas, which were in my First Edition, constitute the third and final part of the section "Hardy and the Novel," designed to give readers a comprehensive account of the background, origins, composition, and publication of the novel.

In the second of the appendices, entitled "Criticism," I have made no change in the selections illustrating "Contemporary Critical Reception," but the little anthology of "Essays in Criticism" has been considerably amended for this Second Edition by my decision to add two essays that are excellent introductions to critical study of the novel: i.e., the interpretations by Dorothy Van Ghent (1953) and by Irving Howe (1967). To make room for them I have neglected all but one of the most recent Hardy critics, have deleted some of the selections included in the First Edition, and have abridged others. But I have retained Lionel Johnson's remarkable essay, published only three years after *Tess* appeared, Virginia Woolf's defense of Hardy and her reasons for calling him "the greatest tragic writer among English novelists," and D. H. Lawrence's exposition of what he saw as the male and female principles in *Tess*. For an understanding of Hardy's place in the English literary tradition I think the essays of Donald Davidson, David Cecil, and Albert J. Guerard most useful, and I continue to be grateful for permission to reprint their work in abridged form.

Finally, I have added to the selection of critical essays two book reviews which together furnish a useful introduction to an increasingly popular idea about how to read Hardy. In a review of Irving

Howe's *Thomas Hardy* (1969), J. Hillis Miller stated briefly his reasons for believing that no one can completely understand a novel of Hardy's without knowing all of Hardy's works—a thesis Miller illustrated in his book *Thomas Hardy: Distance and Desire* (1970). And in a review of that book Hugh Kenner summarized Miller's analysis of Hardy's works, as well as Miller's critical assumptions, in a way that seems to me to be fair and provocative. These two reviews suggest ways of reading and talking about *Tess*, Hardy, and perhaps all literature that many students and teachers have discovered to be rewarding.

The size of the "Selected Bibliography" in this Second Edition suggests the great increase in critical attention that Hardy has attracted during the past fourteen years.

I have indicated sources for some footnotes by initials within brackets, as follows: [W] for Carl J. Weber's edition (New York: Harper and Brothers, 1935; [F] for P. N. Furbank's New Wessex Edition (London: Macmillan, 1974); [EDD] for *The English Dialect Dictionary*, ed. Joseph Wright (London, 1898); and [OED] for the *Oxford English Dictionary*. I am especially indebted to P. N. Furbank for many new footnotes, and to my friend and colleague Daniel Schwarz for expert advice.

My text is that of the Wessex Edition of 1912.

SCOTT ELLEDGE

The Text of
Tess of the d'Urbervilles

A PURE WOMAN
FAITHFULLY PRESENTED BY
THOMAS HARDY

". . . Poor wounded name! My bosom
Shall lodge thee."
—W. Shakespeare *

* *Two Gentlemen of Verona*, I.ii.110.

Explanatory Note to the First Edition

The main portion of the following story appeared—with slight modifications—in the *Graphic* newspaper; other chapters, more especially addressed to adult readers, in the *Fortnightly Review* and the *National Observer*, as episodic sketches. My thanks are tendered to the editors and proprietors of those periodicals for enabling me now to piece the trunk and limbs of the novel together, and print it complete, as originally written two years ago.

I will just add that the story is sent out in all sincerity of purpose, as an attempt to give artistic form to a true sequence of things; and in respect of the book's opinions and sentiments, I would ask any too genteel reader, who cannot endure to have said what everybody nowadays thinks and feels, to remember a well-worn sentence of St. Jerome's: If an offence come out of the truth, better is it that the offence come than that the truth be concealed.

November 1891.   T. H.

Preface to the Fifth and Later Editions

This novel being one wherein the great campaign of the heroine begins after an event in her experience which has usually been treated as fatal to her part of protagonist, or at least as the virtual ending of her enterprises and hopes, it was quite contrary to avowed conventions that the public should welcome the book, and agree with me in holding that there was something more to be said in fiction than had been said about the shaded side of a well-known catastrophe. But the responsive spirit in which *Tess of the d'Urbervilles* has been received by the readers of England and America, would seem to prove that the plan of laying down a story on the lines of tacit opinion, instead of making it to square with the merely vocal formulae of society, is not altogether a wrong one, even when exemplified in so unequal and partial an achievement as the present. For this responsiveness I cannot refrain from expressing my thanks; and my regret is that, in a world where one so often hungers in vain for friendship, where even not to be wilfully misunderstood is felt as a kindness, I shall never meet in person these appreciative readers, male and female, and shake them by the hand.

I include amongst them the reviewers—by far the majority—who have so generously welcomed the tale. Their words show that they,

1

like the others, have only too largely repaired my defects of narration by their own imaginative intuition.

Nevertheless, though the novel was intended to be neither didactic nor aggressive, but in the scenic parts to be representative simply, and in the contemplative to be oftener charged with impressions than with convictions, there have been objectors both to the matter and to the rendering.

The more austere of these maintain a conscientious difference of opinion concerning, among other things, subjects fit for art, and reveal an inability to associate the idea of the sub-title adjective with any but the artificial and derivative meaning which has resulted to it from the ordinances of civilization. They ignore the meaning of the word in Nature, together with all aesthetic claims upon it, not to mention the spiritual interpretation afforded by the finest side of their own Christianity. Others dissent on grounds which are intrinsically no more than an assertion that the novel embodies the views of life prevalent at the end of the nineteenth century, and not those of an earlier and simpler generation—an assertion which I can only hope may be well founded. Let me repeat that a novel is an impression, not an argument; and there the matter must rest; as one is reminded by a passage which occurs in the letters of Schiller to Goethe on judges of this class: 'They are those who seek only their own ideas in a representation, and prize that which should be as higher than what is. The cause of the dispute, therefore, lies in the very first principles, and it would be utterly impossible to come to an understanding with them.' And again: 'As soon as I observe that any one, when judging of poetical representations, considers anything more important than the inner Necessity and Truth, I have done with him.'

In the introductory words to the first edition I suggested the possible advent of the genteel person who would not be able to endure something or other in these pages. That person duly appeared among the aforesaid objectors. In one case he felt upset that it was not possible for him to read the book through three times, owing to my not having made that critical effort which 'alone can prove the salvation of such an one.' In another, he objected to such vulgar articles as the Devil's pitchfork, a lodging-house carving-knife, and a shame-bought parasol, appearing in a respectable story. In another place he was a gentleman who turned Christian for half-an-hour the better to express his grief that a disrespectful phrase about the Immortals should have been used; though the same innate gentility compelled him to excuse the author in words of pity that one cannot be too thankful for: 'He does but give us of his best.' I can assure this great critic[1] that to exclaim illogically against the gods,

1. Andrew Lang. See p. 380.

singular or plural, is not such an original sin of mine as he seems to imagine. True, it may have some local originality; though if Shakespeare were an authority on history, which perhaps he is not, I could show that the sin was introduced into Wessex as early as the Heptarchy itself. Says Glo'ster in *Lear*, otherwise Ina, king of that country:

As flies to wanton boys are we to the gods;
They kill us for their sport.[2]

The remaining two or three manipulators of *Tess* were of the predetermined sort whom most writers and readers would gladly forget; professed literary boxers, who put on their convictions for the occasion; modern 'Hammers of Heretics'; sworn Discouragers, ever on the watch to prevent the tentative half-success from becoming the whole success later on; who pervert plain meanings, and grow personal under the name of practising the great historical method. However, they may have causes to advance, privileges to guard, traditions to keep going; some of which a mere tale-teller, who writes down how the things of the world strike him, without any ulterior intentions whatever, has overlooked, and may by pure inadvertence have run foul of when in the least aggressive mood. Perhaps some passing perception, the outcome of a dream hour, would, if generally acted on, cause such an assailant considerable inconvenience with respect to position, interests, family, servant, ox, ass, neighbour, or neighbour's wife.[3] He therefore valiantly hides his personality behind a publisher's shutters, and cries 'Shame!' So densely is the world thronged that any shifting of positions, even the best warranted advance, galls somebody's kibe.[4] Such shiftings often begin in sentiment, and such sentiment sometimes begins in a novel.

July 1892.

The foregoing remarks were written during the early career of this story, when a spirited public and private criticism of its points was still fresh to the feelings. The pages are allowed to stand for what they are worth, as something once said; but probably they would not have been written now. Even in the short time which has elapsed since the book was first published, some of the critics who provoked the reply have 'gone down into silence,'[5] as if to remind one of the infinite unimportance of both their say and mine.

January 1895.

2. Shakespeare, *King Lear*, IV.i.36-37.
3. Exodus xx:17: "Thou shalt not covet thy neighbor's house * * * thy neighbor's wife, nor his manservant * * * nor his ox, nor his ass * * *."
4. Shakespeare, *Hamlet*, V.i.146: "The age is grown so picked that the toe of the peasant comes so near the heel of the courtier, he galls his kibe."
5. Psalms cxv:17: "The dead praise not the Lord, neither any that go down into silence."

The present edition of this novel contains a few pages[6] that have never appeared in any previous edition. When the detached episodes were collected as stated in the preface of 1891, these pages were overlooked, though they were in the original manuscript. They occur in Chapter X.

Respecting the sub-title, to which allusion was made above, I may add that it was appended at the last moment, after reading the final proofs, as being the estimate left in a candid mind of the heroine's character—an estimate that nobody would be likely to dispute. It was disputed more than anything else in the book. *Melius fuerat non scribere.*[6] But there it stands.

The novel was first published complete, in three volumes, in November 1891.

March 1912.   T. H.

6. Pp. 52–55.
7. It would have been better not to write it.

Phase the First—The Maiden

I

On an evening in the latter part of May a middle-aged man was walking homeward from Shaston to the village of Marlott,[1] in the adjoining Vale of Blakemore or Blackmoor. The pair of legs that carried him were rickety, and there was a bias in his gait which inclined him somewhat to the left of a straight line. He occasionally gave a smart nod, as if in confirmation of some opinion, though he was not thinking of anything in particular. An empty egg-basket was slung upon his arm, the nap of his hat was ruffled, a patch being quite worn away at its brim where his thumb came in taking it off. Presently he was met by an elderly parson astride on a gray mare, who, as he rode, hummed a wandering tune.

'Good night t'ee,' said the man with the basket.

'Good night, Sir John,' said the parson.

The pedestrian, after another pace or two, halted, and turned round.

'Now, sir, begging your pardon; we met last market-day on this road about this time, and I zaid "Good night," and you made reply "*Good night, Sir John*," as now.'

'I did,' said the parson.

'And once before that—near a month ago.'

'I may have.'

'Then what might your meaning be in calling me "Sir John" these different times, when I be plain Jack Durbeyfield, the haggler?'[2]

The parson rode a step or two nearer.

'It was only my whim,' he said; and, after a moment's hesitation: 'It was on account of a discovery I made some little time ago, whilst I was hunting up pedigrees for the new county history. I am Parson Tringham, the antiquary, of Stagfoot Lane. Don't you really know, Durbeyfield, that you are the lineal representative of the ancient and knightly family of the d'Urbervilles, who derive their descent from Sir Pagan d'Urberville, that renowned knight who came from Normandy with William the Conqueror, as appears by Battle Abbey Roll?'[3]

---

1. The real names of these villages in Dorset, a county in the south of England, are Shaftesbury and Marnhull. Hardy began to create the fictional region of "Wessex" in *Far from the Madding Crowd* (1874); and throughout all the Wessex novels the geography is that of Dorset, Somerset, Wiltshire, and Devon, though most of the places were renamed. Dorchester, for example, became "Casterbridge"; and in this novel Salisbury is called "Melchester" and Winchester, "Wintoncester." [W]
2. Peddler.
3. Battle Abbey was a Benedictine abbey founded by William the Conqueror near Hastings.

'Never heard it before, sir!'

'Well it's true. Throw up your chin a moment, so that I may catch the profile of your face better. Yes, that's the d'Urberville nose and chin—a little debased. Your ancestor was one of the twelve knights who assisted the Lord of Estremavilla in Normandy in his conquest of Glamorganshire. Branches of your family held manors over all this part of England; their names appear in the Pipe Rolls[4] in the time of King Stephen. In the reign of King John one of them was rich enough to give a manor to the Knights Hospitallers; and in Edward the Second's time your forefather Brian was summoned to Westminster to attend the great Council there. You declined a little in Oliver Cromwell's time, but to no serious extent, and in Charles the Second's reign you were made Knights of the Royal Oak for your loyalty. Aye, there have been generations of Sir Johns among you, and if knighthood were hereditary, like a baronetcy, as it practically was in old times, when men were knighted from father to son, you would be Sir John now.'

'Ye don't say so!'

'In short,' concluded the parson, decisively smacking his leg with his switch, 'there's hardly such another family in England.'

'Daze my eyes, and isn't there?' said Durbeyfield. 'And here have I been knocking about, year after year, from pillar to post, as if I was no more than the commonest feller in the parish. ... And how long hev this news about me been knowed, Pa'son Tringham?'

The clergyman explained that, as far as he was aware, it had quite died out of knowledge, and could hardly be said to be known at all. His own investigations had begun on a day in the preceding spring when, having been engaged in tracing the vicissitudes of the d'Urberville family, he had observed Durbeyfield's name on his waggon, and had thereupon been led to make inquiries about his father and grandfather till he had no doubt on the subject.

'At first I resolved not to disturb you with such a useless piece of information,' said he. 'However, our impulses are too strong for our judgment sometimes. I thought you might perhaps know something of it all the while.'

'Well, I have heard once or twice, 'tis true, that my family had seen better days afore they came to Blackmoor. But I took no notice o't, thinking it to mean that we had once kept two horses where we now keep only one. I've got a wold[5] silver spoon, and a wold graven seal at home, too; but, Lord, what's a spoon and seal? ... And to think that I and these noble d'Urbervilles were one flesh all the time. 'Twas said that my gr't-grandfer had secrets, and didn't care to

4. The great Rolls of the Exchequer, comprising the various "pipes" or enrolled accounts of sheriffs and others for a financial year.
5. Old.

talk of where he came from. . . . And where do we raise our smoke, now, parson, if I may make so bold; I mean, where do we d'Urbervilles live?'

'You don't live anywhere. You are extinct—as a county family.'

'That's bad.'

'Yes—what the mendacious family chronicles call extinct in the male line—that is, gone down—gone under.'

'Then where do we lie?'

'At Kingsbere-sub-Greenhill: rows and rows of you in your vaults, with your effigies under Purbeck-marble[6] canopies.'

'And where be our family mansions and estates?'

'You haven't any.'

'Oh? No lands neither?'

'None; though you once had 'em in abundance, as I said, for your family consisted of numerous branches. In this county there was a seat of yours at Kingsbere, and another at Sherton, and another at Millpond, and another at Lullstead, and another at Wellbridge.'

'And shall we ever come into our own again?'

'Ah—that I can't tell!'

'And what had I better do about it, sir?' asked Durbeyfield, after a pause.

'Oh—nothing, nothing; except chasten yourself with the thought of "how are the mighty fallen."[7] It is a fact of some interest to the local historian and genealogist, nothing more. There are several families among the cottagers of this county of almost equal lustre. Good night.'

'But you'll turn back and have a quart of beer wi' me on the strength o't, Pa'son Tringham? There's a very pretty brew in tap at The Pure Drop—though, to be sure, not so good as at Rolliver's.'

'No, thank you—not this evening, Durbeyfield. You've had enough already.' Concluding thus the parson rode on his way, with doubts as to his discretion in retailing this curious bit of lore.

When he was gone Durbeyfield walked a few steps in a profound reverie, and then sat down upon the grassy bank by the roadside, depositing his basket before him. In a few minutes a youth appeared in the distance, walking in the same direction as that which had been pursued by Durbeyfield. The latter, on seeing him, held up his hand, and the lad quickened his pace and came near.

'Boy, take up that basket! I want 'ee to go on an errand for me.'

The lath-like stripling frowned. 'Who be you, then, John Durbeyfield, to order me about and call me "boy"? You know my name as well as I know yours!'

6. A hard limestone obtained from Pur-   7. Samuel i:25.
beck, a peninsula on the Dorset coast.

'Do you, do you? That's the secret—that's the secret! Now obey my orders, and take the message I'm going to charge 'ee wi'. . . . Well, Fred, I don't mind telling you that the secret is that I'm one of a noble race—it has been just found out by me this present afternoon, P.M.' And as he made the announcement, Durbeyfield, declining from his sitting position, luxuriously stretched himself out upon the bank among the daisies.

The lad stood before Durbeyfield, and contemplated his length from crown to toe.

'Sir John d'Urberville—that's who I am,' continued the prostrate man. 'That is if knights were baronets—which they be. 'Tis recorded in history all about me. Dost know of such a place, lad, as Kingsbere-sub-Greenhill?'

'Ees. I've been there to Greenhill Fair.'

'Well, under the church of that city there lie——'

' 'Tisn't a city, the place I mean; leastwise 'twaddn' when I was there—'twas a little one-eyed, blinking sort o' place.'

'Never you mind the place, boy, that's not the question before us. Under the church of that there parish lie my ancestors—hundreds of 'em—in coats of mail and jewels, in gr't lead coffins weighing tons and tons. There's not a man in the county o' South-Wessex that's got grander and nobler skillentons in his family than I.'

'Oh?'

'Now take up that basket, and goo on to Marlott, and when you've come to The Pure Drop Inn, tell 'em to send a horse and carriage to me immed'ately, to carry me hwome. And in the bottom o' the carriage they be to put a noggin o' rum in a small bottle, and chalk it up to my account. And when you've done that goo on to my house with the basket, and tell my wife to put away that washing, because she needn't finish it, and wait till I come hwome, as I've news to tell her.'

As the lad stood in a dubious attitude, Durbeyfield put his hand in his pocket, and produced a shilling, one of the chronically few that he possessed.

'Here's for your labour, lad.'

This made a difference in the young man's estimate of the position.

'Yes, Sir John. Thank 'ee. Anything else I can do for 'ee, Sir John?'

'Tell 'em at hwome that I should like for supper,—well, lamb's fry if they can get it; and if they can't, black-pot; and if they can't get that, well, chitterlings[8] will do.'

'Yes, Sir John.'

---

8. Lamb's fry, a product of lambs' castration; black-pot, a sausage made of fat and blood; chitterlings, smaller intestines of pigs, fried.

The boy took up the basket, and as he set out the notes of a brass band were heard from the direction of the village.

'What's that?' said Durbeyfield. 'Not on account o' I?'

' 'Tis the women's club-walking, Sir John. Why, your da'ter is one o' the members.'

'To be sure—I'd quite forgot it in my thoughts of greater things! Well, vamp[9] on to Marlott, will ye, and order that carriage, and maybe I'll drive round and inspect the club.'

The lad departed, and Durbeyfield lay waiting on the grass and daisies in the evening sun. Not a soul passed that way for a long while, and the faint notes of the band were the only human sounds audible within the rim of blue hills.

II

The village of Marlott lay amid the north-eastern undulations of the beautiful Vale of Blakemore or Blackmoor aforesaid, an engirdled and secluded region, for the most part untrodden as yet by tourist or landscape-painter, though within a four hours' journey from London.

It is a vale whose acquaintance is best made by viewing it from the summits of the hills that surround it—except perhaps during the droughts of summer. An unguided ramble into its recesses in bad weather is apt to engender dissatisfaction with its narrow, tortuous, and miry ways.

This fertile and sheltered tract of country, in which the fields are never brown and the springs never dry, is bounded on the south by the bold chalk ridge that embraces the prominences of Hambledon Hill, Bulbarrow, Nettlecombe-Tout, Dogbury, High Stoy, and Bubb Down. The traveller from the coast, who, after plodding northward for a score of miles over calcareous downs and corn-lands, suddenly reaches the verge of one of these escarpments, is surprised and delighted to behold, extended like a map beneath him, a country differing absolutely from that which he has passed through. Behind him the hills are open, the sun blazes down upon fields so large as to give an unenclosed character to the landscape, the lanes are white, the hedges low and plashed,[1] the atmosphere colourless. Here, in the valley, the world seems to be constructed upon a smaller and more delicate scale; the fields are mere paddocks, so reduced that from this height their hedgerows appear a network of dark green threads overspreading the paler green of the grass. The atmosphere beneath is languorous, and is so tinged with azure that what artists call the middle distance partakes also of that hue, while the horizon beyond is of the deepest ultramarine. Arable lands are few and limited; with but slight exceptions the prospect is a broad rich mass of grass

9. Tramp.
1. Artificially interwoven.

and trees, mantling minor hills and dales within the major. Such is the Vale of Blackmoor.

The district is of historic, no less than of topographical interest. The Vale was known in former times as the Forest of White Hart, from a curious legend of King Henry III.'s reign, in which the killing by a certain Thomas de la Lynd of a beautiful white hart which the king had run down and spared, was made the occasion of a heavy fine. In those days, and till comparatively recent times, the country was densely wooded. Even now, traces of its earlier condition are to be found in the old oak copses and irregular belts of timber that yet survive upon its slopes, and the hollow-trunked trees that shade so many of its pastures.

The forests have departed, but some old customs of their shades remain. Many, however, linger only in a metamorphosed or disguised form. The May-Day dance, for instance, was to be discerned on the afternoon under notice, in the guise of the club revel, or 'club-walking,' as it was there called.

It was an interesting event to the younger inhabitants of Marlott, though its real interest was not observed by the participators in the ceremony. Its singularity lay less in the retention of a custom of walking in procession and dancing on each anniversary than in the members being solely women. In men's clubs such celebrations were, though expiring, less uncommon; but either the natural shyness of the softer sex, or a sarcastic attitude on the part of male relatives, had denuded such women's clubs as remained (if any other did) of this their glory and consummation. The club of Marlott alone lived to uphold the local Cerealia.[2] It had walked for hundreds of years, if not as benefit-club, as votive sisterhood of some sort; and it walked still.

The banded ones were all dressed in white gowns—a gay survival from Old Style days, when cheerfulness and May-time were synonyms—days before the habit of taking long views had reduced emotions to a monotonous average. Their first exhibition of themselves was in a processional march of two and two round the parish. Ideal and real clashed slightly as the sun lit up their figures against the green hedges and creeper-laced house-fronts; for, though the whole troop wore white garments, no two whites were alike among them. Some approached pure blanching; some had a bluish pallor; some worn by the older characters (which had possibly lain by folded for many a year) inclined to a cadaverous tint, and to a Georgian[3] style.

In addition to the distinction of a white frock, every woman and girl carried in her right hand a peeled willow wand, and in her left

2. Ceremony in honor of Ceres, the goddess of agriculture.
3. The fashion of the preceding century.

The action in the novel takes place about 1880.

a bunch of white flowers. The peeling of the former, and the selection of the latter, had been an operation of personal care.

There were a few middle-aged and even elderly women in the train, their silver-wiry hair and wrinkled faces, scourged by time and trouble, having almost a grotesque, certainly a pathetic, appearance in such a jaunty situation. In a true view, perhaps, there was more to be gathered and told of each anxious and experienced one, to whom the years were drawing nigh when she should say, 'I have no pleasure in them,'[4] than of her juvenile comrades. But let the elder be passed over here for those under whose bodices the life throbbed quick and warm.

The young girls formed, indeed, the majority of the band, and their heads of luxuriant hair reflected in the sunshine every tone of gold, and black, and brown. Some had beautiful eyes, others a beautiful nose, others a beautiful mouth and figure: few, if any, had all. A difficulty of arranging their lips in this crude exposure to public scrutiny, an inability to balance their heads, and to dissociate self-consciousness from their features, was apparent in them, and showed that they were genuine country girls, unaccustomed to many eyes.

And as each and all of them were warmed without by the sun, so each had a private little sun for her soul to bask in; some dream, some affection, some hobby, at least some remote and distant hope which, though perhaps starving to nothing, still lived on, as hopes will. Thus they were all cheerful, and many of them merry.

They came round by The Pure Drop Inn, and were turning out of the high road to pass through a wicket-gate into the meadows, when one of the women said—

'The Lord-a-Lord! Why, Tess Durbeyfield, if there isn't thy father riding hwome in a carriage!'

A young member of the band turned her head at the exclamation. She was a fine and handsome girl—not handsomer than some others, possibly—but her mobile peony mouth and large innocent eyes added eloquence to colour and shape. She wore a red ribbon in her hair, and was the only one of the white company who could boast of such a pronounced adornment. As she looked round Durbeyfield was seen moving along the road in a chaise belonging to The Pure Drop, driven by a frizzle-headed brawny damsel with her gown-sleeves rolled above her elbows. This was the cheerful servant of that establishment, who, in her part of factotum, turned groom and ostler at times. Durbeyfield, leaning back, and with his eyes closed luxuriously, was waving his hand above his head, and singing in a slow recitative—

'I've-got-a-gr't-family-vault-at-Kingsbere—and knighted-forefathers-in-lead-coffins-there!'

4. Ecclesiastes xii:1, on old age.

The clubbists tittered, except the girl called Tess—in whom a slow heat seemed to rise at the sense that her father was making himself foolish in their eyes.

'He's tired, that's all,' she said hastily, 'and he has got a lift home, because our own horse has to rest to-day.'

'Bless thy simplicity, Tess,' said her companions. 'He's got his market-nitch.[5] Haw-haw!'

'Look here; I won't walk another inch with you, if you say any jokes about him!' Tess cried, and the colour upon her cheeks spread over her face and neck. In a moment her eyes grew moist, and her glance drooped to the ground. Perceiving that they had really pained her they said no more, and order again prevailed. Tess's pride would not allow her to turn her head again, to learn what her father's meaning was, if he had any; and thus she moved on with the whole body to the enclosure where there was to be dancing on the green. By the time the spot was reached she had recovered her equanimity, and tapped her neighbour with her wand and talked as usual.

Tess Durbeyfield at this time of her life was a mere vessel of emotion untinctured by experience. The dialect was on her tongue to some extent, despite the village school: the characteristic intonation of that dialect for this district being the voicing approximately rendered by the syllable UR, probably as rich an utterance as any to be found in human speech. The pouted-up deep red mouth to which this syllable was native had hardly as yet settled into its definite shape, and her lower lip had a way of thrusting the middle of her top one upward, when they closed together after a word.

Phases of her childhood lurked in her aspect still. As she walked along to-day, for all her bouncing handsome womanliness, you could sometimes see her twelfth year in her cheeks, or her ninth sparkling from her eyes; and even her fifth would flit over the curves of her mouth now and then.

Yet few knew, and still fewer considered this. A small minority, mainly strangers, would look long at her in casually passing by, and grow momentarily fascinated by her freshness, and wonder if they would ever see her again: but to almost everybody she was a fine and picturesque country girl, and no more.

Nothing was seen or heard further of Durbeyfield in his triumphal chariot under the conduct of the ostleress, and the club having entered the allotted space, dancing began. As there were no men in the company the girls danced at first with each other, but when the hour for the close of labour drew on, the masculine inhabitants of the village, together with other idlers and pedestrians, gathered round the spot, and appeared inclined to negotiate for a partner.

5. The quantity of ale or spirits drunk after market.

Among these on-lookers were three young men of a superior class, carrying small knapsacks strapped to their shoulders, and stout sticks in their hands. Their general likeness to each other, and their consecutive ages, would almost have suggested that they might be, what in fact they were, brothers. The eldest wore the white tie, high waistcoat, and thin-brimmed hat of the regulation curate; the second was the normal undergraduate; the appearance of the third and youngest would hardly have been sufficient to characterize him; there was an uncribbed, uncabined[6] aspect in his eyes and attire, implying that he had hardly as yet found the entrance to his professional groove. That he was a desultory tentative student of something and everything might only have been predicted of him.

These three brethren told casual acquaintance that they were spending their Whitsun holidays in a walking tour through the Vale of Blackmoor, their course being south-westerly from the town of Shaston on the north-east.

They leant over the gate by the highway, and inquired as to the meaning of the dance and the white-frocked maids. The two elder of the brothers were plainly not intending to linger more than a moment, but the spectacle of a bevy of girls dancing without male partners seemed to amuse the third, and make him in no hurry to move on. He unstrapped his knapsack, put it, with his stick, on the hedge-bank, and opened the gate.

'What are you going to do, Angel?' asked the eldest.

'I am inclined to go and have a fling with them. Why not all of us—just for a minute or two—it will not detain us long?'

'No—no; nonsense!' said the first. 'Dancing in public with a troop of country hoydens—suppose we should be seen! Come along, or it will be dark before we get to Stourcastle, and there's no place we can sleep at nearer than that; besides, we must get through another chapter of *A Counterblast to Agnosticism* before we turn in, now I have taken the trouble to bring the book.'

'All right—I'll overtake you and Cuthbert in five minutes; don't stop; I give my word that I will, Felix.'

The two elder reluctantly left him and walked on, taking their brother's knapsack to relieve him in following, and the youngest entered the field.

'This is a thousand pities,' he said gallantly, to two or three girls nearest him, as soon as there was a pause in the dance. 'Where are your partners, my dears?'

'They've not left off work yet,' answered one of the boldest. 'They'll be here by and by. Till then, will you be one, sir?'

'Certainly. But what's one among so many!'

'Better than none. 'Tis melancholy work facing and footing it to

6. Shakespeare, *Macbeth*, III.iv.24: "I am cabin'd, cribb'd, confin'd."

one of your own sort, and no clipsing and colling[7] at all. Now, pick and choose.'

"Ssh—don't be so for'ard!' said a shyer girl.

The young man, thus invited, glanced them over, and attempted some discrimination; but, as the group were all so new to him, he could not very well exercise it. He took almost the first that came to hand, which was not the speaker, as she had expected; nor did it happen to be Tess Durbeyfield. Pedigree, ancestral skeletons, monumental record, the d'Urberville lineaments, did not help Tess in her life's battle as yet, even to the extent of attracting to her a dancing-partner over the heads of the commonest peasantry. So much for Norman blood unaided by Victorian lucre.

The name of the eclipsing girl, whatever it was, has not been handed down; but she was envied by all as the first who enjoyed the luxury of a masculine partner that evening. Yet such was the force of example that the village young men, who had not hastened to enter the gate while no intruder was in the way, now dropped in quickly, and soon the couples became leavened with rustic youth to a marked extent, till at length the plainest woman in the club was no longer compelled to foot it on the masculine side of the figure.

The church clock struck, when suddenly the student said that he must leave—he had been forgetting himself—he had to join his companions. As he fell out of the dance his eyes lighted on Tess Durbeyfield, whose own large orbs wore, to tell the truth, the faintest aspect of reproach that he had not chosen her. He, too, was sorry then that, owing to her backwardness, he had not observed her; and with that in his mind he left the pasture.

On account of his long delay he started in a flying-run down the lane westward, and had soon passed the hollow and mounted the next rise. He had not yet overtaken his brothers, but he paused to get breath, and looked back. He could see the white figures of the girls in the green enclosure whirling about as they had whirled when he was among them. They seemed to have quite forgotten him already.

All of them, except, perhaps, one. This white shape stood apart by the hedge alone. From her position he knew it to be the pretty maiden with whom he had not danced. Trifling as the matter was, he yet instinctively felt that she was hurt by his oversight. He wished that he had asked her; he wished that he had inquired her name. She was so modest, so expressive, she had looked so soft in her thin white gown that he felt he had acted stupidly.

However, it could not be helped, and turning, and bending himself to a rapid walk, he dismissed the subject from his mind.

---

7. Embracing around the waist and around the neck.

III

As for Tess Durbeyfield, she did not so easily dislodge the incident from her consideration. She had no spirit to dance again for a long time, though she might have had plenty of partners; but, ah! they did not speak so nicely as the strange young man had done. It was not till the rays of the sun had absorbed the young stranger's retreating figure on the hill that she shook off her temporary sadness and answered her would-be partner in the affirmative.

She remained with her comrades till dusk, and participated with a certain zest in the dancing; though, being heart-whole as yet, she enjoyed treading a measure purely for its own sake; little divining when she saw 'the soft torments, the bitter sweets, the pleasing pains, and the agreeable distresses' of those girls who had been wooed and won, what she herself was capable of in that kind. The struggles and wrangles of the lads for her hand in a jig were an amusement to her —no more; and when they became fierce she rebuked them.

She might have stayed even later, but the incident of her father's odd appearance and manner returned upon the girl's mind to make her anxious, and wondering what had become of him she dropped away from the dancers and bent her steps towards the end of the village at which the parental cottage lay.

While yet many score yards off, other rhythmic sounds than those she had quitted became audible to her; sounds that she knew well— so well. They were a regular series of thumpings from the interior of the house, occasioned by the violent rocking of a cradle upon a stone floor, to which movement a feminine voice kept time by singing, in a vigorous gallopade,[8] the favourite ditty of 'The Spotted Cow'—

I saw her lie do'—own in yon'—der green gro'—ove;
Come, love !' and I'll tell' you where !'

The cradle-rocking and the song would cease simultaneously for a moment, and an exclamation at highest vocal pitch would take the place of the melody.

'God bless thy diment[9] eyes! And thy waxen[1] cheeks! And thy cherry mouth! And thy Cubit's[2] thighs! And every bit o' thy blessed body!"

After this invocation the rocking and the singing would recommence, and the 'Spotted Cow' proceed as before. So matters stood when Tess opened the door, and paused upon the mat within it surveying the scene.

The interior, in spite of the melody, struck upon the girl's senses with an unspeakable dreariness. From the holiday gaieties of the field—the white gowns, the nosegays, the willow-wands, the whirling

---

8. "A lively dance. 'The galopade, strange agreeable tramp, / Made of a scrape, a hobble, and stamp.' 1835 L. Hunt, *Capt. Sword* iii 13." [*OED*]

9. Shining.

1. "Waxworks" meant "anything fair, beautiful, or delicate." In Lincolnshire "nurses call babies little waxworks." [*EDD*]

2. Cupid's. [F]

movements on the green, the flash of gentle sentiment towards the stranger—to the yellow melancholy of this one-candled spectacle, what a step! Besides the jar of contrast there came to her a chill self-reproach that she had not returned sooner, to help her mother in these domesticities, instead of indulging herself out-of-doors.

There stood her mother amid the group of children, as Tess had left her, hanging over the Monday washing-tub, which had now, as always, lingered on to the end of the week. Out of that tub had come the day before—Tess felt it with a dreadful sting of remorse—the very white frock upon her back which she had so carelessly greened about the skirt on the damping grass—which had been wrung up and ironed by her mother's own hands.

As usual, Mrs. Durbeyfield was balanced on one foot beside the tub, the other being engaged in the aforesaid business of rocking her youngest child. The cradle-rockers had done hard duty for so many years, under the weight of so many children, on that flagstone floor, that they were worn nearly flat, in consequence of which a huge jerk accompanied each swing of the cot, flinging the baby from side to side like a weaver's shuttle, as Mrs. Durbeyfield, excited by her song, trod the rocker with all the spring that was left in her after a long day's seething in the suds.

Nick-knock, nick-knock, went the cradle; the candle-flame stretched itself tall, and began jigging up and down; the water dribbled from the matron's elbows, and the song galloped on to the end of the verse, Mrs. Durbeyfield regarding her daughter the while. Even now, when burdened with a young family, Joan Durbeyfield was a passionate lover of tune. No ditty floated into Blackmoor Vale from the outer world but Tess's mother caught up its notation in a week.

There still faintly beamed from the woman's features something of the freshness, and even the prettiness, of her youth; rendering it probable that the personal charms which Tess could boast of were in main part her mother's gift, and therefore unknightly, unhistorical.

'I'll rock the cradle for 'ee, mother,' said the daughter gently. 'Or I'll take off my best frock and help you wring up? I thought you had finished long ago.'

Her mother bore Tess no ill-will for leaving the house-work to her single-handed efforts for so long; indeed, Joan seldom upbraided her thereon at any time, feeling but slightly the lack of Tess's assistance whilst her instinctive plan for relieving herself of her labours lay in postponing them. To-night, however, she was even in a blither mood than usual. There was a dreaminess, a preoccupation, an exaltation, in the maternal look which the girl could not understand.

'Well, I'm glad you've come,' her mother said, as soon as the last note had passed out of her. 'I want to go and fetch your father; but what's more'n that, I want to tell 'ee what have happened. Y'll be fess[3] enough, my poppet, when th'st know!' (Mrs. Durbeyfield habitually spoke the dialect; her daughter, who had passed the Sixth Standard in the National School[4] under a London-trained mistress, spoke two languages; the dialect at home, more or less; ordinary English abroad and to persons of quality.)

'Since I've been away?' Tess asked.

'Ay!'

'Had it anything to do with father's making such a mommet[5] of himself in thik carriage this afternoon? Why did 'er? I felt inclined to sink into the ground with shame!'

'That wer all a part of the larry![6] We've been found to be the greatest gentlefolk in the whole county—reaching all back long before Oliver Grumble's[7] time—to the days of the Pagan Turks—with monuments, and vaults, and crests, and 'scutcheons, and the Lord knows what all. In Saint Charles's days we was made Knights o' the Royal Oak, our real name being d'Urberville! . . . Don't that make your bosom plim?[8] 'Twas on this account that your father rode home in the vlee;[9] not because he'd been drinking, as people supposed.'

'I'm glad of that. Will it do us any good, mother?'

'O yes! 'Tis thoughted that great things may come o't. No doubt a mampus[1] of volk of our own rank will be down here in their carriages as soon as 'tis known. Your father learnt it on his way hwome from Shaston, and he has been telling me the whole pedigree of the matter.'

'Where is father now?' asked Tess suddenly.

Her mother gave irrelevant information by way of answer: 'He called to see the doctor to-day in Shaston. It is not consumption at all, it seems. It is fat round his heart, 'a says. There, it is like this.' Joan Durbeyfield, as she spoke, curved a sodden thumb and forefinger to the shape of the letter C, and used the other forefinger as a pointer. ' "At the present moment," he says to your father, "your heart is enclosed all round there, and all round there; this space is still open," 'a says. "As soon as it do meet, so," '—Mrs. Durbeyfield closed her fingers into a circle complete—"off you will go like a shadder, Mr. Durbeyfield," 'a says. "You mid last ten years; you mid go off in ten months, or ten days." '

Tess looked alarmed. Her father possibly to go behind the eternal cloud so soon, notwithstanding this sudden greatness!

'But where *is* father?' she asked again.

3. Conceited, proud, stuck-up.
4. The National Schools were founded in 1811 to promote the education of the poor. A Standard was a level of proficiency according to which school children were classified.
5. From mummer, an actor who wore grotesque masks.
6. Hubbub.
7. Cromwell's. [F]
8. Swell.
9. Carriage.
1. Crowd.

Her mother put on a deprecating look. 'Now don't you be burst-ing out angry! The poor man—he felt so rafted[2] after his uplifting by the pa'son's news—that he went up to Rolliver's half an hour ago. He do want to get up his strength for his journey tomorrow with that load of beehives, which must be delivered, family or no. He'll have to start shortly after twelve to-night, as the distance is so long.'

'Get up his strength!' said Tess impetuously, the tears welling to her eyes. 'O my God! Go to a public-house to get up his strength! And you as well agreed as he, mother!'

Her rebuke and her mood seemed to fill the whole room, and to impart a cowed look to the furniture, and candle, and children play-ing about, and to her mother's face.

'No,' said the latter touchily, 'I be not agreed. I have been waiting for 'ee to bide and keep house while I go to fetch him.'

'I'll go.'

'O no, Tess. You see, it would be no use.'

Tess did not expostulate. She knew what her mother's objection meant. Mrs. Durbeyfield's jacket and bonnet were already hanging slily upon a chair by her side, in readiness for this contemplat-ed jaunt, the reason for which the matron deplored more than its necessity.

'And take the *Compleat Fortune-Teller* to the outhouse,' Joan continued, rapidly wiping her hands, and donning the garments.

The *Compleat Fortune-Teller* was an old thick volume, which lay on a table at her elbow, so worn by pocketing that the margins had reached the edge of the type. Tess took it up, and her mother started.

This going to hunt up her shiftless husband at the inn was one of Mrs. Durbeyfield's still extant enjoyments in the muck and muddle of rearing children. To discover him at Rolliver's, to sit there for an hour or two by his side and dismiss all thought and care of the chil-dren during the interval, made her happy. A sort of halo, an occiden-tal glow, came over life then. Troubles and other realities took on themselves a metaphysical impalpability, sinking to mere mental phenomena for serene contemplation, and no longer stood as press-ing concretions which chafed body and soul. The youngsters, not im-mediately within sight, seemed rather bright and desirable appurte-nances than otherwise; the incidents of daily life were not without humorousness and jollity in their aspect there. She felt a little as she had used to feel when she sat by her now wedded husband in the same spot during his wooing, shutting her eyes to his defects of character, and regarding him only in his ideal presentation as lover.

Tess, being left alone with the younger children, went first to the outhouse with the fortune-telling book, and stuffed it into the thatch. A curious fetichistic fear of this grimy volume on the part of her

2. Disturbed.

mother prevented her ever allowing it to stay in the house all night, and hither it was brought back whenever it had been consulted. Between the mother, with her fast-perishing lumber of superstitions, folk-lore dialect, and orally transmitted ballads, and the daughter, with her trained National teachings and Standard knowledge under an infinitely Revised Code,[3] there was a gap of two hundred years as ordinarily understood. When they were together the Jacobean and the Victorian ages were juxtaposed.

Returning along the garden path Tess mused on what the mother could have wished to ascertain from the book on this particular day. She guessed the recent ancestral discovery to bear upon it, but did not divine that it solely concerned herself. Dismissing this, however, she busied herself with sprinkling the linen dried during the daytime, in company with her nine-year-old brother Abraham, and her sister Eliza-Louisa of twelve and a half, called ' 'Liza-Lu,' the youngest ones being put to bed. There was an interval of four years and more between Tess and the next of the family, the two who had filled the gap having died in their infancy, and this lent her a deputy-maternal attitude when she was alone with her juniors. Next in juvenility to Abraham came two more girls, Hope and Modesty; then a boy of three, and then the baby, who had just completed his first year.

All these young souls were passengers in the Durbeyfield ship—entirely dependent on the judgment of the two Durbeyfield adults for their pleasures, their necessities, their health, even their existence. If the heads of the Durbeyfield household chose to sail into difficulty, disaster, starvation, disease, degradation, death, thither were these half-dozen little captives under hatches compelled to sail with them —six helpless creatures, who had never been asked if they wished for life on any terms, much less if they wished for it on such hard conditions as were involved in being of the shiftless house of Durbeyfield. Some people would like to know whence the poet whose philosophy is in these days deemed as profound and trustworthy as his song is breezy and pure, gets his authority for speaking of 'Nature's holy plan.'[4]

It grew later, and neither father nor mother reappeared. Tess looked out of the door, and took a mental journey through Marlott. The village was shutting its eyes. Candles and lamps were being put out everywhere: she could inwardly behold the extinguisher and the extended hand.

Her mother's fetching simply meant one more to fetch. Tess began to perceive that a man in indifferent health, who proposed to

3. The Revised Code of 1862, revised again in 1867, provided for the payment of teachers according to the success of their students in standard examinations.
4. Wordsworth, "Lines Written in Early Spring," line 22.

start on a journey before one in the morning, ought not to be at an inn at this late hour celebrating his ancient blood.

'Abraham,' she said to her little brother, 'do you put on your hat —you bain't afraid?—and go up to Rolliver's and see what has gone wi' father and mother.'

The boy jumped promptly from his seat, and opened the door, and the night swallowed him up. Half an hour passed yet again; neither man, woman, nor child returned. Abraham, like his parents, seemed to have been limed and caught by the ensnaring inn.

'I must go myself,' she said.

'Liza-Lu then went to bed, and Tess, locking them all in, started on her way up the dark and crooked lane or street not made for hasty progress; a street laid out before inches of land had value, and when one-handed clocks sufficiently subdivided the day.

IV

Rolliver's inn, the single alehouse at this end of the long and broken village, could only boast of an off-license; hence, as nobody could legally drink on the premises, the amount of overt accommodation for consumers was strictly limited to a little board about six inches wide and two yards long, fixed to the garden palings by pieces of wire, so as to form a ledge. On this board thirsty strangers deposited their cups as they stood in the road and drank, and threw the dregs on the dusty ground to the pattern of Polynesia, and wished they could have a restful seat inside.

Thus the strangers. But there were also local customers who felt the same wish; and where there's a will there's a way.

In a large bedroom upstairs, the window of which was thickly curtained with a great woollen shawl lately discarded by the landlady Mrs. Rolliver, were gathered on this evening nearly a dozen persons, all seeking beatitude; all old inhabitants of the nearer end of Marlott, and frequenters of this retreat. Not only did the distance to The Pure Drop, the fully-licensed tavern at the further part of the dispersed village, render its accommodation practically unavailable for dwellers at this end; but the far more serious question, the quality of the liquor, confirmed the prevalent opinion that it was better to drink with Rolliver in a corner of the housetop than with the other landlord in a wide house.[5]

A gaunt four-post bedstead which stood in the room afforded sitting-space for several persons gathered round three of its sides; a couple more men had elevated themselves on a chest of drawers; another rested on the oak-carved 'cwoffer'; [6] two on the wash-stand; another on the stool; and thus all were, somehow, seated at their ease. The stage of mental comfort to which they had arrived at this hour was

---

5. Proverbs xxi:9: "It is better to dwell in a corner of the housetop, than with a brawling woman in a whole house."
6. Coffer, *i.e.*, a chest.

one wherein their souls expanded beyond their skins, and spread their personalities warmly through the room. In this process the chamber and its furniture grew more and more dignified and luxurious; the shawl hanging at the window took upon itself the richness of tapestry; the brass handles of the chest of drawers were as golden knockers; and the carved bed-posts seemed to have some kinship with the magnificent pillars of Solomon's temple.

Mrs. Durbeyfield, having quickly walked hitherward after parting from Tess, opened the front door, crossed the downstairs room, which was in deep gloom, and then unfastened the stair-door like one whose fingers knew the tricks of the latches well. Her ascent of the crooked staircase was a slower process, and her face, as it rose into the light above the last stair, encountered the gaze of all the party assembled in the bedroom.

'——Being a few private friends I've asked in to keep up club-walking at my own expense,' the landlady exclaimed at the sound of footsteps, as glibly as a child repeating the Catechism, while she peered over the stairs. 'Oh, 'tis you, Mrs. Durbeyfield—Lard—how you frightened me!—I thought it might be some gaffer[7] sent by Gover'ment.'

Mrs. Durbeyfield was welcomed with glances and nods by the remainder of the conclave, and turned to where her husband sat. He was humming absently to himself, in a low tone: 'I be as good as some folks here and there! I've got a great family vault at Kingsbere-sub-Greenhill, and finer skillentons than any man in Wessex!'

'I've something to tell 'ee that's come into my head about that—a grand projick!' whispered his cheerful wife. 'Here, John, don't 'ee see me?' She nudged him, while he, looking through her as through a window-pane, went on with his recitative.

'Hush! Don't 'ee sing so loud, my good man,' said the landlady; 'in case any member of the Gover'ment should be passing, and take away my licends.'

'He's told 'ee what's happened to us, I suppose?' asked Mrs. Durbeyfield.

'Yes—in a way. D'ye think there's any money hanging by it?'

'Ah, that's the secret,' said Joan Durbeyfield sagely. 'However, 'tis well to be kin to a coach, even if you don't ride in 'en.' She dropped her public voice, and continued in a low tone to her husband: 'I've been thinking since you brought the news that there's a great rich lady out by Trantridge, on the edge o' The Chase, of the name of d'Urberville.'

'Hey—what's that?' said Sir John.

She repeated the information. 'That lady must be our relation,' she said. 'And my projick is to send Tess to claim kin.'

7. Official. [F]

'There *is* a lady of the name, now you mention it,' said Durbeyfield. 'Pa'son Tringham didn't think of that. But she's nothing beside we—a junior branch of us, no doubt, hailing[8] long since King Norman's day.'

While this question was being discussed neither of the pair noticed, in their preoccupation, that little Abraham had crept into the room, and was awaiting an opportunity of asking them to return.

'She is rich, and she'd be sure to take notice o' the maid,' continued Mrs. Durbeyfield; 'and 'twill be a very good thing. I don't see why two branches o' one family should not be on visiting terms.'

'Yes; and we'll all claim kin!' said Abraham brightly from under the bedstead. 'And we'll all go and see her when Tess has gone to live with her; and we'll ride in her coach and wear black clothes!'

'How do you come here, child? What nonsense be ye talking! Go away, and play on the stairs till father and mother be ready! . . . Well, Tess ought to go to this other member of our family. She'd be sure to win the lady—Tess would; and likely enough 'twould lead to some noble gentleman marrying her. In short, I know it.'

'How?'

'I tried her fate in the *Fortune-Teller*, and it brought out that very thing! . . . You should ha' seen how pretty she looked to-day; her skin is as sumple[9] as a duchess's.'

'What says the maid herself to going?'

'I've not asked her. She don't know there is any such lady-relation yet. But it would certainly put her in the way of a grand marriage, and she won't say nay to going.'

'Tess is queer.'

'But she's tractable at bottom. Leave her to me.'

Though this conversation had been private, sufficient of its import reached the understandings of those around to suggest to them that the Durbeyfields had weightier concerns to talk of now than common folks had, and that Tess, their pretty eldest daughter, had fine prospects in store.

'Tess is a fine figure o' fun, as I said to myself to-day when I zeed her vamping round parish with the rest,' observed one of the elderly boozers in an undertone. 'But Joan Durbeyfield must mind that she don't get green malt in floor.'[1] It was a local phrase which had a peculiar meaning, and there was no reply.

The conversation became inclusive, and presently other footsteps were heard crossing the room below.

'——Being a few private friends asked in to-night to keep up club-walking at my own expense.' The landlady had rapidly re-used the formula she kept on hand for intruders before she recognized that the newcomer was Tess.

8. "Durbeyfield means 'hailing from.'" [F]

9. Supple.

1. "I.e., get herself pregnant." [F]

Even to her mother's gaze the girl's young features looked sadly out of place amid the alcoholic vapours which floated here as no unsuitable medium for wrinkled middle-age; and hardly was a reproachful flash from Tess's dark eyes needed to make her father and mother rise from their seats, hastily finish their ale, and descend the stairs behind her, Mrs. Rolliver's caution following their footsteps.

'No noise, please, if ye'll be so good, my dears; or I mid lose my licends, and be summons'd, and I don't know what all! 'Night t'ye!'

They went home together, Tess holding one arm of her father, and Mrs. Durbeyfield the other. He had, in truth, drunk very little—not a fourth of the quantity which a systematic tippler could carry to church on a Sunday afternoon without a hitch in his eastings[2] or genuflections; but the weakness of Sir John's constitution made mountains of his petty sins in this kind. On reaching the fresh air he was sufficiently unsteady to incline the row of three at one moment as if they were marching to London, and at another as if they were marching to Bath—which produced a comical effect, frequent enough in families on nocturnal homegoings; and, like most comical effects, not quite so comic after all. The two women valiantly disguised these forced excursions and countermarches as well as they could from Durbeyfield their cause, and from Abraham, and from themselves; and so they approached by degrees their own door, the head of the family bursting suddenly into his former refrain as he drew near, as if to fortify his soul at sight of the smallness of his present residence—

'I've got a fam—ily vault at Kingsbere!'

'Hush—don't be so silly, Jacky,' said his wife. 'Yours is not the only family that was of 'count in wold days. Look at the Anktells, and Horseys, and the Tringhams themselves—gone to seed a'most as much as you—though you was bigger folks than they, that's true. Thank God, I was never of no family, and have nothing to be ashamed of in that way!'

'Don't you be so sure o' that. From your nater 'tis my belief you've disgraced yourselves more than any o' us, and was kings and queens outright at one time.'

Tess turned the subject by saying what was far more prominent in her own mind at the moment than thoughts of her ancestry—

'I am afraid father won't be able to take the journey with the beehives to-morrow so early.'

'I? I shall be all right in an hour or two,' said Durbeyfield.

It was eleven o'clock before the family were all in bed, and two o'clock next morning was the latest hour for starting with the beehives if they were to be delivered to the retailers in Casterbridge before the Saturday market began, the way thither lying by bad roads

2. **Turnings towards the altar.**

over a distance of between twenty and thirty miles, and the horse and waggon being of the slowest. At half-past one Mrs. Durbeyfield came into the large bedroom where Tess and all her little brothers and sisters slept.

'The poor man can't go,' she said to her eldest daughter, whose great eyes had opened the moment her mother's hand touched the door.

Tess sat up in bed, lost in a vague interspace between a dream and this information.

'But somebody must go,' she replied. 'It is late for the hives already. Swarming will soon be over for the year; and if we put off taking 'em till next week's market the call for 'em will be past, and they'll be thrown on our hands.'

Mrs. Durbeyfield looked unequal to the emergency. 'Some young feller, perhaps, would go? One of them who were so much after dancing with 'ee yesterday,' she presently suggested.

'O no—I wouldn't have it for the world!' declared Tess proudly. 'And letting everybody know the reason—such a thing to be ashamed of! I think I could go if Abraham could go with me to kip me company.'

Her mother at length agreed to this arrangement. Little Abraham was aroused from his deep sleep in a corner of the same apartment, and made to put on his clothes while still mentally in the other world. Meanwhile Tess had hastily dressed herself; and the twain, lighting a lantern, went out to the stable. The rickety little waggon was already laden, and the girl led out the horse Prince, only a degree less rickety than the vehicle.

The poor creature looked wonderingly round at the night, at the lantern, at their two figures, as if he could not believe that at that hour, when every living thing was intended to be in shelter and at rest, he was called upon to go out and labour. They put a stock of candle-ends into the lantern, hung the latter to the off-side of the load, and directed the horse onward, walking at his shoulder at first during the uphill parts of the way, in order not to overload an animal of so little vigour. To cheer themselves as well as they could, they made an artificial morning with the lantern, some bread and butter, and their own conversation, the real morning being far from come. Abraham, as he more fully awoke (for he had moved in a sort of trance so far), began to talk of the strange shapes assumed by the various dark objects against the sky; of this tree that looked like a raging tiger springing from a lair; of that which resembled a giant's head.

When they had passed the little town of Stourcastle, dumbly somnolent under its thick brown thatch, they reached higher ground. Still higher, on their left, the elevation called Bulbarrow or Bealbarrow, wel-nigh the highest in South Wessex, swelled into the sky, engirdled by its earthen trenches. From hereabout the long road was fairly level for some distance onward. They mounted in front of the waggon, and Abraham grew reflective.

'Tess!' he said in a preparatory tone, after a silence.

'Yes, Abraham.'

'Bain't you glad that we've become gentlefolk?'

'Not particular glad.'

'But you be glad that you 'm going to marry a gentleman?'

'What?' said Tess, lifting her face.

'That our great relation will help 'ee to marry a gentleman.'

'I? Our great relation? We have no such relation. What has put that into your head?'

'I heard 'em talking about it up at Rolliver's when I went to find father. There's a rich lady of our family out at Trantridge, and mother said that if you claimed kin with the lady, she'd put 'ee in the way of marrying a gentleman.'

His sister became abruptly still, and lapsed into a pondering silence. Abraham talked on, rather for the pleasure of utterance than for audition, so that his sister's abstraction was of no account. He leant back against the hives, and with upturned face made observations on the stars, whose cold pulses were beating amid the black hollows above, in serene dissociation from these two wisps of human life. He asked how far away those twinklers were, and whether God was on the other side of them. But ever and anon his childish prattle recurred to what impressed his imagination even more deeply than the wonders of creation. If Tess were made rich by marrying a gentleman, would she have money enough to buy a spy-glass so large that it would draw the stars as near to her as Nettlecombe-Tout?

The renewed subject, which seemed to have impregnated the whole family, filled Tess with impatience.

'Never mind that now!' she exclaimed.

'Did you say the stars were worlds, Tess?'

'Yes.'

'All like ours?'

'I don't know; but I think so. They sometimes seem to be like the apples on our stubbard-tree.[3] Most of them splendid and sound—a few blighted.'

'Which do we live on—a splendid one or a blighted one?'

'A blighted one.'

' 'Tis very unlucky that we didn't pitch on a sound one, when there were so many more of 'em!'

'Yes.'

3. A stubbard is an English variety of apple.

'Is it like that *really*, Tess?' said Abraham, turning to her much impressed, on reconsideration of this rare information. 'How would it have been if we had pitched on a sound one?'

'Well, father wouldn't have coughed and creeped about as he does, and wouldn't have got too tipsy to go this journey; and mother wouldn't have been always washing, and never getting finished.'

'And you would have been a rich lady ready-made, and not have had to be made rich by marrying a gentleman?'

'O Aby, don't—don't talk of that any more!'

Left to his reflections Abraham soon grew drowsy. Tess was not skilful in the management of a horse, but she thought that she could take upon herself the entire conduct of the load for the present, and allow Abraham to go to sleep if he wished to do so. She made him a sort of nest in front of the hives, in such a manner that he could not fall, and, taking the reins into her own hands, jogged on as before.

Prince required but slight attention, lacking energy for super-fluous movements of any sort. With no longer a companion to dis-tract her, Tess fell more deeply into reverie than ever, her back lean-ing against the hives. The mute procession past her shoulders of trees and hedges became attached to fantastic scenes outside reality, and the occasional heave of the wind became the sigh of some im-mense sad soul, conterminous with the universe in space, and with history in time.

Then, examining the mesh of events in her own life, she seemed to see the vanity of her father's pride; the gentlemanly suitor await-ing herself in her mother's fancy; to see him as a grimacing person-age, laughing at her poverty, and her shrouded knightly ancestry. Everything grew more and more extravagant, and she no longer knew how time passed. A sudden jerk shook her in her seat, and Tess awoke from the sleep into which she, too, had fallen.

They were a long way further on than when she had lost con-sciousness, and the waggon had stopped. A hollow groan, unlike anything she had ever heard in her life, came from the front, fol-lowed by a shout of 'Hoi there!'

The lantern hanging at her waggon had gone out, but another was shining in her face—much brighter than her own had been. Something terrible had happened. The harness was entangled with an object which blocked the way.

In consternation Tess jumped down, and discovered the dreadful truth. The groan had proceeded from her father's poor horse Prince. The morning mail-cart, with its two noiseless wheels, speeding along these lanes like an arrow, as it always did, had driven into her slow and unlighted equipage. The pointed shaft of the cart had entered the breast of the unhappy Prince like a sword, and from the wound his life's blood was spouting in a stream, and falling with a hiss into the road.

In her despair Tess sprang forward and put her hand upon the hole, with the only result that she became splashed from face to skirt with the crimson drops. Then she stood helplessly looking on. Prince also stood firm and motionless as long as he could; till he suddenly sank down in a heap.

By this time the mail-cart man had joined her, and began dragging and unharnessing the hot form of Prince. But he was already dead, and, seeing that nothing more could be done immediately, the mail-cart man returned to his own animal, which was uninjured.

'You was on the wrong side,' he said. 'I am bound to go on with the mail-bags, so that the best thing for you to do is to bide here with your load. I'll send somebody to help you as soon as I can. It is getting daylight, and you have nothing to fear.'

He mounted and sped on his way; while Tess stood and waited. The atmosphere turned pale, the birds shook themselves in the hedges, arose, and twittered; the lane showed all its white features, and Tess showed hers, still whiter. The huge pool of blood in front of her was already assuming the iridescence of coagulation; and when the sun rose a hundred prismatic hues were reflected from it. Prince lay alongside still and stark; his eyes half open, the hole in his chest looking scarcely large enough to have let out all that had animated him.

' 'Tis all my doing—all mine!' the girl cried, gazing at the spectacle. 'No excuse for me—none. What will mother and father live on now? Aby, Aby!' She shook the child, who had slept soundly through the whole disaster. 'We can't go on with our load—Prince is killed!'

When Abraham realized all, the furrows of fifty years were extemporized on his young face.

'Why, I danced and laughed only yesterday!' she went on to herself. 'To think that I was such a fool!'

' 'Tis because we be on a blighted star, and not a sound one, isn't it, Tess?' murmured Abraham through his tears.

In silence they waited through an interval which seemed endless. At length a sound, and an approaching object, proved to them that the driver of the mail-cart had been as good as his word. A farmer's man from near Stourcastle came up, leading a strong cob. He was harnessed to the waggon of beehives in the place of Prince, and the load taken on towards Casterbridge.

The evening of the same day saw the empty waggon reach again the spot of the accident. Prince had lain there in the ditch since the morning; but the place of the blood-pool was still visible in the middle of the road, though scratched and scraped over by passing vehicles. All that was left of Prince was now hoisted into the waggon he had formerly hauled, and with his hoofs in the air, and his shoes shining in the setting sunlight, he retraced the eight or nine miles to Marlott.

Tess had gone back earlier. How to break the news was more than she could think. It was a relief to her tongue to find from the faces of her parents that they already knew of their loss, though this did not lessen the self-reproach which she continued to heap upon herself for her negligence.

But the very shiftlessness of the household rendered the misfortune a less terrifying one to them than it would have been to a striving family, though in the present case it meant ruin, and in the other it would only have meant inconvenience. In the Durbeyfield countenances there was nothing of the red wrath that would have burnt upon the girl from parents more ambitious for her welfare. Nobody blamed Tess as she blamed herself.

When it was discovered that the knacker[4] and tanner would give only a very few shillings for Prince's carcase because of his decrepitude, Durbeyfield rose to the occasion.

'No,' said he stoically, 'I won't sell his old body. When we d'Urbervilles was knights in the land, we didn't sell our chargers for cat's meat. Let 'em keep their shillings! He've served me well in his lifetime, and I won't part from him now.'

He worked harder the next day in digging a grave for Prince in the garden than he had worked for months to grow a crop for his family. When the hole was ready, Durbeyfield and his wife tied a rope round the horse and dragged him up the path towards it, the children following in funeral train. Abraham and 'Liza-Lu sobbed, Hope and Modesty discharged their griefs in loud blares which echoed from the walls; and when Prince was tumbled in they gathered round the grave. The bread-winner had been taken away from them; what would they do?

'Is he gone to heaven?' asked Abraham, between the sobs.

Then Durbeyfield began to shovel in the earth, and the children cried anew. All except Tess. Her face was dry and pale, as though she regarded herself in the light of a murderess.

V

The haggling business, which had mainly depended on the horse, became disorganized forthwith. Distress, if not penury, loomed in the distance. Durbeyfield was what was locally called a slack-twisted fellow; he had good strength to work at times; but the times could not be relied on to coincide with the hours of requirement; and, having been unaccustomed to the regular toil of the day-labourer, he was not particularly persistent when they did so coincide.

Tess, meanwhile, as the one who had dragged her parents into

4. Buyer of worn-out horses.

this quagmire, was silently wondering what she could do to help them out of it; and then her mother broached her scheme.

'We must take the ups wi' the downs, Tess,' said she; 'and never could your high blood have been found out at a more called-for moment. You must try your friends. Do ye know that there is a very rich Mrs. d'Urberville living on the outskirts o' The Chase, who must be our relation? You must go to her and claim kin, and ask for some help in our trouble.'

'I shouldn't care to do that,' says Tess. 'If there is such a lady, 'twould be enough for us if she were friendly—not to expect her to give us help.'

'You could win her round to do anything, my dear. Besides, perhaps there's more in it than you know of. I've heard what I've heard, good-now.'[5]

The oppressive sense of the harm she had done led Tess to be more deferential than she might otherwise have been to the maternal wish; but she could not understand why her mother should find such satisfaction in contemplating an enterprise of, to her, such doubtful profit. Her mother might have made inquiries, and have discovered that this Mrs. d'Urberville was a lady of unequalled virtues and charity. But Tess's pride made the part of poor relation one of particular distaste to her.

'I'd rather try to get work,' she murmured.

'Durbeyfield, you can settle it,' said his wife, turning to where he sat in the background. 'If you say she ought to go, she will go.'

'I don't like my children going and making themselves beholden to strange kin,' murmured he. 'I'm the head of the noblest branch o' the family, and I ought to live up to it.'

His reasons for staying away were worse to Tess than her own objection to going. 'Well, as I killed the horse, mother,' she said mournfully, 'I suppose I ought to do something. I don't mind going and seeing her, but you must leave it to me about asking for help. And don't go thinking about her making a match for me—it is silly.'

'Very well said, Tess!' observed her father sententiously.

'Who said I had such a thought?' asked Joan.

'I fancy it is in your mind, mother. But I'll go.'

Rising early next day she walked to the hill-town called Shaston, and there took advantage of a van which twice in the week ran from Shaston eastward to Chaseborough, passing near Trantridge, the parish in which the vague and mysterious Mrs. d'Urberville had her residence.

Tess Durbeyfield's route on this memorable morning lay amid the north-eastern undulations of the Vale in which she had been born, and in which her life had unfolded. The Vale of Blackmoor was to her the world, and its inhabitants the races thereof. From the gates

5. "According to Hardy this phrase is equivalent to the American 'I guess.'"[F]

and stiles of Marlott she had looked down its length in the wondering days of infancy, and what had been mystery to her then was not much less than mystery to her now. She had seen daily from her chamber-window towers, villages, faint white mansions; above all the town of Shaston standing majestically on its height; its windows shining like lamps in the evening sun. She had hardly ever visited the place, only a small tract even of the Vale and its environs being known to her by close inspection. Much less had she been far outside the valley. Every contour of the surrounding hills was as personal to her as that of her relatives' faces; but for what lay beyond her judgment was dependent on the teaching of the village school, where she had held a leading place at the time of her leaving, a year or two before this date.

In those early days she had been much loved by others of her own sex and age, and had used to be seen about the village as one of three—all nearly of the same year—walking home from school side by side; Tess the middle one—in a pink print pinafore, of a finely reticulated pattern, worn over a stuff frock that had lost its original colour for a nondescript tertiary—marching on upon long stalky legs, in tight stockings which had little ladder-like holes at the knees, torn by kneeling in the roads and banks in search of vegetable and mineral treasures; her then earth-coloured hair hanging like pothooks; the arms of the two outside girls resting round the waist of Tess; her arms on the shoulders of the two supporters.

As Tess grew older, and began to see how matters stood, she felt quite a Malthusian[6] towards her mother for thoughtlessly giving her so many little sisters and brothers, when it was such a trouble to nurse and provide for them. Her mother's intelligence was that of a happy child: Joan Durbeyfield was simply an additional one, and that not the eldest, to her own long family of waiters on Providence.

However, Tess became humanely beneficent towards the small ones, and to help them as much as possible she used, as soon as she left school, to lend a hand at haymaking or harvesting on neighbouring farms; or, by preference, at milking or butter-making processes, which she had learnt when her father had owned cows; and being deft-fingered it was a kind of work in which she excelled.

Every day seemed to throw upon her young shoulders more of the family burdens, and that Tess should be the representative of the Durbeyfields at the d'Urberville mansion came as a thing of course. In this instance it must be admitted that the Durbeyfields were putting their fairest side outward.

She alighted from the van at Trantridge Cross, and ascended on foot a hill in the direction of the district known as The Chase, on the borders of which, as she had been informed, Mrs. d'Urberville's

6. One who agreed with Robert Malthus (d. 1834), the English economist, who wrote on the evils of overpopulation.

seat, The Slopes, would be found. It was not a manorial home in the ordinary sense, with fields, and pastures, and a grumbling farmer, out of whom the owner had to squeeze an income for himself and his family by hook or by crook. It was more, far more; a country-house built for enjoyment pure and simple, with not an acre of troublesome land attached to it beyond what was required for residential purposes, and for a little fancy farm kept in hand by the owner, and tended by a bailiff.

The crimson brick lodge came first in sight, up to its eaves in dense evergreens. Tess thought this was the mansion itself till, passing through the side wicket with some trepidation, and onward to a point at which the drive took a turn, the house proper stood in full view. It was of recent erection—indeed almost new—and of the same rich red colour that formed such a contrast with the evergreens of the lodge. Far behind the corner of the house—which rose like a geranium bloom against the subdued colours around—stretched the soft azure landscape of The Chase—a truly venerable tract of forest land, one of the few remaining woodlands in England of undoubted primeval date, wherein Druidical mistletoe was still found on aged oaks,[7] and where enormous yew-trees, not planted by the hand of man, grew as they had grown when they were pollarded[8] for bows. All this sylvan antiquity, however, though visible from The Slopes, was outside the immediate boundaries of the estate.

Everything on this snug property was bright, thriving, and well kept; acres of glass-houses stretched down the inclines to the copses at their feet. Everything looked like money—like the last coin issued from the Mint. The stables, partly screened by Austrian pines and evergreen oaks, and fitted with every late appliance, were as dignified as Chapels-of-Ease.[9] On the extensive lawn stood an ornamental tent, its door being towards her.

Simple Tess Durbeyfield stood at gaze, in a half-alarmed attitude, on the edge of the gravel sweep. Her feet had brought her onward to this point before she had quite realized where she was; and now all was contrary to her expectation.

'I thought we were an old family; but this is all new!' she said, in her artlessness. She wished that she had not fallen in so readily with her mother's plans for 'claiming kin,' and had endeavoured to gain assistance nearer home.

The d'Urbervilles—or Stoke-d'Urbervilles, as they at first called themselves—who owned all this, were a somewhat unusual family to find in such an old-fashioned part of the country. Parson Tringham

---

7. Mistletoe was "held in veneration by the Druids, esp. when found growing [as it rarely does] on the oak." [*OED*]

8. Cut back to the trunk to promote the growth of boughs.

9. "Built for the convenience of parishioners who live far from the parish church." [*OED*]

had spoken truly when he said that our shambling John Durbeyfield was the only really lineal representative of the old d'Urberville family existing in the county, or near it; he might have added, what he knew very well, that the Stoke-d'Urbervilles were no more d'Urbervilles of the true tree than he was himself. Yet it must be admitted that this family formed a very good stock whereon to regraft a name which sadly wanted such renovation.

When old Mr. Simon Stoke, latterly deceased, had made his fortune as an honest merchant (some said money-lender) in the North, he decided to settle as a county man in the South of England, out of hail of his business district; and in doing this he felt the necessity of recommencing with a name that would not too readily identify him with the smart tradesman of the past, and that would be less commonplace than the original bald stark words. Conning for an hour in the British Museum the pages of works devoted to extinct, half-extinct, obscured, and ruined families appertaining to the quarter of England in which he proposed to settle, he considered that *d'Urberville* looked and sounded as well as any of them: and d'Urberville accordingly was annexed to his own name for himself and his heirs eternally. Yet he was not an extravagant-minded man in this, and in constructing his family tree on the new basis was duly reasonable in framing his intermarriages and aristocratic links, never inserting a single title above a rank of strict moderation.

Of this work of imagination poor Tess and her parents were naturally in ignorance—much to their discomfiture; indeed, the very possibility of such annexations was unknown to them; who supposed that, though to be well-favoured might be the gift of fortune, a family name came by nature.[1]

Tess still stood hesitating like a bather about to make his plunge, hardly knowing whether to retreat or to persevere, when a figure came forth from the dark triangular door of the tent. It was that of a tall young man, smoking.

He had an almost swarthy complexion, with full lips, badly moulded, though red and smooth, above which was a well-groomed black moustache with curled points, though his age could not be more than three or four-and-twenty. Despite the touches of barbarism in his contours, there was a singular force in the gentleman's face, and in his bold rolling eye.

'Well, my Beauty, what can I do for you?' said he, coming forward. And perceiving that she stood quite confounded: 'Never mind me. I am Mr. d'Urberville. Have you come to see me or my mother?'

This embodiment of a d'Urberville and a namesake differed even more from what Tess had expected than the house and grounds had

1. See Shakespeare's *Much Ado About Nothing*, III.ii: 'To be a well-favoured man is the gift of fortune; but to write and read comes by nature.' " [F]

differed. She had dreamed of an aged and dignified face, the sublimation of all the d'Urberville lineaments, furrowed with incarnate memories representing in hieroglyphic the centuries of her family's and England's history. But she screwed herself up to the work in hand, since she could not get out of it, and answered—

'I came to see your mother, sir.'

'I am afraid you cannot see her—she is an invalid,' replied the present representative of the spurious house; for this was Mr. Alec, the only son of the lately deceased gentleman. 'Cannot I answer your purpose? What is the business you wish to see her about?'

'It isn't business—it is—I can hardly say what!'

'Pleasure?'

'Oh no. Why, sir, if I tell you, it will seem——'

Tess's sense of a certain ludicrousness in her errand was now so strong that, notwithstanding her awe of him, and her general discomfort at being here, her rosy lips curved towards a smile, much to the attraction of the swarthy Alexander.

'It is so very foolish,' she stammered; 'I fear I can't tell you!'

'Never mind; I like foolish things. Try again, my dear,' said he kindly.

'Mother asked me to come,' Tess continued; 'and, indeed, I was in the mind to do so myself likewise. But I did not think it would be like this. I came, sir, to tell you that we are of the same family as you.'

'Ho! Poor relations?'

'Yes.'

'Stokes?'

'No; d'Urbervilles.'

'Ay, ay; I mean d'Urbervilles.'

'Our names are worn away to Durbeyfield; but we have several proofs that we are d'Urbervilles. Antiquarians hold we are,—and—and we have an old seal, marked with a ramping lion on a shield, and a castle over him. And we have a very old silver spoon, round in the bowl like a little ladle, and marked with the same castle. But it is so worn that mother uses it to stir the pea-soup.'

'A castle argent is certainly my crest,' said he blandly. 'And my arms a lion rampant.'

'And so mother said we ought to make ourselves beknown to you —as we've lost our horse by a bad accident, and are the oldest branch o' the family.'

'Very kind of your mother, I'm sure. And I, for one, don't regret her step.' Alec looked at Tess as he spoke, in a way that made her blush a little. 'And so, my pretty girl, you've come on a friendly visit to us, as relations?'

'I suppose I have,' faltered Tess, looking uncomfortable again.

'Well—there's no harm in it. Where do you live? What are you?'

She gave him brief particulars; and responding to further inquiries told him that she was intending to go back by the same carrier who had brought her.

'It is a long while before he returns past Trantridge Cross. Supposing we walk round the grounds to pass the time, my pretty Coz?'[2]

Tess wished to abridge her visit as much as possible; but the young man was pressing, and she consented to accompany him. He conducted her about the lawns, and flower-beds, and conservatories; and thence to the fruit-garden and green-houses, where he asked her if she liked strawberries.

'Yes,' said Tess, 'when they come.'

'They are already here.' D'Urberville began gathering specimens of the fruit for her, handing them back to her as he stooped; and, presently, selecting a specially fine product of the 'British Queen' variety, he stood up and held it by the stem to her mouth.

'No—no!' she said quickly, putting her fingers between his hand and her lips. 'I would rather take it in my own hand.'

'Nonsense!' he insisted; and in a slight distress she parted her lips and took it in.

They had spent some time wandering desultorily thus, Tess eating in a half-pleased, half-reluctant state whatever d'Urberville offered her. When she could consume no more of the strawberries he filled her little basket with them; and then the two passed round to the rose trees, whence he gathered blossoms and gave her to put in her bosom. She obeyed like one in a dream, and when she could affix no more he himself tucked a bud or two into her hat, and heaped her basket with others in the prodigality of his bounty. At last, looking at his watch, he said, 'Now, by the time you have had something to eat, it will be time for you to leave, if you want to catch the carrier to Shaston. Come here, and I'll see what grub I can find.'

Stoke-d'Urberville took her back to the lawn and into the tent, where he left her, soon reappearing with a basket of light luncheon, which he put before her himself. It was evidently the gentleman's wish not to be disturbed in this pleasant *tête-á-tête* by the servantry.

'Do you mind my smoking?' he asked.

'Oh, not at all, sir.'

He watched her pretty and unconscious munching through the skeins of smoke that pervaded the tent, and Tess Durbeyfield did not divine, as she innocently looked down at the roses in her bosom, that there behind the blue narcotic haze was potentially the 'tragic mischief' of her drama—one who stood fair to be the blood-red ray in the spectrum of her young life. She had an attribute which amounted to

---

2. Perhaps an echo of another romantic comedy of Shakespeare's, *As You Like It*, in which cousins Rosalind and Celia (who to "pass the time" discuss the difference between Fortune and Nature) call one another "sweet my coz" and "my pretty little coz."

a disadvantage just now; and it was this that caused Alec d'Urberville's eyes to rivet themselves upon her. It was a luxuriance of aspect, a fulness of growth, which made her appear more of a woman than she really was. She had inherited the feature from her mother without the quality it denoted. It had troubled her mind occasionally, till her companions had said that it was a fault which time would cure.

She soon had finished her lunch. 'Now I am going home, sir,' she said, rising.

'And what do they call you?' he asked, as he accompanied her along the drive till they were out of sight of the house.

'Tess Durbeyfield, down at Marlott.'

'And you say your people have lost their horse?'

'I—killed him!' she answered, her eyes filling with tears as she gave particulars of Prince's death. 'And I don't know what to do for father on account of it!'

'I must think if I cannot do something. My mother must find a berth for you. But, Tess, no nonsense about "d'Urberville";—"Durbeyfield" only, you know—quite another name.'

'I wish for no better, sir,' said she with something of dignity.

For a moment—only for a moment—when they were in the turning of the drive, between the tall rhododendrons and conifers, before the lodge became visible, he inclined his face towards her as if— but, no: he thought better of it, and let her go.

Thus the thing began. Had she perceived this meeting's import she might have asked why she was doomed to be seen and coveted that day by the wrong man, and not by some other man, the right and desired one in all respects—as nearly as humanity can supply the right and desired; yet to him who amongst her acquaintance might have approximated to this kind, she was but a transient impression, half forgotten.

In the ill-judged execution of the well-judged plan of things the call seldom produces the comer, the man to love rarely coincides with the hour for loving. Nature does not often say 'See!' to her poor creature at a time when seeing can lead to happy doing; or reply 'Here!' to a body's cry of 'Where?' till the hide-and-seek has become an irksome, outworn game. We may wonder whether at the acme and summit of the human progress these anachronisms will be corrected by a finer intuition, a closer interaction of the social machinery than that which now jolts us round and along; but such completeness is not to be prophesied, or even conceived as possible. Enough that in the present case, as in millions, it was not the two halves of a perfect whole that confronted each other at the perfect moment; a missing counterpart wandered independently about the earth waiting in crass obtuseness till the late time came. Out of which maladroit delay sprang anxieties, disappointments, shocks, catastrophes, and passing-strange destinies.

When d'Urberville got back to the tent he sat down astride on a chair reflecting, with a pleased gleam in his face. Then he broke into a loud laugh.

'Well, I'm damned! What a funny thing! Ha-ha-ha! And what a crumby [3] girl!'

VI

Tess went down the hill to Trantridge Cross, and inattentively waited to take her seat in the van returning from Chaseborough to Shaston. She did not know what the other occupants said to her as she entered, though she answered them; and when they had started anew she rode along with an inward and not an outward eye.

One among her fellow-travellers addressed her more pointedly than any had spoken before: 'Why, you be quite a posy! And such roses in early June!'

Then she became aware of the spectacle she presented to their surprised vision: roses at her breast; roses in her hat; roses and strawberries in her basket to the brim. She blushed, and said confusedly that the flowers had been given to her. When the passengers were not looking she stealthily removed the more prominent blooms from her hat and placed them in the basket, where she covered them with her handkerchief. Then she fell to reflecting again, and in looking downwards a thorn of the rose remaining in her breast accidentally pricked her chin. Like all the cottagers in Blackmoor Vale, Tess was steeped in fancies and prefigurative superstitions; she thought this an ill omen—the first she had noticed that day.

The van travelled only so far as Shaston, and there were several miles of pedestrian descent from that mountain-town into the vale to Marlott. Her mother had advised her to stay here for the night, at the house of a cottage-woman they knew, if she should feel too tired to come on; and this Tess did, not descending to her home till the following afternoon.

When she entered the house she perceived in a moment from her mother's triumphant manner that something had occurred in the interim.

'Oh yes; I know all about it! I told 'ee it would be all right, and now 'tis proved!'

'Since I've been away? What has?' said Tess rather wearily.

Her mother surveyed the girl up and down with arch approval, and went on banteringly: 'So you've brought 'em round!'

'How do you know, mother?'

'I've had a letter.'

Tess then remembered that there would have been time for this.

'They say—Mrs. d'Urberville says—that she wants you to look after

3. Plump, comely, attractive.

a little fowl-farm which is her hobby. But this is only her artful way of getting 'ee there without raising your hopes. She's going to own 'ee as kin—that's the meaning o't.'

'But I didn't see her.'

'You zid somebody, I suppose?'

'I saw her son.'

'And did he own 'ee?'

'Well—he called me Coz.'

'An' I knew it! Jacky—he called her Coz!' cried Joan to her husband. 'Well, he spoke to his mother, of course, and she do want 'ee there.'

'But I don't know that I am apt at tending fowls,' said the dubious Tess.

'Then I don't know who is apt. You've be'n born in the business, and brought up in it. They that be born in a business always know more about it than any 'prentice. Besides, that's only just a show of something for you to do, that you midn't feel beholden.'

'I don't altogether think I ought to go,' said Tess thoughtfully. 'Who wrote the letter? Will you let me look at it?'

'Mrs. d'Urberville wrote it. Here it is.'

The letter was in the third person, and briefly informed Mrs. Durbeyfield that her daughter's services would be useful to that lady in the management of her poultry-farm, that a comfortable room would be provided for her if she could come, and that the wages would be on a liberal scale if they liked her.

'Oh—that's all!' said Tess.

'You couldn't expect her to throw her arms round 'ee, an' to kiss and to coll 'ee all at once.'

Tess looked out of the window.

'I would rather stay here with father and you,' she said.

'But why?'

'I'd rather not tell you why, mother; indeed, I don't quite know why.'

A week afterwards she came in one evening from an unavailing search for some light occupation in the immediate neighbourhood. Her idea had been to get together sufficient money during the summer to purchase another horse. Hardly had she crossed the threshold before one of the children danced across the room, saying, 'The gentleman's been here!'

Her mother hastened to explain, smiles breaking from every inch of her person. Mrs. d'Urberville's son had called on horseback, having been riding by chance in the direction of Marlott. He had wished to know, finally, in the name of his mother, if Tess could really come to manage the old lady's fowl-farm or not; the lad who had hitherto superintended the birds having proved untrustworthy. 'Mr. d'Urberville says you must be a good girl if you are at all as you appear; he knows you must be worth your weight in gold. He is very much interested in 'ee—truth to tell.'

Tess seemed for the moment really pleased to hear that she had won such high opinion from a stranger when, in her own esteem, she had sunk so low.

'It is very good of him to think that,' she murmured; 'and if I was quite sure how it would be living there, I would go any-when.'

'He is a mighty handsome man!'

'I don't think so,' said Tess coldly.

'Well, there's your chance, whether or no; and I'm sure he wears a beautiful diamond ring!'

'Yes,' said little Abraham, brightly, from the window-bench; 'and I seed it! and it did twinkle when he put his hand up to his mistarshers. Mother, why did our grand relation keep on putting his hand up to his mistarshers?'

'Hark at that child!' cried Mrs. Durbeyfield, with parenthetic admiration.

'Perhaps to show his diamond ring,' murmured Sir John, dreamily, from his chair.

'I'll think it over,' said Tess, leaving the room.

'Well, she's made a conquest o' the younger branch of us, straight off,' continued the matron to her husband, 'and she's a fool if she don't follow it up.'

'I don't quite like my children going away from home,' said the haggler. 'As the head of the family, the rest ought to come to me.'

'But do let her go, Jacky,' coaxed his poor witless wife. 'He's struck wi' her—you can see that. He called her Coz! He'll marry her, most likely, and make a lady of her; and then she'll be what her forefathers was.'

John Durbeyfield had more conceit than energy or health, and this supposition was pleasant to him.

'Well, perhaps, that's what young Mr. d'Urberville means,' he admitted; 'and sure enough he mid have serious thoughts about improving his blood by linking on to the old line. Tess, the little rogue! And have she really paid 'em a visit to such an end as this?'

Meanwhile Tess was walking thoughtfully among the gooseberry-bushes in the garden, and over Prince's grave. When she came in her mother pursued her advantage.

'Well, what be you going to do?' she asked.

'I wish I had seen Mrs. d'Urberville,' said Tess.

'I think you mid as well settle it. Then you'll see her soon enough.'

Her father coughed in his chair.

'I don't know what to say!' answered the girl restlessly. 'It is for you to decide. I killed the old horse, and I suppose I ought to do something to get ye a new one. But—but—I don't quite like Mr. d'Urberville being there!'

The children, who had made use of this idea of Tess being taken up by their wealthy kinsfolk (which they imagined the other family to be) as a species of dolorifuge[4] after the death of the horse, began to cry at Tess's reluctance, and teased and reproached her for hesitating.

'Tess won't go—o—o and be made a la—a—dy of!—no, she says she wo—o—on't!' they wailed, with square mouths. 'And we shan't have a nice new horse, and lots o' golden money to buy fairlings![5] And Tess won't look pretty in her best cloze no mo—o—ore!'

Her mother chimed in to the same tune: a certain way she had of making her labours in the house seem heavier than they were by prolonging them indefinitely, also weighed in the argument. Her father alone preserved an attitude of neutrality.

'I will go,' said Tess at last.

Her mother could not repress her consciousness of the nuptial Vision conjured up by the girl's consent.

'That's right! For such a pretty maid as 'tis, this is a fine chance!'

Tess smiled crossly.

'I hope it is a chance for earning money. It is no other kind of chance. You had better say nothing of that silly sort about parish.'

Mrs. Durbeyfield did not promise. She was not quite sure that she did not feel proud enough, after the visitor's remarks, to say a good deal.

Thus it was arranged; and the young girl wrote, agreeing to be ready to set out on any day on which she might be required. She was duly informed that Mrs. d'Urberville was glad of her decision, and that a spring-cart should be sent to meet her and her luggage at the top of the Vale on the day after the morrow, when she must hold herself prepared to start. Mrs. d'Urberville's handwriting seemed rather masculine.

'A cart?' murmured Joan Durbeyfield doubtingly. 'It might have been a carriage for her own kin!'

Having at last taken her course Tess was less restless and abstracted, going about her business with some self-assurance in the thought of acquiring another horse for her father by an occupation which would not be onerous. She had hoped to be a teacher at the school, but the fates seemed to decide otherwise. Being mentally older than her mother she did not regard Mrs. Durbeyfield's matrimonial hopes for her in a serious aspect for a moment. The light-minded woman had been discovering good matches for her daughter almost from the year of her birth.

---

4. An agent for relieving pain.   5. Presents bought at a fair.

VII

On the morning appointed for her departure Tess was awake before dawn—at the marginal minute of the dark when the grove is still mute, save for one prophetic bird who sings with a clear-voiced conviction that he at least knows the correct time of day, the rest preserving silence as if equally convinced that he is mistaken. She remained upstairs packing till breakfast-time, and then came down in her ordinary weekday clothes, her Sunday apparel being carefully folded in her box.

Her mother expostulated. 'You will never set out to see your folks without dressing up more the dand[6] than that?'

'But I am going to work!' said Tess.

'Well, yes,' said Mrs. Durbeyfield; and in a private tone, 'at first there mid be a little pretence o't. . . . But I think it will be wiser of 'ee to put your best side outward,' she added.

'Very well; I suppose you know best,' replied Tess with calm abandonment.

And to please her parent the girl put herself quite in Joan's hands, saying serenely—'Do what you like with me, mother.'

Mrs. Durbeyfield was only too delighted at this tractability. First she fetched a great basin, and washed Tess's hair with such thoroughness that when dried and brushed it looked twice as much as at other times. She tied it with a broader pink ribbon than usual. Then she put upon her the white frock that Tess had worn at the club-walking, the airy fulness of which, supplementing her enlarged *coiffure*, imparted to her developing figure an amplitude which belied her age, and might cause her to be estimated as a woman when she was not much more than a child.

'I declare there's a hole in my stocking-heel!' said Tess.

'Never mind holes in your stockings—they don't speak! When I was a maid, so long as I had a pretty bonnet the devil might ha' found me in heels.'

Her mother's pride in the girl's appearance led her to step back, like a painter from his easel, and survey her work as a whole.

'You must zee yourself!' she cried. 'It is much better than you was t'other day.'

As the looking-glass was only large enough to reflect a very small portion of Tess's person at one time, Mrs. Durbeyfield hung a black cloak outside the casement, and so made a large reflector of the panes, as it is the wont of bedecking cottagers to do. After this she went downstairs to her husband, who was sitting in the lower room.

'I'll tell 'ee what 'tis, Durbeyfield,' said she exultingly; 'he'll never have the heart not to love her. But whatever you do, don't zay too much to Tess of his fancy for her, and this chance she has got. She is

6. Dandy; an elegant woman.

such an odd maid that it mid zet her against him, or against going there, even now. If all goes well, I shall certainly be for making some return to that pa'son at Stagfoot Lane for telling us—dear, good man!'

However, as the moment for the girl's setting out drew nigh, when the first excitement of the dressing had passed off, a slight misgiving found place in Joan Durbeyfield's mind. It prompted the matron to say that she would walk a little way—as far as to the point where the acclivity from the valley began its first steep ascent to the outer world. At the top Tess was going to be met with the spring-cart sent by the Stoke-d'Urbervilles, and her box had already been wheeled ahead towards this summit by a lad with trucks,[7] to be in readiness.

Seeing their mother put on her bonnet the younger children clamoured to go with her.

'I do want to walk a little-ways wi' Sissy, now she's going to marry our gentleman-cousin, and wear fine cloze!'

'Now,' said Tess, flushing and turning quickly, 'I'll hear no more o' that! Mother, how could you ever put such stuff into their heads?'

'Going to work, my dears, for our rich relation, and help get enough money for a new horse,' said Mrs. Durbeyfield pacifically.

'Good-bye, father,' said Tess, with a lumpy throat.

'Good-bye, my maid,' said Sir John, raising his head from his breast as he suspended his nap, induced by a slight excess this morning in honour of the occasion. 'Well, I hope my young friend will like such a comely sample of his own blood. And tell'n, Tess, that being sunk, quite, from our former grandeur, I'll sell him the title—yes, sell it—and at no onreasonable figure.'

'Not for less than a thousand pound!' cried Lady Durbeyfield.

'Tell'n—I'll take a thousand pound. Well, I'll take less, when I come to think o't. He'll adorn it better than a poor lammicken[8] feller like myself can. Tell'n he shall hae it for a hundred. But I won't stand upon trifles—tell'n he shall hae it for fifty—for twenty pound! Yes, twenty pound—that's the lowest. Dammy, family honour is family honour, and I won't take a penny less!'

Tess's eyes were too full and her voice too choked to utter the sentiments that were in her. She turned quickly, and went out.

So the girls and their mother all walked together, a child on each side of Tess, holding her hand, and looking at her meditatively from time to time, as at one who was about to do great things; her mother just behind with the smallest; the group forming a picture of honest beauty flanked by innocence, and backed by simple-souled vanity. They followed the way till they reached the beginning of the ascent, on the crest of which the vehicle from Trantridge was to re-

7. A wheelbarrow.   8. Clumsy. [F]

ceive her, this limit having been fixed to save the horse the labour of the last slope. Far away behind the first hills the cliff-like dwellings of Shaston broke the line of the ridge. Nobody was visible in the elevated road which skirted the ascent save the lad whom they had sent on before them, sitting on the handle of the barrow that contained all Tess's worldly possessions.

'Bide here a bit, and the cart will soon come, no doubt,' said Mrs. Durbeyfield. 'Yes, I see it yonder!'

It had come—appearing suddenly from behind the forehead of the nearest upland, and stopping beside the boy with the barrow. Her mother and the children thereupon decided to go no farther, and bidding them a hasty good-bye Tess bent her steps up the hill.

They saw her white shape draw near to the spring-cart, on which her box was already placed. But before she had quite reached it another vehicle shot out from a clump of trees on the summit, came round the bend of the road there, passed the luggage-cart, and halted beside Tess, who looked up as if in great surprise.

Her mother perceived, for the first time, that the second vehicle was not a humble conveyance like the first, but a spick-and-span gig or dog-cart,[9] highly varnished and equipped. The driver was a young man of three- or four-and-twenty, with a cigar between his teeth; wearing a dandy cap, drab jacket, breeches of the same hue, white neckcloth, stick-up collar, and brown driving-gloves—in short, he was the handsome, horsey young buck who had visited Joan a week or two before to get her answer about Tess.

Mrs. Durbeyfield clapped her hands like a child. Then she looked down, then stared again. Could she be deceived as to the meaning of this?

'Is dat the gentleman-kinsman who'll make Sissy a lady?' asked the youngest child.

Meanwhile the muslined form of Tess could be seen standing still, undecided, beside this turn-out, whose owner was talking to her. Her seeming indecision was, in fact, more than indecision: it was misgiving. She would have preferred the humble cart. The young man dismounted, and appeared to urge her to ascend. She turned her face down the hill to her relatives, and regarded the little group. Something seemed to quicken her to a determination; possibly the thought that she had killed Prince. She suddenly stepped up; he mounted beside her, and immediately whipped on the horse. In a moment they had passed the slow cart with the box, and disappeared behind the shoulder of the hill.

Directly Tess was out of sight, and the interest of the matter as a drama was at an end, the little ones' eyes filled with tears. The youngest child said, 'I wish poor, poor Tess wasn't gone away to be a lady!' and, lowering the corners of his lips, burst out crying. The new

9. Two-wheeled, one-horse carriage.

point of view was infectious, and the next child did likewise, and then the next, till the whole three of them wailed loud.

There were tears also in Joan Durbeyfield's eyes as she turned to go home. But by the time she had got back to the village she was passively trusting to the favour of accident. However, in bed that night she sighed, and her husband asked her what was the matter.

'Oh, I don't know exactly,' she said. 'I was thinking that perhaps it would ha' been better if Tess had not gone.'

'Oughtn't ye to have thought of that before?'

'Well, 'tis a chance for the maid—— Still, if 'twere the doing again, I wouldn't let her go till I had found out whether the gentleman is really a good-hearted young man and choice over her[1] as his kinswoman.'

'Yes, you ought, perhaps, to ha' done that,' snored Sir John.

Joan Durbeyfield always managed to find consolation somewhere: 'Well, as one of the genuine stock, she ought to make her way with 'en, if she plays her trump card aright. And if he don't marry her afore he will after. For that he's all afire wi' love for her any eye can see.'

'What's her trump card? Her d'Urberville blood, you mean?'

'No, stupid; her face—as 'twas mine.'

VIII

Having mounted beside her, Alec d'Urberville drove rapidly along the crest of the first hill, chatting compliments to Tess as they went, the cart with her box being left far behind. Rising still, an immense landscape stretched around them on every side; behind, the green valley of her birth, before, a gray country of which she knew nothing except from her first brief visit to Trantridge. Thus they reached the verge of an incline down which the road stretched in a long straight descent of nearly a mile.

Ever since the accident with her father's horse Tess Durbeyfield, courageous as she naturally was, had been exceedingly timid on wheels; the least irregularity of motion startled her. She began to get uneasy at a certain recklessness in her conductor's driving.

'You will go down slow, sir, I suppose?' she said with attempted unconcern.

D'Urberville looked round upon her, nipped his cigar with the tips of his large white centre-teeth, and allowed his lips to smile slowly of themselves.

'Why, Tess,' he answered, after another whiff or two, 'it isn't a brave bouncing girl like you who asks that? Why, I always go down at full gallop. There's nothing like it for raising your spirits.'

'But perhaps you need not now?'

'Ah,' he said, shaking his head, 'there are two to be reckoned with.

---

1. Sets great store by her.

It is not me alone. Tib has to be considered, and she has a very queer temper.'

'Who?'

'Why, this mare. I fancy she looked round at me in a very grim way just then. Didn't you notice it?'

'Don't try to frighten me, sir,' said Tess stiffly.

'Well, I don't. If any living man can manage this horse I can:—I won't say any living man can do it—but if such has the power, I am he.'

'Why do you have such a horse?'

'Ah, well may you ask it! It was my fate, I suppose. Tib has killed one chap; and just after I bought her she nearly killed me. And then, take my word for it, I nearly killed her. But she's touchy still, very touchy; and one's life is hardly safe behind her sometimes.'

They were just beginning to descend; and it was evident that the horse, whether of her own will or of his (the latter being the more likely), knew so well the reckless performance expected of her that she hardly required a hint from behind.

Down, down, they sped, the wheels humming like a top, the dog-cart rocking right and left, its axis acquiring a slightly oblique set in relation to the line of progress; the figure of the horse rising and falling in undulations before them. Sometimes a wheel was off the ground, it seemed, for many yards; sometimes a stone was sent spinning over the hedge, and flinty sparks from the horse's hoofs out-shone the daylight. The aspect of the straight road enlarged with their advance, the two banks dividing like a splitting stick; one rushing past at each shoulder.

The wind blew through Tess's white muslin to her very skin, and her washed hair flew out behind. She was determined to show no open fear, but she clutched d'Urberville's rein-arm.

'Don't touch my arm! We shall be thrown out if you do! Hold on round my waist!'

She grasped his waist, and so they reached the bottom.

'Safe, thank God, in spite of your fooling!' said she, her face on fire.

'Tess—fie! that's temper!' said d'Urberville.

' 'Tis truth.'

'Well, you need not let go your hold of me so thanklessly the moment you feel yourself out of danger.'

She had not considered what she had been doing; whether he were man or woman, stick or stone, in her involuntary hold on him. Recovering her reserve she sat without replying, and thus they reached the summit of another declivity.

'Now then, again!' said d'Urberville.

'No, no!' said Tess. 'Show more sense, do, please.'

'But when people find themselves on one of the highest points in the county, they must get down again,' he retorted.

He loosened rein, and away they went a second time. D'Urberville turned his face to her as they rocked, and said, in playful raillery: 'Now then, put your arms round my waist again, as you did before, my Beauty.'

'Never!' said Tess independently, holding on as well as she could without touching him.

'Let me put one little kiss on those holmberry[2] lips, Tess, or even on that warmed cheek, and I'll stop—on my honour, I will!'

Tess, surprised beyond measure, slid farther back still on her seat, at which he urgd the horse anew, and rocked her the more.

'Will nothing else do?' she cried at length, in desperation, her large eyes staring at him like those of a wild animal. This dressing her up so prettily by her mother had apparently been to lamentable purpose.

'Nothing, dear Tess,' he replied.

'Oh, I don't know—very well; I don't mind!' she panted miserably.

He drew rein, and as they slowed he was on the point of imprinting the desired salute, when, as if hardly yet aware of her own modesty, she dodged aside. His arms being occupied with the reins there was left him no power to prevent her maneuvre.

'Now, damn it—I'll break both our necks!' swore her capriciously passionate companion. 'So you can go from your word like that, you young witch, can you?'

'Very well,' said Tess, 'I'll not move since you be so determined! But I—thought you would be kind to me, and protect me, as my kinsman!'

'Kinsman be hanged! Now!'

'But I don't want anybody to kiss me, sir!' she implored, a big tear beginning to roll down her face, and the corners of her mouth trembling in her attempts not to cry. 'And I wouldn't ha' come if I had known!'

He was inexorable, and she sat still, and d'Urberville gave her the kiss of mastery. No sooner had he done so than she flushed with shame, took out her handkerchief, and wiped the spot on her cheek that had been touched by his lips. His ardour was nettled at the sight, for the act on her part had been unconsciously done.

'You are mighty sensitive for a cottage girl!' said the young man.

Tess made no reply to this remark, of which, indeed, she did not quite comprehend the drift, unheeding the snub she had administered by her instinctive rub upon her cheek. She had, in fact, undone the kiss, as far as such a thing was physically possible. With a dim sense that he was vexed she looked steadily ahead as they trotted

2. Hollyberry.

on near Melbury Down and Wingreen, till she saw, to her consternation, that there was yet another descent to be undergone.

'You shall be made sorry for that!' he resumed, his injured tone
still remaining, as he flourished the whip anew. 'Unless, that is, you
agree willingly to let me do it again, and no handkerchief.'

She sighed. 'Very well, sir!' she said. 'Oh—let me get my hat!'

At the moment of speaking her hat had blown off into the road,
their present speed on the upland being by no means slow. D'Urberville pulled up, and said he would get it for her, but Tess was down
on the other side.

She turned back and picked up the article.

'You look prettier with it off, upon my soul, if that's possible,' he
said, contemplating her over the back of the vehicle. 'Now then, up
again! What's the matter?'

The hat was in place and tied, but Tess had not stepped forward.

'No, sir,' she said, revealing the red and ivory of her mouth as her
eye lit in defiant triumph; 'not again, if I know it!'

'What—you won't get up beside me?'

'No; I shall walk.'

' 'Tis five or six miles yet to Trantridge.'

'I don't care if 'tis dozens. Besides, the cart is behind.'

'You artful hussy! Now, tell me—didn't you make that hat blow
off on purpose? I'll swear you did!'

Her strategic silence confirmed his suspicion.

Then d'Urberville cursed and swore at her, and called her everything he could think of for the trick. Turning the horse suddenly he
tried to drive back upon her, and so hem her in between the gig and
the hedge. But he could not do this short of injuring her.

'You ought to be ashamed of yourself for using such wicked
words!' cried Tess with spirit, from the top of the hedge into which
she had scrambled. 'I don't like 'ee at all! I hate and detest you! I'll
go back to mother, I will!'

D'Urberville's bad temper cleared up at sight of hers; and he
laughed heartily.

'Well, I like you all the better,' he said. 'Come, let there be
peace. I'll never do it any more against your will. My life upon it
now!'

Still Tess could not be induced to remount. She did not, however,
object to his keeping his gig alongside her; and in this manner, at a
slow pace, they advanced towards the village of Trantridge. From
time to time d'Urberville exhibited a sort of fierce distress at the
sight of the tramping he had driven her to undertake by his mis-
demeanour. She might in truth have safely trusted him now; but he
had forfeited her confidence for the time, and she kept on the
ground, progressing thoughtfully, as if wondering whether it would

be wiser to return home. Her resolve, however, had been taken, and it seemed vacillating even to childishness to abandon it now, unless for graver reasons. How could she face her parents, get back her box, and disconcert the whole scheme for the rehabilitation of her family on such sentimental grounds?

A few minutes later the chimneys of The Slopes appeared in view, and in a snug nook to the right the poultry-farm and cottage of Tess's destination.

IX

The community of fowls to which Tess had been appointed as supervisor, purveyor, nurse, surgeon, and friend, made its headquarters in an old thatched cottage standing in an enclosure that had once been a garden, but was now a trampled and sanded square. The house was overrun with ivy, its chimney being enlarged by the boughs of the parasite to the aspect of a ruined tower. The lower rooms were entirely given over to the birds, who walked about them with a proprietary air, as though the place had been built by themselves, and not by certain dusty copyholders[3] who now lay east and west in the churchyard. The descendants of these bygone owners felt it almost as a slight to their family when the house which had so much of their affection, had cost so much of their forefathers' money, and had been in their possession for several generations before the d'Urbervilles came and built here, was indifferently turned into a fowl-house by Mrs. Stoke-d'Urberville as soon as the property fell into hand according to law. ' 'Twas good enough for Christians in grandfather's time,' they said.

The rooms wherein dozens of infants had wailed at their nursing now resounded with the tapping of nascent chicks. Distracted hens in coops occupied spots where formerly stood chairs supporting sedate agriculturists. The chimney-corner and once blazing hearth was now filled with inverted beehives, in which the hens laid their eggs; while out of doors the plots that each succeeding householder had carefully shaped with his spade were torn by the cocks in wildest fashion.

The garden in which the cottage stood was surrounded by a wall, and could only be entered through a door.

When Tess had occupied herself about an hour the next morning in altering and improving the arrangements, according to her skilled ideas as the daughter of a professed poulterer, the door in the wall opened and a servant in white cap and apron entered. She had come from the manor-house.

'Mrs. d'Urberville wants the fowls as usual,' she said; but perceiv-

3. Tenants for life, or "owners," as in the following line.

ing that Tess did not quite understand, she explained, 'Mis'ess is a old lady, and blind.'

'Blind!' said Tess.

Almost before her misgiving at the news could find time to shape itself she took, under her companion's direction, two of the most beautiful of the Hamburghs in her arms, and followed the maid-servant, who had likewise taken two, to the adjacent mansion, which, though ornate and imposing, showed traces everywhere on this side that some occupant of its chambers could bend to the love of dumb creatures—feathers floating within view of the front, and hen-coops standing on the grass.

In a sitting-room on the ground-floor, ensconced in an armchair with her back to the light, was the owner and mistress of the estate, a white-haired woman of not more than sixty, or even less, wearing a large cap. She had the mobile face frequent in those whose sight has decayed by stages, has been laboriously striven after, and reluctantly let go, rather than the stagnant mien apparent in persons long sightless or born blind. Tess walked up to this lady with her feathered charges—one sitting on each arm.

'Ah, you are the young woman come to look after my birds?' said Mrs. d'Urberville, recognizing a new footstep. 'I hope you will be kind to them. My bailiff tells me you are quite the proper person. Well, where are they? Ah, this is Strut! But he is hardly so lively to-day, is he? He is alarmed at being handled by a stranger, I suppose. And Phena too—yes, they are a little frightened—aren't you, dears? But they will soon get used to you.'

While the old lady had been speaking Tess and the other maid, in obedience to her gestures, had placed the fowls severally in her lap, and she had felt them over from head to tail, examining their beaks, their combs, the manes of the cocks, their wings, and their claws. Her touch enabled her to recognize them in a moment, and to discover if a single feather were crippled or draggled. She handled their crops, and knew what they had eaten, and if too little or too much; her face enacting a vivid pantomine of the criticisms passing in her mind.

The birds that the two girls had brought in were duly returned to the yard, and the process was repeated till all the pet cocks and hens had been submitted to the old woman—Hamburghs, Bantams, Cochins, Brahmas, Dorkings, and such other sorts as were in fashion just then—her perception of each visitor being seldom at fault as she received the bird upon her knees.

It reminded Tess of a Confirmation, in which Mrs. d'Urberville was the bishop, the fowls the young people presented, and herself and the maid-servant the parson and curate of the parish bringing them up. At the end of the ceremony Mrs. d'Urberville abruptly asked Tess, wrinkling and twitching her face into undulations, 'Can you whistle?'

'Whistle, Ma'am?'

'Yes, whistle tunes.'

Tess could whistle like most other country girls, though the accomplishment was one which she did not care to profess in genteel company. However, she blandly admitted that such was the fact.

'Then you will have to practise it every day. I had a lad who did it very well, but he has left. I want you to whistle to my bullfinches; as I cannot see them I like to hear them, and we teach 'em airs that way. Tell her where the cages are, Elizabeth. You must begin tomorrow, or they will go back in their piping. They have been neglected these several days.'

'Mr. d'Urberville whistled to 'em this morning, ma'am,' said Elizabeth.

'He! Pooh!'

The old lady's face creased into furrows of repugnance, and she made no further reply.

Thus the reception of Tess by her fancied kinswoman terminated, and the birds were taken back to their quarters. The girl's surprise at Mrs. d'Urberville's manner was not great; for since seeing the size of the house she had expected no more. But she was far from being aware that the old lady had never heard a word of the so-called kinship. She gathered that no great affection flowed between the blind woman and her son. But in that, too, she was mistaken. Mrs. d'Urberville was not the first mother compelled to love her offspring resentfully, and to be bitterly fond.

In spite of the unpleasant initiation of the day before, Tess inclined to the freedom and novelty of her new position in the morning when the sun shone, now that she was once installed there; and she was curious to test her powers in the unexpected direction asked of her, so as to ascertain her chance of retaining her post. As soon as she was alone within the walled garden she sat herself down on a coop, and seriously screwed up her mouth for the long-neglected practice. She found her former ability to have degenerated to the production of a hollow rush of wind through the lips, and no clear note at all.

She remained fruitlessly blowing and blowing, wondering how she could have so grown out of the art which had come by nature, till she became aware of a movement among the ivy-boughs which cloaked the garden-wall no less than the cottage. Looking that way she beheld a form springing from the coping to the plot. It was

Alec d'Urberville, whom she had not set eyes on since he had conducted her the day before to the door of the gardener's cottage where she had lodgings.

'Upon my honour!' cried he, 'there was never before such a beautiful thing in Nature or Art as you look, "Cousin" Tess ["Cousin" had a faint ring of mockery]. I have been watching you from over the wall—sitting like *Im*-patience on a monument,[4] and pouting up that pretty red mouth to whistling shape, and whooing and whooing, and privately swearing, and never being able to produce a note. Why, you are quite cross because you can't do it.'

'I may be cross, but I didn't swear.'

'Ah! I understand why you are trying—those bullies! My mother wants you to carry on their musical education. How selfish of her! As if attending to these curst cocks and hens here were not enough work for any girl. I would flatly refuse, if I were you.'

'But she wants me particularly to do it, and to be ready by to-morrow morning.'

'Does she? Well then—I'll give you a lesson or two.'

'Oh no, you won't!' said Tess, withdrawing towards the door.

'Nonsense; I don't want to touch you. See—I'll stand on this side of the wire-netting, and you can keep on the other; so you may feel quite safe. Now, look here; you screw up your lips too harshly. There 'tis—so.'

He suited the action to the word, and whistled a line of 'Take, O take those lips away.'[5] But the allusion was lost upon Tess.

'Now try,' said d'Urberville.

She attempted to look reserved; her face put on a sculptural severity. But he persisted in his demand, and at last, to get rid of him, she did put up her lips as directed for producing a clear note; laughing distressfully, however, and then blushing with vexation that she had laughed.

He encouraged her with 'Try again!'

Tess was quite serious, painfully serious by this time; and she tried—ultimately and unexpectedly emitting a real round sound. The momentary pleasure of success got the better of her; her eyes enlarged, and she involuntarily smiled in his face.

'That's it! Now I have started you—you'll go on beautifully. There —I said I would not come near you; and, in spite of such temptation as never before fell to mortal man, I'll keep my word. . . . Tess, do you think my mother a queer old soul?'

'I don't know much of her yet, sir.'

'You'll find her so; she must be, to make you learn to whistle to her bullfinches. I am rather out of her books just now, but you will be quite in favour if you treat her live-stock well. Good morning. If

4. An echo of Shakespeare, *Twelfth Night*, II.iv.117.

5. Shakespeare, *Measure for Measure*, IV.i.1.

you meet with any difficulties and want help here, don't go to the bailiff, come to me.'

It was in the economy of this *régime* that Tess Durbeyfield had undertaken to fill a place. Her first day's experiences were fairly typical of those which followed through many succeeding days. A familiarity with Alec d'Urberville's presence—which that young man carefully cultivated in her by playful dialogue, and by jestingly calling her his cousin when they were alone—removed much of her original shyness of him, without, however, implanting any feeling which could engender shyness of a new and tenderer kind. But she was more pliable under his hands than a mere companionship would have made her, owing to her unavoidable dependence upon his mother, and, through that lady's comparative helplessness, upon him.

She soon found that whistling to the bullfinches in Mrs. d'Urberville's room was no such onerous business when she had regained the art, for she had caught from her musical mother numerous airs that suited those songsters admirably. A far more satisfactory time than when she practised in the garden was this whistling by the cages each morning. Unrestrained by the young man's presence she threw up her mouth, put her lips near the bars, and piped away in easeful grace to the attentive listeners.

Mrs. d'Urberville slept in a large four-post bedstead hung with heavy damask curtains, and the bullfinches occupied the same apartment, where they flitted about freely at certain hours, and made little white spots on the furniture and upholstery. Once while Tess was at the window where the cages were ranged, giving her lesson as usual, she thought she heard a rustling behind the bed. The old lady was not present, and turning round the girl had an impression that the toes of a pair of boots were visible below the fringe of the curtains. Thereupon her whistling became so disjointed that the listener, if such there were, must have discovered her suspicion of his presence. She searched the curtains every morning after that, but never found anybody within them. Alec d'Urberville had evidently thought better of his freak to terrify her by an ambush of that kind.[6]

X

Every village has its idiosyncrasy, its constitution, often its own code of morality. The levity of some of the younger women in and about Trantridge was marked, and was perhaps symptomatic of the choice spirit who ruled The Slopes in that vicinity. The place had also a more abiding defect; it drank hard. The staple conversation on the

6. In the serial version of the novel, published in the *National Graphic* magazine before the book appeared (for details see pp. 364-65), the last two paragraphs of this chapter and all of the next two chapters were omitted, except for a few sentences at the end of Chapter XI. [W]

farms around was on the uselessness of saving money; and smock-frocked arithmeticians, leaning on their ploughs or hoes, would enter into calculations of great nicety to prove that parish relief was a fuller provision for a man in his old age than any which could result from savings out of their wages during a whole lifetime.

The chief pleasure of these philosophers lay in going every Saturday night, when work was done, to Chaseborough, a decayed market-town two or three miles distant; and, returning in the small hours of the next morning, to spend Sunday in sleeping off the dyspeptic effects of the curious compounds sold to them as beer by the monopolizers of the once independent inns.

For a long time Tess did not join in the weekly pilgrimages. But under pressure from matrons not much older than herself—for a field-man's wages being as high at twenty-one as at forty, marriage was early here—Tess at length consented to go. Her first experience of the journey afforded her more enjoyment than she had expected, the hilariousness of the others being quite contagious after her monotonous attention to the poultry-farm all the week. She went again and again. Being graceful and interesting,. standing moreover on the momentary threshold of womanhood, her appearance drew down upon her some sly regards from loungers in the streets of Chaseborough; hence, though sometimes her journey to the town was made independently, she always searched for her fellows at nightfall, to have the protection of their companionship homeward.

This had gone on for a month or two when there came a Saturday in September, on which a fair and a market coincided; and the pilgrims from Trantridge sought double delights at the inns on that account.[7] Tess's occupations made her late in setting out, so that her comrades reached the town long before her. It was a fine September evening, just before sunset, when yellow lights struggle with blue shades in hair-like lines, and the atmosphere itself forms a prospect without aid from more solid objects, except the innumerable winged insects that dance in it. Through this low-lit mistiness Tess walked leisurely along.

She did not discover the coincidence of the market with the fair till she had reached the place, by which time it was close upon dusk. Her limited marketing was soon completed; and then as usual she began to look about for some of the Trantridge cottagers.

At first she could not find them, and she was informed that most of them had gone to what they called a private little jig at the house of a hay-trusser and peat-dealer who had transactions with their farm. He lived in an out-of-the-way nook of the townlet, and in try-

<hr />

7. The following episode, the dance at the hay-trusser's, though in the original MS., was omitted from the novel until the Wessex Edition appeared in 1912. See Hardy's Preface, p. 4.

ing to find her course thither her eyes fell upon Mr. d'Urberville standing at a street corner.

'What—my Beauty? You here so late?' he said.

She told him that she was simply waiting for company homeward.

'I'll see you again,' said he over her shoulder as she went on down the back lane.

Approaching the hay-trussers she could hear the fiddled notes of a reel proceeding from some building in the rear; but no sound of dancing was audible—an exceptional state of things for these parts, where as a rule the stamping drowned the music. The front door being open she could see straight through the house into the garden at the back as far as the shades of night would allow; and nobody appearing to her knock she traversed the dwelling and went up the path to the outhouse whence the sound had attracted her.

It was a windowless erection used for storage, and from the open door there floated into the obscurity a mist of yellow radiance, which at first Tess thought to be illuminated smoke. But on drawing nearer she perceived that it was a cloud of dust, lit by candles within the outhouse, whose beams upon the haze carried forward the outline of the doorway into the wide night of the garden.

When she came close and looked in she beheld indistinct forms racing up and down to the figure of the dance, the silence of their footfalls arising from their being overshoe in 'scroff'—that is to say, the powdery residuum from the storage of peat and other products, the stirring of which by their turbulent feet created the nebulosity that involved the scene. Through this floating, fusty *débris* of peat and hay, mixed with the perspirations and warmth of the dancers, and forming together a sort of vegeto-human pollen, the muted fiddles feebly pushed their notes, in marked contrast to the spirit with which the measure was trodden out. They coughed as they danced, and laughed as they coughed. Of the rushing couples there could barely be discerned more than the high lights—the indistinctness shaping them to satyrs clasping nymphs—a multiplicity of Pans whirling a multiplicity of Syrinxes; Lotis attempting to elude Priapus,[8] and always failing.

At intervals a couple would approach the doorway for air, and the haze no longer veiling their features, the demigods resolved themselves into the homely personalities of her own next-door neighbours. Could Trantridge in two or three short hours have metamorphosed itself thus madly!

---

8. Syrinx, a nymph pursued by Pan, turned into an armful of reeds when she was caught. Lotis, another nymph, in a similar situation turned into a lotus plant. Priapus, a Roman god of male generative power, was worshipped in orgiastic rites. "Sileni" (below): plural of Silenus, the name of a son of Pan who became a fat old satyr, fond of drink.

Some Sileni of the throng sat on benches and hay-trusses by the wall; and one of them recognized her.

'The maids don't think it respectable to dance at "The Flower-de-Luce," ' he explained. 'They don't like to let everybody see which be their fancy-men. Besides, the house sometimes shuts up just when their jints begin to get greased. So we come here and send out for liquor.'

'But when be any of you going home?' asked Tess with some anxiety.

'Now—a'most directly. This is all but the last jig.'

She waited. The reel drew to a close, and some of the party were in the mind for starting. But others would not, and another dance was formed. This surely would end it, thought Tess. But it merged in yet another. She became restless and uneasy; yet, having waited so long, it was necessary to wait longer; on account of the fair the roads were dotted with roving characters of possibly ill intent; and, though not fearful of measurable dangers, she feared the unknown. Had she been near Marlott she would have had less dread.

'Don't ye be nervous, my dear good soul,' expostulated, between his coughs, a young man with a wet face, and his straw hat so far back upon his head that the brim encircled it like the nimbus of a saint. 'What's yer hurry? To-morrow is Sunday, thank God, and we can sleep it off in church-time. Now, have a turn with me?'

She did not abhor dancing, but she was not going to dance here. The movement grew more passionate: the fiddlers behind the luminous pillar of cloud now and then varied the air by playing on the wrong side of the bridge or with the back of the bow. But it did not matter; the panting shapes spun onwards.

They did not vary their partners if their inclination were to stick to previous ones. Changing partners simply meant that a satisfactory choice had not as yet been arrived at by one or other of the pair, and by this time every couple had been suitably matched. It was then that the ecstasy and the dream began, in which emotion was the matter of the universe, and matter but an adventitious intrusion likely to hinder you from spinning where you wanted to spin.

Suddenly there was a dull thump on the ground: a couple had fallen, and lay in a mixed heap. The next couple, unable to check its progress, came toppling over the obstacle. An inner cloud of dust rose around the prostrate figures amid the general one of the room, in which a twitching entanglement of arms and legs was discernible.

'You shall catch it for this, my gentleman, when you get home!' burst in female accents from the human heap—those of the unhappy partner of the man whose clumsiness had caused the mishap; she happened also to be his recently married wife, in which assortment there was nothing unusual at Trantridge as long as any affection remained between wedded couples; and, indeed, it was not uncustomary in their later lives, to avoid making odd lots of the single people between whom there might be a warm understanding.

A loud laugh from behind Tess's back, in the shade of the garden, united with the titter within the room. She looked round, and saw the red coal of a cigar: Alec d'Uberville was standing there alone. He beckoned to her, and she reluctantly retreated towards him.

'Well, my Beauty, what are you doing here?'

She was so tired after her long day and her walk that she confided her trouble to him—that she had been waiting ever since he saw her to have their company home, because the road at night was strange to her. 'But it seems they will never leave off, and I really think I will wait no longer.'

'Certainly do not. I have only a saddle-horse here to-day; but come to "The Flower-de-Luce," and I'll hire a trap, and drive you home with me.'

Tess, though flattered, had never quite got over her original mistrust of him, and, despite their tardiness, she preferred to walk home with the work-fòlk. So she answered that she was much obliged to him, but would not trouble him. 'I have said that I will wait for 'em, and they will expect me to now.'

'Very well, Miss Independence. Please yourself. . . . Then I shall not hurry . . . My good Lord, what a kick-up they are having there!'

He had not put himself forward into the light, but some of them had perceived him, and his presence led to a slight pause and a consideration of how the time was flying. As soon as he had re-lit a cigar and walked away the Trantridge people began to collect themselves from amid those who had come in from other farms, and prepared to leave in a body. Their bundles and baskets were gathered up, and half an hour later, when the clock-chime sounded a quarter past eleven, they were straggling along the lane which led up the hill towards their homes.

It was a three-mile walk, along a dry white road, made whiter to-night by the light of the moon.

Tess soon perceived as she walked in the flock, sometimes with this one, sometimes with that, that the fresh night air was producing staggerings and serpentine courses among the men who had partaken too freely; some of the more careless women also were wandering in their gait—to wit, a dark virago, Car Darch, dubbed Queen of Spades, till lately a favourite of d'Urberville's; Nancy, her sister, nicknamed the Queen of Diamonds; and the young married woman who had already tumbled down. Yet however terrestrial and lumpy their appearance just now to the mean unglamoured eye, to themselves the case was different. They followed the road with a sensa-

tion that they were soaring along in a supporting medium, possessed of original and profound thoughts, themselves and surrounding
nature forming an organism of which all the parts harmoniously
and joyously interpenetrated each other. They were as sublime as
the moon and stars above them, and the moon and stars were as ardent as they.

Tess, however, had undergone such painful experiences of this
kind in her father's house, that the discovery of their condition spoilt the pleasure she was beginning to feel in the moonlight
journey. Yet she stuck to the party, for reasons above given.

In the open highway they had progressed in scattered order; but
now their route was through a field-gate, and the foremost finding
a difficulty in opening it they closed up together.

This leading pedestrian was Car the Queen of Spades, who carried a wicker-basket containing her mother's groceries, her own
draperies, and other purchases for the week. The basket being large
and heavy, Car had placed it for convenience of porterage on the
top of her head, where it rode on in jeopardized balance as she walked with arms akimbo.

'Well—whatever is that a-creeping down thy back, Car Darch?'
said one of the group suddenly.

All looked at Car. Her gown was a light cotton print, and from
the back of her head a kind of rope could be seen descending to some
distance below her waist, like a Chinaman's queue.

' 'Tis her hair falling down,' said another.

No; it was not her hair: it was a black stream of something oozing
from her basket, and it glistened like a slimy snake in the cold still
rays of the moon.

' 'Tis treacle,' said an observant matron.

Treacle it was. Car's poor old grandmother had a weakness for
the sweet stuff. Honey she had in plenty out of her own hives, but
treacle was what her soul desired, and Car had been about to give
her a treat of surprise. Hastily lowering the basket the dark girl found
that the vessel containing the syrup had been smashed within.

By this time there had arisen a shout of laughter at the extraordinary appearance of Car's back, which irritated the dark queen
into getting rid of the disfigurement by the first sudden means available, and independently of the help of the scoffers. She rushed ex-
citedly into the field they were about to cross, and flinging herself flat
on her back upon the grass, began to wipe her gown as well as she
could by spinning horizontally on the herbage and dragging herself
over it upon her elbows.

The laughter rang louder; they clung to the gate, to the posts,
rested on their staves, in the weakness engendered by their convul-
sions at the spectacle of Car. Our heroine, who had hitherto held

her peace, at this wild moment could not help joining in with the rest.

It was a misfortune—in more ways than one. No sooner did the dark queen hear the soberer richer note of Tess among those of the other work-people than a long smouldering sense of rivalry inflamed her to madness. She sprang to her feet and closely faced the object of her dislike.

'How darest th' laugh at me, hussy!' she cried.

'I couldn't really help it when t'others did,' apologized Tess, still tittering.

'Ah, th'st think th' beest everybody, dostn't, because th' beest first favourite with He just now! But stop a bit, my lady, stop a bit! I'm as good as two of such! Look here—here's at 'ee!'

To Tess's horror the dark queen began stripping off the bodice of her gown—which for the added reason of its ridiculed condition she was only too glad to be free of—till she had bared her plump neck, shoulders, and arms to the moonshine, under which they looked as luminous and beautiful as some Praxitelean[9] creation, in their possession of the faultless rotundities of a lusty country girl. She closed her fists and squared up at Tess.

'Indeed, then, I shall not fight!' said the latter majestically; 'and if I had known you was of that sort, I wouldn't have so let myself down as to come with such a whorage as this is!'

The rather too inclusive speech brought down a torrent of vituperation from other quarters upon fair Tess's unlucky head, particularly from the Queen of Diamonds, who having stood in the relations to d'Urberville that Car had also been suspected of, united with the latter against the common enemy. Several other women also chimed in, with an animus which none of them would have been so fatuous as to show but for the rollicking evening they had passed. Thereupon, finding Tess unfairly browbeaten, the husbands and lovers tried to make peace by defending her; but the result of that attempt was directly to increase the war.

Tess was indignant and ashamed. She no longer minded the loneliness of the way and the lateness of the hour; her one object was to get away from the whole crew as soon as possible. She knew well enough that the better among them would repent of their passion next day. They were all now inside the field, and she was edging back to rush off alone when a horseman emerged almost silently from the corner of the hedge that screened the road, and Alec d'Urberville looked round upon them.

'What the devil is all this row about, work-folk?' he asked.

The explanation was not readily forthcoming; and, in truth, he did not require any. Having heard their voices while yet some way

9. Praxiteles was a Greek sculptor of the fourth century B.C.

off he had ridden creepingly forward, and learnt enough to satisfy himself.

Tess was standing apart from the rest, near the gate. He bent over towards her. 'Jump up behind me,' he whispered, 'and we'll get shot of the screaming cats in a jiffy!'

She felt almost ready to faint, so vivid was her sense of the crisis. At almost any other moment of her life she would have refused such proffered aid and company, as she had refused them several times before; and now the loneliness would not of itself have forced her to do otherwise. But coming as the invitation did at the particular juncture when fear and indignation at these adversaries could be transformed by a spring of the foot into a triumph over them, she abandoned herself to her impulse, climbed the gate, put her toe upon his instep, and scrambled into the saddle behind him. The pair were speeding away into the distant gray by the time that the contentious revellers became aware of what had happened.

The Queen of Spades forgot the stain on her bodice, and stood beside the Queen of Diamonds and the new-married, staggering young woman—all with a gaze of fixity in the direction in which the horse's tramp was diminishing into silence on the road.

'What be ye looking at?' asked a man who had not observed the incident.

'Ho-ho-ho!' laughed dark Car.

'Hee-hee-hee!' laughed the tippling bride, as she steadied herself on the arm of her fond husband.

'Heu-heu-heu!' laughed dark Car's mother, stroking her moustache as she explained laconically: 'Out of the frying-pan into the fire!'

Then these children of the open air, whom even excess of alcohol could scarce injure permanently, betook themselves to the field-path; and as they went there moved onward with them, around the shadow of each one's head, a circle of opalized light, formed by the moon's rays upon the glistening sheet of dew. Each pedestrian could see no halo but his or her own, which never deserted the head-shadow, whatever its vulgar unsteadiness might be; but adhered to it, and persistently beautified it; till the erratic motions seemed an inherent part of the irradiation, and the fumes of their breathing a component of the night's mist; and the spirit of the scene, and of the moonlight, and of Nature, seemed harmoniously to mingle with the spirit of wine.

XI

The twain cantered along for some time without speech, Tess as she clung to him still panting in her triumph, yet in other respects dubious. She had perceived that the horse was not the spirited one he sometimes rode, and felt no alarm on that score, though her seat was precarious enough despite her tight hold of him. She begged him to slow the animal to a walk, which Alec accordingly did.

'Neatly done, was it not, dear Tess?' he said by and by.

'Yes!' said she. 'I am sure I ought to be much obliged to you.'

'And are you?'

She did not reply.

'Tess, why do you always dislike my kissing you?'

'I suppose——because I don't love you.'

'You are quite sure?'

'I am angry with you sometimes!'

'Ah, I half feared as much.' Nevertheless, Alec did not object to that confession. He knew that anything was better than frigidity. 'Why haven't you told me when I have made you angry?'

'You know very well why. Because I cannot help myself here.'

'I haven't offended you often by love-making?'

'You have sometimes.'

'How many times?'

'You know as well as I—too many times.'

'Every time I have tried?'

She was silent, and the horse ambled along for a considerable distance, till a faint luminous fog, which had hung in the hollows all the evening, became general and enveloped them. It seemed to hold the moonlight in suspension, rendering it more pervasive than in clear air. Whether on this account, or from absent-mindedness, or from sleepiness, she did not perceive that they had long ago passed the point at which the lane to Trantridge branched from the highway, and that her conductor had not taken the Trantridge track.

She was inexpressibly weary. She had risen at five o'clock every morning of that week, had been on foot the whole of each day, and on this evening had in addition walked the three miles to Chaseborough, waited three hours for her neighbours without eating or drinking, her impatience to start them preventing either; she had then walked a mile of the way home, and had undergone the excitement of the quarrel, till, with the slow progress of their steed, it was now nearly one o'clock. Only once, however, was she overcome by actual drowsiness. In that moment of oblivion her head sank gently against him.

D'Urberville stopped the horse, withdrew his feet from the stirrups, turned sideways on the saddle, and enclosed her waist with his arm to support her.

This immediately put her on the defensive, and with one of those sudden impulses of reprisal to which she was liable she gave him a little push from her. In his ticklish position he nearly lost his balance and only just avoided rolling over into the road, the horse, though a powerful one, being fortunately the quietest he rode.

'That is devilish unkind!' he said. 'I mean no harm—only to keep you from falling.'

She pondered suspiciously; till, thinking that this might after all be true, she relented, and said quite humbly, 'I beg your pardon, sir.'

'I won't pardon you unless you show some confidence in me. Good God!' he burst out, 'what am I, to be repulsed so by a mere chit like you? For near three mortal months have you trifled with my feelings, eluded me, and snubbed me; and I won't stand it!'

'I'll leave you to-morrow, sir.'

'No, you will not leave me to-morrow! Will you, I ask once more, show your belief in me by letting me clasp you with my arm? Come, between us two and nobody else, now. We know each other well; and you know that I love you, and think you the prettiest girl in the world, which you are. Mayn't I treat you as a lover?'

She drew a quick pettish breath of objection, writhing uneasily on her seat, looked far ahead, and murmured, 'I don't know—I wish —how can I say yes or no when——'

He settled the matter by clasping his arm round her as he desired, and Tess expressed no further negative. Thus they sidled slowly onward till it struck her they had been advancing for an unconscionable time—far longer than was usually occupied by the short journey from Chaseborough, even at this walking pace, and that they were no longer on hard road, but in a mere trackway.

'Why, where be we?' she exclaimed.

'Passing by a wood.'

'A wood—what wood? Surely we are quite out of the road?'

'A bit of The Chase—the oldest wood in England. It is a lovely night, and why should we not prolong our ride a little?'

'How could you be so treacherous!' said Tess, between archness and real dismay, and getting rid of his arm by pulling open his fingers one by one, though at the risk of slipping off herself. 'Just when I've been putting such trust in you, and obliging you to please you, because I thought I had wronged you by that push! Please set me down, and let me walk home.'

'You cannot walk home, darling, even if the air were clear. We are miles away from Trantridge, if I must tell you, and in this growing fog you might wander for hours among these trees.'

'Never mind that,' she coaxed. 'Put me down, I beg you. I don't mind where it is; only let me get down, sir, please!'

'Very well, then, I will—on one condition. Having brought you here to this out-of-the-way place, I feel myself responsible for your safe-conduct home, whatever you may yourself feel about it. As to your getting to Trantridge without assistance, it is quite impossible; for, to tell the truth, dear, owing to this fog, which so disguises everything, I don't quite know where we are myself. Now, if you will promise to wait beside the horse while I walk through the bushes till I come to some road or house, and ascertain exactly our whereabouts, I'll deposit you here willingly. When I come back I'll give you full directions, and if you insist upon walking you may; or you may ride—at your pleasure.'

She accepted these terms, and slid off on the near side, though not till he had stolen a cursory kiss. He sprang down on the other side.

'I suppose I must hold the horse?' said she.

'Oh no; it's not necessary,' replied Alec, patting the panting creature. 'He's had enough of it for to-night.'

He turned the horse's head into the bushes, hitched him on to a bough, and made a sort of couch or nest for her in the deep mass of dead leaves.

'Now, you sit there,' he said. 'The leaves have not got damp as yet. Just give an eye to the horse—it will be quite sufficient.'

He took a few steps away from her, but, returning, said, 'By the bye, Tess, your father has a new cob to-day. Somebody gave it to him.'

'Somebody? You!'

D'Urberville nodded.

'O how very good of you that is!' she exclaimed, with a painful sense of the awkwardness of having to thank him just then.

'And the children have some toys.'

'I didn't know—you ever sent them anything!' she murmured, much moved. 'I almost wish you had not—yes, I almost wish it!'

'Why, dear?'

'It—hampers me so.'

'Tessy—don't you love me ever so little now?'

'I'm grateful,' she reluctantly admitted. 'But I fear I do not——' The sudden vision of his passion for herself as a factor in this result so distressed her that, beginning with one slow tear, and then following with another, she wept outright.

'Don't cry, dear, dear one! Now sit down here, and wait till I come.' She passively sat down amid the leaves he had heaped, and shivered slightly. 'Are you cold?' he asked.

'Not very—a little.'

He touched her with his fingers, which sank into her as into down. 'You have only that puffy muslin dress on—how's that?'

'It's my best summer one. 'Twas very warm when I started, and I didn't know I was going to ride, and that it would be night.'

'Nights grow chilly in September. Let me see.' He pulled off a light overcoat that he had worn, and put it round her tenderly. 'That's it—now you'll feel warmer,' he continued. 'Now, my pretty, rest there; I shall soon be back again.'

Having buttoned the overcoat round her shoulders he plunged into the webs of vapour which by this time formed veils between the trees. She could hear the rustling of the branches as he ascended the adjoining slope, till his movements were no louder than the hopping of a bird, and finally died away. With the setting of the moon the pale light lessened, and Tess became invisible as she fell into reverie upon the leaves where he had left her.

In the meantime Alec d'Urberville had pushed on up the slope to clear his genuine doubt as to the quarter of The Chase they were in. He had, in fact, ridden quite at random for over an hour, taking any turning that came to hand in order to prolong companionship with her, and giving far more attention to Tess's moonlit person than to any wayside object. A little rest for the jaded animal being desirable, he did not hasten his search for landmarks. A clamber over the hill into the adjoining vale brought him to the fence of a highway whose contours he recognized, which settled the question of their whereabouts. D'Urberville thereupon turned back; but by this time the moon had quite gone down, and partly on account of the fog The Chase was wrapped in thick darkness, although morning was not far off. He was obliged to advance with outstretched hands to avoid contact with the boughs, and discovered that to hit the exact spot from which he had started was at first entirely beyond him. Roaming up and down, round and round, he at length heard a slight movement of the horse close at hand; and the sleeve of his overcoat unexpectedly caught his foot.

'Tess!' said d'Urberville.

There was no answer. The obscurity was now so great that he could see absolutely nothing but a pale nebulousness at his feet, which represented the white muslin figure he had left upon the dead leaves. Everything else was blackness alike. D'Urberville stooped; and heard a gentle regular breathing. He knelt and bent lower, till her breath warmed his face, and in a moment his cheek was in contact with hers. She was sleeping soundly, and upon her eyelashes there lingered tears.

Darkness and silence ruled everywhere around. Above them rose the primeval yews and oaks of The Chase, in which were poised gentle roosting birds in their last nap; and about them stole the hopping rabbits and hares. But, might some say, where was Tess's guardian angel? where was the providence of her simple faith? Perhaps, like that other god of whom the ironical Tishbite spoke, he was talking, or he was pursuing, or he was in a journey, or he was sleeping and not to be awaked.[1]

Why it was that upon this beautiful feminine tissue, sensitive as

1. I Kings xviii:27: "Elijah mocked them, and said, Cry aloud: for he is a god; either he is talking, or he is pursuing, or he is in a journey, or peradventure he sleepeth, and must be awaked."

gossamer, and practically blank as snow as yet, there should have been traced such a coarse pattern as it was doomed to receive; why so often the coarse appropriates the finer thus, the wrong man the woman, the wrong woman the man, many thousand years of analytical philosophy have failed to explain to our sense of order. One may, indeed, admit the possibility of a retribution lurking in the present catastrophe. Doubtless some of Tess d'Urberville's mailed ancestors rollicking home from a fray had dealt the same measure even more ruthlessly towards peasant girls of their time. But though to visit the sins of the fathers upon the children may be a morality good enough for divinities,[2] it is scorned by average human nature; and it therefore does not mend the matter.

As Tess's own people down in those retreats are never tired of saying among each other in their fatalistic way: 'It was to be.' There lay the pity of it. An immeasurable social chasm was to divide our heroine's personality thereafter from that previous self of hers who stepped from her mother's door to try her fortune at Trantridge poultry-farm.

END OF PHASE THE FIRST

Phase the Second—Maiden No More

XII

The basket was heavy and the bundle was large, but she lugged them along like a person who did not find her especial burden in material things. Occasionally she stopped to rest in a mechanical way by some gate or post; and then, giving the baggage another hitch upon her full round arm, went steadily on again.

It was a Sunday morning in late October, about four months after Tess Durbeyfield's arrival at Trantridge, and some few weeks subsequent to the night ride in The Chase. The time was not long past daybreak, and the yellow luminosity upon the horizon behind her back lighted the ridge towards which her face was set—the barrier of the vale wherein she had of late been a stranger—which she would have to climb over to reach her birthplace. The ascent was gradual on this side, and the soil and scenery differed much from those within Blakemore Vale. Even the character and accent of the two peoples had shades of difference, despite the amalgamating effects of a roundabout railway; so that, though less than twenty miles from the place of her sojourn at Trantridge, her native village had

2. **Exodus xx:5:** "I the Lord thy God am a jealous God, visiting the iniquity of the fathers upon the children unto the third and fourth generation of them that hate me."

seemed a far-away spot. The field-folk shut in there traded north-ward and westward, travelled, courted, and married northward and westward, thought northward and westward; those on this side main-ly directed their energies and attention to the east and south.

The incline was the same down which d'Urberville had driven with her so wildly on that day in June. Tess went up the remainder of its length without stopping, and on reaching the edge of the es-carpment gazed over the familiar green world beyond, now half-veiled in mist. It was always beautiful from here; it was terribly beautiful to Tess to-day, for since her eyes last fell upon it she had learnt that the serpent hisses where the sweet birds sing, and her views of life had been totally changed for her by the lesson. Verily another girl than the simple one she had been at home was she who, bowed by the thought, stood still here, and turned to look behind her. She could not bear to look forward into the Vale.

Ascending by the long white road that Tess herself had just la-boured up, she saw a two-wheeled vehicle, beside which walked a man, who held up his hand to attract her attention.

She obeyed the signal to wait for him with unspeculative repose, and in a few minutes man and horse stopped beside her.

'Why did you slip away by stealth like this?' said d'Urberville, with upbraiding breathlessness; 'on a Sunday morning, too, when people were all in bed! I only discovered it by accident, and I have been driving like the deuce to overtake you. Just look at the mare. Why go off like this? You know that nobody wished to hinder your going. And how unnecessary it has been for you to toil along on foot, and encumber yourself with this heavy load! I have followed like a mad-man, simply to drive you the rest of the distance, if you won't come back.'

'I shan't come back,' said she.

'I thought you wouldn't—I said so! Well, then, put up your bas-kets, and let me help you on.'

She listlessly placed her basket and bundle within the dog-cart, and stepped up, and they sat side by side. She had no fear of him now, and in the cause of her confidence her sorrow lay.

D'Urberville mechanically lit a cigar, and the journey was con-tinued with broken unemotional conversation on the commonplace objects by the wayside. He had quite forgotten his struggle to kiss her when, in the early summer, they had driven in the opposite di-rection along the same road. But she had not, and she sat now, like a puppet, replying to his remarks in monosyllables. After some miles they came in view of the clump of trees beyond which the village of Marlott stood. It was only then that her still face showed the least emotion, a tear or two beginning to trickle down.

'What are you crying for?' he coldly asked.

'I was only thinking that I was born over there,' murmured Tess.

'Well—we must all be born somewhere.'

'I wish I had never been born—there or anywhere else!'

'Pooh! Well, if you didn't wish to come to Trantridge why did you come?'

She did not reply.

'You didn't come for love of me, that I'll swear.'

' 'Tis quite true. If I had gone for love o' you, if I had ever sincerely loved you, if I loved you still, I should not so loathe and hate myself for my weakness as I do now! . . . My eyes were dazed by you for a little, and that was all.'

He shrugged his shoulders. She resumed—

'I didn't understand your meaning till it was too late.'

'That's what every woman says.'

'How can you dare to use such words!' she cried, turning impetuously upon him, her eyes flashing as the latent spirit (of which he was to see more some day) awoke in her. 'My God! I could knock you out of the gig! Did it never strike your mind that what every woman says some women may feel?'

'Very well,' he said, laughing; 'I am sorry to wound you. I did wrong—I admit it.' He dropped into some little bitterness as he continued: 'Only you needn't be so everlastingly flinging it in my face. I am ready to pay to the uttermost farthing. You know you need not work in the fields or the dairies again. You know you may clothe yourself with the best, instead of in the bald plain way you have lately affected, as if you couldn't get a ribbon more than you earn.'

Her lip lifted slightly, though there was little scorn, as a rule, in her large and impulsive nature.

'I have said I will not take anything more from you, and I will not—I cannot! I *should* be your creature to go on doing that, and I won't!'

'One would think you were a princess from your manner, in addition to a true and original d'Urberville—ha! ha! Well, Tess, dear, I can say no more. I suppose I am a bad fellow—a damn bad fellow. I was born bad, and I have lived bad, and I shall die bad in all probability. But, upon my lost soul, I won't be bad towards you again, Tess. And if certain circumstances should arise—you understand—in which you are in the least need, the least difficulty, send me one line, and you shall have by return whatever you require. I may not be at Trantridge—I am going to London for a time—I can't stand the old woman. But all letters will be forwarded.'

She said that she did not wish him to drive her further, and they stopped just under the clump of trees. D'Urberville alighted, and lifted her down bodily in his arms, afterwards placing her articles on the ground beside her. She bowed to him slightly, her eye just lingering in his; and then she turned to take the parcels for departure.

Alec d'Urberville removed his cigar, bent towards her, and said—

'You are not going to turn away like that, dear? Come!'

'If you wish,' she answered indifferently. 'See how you've mastered me!'

She thereupon turned round and lifted her face to his, and remained like a marble term[3] while he imprinted a kiss upon her cheek —half perfunctorily, half as if zest had not yet quite died out. Her eyes vaguely rested upon the remotest trees in the lane while the kiss was given, as though she were nearly unconscious of what he did.

'Now the other side, for old acquaintance' sake.'

She turned her head in the same passive way, as one might turn at the request of a sketcher or hairdresser, and he kissed the other side, his lips touching cheeks that were damp and smoothly chill as the skin of the mushrooms in the fields around.

'You don't give me your mouth and kiss me back. You never willingly do that—you'll never love me, I fear.'

'I have said so, often. It is true. I have never really and truly loved you, and I think I never can.' She added mournfully, 'Perhaps, of all things, a lie on this thing would do the most good to me now; but I have honour enough left, little as 'tis, not to tell that lie. If I did love you I may have the best o' causes for letting you know it. But I don't.'

He emitted a laboured breath, as if the scene were getting rather oppressive to his heart, or to his conscience, or to his gentility.

'Well, you are absurdly melancholy, Tess. I have no reason for flattering you now, and I can say plainly that you need not be so sad. You can hold your own for beauty against any woman of these parts, gentle or simple; I say it to you as a practical man and well-wisher. If you are wise you will show it to the world more than you do before it fades. . . . And yet, Tess, will you come back to me? Upon my soul I don't like to let you go like this!'

'Never, never! I made up my mind as soon as I saw—what I ought to have seen sooner; and I won't come.'

'Then good morning, my four months' cousin—good-bye!'

He leapt up lightly, arranged the reins, and was gone between the tall red-berried hedges.

Tess did not look after him, but slowly wound along the crooked lane. It was still early, and though the sun's lower limb was just free

3. "*Arch.* A statue or bust like those of the god Terminus, representing the upper part of the body, sometimes without the arms, and terminating below in a pillar." [*OED*]

of the hill, his rays, ungenial and peering, addressed the eye rather than the touch as yet. There was not a human soul near. Sad October and her sadder self seemed the only two existences haunting that lane.

As she walked, however, some footsteps approached behind her, the footsteps of a man;[4] and owing to the briskness of his advance he was close at her heels and had said 'Good morning' before she had been long aware of his propinquity. He appeared to be an artisan of some sort, and carried a tin pot of red paint in his hand. He asked in a business-like manner if he should take her basket, which she permitted him to do, walking beside him.

'It is early to be astir this Sabbath morn!' he said cheerfully.

'Yes,' said Tess.

'When most people are at rest from their week's work.'

She also assented to this.

'Though I do more real work to-day than all the week besides.'

'Do you?'

'All the week I work for the glory of man, and on Sunday for the glory of God. That's more real than the other—hey? I have a little to do here at this stile.' The man turned as he spoke to an opening at the roadside leading into a pasture. 'If you'll wait a moment,' he added, 'I shall not be long.'

As he had her basket she could not well do otherwise; and she waited, observing him. He set down her basket and the tin pot, and stirring the paint with the brush that was in it began painting large square letters on the middle board of the three composing the stile, placing a comma after each word, as if to give pause while that word was driven well home to the reader's heart—

THY, DAMNATION, SLUMBERETH, NOT.
2 PET. ii. 3.

Against the peaceful landscape, the pale, decaying tints of the copses, the blue air of the horizon, and the lichened stile-boards, these staring vermilion words shone forth. They seemed to shout themselves out and make the atmosphere ring. Some people might have cried 'Alas, poor Theology!' at the hideous defacement—the last grotesque phase of a creed which had served mankind well in its time. But the words entered Tess with accusatory horror. It was as if this man had known her recent history; yet he was a total stranger.

Having finished his text he picked up her basket, and she mechanically resumed her walk beside him.

'Do you believe what you paint?' she asked in low tones.

'Believe that tex? Do I believe in my own existence!'

4. The episode of the text-painter was omitted in the serial version. [W]

'But,' said she tremulously, 'suppose your sin was not of your own seeking?'

He shook his head.

'I cannot split hairs on that burning query,' he said. 'I have walked hundreds of miles this past summer, painting these texes on every wall, gate, and stile in the length and breadth of this district. I leave their application to the hearts of the people who read 'em.'

'I think they are horrible,' said Tess. 'Crushing! killing!'

'That's what they are meant to be!' he replied in a trade voice. 'But you should read my hottest ones—them I kips for slums and seaports. They'd make ye wriggle! Not but what this is a very good tex for rural districts. . . . Ah—there's a nice bit of blank wall up by that barn standing to waste. I must put one there—one that it will be good for dangerous young females like yerself to heed. Will ye wait, missy?'

'No,' said she; and taking her basket Tess trudged on. A little way forward she turned her head. The old gray wall began to advertise a similar fiery lettering to the first, with a strange and unwonted mien, as if distressed at duties it had never before been called upon to perform. It was with a sudden flush that she read and realized what was to be the inscription he was now half-way through—

THOU, SHALT, NOT, COMMIT——

Her cheerful friend saw her looking, stopped his brush, and shouted—

'If you want to ask for edification on these things of moment, there's a very earnest good man going to preach a charity-sermon to-day in the parish you are going to—Mr. Clare of Emminster. I'm not of his persuasion now, but he's a good man, and he'll expound as well as any parson I know. 'Twas he began the work in me.'

But Tess did not answer; she throbbingly resumed her walk, her eyes fixed on the ground. 'Pooh—I don't believe God said such things!' she murmured contemptuously when her flush had died away.

A plume of smoke soared up suddenly from her father's chimney, the sight of which made her heart ache. The aspect of the interior, when she reached it, made her heart ache more. Her mother, who had just come down stairs, turned to greet her from the fireplace, where she was kindling barked-oak twigs[5] under the breakfast kettle. The young children were still above, as was also her father, it being Sunday morning, when he felt justified in lying an additional half-hour.

---

5. Twigs of an oak killed by removing the bark, used for tanning.

'Well!—my dear Tess!' exclaimed her surprised mother, jump-ing up and kissing the girl. 'How be ye? I didn't see you till you was in upon me! Have you come home to be married?'

'No, I have not come for that, mother.'

'Then for a holiday?'

'Yes—for a holiday; for a long holiday,' said Tess.

'What, isn't your cousin going to do the handsome thing?'

'He's not my cousin, and he's not going to marry me.'

Her mother eyed her narrowly.

'Come, you have not told me all,' she said.

Then Tess went up to her mother, put her face upon Joan's neck, and told.[6]

'And yet th'st not got him to marry 'ee!' reiterated her mother. 'Any woman would have done it but you, after that!'

'Perhaps any woman would except me.'

'It would have been something like a story to come back with, if you had!' continued Mrs. Durbeyfield, ready to burst into tears of vexation. 'After all the talk about you and him which has reach-ed us here, who would have expected it to end like this! Why didn't ye think of doing some good for your family instead o' thinking only of yourself? See how I've got to teave[7] and slave, and your poor weak father with his heart clogged like a dripping-pan. I did hope for something to come out o' this! To see what a pretty pair you and he made that day when you drove away together four months ago! See what he has given us—all, as we thought, because we were his kin. But if he's not, it must have been done because of his love for 'ee. And yet you've not got him to marry!'

Get Alec d'Urberville in the mind to marry her! He marry *her*! On matrimony he had never once said a word. And what if he had? How a convulsive snatching at social salvation might have impelled her to answer him she could not say. But her poor foolish mother little knew her present feeling towards this man. Perhaps it was un-usual in the circumstances, unlucky, unaccountable; but there it was; and this, as she had said, was what made her detest herself. She had never wholly cared for him, she did not at all care for him now. She had dreaded him, winced before him, succumbed to adroit advan-tages he took of her helplessness; then, temporarily blinded by his ardent manners, had been stirred to confused surrender awhile: had suddenly despised and disliked him, and had run away. That was all. Hate him she did not quite; but he was dust and ashes[8] to her, and even for her name's sake she scarcely wished to marry him.

---

6. In the serial version, Tess's account (from here to the end of the chapter) was altered. In it Alec persuaded Tess to marry him, took her to a "private room" of a man he said was a registrar, and pre-tended to go through the form of marriage. A few weeks later Alec told Tess he had deceived her.

7. Toil.

8. Job xlii:6: "Wherefore I abhor my-self, and repent in dust and ashes."

'You ought to have been more careful if you didn't mean to get him to make you his wife!'

'O mother, my mother!' cried the agonized girl, turning passionately upon her parent as if her poor heart would break. 'How could I be expected to know? I was a child when I left this house four months ago. Why didn't you tell me there was danger in men-folk? Why didn't you warn me? Ladies know what to fend hands[9] against, because they read novels that tell them of these tricks; but I never had the chance o' learning in that way, and you did not help me!'

Her mother was subdued.

'I thought if I spoke of his fond feelings and what they might lead to, you would be hontish[1] wi' him and lose your chance,' she murmured, wiping her eyes with her apron. 'Well, we must make the best of it, I suppose. 'Tis nater, after all, and what do please God!'

XIII

The event of Tess Durbeyfield's return from the manor of her bogus kinsfolk was rumoured abroad, if rumour be not too large a word for a space of a square mile. In the afternoon several young girls of Marlott, former schoolfellows and acquaintances of Tess, called to see her, arriving dressed in their best starched and ironed, as became visitors to a person who had made a transcendent conquest (as they supposed), and sat round the room looking at her with great curiosity. For the fact that it was this said thirty-first cousin, Mr. d'Urberville, who had fallen in love with her, a gentleman not altogether local, whose reputation as a reckless gallant and heart-breaker was beginning to spread beyond the immediate boundaries of Trantridge, lent Tess's supposed position, by its fearsomeness, a far higher fascination than it would have exercised if unhazardous.

Their interest was so deep that the younger ones whispered when her back was turned—

'How pretty she is; and how that best frock do set her off! I believe it cost an immense deal, and that it was a gift from him.'

Tess, who was reaching up to get the tea-things from the corner-cupboard, did not hear these commentaries. If she had heard them, she might soon have set her friends right on the matter. But her mother heard, and Joan's simple vanity, having been denied the hope of a dashing marriage, fed itself as well as it could upon the sensation of a dashing flirtation. Upon the whole she felt gratified, even though such a limited and evanescent triumph should involve her daughter's reputation; it might end in marriage yet, and in the warmth of her responsiveness to their admiration she invited her visitors to stay to tea.

9. Guard.   1. Haughty.

Their chatter, their laughter, their good-humoured innuendoes, above all, their flashes and flickerings of envy, revived Tess's spirits also; and, as the evening wore on, she caught the infection of their excitement, and grew almost gay. The marble hardness left her face, she moved with something of her old bounding step, and flushed in all her young beauty.

At moments, in spite of thought, she would reply to their inquiries with a manner of superiority, as if recognizing that her experiences in the field of courtship had, indeed, been slightly enviable. But so far was she from being, in the words of Robert South,[2] 'in love with her own ruin,' that the illusion was transient as lightning; cold reason came back to mock her spasmodic weakness; the ghastliness of her momentary pride would convict her, and recall her to reserved listlessness again.

And the despondency of the next morning's dawn, when it was no longer Sunday, but Monday; and no best clothes; and the laughing visitors were gone, and she awoke alone in her old bed, the innocent younger children breathing softly around her. In place of the excitement of her return, and the interest it had inspired, she saw before her a long and stony highway which she had to tread, without aid, and with little sympathy. Her depression was then terrible, and she could have hidden herself in a tomb.

In the course of a few weeks Tess revived sufficiently to show herself so far as was necessary to get to church one Sunday morning. She liked to hear the chanting—such as it was—and the old Psalms, and to join in the Morning Hymn.[3] That innate love of melody, which she had inherited from her ballad-singing mother, gave the simplest music a power over her which could well-nigh drag her heart out of her bosom at times.

To be as much out of observation as possible for reasons of her own, and to escape the gallantries of the young men, she set out before the chiming began, and took a back seat under the gallery, close to the lumber,[4] where only old men and women came, and where the bier stood on end among the churchyard tools.

Parishioners dropped in by twos and threes, deposited themselves in rows before her, rested three-quarters of a minute on their foreheads as if they were praying, though they were not; then sat up, and looked around. When the chants came on one of her favourites happened to be chosen among the rest—the old double chant 'Langdon'[5]—but she did not know what it was

---

2. Whose *Sermons* (1692) were still widely read in Hardy's day.

3. "The hymn 'Awake, my soul, and with the sun . . .' by Bishop Thomas Ken, the words of which were first published in 1674." [F]

4. Miscellaneous stored objects, such as the "bier" and "churchyard tools."

5. A double chant is twice the length of the standard Anglican chant. Richard Langdon (1730-1803) was an English organist and composer.

called, though she would much have liked to know. She thought, without exactly wording the thought, how strange and godlike was a composer's power, who from the grave could lead through sequences of emotion, which he alone had felt at first, a girl like her who had never heard of his name, and never would have a clue to his personality.

The people who had turned their heads turned them again as the service proceeded; and at last observing her they whispered to each other. She knew what their whispers were about, grew sick at heart, and felt that she could come to church no more.

The bedroom which she shared with some of the children formed her retreat more continually than ever. Here, under her few square yards of thatch, she watched winds, and snows, and rains, gorgeous sunsets, and successive moons at their full. So close kept she that at length almost everybody thought she had gone away.

The only exercise that Tess took at this time was after dark; and it was then, when out in the woods, that she seemed least solitary. She knew how to hit to a hair's-breadth that moment of evening when the light and the darkness are so evenly balanced that the constraint of day and the suspense of night neutralize each other, leaving absolute mental liberty. It is then that the plight of being alive becomes attenuated to its least possible dimensions. She had no fear of the shadows; her sole idea seemed to be to shun mankind—or rather that cold accretion called the world, which, so terrible in the mass, is so unformidable, even pitiable, in its units.

On these lonely hills and dales her quiescent glide was of a piece with the element she moved in. Her flexuous and stealthy figure became an integral part of the scene. At times her whimsical fancy would intensify natural processes around her till they seemed a part of her own story. Rather they became a part of it; for the world is only a psychological phenomenon, and what they seemed they were. The midnight airs and gusts, moaning amongst the tightly-wrapped buds and bark of the winter twigs, were formulae of bitter reproach. A wet day was the expression of irremediable grief at the weakness in the mind of some vague ethical being whom she could not class definitely as the God of her childhood, and could not comprehend as any other.

But this encompassment of her own characterization, based on shreds of convention, peopled by phantoms and voices antipathetic to her, was a sorry and mistaken creation of Tess's fancy —a cloud of moral hobgoblins by which she was terrified without reason. It was they that were out of harmony with the actual world, not she. Walking among the sleeping birds in the hedges, watching the skipping rabbits on a moonlit warren, or standing under a pheasant-laden bough, she looked upon herself as a figure of Guilt intruding into the haunts of Innocence. But all the while she was making a distinction where there was no difference. Feeling herself in antagonism she was quite in accord. She had been made to break an accepted social law, but no law known to the environment in which she fancied herself such an anomaly.

XIV[6]

It was a hazy sunrise in August. The denser nocturnal vapours, attacked by the warm beams, were dividing and shrinking into isolated fleeces within hollows and coverts, where they waited till they should be dried away to nothing.

The sun, on account of the mist, had a curious sentient, personal look, demanding the masculine pronoun for its adequate expression. His present aspect, coupled with the lack of all human forms in the scene, explained the old-time heliolatries in a moment. One could feel that a saner religion had never prevailed under the sky. The luminary was a golden-haired, beaming, mild-eyed, God-like creature, gazing down in the vigour and intentness of youth upon an earth that was brimming with interest for him.

His light, a little later, broke through chinks of cottage shutters, throwing stripes like red-hot pokers upon cupboards, chests of drawers, and other furniture within; and awakening harvesters who were not already astir.

But of all ruddy things that morning the brightest were two broad arms of painted wood, which rose from the margin of a yellow cornfield hard by Marlott village. They, with two others below, formed the revolving Maltese cross of the reaping-machine, which had been brought to the field on the previous evening to be ready for operations this day. The paint with which they were smeared, intensified in hue by the sunlight, imparted to them a look of having been dipped in liquid fire.

The field had already been 'opened'; that is to say, a lane a few feet wide had been hand-cut through the wheat along the whole circumference of the field, for the first passage of the horses and machine.

Two groups, one of men and lads, the other of women, had come down the lane just at the hour when the shadows of the eastern hedge-top struck the west hedge midway, so that the heads of the groups were enjoying sunrise while their feet were still in the dawn. They disappeared from the lane between the two stone posts which flanked the nearest field-gate.

6. This chapter and all references to Tess's baby were omitted in the serial version. [W]

Presently there arose from within a ticking like the love-making of the grasshopper. The machine had begun, and a moving concatenation of three horses and the aforesaid long rickety machine was visible over the gate, a driver sitting upon one of the hauling horses, and an attendant on the seat of the implement. Along one side of the field the whole wain went, the arms of the mechanical reaper revolving slowly, till it passed down the hill quite out of sight. In a minute it came up on the other side of the field at the same equable pace; the glistening brass star in the forehead of the fore horse first catching the eye as it rose into view over the stubble, then the bright arms, and then the whole machine.

The narrow lane of stubble encompassing the field grew wider with each circuit, and the standing corn was reduced to smaller area as the morning wore on. Rabbits, hares, snakes, rats, mice, retreated inwards as into a fastness, unaware of the ephemeral nature of their refuge, and of the doom that awaited them later in the day when, their covert shrinking to a more and more horrible narrowness, they were huddled together, friends and foes, till the last few yards of upright wheat fell also under the teeth of the unerring reaper, and they were every one put to death by the sticks and stones of the harvesters.

The reaping-machine left the fallen corn behind it in little heaps, each heap being of the quantity for a sheaf; and upon these the active binders in the rear laid their hands—mainly women, but some of them men in print shirts, and trousers supported round their waists by leather straps, rendering useless the two buttons behind, which twinkled and bristled with sunbeams at every movement of each wearer, as if they were a pair of eyes in the small of his back.

But those of the other sex were the most interesting of this company of binders, by reason of the charm which is acquired by woman when she becomes part and parcel of outdoor nature, and is not merely an object set down therein as at ordinary times. A field-man is a personality afield; a field-woman is a portion of the field; she has somehow lost her own margin, imbibed the essence of her surrounding, and assimilated herself with it.

The women—or rather girls, for they were mostly young—wore drawn[7] cotton bonnets with great flapping curtains to keep off the sun, and gloves to prevent their hands being wounded by the stubble. There was one wearing a pale pink jacket, another in a cream-coloured tight-sleeved gown, another in a petticoat as red as the arms of the reaping-machine; and others, older, in the brown-rough 'wropper' or over-all—the old-established and most

7. In drawn work some of the threads of warp and woof are pulled to make designs.

appropriate dress of the field-woman, which the young ones were abandoning. This morning the eye returns involuntarily to the girl in the pink cotton jacket, she being the most flexuous and finely-drawn figure of them all. But her bonnet is pulled so far over her brow that none of her face is disclosed while she binds, though her complextion may be guessed from a stray twine or two of dark brown hair which extends below the curtain of her bonnet. Perhaps one reason why she seduces casual attention is that she never courts it, though the other women often gaze around them.

Her binding proceeds with clock-like monotony. From the sheaf last finished she draws a handful of ears, patting their tips with her left palm to bring them even. Then stooping low she moves forward, gathering the corn with both hands against her knees, and pushing her left gloved hand under the bundle to meet the right on the other side, holding the corn in an embrace like that of a lover. She brings the ends of the bond together, and kneels on the sheaf while she ties it, beating back her skirts now and then when lifted by the breeze. A bit of her naked arm is visible between the buff leather of the gauntlet and the sleeve of her gown; and as the day wears on its feminine smoothness becomes scarified by the stubble, and bleeds.

At intervals she stands up to rest, and to retie her disarranged apron, or to pull her bonnet straight. Then one can see the oval face of a handsome young woman with deep dark eyes and long heavy clinging tresses, which seem to clasp in a beseeching way anything they fall against. The cheeks are paler, the teeth more regular, the red lips thinner than is usual in a country-bred girl.

It is Tess Durbeyfield, otherwise d'Urberville, somewhat changed—the same, but not the same; at the present stage of her existence living as a stranger and an alien here, though it was no strange land that she was in. After a long seclusion she had come to a resolve to undertake outdoor work in her native village, the busiest season of the year in the agricultural world having arrived, and nothing that she could do within the house being so remunerative for the time as harvesting in the fields.

The movements of the other women were more or less similar to Tess's, the whole bevy of them drawing together like dancers in a quadrille at the completion of a sheaf by each, every one placing her sheaf on end against those of the rest, till a shock, or 'stitch' as it was here called, of ten or a dozen was formed.

They went to breakfast, and came again, and the work proceeded as before. As the hour of eleven drew near a person watching her might have noticed that every now and then Tess's glance flitted wistfully to the brow of the hill, though she did not pause in her sheafing. On the verge of the hour the heads of a group of children, of ages ranging from six to fourteen, rose above the stubbly convexity of the hill.

The face of Tess flushed slightly, but still she did not pause.

The eldest of the comers, a girl who wore a triangular shawl, its corner draggling on the stubble, carried in her arms what at first sight seemed to be a doll, but proved to be an infant in long clothes. Another brought some lunch. The harvesters ceased working, took their provisions, and sat down against one of the shocks. Here they fell to, the men plying a stone jar freely, and passing round a cup.

Tess Durbeyfield had been one of the last to suspend her labours. She sat down at the end of the shock, her face turned somewhat away from her companions. When she had deposited herself a man in a rabbit-skin cap and with a red handkerchief tucked into his belt, held the cup of ale over the top of the shock for her to drink. But she did not accept his offer. As soon as her lunch was spread she called up the big girl her sister, and took the baby of her, who, glad to be relieved of the burden, went away to the next shock and joined the other children playing there. Tess, with a curiously stealthy yet courageous movement, and with a still rising colour, unfastened her frock and began suckling the child.

The men who sat nearest considerately turned their faces towards the other end of the field, some of them beginning to smoke; one, with absent-minded fondness, regretfully stroking the jar that would no longer yield a stream. All the women but Tess fell into animated talk, and adjusted the disarranged knots of their hair.

When the infant had taken its fill the young mother sat it upright in her lap, and looking into the far distance dandled it with a gloomy indifference that was almost dislike; then all of a sudden she fell to violently kissing it some dozens of times, as if she could never leave off, the child crying at the vehemence of an onset which strangely combined passionateness with contempt.

'She's fond of that there child, though she mid pretend to hate en, and say she wishes the baby and her too were in the churchyard,' observed the woman in the red petticoat.

'She'll soon leave off saying that,' replied the one in buff. 'Lord, 'tis wonderful what a body can get used to o' that sort in time!'

'A little more than persuading had to do wi' the coming o't, I reckon. There were they that heard a sobbing one night last year in The Chase; and it mid ha' gone hard wi' a certain party if folks had come along.'

'Well, a little more, or a little less, 'twas a thousand pities that it should have happened to she, of all others. But 'tis always the comeliest! The plain ones be as safe as churches—hey, Jenny?' The speaker turned to one of the group who certainly was not ill-defined as plain.

It was a thousand pities, indeed; it was impossible for even an enemy to feel otherwise on looking at Tess as she sat there, with her flower-like mouth and large tender eyes, neither black nor blue nor gray nor violet; rather all those shades together, and a hundred others, which could be seen if one looked into their irises— shade behind shade—tint beyond tint—around pupils that had no bottom; an almost standard woman, but for the slight incautiousness of character inherited from her race.

A resolution which had surprised herself had brought her into the fields this week for the first time during many months. After wearing and wasting her palpitating heart with every engine of regret that lonely inexperience could devise, common-sense had illumined her. She felt that she would do well to be useful again —to taste anew sweet independence at any price. The past was past; whatever it had been it was no more at hand. Whatever its consequences, time would close over them; they would all in a few years be as if they had never been, and she herself grassed down and forgotten. Meanwhile the trees were just as green as before; the birds sang and the sun shone as clearly now as ever. The familiar surroundings had not darkened because of her grief, nor sickened because of her pain.

She might have seen that what had bowed her head so profoundly—the thought of the world's concern at her situation— was founded on an illusion. She was not an existence, an experience, a passion, a structure of sensations, to anybody but herself. To all humankind besides Tess was only a passing thought. Even to friends she was no more than a frequently passing thought. If she made herself miserable the livelong night and day it was only this much to them—'Ah, she makes herself unhappy.' If she tried to be cheerful, to dismiss all care, to take pleasure in the daylight, the flowers, the baby, she could only be this idea to them—'Ah, she bears it very well.' Moreover, alone in a desert island would she have been wretched at what had happened to her? Not greatly. If she could have been but just created, to discover herself as a spouseless mother, with no experience of life except as the parent of a nameless child, would the position have caused her to despair? No, she would have taken it calmly, and found pleasures therein. Most of the misery had been generated by her conventional aspect, and not by her innate sensations.

Whatever Tess's reasoning, some spirit had induced her to dress herself up neatly as she had formerly done, and come out into the fields, harvest-hands being greatly in demand just then. This was why she had borne herself with dignity, and had looked people calmly in the face at times, even when holding the baby in her arms.

The harvest-men rose from the shock of corn, and stretched their limbs, and extinguished their pipes. The horses, which had been unharnessed and fed, were again attached to the scarlet machine. Tess, having quickly eaten her own meal, beckoned to her eldest sister to come and take away the baby, fastened her dress, put on the buff gloves again, and stooped anew to draw a bond from the last completed sheaf for the tying of the next.

In the afternoon and evening the proceedings of the morning were continued, Tess staying on till dusk with the body of harvesters. Then they all rode home in one of the largest wagons, in the company of a broad tarnished moon that had risen from the ground to the eastwards, its face resembling the outworn gold-leaf halo of some worm-eaten Tuscan saint.[8] Tess's female companions sang songs, and showed themselves very sympathetic and glad at her reappearance out of doors, though they could not refrain from mischievously throwing in a few verses of the ballad about the maid who went to the merry green wood and came back a changed state. There are counterpoises and compensations in life; and the event which had made of her a social warning had also for the moment made her the most interesting personage in the village to many. Their friendliness won her still farther away from herself, their lively spirits were contagious, and she became almost gay.

But now that her moral sorrows were passing away a fresh one arose on the natural side of her which knew no social law. When she reached home it was to learn to her grief that the baby had been suddenly taken ill since the afternoon. Some such collapse had been probable, so tender and puny was its frame; but the event came as a shock nevertheless.

The baby's offence against society in coming into the world was forgotten by the girl-mother; her soul's desire was to continue that offence by preserving the life of the child. However, it soon grew clear that the hour of emancipation for that little prisoner of the flesh was to arrive earlier than her worst misgivings had conjectured. And when she had discovered this she was plunged into a misery which transcended that of the child's simple loss. Her baby had not been baptized.

Tess had drifted into a frame of mind which accepted passively the consideration that if she should have to burn for what she had done, burn she must, and there was an end of it. Like all

8. Florentine (Tuscan) painters in the time of Giotto painted in tempera on canvas-covered, wooden panels.

village girls she was well grounded in the Holy Scriptures, and had dutifully studied the histories of Aholah and Aholibah,[9] and knew the inferences to be drawn therefrom. But when the same question arose with regard to the baby, it had a very different colour. Her darling was about to die, and no salvation.

It was nearly bedtime, but she rushed downstairs and asked if she might send for the parson. The moment happened to be one at which her father's sense of the antique nobility of his family was highest, and his sensitiveness to the smudge which Tess had set upon that nobility most pronounced, for he had just returned from his weekly booze at Rolliver's Inn. No parson should come inside his door, he declared, prying into his affairs, just then, when, by her shame, it had become more necessary than ever to hide them. He locked the door and put the key in his pocket.

The household went to bed, and, distressed beyond measure, Tess retired also. She was continually waking as she lay, and in the middle of the night found that the baby was still worse. It was obviously dying — quietly and painlessly, but none the less surely.

In her misery she rocked herself upon the bed. The clock struck the solemn hour of one, that hour when fancy stalks outside reason, and malignant possibilities stand rock-firm as facts. She thought of the child consigned to the nethermost corner of hell, as its double doom for lack of baptism and lack of legitimacy; saw the arch-fiend tossing it with his three-pronged fork, like the one they used for heating the oven on baking days; to which picture she added many other quaint and curious details of torment sometimes taught the young in this Christian country. The lurid presentment so powerfully affected her imagination in the silence of the sleeping house that her nightgown became damp with perspiration, and the bedstead shook with each throb of her heart.

The infant's breathing grew more difficult, and the mother's mental tension increased. It was useless to devour the little thing with kisses; she could stay in bed no longer, and walked feverishly about the room.

'O merciful God, have pity; have pity upon my poor baby!' she cried. 'Heap as much anger as you want to upon me, and welcome; but pity the child!'

She leant against the chest of drawers, and murmured incoherent supplications for a long while, till she suddenly started up.

'Ah! perhaps baby can be saved! Perhaps it will be just the same!'

She spoke so brightly that it seemed as though her face might have shone in the gloom surrounding her.

She lit a candle, and went to a second and a third bed under

9. In Ezekiel xxiii:2-35 is told the story of these two prostitutes upon whom the Lord wreaked a terrible vengeance.

the wall, where she awoke her young sisters and brothers, all of whom occupied the same room. Pulling out the washing-stand so that she could get behind it, she poured some water from a jug, and made them kneel around, putting their hands together with fingers exactly vertical. While the children, scarcely awake, awe-stricken at her manner, their eyes growing larger and larger, re-mained in this position, she took the baby from her bed—a child's child—so immature as scarce to seem a sufficient personality to endow its producer with the maternal title. Tess then stood erect with the infant on her arm beside the basin, the next sister held the Prayer-Book open before her, as the clerk at church held it before the parson; and thus the girl set about baptizing her child.

Her figure looked singularly tall and imposing as she stood in her long white nightgown, a thick cable of twisted dark hair hang-ing straight down her back to her waist. The kindly dimness of the weak candle abstracted from her form and features the little blemishes which sunlight might have revealed—the stubble scratches upon her wrists, and the weariness of her eyes—her high enthusiasm having a transfiguring effect upon the face which had been her undoing, showing it as a thing of immaculate beauty, with a touch of dignity which was almost regal. The lit-tle ones kneeling round, their sleepy eyes blinking and red, awaited her preparations full of a suspended wonder which their physical heaviness at that hour would not allow to become active.

The most impressed of them said:

'Be you really going to christen him, Tess?'

The girl-mother replied in a grave affirmative.

'What's his name going to be?'

She had not thought of that, but a name suggested by a phrase in the book of Genesis[1] came into her head as she pro-ceeded with the baptismal service, and now she pronounced it:

'Sorrow, I baptize thee in the name of the Father, and of the Son, and of the Holy Ghost.'

She sprinkled the water, and there was silence.

'Say "Amen," children.'

The tiny voices piped in obedient response 'Amen!'

Tess went on:

'We receive this child'—and so forth—'and do sign him with the sign of the Cross.'

Here she dipped her hand into the basin, and fervently drew an immense cross upon the baby with her forefinger, continuing with the customary sentences as to his manfully fighting against

---

1. Genesis xxxv:18: "And it came to pass, as her [Rachel's] soul was in de-parting, (for she died) that she called his name Ben-oni [son of sorrow]: but his father called him Benjamin."

sin, the world, and the devil, and being a faithful soldier and servant unto his life's end. She duly went on with the Lord's Prayer, the children lisping it after her in a thin gnat-like wail, till, at the conclusion, raising their voices to clerk's pitch, they again piped into the silence, 'Amen!'

Then their sister, with much augmented confidence in the efficacy of this sacrament, poured forth from the bottom of her heart the thanksgiving that follows, uttering it boldly and triumphantly in the stopt-diapason note[2] which her voice acquired when her heart was in her speech, and which will never be forgotten by those who knew her. The ecstasy of faith almost apotheosized her; it set upon her face a glowing irradiation, and brought a red spot into the middle of each cheek; while the miniature candle-flame inverted in her eye-pupils shone like a diamond. The children gazed up at her with more and more reverence, and no longer had a will for questioning. She did not look like Sissy to them now, but as a being large, towering, and awful—a divine personage with whom they had nothing in common.

Poor Sorrow's campaign against sin, the world, and the devil was doomed to be of limited brilliancy—luckily perhaps for himself, considering his beginnings. In the blue of the morning that fragile soldier and servant breathed his last, and when the other children awoke they cried bitterly, and begged Sissy to have another pretty baby.

The calmness which had possessed Tess since the christening remained with her in the infant's loss. In the daylight, indeed, she felt her terrors about his soul to have been somewhat exaggerated; whether well founded or not she had no uneasiness now, reasoning that if Providence would not ratify such an act of approximation she, for one, did not value the kind of heaven lost by the irregularity—either for herself or for her child.

So passed away Sorrow the Undesired—that intrusive creature, that bastard gift of shameless Nature who respects not the social law; a waif to whom eternal Time had been a matter of days merely, who knew not that such things as years and centuries ever were; to whom the cottage interior was the universe, the week's weather climate, new-born babyhood human existence, and the instinct to suck human knowledge.

Tess, who mused on the christening a good deal, wondered if it were doctrinally sufficient to secure a Christian burial for the child. Nobody could tell this but the parson of the parish, and he was a new-comer, and did not know her. She went to his house after dusk, and stood by the gate, but could not summon courage

2. "A diapason is the basic, untempered note made by an organ-pipe When it is stopped it sounds an octave higher, which gives it a softer, gentler, muffled quality." [F]

to go in. The enterprise would have been abandoned if she had not by accident met him coming homeward as she turned away. In the gloom she did not mind speaking freely.

'I should like to ask you something, sir.'

He expressed his willingness to listen, and she told the story of the baby's illness and the extemporized ordinance.

'And now, sir,' she added earnestly, 'can you tell me this—will it be just the same for him as if you had baptized him?'

Having the natural feelings of a tradesman at finding that a job he should have been called in for had been unskilfully botched by his customers among themselves, he was disposed to say no. Yet the dignity of the girl, the strange tenderness in her voice, combined to affect his nobler impulses—or rather those that he had left in him after ten years of endeavour to graft technical belief on actual scepticism. The man and the ecclesiastic fought within him, and the victory fell to the man.

'My dear girl,' he said, 'it will be just the same.'

'Then will you give him a Christian burial?' she asked quickly.

The Vicar felt himself cornered. Hearing of the baby's illness, he had conscientiously gone to the house after nightfall to perform the rite, and, unaware that the refusal to admit him had come from Tess's father and not from Tess, he could not allow the plea of necessity for its irregular administration.

'Ah—that's another matter,' he said.

'Another matter—why?' asked Tess, rather warmly.

'Well—I would willingly do so if only we two were concerned. But I must not—for certain reasons.'

'Just for once, sir!'

'Really I must not.'

'O sir!' She seized his hand as she spoke.

He withdrew it, shaking his head.

'Then I don't like you!' she burst out, 'and I'll never come to your church no more!'

'Don't talk so rashly.'

'Perhaps it will be just the same to him if you don't? . . . Will it be just the same? Don't for God's sake speak as saint to sinner, but as you yourself to me myself—poor me!'

How the Vicar reconciled his answer with the strict notions he supposed himself to hold on these subjects it is beyond a layman's power to tell, though not to excuse. Somewhat moved, he said in this case also—

'It will be just the same.'

So the baby was carried in a small deal box, under an ancient woman's shawl, to the churchyard that night, and buried by lantern-light, at the cost of a shilling and a pint of beer to the sexton, in that shabby corner of God's allotment where He lets the nettles grow, and where all unbaptized infants, notorious drunkards, suicides, and others of the conjecturally damned are laid. In spite of the untoward surroundings, however, Tess bravely made a little cross of two laths and a piece of string, and having bound it with flowers, she stuck it up at the head of the grave one evening when she could enter the churchyard without being seen, putting at the foot also a bunch of the same flowers in a little jar of water to keep them alive. What matter was it that on the outside of the jar the eye of mere observation noted the words 'Keelwell's Marmalade'? The eye of maternal affection did not see them in its vision of higher things.

XV

'By experience,' says Roger Ascham, 'we find out a short way by a long wandering.'[3] Not seldom that long wandering unfits us for further travel, and of what use is our experience to us then? Tess Durbeyfield's experience was of this incapacitating kind. At last she had learned what to do; but who would now accept her doing?

If before going to the d'Urbervilles' she had vigorously moved under the guidance of sundry gnomic texts and phrases known to her and to the world in general, no doubt she would never have been imposed on. But it had not been in Tess's power—nor is it in anybody's power—to feel the whole truth of golden opinions while it is possible to profit by them. She—and how many more—might have ironically said to God with Saint Augustine: 'Thou hast counselled a better course than Thou hast permitted.'

She remained in her father's house during the winter months, plucking fowls, or cramming turkeys and geese, or making clothes for her sisters and brothers out of some finery which d'Urberville had given her, and she had put by with contempt. Apply to him she would not. But she would often clasp her hands behind her head and muse when she was supposed to be working hard.

She philosophically noted dates as they came past in the revolution of the year; the disastrous night of her undoing at Trantridge with its dark background of The Chase; also the dates of the baby's birth and death; also her own birthday; and every other day individualized by incidents in which she had taken some share. She suddenly thought one afternoon, when looking in the glass at her fairness, that there was yet another

3. In the First Book of Ascham's *Schoolmaster* (1570), the sentence reads: "We know by experience itself that it is a marvelous pain to find out but a short way by long wandering."

date, of greater importance to her than those; that of her own death, when all these charms would have disappeared; a day which lay sly and unseen among all the other days of the year, giving no sign or sound when she annually passed over it; but not the less surely there. When was it? Why did she not feel the chill of each yearly encounter with such a cold relation? She had Jeremy Taylor's[4] thought that some time in the future those who had known her would say: 'It is the—th, the day that poor Tess Durbeyfield died'; and there would be nothing singular to their minds in the statement. Of that day, doomed to be her terminus in time through all the ages, she did not know the place in month, week, season, or year.

Almost at a leap Tess thus changed from simple girl to complex woman. Symbols of reflectiveness passed into her face, and a note of tragedy at times into her voice. Her eyes grew larger and more eloquent. She became what would have been called a fine creature; her aspect was fair and arresting; her soul that of a woman whom the turbulent experiences of the last year or two had quite failed to demoralize. But for the world's opinion those experiences would have been simply a liberal education.

She had held so aloof of late that her trouble, never generally known, was nearly forgotten in Marlott. But it became evident to her that she could never be really comfortable again in a place which had seen the collapse of her family's attempt to 'claim kin'—and, through her, even closer union—with the rich d'Urbervilles. At least she could not be comfortable there till long years should have obliterated her keen consciousness of it. Yet even now Tess felt the pulse of hopeful life still warm within her; she might be happy in some nook which had no memories. To escape the past and all that appertained thereto was to annihilate it, and to do that she would have to get away.

Was once lost always lost really true of chastity? she would ask herself. She might prove it false if she could veil bygones. The recuperative power which pervaded organic nature was surely not denied to maidenhood alone.

She waited a long time without finding opportunity for a new departure. A particularly fine spring came round, and the stir of germination was almost audible in the buds; it moved her, as it moved the wild animals, and made her passionate to go. At last, one day in early May, a letter reached her from a former friend of her mother's, to whom she had addressed inquiries long before—a person whom she had never seen—that a skilful milkmaid was required at a dairy-house many miles to the south-

4. A famous seventeenth-century preacher, whose *Holy Living* (1650) and *Holy* *Dying* (1651) continue to be admired for their style.

ward, and that the dairyman would be glad to have her for the summer months.

It was not quite so far off as could have been wished; but it was probably far enough, her radius of movement and repute having been so small. To persons of limited spheres, miles are as geographical degrees, parishes as counties, counties as provinces and kingdoms.

On one point she was resolved: there should be no more d'Urberville air-castles in the dreams and deeds of her new life. She would be the dairymaid Tess, and nothing more. Her mother knew Tess's feeling on this point so well, though no words had passed between them on the subject, that she never alluded to the knightly ancestry now.

Yet such is human inconsistency that one of the interests of the new place to her was the accidental virtue of its lying near her forefathers' country (for they were not Blakemore men, though her mother was Blakemore to the bone). The dairy called Talbothays, for which she was bound, stood not remotely from some of the former estates of the d'Urbervilles, near the great family vaults of her granddames and their powerful husbands. She would be able to look at them, and think not only that d'Urberville, like Babylon, had fallen,[5] but that the individual innocence of a humble descendant could lapse as silently. All the while she wondered if any strange good thing might come of her being in her ancestral land; and some spirit within her rose automatically as the sap in the twigs. It was unexpended youth, surging up anew after its temporary check, and bringing with it hope, and the invincible instinct towards self-delight.

END OF PHASE THE SECOND

Phase the Third—The Rally

XVI

On a thyme-scented, bird-hatching morning in May, between two and three years after the return from Trantridge—silent reconstructive years for Tess Durbeyfield—she left her home for the second time.

Having packed up her luggage so that it could be sent to her later, she started in a hired trap for the little town of Stourcastle, through which it was necessary to pass on her journey, now in a direction almost opposite to that of her first adventuring. On the curve of the nearest hill she looked back regretfully at Mar-

5. Isaiah xxi:9: "Babylon is fallen, is fallen."

lott and her father's house, although she had been so anxious to get away.

Her kindred dwelling there would probably continue their daily lives as heretofore, with no great diminution of pleasure in their consciousness, although she would be far off, and they deprived of her smile. In a few days the children would engage in their games as merrily as ever without the sense of any gap left by her departure. This leaving of the younger children she had decided to be for the best; were she to remain they would probably gain less good by her precepts than harm by her example.

She went through Stourcastle without pausing, and onward to a junction of highways, where she could await a carrier's van that ran to the south-west; for the railways which engirdled this interior tract of country had never yet struck across it. While waiting, however, there came along a farmer in his spring cart, driving approximately in the direction that she wished to pursue. Though he was a stranger to her she accepted his offer of a seat beside him, ignoring that its motive was a mere tribute to her countenance. He was going to Weatherbury, and by accompanying him thither she could walk the remainder of the distance instead of travelling in the van by way of Casterbridge.

Tess did not stop at Weatherbury, after this long drive, further than to make a slight nondescript meal at noon at a cottage to which the farmer recommended her. Thence she started on foot, basket in hand, to reach the wide upland of heath dividing this district from the low-lying meads of a further valley in which the dairy stood that was the aim and end of her day's pilgrimage.

Tess had never before visited this part of the country, and yet she felt akin to the landscape. Not so very far to the left of her she could discern a dark patch in the scenery, which inquiry confirmed her in supposing to be trees marking the environs of Kingsbere—in the church of which parish the bones of her ancestors—her useless ancestors—lay entombed.[6]

She had no admiration for them now; she almost hated them for the dance they had led her; not a thing of all that had been theirs did she retain but the old seal and spoon. 'Pooh—I have as much of mother as father in me!' she said. 'All my prettiness comes from her, and she was only a dairymaid.'

The journey over the intervening uplands and lowlands of Egdon, when she reached them, was a more troublesome walk than she had anticipated, the distance being actually but a few miles. It was two hours, owing to sundry wrong turnings, ere she found herself on a summit commanding the long-sought-for vale,

6. In the serial version Hardy had put here the account (later moved to Chapter LII) of Tess's visit to the tomb of her ancestors. [W]

the Valley of the Great Dairies, the valley in which milk and butter grew to rankness, and were produced more profusely, if less delicately, than at her home—the verdant plain so well watered by the river Var or Froom.

It was intrinsically different from the Vale of Little Dairies, Blackmoor Vale, which, save during her disastrous sojourn at Trantridge, she had exclusively known till now. The world was drawn to a larger pattern here. The enclosures numbered fifty acres instead of ten, the farmsteads were more extended, the groups of cattle formed tribes hereabout; there only families. These myriads of cows stretching under her eyes from the far east to the far west outnumbered any she had ever seen at one glance before. The green lea was speckled as thickly with them as a canvas by Van Alsloot or Sallaert with burghers.[7] The ripe hues of the red and dun kine absorbed the evening sunlight, which the white-coated animals returned to the eye in rays almost dazzling, even at the distant elevation on which she stood.

The bird's-eye perspective before her was not so luxuriantly beautiful, perhaps, as that other one which she knew so well; yet it was more cheering. It lacked the intensely blue atmosphere of the rival vale, and its heavy soils and scents; the new air was clear, bracing, ethereal. The river itself, which nourished the grass and cows of these renowned dairies, flowed not like the streams in Blackmoor. Those were slow, silent, often turbid; flowing over beds of mud into which the incautious wader might sink and vanish unawares. The Froom waters were clear as the pure River of Life shown to the Evangelist,[8] rapid as the shadow of a cloud, with pebbly shallows that prattled to the sky all day long. There the water-flower was the lily; the crowfoot here.

Either the change in the quality of the air from heavy to light, or the sense of being amid new scenes where there were no invidious eyes upon her, sent up her spirits wonderfully. Her hopes mingled with the sunshine in an ideal photosphere which surrounded her as she bounded along against the soft south wind. She heard a pleasant voice in every breeze, and in every bird's note seemed to lurk a joy.

Her face had latterly changed with changing states of mind, continually fluctuating between beauty and ordinariness, according as the thoughts were gay or grave. One day she was pink and flawless; another pale and tragical. When she was pink she was feeling less than when pale; her more perfect beauty accorded with her less elevated mood; her more intense mood with

7. Minor seventeenth-century Flemish painters, whose work Hardy may have seen in Brussels.

8. St. John. Revelation xxii:1: "And he shewed me a pure river of water of life, clear as crystal * * *."

her less perfect beauty. It was her best face physically that was now set against the south wind.

The irresistible, universal, automatic tendency to find sweet pleasure somewhere, which pervades all life, from the meanest to the highest, had at length mastered Tess. Being even now only a young woman of twenty, one who mentally and sentimentally had not finished growing, it was impossible that any event should have left upon her an impression that was not in time capable of transmutation.

And thus her spirits, and her thankfulness, and her hopes, rose higher and higher. She tried several ballads, but found them inadequate; till, recollecting the psalter that her eyes had so often wandered over of a Sunday morning before she had eaten of the tree of knowledge, she chanted: 'O ye Sun and Moon . . . O ye Stars . . . ye Green Things upon the Earth . . . ye Fowls of the Air . . . Beasts and Cattle . . . Children of Men . . . bless ye the Lord, praise Him and magnify Him for ever!'[9]

She suddenly stopped and murmured: 'But perhaps I don't quite know the Lord as yet.'

And probably the half-unconscious rhapsody was a Fetichistic utterance in a Monotheistic setting; women whose chief companions are the forms and forces of outdoor Nature retain in their souls far more of the Pagan fantasy of their remote forefathers than of the systematized religion taught their race at later date. However, Tess found at least approximate expression for her feelings in the old *Benedicite* that she had lisped from infancy; and it was enough. Such high contentment with such a slight initial performance as that of having started towards a means of independent living was a part of the Durbeyfield temperament. Tess really wished to walk uprightly, while her father did nothing of the kind; but she resembled him in being content with immediate and small achievements, and in having no mind for laborious effort towards such petty social advancement as could alone be effected by a family so heavily handicapped as the once powerful d'Urbervilles were now.

There was, it might be said, the energy of her mother's unexpended family, as well as the natural energy of Tess's years, rekindled after the experience which had so overwhelmed her for the time. Let the truth be told—women do as a rule live through such humiliations, and regain their spirits, and again look about them with an interested eye. While there's life there's hope is a conviction not so entirely unknown to the 'betrayed' as some amiable theorists would have us believe.

9. Not in the Psalter; it is from the canticle *Benedicite*, one of the liturgical songs sometimes chanted in the daily Morning Prayer service in the Church of England. [W]

Tess Durbeyfield, then, in good heart, and full of zest for life, descended the Egdon slopes lower and lower towards the dairy of her pilgrimage.

The marked difference, in the final particular, between the rival vales now showed itself. The secret of Blackmoor was best discovered from the heights around; to read aright the valley before her it was necessary to descend into its midst. When Tess had accomplished this feat she found herself to be standing on a carpeted level, which stretched to the east and west as far as the eye could reach.

The river had stolen from the higher tracts and brought in particles to the vale all this horizontal land; and now, exhausted, aged, and attenuated, lay serpentining along through the midst of its former spoils.

Not quite sure of her direction Tess stood still upon the hemmed expanse of verdant flatness, like a fly on a billiard-table of indefinite length, and of no more consequence to the surroundings than that fly. The sole effect of her presence upon the placid valley so far had been to excite the mind of a solitary heron, which, after descending to the ground not far from her path, stood with neck erect, looking at her.

Suddenly there arose from all parts of the lowland a prolonged and repeated call—

'Waow! waow! waow!'

From the furthest east to the furthest west the cries spread as if by contagion, accompanied in some cases by the barking of a dog. It was not the expression of the valley's consciousness that beautiful Tess had arrived, but the ordinary announcement of milking-time—half-past four o'clock, when the dairymen set about getting in the cows.

The red and white herd nearest at hand, which had been phlegmatically waiting for the call, now trooped towards the steading in the background, their great bags of milk swinging under them as they walked. Tess followed slowly in their rear, and entered the barton by the open gate through which they had entered before her. Long thatched sheds stretched round the enclosure, their slopes encrusted with vivid green moss, and their eaves supported by wooden posts rubbed to a glossy smoothness by the flanks of infinite cows and calves of bygone years, now passed to an oblivion almost inconceivable in its profundity. Between the posts were ranged the milchers, each exhibiting herself at the present moment to a whimsical eye in the rear as a circle on two stalks, down the centre of which a switch moved pendulum-wise; while the sun, lowering itself behind this patient row, threw their shadows accurately inwards upon the wall. Thus it threw shadows of these obscure and homely figures every evening with as much care over each contour as if it had been the profile of a

Court beauty on a palace wall; copied them as diligently as it had copied Olympian shapes on marble *façades* long ago, or the outline of Alexander, Caesar, and the Pharaohs.

They were the less restful cows that were stalled. Those that would stand still of their own will were milked in the middle of the yard, where many of such better behaved ones stood waiting now—all prime milchers, such as were seldom seen out of this valley, and not always within it; nourished by the succulent feed which the water-meads supplied at this prime season of the year. Those of them that were spotted with white reflected the sunshine in dazzling brilliancy, and the polished brass knobs on their horns glittered with something of military display. Their large-veined udders hung ponderous as sandbags, the teats sticking out like the legs of a gipsy's crock; and as each animal lingered for her turn to arrive the milk oozed forth and fell in drops to the ground.

XVII

The dairymaids and men had flocked down from their cottages and out of the dairy-house with the arrival of the cows from the meads; the maids walking in pattens, not on account of the weather, but to keep their shoes above the mulch of the barton. Each girl sat down on her three-legged stool, her face sideways, her right cheek resting against the cow; and looked musingly along the animal's flank at Tess as she approached. The male milkers, with hat-brims turned down, resting flat on their foreheads and gazing on the ground, did not observe her.

One of these was a sturdy middle-aged man—whose long white 'pinner'[1] was somewhat finer and cleaner than the wraps of the others, and whose jacket underneath had a presentable marketing aspect—the master-dairyman, of whom she was in quest, his double character as a working milker and butter-maker here during six days, and on the seventh as a man in shining broadcloth in his family pew at church, being so marked as to have inspired a rhyme—

> Dairyman Dick
> All the week:—
> On Sundays Mister Richard Crick.

Seeing Tess standing at gaze he went across to her.

The majority of dairymen have a cross manner at milking-time, but it happened that Mr. Crick was glad to get a new hand—for the days were busy ones now—and he received her warmly; inquiring for her mother and the rest of the family—(through this as a matter of form merely, for in reality he had

1. Pinafore.

not been aware of Mrs. Durbeyfield's existence till apprised of the fact by a brief business-letter about Tess).

'Oh—ay, as a lad I knowed your part o' the country very well,' he said terminatively. 'Though I've never been there since. And a aged woman of ninety that used to live nigh here, but is dead and gone long ago, told me that a family of some such name as yours in Blackmoor Vale came originally from these parts, and that 'twere a old ancient race that had all but perished off the earth—though the new generations didn't know it. But, Lord, I took no notice of the old woman's ramblings, not I.'

'Oh no— it is nothing,' said Tess.

Then the talk was of business only.

'You can milk 'em clean, my maidy? I don't want my cows going azew[2] at this time o' year.'

She reassured him on that point, and he surveyed her up and down. She had been staying indoors a good deal, and her complexion had grown delicate.

'Quite sure you can stand it? 'Tis comfortable enough here for rough folk; but we don't live in a cowcumber frame.'[3]

She declared that she could stand it, and her zest and willingness seemed to win him over.

'Well, I suppose you'll want a dish o' tay, or victuals of some sort, hey? Not yet? Well, do as ye like about it. But faith, if 'twas I, I should be as dry as a kex[4] wi' travelling so far.'

'I'll begin milking now, to get my hand in,' said Tess.

She drank a little milk as temporary refreshment—to the surprise—indeed, slight contempt—of Dairyman Crick, to whose mind it had apparently never occurred that milk was good as a beverage.

'Oh, if ye can swaller that, be it so,' he said indifferently, while one held up the pail that she sipped from. ' 'Tis what I hain't touched for years—not I. Rot the stuff; it would lie in my innerds like lead. You can try your hand upon she,' he pursued, nodding to the nearest cow. 'Not but what she do milk rather hard. We've hard ones and we've easy ones, like other folks. However, you'll find out that soon enough.'

When Tess had changed her bonnet for a hood, and was really on her stool under the cow, and the milk was squirting from her fists into the pail, she appeared to feel that she really had laid a new foundation for her future. The conviction bred serenity, her pulse slowed, and she was able to look about her.

The milkers formed quite a little battalion of men and maids,

2. Dry.
3. Hothouse.
4. The dry, hollow stem of such plants as cow parsnips. "Dry as a kex," *i.e.*, thirsty.

the men operating on the hard-teated animals, the maids on the kindlier natures. It was a large dairy. There were nearly a hundred milchers under Crick's management, all told; and of the herd the master-dairyman milked six or eight with his own hands, unless away from home. These were the cows that milked hardest of all; for his journey-milkmen[5] being more or less casually hired, he would not entrust this half-dozen to their treatment, lest, from indifference, they should not milk them fully; nor to the maids, lest they should fail in the same way for lack of finger-grip; with the result that in course of time the cows would 'go azew'—that is, dry up. It was not the loss for the moment that made slack milking so serious, but that with the decline of demand there came decline, and ultimately cessation, of supply.

After Tess had settled down to her cow there was for a time no talk in the barton,[6] and not a sound interfered with the purr of the milk-jets into the numerous pails, except a momentary exclamation to one or other of the beasts requesting her to turn round or stand still. The only movements were those of the milkers' hands up and down, and the swing of the cows' tails. Thus they all worked on, encompassed by the vast flat mead which extended to either slope of the valley—a level landscape compounded of old landscapes long forgotten, and, no doubt, differing in character very greatly from the landscape they composed now.

'To my thinking,' said the dairyman, rising suddenly from a cow he had just finished off, snatching up his three-legged stool in one hand and the pail in the other, and moving on to the next hard-yielder in his vicinity; 'to my thinking, the cows don't gie down their milk to-day as usual. Upon my life, if Winker do begin keeping back like this, she'll not be worth going under by midsummer.'

''Tis because there's a new hand come among us,' said Jonathan Kail. 'I've noticed such things afore.'

'To be sure. It may be so. I didn't think o't.'

'I've been told that it goes up into their horns at such times,' said a dairymaid.

'Well, as to going up into their horns,' replied Dairyman Crick dubiously, as though even witchcraft might be limited by anatomical possibilities, 'I couldn't say; I certainly could not. But as nott cows will keep it back as well as the horned ones, I don't quite agree to it. Do ye know that riddle about the nott cows, Jonathan? Why do nott[7] cows give less milk in a year than horned?'

'I don't!' interposed the milkmaid. 'Why do they?'

'Because there bain't so many of 'em,' said the dairyman. 'Howsomever, these gam'sters[8] do certainly keep back their milk to-day. Folks, we must lift up a stave or two—that's the only cure for't.'

Songs were often resorted to in dairies hereabout as an entice-ment to the cows when they showed signs of withholding their usual yield; and the band of milkers at this request burst into melody—in purely business-like tones, it is true, and with no great spontaneity; the result, according to their own belief, being a de-cided improvement during the song's continuance. When they had gone through fourteen or fifteen verses of a cheerful ballad about a murderer who was afraid to go to bed in the dark because he saw certain brimstone flames around him, one of the male milkers said—

'I wish singing on the stoop didn't use up so much of a man's wind! You should get your harp, sir; not but what a fiddle is best.'

Tess, who had given ear to this, thought the words were ad-dressed to the dairyman, but she was wrong. A reply, in the shape of 'Why?' came as it were out of the belly of a dun cow in the stalls; it had been spoken by a milker behind the animal, whom she had not hitherto perceived.

'Oh yes; there's nothing like a fiddle,' said the dairyman. 'Though I do think that bulls are more moved by a tune than cows — at least that's my experience. Once there was a old aged man over at Mellstock—William Dewy by name—one of the family that used to do a good deal of business as tranters[9] over there, Jonathan, do ye mind?—I knowed the man by sight as well as I know my own brother, in a manner of speaking. Well, this man was a-coming home-along from a wedding where he had been playing his fiddle, one fine moonlight night, and for shortness' sake he took a cut across Forty-acres, a field lying that way, where a bull was out to grass. The bull seed William, and took after him, horns aground, begad; and though William runned his best, and hadn't *much* drink in him (considering 'twas a wedding, and the folks well off), he found he'd never reach the fence and get over in time to save himself. Well, as a last thought, he pulled out his fiddle as he runned, and struck up a jig, turning to the bull, and backing towards the corner. The bull softened down, and stood still, looking hard at William Dewy, who fiddled on and on; till a sort of a smile stole over the bull's face. But no sooner did William stop his playing and turn to get over hedge than the bull would stop his smiling and lower his horns towards the seat of William's breeches. Well, William had to turn about and play on, willy-nilly; and 'twas only

8. Jokers.   9. Haulers.

three o'clock in the world, and 'a knowed that nobody would come that way for hours, and he so leery[1] and tired that 'a didn't know what to do. When he had scraped till about four o'clock he felt that he verily would have to give over soon, and he said to himself, "There's only this last tune between me and eternal welfare! Heaven save me, or I'm a done man." Well, then he called to mind how he'd seen the cattle kneel o' Christmas Eves in the dead o' night. It was not Christmas Eve then, but it came into his head to play a trick upon the bull. So he broke into the 'Tivity Hymn, just as at Christmas carol-singing; when, lo and behold, down went the bull on his bended knees, in his ignorance, just as if 'twere the true 'Tivity night and hour. As soons as his horned friend were down, William turned, clinked off like a long-dog,[2] and jumped safe over hedge, before the praying bull had got on his feet again to take after him. William used to say that he'd seen a man look a fool a good many times, but never such a fool as that bull looked when he found his pious feelings had been played upon, and 'twas not Christmas Eve. . . . Yes, William Dewy, that was the man's name; and I can tell you to a foot where's he a-lying in Mellstock Churchyard at this very moment —just between the second yew-tree and the north aisle.'

'It's a curious story; it carries us back to medieval times, when faith was a living thing!'

The remark, singular for a dairy-yard, was murmured by the voice behind the dun cow; but as nobody understood the reference no notice was taken, except that the narrator seemed to think it might imply scepticism as to his tale.

'Well, 'tis quite true, sir, whether or no. I knowed the man well.'

'Oh yes; I have no doubt of it,' said the person behind the dun cow.

Tess's attention was thus attracted to the dairyman's interlocutor, of whom she could see but the merest patch, owing to his burying his head so persistently in the flank of the milcher. She could not understand why he should be addressed as 'sir' even by the dairyman himself. But no explanation was discernible; he remained under the cow long enough to have milked three, uttering a private ejaculation now and then, as if he could not get on.

'Take it gentle, sir; take it gentle,' said the dairyman. ' 'Tis knack, not strength that does it.'

'So I find,' said the other, standing up at last and stretching his arms. 'I think I have finished her, however, though she made my fingers ache.'

Tess could then see him at full length. He wore the ordinary

---

1. Empty.   2. A fast walker; a greyhound.

white pinner and leather leggings of a dairy-farmer when milk-ing, and his boots were clogged with the mulch of the yard; but this was all his local livery. Beneath it was something educated, reserved, subtle, sad, differing.

But the details of his aspect were temporarily thrust aside by the discovery that he was one whom she had seen before. Such vicissitudes had Tess passed through since that time that for a moment she could not remember where she had met him; and then it flashed upon her that he was the pedestrian who had joined in the club-dance at Marlott—the passing stranger who had come she knew not whence, had danced with others but not with her, had slightingly left her, and gone on his way with his friends.

The flood of memories brought back by this revival of an inci-dent anterior to her troubles produced a momentary dismay lest, recognizing her also, he should by some means discover her story. But it passed away when she found no sign of remembrance in him. She saw by degrees that since their first and only encounter his mobile face had grown more thoughtful, and had acquired a young man's shapely moustache and beard—the latter of the palest straw colour where it began upon his cheeks, and deepen-ing to a warm brown farther from its root. Under his linen milk-ing-pinner he wore a dark velveteen jacket, cord breeches and gaiters, and a starched white shirt. Without the milking-gear no-body could have guessed what he was. He might with equal prob-ability have been an eccentric landowner or a gentlemanly ploughman. That he was but a novice at dairy-work she had realized in a moment, from the time he had spent upon the milk-ing of one cow.

Meanwhile many of the milkmaids had said to one another of the new-comer, 'How pretty she is!' with something of real gen-erosity and admiration, though with a half hope that the audi-tors would qualify the assertion—which, strictly speaking, they might have done, prettiness being an inexact definition of what struck the eye in Tess. When the milking was finished for the eve-ning they straggled indoors, where Mrs. Crick, the dairyman's wife—who was too respectable to go out milking herself, and wore a hot stuff gown in warm weather because the dairymaids wore prints—was giving an eye to the leads[3] and things.

Only two or three of the maids, Tess learnt, slept in the dairy-house besides herself; most of the helpers going to their homes. She saw nothing at supper-time of the superior milker who had com-mented on the story, and asked no questions about him, the re-mainder of the evening being occupied in arranging her place in

3. Leaden milk-pans.

the bed-chamber. It was a large room over the milk-house, some thirty feet long; the sleeping-cots of the other three indoor milk-maids being in the same apartment. They were blooming young women, and, except one, rather older than herself. By bedtime Tess was thoroughly tired, and fell asleep immediately.

But one of the girls who occupied an adjoining bed was more wakeful than Tess, and would insist upon relating to the latter various particulars of the homestead into which she had just entered. The girl's whispered words mingled with the shades, and, to Tess's drowsy mind, they seemed to be generated by the darkness in which they floated.

'Mr. Angel Clare—he that is learning milking, and that plays the harp—never says much to us. He is a pa'son's son, and is too much taken up wi' his own thoughts to notice girls. He is the dairy man's pupil—learning farming in all its branches. He has learnt sheep-farming at another place, and he's now mastering dairy-work. . . . Yes, he is quite the gentleman-born. His father is the Reverent Mr. Clare at Emminster—a good many miles from here.'

'Oh—I have heard of him,' said her companion, now awake. 'A very earnest clergyman, is he not?'

'Yes—that he is—the earnestest man in all Wessex, they say —the last of the old Low Church sort, they tell me—for all about here be what they call High. All his sons, except our Mr. Clare, be made pa'sons too.'

Tess had not at this hour the curiosity to ask why the present Mr. Clare was not made a parson like his brethren, and gradually fell asleep again, the words of her informant coming to her along with the smell of the cheeses in the adjoining cheese-loft, and the measured dripping of the whey from the wrings[4] downstairs.

XVIII

Angel Clare rises out of the past not altogether as a distinct figure, but as an appreciative voice, a long regard of fixed, abstracted eyes, and a mobility of mouth somewhat too small and delicately lined for a man's, though with an unexpectedly firm close of the lower lip now and then; enough to do away with any inference of indecision. Nevertheless, something nebulous, preoccupied, vague, in his bearing and regard, marked him as one who probably had no very definite aim or concern about his material future. Yet as a lad people had said of him that he was one who might do anything if he tried.

He was the youngest son of his father, a poor parson at the

4. Presses.

other end of the county, and had arrived at Talbothays Dairy as a six months' pupil, after going the round of some other farms, his object being to acquire a practical skill in the various processes of farming, with a view either to the Colonies, or the tenure of a home-farm, as circumstances might decide.

His entry into the ranks of the agriculturists and breeders was a step in the young man's career which had been anticipated neither by himself nor by others.

Mr. Clare the elder, whose first wife had died and left him a daughter, married a second late in life. This lady had somewhat unexpectedly brought him three sons, so that between Angel, the youngest, and his father the vicar there seemed to be almost a missing generation. Of these boys the aforesaid Angel, the child of his old age, was the only son who had not taken a University degree, though he was the single one of them whose early promise might have done full justice to an academical training.

Some two or three years before Angel's appearance at the Marlott dance, on a day when he had left school and was pursuing his studies at home, a parcel came to the vicarage from the local bookseller's, directed to the Reverend James Clare. The vicar having opened it and found it to contain a book, read a few pages; whereupon he jumped up from his seat and went straight to the shop with the book under his arm.

'Why has this been sent to my house?' he asked peremptorily, holding up the volume.

'It was ordered, sir.'

'Not by me, or any one belonging to me, I am happy to say.'

The shopkeeper looked into his order-book.

'Oh, it has been misdirected, sir,' he said. 'It was ordered by Mr. Angel Clare, and should have been sent to him.'

Mr. Clare winced as if he had been struck. He went home pale and dejected, and called Angel into his study.

'Look into this book, my boy,' he said. 'What do you know about it?'

'I ordered it,' said Angel simply.

'What for?'

'To read.'

'How can you think of reading it?'

'How can I? Why—it is a system of philosophy. There is no more moral, or even religious, work published.'

'Yes—moral enough; I don't deny that. But religious!—and for *you*, who intend to be a minister of the Gospel!'

'Since you have alluded to the matter, father,' said the son, with anxious thought upon his face, 'I should like to say, once for all, that I should prefer not to take Orders.[5] I fear I could not conscientiously do so. I love the Church as one loves a parent. I shall always have the warmest affection for her. There is no institution for whose history I have a deeper admiration; but I cannot honestly be ordained her minister, as my brothers are, while she refuses to liberate her mind from an untenable redemptive theolatry.'

It had never occurred to the straightforward and simple-minded Vicar that one of his own flesh and blood could come to this! He was stultified, shocked, paralyzed. And if Angel were not going to enter the Church, what was the use of sending him to Cambridge? The University as a step to anything but ordination seemed, to this man of fixed ideas, a preface without a volume. He was a man not merely religious, but devout; a firm believer —not as the phrase is now elusively construed by theological thimble-riggers in the Church and out of it, but in the old and ardent sense of the Evangelical school: one who could

> Indeed opine
> That the Eternal and Divine
> Did, eighteen centuries ago
> In very truth . . .[6]

Angel's father tried argument, persuasion, entreaty.

'No, father; I cannot underwrite Article Four[7] (leave alone the rest), taking it "in the literal and grammatical sense" as required by the Declaration; and, therefore, I can't be a parson in the present state of affairs,' said Angel. 'My whole instinct in matters of religion is towards reconstruction; to quote your favourite Epistle to the Hebrews, "*the removing of those things that are shaken, as of things that are made, that those things which cannot be shaken may remain.*" '[8]

His father grieved so deeply that it made Angel quite ill to see him.

'What is the good of your mother and me economizing and stinting ourselves to give you a University education, if it is not to be used for the honour and glory of God?' his father repeated.

'Why, that it may be used for the honour and glory of man, father.'

Perhaps if Angel had persevered he might have gone to Cambridge like his brothers. But the Vicar's view of that seat of learning as a stepping-stone to Orders alone was quite a family tradition; and so rooted was the idea in his mind that perseverance began to appear to the sensitive son akin to an intent to misap-

5. To be ordained, to enter the ministry.
6. Browning, "Easter Day," viii.
7. Of the 39 Articles of Religion. To "underwrite" it he would have had to believe that "Christ did truly rise again from death, and took again his body, with flesh, bones, and all things appertaining to the perfection of man's nature." [W]
8. Hebrews xii:27.

propriate a trust, and wrong the pious heads of the household, who had been and were, as his father had hinted, compelled to exercise much thrift to carry out this uniform plan of education for the three young men.

'I will do without Cambridge,' said Angel at last. 'I feel that I have no right to go there in the circumstances.'

The effects of this decisive debate were not long in showing themselves. He spent years and years in desultory studies, undertakings, and meditations; he began to evince considerable indifference to social forms and observances. The material distinctions of rank and wealth he increasingly despised. Even the 'good old family' (to use a favourite phrase of a late local worthy) had no aroma for him unless there were good new resolutions in its representatives. As a balance to these austerities, when he went to live in London to see what the world was like, and with a view to practising a profession or business there, he was carried off his head, and nearly entrapped by a woman much older than himself, though luckily he escaped not greatly the worse for the experience.

Early association with country solitudes had bred in him an unconquerable, and almost unreasonable, aversion to modern town life, and shut him out from such success as he might have aspired to by following a mundane calling in the impracticability of the spiritual one. But something had to be done; he had wasted many valuable years; and having an acquaintance who was starting on a thriving life as a Colonial farmer, it occurred to Angel that this might be a lead in the right direction. Farming, either in the Colonies, America, or at home—farming, at any rate, after becoming well qualified for the business by a careful apprenticeship—that was a vocation which would probably afford an independence without the sacrifice of what he valued even more than a competency—intellectual liberty.

So we find Angel Clare at six-and-twenty here at Talbothays as a student of kine, and, as there were no houses near at hand in which he could get a comfortable lodging, a boarder at the dairyman's.

His room was an immense attic which ran the whole length of the dairy-house. It could only be reached by a ladder from the cheese-loft, and had been closed up for a long time till he arrived and selected it as his retreat. Here Clare had plenty of space, and could often be heard by the dairy-folk pacing up and down when the household had gone to rest. A portion was divided off at one end by a curtain, behind which was his bed, the outer part being furnished as a homely sitting-room.

At first he lived up above entirely, reading a good deal, and strumming upon an old harp which he had bought at a sale, saying when in a bitter humour that he might have to get his living by it in the streets some day. But he soon preferred to read human nature by taking his meals downstairs in the general dining-kitchen, with the dairyman and his wife, and the maids and men, who all together formed a lively assembly; for though but few milking hands slept in the house, several joined the family at meals. The longer Clare resided here the less objection had he to his company, and the more did he like to share quarters with them in common.

Much to his surprise he took, indeed, a real delight in their companionship. The conventional farm-folk of his imagination—personified in the newspaper-press by the pitiable dummy known as Hodge—were obliterated after a few days' residence. At close quarters no Hodge[9] was to be seen. At first, it is true, when Clare's intelligence was fresh from a contrasting society, these friends with whom he now hobnobbed seemed a little strange. Sitting down as a level member of the dairyman's household seemed at the outset an undignified proceeding. The ideas, the modes, the surroundings, appeared retrogressive and unmeaning. But with living on there, day after day, the acute sojourner became conscious of a new aspect in the spectacle. Without any objective change whatever, variety had taken the place of monotonousness. His host and his host's household, his men and his maids, as they became intimately known to Clare, began to differentiate themselves as in a chemical process. The thought of Pascal's was brought home to him: 'A mesure qu'on a plus d'esprit, on trouve qu'il y a plus d'hommes originaux. Les gens du commun ne trouvent pas de différence entre les hommes.'[1] The typical and unvarying Hodge ceased to exist. He had been disintegrated into a number of varied fellow-creatures—beings of many minds, beings infinite in difference; some happy, many serene, a few depressed, one here and there bright even to genius, some stupid, others wanton, others austere; some mutely Miltonic, some potentially Cromwellian;[2] into men who had private views of each other, as he had of his friends; who could applaud or condemn each other, amuse or sadden themselves by the contemplation of each other's foibles or vices; men every one of whom walked in his own individual way the road to dusty death.[3]

Unexpectedly he began to like the outdoor life for its own sake, and for what it brought, apart from its bearing on his own proposed career. Considering his position he became wonderfully free from the chronic melancholy which is taking hold of the civilized

---

9. A typical name for a rustic.
1. "The more intelligence one has, the more one sees how unique every man is. Common people do not see what distinguishes one man from another."
2. An echo of Gray's *Elegy*, lines 59–60.
3. Cf. Macbeth's "way to dusty death."

races with the decline of belief in a beneficent Power. For the first time of late years he could read as his musings inclined him, without any eye to cramming for a profession, since the few farming handbooks which he deemed it desirable to master occupied him but little time.

He grew away from old associations, and saw something new in life and humanity. Secondarily, he made close acquaintance with phenomena which he had before known but darkly—the seasons in their moods, morning and evening, night and noon, winds in their different tempers, trees, waters and mists, shades and silences, and the voices of inanimate things.

The early mornings were still sufficiently cool to render a fire acceptable in the large room wherein they breakfasted; and, by Mrs. Crick's orders, who held that he was too genteel to mess at their table, it was Angel Clare's custom to sit in the yawning chimney-corner during the meal, his cup-and-saucer and plate being placed on a hinged flap at his elbow. The light from the long, wide, mullioned window opposite shone in upon his nook, and, assisted by a secondary light of cold blue quality which shone down the chimney, enabled him to read there easily whenever disposed to do so. Between Clare and the window was the table at which his companions sat, their munching profiles rising sharp against the panes; while to the side was the milk-house door, through which were visible the rectangular leads in rows, full to the brim with the morning's milk. At the further end the great churn could be seen revolving, and its slip-slopping heard— the moving power being discernible through the window in the form of a spiritless horse walking in a circle and driven by a boy.

For several days after Tess's arrival Clare, sitting abstractedly reading from some book, periodical, or piece of music just come by post, hardly noticed that she was present at table. She talked so little, and the other maids talked so much, that the babble did not strike him as possessing a new note, and he was ever in the habit of neglecting the particulars of an outward scene for the general impression. One day, however, when he had been conning one of his music-scores, and by force of imagination was hearing the tune in his head, he lapsed into listlessness, and the music-sheet rolled to the hearth. He looked at the fire of logs, with its one flame pirouetting on the top in a dying dance after the breakfast-cooking and boiling, and it seemed to jig to his inward tune; also at the two chimney crooks dangling down from the cotterel or cross-bar, plumed with soot which quivered to the same melody; also at the half-empty kettle whining an accompaniment. The conversation at the table mixed in with his phantasmal orchestra till he thought: 'What a fluty voice one of those milkmaids has! I suppose it is the new one.'

Clare looked round upon her, seated with the others.

She was not looking towards him. Indeed, owing to his long silence, his presence in the room was almost forgotten.

'I don't know about ghosts,' she was saying; 'but I do know that our souls can be made to go outside our bodies when we are alive.'

The dairyman turned to her with his mouth full, his eyes charged with serious inquiry, and his great knife and fork (breakfasts were breakfasts here) planted erect on the table, like the beginning of a gallows.

'What—really now? And is it so, maidy?' he said.

'A very easy way to feel 'em go,' continued Tess, 'is to lie on the grass at night and look straight up at some big bright star; and, by fixing your mind upon it, you will soon find that you are hundreds and hundreds o' miles away from your body, which you don't seem to want at all.'

The dairyman removed his hard gaze from Tess, and fixed it on his wife.

'Now that's a rum thing, Christianner—hey? To think o' the miles I've vamped o' starlight nights these last thirty year, courting, or trading, or for doctor, or for nurse, and yet never had the least notion o' that till now, or feeled my soul rise so much as an inch above my shirt-collar.'

The general attention being drawn to her, including that of the dairyman's pupil, Tess flushed, and remarking evasively that it was only a fancy, resumed her breakfast.

Clare continued to observe her. She soon finished her eating, and having a consciousness that Clare was regarding her, began to trace imaginary patterns on the tablecloth with her forefinger with the constraint of a domestic animal that perceives itself to be watched.

'What a fresh and virginal daughter of Nature that milkmaid is!' he said to himself.

And then he seemed to discern in her something that was familiar, something which carried him back into a joyous and unforeseeing past, before the necessity of taking thought had made the heavens gray. He concluded that he had beheld her before; where he could not tell. A casual encounter during some country ramble it certainly had been, and he was not greatly curious about it. But the circumstance was sufficient to lead him to select Tess in preference to the other pretty milkmaids when he wished to contemplate contiguous womankind.

XIX

In general the cows were milked as they presented themsleves, without fancy or choice. But certain cows will show a fondness for a particular pair of hands, sometimes carrying this predilection so far as to refuse to stand at all except to their favourite, the pail of a stranger being unceremoniously kicked over.

It was Dairyman Crick's rule to insist on breaking down these partialities and aversions by constant interchange, since otherwise, in the event of a milkman or maid going away from the dairy, he was placed in a difficulty. The maids' private aims, however, were the reverse of the dairyman's rule, the daily selection by each damsel of the eight or ten cows to which she had grown accustomed rendering the operation on their willing udders surprisingly easy and effortless.

Tess, like her compeers, soon discovered which of the cows had a preference for her style of manipulation, and her fingers having become delicate from the long domiciliary imprisonments to which she had subjected herself at intervals during the last two or three years, she would have been glad to meet the milchers' views in this respect. Out of the whole ninety-five there were eight in particular—Dumpling, Fancy, Lofty, Mist, Old Pretty, Young Pretty, Tidy, and Loud—who, though the teats of one or two were as hard as carrots, gave down to her with a readiness that made her work on them a mere touch of the fingers. Knowing, however, the dairyman's wish, she endeavoured conscientiously to take the animals just as they came, excepting the very hard yielders which she could not yet manage.

But she soon found a curious correspondence between the ostensibly chance position of the cows and her wishes in this matter, till she felt that their order could not be the result of accident. The dairyman's pupil had lent a hand in getting the cows together of late, and at the fifth or sixth time she turned her eyes, as she rested against the cow, full of sly inquiry upon him.

'Mr. Clare, you have ranged the cows!' she said, blushing; and in making the accusation symptoms of a smile gently lifted her upper lip in spite of her, so as to show the tips of her teeth, the lower lip remaining severely still.

'Well, it makes no difference,' said he. 'You will always be here to milk them.'

'Do you think so? I *hope* I shall! But I don't *know*.'

She was angry with herself afterwards, thinking that he, unaware of her grave reasons for liking this seclusion, might have mistaken her meaning. She had spoken so earnestly to him, as if his presence were somehow a factor in her wish. Her misgiving was such that at dusk, when the milking was over, she walked in the garden alone, to continue her regrets that she had disclosed to him her discovery of his considerateness.

It was a typical summer evening in June, the atmosphere being in such delicate equilibrium and so transmissive that inanimate objects seemed endowed with two or three senses, if not five. There was no distinction between the near and the far, and an auditor felt close to everything within the horizon. The soundlessness impressed her as a positive entity rather than as the mere negation of noise. It was broken by the strumming of strings.

Tess had heard those notes in the attic above her head. Dim, flattened, constrained by their confinement, they had never appealed to her as now, when they wandered in the still air with a stark quality like that of nudity. To speak absolutely, both instrument and execution were poor; but the relative is all, and as she listened Tess, like a fascinated bird, could not leave the spot. Far from leaving she drew up towards the performer, keeping behind the hedge that he might not guess her presence.

The outskirt of the garden in which Tess found herself had been left uncultivated for some years, and was now damp and rank with juicy grass which sent up mists of pollen at a touch; and with tall blooming weeds emitting offensive smells—weeds whose red and yellow and purple hues formed a polychrome as dazzling as that of cultivated flowers. She went stealthily as a cat through this profusion of growth, gathering cuckoo-spittle on her skirts, cracking snails that were underfoot, staining her hands with thistle-milk and slug-slime, and rubbing off upon her naked arms sticky blights which, though snow-white on the apple-tree trunks, made madder stains on her skin; thus she drew quite near to Clare, still unobserved of him.

Tess was conscious of neither time nor space. The exaltation which she had described as being producible at will by gazing at a star, came now without any determination of hers; she undulated upon the thin notes of the second-hand harp, and their harmonies passed like breezes through her, bringing tears into her eyes. The floating pollen seemed to be his notes made visible, and the dampness of the garden the weeping of the garden's sensibility. Though near nightfall, the rank-smelling weed-flowers glowed as if they would not close for intentness, and the waves of colour mixed with the waves of sound.

The light which still shone was derived mainly from a large hole in the western bank of cloud; it was like a piece of day left behind by accident, dusk having closed in elsewhere. He concluded his plaintive melody, a very simple performance, demanding no great skill; and she waited, thinking another might be begun. But, tired of playing, he had desultorily come round the fence, and was rambling up behind her. Tess, her cheeks on fire, moved away furtively, as if hardly moving at all.

Angel, however, saw her light summer gown, and he spoke; his low tones reaching her, though he was some distance off.

'What makes you draw off in that way, Tess?' said he. 'Are you afraid?'

'Oh no, sir . . . not of outdoor things; especially just now when the apple-blooth is falling, and everything so green.'

'But you have your indoor fears—eh?'

'Well—yes, sir.'

'What of?'

'I couldn't quite say.'

'The milk turning sour?'

'No.'

'Life in general?'

'Yes, sir.'

'Ah—so have I, very often. This hobble of being alive is rather serious, don't you think so?'

'It is—now you put it that way.'

'All the same, I shouldn't have expected a young girl like you to see it so just yet. How is it you do?'

She maintained a hesitating silence.

'Come, Tess, tell me in confidence.'

She thought that he meant what were the aspects of things to her, and replied shyly—

'The trees have inquisitive eyes, haven't they?—that is, seem as if they had. And the river says,—"Why do ye trouble me with your looks?" And you seem to see numbers of to-morrows just all in a line, the first of them the biggest and clearest, the others getting smaller and smaller as they stand farther away; but they all seem very fierce and cruel and as if they said, "I'm coming! Beware of me! Beware of me!" . . . But *you*, sir, can raise up dreams with your music, and drive all such horrid fancies away!'

He was surprised to find this young woman—who though but a milkmaid had just that touch of rarity about her which might make her the envied of her housemates—shaping such sad imaginings. She was expressing in her own native phrases—assisted a little by her Sixth Standard training—feelings which might almost have been called those of the age—the ache of modernism. The perception arrested him less when he reflected that what are called advanced ideas are really in great part but the latest fashion in definition—a more accurate expression, by words in *logy* and *ism*, of sensations which men and women have vaguely grasped for centuries.

Still, it was strange that they should have come to her while yet so young; more than strange; it was impressive, interesting, pathetic. Not guessing the cause, there was nothing to remind him that experience is as to intensity, and not as to duration. Tess's passing corporeal blight had been her mental harvest.

Tess, on her part, could not understand why a man of clerical family and good education, and above physical want, should look upon it as a mishap to be alive. For the unhappy pilgrim herself there was very good reason. But how could this admirable and poetic man ever have descended into the Valley of Humiliation,[4] have felt with the man of Uz—as she herself had felt two or three years ago—'My soul chooseth strangling and death rather than my life. I loathe it; I would not live alway.'[5]

It was true that he was at present out of his class. But she knew that was only because, like Peter the Great[6] in a shipwright's yard, he was studying what he wanted to know. He did not milk cows because he was obliged to milk cows, but because he was learning how to be a rich and prosperous dairyman, landowner, agriculturist, and breeder of cattle. He would become an American or Australian Abraham, commanding like a monarch his flocks and his herds, his spotted and his ring-straked, his menservants and his maids. At times, nevertheless, it did seem unaccountable to her that a decidedly bookish, musical, thinking young man should have chosen deliberately to be a farmer, and not a clergyman, like his father and brothers.

Thus, neither having the clue to the other's secret, they were respectively puzzled at what each revealed, and awaited new knowledge of each other's character and moods without attempting to pry into each other's history.

Every day, every hour, brought to him one more little stroke of her nature, and to her one more of his. Tess was trying to lead a repressed life, but she little divined the strength of her own vitality.

At first Tess seemed to regard Angel Clare as an intelligence rather than as a man. As such she compared him with herself; and at every discovery of the abundance of his illuminations, of the distance between her own modest mental standpoint and the unmeasurable, Andean altitude of his, she became quite dejected, disheartened from all further effort on her own part whatever.

He observed her dejection one day, when he had casually mentioned something to her about pastoral life in ancient Greece. She was gathering the buds called 'lords and ladies'[7] from the bank while he spoke.

'Why do you look so woebegone all of a sudden?' he asked.

'Oh, 'tis only—about my own self,' she said, with a frail laugh of sadness, fitfully beginning to peel 'a lady' meanwhile. 'Just a sense of what might have been with me! My life looks as if it had been wasted for want of chances! When I see what you

---

4. In Bunyan's *Pilgrim's Progress*, I.
5. Job vii:15, 16.
6. Peter I (1672-1725), Emperor of Russia.
7. Popular name for the wild arum.

know, what you have read, and seen, and thought, I feel what a nothing I am! I'm like the poor Queen of Sheba who lived in the Bible. There is no more spirit in me.'[8]

'Bless my soul, don't go troubling about that! Why,' he said with some enthusiasm, 'I should be only too glad, my dear Tess, to help you to anything in the way of history, or any line of reading you would like to take up——'

'It is a lady again,' interrupted she, holding out the bud she had peeled.

'What?'

'I meant that there are always more ladies than lords when you come to peel them.'

'Never mind about the lords and ladies. Would you like to take up any course of study—history, for example?'

'Sometimes I feel I don't want to know anything more about it than I know already.'

'Why not?'

'Because what's the use of learning that I am one of a long row only—finding out that there is set down in some old book somebody just like me, and to know that I shall only act her part; making me sad, that's all. The best is not to remember that your nature and your past doings have been just like thousands' and thousands', and that your coming life and doings'll be like thousands' and thousands'.'

'What, really, then, you don't want to learn anything?'

'I shouldn't mind learning why—why the sun do shine on the just and the unjust alike,'[9] she answered, with a slight quaver in her voice. 'But that's what books will not tell me.'

'Tess, fie for such bitterness!' Of course he spoke with a conventional sense of duty only, for that sort of wondering had not been unknown to himself in bygone days. And as he looked at the unpractised mouth and lips, he thought that such a daughter of the soil could only have caught up the sentiment by rote. She went on peeling the lords and ladies till Clare, regarding for a moment the wave-like curl of her lashes as they drooped with her bent gaze on her soft cheek, lingeringly went away. When he was gone she stood awhile, thoughtfully peeling the last bud; and then, awakening from her reverie, flung it and all the crowd of floral nobility impatiently on the ground, in an ebullition of displeasure with herself for her *niaiseries*,[1] and with a quickening warmth in her heart of hearts.

How stupid he must think her! In an access of hunger for his good opinion she bethought herself of what she had latterly

8. An echo of I Kings x:5.
9. Matthew v:45: "For he maketh his sun to rise on the evil and on the good, and sendeth rain on the just and on the unjust."
1. Silliness.

endeavoured to forget, so unpleasant had been its issues—the identity of her family with that of the knightly d'Urbervilles. Barren attribute as it was, disastrous as its discovery had been in many ways to her, perhaps Mr. Clare, as a gentleman and a student of history, would respect her sufficiently to forget her childish conduct with the lords and ladies if he knew that those Purbeck-marble and alabaster people in Kingsbere Church really represented her own lineal forefathers; that she was no spurious d'Urberville, compounded of money and ambition like those at Trantridge, but true d'Urberville to the bone.

But, before venturing to make the revelation, dubious Tess indirectly sounded the dairyman as to its possible effect upon Mr. Clare, by asking the former if Mr. Clare had any great respect for old county families when they had lost all their money and land.

'Mr. Clare,' said the dairyman emphatically, 'is one of the most rebellest rozums[2] you ever knowed—not a bit like the rest of his family; and if there's one thing that he do hate more than another 'tis the notion of what's called a' old family. He says that it stands to reason that old families have done their spurt of work in past days, and can't have anything left in 'em now. There's the Billetts and the Drenkhards and the Greys and the St. Quintins and the Hardys[3] and the Goulds, who used to own the lands for miles down this valley; you could buy 'em all up now for an old song a'most. Why, our little Retty Priddle here, you know, is one of the Paridelles—the old family that used to own lots o' the lands out by King's-Hintock now owned by the Earl o' Wessex, afore even he or his was heard of. Well, Mr. Clare found this out, and spoke quite scornful to the poor girl for days. "Ah!" he says to her, "you'll never make a good dairymaid! All your skill was used up ages ago in Palestine, and you must lie fallow for a thousand years to git strength for more deeds!" A boy came here t'other day asking for a job, and said his name was Matt, and when we asked him his surname he said he'd never heard that 'a had any surname, and when we asked why, he said he supposed his folks hadn't been 'stablished long enough. "Ah! you're the very boy I want!" says Mr. Clare, jumping up and shaking hands wi'en; "I've great hopes of you"; and gave him half-a-crown. O no! He can't stomach old families!'

After hearing this caricature of Clare's opinions poor Tess was glad that she had not said a word in a weak moment about her family—even though it was so unusually old as almost to have gone round the circle and become a new one. Besides,

2. People with "strange ideas or quaint   3. Cf. p. 343, below.
notions." [W]

another dairy-girl was as good as she, it seemed, in that respect. She held her tongue about the d'Urberville vault, and the Knight of the Conqueror whose name she bore. The insight afforded into Clare's character suggested to her that it was largely owing to her supposed untraditional newness that she had won interest in his eyes.

XX

The season developed and matured. Another year's instalment of flowers, leaves, nightingales, thrushes, finches, and such ephemeral creatures, took up their positions where only a year ago others had stood in their place when these were nothing more than germs and inorganic particles. Rays from the sunrise drew forth the buds and stretched them into long stalks, lifted up sap in noiseless streams, opened petals, and sucked out scents in invisible jets and breathings.

Dairyman Crick's household of maids and men lived on comfortably, placidly, even merrily. Their position was perhaps the happiest of all positions in the social scale, being above the line at which neediness ends, and below the line at which the *convenances*[4] begin to cramp natural feeling, and the stress of threadbare modishness makes too little of enough.

Thus passed the leafy time when arborescence seems to be the one thing aimed at out of doors. Tess and Clare unconsciously studied each other, ever balanced on the edge of a passion, yet apparently keeping out of it. All the while they were converging, under an irresistible law, as surely as two streams in one vale.

Tess had never in her recent life been so happy as she was now, possibly never would be so happy again. She was, for one thing, physically and mentally suited among these new surroundings. The sapling which had rooted down to a poisonous stratum on the spot of its sowing had been transplanted to a deeper soil. Moreover she, and Clare also, stood as yet on the debatable land between predilection and love; where no profundities have been reached; no reflections have set in, awkwardly inquiring, 'Whither does this new current tend to carry me? What does it mean to my future? How does it stand towards my past?'

Tess was the merest stray phenomenon to Angel Clare as yet —a rosy warming apparition which had only just acquired the attribute of persistence in his consciousness. So he allowed his mind to be occupied with her, deeming his preoccupation to be no more than a philosopher's regard of an exceedingly novel, fresh, and interesting specimen of womankind.

They met continually; they could not help it. They met daily in that strange and solemn interval, the twilight of the morning,

4. Social conventions.

in the violet or pink dawn; for it was necessary to rise early, so very early, here. Milking was done betimes; and before the milking came the skimming, which began at a little past three. It usually fell to the lot of some one or other of them to wake the rest, the first being aroused by an alarm-clock; and, as Tess was the latest arrival, and they soon discovered that she could be depended upon not to sleep through the alarm as the others did, this task was thrust most frequently upon her. No sooner had the hour of three struck and whizzed, than she left her room and ran to the dairyman's door; then up the ladder to Angel's, calling him in a loud whisper; then woke her fellow-milkmaids. By the time that Tess was dressed Clare was downstairs and out in the humid air. The remaining maids and the dairyman usually gave themselves another turn on the pillow, and did not appear till a quarter of an hour later.

The gray half-tones of daybreak are not the gray half-tones of the day's close, though the degree of their shade may be the same. In the twilight of the morning light seems active, darkness passive; in the twilight of evening it is the darkness which is active and crescent, and the light which is the drowsy reverse.

Being so often—possibly not always by chance—the first two persons to get up at the dairy-house, they seemed to themselves the first persons up of all the world. In these early days of her residence here Tess did not skim, but went out of doors at once after rising, where he was generally awaiting her. The spectral, half-compounded, aqueous light which pervaded the open mead, impressed them with a feeling of isolation, as if they were Adam and Eve. At this dim inceptive stage of the day Tess seemed to Clare to exhibit a dignified largeness both of disposition and physique, an almost regnant power, possibly because he knew that at that preternatural time hardly any woman so well endowed in person as she was likely to be walking in the open air within the boundaries of his horizon; very few in all England. Fair women are usually asleep at midsummer dawns. She was close at hand, and the rest were nowhere.

The mixed, singular, luminous gloom in which they walked along together to the spot where the cows lay, often made him think of the Resurrection hour. He little thought that the Magdalen might be at his side.[5] Whilst all the landscape was in neutral shade his companion's face, which was the focus of his eyes, rising above the mist stratum, seemed to have a sort of phosphorescence upon it. She looked ghostly, as if she were merely a soul at large. In reality her face, without appearing to do

5. Mary Magdalen was the first person to whom Christ appeared after his resurrection. Mark xvi:9.

so, had caught the cold gleam of day from the north-east; his own face, though he did not think of it, wore the same aspect to her.

It was then, as has been said, that she impressed him most deeply. She was no longer the milkmaid, but a visionary essence of woman—a whole sex condensed into one typical form. He called her Artemis, Demeter, and other fanciful names half teasingly, which she did not like because she did not understand them.

'Call me Tess,' she would say askance; and he did.

Then it would grow lighter, and her features would become simply feminine; they had changed from those of a divinity who could confer bliss to those of a being who craved it.

At these non-human hours they could get quite close to the waterfowl. Herons came, with a great bold noise as of opening doors and shutters, out of the boughs of a plantation which they frequented at the side of the mead; or, if already on the spot, hardily maintained their standing in the water as the pair walked by, watching them by moving their heads round in a slow, horizontal, passionless wheel, like the turn of puppets by clockwork.

They could then see the faint summer fogs in layers, woolly, level, and apparently no thicker than counterpanes, spread about the meadows in detached remnants of small extent. On the gray moisture of the grass were marks where the cows had lain through the night—dark-green islands of dry herbage the size of their carcases, in the general sea of dew. From each island proceeded a serpentine trail, by which the cow had rambled away to feed after getting up, at the end of which trail they found her; the snoring puff from her nostrils, when she recognized them, making an intenser little fog of her own amid the prevailing one. Then they drove the animals back to the barton, or sat down to milk them on the spot, as the case might require.

Or perhaps the summer fog was more general, and the meadows lay like a white sea, out of which the scattered trees rose like dangerous rocks. Birds would soar through it into the upper radiance, and hang on the wing sunning themselves, or alight on the wet rails subdividing the mead, which now shone like glass rods. Minute diamonds of moisture from the mist hung, too, upon Tess's eyelashes, and drops upon her hair, like seed pearls. When the day grew quite strong and commonplace these dried off her; moreover, Tess then lost her strange and ethereal beauty; her teeth, lips, and eyes scintillated in the sunbeams, and she was again the dazzlingly fair dairymaid only, who had to hold her own against the other women of the world.

About this time they would hear Dairyman Crick's voice, lecturing the non-resident milkers for arriving late, and speaking sharply to old Deborah Fyander for not washing her hands.

'For Heaven's sake, pop thy hands under the pump, Deb! Upon my soul, if the London folk only knowed of thee and thy slovenly ways, they'd swaller their milk and butter more mincing than they do a'ready; and that's saying a good deal.'

The milking progressed, till towards the end Tess and Clare, in common with the rest, could hear the heavy breakfast table dragged out from the wall in the kitchen by Mrs. Crick, this being the invariable preliminary to each meal; the same horrible scrape accompanying its return journey when the table had been cleared.

XXI

There was a great stir in the milk-house just after breakfast. The churn revolved as usual, but the butter would not come. Whenever this happened the dairy was paralyzed. Squish, squash, echoed the milk in the great cylinder, but never arose the sound they waited for.

Dairyman Crick and his wife, the milkmaids Tess, Marian, Retty Priddle, Izz Huett, and the married ones from the cottages; also Mr. Clare, Jonathan Kail, old Deborah, and the rest, stood gazing hopelessly at the churn; and the boy who kept the horse going outside put on moon-like eyes to show his sense of the situation. Even the melancholy horse himself seemed to look in at the window in inquiring despair at each walk round.

' 'Tis years since I went to Conjuror Trendle's son in Egdon—years!' said the dairyman bitterly. 'And he was nothing to what his father had been. I have said fifty times, if I have said once, that I don't believe in en. And I *don't* believe in en. But I shall have to go to 'n if he's alive. O yes, I shall have to go to 'n, if this sort of thing continnys!'

Even Mr. Clare began to feel tragical at the dairyman's desperation.

'Conjuror Fall, t'other side of Casterbridge, that they used to call "Wide-O," was a very good man when I was a boy,' said Jonathan Kail. 'But he's rotten as touchwood by now.'

'My grandfather used to go to Conjuror Mynterne, out at Owlscombe, and a clever man a' were, so I've heard grandf'er say,' continued Mr. Crick. 'But there's no such genuine folk about nowadays!'

Mrs. Crick's mind kept nearer to the matter in hand.

'Perhaps somebody in the house is in love,' she said tentatively. 'I've heard tell in my younger days that that will cause it. Why, Crick

—that maid we had years ago, do ye mind, and how the butter didn't come then——'

'Ah yes, yes!—but that isn't the rights o't. It had nothing to do with the love-making. I can mind all about it—'twas the damage to the churn.'

He turned to Clare.

'Jack Dollop, a 'hore's-bird[6] of a fellow we had here as milker at one time, sir, courted a young woman over at Mellstock, and deceived her as he had deceived many afore. But he had another sort o' woman to reckon wi' this time, and it was not the girl herself. One Holy Thursday, of all days in the almanack, we was here as we mid be now, only there was no churning in hand, when we zid the girl's mother coming up to the door, wi' a great brass-mounted umbrella in her hand that would ha' felled an ox, and saying "Do Jack Dollop work here?—because I want him! I have a big bone to pick with he, I can assure 'n!" And some way behind her mother walked Jack's young woman, crying bitterly into her handkercher. "O Lard, here's a time!" said Jack, looking out o' winder at 'em. "She'll murder me! Where shall I get—where shall I——? Don't tell her where I be!" And with that he scrambled into the churn through the trap-door, and shut himself inside, just as the young woman's mother busted into the milk-house. "The villain—where is he?" says she, "I'll claw his face for'n, let me only catch him!" Well, she hunted about everywhere, ballyragging Jack by side and by seam,[7] Jack lying a'most stifled inside the churn, and the poor maid—or young woman rather—standing at the door crying her eyes out. I shall never forget it, never! 'Twould have melted a marble stone! But she couldn't find him nowhere at all.'

The dairyman paused, and one or two words of comment came from the listeners.

Dairyman Crick's stories often seemed to be ended when they were not really so, and strangers were betrayed into premature interjections of finality; though old friends knew better. The narrator went on——

'Well, how the old woman should have had the wit to guess it I could never tell, but she found out that he was inside that there churn. Without saying a word she took hold of the winch (it was turned by handpower then), and round she swung him, and Jack began to flop about in side. "O Lard! stop the churn! let me out!" says he, popping out his head, "I shall be churned into a pummy!"[8] (he was a cowardly chap in his heart, as such men

6. The child of a whore; a vulgar term of abuse.
7. Probably, "'outside and inside''—

thoroughly.
8. Apple pulp from a cider press.

mostly be). "Not till ye make amends for ravaging her virgin innocence!" says the old woman. "Stop the churn, you old witch!" screams he. "You call me old witch, do ye, you deceiver!" says she, "when ye ought to ha' been calling me mother-law these last five months!" And on went the churn, and Jack's bones rattled round again. Well, none of us ventured to interfere; and at last 'a promised to make it right wi' her. "Yes—I'll be as good as my word!" he said. And so it ended that day.'

While the listeners were smiling their comments there was a quick movement behind their backs, and they looked round. Tess, pale-faced, had gone to the door.

'How warm 'tis to-day!' she said, almost inaudibly.

It was warm, and none of them connected her withdrawal with the reminiscences of the dairyman. He went forward, and opened the door for her, saying with tender raillery—

'Why, maidy' (he frequently, with unconscious irony, gave her this pet name), 'the prettiest milker I've got in my dairy; you mustn't get so fagged as this at the first breath of summer weather, or we shall be finely put to for want of 'ee by dog-days, shan't we, Mr. Clare?'

'I was faint—and—I think I am better out o' doors,' she said mechanically; and disappeared outside.

Fortunately for her the milk in the revolving churn at that moment changed its squashing for a decided flick-flack.

' 'Tis coming!' cried Mrs. Crick, and the attention of all was called off from Tess.

That fair sufferer soon recovered herself externally; but she remained much depressed all the afternoon. When the evening milking was done she did not care to be with the rest of them, and went out of doors wandering along she knew not whither. She was wretched—O so wretched—at the perception that to her companions the dairyman's story had been rather a humorous narration than otherwise; none of them but herself seemed to see the sorrow of it; to a certainty, not one knew how cruelly it touched the tender place in her experience. The evening sun was now ugly to her, like a great inflamed wound in the sky. Only a solitary cracked-voiced reed-sparrow greeted her from the bushes by the river, in a sad, machine-made tone, resembling that of a past friend whose friendship she had outworn.

In these long June days the milkmaids, and, indeed, most of the household, went to bed at sunset or sooner, the morning work before milking being so early and heavy at a time of full pails. Tess usually accompanied her fellows upstairs. To-night, however, she was the first to go to their common chamber; and she had dozed when the other girls came in. She saw them undressing in the orange light of the vanished sun, which flushed their forms with its colour; she dozed again, but she was reawakened by their voices, and quietly turned her eyes towards them.

Neither of her three chamber-companions had got into bed. They were standing in a group, in their nightgowns, barefooted, at the window, the last red rays of the west still warming their faces and necks, and the walls around them. All were watching somebody in the garden with deep interest, their three faces close together: a jovial and round one, a pale one with dark hair, and a fair one whose tresses were auburn.

'Don't push! You can see as well as I,' said Retty, the auburn-haired and youngest girl, without removing her eyes from the window.

' 'Tis no use for you to be in love with him any more than me, Retty Priddle,' said jolly-faced Marian, the eldest, slily. 'His thoughts be of other cheeks than thine!'

Retty Priddle still looked, and the others looked again.

'There he is again!' cried Izz Huett, the pale girl with dark damp hair and keenly cut lips.

'You needn't say anything, Izz,' answered Retty. 'For I zid you kissing his shade.'

'*What* did you see her doing?' asked Marian.

'Why—he was standing over the whey-tub to let off the whey, and the shade of his face came upon the wall behind, close to Izz, who was standing there filling a vat. She put her mouth against the wall and kissed the shade of his mouth; I zid her, though he didn't.'

'O Izz Huett!' said Marian.

A rosy spot came into the middle of Izz Huett's cheek.

'Well, there was no harm in it,' she declared, with attempted coolness. 'And if I be in love wi'en, so is Retty, too; and so be you, Marian, come to that.'

Marian's full face could not blush past its chronic pinkness.

'I!' she said. 'What a tale! Ah, there he is again! Dear eyes —dear face—dear Mr. Clare!'

'There—you've owned it!'

'So have you—so have we all,' said Marian, with the dry frankness of complete indifference to opinion. 'It is silly to pretend otherwise amongst ourselves, though we need not own it to other folks. I would just marry'n to-morrow!'

'So would I—and more,' murmured Izz Huett.

'And I too,' whispered the more timid Retty.

The listener grew warm.

'We can't all marry him,' said Izz.

'We shan't, either of us; which is worse still,' said the eldest.

'There he is again!'

They all three blew him a silent kiss.

'Why?' asked Retty quickly.

'Because he likes Tess Durbeyfield best,' said Marian, lowering her voice. 'I have watched him every day, and have found it out.'

There was a reflective silence.

'But she don't care anything for 'n?' at length breathed Retty.

'Well—I sometimes think that too.'

'But how silly all this is!' said Izz Huett impatiently. 'Of course he won't marry any one of us, or Tess either—a gentleman's son, who's going to be a great landowner and farmer abroad! More likely to ask us to come wi'en as farm-hands at so much a year!'

One sighed, and another sighed, and Marian's plump figure sighed biggest of all. Somebody in bed hard by sighed too. Tears came into the eyes of Retty Priddle, the pretty red-haired youngest—the last bud of the Paridelles, so important in the county annals. They watched silently a little longer, their three faces still close together as before, and the triple hues of their hair mingling. But the unconscious Mr. Clare had gone indoors, and they saw him no more; and, the shades beginning to deepen, they crept into their beds. In a few minutes they heard him ascend the ladder to his own room. Marian was soon snoring, but Izz did not drop into forgetfulness for a long time. Retty Priddle cried herself to sleep.

The deeper-passioned Tess was very far from sleeping even then. This conversation was another of the bitter pills she had been obliged to swallow that day. Scarce the least feeling of jealousy arose in her breast. For that matter she knew herself to have the preference. Being more finely formed, better educated, and, though the youngest except Retty, more woman than either, she perceived that only the slightest ordinary care was necessary for holding her own in Angel Clare's heart against these her candid friends. But the grave question was, ought she to do this? There was, to be sure, hardly a ghost of a chance for either of them, in a serious sense; but there was, or had been a chance of one or the other inspiring him with a passing fancy for her, and enjoying the pleasure of his attentions while he stayed here. Such unequal attachments had led to marriage; and she had heard from Mrs. Crick that Mr. Clare had one day asked, in a laughing way, what would be the use of his marrying a fine lady, and all the while ten thousand acres of Colonial pasture to feed, and cattle to rear, and corn to reap. A farm-woman would be the only sensible kind of wife for him. But whether Mr.

Clare had spoken seriously or not, why should she, who could never conscientiously allow any man to marry her now, and who had religiously determined that she never would be tempted to do so, draw off Mr. Clare's attention from other women, for the brief happiness of sunning herself in his eyes while he remained at Talbothays?

XXII

They came downstairs yawning next morning; but skimming and milking were proceeded with as usual, and they went indoors to breakfast. Dairyman Crick was discovered stamping about the house. He had received a letter, in which a customer had complained that the butter had a twang.

'And begad, so 't have!' said the dairyman, who held in his left hand a wooden slice on which a lump of butter was stuck. 'Yes—taste for yourself!'

Several of them gathered round him; and Mr. Clare tasted, Tess tasted, also the other indoor milkmaids, one or two of the milking-men, and last of all Mrs. Crick, who came out from the waiting breakfast-table. There certainly was a twang.

The dairyman, who had thrown himself into abstraction to better realize the taste, and so divine the particular species of noxious weed to which it appertained, suddenly exclaimed—

' 'Tis garlic! and I thought there wasn't a blade left in that mead!'

Then all the old hands remembered that a certain dry mead, into which a few of the cows had been admitted of late, had, in years gone by, spoilt the butter in the same way. The dairyman had not recognized the taste at that time, and thought the butter bewitched.

'We must overhaul that mead,' he resumed; 'this mustn't continny!'

All having armed themselves with old pointed knives they went out together. As the inimical plant could only be present in very microscopic dimensions to have escaped ordinary observation, to find it seemed rather a hopeless attempt in the stretch of rich grass before them. However, they formed themselves into line, all assisting, owing to the importance of the search; the dairyman at the upper end with Mr. Clare, who had volunteered to help; then Tess, Marian, Izz Huett, and Retty; the Bill Lewell, Jonathan, and the married dairywomen—Beck Knibbs, with her woolly black hair and rolling eyes; and flaxen Frances, consumptive from the winter damps of the water-meads—who lived in their respective cottages.

With eyes fixed upon the ground they crept slowly across a strip of the field, returning a little further down in such a manner that, when they should have finished, not a single inch of the pasture but would have fallen under the eye of some one of them. It was a most tedious business, not more than half a dozen shoots of garlic being discoverable in the whole field; yet such was the herb's pungency that probably one bite of it by one cow had been sufficient to season the whole dairy's produce for the day.

Differing one from another in natures and moods so greatly as they did, they yet formed, bending, a curiously uniform row—automatic, noiseless; and an alien observer passing down the neighbouring lane might well have been excused for massing them as 'Hodge.' As they crept along, stooping low to discern the plant, a soft yellow gleam was reflected from the buttercups into their shaded faces, giving them an elfish, moonlit aspect, though the sun was pouring upon their backs in all the strength of noon.

Angel Clare, who communistically[9] stuck to his rule of taking part with the rest in everything, glanced up now and then. It was not, of course, by accident that he walked next to Tess.

'Well, how are you?' he murmured.

'Very well, thank you, sir,' she replied demurely.

As they had been discussing a score of personal matters only half-an-hour before, the introductory style seemed a little superfluous. But they got no further in speech just then. They crept and crept, the hem of her petticoat just touching his gaiter, and his elbow sometimes brushing hers. At last the dairyman, who came next, could stand it no longer.

'Upon my soul and body, this here stooping do fairly make my back open and shut!' he exclaimed, straightening himself slowly with an excruciated look till quite upright. 'And you, maidy Tess, you wasn't well a day or two ago—this will make your head ache finely! Don't do any more, if you feel fainty; leave the rest to finish it.'

Dairyman Crick withdrew, and Tess dropped behind. Mr. Clare also stepped out of line, and began privateering about for the weed. When she found him near her, her very tension at what she had heard the night before made her the first to speak.

'Don't they look pretty?' she said.

'Who?'

'Izzy Huett and Retty.'

Tess had moodily decided that either of these maidens would make a good farmer's wife, and that she ought to recommend them, and obscure her own wretched charms.

'Pretty? Well, yes—they are pretty girls—fresh looking. I have often thought so.'

'Though, poor dears, prettiness won't last long!'

'O no, unfortunately.'

9. The word was first used about 1850.

'They are excellent dairywomen.'

'Yes: though not better than you.'

'They skim better than I.'

'Do they?'

Clare remained observing them—not without their observing him.

'She is colouring up,' continued Tess heroically.

'Who?'

'Retty Priddle.'

'Oh! Why is that?'

'Because you are looking at her.'

Self-sacrificing as her mood might be Tess could not well go further and cry, 'Marry one of them, if you really do want a dairywoman and not a lady; and don't think of marrying me!' She followed Dairyman Crick, and had the mournful satisfaction of seeing that Clare remained behind.

From this day she forced herself to take pains to avoid him— never allowing herself, as formerly, to remain long in his company, even if their juxtaposition were purely accidental. She gave the other three every chance.

Tess was woman enough to realize from their avowals to herself that Angel Clare had the honour of all the dairymaids in his keeping, and her perception of his care to avoid compromising the happiness of either in the least degree bred a tender respect in Tess for what she deemed, rightly or wrongly, the self-controlling sense of duty shown by him, a quality which she had never expected to find in one of the opposite sex, and in the absence of which more than one of the simple hearts who were his housemates might have gone weeping on her pilgrimage.

XXIII

The hot weather of July had crept upon them unawares, and the atmosphere of the flat vale hung heavy as an opiate over the dairy-folk, the cows, and the trees. Hot steaming rains fell frequently, making the grass where the cows fed yet more rank, and hindering the late haymaking in the other meads.

It was Sunday morning; the milking was done; the outdoor milkers had gone home. Tess and the other three were dressing themselves rapidly, the whole bevy having agreed to go together to Mellstock Church, which lay some three or four miles distant from the dairy-house. She had now been two months at Talbothays, and this was her first excursion.

All the preceding afternoon and night heavy thunderstorms had hissed down upon the meads, and washed some of the hay into the river; but this morning the sun shone out all the more brilliantly for the deluge, and the air was balmy and clear.

The crooked lane leading from their own parish to Mellstock

ran along the lowest levels in a portion of its length, and when the girls reached the most depressed spot they found that the result of the rain had been to flood the lane over-shoe to a distance of some fifty yards. This would have been no serious hindrance on a week-day; they would have clicked through it in their high pattens and boots quite unconcerned; but on this day of vanity, this Sun's-day, when flesh went forth to coquet with flesh while hypocritically affecting business with spiritual things; on this occasion for wearing their white stockings and thin shoes, and their pink, white, and lilac gowns, on which every mud spot would be visible, the pool was an awkward impediment. They could hear the church-bell calling—as yet nearly a mile off.

'Who would have expected such a rise in the river in summertime!' said Marian, from the top of the roadside-bank on which they had climbed, and were maintaining a precarious footing in the hope of creeping along its slope till they were past the pool.

'We can't get there anyhow, without walking right through it, or else going round the Turnpike way; and that would make us so very late!' said Retty, pausing hopelessly.

'And I do colour up so hot, walking into church late, and all the people staring round,' said Marian, 'that I hardly cool down again til we get into the That-it-may-please-Thees.'[1]

While they stood clinging to the bank they heard a splashing round the bend of the road, and presently appeared Angel Clare, advancing along the lane towards them through the water.

Four hearts gave a big throb simultaneously.

His aspect was probably as un-Sabbatarian a one as a dogmatic parson's son often presented; his attire being his dairy clothes, long wading boots, a cabbage-leaf inside his hat to keep his head cool, with a thistle-spud to finish him off.

'He's not going to church,' said Marian.

'No—I wish he was!' murmured Tess.

Angel, in fact, rightly or wrongly (to adopt the safe phrase of evasive controversialists), preferred sermons in stones to sermons[2] in churches and chapels on fine summer days. This morning, moreover, he had gone out to see if the damage to the hay by the flood was considerable or not. On his walk he observed the girls from a long distance, though they had been so occupied with their difficulties of passage as not to notice him. He knew that the water had risen at that spot, and that it would quite check their progress. So he had hastened on, with a dim idea of how he could help them—one of them in particular.

The rosy-cheeked, bright-eyed quartet looked so charming in

1. A response repeated in the Litany, in   2. Shakespeare, *As You Like It*, II.i.17.
the church service.

their light summer attire, clinging to the roadside bank like pigeons on a roof-slope, that he stopped a moment to regard them before coming close. Their gauzy skirts had brushed up from the grass innumerable flies and butterflies which, unable to escape, remained caged in the transparent tissue as in an aviary. Angel's eye at last fell upon Tess, the hindmost of the four; she, being full of suppressed laughter at their dilemma, could not help meeting his glance radiantly.

He came beneath them in the water, which did not rise over his long boots; and stood looking at the entrapped flies and butterflies.

'Are you trying to get to church?' he said to Marian, who was in front, including the next two in his remark, but avoiding Tess.

'Yes, sir; and 'tis getting late; and my colour do come up so——'

'I'll carry you through the pool—every Jill of you.'[3]

The whole four flushed as if one heart beat through them.

'I think you can't, sir,' said Marian.

'It is the only way for you to get past. Stand still. Nonsense—you are not too heavy! I'd carry you all four together. Now, Marian, attend,' he continued, 'and put your arms round my shoulders, so. Now! Hold on. That's well done.'

Marian had lowered herself upon his arm and shoulder as directed, and Angel strode off with her, his slim figure, as viewed from behind, looking like the mere stem to the great nosegay suggested by hers. They disappeared round the curve of the road, and only his sousing footsteps and the top ribbon of Marian's bonnet told where they were. In a few minutes he reappeared. Izz Huett was the next in order upon the bank.

'Here he comes,' she murmured, and they could hear that her lips were dry with emotion. 'And I have to put my arms round his neck and look into his face as Marian did.'

'There's nothing in that,' said Tess quickly.

'There's a time for everything,' continued Izz, unheeding. 'A time to embrace, and a time to refrain from embracing;[4] the first is now going to be mine.'

'Fie—it is Scripture, Izz!'

'Yes,' said Izz, 'I've always a' ear at church for pretty verses.'

Angel Clare, to whom three-quarters of this performance was a commonplace act of kindness, now approached Izz. She quietly and dreamily lowered herself into his arms, and Angel methodically marched off with her. When he was heard return-

---

3. In the serial version Clare carries the girls across in a wheelbarrow.
4. Ecclesiastes iii:5: "A time to embrace, and a time to refrain from embracing."

ing for the third time Retty's throbbing heart could be almost seen to shake her. He went up to the red-haired girl, and while he was seizing her he glanced at Tess. His lips could not have pronounced more plainly, 'It will soon be you and I.' Her comprehension appeared in her face; she could not help it. There was an understanding between them.

Poor little Retty, though by far the lightest weight, was the most troublesome of Clare's burdens. Marian had been like a sack of meal, a dead weight of plumpness under which he had literally staggered. Izz had ridden sensibly and calmly. Retty was a bunch of hysterics.

However, he got through with the disquieted creature, deposited her, and returned. Tess could see over the hedge the distant three in a group, standing as he had placed them on the next rising ground. It was now her turn. She was embarrassed to discover that excitement at the proximity of Mr. Clare's breath and eyes, which she had contemned in her companions, was intensified in herself; and as if fearful of betraying her secret she paltered with him at the last moment.

'I may be able to clim' along the bank perhaps—I can clim' better than they. You must be so tired, Mr. Clare!'

'No, no, Tess,' said he quickly. And almost before she was aware she was seated in his arms and resting against his shoulder.

'Three Leahs to get one Rachel,'[5] he whispered.

'They are better women than I,' she replied, magnanimously sticking to her resolve.

'Not to me,' said Angel.

He saw her grow warm at this; and they went some steps in silence.

'I hope I am not too heavy?' she said timidly.

'O no. You should lift Marian! Such a lump. You are like an undulating billow warmed by the sun. And all this fluff of muslin about you is the froth.'

'It is very pretty—if I seem like that to you.'

'Do you know that I have undergone three-quarters of this labour entirely for the sake of the fourth quarter?'

'No.'

'I did not expect such an event to-day.'

'Nor I. . . . The water came up so sudden.'

That the rise in the water was what she understood him to refer to, the state of her breathing belied. Clare stood still and inclined his face towards hers.

5. Jacob agreed to work seven years for Rachel's hand in marriage, but at the end of the seven years he was given Leah, Rachel's sister, and had to work seven more years to win Rachel.

'O Tessy!' he exclaimed.

The girl's cheeks burned to the breeze, and she could not look into his eyes for her emotion. It reminded Angel that he was somewhat unfairly taking advantage of an accidental position; and he went no further with it. No definite words of love had crossed their lips as yet, and suspension at this point was desirable now. However, he walked slowly, to make the remainder of the distance as long as possible; but at last they came to the bend, and the rest of their progress was in full view of the other three. The dry land was reached, and he set her down.

Her friends were looking with round thoughtful eyes at her and him, and she could see that they had been talking of her. He hastily bade them farewell, and splashed back along the stretch of submerged road.

The four moved on together as before, till Marian broke the silence by saying—

'No—in all truth; we have no chance against her!' She looked joylessly at Tess.

'What do you mean?' asked the latter.

'He likes 'ee best—the very best! We could see it as he brought 'ee. He would have kissed 'ee, if you had encouraged him to do it, ever so little.'

'No, no,' said she.

The gaiety with which they had set out had somehow vanished; and yet there was no enmity or malice between them. They were generous young souls; they had been reared in the lonely country nooks where fatalism is a strong sentiment, and they did not blame her. Such supplanting was to be.

Tess's heart ached. There was no concealing from herself the fact that she loved Angel Clare, perhaps all the more passionately from knowing that the others had also lost their hearts to him. There is contagion in this sentiment, especially among women. And yet that same hungry heart of hers compassionated her friends. Tess's honest nature had fought against this, but too feebly, and the natural result had followed.

'I will never stand in your way, nor in the way of either of you!' she declared to Retty that night in the bedroom (her tears running down). 'I can't help this, my dear! I don't think marrying is in his mind at all; but if he were even to ask me I should refuse him, as I should refuse any man.'

'Oh! would you? Why?' said wondering Retty.

'It cannot be! But I will be plain. Putting myself quite on one side, I don't think he will choose either of you.'

'I have never expected it—thought of it!' moaned Retty. 'But O! I wish I was dead!'

The poor child, torn by a feeling which she hardly understood, turned to the other two girls who came upstairs just then.

'We be friends with her again,' she said to them. 'She thinks no more of his choosing her than we do.'

So the reserve went off, and they were confiding and warm.

'I don't seem to care what I do now,' said Marian, whose mood was tuned to its lowest bass. 'I was going to marry a dairy-man at Stickleford, who's asked me twice; but—my soul—I would put an end to myself rather'n be his wife now! Why don't ye speak, Izz?'

'To confess, then,' murmured Izz, 'I made sure to-day that he was going to kiss me as he held me; and I lay still against his breast, hoping and hoping, and never moved at all. But he did not. I don't like biding here at Talbothays any longer! I shall go hwome.'

The air of the sleeping-chamber seemed to palpitate with the hopeless passion of the girls. They writhed feverishly under the oppressiveness of an emotion thrust on them by cruel Nature's law —an emotion which they had neither expected nor desired. The incident of the day had fanned the flame that was burning the inside of their hearts out, and the torture was almost more than they could endure. The differences which distinguished them as individuals were abstracted by this passion, and each was but portion of one organism called sex. There was so much frankness and so little jealousy because there was no hope. Each one was a girl of fair common sense, and she did not delude herself with any vain conceits, or deny her love, or give herself airs, in the idea of outshining the others. The full recognition of the futility of their infatuation, from a social point of view; its purposeless beginning; its self-bounded outlook; its lack of everything to justify its existence in the eye of civilization (while lacking nothing in the eye of Nature); the one fact that it did exist, ecstasizing them to a killing joy; all this imparted to them a resignation, a dignity, which a practical and sordid expectation of winning him as a husband would have destroyed.

They tossed and turned on their little beds, and the cheese-wring dripped monotonously downstairs.

'B' you awake, Tess?' whispered one, half-an-hour later.

It was Izz Huett's voice.

Tess replied in the affirmative, whereupon also Retty and Marian suddenly flung the bedclothes off them, and sighed—

'So be we!'

'I wonder what she is like—the lady they say his family have looked out for him!'

'I wonder,' said Izz.

'Some lady looked out for him?' gasped Tess, starting. 'I have never heard o' that!'

'O yes—'tis whispered; a young lady of his own rank, chosen by his family; a Doctor of Divinity's daughter near his father's parish of Emminster; he don't much care for her, they say. But he is sure to marry her.'

They had heard so very little of this; yet it was enough to build up wretched dolorous dreams upon, there in the shade of the night. They pictured all the details of his being won round to consent, of the wedding preparations, of the bride's happiness, of her dress and veil, of her blissful home with him, when oblivion would have fallen upon themselves as far as he and their love were concerned. Thus they talked, and ached, and wept till sleep charmed their sorrow away.

After this disclosure Tess nourished no further foolish thought that there lurked any grave and deliberate import in Clare's attentions to her. It was a passing summer love of her face, for love's own temporary sake—nothing more. And the thorny crown of this sad conception was that she whom he really did prefer in a cursory way to the rest, she who knew herself to be more impassioned in nature, cleverer, more beautiful than they, was in the eyes of propriety far less worthy of him than the homelier ones whom he ignored.

XXIV

Amid the oozing fatness and warm ferments of the Froom Vale, at a season when the rush of juices could almost be heard below the hiss of fertilization, it was impossible that the most fanciful love should not grow passionate. The ready bosoms existing there were impregnated by their surroundings.

July passed over their heads, and the Thermidorean[6] weather which came in its wake seemed an effort on the part of Nature to match the state of hearts at Talbothays Dairy. The air of the place, so fresh in the spring and early summer, was stagnant and enervating now. Its heavy scents weighed upon them, and at mid-day the landscape seemed lying in a swoon. Ethiopic scorchings browned the upper slopes of the pastures, but there was still bright green herbage here where the watercourses purled. And as Clare was oppressed by the outward heats, so was he burdened inwardly by waxing fervour of passion for the soft and silent Tess.

6. In the new calendar of the first French republic the month of Thermidor (Greek *therm*, heat, + *dor*, gift) ran from July 19 to August 17. But Hardy may allude also to the day (July 27, 1794), in a very hot summer, when the climax of the bloody Reign of Terror occurred with the fall of Robespierre.

The rains having passed the uplands were dry. The wheels of the dairyman's spring cart, as he sped home from market, licked up the pulverized surface of the highway, and were followed by white ribands of dust, as if they had set a thin powder-train on fire. The cows jumped wildly over the five-barred barton-gate, maddened by the gad-fly; Dairyman Crick kept his shirt-sleeves permanently rolled up from Monday to Saturday: open windows had no effect in ventilation without open doors, and in the dairy-garden the blackbirds and thrushes crept about under the currant-bushes, rather in the manner of quadrupeds than of winged creatures. The flies in the kitchen were lazy, teasing, and familiar, crawling about in unwonted places, on the floor, into drawers, and over the backs of the milkmaids' hands. Conversations were concerning sunstroke; while butter-making, and still more butter-keeping, was a despair.

They milked entirely in the meads for coolness and convenience, without driving in the cows. During the day the animals obsequiously followed the shadow of the smallest tree as it moved round the stem with the diurnal roll; and when the milkers came they could hardly stand still for the flies.

On one of these afternoons four or five unmilked cows chanced to stand apart from the general herd, behind the corner of a hedge, among them being Dumpling and Old Pretty, who loved Tess's hands above those of any other maid. When she rose from her stool under a finished cow Angel Clare, who had been observing her for some time, asked her if she would take the aforesaid creatures next. She silently assented, and with her stool at arm's length, and the pail against her knee, went round to where they stood. Soon the sound of Old Pretty's milk fizzing into the pail came through the hedge, and then Angel felt inclined to go round the corner also, to finish off a hard-yielding milcher who had strayed there, he being now as capable of this as the dairyman himself.

All the men, and some of the women, when milking, dug their foreheads into the cows and gazed into the pail. But a few— mainly the younger ones—rested their heads sideways. This was Tess Durbeyfield's habit, her temple pressing the milcher's flank, her eyes fixed on the far end of the meadow with the quiet of one lost in meditation. She was milking Old Pretty thus, and the sun chancing to be on the milking-side it shone flat upon her pink-gowned form and her white curtain-bonnet, and upon her profile, rendering it keen as a cameo cut from the dun background of the cow.

She did not know that Clare had followed her round, and that he sat under his cow watching her. The stillness of her head and features was remarkable: she might have been in a trance, her eyes open, yet unseeing. Nothing in the picture moved but Old Pretty's tail and Tess's pink hands, the latter so gently as to be a rhythmic pulsation only, as if they were obeying a reflex stimulus, like a beating heart.

How very lovable her face was to him. Yet there was nothing ethereal about it; all was real vitality, real warmth, real incarnation. And it was in her mouth that this culminated. Eyes almost as deep and speaking he had seen before, and cheeks perhaps as fair; brows as arched, a chin and throat almost as shapely; her mouth he had seen nothing to equal on the face of the earth. To a young man with the least fire in him that little upward lift in the middle of her red top lip was distracting, infatuating, maddening. He had never before seen a woman's lips and teeth which forced upon his mind with such persistent iteration the old Elizabethan simile of roses filled with snow.[7] Perfect, he, as a lover, might have called them off-hand. But no— they were not perfect. And it was the touch of the imperfect upon the would-be perfect that gave the sweetness, because it was that which gave the humanity.

Clare had studied the curves of those lips so many times that he could reproduce them mentally with ease: and now, as they again confronted him, clothed with colour and life, they sent an *aura* over his flesh, a breeze through his nerves, which wellnigh produced a qualm; and actually produced, by some mysterious physiological process, a prosaic sneeze.

She then became conscious that he was observing her; but she would not show it by any change of position, though the curious dream-like fixity disappeared, and a close eye might easily have discerned that the rosiness of her face deepened, and then faded till only a tinge of it was left.

The influence that had passed into Clare like an excitation from the sky did not die down. Resolutions, reticences, prudences, fears, fell back like a defeated battalion. He jumped up from his seat, and, leaving his pail to be kicked over if the milcher had such a mind, went quickly towards the desire of his eyes, and, kneeling down beside her, clasped her in his arms.

Tess was taken completely by surprise, and she yielded to his embrace with unreflecting inevitableness. Having seen that it was really her lover who had advanced, and no one else, her lips parted, and she sank upon him in her momentary joy, with something very like an ecstatic cry.

7. On July 23, 1889, Hardy made this entry in his note book: "Of the people I have met this summer, the lady whose mouth recalls more fully than any other beauty's the Elizabethan metaphor 'Her lips are roses full of snow' (or is it Lodge's?) is Mrs. Hamo Thornycroft —whom I talked to at Gosse's dinner" (*The Early Life*, pp. 288-89). The lines are from Thomas Campion's "There is a Garden in Her Face": "They look like rosebuds filled with snow." [W]

He had been on the point of kissing that too tempting mouth, but he checked himself, for tender conscience' sake.

'Forgive me, Tess dear!' he whispered. 'I ought to have asked. I—did not know what I was doing. I do not mean it as a liberty. I am devoted to you, Tessy, dearest, in all sincerity!'

Old Pretty by this time had looked round, puzzled; and seeing two people crouching under her where, by immemorial custom, there should have been only one, lifted her hind leg crossly.

'She is angry—she doesn't know what we mean—she'll kick over the milk!' exclaimed Tess, gently striving to free herself, her eyes concerned with the quadruped's actions, her heart more deeply concerned with herself and Clare.

She slipped up from her seat, and they stood together, his arm still encircling her. Tess's eyes, fixed on distance, began to fill.

'Why do you cry, my darling?' he said.

'O—I don't know!' she murmured.

As she saw and felt more clearly the position she was in she became agitated and tried to withdraw.

'Well, I have betrayed my feeling, Tess, at last,' said he, with a curious sigh of desperation, signifying unconsciously that his heart had outrun his judgment. 'That I—love you dearly and truly I need not say. But I—it shall go no further now—it distresses you—I am as surprised as you are. You will not think I have presumed upon your defencelessness—been too quick and unreflecting, will you?'

'N'—I can't tell.'

He had allowed her to free herself; and in a minute or two the milking of each was resumed. Nobody had beheld the gravitation of the two into one; and when the dairyman came round by that screened nook a few minutes later there was not a sign to reveal that the markedly sundered pair were more to each other than mere acquaintance. Yet in the interval since Crick's last view of them something had occurred which changed the pivot of the universe for their two natures; something which, had he known its quality, the dairyman would have despised, as a practical man; yet which was based upon a more stubborn and resistless tendency than a whole heap of so-called practicalities. A veil had been whisked aside; the tract of each one's outlook was to have a new horizon thenceforward—for a short time or for a long.

END OF PHASE THE THIRD

Phase the Fourth—The Consequence

XXV

Clare, restless, went out into the dusk when evening drew on, she who had won him having retired to her chamber.

The night was as sultry as the day. There was no coolness after dark unless on the grass. Roads, garden-paths, the house-fronts, the barton-walls were warm as hearths, and reflected the noontide temperature into the noctambulist's face.

He sat on the east gate of the dairy-yard, and knew not what to think of himself. Feeling had indeed smothered judgment that day.

Since the sudden embrace, three hours before, the twain had kept apart. She seemed stilled, almost alarmed, at what had occurred, while the novelty, unpremeditation, mastery of circumstance disquieted him—palpitating, contemplative being that he was. He could hardly realize their true relations to each other as yet, and what their mutual bearing should be before third parties thenceforward.

Angel had come as pupil to this dairy in the idea that his temporary existence here was to be the merest episode in his life, soon passed through and early forgotten; he had come as to a place from which as from a screened alcove he could calmly view the absorbing world without, and, apostrophizing it with Walt Whitman—

> Crowds of men and women attired in the usual costumes,
> How curious you are to me!—[8]

resolve upon a plan for plunging into that world anew. But, behold, the absorbing scene had been imported hither. What had been the engrossing world had dissolved into an uninteresting outer dumb-show; while here, in this apparently dim and unimpassioned place, novelty had volcanically started up, as it had never, for him, started up elsewhere.

Every window of the house being open Clare could hear across the yard each trivial sound of the retiring household. That dairy-house, so humble, so insignificant, so purely to him a place of constrained sojourn that he had never hitherto deemed it of sufficient importance to be reconnoitred as an object of any quality whatever in the landscape; what was it now? The aged and lichened brick gables breathed forth 'Stay!' The windows

8. Walt Whitman, "Crossing Brooklyn Ferry" (1856), line 3.

smiled, the door coaxed and beckoned, the creeper blushed confederacy. A personality within it was so far-reaching in her influence as to spread into and make the bricks, mortar, and whole overhanging sky throb with a burning sensibility. Whose was this mighty personality? A milkmaid's.

It was amazing, indeed, to find how great a matter the life of the obscure dairy had become to him. And though new love was to be held partly responsible for this it was not solely so. Many besides Angel have learnt that the magnitude of lives is not as to their external displacements, but as to their subjective experiences. The impressionable peasant leads a larger, fuller, more dramatic life than the pachydermatous king. Looking at it thus he found that life was to be seen of the same magnitude here as elsewhere.

Despite his heterodoxy, faults, and weaknesses, Clare was a man with a conscience. Tess was no insignificant creature to toy with and dismiss; but a woman living her precious life—a life which, to herself who endured or enjoyed it, possessed as great a dimension as the life of the mightiest to himself. Upon her sensations the whole world depended to Tess; through her existence all her fellow-creatures existed, to her. The universe itself only came into being for Tess on the particular day in the particular year in which she was born.

This consciousness upon which he had intruded was the single opportunity of existence ever vouchsafed to Tess by an unsympathetic First Cause—her all; her every and only chance. How then should he look upon her as of less consequence than himself; as a pretty trifle to caress and grow weary of; and not deal in the greatest seriousness with the affection which he knew that he had awakened in her—so fervid and so impressionable as she was under her reserve; in order that it might not agonize and wreck her?

To encounter her daily in the accustomed manner would be to develop what had begun. Living in such close relations, to meet meant to fall into endearment; flesh and blood could not resist it; and, having arrived at no conclusion as to the issue of such a tendency, he decided to hold aloof for the present from occupations in which they would be mutually engaged. As yet the harm done was small.

But it was not easy to carry out the resolution never to approach her. He was driven towards her by every heave of his pulse.

He thought he would go and see his friends. It might be possible to sound them upon this. In less than five months his term here would have ended, and after a few additional months spent upon other farms he would be fully equipped in agricultural knowledge, and in a position to start on his own account. Would not a farmer want a wife, and should a farmer's wife be a drawing-room wax-figure, or a woman who understood farming? Notwithstanding the pleasing answer returned to him by the silence he resolved to go his journey.

One morning when they sat down to breakfast at Talbothays Dairy some maid observed that she had not seen anything of Mr. Clare that day.

'O no,' said Dairyman Crick. 'Mr. Clare has gone hwome to Emminster to spend a few days wi' his kinsfolk.'

For four impassioned ones around that table the sunshine of the morning went out at a stroke, and the birds muffled their song. But neither girl by word or gesture revealed her blankness.

'He's getting on towards the end of his time wi' me,' added the dairyman, with a phlegm which unconsciously was brutal; 'and so I suppose he is beginning to see about his plans elsewhere.'

'How much longer is he to bide here?' asked Izz Huett, the only one of the gloom-stricken bevy who could trust her voice with the question.

The others waited for the dairyman's answer as if their lives hung upon it; Retty, with parted lips, gazing on the table-cloth, Marian with heat added to her redness, Tess throbbing and looking out at the meads.

'Well, I can't mind the exact day without looking at my memorandum-book,' replied Crick, with the same intolerable unconcern. 'And even that may be altered a bit. He'll bide to get a little practice in the calving out at the straw-yard, for certain. He'll hang on till the end of the year I should say.'

Four months or so of torturing ecstasy in his society—of 'pleasure girdled about with pain.'[9] After that the blackness of unutterable night.

At this moment of the morning Angel Clare was riding along a narrow lane ten miles distant from the breakfasters, in the direction of his father's vicarage at Emminster, carrying, as well as he could, a little basket which contained some black-puddings and a bottle of mead, sent by Mrs. Crick, with her kind respects, to his parents. The white lane stretched before him, and his eyes were upon it; but they were staring into next year, and not at the lane. He loved her; ought he to marry her? Dared he to marry her? What would his mother and his brothers say? What would he himself say a couple of years after the event? That would depend upon whether the germs of staunch comradeship underlay the temporary emotion, or whether it were a sensuous joy in her form only, with no substratum of everlastingness.

His father's hill-surrounded little town, the Tudor church-tower of red stone, the clump of trees near the vicarage, came at last into view beneath him, and he rode down towards the well-known gate. Casting a glance in the direction of the church before entering his home, he beheld standing by the vestry-door a group of girls, of ages between twelve and sixteen, apparently awaiting the arrival of some other one, who in a moment became visible; a figure somewhat older than the school-girls, wearing a broad-brimmed hat and highly-starched cambric morning-gown, with a couple of books in her hand.

Clare knew her well. He could not be sure that she observed him; he hoped she did not, so as to render it unnecessary that he should go and speak to her, blameless creature that she was. An overpowering reluctance to greet her made him decide that she had not seen him. The young lady was Miss Mercy Chant, the only daughter of his father's neighbour and friend, whom it was his parents' quiet hope that he might wed some day. She was great at Antinomianism[1] and Bible-classes, and was plainly going to hold a class now. Clare's mind flew to the impassioned, summer-steeped heathens in the Var Vale, their rosy faces court-patched[2] with cow-droppings; and to one the most impassioned of them all.

It was on the impulse of the moment that he had resolved to trot over to Emminster, and hence had not written to apprise his mother and father, aiming, however, to arrive about the breakfast hour, before they should have gone out to their parish duties. He was a little late, and they had already sat down to the morning meal. The group at table jumped up to welcome him as soon as he entered. They were his father and mother, his brother the Reverend Felix—curate at a town in the adjoining county, home for the inside of a fortnight—and his other brother, the Reverend Cuthbert, the classical scholar, and Fellow and Dean of his College, down from Cambridge for the long vacation. His mother appeared in a cap and silver spectacles, and his father looked what in fact he was—an earnest, God-fearing man, somewhat gaunt, in years about sixty-five, his pale face lined with thought and purpose. Over their heads hung the picture of Angel's sister, the eldest of the family, sixteen years his senior, who had married a missionary and gone out to Africa.

Old Mr. Clare was a clergyman of a type which, within the

1. The doctrine that salvation depends not on good works or on obedience to God's laws but simply on faith in Jesus Christ.
2. "Spotted, as if with the patches [of black, adhesive 'court-plaster'] worn by ladies of fashion in the seventeenth and eighteenth centuries." [F] Hardy may pun on *court*, which may also mean farmyard.

last twenty years, has wellnigh dropped out of contemporary life. A spiritual descendant in the direct line from Wycliff, Huss, Luther, Calvin; an Evangelical of the Evangelicals, a Conversionist, a man of Apostolic simplicity in life and thought, he had in his raw youth made up his mind once for all on the deeper questions of existence, and admitted no further reasoning on them thenceforward. He was regarded even by those of his own date and school of thinking as extreme; while, on the other hand, those totally opposed to him were unwillingly won to admiration for his thoroughness, and for the remarkable power he showed in dismissing all question as to principles in his energy for applying them. He loved Paul of Tarsus, liked St. John, hated St. James as much as he dared, and regarded with mixed feelings Timothy, Titus, and Philemon. The New Testament was less a Christiad than a Pauliad to his intelligence—less an argument than an intoxication. His creed of determinism was such that it almost amounted to a vice, and quite amounted, on its negative side, to a renunciative philosophy which had cousinship with that of Schopenhauer and Leopardi. He despised the Canons and Rubric, swore by the Articles,[3] and deemed himself consistent through the whole category—which in a way he might have been. One thing he certainly was—sincere.

To the aesthetic, sensuous, pagan pleasure in natural life and lush womanhood which his son Angel had lately been experiencing in Var Vale, his temper would have been antipathetic in a high degree, had he either by inquiry or imagination been able to apprehend it. Once upon a time Angel had been so unlucky as to say to his father, in a moment of irritation, that it might have resulted far better for mankind if Greece had been the source of the religion of modern civilization, and not Palestine; and his father's grief was of that blank description which could not realize that there might lurk a thousandth part of a truth, much less a half truth or a whole truth, in such a proposition. He had simply preached austerely at Angel for some time after. But the kindness of his heart was such that he never resented anything for long, and welcomed his son to-day with a smile which was as candidly sweet as a child's.

Angel sat down, and the place felt like home; yet he did not so much as formerly feel himself one of the family gathered there. Every time that he returned hither he was conscious of this divergence, and since he had last shared in the Vicarage life it had

3. The "Canons," in the Church of England, are the "Constitutions and Canons Ecclesiastical" agreed upon by Convocation, and ratified by King James I in 1603. The "Rubric" is the direction for the conduct of divine service, printed in red in liturgical books. The Thirty-nine Articles of Religion are the statements to which all men ordained in the Church of England must subscribe.

grown even more distinctly foreign to his own than usual. Its transcendental aspirations—still unconsciously based on the geocentric view of things, a zenithal paradise, a nadiral hell—were as foreign to his own as if they had been the dreams of people on another planet. Latterly he had seen only Life, felt only the great passionate pulse of existence, unwarped, uncontorted, untrammelled by those creeds which futilely attempt to check what wisdom would be content to regulate.

On their part they saw a great difference in him, a growing divergence from the Angel Clare of former times. It was chiefly a difference in his manner that they noticed just now, particularly his brothers. He was getting to behave like a farmer; he flung his legs about; the muscles of his face had grown more expressive; his eyes looked as much information as his tongue spoke, and more. The manner of the scholar had nearly disappeared; still more the manner of the drawing-room young man. A prig would have said that he had lost culture, and a prude that he had become coarse. Such was the contagion of domiciliary fellowship with the Talbothays nymphs and swains.

After breakfast he walked with his two brothers, non-evangelical, well-educated, hall-marked young men, correct to their remotest fibre; such unimpeachable models as are turned out yearly by the lathe of a systematic tuition. They were both somewhat short-sighted, and when it was the custom to wear a single eyeglass and string they wore a single eyeglass and string; when it was the custom to wear a double glass they wore a double glass; when it was the custom to wear spectacles they wore spectacles straightway, all without reference to the particular variety of defect in their own vision. When Wordsworth was enthroned they carried pocket copies; and when Shelley was belittled they allowed him to grow dusty on their shelves. When Correggio's Holy Families were admired, they admired Correggio's Holy Families; when he was decried in favour of Velasquez, they sedulously followed suit without any personal objection.[4]

If these two noticed Angel's growing social ineptness, he noticed their growing mental limitations. Felix seemed to him all Church; Cuthbert all College. His Diocesan Synod and Visitations were the mainsprings of the world to the one; Cambridge to the other. Each brother candidly recognized that there were a few unimportant scores of millions of outsiders in civilized society, persons who were neither University men nor churchmen; but they were to be tolerated rather than reckoned with and respected.

They were both dutiful and attentive sons, and were regular

4. Correggio, a famous Italian painter of the sixteenth century; Velasquez, a great seventeenth-century Spanish painter.

in their visits to their parents. Felix, though an offshoot from a far more recent point in the devolution of theology than his father, was less self-sacrificing and disinterested. More tolerant than his father of a contradictory opinion, in its aspect as a danger to its holder, he was less ready than his father to pardon it as a slight to his own teaching. Cuthbert was, upon the whole, the more liberal-minded, though, with greater subtlety, he had not so much heart.

As they walked along the hillside Angel's former feeling revived in him—that whatever their advantages by comparison with himself, neither saw or set forth life as it really was lived. Perhaps, as with many men, their opportunities of observation were not so good as their opportunities of expression. Neither had an adequate conception of the complicated forces at work outside the smooth and gentle current in which they and their associates floated. Neither saw the difference between local truth and universal truth; that what the inner world said in their clerical and academic hearing was quite a different thing from what the outer world was thinking.

'I suppose it is farming or nothing for you now, my dear fellow,' Felix was saying, among other things, to his youngest brother, as he looked through his spectacles at the distant fields with sad austerity. 'And, therefore, we must make the best of it. But I do entreat you to endeavour to keep as much as possible in touch with moral ideals. Farming, of course, means roughing it externally; but high thinking may go with plain living, nevertheless.'

'Of course it may,' said Angel. 'Was it not proved nineteen hundred years ago—if I may trespass upon your domain a little? Why should you think, Felix, that I am likely to drop my high thinking and my moral ideals?'

'Well, I fancied, from the tone of your letters and our conversation—it may be fancy only—that you were somehow losing intellectual grasp. Hasn't it struck you, Cuthbert?'

'Now, Felix,' said Angel drily, 'we are very good friends, you know; each of us treading our allotted circles; but if it comes to intellectual grasp, I think you, as a contented dogmatist, had better leave mine alone, and inquire what has become of yours.'

They returned down the hill to dinner, which was fixed at any time at which their father's and mother's morning work in the parish usually concluded. Convenience as regarded afternoon callers was the last thing to enter into the consideration of unselfish Mr. and Mrs. Clare; though the three sons were sufficiently in unison on this matter to wish that their parents would conform a little to modern notions.

The walk had made them hungry, Angel in particular, who

was now an outdoor man, accustomed to the profuse *dapes inemptae*[5] of the dairyman's somewhat coarsely-laden table. But neither of the old people had arrived, and it was not till the sons were almost tired of waiting that their parents entered. The self-denying pair had been occupied in coaxing the appetites of some of their sick parishioners, whom they, somewhat inconsistently, tried to keep imprisoned in the flesh, their own appetites being quite forgotten.

The family sat down to table, and a frugal meal of cold viands was deposited before them. Angel looked round for Mrs. Crick's black-puddings,[6] which he had directed to be nicely grilled, as they did them at the dairy, and of which he wished his father and mother to appreciate the marvellous herbal savours as highly as he did himself.

'Ah! you are looking for the black-puddings, my dear boy,' observed Clare's mother. 'But I am sure you will not mind doing without them, as I am sure your father and I shall not, when you know the reason. I suggested to him that we should take Mrs. Crick's kind present to the children of the man who can earn nothing just now because of his attacks of delirium tremens; and he agreed that it would be a great pleasure to them; so we did.'

'Of course,' said Angel cheerfully, looking round for the mead.

'I found the mead so extremely alcoholic,' continued his mother, 'that it was quite unfit for use as a beverage, but as valuable as rum or brandy in an emergency; so I have put it in my medicine-closet.'

'We never drink spirits at this table, on principle,' added his father.

'But what shall I tell the dairyman's wife?' said Angel.

'The truth, of course,' said his father.

'I rather wanted to say we enjoyed the mead and the black-puddings very much. She is a kind, jolly sort of body, and is sure to ask me directly I return.'

'You cannot, if we did not,' Mr. Clare answered lucidly.

'Ah—no; though that mead was a drop of pretty tipple.'

'A what?' said Cuthbert and Felix both.

'Oh—'tis an expression they use down at Talbothays,' replied Angel, blushing. He felt that his parents were right in their practice if wrong in their want of sentiment, and said no more.

XXVI

It was not till the evening, after family prayers, that Angel found opportunity of broaching to his father one or two subjects near his heart. He had strung himself up to the purpose while

5. "Unpurchased feast" (Virgil, *Georgics*, iv. 133).   6. Sausage made of blood and suet.

kneeling behind his brothers on the carpet, studying the little nails in the heels of their walking boots. When the service was over they went out of the room with their mother, and Mr. Clare and himself were left alone.

The young man first discussed with the elder his plans for the attainment of his position as a farmer on an extensive scale—either in England or in the Colonies. His father then told him that, as he had not been put to the expense of sending Angel up to Cambridge, he had felt it his duty to set by a sum of money every year towards the purchase or lease of land for him some day, that he might not feel himself unduly slighted.

'As far as worldly wealth goes,' continued his father, 'you will no doubt stand far superior to your brothers in a few years.'

This considerateness on old Mr. Clare's part led Angel onward to the other and dearer subject. He observed to his father that he was then six-and-twenty, and that when he should start in the farming business he would require eyes in the back of his head to see to all matters—some one would be necessary to superintend the domestic labours of his establishment whilst he was afield. Would it not be well, therefore, for him to marry?

His father seemed to think this idea not unreasonable; and then Angel put the question—

'What kind of wife do you think would be best for me as a thrifty hard-working farmer?'

'A truly Christian woman, who will be a help and a comfort to you in your goings-out and your comings-in.[7] Beyond that, it really matters little. Such an one can be found; indeed, my earnest-minded friend and neighbour, Dr. Chant——'

'But ought she not primarily to be able to milk cows, churn good butter, make immense cheeses; know how to sit hens and turkeys, and rear chickens, to direct a field of labourers in an emergency, and estimate the value of sheep and calves?'

'Yes; a farmer's wife; yes, certainly. It would be desirable.' Mr. Clare, the elder, had plainly never thought of these points before. 'I was going to add,' he said, 'that for a pure and saintly woman you will not find one more to your true advantage, and certainly not more to your mother's mind and my own, than your friend Mercy, whom you used to show a certain interest in. It is true that my neighbour Chant's daughter has lately caught up the fashion of the younger clergy round about us for decorating the Communion-table—altar, as I was shocked to hear her call it one day—with flowers and other stuff on festival occasions. But her father, who is quite as opposed to such flummery as I, says that can be cured. It is a mere girlish outbreak which, I am sure, will not be permanent.'

7. Psalms cxxi:8: "The Lord shall preserve thy going out and thy coming in."

'Yes, yes; Mercy is good and devout, I know. But, father, don't you think that a young woman equally pure and virtuous as Miss Chant, but one who, in place of that lady's ecclesiastical accomplishments, understands the duties of farm life as well as a farmer himself, would suit me infinitely better?'

His father persisted in his conviction that a knowledge of a farmer's wife's duties came second to a Pauline view of humanity; and the impulsive Angel, wishing to honour his father's feelings and to advance the cause of his heart at the same time, grew specious. He said that fate or Providence had thrown in his way a woman who possessed every qualification to be the helpmate of an agriculturist, and was decidedly of a serious turn of mind. He would not say whether or not she had attached herself to the sound Low Church School of his father; but she would probably be open to conviction on that point; she was a regular church-goer of simple faith; honest-hearted, receptive, intelligent, graceful to a degree, chaste as a vestal, and, in personal appearance, exceptionally beautiful.

'Is she of a family such as you would care to marry into—a lady, in short?' asked his startled mother, who had come softly into the study during the conversation.

'She is not what in common parlance is called a lady,' said Angel, unflinchingly, 'for she is a cottager's daughter, as I am proud to say. But she *is* a lady, nevertheless—in feeling and nature.'

'Mercy Chant is of a very good family.'

'Pooh!—what's the advantage of that, mother?' said Angel quickly. 'How is family to avail the wife of a man who has to rough it as I have, and shall have to do?'

'Mercy is accomplished. And accomplishments have their charm,' returned his mother, looking at him through her silver spectacles.

'As to external accomplishments, what will be the use of them in the life I am going to lead?—while as to her reading, I can take that in hand. She'll be apt pupil enough, as you would say if you knew her. She's brim full of poetry—actualized poetry, if I may use the expression. She *lives* what paper-poets only write. ...And she is an unimpeachable Christian, I am sure; perhaps of the very tribe, genus, and species you desire to propagate.'

'O Angel, you are mocking!'

'Mother, I beg pardon. But as she really does attend Church almost every Sunday morning, and is a good Christian girl, I am sure you will tolerate any social shortcomings for the sake of that quality, and feel that I may do worse than choose her.'

Angel waxed quite earnest on that rather automatic orthodoxy in his beloved Tess which (never dreaming that it might stand him in such good stead) he had been prone to slight when observing it practised by her and the other milkmaids, because of its obvious unreality amid beliefs essentially naturalistic.

In their sad doubts as to whether their son had himself any right whatever to the title he claimed for the unknown young woman, Mr. and Mrs. Clare began to feel it as an advantage not to be overlooked that she at least was sound in her views; especially as the conjunction of the pair must have arisen by an act of Providence; for Angel never would have made orthodoxy a condition of his choice. They said finally that it was better not to act in a hurry, but that they would not object to see her.

Angel therefore refrained from declaring more particulars now. He felt that, single-minded and self-sacrificing as his parents were, there yet existed certain latent prejudices of theirs, as middle-class people, which it would require some tact to overcome. For though legally at liberty to do as he chose, and though their daughter-in-law's qualifications could make no practical difference to their lives, in the probability of her living far away from them, he wished for affection's sake not to wound their sentiment in the most important decision of his life.

He observed his own inconsistencies in dwelling upon accidents in Tess's life as if they were vital features. It was for herself that he loved Tess; her soul, her heart, her substance—not for her skill in the dairy, her aptness as his scholar, and certainly not for her simple formal faith-professions. Her unsophisticated open-air existence required no varnish of conventionality to make it palatable to him. He held that education had as yet but little affected the beats of emotion and impulse on which domestic happiness depends. It was probable that, in the lapse of ages, improved systems of moral and intellectual training would appreciably, perhaps considerably, elevate the involuntary and even the unconscious instincts of human nature; but up to the present day culture, as far as he could see, might be said to have affected only the mental epiderm of those lives which had been brought under its influence. This belief was confirmed by his experience of women, which, having latterly been extended from the cultivated middle-class into the rural community, had taught him how much less was the intrinsic difference between the good and wise woman of one social stratum and the good and wise woman of another social stratum, than between the good and bad, the wise and the foolish, of the same stratum or class.

It was the morning of his departure. His brothers had already left the vicarage to proceed on a walking tour in the north, whence one was to return to his college, and the other to his curacy. Angel might have accompanied them, but preferred to rejoin his sweetheart at Talbothays. He would have been an awkward member of the party; for, though the most appreciative humanist, the most ideal religionist, even the best-versed Christologist of the three, there was alienation in the standing consciousness that his squareness would not fit the round hole that had been prepared for him. To neither Felix nor Cuthbert had he ventured to mention Tess.

His mother made him sandwiches, and his father accompanied him, on his own mare, a little way along the road. Having fairly well advanced his own affairs Angel listened in a willing silence, as they jogged on together through the shady lanes, to his father's account of his parish difficulties, and the coldness of brother clergymen whom he loved, because of his strict interpretations of the New Testament by the light of what they deemed a pernicious Calvinistic doctrine.

'Pernicious!' said Mr. Clare, with genial scorn; and he proceeded to recount experiences which would show the absurdity of that idea. He told of wondrous conversions of evil livers of which he had been the instrument, not only amongst the poor, but amongst the rich and well-to-do; and he also candidly admitted many failures.

As an instance of the latter, he mentioned the case of a young upstart squire named d'Urberville, living some forty miles off, in the neighbourhood of Trantridge.

'Not one of the ancient d'Urbervilles of Kingsbere and other places?' asked his son. 'That curiously historic worn-out family with its ghostly legend of the coach-and-four?'

'O no. The original d'Urbervilles decayed and disappeared sixty or eighty years ago—at least, I believe so. This seems to be a new family which has taken the name; for the credit of the former knightly line I hope they are spurious, I'm sure. But it is odd to hear you express interest in old families. I thought you set less store by them even than I.'

'You misapprehend me, father; you often do,' said Angel with a little impatience. 'Politically I am sceptical as to the virtue of their being old. Some of the wise even among themselves "exclaim against their own succession," as Hamlet puts it;[8] but lyrically, dramatically, and even historically, I am tenderly attached to them.'

This distinction, though by no means a subtle one, was yet too subtle for Mr. Clare the elder, and he went on with the story he had been about to relate; which was that after the death of

8. *Hamlet*, II.ii.368.

the senior so-called d'Urberville the young man developed the most culpable passions, though he had a blind mother, whose condition should have made him know better. A knowledge of his career having come to the ears of Mr. Clare, when he was in that part of the country preaching missionary sermons, he boldly took occasion to speak to the delinquent on his spiritual state. Though he was a stranger, occupying another's pulpit, he had felt this to be his duty, and took for his text the words from St. Luke: 'Thou fool, this night thy soul shall be required of thee!'[9] The young man much resented this directness of attack, and in the war of words which followed when they met he did not scruple publicly to insult Mr. Clare, without respect for his gray hairs.

Angel flushed with distress.

'Dear father,' he said sadly, 'I wish you would not expose yourself to such gratuitous pain from scoundrels!'

'Pain?' said his father, his rugged face shining in the ardour of self-abnegation. 'The only pain to me was pain on his account, poor, foolish young man. Do you suppose his incensed words could give me any pain, or even his blows? "Being reviled we bless; being persecuted we suffer it; being defamed we entreat; we are made as the filth of the world, and as the offscouring of all things unto this day."[1] Those ancient and noble words to the Corinthians are strictly true at this present hour.'

'Not blows, father? He did not proceed to blows?'

'No, he did not. Though I have borne blows from men in a mad state of intoxication.'

'No!'

'A dozen times, my boy. What then? I have saved them from the guilt of murdering their own flesh and blood thereby; and they have lived to thank me, and praise God.'

'May this young man do the same!' said Angel fervently. 'But I fear otherwise, from what you say.'

'We'll hope, nevertheless,' said Mr. Clare. 'And I continue to pray for him, though on this side of the grave we shall probably never meet again. But, after all, one of those poor words of mine may spring up in his heart as a good seed some day.'

Now, as always, Clare's father was sanguine as a child; and though the younger could not accept his parent's narrow dogma he revered his practice, and recognized the hero under the pietist. Perhaps he revered his father's practice even more now than ever, seeing that, in the question of making Tessy his wife, his father had not once thought of inquiring whether she were well provided or penniless. The same unworldliness was what had necessitated Angel's getting a living as a farmer, and would probably keep his brothers in the position of poor parsons for the

9. Luke xii:20.   1. I Corinthians iv:12.

term of their activitites; yet Angel admired it none the less. Indeed, despite his own heterodoxy, Angel often felt that he was nearer to his father on the human side than was either of his brethren.

XXVII

An up-hill and down-dale ride of twenty-odd miles through a garish mid-day atmosphere brought him in the afternoon to a detached knoll a mile or two west of Talbothays, whence he again looked into that green trough of sappiness and humidity, the valley of the Var or Froom. Immediately he began to descend from the upland to the fat alluvial soil below, the atmosphere grew heavier; the languid perfume of the summer fruits, the mists, the hay, the flowers, formed therein a vast pool of odour which at this hour seemed to make the animals, the very bees and butterflies, drowsy. Clare was now so familiar with the spot that he knew the individual cows by their names when, a long distance off, he saw them dotted about the meads. It was with a sense of luxury that he recognized his power of viewing life here from its inner side, in a way that had been quite foreign to him in his student-days; and, much as he loved his parents, he could not help being aware that to come here, as now, after an experience of home-life, affected him like throwing off splints and bandages; even the one customary curb on the humours of English rural societies being absent in this place, Talbothays having no resident landlord.

Not a human being was out of doors at the dairy. The denizens were all enjoying the usual afternoon nap of an hour or so which the exceedingly early hours kept in summer-time rendered a necessity. At the door the wood-hooped pails, sodden and bleached by infinite scrubbings, hung like hats on a stand upon the forked and peeled limb of an oak fixed there for that purpose; all of them ready and dry for the evening milking. Angel entered, and went through the silent passages of the house to the back quarters, where he listened for a moment. Sustained snores came from the cart-house, where some of the men were lying down; the grunt and squeal of sweltering pigs arose from the still further distance. The large-leaved rhubarb and cabbage plants slept too, their broad limp surfaces hanging in the sun like half-closed umbrellas.

He unbridled and fed his horse, and as he re-entered the house the clock struck three. Three was the afternoon skimming-hour; and, with the stroke, Clare heard the creaking of the floor-boards above, and then the touch of a descending foot on the stairs. It was Tess's, who in another moment came down before his eyes.

She had not heard him enter, and hardly realized his presence there. She was yawning, and he saw the red interior of her mouth as if it had been a snake's. She had stretched one arm so high above her coiled-up cable of hair that he could see its satin delicacy above the sunburn; her face was flushed with sleep, and her eyelids hung heavy over their pupils. The brim-fulness of her nature breathed from her. It was a moment when a woman's soul is more incarnate than at any other time; when the most spiritual beauty bespeaks itself flesh; and sex takes the outside place in the presentation.

Then those eyes flashed brightly through their filmy heaviness, before the remainder of her face was well awake. With an oddly compounded look of gladness, shyness, and surprise, she exclaimed—

'O Mr. Clare! How you frightened me— I——'

There had not at first been time for her to think of the changed relations which his declaration had introduced; but the full sense of the matter rose up in her face when she encountered Clare's tender look as he stepped forward to the bottom stair.

'Dear, darling Tessy!' he whispered, putting his arm round her, and his face to her flushed cheek. 'Don't, for Heaven's sake, Mister me any more. I have hastened back so soon because of you!'

Tess's excitable heart beat against his by way of reply; and there they stood upon the red-brick floor of the entry, the sun slanting in by the window upon his back, as he held her tightly to his breast; upon her inclining face, upon the blue veins of her temple, upon her naked arm, and her neck, and into the depths of her hair. Having been lying down in her clothes she was warm as a sunned cat. At first she would not look straight up at him, but her eyes soon lifted, and his plumbed the deepness of the ever-varying pupils, with their radiating fibrils of blue, and black, and gray, and violet, while she regarded him as Eve at her second waking might have regarded Adam.

'I've got to go a-skimming,' she pleaded, 'and I have on'y old Deb to help me to-day. Mrs. Crick is gone to market with Mr. Crick, and Retty is not well, and the others are gone out somewhere, and won't be home till milking.'

As they retreated to the milk-house Deborah Fyander appeared on the stairs.

'I have come back, Deborah,' said Mr. Clare, upwards, 'So I can help Tess with the skimming; and, as you are very tired, I am sure, you needn't come down till milking-time.'

Possibly the Talbothays milk was not very thoroughly skimmed that afternoon. Tess was in a dream wherein familiar objects appeared as having light and shade and position, but no particular outline. Every time she held the skimmer under the pump to cool it for the work her hand trembled, the ardour of his affection being so palpable that she seemed to flinch under it like a plant in too burning a sun.

Then he pressed her again to his side, and when she had done running her forefinger round the leads to cut off the cream-edge, he cleaned it in nature's way; for the unconstrained manners of Talbothays dairy came convenient now.

'I may as well say it now as later, dearest,' he resumed gently. 'I wish to ask you something of a very practical nature, which I have been thinking of ever since that day last week in the meads. I shall soon want to marry, and, being a farmer, you see I shall require for my wife a woman who knows all about the management of farms. Will you be that woman, Tessy?'

He put it in that way that she might not think he had yielded to an impulse of which his head would disapprove.

She turned quite careworn. She had bowed to the inevitable result of proximity, the necessity of loving him; but she had not calculated upon this sudden corollary, which, indeed, Clare had put before her without quite meaning himself to do it so soon. With pain that was like the bitterness of dissolution she murmured the words of her indispensable and sworn answer as an honourable woman.

'O Mr. Clare—I cannot be your wife—I cannot be!'

The sound of her own decision seemed to break Tess's very heart, and she bowed her face in her grief.

'But, Tess!' he said, amazed at her reply, and holding her still more greedily close. 'Do you say no? Surely you love me?'

'O yes, yes! And I would rather be yours than anybody's in the world,' returned the sweet and honest voice of the distressed girl. 'But I *cannot* marry you!'

'Tess,' he said, holding her at arm's length, 'you are engaged to marry some one else!'

'No, no!'

'Then why do you refuse me?'

'I don't want to marry! I have not thought of doing it. I cannot! I only want to love you.'

'But why?'

Driven to subterfuge, she stammered—

'Your father is a parson, and your mother wouldn' like you to marry such as me. She will want you to marry a lady.'

'Nonsense—I have spoken to them both. That was partly why I went home.'

'I feel I cannot—never, never!' she echoed.

'Is it too sudden to be asked thus, my Pretty?'

'Yes—I did not expect it.'

'If you will let it pass, please, Tessy, I will give you time,' he said. 'It was very abrupt to come home and speak to you all at once. I'll not allude to it again for a while.'

She again took up the shining skimmer, held it beneath the pump, and began anew. But she could not, as at other times, hit the exact under-surface of the cream with the delicate dexterity required, try as she might: sometimes she was cutting down into the milk, sometimes in the air. She could hardly see, her eyes having filled with two blurring tears drawn forth by a grief which, to this her best friend and dear advocate, she could never explain.

'I can't skim—I can't!' she said, turning away from him.

Not to agitate and hinder her longer the considerate Clare began talking in a more general way:

'You quite misapprehend my parents. They are the most simple-mannered people alive, and quite unambitious. They are two of the few remaining Evangelical school. Tessy, are you an Evangelical?'

'I don't know.'

'You go to church very regularly, and our parson here is not very High, they tell me.'

Tess's ideas on the views of the parish clergyman, whom she heard every week, seemed to be rather more vague than Clare's, who had never heard him at all.

'I wish I could fix my mind on what I hear there more firmly than I do,' she remarked as a safe generality. 'It is often a great sorrow to me.'

She spoke so unaffectedly that Angel was sure in his heart that his father could not object to her on religious grounds, even though she did not know whether her principles were High, Low, or Broad. He himself knew that, in reality, the confused beliefs which she held, apparently imbibed in childhood, were, if any thing, Tractarian as to phraseology, and Pantheistic as to essence. Confused or otherwise, to disturb them was his last desire:

> Leave thou thy sister, when she prays,
>> Her early Heaven, her happy views;
>> Nor thou with shadow'd hint confuse
> A life that leads melodious days.[2]

He had occasionally thought the counsel less honest than musical; but he gladly conformed to it now.

He spoke further of the incidents of his visit, of his father's mode of life, of his zeal for his principles; she grew serener, and the undulations disappeared from her skimming; as she finished one

2. Tennyson, *In Memoriam*, xxxiii.5.

lead after another he followed her, and drew the plugs for letting down the milk.

'I fancied you looked a little downcast when you came in,' she ventured to observe, anxious to keep away from the subject of herself.

'Yes—well, my father has been talking a good deal to me of his troubles and difficulties, and the subject always tends to depress me. He is so zealous that he gets many snubs and buffetings from people of a different way of thinking from himself, and I don't like to hear of such humiliations to a man of his age, the more particularly as I don't think earnestness does any good when carried so far. He has been telling me of a very unpleasant scene in which he took part quite recently. He went as the deputy of some missionary society to preach in the neighbourhood of Trantridge, a place forty miles from here, and made it his business to expostulate with a lax young cynic he met with somewhere about there—son of some landowner up that way—and who has a mother afflicted with blindness. My father addressed himself to the gentleman point-blank, and there was quite a disturbance. It was very foolish of my father, I must say, to intrude his conversation upon a stranger when the probabilities were so obvious that it would be useless. But whatever he thinks to be his duty, that he'll do, in season or out of season; and, of course, he makes many enemies, not only among the absolutely vicious, but among the easy-going, who hate being bothered. He says he glories in what happened, and that good may be done indirectly; but I wish he would not so wear himself out now he is getting old, and would leave such pigs to their wallowing.'

Tess's look had grown hard and worn, and her ripe mouth tragical; but she no longer showed any tremulousness. Clare's revived thoughts of his father prevented his noticing her particularly; and so they went on down the white row of liquid rectangles till they had finished and drained them off, when the other maids returned, and took their pails, and Deb came to scald out the leads for the new milk. As Tess withdrew to go afield to the cows he said to her softly—

'And my question, Tessy?'

'O no—no!' replied she with grave hopelessness, as one who had heard anew the turmoil of her own past in the allusion to Alec d'Urberville. 'It *can't* be!'

She went out towards the mead, joining the other milkmaids with a bound, as if trying to make the open air drive away her sad constraint. All the girls drew onward to the spot where the cows were grazing in the farther mead, the bevy advancing with the bold grace of wild animals—the reckless unchastened motion

of women accustomed to unlimited space—in which they abandoned themselves to the air as a swimmer to the wave. It seemed
natural enough to him now that Tess was again in sight to choose
a mate from unconstrained Nature, and not from the abodes of Art.

XXVIII

Her refusal, though unexpected, did not permanently daunt
Clare. His experience of women was great enough for him to be
aware that the negative often meant nothing more than the preface to the affirmative; and it was little enough for him not to
know that in the manner of the present negative there lay a great
exception to the dallyings of coyness. That she had already permitted him to make love to her he read as an additional assurance, not fully trowing that in the fields and pastures to 'sigh
gratis'[3] is by no means deemed waste; love-making being here
more often accepted inconsiderately and for its own sweet sake
than in the carking anxious homes of the ambitious, where a
girl's craving for an establishment paralyzes her healthy thought
of a passion as an end.

'Tess, why did you say "no" in such a positive way?' he asked
her in the course of a few days.

She started.

'Don't ask me, I told you why—partly. I am not good enough
—not worthy enough.'

'How? Not fine lady enough?'

'Yes—something like that,' murmured she. 'Your friends would
scorn me.'

'Indeed, you mistake them—my father and mother. As for my
brothers, I don't care——' He clasped his fingers behind her back
to keep her from slipping away. 'Now—you did not mean it,
sweet?—I am sure you did not! You have made me so restless
that I cannot read, or play, or do anything. I am in no hurry,
Tess, but I want to know—to hear from your own warm lips—that
you will some day be mine—any time you may choose; but some
day?'

She could only shake her head and look away from him.

Clare regarded her attentively, conned the characters of her
face as if they had been hieroglyphics. The denial seemed real.

'Then I ought not to hold you in this way—ought I? I have no
right to you—no right to seek out where you are, or to walk with
you! Honestly, Tess, do you love any other man?'

'How can you ask?' she said, with continued self-suppression.

'I almost know that you do not. But then, why do you repulse
me?'

'I don't repulse you. I like you to—tell me you love me; and you

3. *Hamlet*, II.ii.308: "The lover shall not sigh gratis."

may always tell me so as you go about with me—and never offend me.'

'But you will not accept me as a husband?'

'Ah—that's different—it is for your good, indeed my dearest! O, believe me, it is only for your sake! I don't like to give myself the great happiness o' promising to be yours in that way—because—because I am *sure* I ought not to do it.'

'But you will make me happy!'

'Ah—you think so, but you don't know!'

At such times as this, apprehending the grounds of her refusal to be her modest sense of incompetence in matters social and polite, he would say that she was wonderfully well-informed and versatile—which was certainly true, her natural quickness, and her admiration for him, having led her to pick up his vocabulary, his accent, and fragments of his knowledge, to a surprising extent. After these tender contests and her victory she would go away by herself under the remotest cow, if at milking-time, or into the sedge, or into her room, if at a leisure interval, and mourn silently, not a minute after an apparently phlegmatic negative.

The struggle was so fearful; her own heart was so strongly on the side of his—two ardent hearts against one poor little conscience—that she tried to fortify her resolution by every means in her power. She had come to Talbothays with a made-up mind. On no account could she agree to a step which might afterwards cause bitter rueing to her husband for his blindness in wedding her. And she held that what her conscience had decided for her when her mind was unbiassed ought not to be overruled now.

'Why don't somebody tell him all about me?' she said. 'It was only forty miles off—why hasn't it reached here? Somebody must know!'

Yet nobody seemed to know; nobody told him.

For two or three days no more was said. She guessed from the sad countenances of her chamber companions that they regarded her not only as the favourite, but as the chosen; but they could see for themselves that she did not put herself in his way.

Tess had never before known a time in which the thread of her life was so distinctly twisted of two strands, positive pleasure and positive pain. At the next cheese-making the pair were again left alone together. The dairyman himself had been lending a hand; but Mr. Crick, as well as his wife, seemed latterly to have acquired a suspicion of mutual interest between these two; though they walked so circumspectly that suspicion was but of the faintest. Anyhow, the dairyman left them to themselves.

They were breaking up the masses of curd before putting them into the vats. The operation resembled the act of crumbling bread on a large scale; and amid the immaculate whiteness of the curds Tess Durbeyfield's hands showed themselves of the pinkness of the rose. Angel, who was filling the vats with his handfuls, suddenly ceased, and laid his hands flat upon hers. Her sleeves were rolled far above the elbow, and bending lower he kissed the inside vein of her soft arm.

Although the early September weather was sultry, her arm, from her dabbling in the curds, was as cold and damp to his mouth as a new-gathered mushroom, and tasted of the whey. But she was such a sheaf of susceptibilities that her pulse was accelerated by the touch, her blood driven to her finger-ends, and the cool arms flushed hot. Then, as though her heart had said, 'Is coyness longer necessary? Truth is truth between man and woman, as between man and man,' she lifted her eyes, and they beamed devotedly into his, as her lip rose in a tender half-smile.

'Do you know why I did that, Tess?' he said.

'Because you love me very much!'

'Yes, and as a preliminary to a new entreaty.'

'Not *again!*'

She looked a sudden fear that her resistance might break down under her own desire.

'O, Tessy!' he went on, 'I *cannot* think why you are so tantalizing. Why do you disappoint me so? You seem almost like a coquette, upon my life you do—a coquette of the first urban water! They blow hot and blow cold, just as you do; and it is the very last sort of thing to expect to find in a retreat like Talbothays. . . . And yet, dearest,' he quickly added, observing how the remark had cut her, 'I know you to be the most honest, spotless creature that ever lived. So how can I suppose you a flirt? Tess, why don't you like the idea of being my wife, if you love me as you seem to do?'

'I have never said I don't like the idea, and I never could say it; because—it isn't true!'

The stress now getting beyond endurance her lip quivered, and she was obliged to go away. Clare was so pained and perplexed that he ran after and caught her in the passage.

'Tell me, tell me!' he said, passionately clasping her, in forgetfulness of his curdy hands: 'do tell me that you won't belong to anybody but me!'

'I will, I will tell you!' she exclaimed. 'And I will give you a complete answer, if you will let me go now. I will tell you my experiences—all about myself—all!'

'Your experiences, dear; yes, certainly; any number.' He expressed assent in loving satire, looking into her face. 'My Tess has, no doubt, almost as many experiences as that wild convolvulus out there on the garden hedge, that opened itself this morning for the first time. Tell me anything, but don't use that wretched expression any more about not being worthy of me.'

'I will try—not! And I'll give you my reasons to-morrow—next week.'

'Say on Sunday?'

'Yes, on Sunday.'

At last she got away, and did not stop in her retreat till she was in the thicket of pollard willows at the lower side of the barton, where she could be quite unseen. Here, Tess flung herself down upon the rustling undergrowth of spear-grass, as upon a bed, and remained crouching in palpitating misery broken by momentary shoots of joy, which her fears about the ending could not altogether suppress.

In reality, she was drifting into acquiescence. Every see-saw of her breath, every wave of her blood, every pulse singing in her ears, was a voice that joined with nature in revolt against her scrupulousness. Reckless, inconsiderate acceptance of him; to close with him at the altar, revealing nothing, and chancing discovery; to snatch ripe pleasure before the iron teeth of pain could have time to shut upon her: that was what love counselled; and in almost a terror of ecstasy Tess divined that, despite her many months of lonely self-chastisement, wrestlings, communings, schemes to lead a future of austere isolation, love's counsel would prevail.

The afternoon advanced, and still she remained among the willows. She heard the rattle of taking down the pails from the forked stands; the 'waow-waow!' which accompanied the getting together of the cows. But she did not go to the milking. They would see her agitation; and the dairyman, thinking the cause to be love alone, would good-naturedly tease her; and that harassment could not be borne.

Her lover must have guessed her overwrought state, and invented some excuse for her non-appearance, for no inquiries were made or calls given. At half-past six the sun settled down upon the levels, with the aspect of a great forge in the heavens, and presently a monstrous pumpkin-like moon arose on the other hand. The pollard willows, tortured out of their natural shape by incessant choppings, because spiny-haired monsters as they stood up against it. She went in, and upstairs without a light.

It was now Wednesday. Thursday came, and Angel looked thoughtfully at her from a distance, but intruded in no way upon her. The indoor milkmaids, Marian and the rest, seemed to guess that something definite was afoot, for they did not force any remarks upon her in the bedchamber. Friday passed; Saturday. To-morrow was the day.

'I shall give way—I shall say yes—I shall let myself marry

him—I cannot help it!' she jealously panted, with her hot face to the pillow that night, on hearing one of the other girls sigh his name in her sleep. 'I can't bear to let anybody have him but me! Yet it is a wrong to him, and may kill him when he knows! O my heart—O—O—O!'

XXIX

'Now, who mid ye think I've heard news o' this morning?' said Dairyman Crick, as he sat down to breakfast next day, with a riddling gaze round upon the munching men and maids. 'Now, just who mid ye think?'

One guessed, and another guessed. Mrs. Crick did not guess, because she knew already.

'Well,' said the dairyman, ' 'tis that slack-twisted 'hore's-bird of a feller, Jack Dollop. He's lately got married to a widow-woman.'

'Not Jack Dollop? A villain—to think o' that!' said a milker.

The name entered quickly into Tess Durbeyfield's consciousness, for it was the name of the lover who had wronged his sweetheart, and had afterwards been so roughly used by the young woman's mother in the butter-churn.

'And has he married the valiant matron's daughter, as he promised?' asked Angel Clare absently, as he turned over the newspaper he was reading at the little table to which he was always banished by Mrs. Crick, in her sense of his gentility.

'Not he, sir. Never meant to,' replied the dairyman. 'As I say, 'tis a widow-woman, and she had money, it seems—fifty poun' a year or so; and that was all he was after. They were married in a great hurry; and then she told him that by marrying she had lost her fifty poun' a year. Just fancy the state o' my gentleman's mind at that news! Never such a cat-and-dog life as they've been leading ever since! Serves him well beright. But onluckily the poor woman gets the worst o't.'

'Well, the silly body should have told en sooner that the ghost of her first man would trouble him,' said Mrs. Crick.

'Ay; ay,' responded the dairyman indecisively. 'Still, you can see exactly how 'twas. She wanted a home, and didn't like to run the risk of losing him. Don't ye think that was something like it, maidens?'

He glanced towards the row of girls.

'She ought to ha' told him just before they went to church, when he could hardly have backed out,' exclaimed Marian.

'Yes, she ought,' agreed Izz.

'She must have seen what he was after, and should ha' refused him,' cried Retty spasmodically.

'And what do you say, my dear?' asked the dairyman of Tess.

'I think she ought—to have told him the true state of things—or else refused him—I don't know,' replied Tess, the bread-and-butter choking her.

'Be cust if I'd have done either o't,' said Beck Knibbs, a married helper from one of the cottages. 'All's fair in love and war. I'd ha' married en just as she did, and if he'd said two words to me about not telling him beforehand anything whatsomdever about my first chap that I hadn't chose to tell, I'd ha' knocked him down wi' the rolling-pin—a scram[4] little feller like he! Any woman could do it.'

The laughter which followed this sally was supplemented only by a sorry smile, for form's sake, from Tess. What was comedy to them was tragedy to her; and she could hardly bear their mirth. She soon rose from table, and, with an impression that Clare would follow her, went along a little wriggling path, now stepping to one side of the irrigating channels, and now to the other, till she stood by the main stream of the Var. Men had been cutting the water-weeds higher up the river, and masses of them were floating past her—moving islands of green crow-foot, whereon she might almost have ridden; long locks of which weed had lodged against the piles driven to keep the cows from crossing.

Yes, there was the pain of it. This question of a woman telling her story—the heaviest of crosses to herself—seemed but amusement to others. It was as if people should laugh at martyrdom.

'Tessy!' came from behind her, and Clare sprang across the gully, alighting beside her feet. 'My wife—soon!'

'No, no; I cannot. For your sake, O Mr. Clare; for your sake, I say no!'

'Tess!'

'Still I say no!' she repeated.

Not expecting this he had put his arm lightly round her waist the moment after speaking, beneath her hanging tail of hair. (The younger dairymaids, including Tess, breakfasted with their hair loose on Sunday mornings before building it up extra high for attending church, a style they could not adopt when milking with their heads against the cows.) If she had said 'Yes' instead of 'No' he would have kissed her; it had evidently been his intention; but her determined negative deterred his scrupulous heart. Their condition of domiciliary comradeship put her, as the woman, to such disadvantage by its enforced intercourse, that he felt it unfair to her to exercise any pressure of blandishment which he might have honestly employed had she been better able to avoid him. He released her momentarily-imprisoned waist, and withheld the kiss.

4. Withered.

It all turned on that release. What had given her strength to refuse him this time was solely the tale of the widow told by the dairyman; and that would have been overcome in another moment. But Angel said no more; his face was perplexed; he went away.

Day after day they met—somewhat less constantly than before; and thus two or three weeks went by. The end of September drew near, and she could see in his eye that he might ask her again.

His plan of procedure was different now—as though he had made up his mind that her negatives were, after all, only coyness and youth startled by the novelty of the proposal. The fitful evasiveness of her manner when the subject was under discussion countenanced the idea. So he played a more coaxing game; and while never going beyond words, or attempting the renewal of caresses, he did his utmost orally.

In this way Clare persistently wooed her in undertones like that of the purling milk—at the cow's side, at skimmings, at buttermakings, at cheese-makings, among broody poultry, and among farrowing pigs—as no milkmaid was ever wooed before by such a man.

Tess knew that she must break down. Neither a religious sense of a certain moral validity in the previous union nor a conscientious wish for candour could hold out against it much longer. She loved him so passionately, and he was so godlike in her eyes; and being, though untrained, instinctively refined, her nature cried for his tutelary guidance. And thus, though Tess kept repeating to herself, 'I can never be his wife,' the words were vain. A proof of her weakness lay in the very utterance of what calm strength would not have taken the trouble to formulate. Every sound of his voice beginning on the old subject stirred her with a terrifying bliss, and she coveted the recantation she feared.

His manner was—what man's is not?—so much that of one who would love and cherish and defend her under any conditions, changes, charges, or revelations, that her gloom lessened as she basked in it. The season meanwhile was drawing onward to the equinox, and though it was still fine, the days were much shorter. The dairy had again worked by morning candle-light for a long time; and a fresh renewal of Clare's pleading occurred one morning between three and four.

She had run up in her bedgown to his door to call him as usual; then had gone back to dress and call the others; and in ten minutes was walking to the head of the stairs with the candle in her hand. At the same moment he came down his steps from above in his shirt-sleeves and put his arm across the stairway.

'Now, Miss Flirt, before you go down,' he said peremptorily. 'It is a fortnight since I spoke, and this won't do any longer. You *must* tell me what you mean, or I shall have to leave this house. My door was ajar just now, and I saw you. For your own safety I must go. You don't know. Well? Is it to be yes at last?'

'I am only just up, Mr. Clare, and it is too early to take me to task!' she pouted. 'You need not call me Flirt. 'Tis cruel and untrue. Wait till by and by. Please wait till by and by! I will really think seriously about it between now and then. Let me go downstairs!'

She looked a little like what he said she was as, holding the candle sideways, she tried to smile away the seriousness of her words.

'Call me Angel, then, and not Mr. Clare.'

'Angel.'

'Angel dearest—why not?'

' 'Twould mean that I agree, wouldn't it?'

'It would only mean that you love me, even if you cannot marry me; and you were so good as to own that long ago.'

'Very well, then, "Angel dearest," if I *must*,' she murmured, looking at her candle, a roguish curl coming upon her mouth, notwithstanding her suspense.

Clare had resolved never to kiss her until he had obtained her promise; but somehow, as Tess stood there in her prettily tucked-up milking gown, her hair carelessly heaped upon her head till there should be leisure to arrange it when skimming and milking were done, he broke his resolve, and brought his lips to her cheek for one moment. She passed downstairs very quickly, never looking back at him or saying another word. The other maids were already down, and the subject was not pursued. Except Marian they all looked wistfully and suspiciously at the pair, in the sad yellow rays which the morning candles emitted in contrast with the first cold signals of the dawn without.

When skimming was done—which, as the milk diminished with the approach of autumn, was a lessening process day by day—Retty and the rest went out. The lovers followed them.

'Our tremulous lives are so different from theirs, are they not?' he musingly observed to her, as he regarded the three figures tripping before him through the frigid pallor of opening day.

'Not so very different, I think,' she said.

'Why do you think that?'

'There are very few women's lives that are not—tremulous,' Tess replied, pausing over the new word as if it impressed her. 'There's more in those three than you think.'

'What is in them?'

'Almost either of 'em,' she began, 'would make—perhaps would make—a properer wife than I. And perhaps they love you as well as I—almost.'

'O, Tessy!'

There were signs that it was an exquisite relief to her to hear the impatient exclamation, though she had resolved so intrepidly to let generosity make one bid against herself. That was now done, and she had not the power to attempt self-immolation a second time then. They were joined by a milker from one of the cottages, and no more was said on that which concerned them so deeply. But Tess knew that this day would decide it.

In the afternoon several of the dairyman's household and assistants went down to the meads as usual, a long way from the dairy, where many of the cows were milked without being driven home. The supply was getting less as the animals advanced in calf, and the supernumerary milkers of the lush green season had been dismissed.

The work progressed leisurely. Each pailful was poured into tall cans that stood in a large spring-waggon which had been brought upon the scene; and when they were milked the cows trailed away.

Dairyman Crick, who was there with the rest, his wrapper gleaming miraculously white against a leaden evening sky, suddenly looked at his heavy watch.

'Why, 'tis later than I thought,' he said. 'Begad! We shan't be soon enough with this milk at the station, if we don't mind. There's no time to-day to take it home and mix it with the bulk afore sending off. It must go to station straight from here. Who'll drive it across?'

Mr. Clare volunteered to do so, though it was none of his business, asking Tess to accompany him. The evening, though sunless, had been warm and muggy for the season, and Tess had come out with her milking-hood only, naked-armed and jacketless; certainly not dressed for a drive. She therefore replied by glancing over her scant habiliments; but Clare gently urged her. She assented by relinquishing her pail and stool to the dairyman to take home; and mounted the spring-waggon beside Clare.

XXX

In the diminishing daylight they went along the level roadway through the meads, which stretched away into gray miles, and were backed in the extreme edge of distance by the swarthy and abrupt slopes of Egdon Heath. On its summit stood clumps and stretches of fir-trees, whose notched tips appeared like battlemented towers crowning black-fronted castles of enchantment.

They were so absorbed in the sense of being close to each other that they did not begin talking for a long while, the silence being broken only by the clucking of the milk in the tall cans behind them. The lane they followed was so solitary that the hazel nuts had remained on the boughs till they slipped from their shells, and the blackberries hung in heavy clusters. Every now and then Angel would fling the lash of his whip round one of these, pluck it off, and give it to his companion.

The dull sky soon began to tell its meaning by sending down herald-drops of rain, and the stagnant air of the day changed into a fitful breeze which played about their faces. The quicksilvery glaze on the rivers and pools vanished; from broad mirrors of light they changed to lustreless sheets of lead, with a surface like a rasp. But that spectacle did not affect her preoccupation. Her countenance, a natural carnation slightly embrowned by the season, had deepened its tinge with the beating of the rain-drops; and her hair, which the pressure of the cows' flanks had, as usual, caused to tumble down from its fastenings and stray beyond the curtain of her calico bonnet, was made clammy by the moisture, till it hardly was better than seaweed.

'I ought not to have come, I suppose,' she murmured, looking at the sky.

'I am sorry for the rain,' said he. 'But how glad I am to have you here!'

Remote Egdon disappeared by degrees behind the liquid gauze. The evening grew darker, and the roads being crossed by gates it was not safe to drive faster than at a walking pace. The air was rather chill.

'I am so afraid you will get cold, with nothing upon your arms and shoulders,' he said. 'Creep close to me, and perhaps the drizzle won't hurt you much. I should be sorrier still if I did not think that the rain might be helping me.'

She imperceptibly crept closer, and he wrapped round them both a large piece of sail-cloth, which was sometimes used to keep the sun off the milk-cans. Tess held it from slipping off him as well as herself, Clare's hands being occupied.

'Now we are all right again. Ah—no we are not! It runs down into my neck a little, and it must still more into yours. That's better. Your arms are like wet marble, Tess. Wipe them in the cloth. Now, if you stay quiet, you will not get another drop. Well, dear—about that question of mine—that long-standing question?'

The only reply that he could hear for a little while was the smack of the horse's hoofs on the moistening road, and the cluck of the milk in the cans behind them.

'Do you remember what you said?'

'I do,' she replied.

'Before we get home, mind.'

'I'll try.'

He said no more then. As they drove on the fragment of an old manor house of Caroline[5] date rose against the sky, and was in due course passed and left behind.

'That,' he observed, to entertain her, 'is an interesting old place —one of the several seats which belonged to an ancient Norman family formerly of great influence in this county, the d'Urbervilles. I never pass one of their residences without thinking of them. There is something very sad in the extinction of a family of renown, even if it was fierce, domineering, feudal renown.'

'Yes,' said Tess.

They crept along towards a point in the expanse of shade just at hand at which a feeble light was beginning to assert its presence, a spot where, by day, a fitful white streak of steam at intervals upon the dark green background denoted intermittent moments of contact between their secluded world and modern life. Modern life stretched out its steam feeler to this point three or four times a day, touched the native existences, and quickly withdrew its feeler again, as if what it touched had been uncongenial.

They reached the feeble light, which came from the smoky lamp of a little railway station; a poor enough terrestrial star, yet in one sense of more importance to Talbothays Dairy and mankind than the celestial ones to which it stood in such humiliating contrast. The cans of new milk were unladen in the rain, Tess getting a little shelter from a neighbouring holly tree.

Then there was the hissing of a train, which drew up almost silently upon the wet rails, and the milk was rapidly swung can by can into the truck. The light of the engine flashed for a second upon Tess Durbeyfield's figure, motionless under the great holly tree. No object could have looked more foreign to the gleaming cranks and wheels than this unsophisticated girl, with the round bare arms, the rainy face and hair, the suspended attitude of a friendly leopard at pause, the print gown of no date or fashion, and the cotton bonnet drooping on her brow.

She mounted again beside her lover, with a mute obedience characteristic of impassioned natures at times, and when they had wrapped themselves up over head and ears in the sail-cloth again, they plunged back into the now thick night. Tess was so receptive that the few minutes of contact with the whirl of material progress lingered in her thought.

'Londoners will drink it at their breakfasts to-morrow, won't they?' she asked. 'Strange people that we have never seen.'

5. Of the period of Charles I or Charles II, *i.e.*, roughly seventeenth-century.

'Yes—I suppose they will. Though not as we send it. When its strength has been lowered, so that it may not get up into their heads.'

'Noble men and noble women, ambassadors and centurions, ladies and tradeswomen, and babies who have never seen a cow.'

'Well, yes; perhaps; particularly centurions.'

'Who don't know anything of us, and where it comes from; or think how we two drove miles across the moor to-night in the rain that it might reach 'em in time?'

'We did not drive entirely on account of these precious Londoners; we drove a little on our own—on account of that anxious matter which you will, I am sure, set at rest, dear Tess. Now, permit me to put it in this way. You belong to me already, you know; your heart, I mean. Does it not?'

'You know as well as I. O yes—yes!'

'Then, if your heart does, why not your hand?'

'My only reason was on account of you—on account of a question. I have something to tell you——'

'But suppose it to be entirely for my happiness, and my worldly convenience also?'

'O yes; if it is for your happiness and worldly convenience. But my life before I came here—I want——'

'Well, it is for my convenience as well as my happiness. If I have a very large farm, either English or colonial, you will be invaluable as a wife to me; better than a woman out of the largest mansion in the country. So please—please, dear Tessy, disabuse your mind of the feeling that you will stand in my way.'

'But my history. I want you to know it—you must let me tell you—you will not like me so well!'

'Tell it if you wish to, dearest. This precious history then. Yes, I was born at so and so, Anno Domini——'

'I was born at Marlott,' she said, catching at his words as a help, lightly as they were spoken. 'And I grew up there. And I was in the Sixth Standard when I left school, and they said I had great aptness, and should make a good teacher, so it was settled that I should be one. But there was trouble in my family; father was not very industrious, and he drank a little.'

'Yes, yes. Poor child! Nothing new.' He pressed her more closely to his side.

'And then—there is something very unusual about it—about me. I—I was——'

Tess's breath quickened.

'Yes, dearest. Never mind.'

'I—I—am not a Durbeyfield, but a d'Urberville—a descendant

of the same family as those that owned the old house we passed. And—we are all gone to nothing!'

'A d'Urberville!—Indeed! And is that all the trouble, dear Tess?'

'Yes,' she answered faintly.

'Well—why should I love you less after knowing this?'

'I was told by the dairyman that you hated old families.'

He laughed.

'Well, it is true, in one sense. I do hate the aristocratic principle of blood before everything, and do think that as reasoners the only pedigrees we ought to respect are those spiritual ones of the wise and virtuous, without regard to corporeal paternity. But I am extremely interested in this news—you can have no idea how interested I am! Are not you interested yourself in being one of that well-known line?'

'No. I have thought it sad—especially since coming here, and knowing that many of the hills and fields I see once belonged to my father's people. But other hills and fields belonged to Retty's people, and perhaps others to Marian's, so that I don't value it particularly.'

'Yes—it is surprising how many of the present tillers of the soil were once owners of it, and I sometimes wonder that a certain school of politicians don't make capital of the circumstance; but they don't seem to know it. . . . I wonder that I did not see the resemblance of your name to d'Urberville, and trace the manifest corruption. And this was the carking secret!'

She had not told. At the last moment her courage had failed her, she feared his blame for not telling him sooner; and her instinct of self-preservation was stronger than her candour.

'Of course,' continued the unwitting Clare, 'I should have been glad to know you to be descended exclusively from the long-suffering, dumb, unrecorded rank and file of the English nation, and not from the self-seeking few who made themselves powerful at the expense of the rest. But I am corrupted away from that by my affection for you, Tess [he laughed as he spoke], and made selfish likewise. For your own sake I rejoice in your descent. Society is hopelessly snobbish, and this fact of your extraction may make an appreciable difference to its acceptance of you as my wife, after I have made you the well-read woman that I mean to make you. My mother too, poor soul, will think so much better of you on account of it. Tess, you must spell your name correctly—d'Urberville—from this very day.'

'I like the other way rather best.'

'But you *must*, dearest! Good heavens, why dozens of mushroom millionaires would jump at such a possession! By the bye, there's one of that kidney who has taken the name—where have I heard of him?—Up in the neighbourhood of The Chase, I think. Why, he is the very man who had that rumpus with my father I told you of. What an odd coincidence!'

'Angel, I think I would rather not take the name! It is unlucky, perhaps!'

She was agitated.

'Now then, Mistress Teresa d'Urberville, I have you. Take my name, and so you will escape yours! The secret is out, so why should you any longer refuse me?'

'If it is *sure* to make you happy to have me as your wife, and you feel that you do wish to marry me, *very, very* much——'

'I do, dearest, of course!'

'I mean, that it is only your wanting me very much, and being hardly able to keep alive without me, whatever my offences, that would make me feel I ought to say I will.'

'You will—you do say it, I know! You will be mine for ever and ever.'

He clasped her close and kissed her.

'Yes!'

She had no sooner said it than she burst into a dry hard sobbing, so violent that it seemed to rend her. Tess was not a hysterical girl by any means, and he was surprised.

'Why do you cry, dearest?'

'I can't tell—quite!—I am so glad to think—of being yours, and making you happy!'

'But this does not seem very much like gladness, my Tessy!'

'I mean—I cry because I have broken down in my vow! I said I would die unmarried!'

'But, if you love me you would like me to be your husband?'

'Yes, yes, yes! But O, I sometimes wish I had never been born!'

'Now, my dear Tess, if I did not know that you are very much excited, and very inexperienced, I should say that remark was not very complimentary. How came you to wish that if you care for me? Do you care for me? I wish you would prove it in some way.

'How can I prove it more than I have done?' she cried, in a distraction of tenderness. 'Will this prove it more?'

She clasped his neck, and for the first time Clare learnt what an impassioned woman's kisses were like upon the lips of one whom she loved with all her heart and soul, as Tess loved him.

'There—now do you believe?' she asked, flushed, and wiping her eyes.

'Yes. I never really doubted—never, never!'

So they drove on through the gloom, forming one bundle inside the sail-cloth, the horse going as he would, and the rain driving against them. She had consented. She might as well have agreed at first. The 'appetite for joy' which pervades all creation, that tremendous force which sways humanity to its purpose, as the tide sways the helpless weed, was not to be controlled by vague lucubrations over the social rubric.

'I must write to my mother,' she said. 'You don't mind my doing that?'

'Of course not, dear child. You are a child to me, Tess, not to know how very proper it is to write to your mother at such a time, and how wrong it would be in me to object. Where does she live?'

'At the same place—Marlott. On the further side of Blackmoor Vale.'

'Ah, then I *have* seen you before this summer——'

'Yes; at that dance on the green; but you would not dance with me. O, I hope that is of no ill-omen for us now!'

XXXI

Tess wrote a most touching and urgent letter to her mother the very next day, and by the end of the week a response to her communication arrived in Joan Durbeyfield's wandering last-century hand.

Dear Tess,—J write these few lines Hoping they will find you well, as they leave me at Present, thank God for it. Dear Tess, we are all glad to Hear that you are going really to be married soon. But with respect to your question, Tess, J say between ourselves, quite private but very strong, that on no account do you say a word of your Bygone Trouble to him. J did not tell everything to your Father, he being so Proud on account of his Respectability, which, perhaps, your Intended is the same. Many a woman—some of the Highest in the Land —have had a Trouble in their time; and why should you Trumpet yours when others don't Trumpet theirs? No girl would be such a Fool, specially as it is so long ago, and not your Fault at all. J shall answer the same if you ask me fifty times. Besides, you must bear in mind that, knowing it to be your Childish Nature to tell all that's in your heart—so simple!—J made you promise me never to let it out by Word or Deed, having your Welfare in my Mind; and you most solemnly did promise it going from this Door. J have not named either that Question or your coming marriage to your Father, as he would blab it everywhere, poor Simple Man.

Dear Tess, keep up your Spirits, and we mean to send you a Hogshead of Cyder for your Wedding, knowing there is not much in your parts, and thin Sour Stuff what there is. So no more at present, and with kind love to your Young Man.—From your affectte. Mother,

J. DURBEYFIELD.

'O mother, mother!' murmured Tess.

She was recognizing how light was the touch of events the most oppressive upon Mrs. Durbeyfield's elastic spirit. Her mother did not see life as Tess saw it. That haunting episode of bygone days was to her mother but a passing accident. But perhaps her mother was right as to the course to be followed, whatever she might be in her reasons. Silence seemed, on the face of it, best for her adored one's happiness: silence it should be.

Thus steadied by a command from the only person in the world who had any shadow of right to control her action, Tess grew calmer. The responsibility was shifted, and her heart was lighter than it had been for weeks. The days of declining autumn which followed her assent, beginning with the month of October, formed a season through which she lived in spiritual altitudes more nearly approaching ecstasy than any other period of her life.

There was hardly a touch of earth in her love for Clare. To her sublime trustfulness he was all that goodness could be—knew all that a guide, philosopher, and friend[6] should know. She thought every line in the contour of his person the perfection of masculine beauty, his soul the soul of a saint, his intellect that of a seer. The wisdom of her love for him, as love, sustained her dignity; she seemed to be wearing a crown. The compassion of his love for her, as she saw it, made her lift up her heart to him in devotion. He would sometimes catch her large, worshipful eyes, that had no bottom to them, looking at him from their depths, as if she saw something immortal before her.

She dismissed the past—trod upon it and put it out, as one treads on a coal that is smouldering and dangerous.

She had not known that men could be so disinterested, chivalrous, protective, in their love for women as he. Angel Clare was far from all that she thought him in this respect; absurdly far, indeed; but he was, in truth, more spiritual than animal; he had himself well in hand, and was singularly free from grossness. Though not cold-natured, he was rather bright than hot—less Byronic than Shelleyan; could love desperately, but with a love more especially inclined to the imaginative and ethereal; it was a fastidious emotion which could jealously guard the loved one against his very self. This amazed and enraptured Tess, whose slight experiences had been so infelicitous till now; and in her reaction from indignation against the male sex she swerved to excess of honour for Clare.

They unaffectedly sought each other's company; in her honest faith she did not disguise her desire to be with him. The sum of her instincts on this matter, if clearly stated, would have been

6. An echo of Pope's *Essay on Man*, iv.390.

that the elusive quality in her sex which attracts men in general might be distasteful to so perfect a man after an avowal of love, since it must in its very nature carry with it a suspicion of art.

The country custom of unreserved comradeship out of doors during betrothal was the only custom she knew, and to her it had no strangeness; though it seemed oddly anticipative to Clare till he saw how normal a thing she, in common with all the other dairy-folk, regarded it. Thus, during this October month of wonderful afternoons they roved along the meads by creeping paths which followed the brinks of trickling tributary brooks, hopping across by little wooden bridges to the other side, and back again. They were never out of the sound of some purling weir, whose buzz accompanied their own murmuring, while the beams of the sun, almost as horizontal as the mead itself, formed a pollen of radiance over the landscape. They saw tiny blue fogs in the shadows of trees and hedges, all the time that there was bright sunshine elsewhere. The sun was so near the ground, and the sward so flat, that the shadows of Clare and Tess would stretch a quarter of a mile ahead of them, like two long fingers pointing afar to where the green alluvial reaches abutted against the sloping sides of the vale.

Men were at work here and there—for it was the season for 'taking up' the meadows, or digging the little waterways clear for the winter irrigation, and mending their banks where trodden down by the cows. The shovelfuls of loam, black as jet, brought there by the river when it was as wide as the whole valley, were an essence of soils, pounded champaigns of the past, steeped, refined, and subtilized to extraordinary richness, out of which came all the fertility of the mead, and of the cattle grazing there.

Clare hardily kept his arm round her waist in sight of these watermen, with the air of a man who was accustomed to public dalliance, though actually as shy as she who, with lips parted and eyes askance on the labourers, wore the look of a wary animal the while.

'You are not ashamed of owning me as yours before them!' she said gladly.

'O no!'

'But if it should reach the ears of your friends at Emminster that you are walking about like this with me, a milkmaid——'

'The most bewitching milkmaid ever seen.'

'They might feel it a hurt to their dignity.'

'My dear girl—a d'Urberville hurt the dignity of a Clare! It is a grand card to play—that of your belonging to such a family, and I am reserving it for a grand effect when we are married, and have the proofs of your descent from Parson Tringham. Apart from that, my future is to be totally foreign to my family —it will not affect even the surface of their lives. We shall leave this part of England—perhaps England itself—and what does it matter how people regard us here? You will like going, will you not?'

She could answer no more than a bare affirmative, so great was the emotion aroused in her at the thought of going through the world with him as his own familiar friend. Her feelings almost filled her ears like a babble of waves, and surged up to her eyes. She put her hand in his, and thus they went on, to a place where the reflected sun glared up from the river, under a bridge, with a molten-metallic glow that dazzled their eyes, though the sun itself was hidden by the bridge. They stood still, whereupon little furred and feathered heads popped up from the smooth surface of the water; but, finding that the disturbing presences had paused, and not passed by, they disappeared again. Upon this river-brink they lingered till the fog began to close round them—which was very early in the evening at this time of the year—settling on the lashes of her eyes, where it rested like crystals, and on his brows and hair.

They walked later on Sundays, when it was quite dark. Some of the dairy-people, who were also out of doors on the first Sunday evening after their engagement, heard her impulsive speeches, ecstasized to fragments, though they were too far off to hear the words discoursed; noted the spasmodic catch in her remarks, broken into syllables by the leapings of her heart, as she walked leaning on his arm; her contented pauses, the occasional little laugh upon which her soul seemed to ride—the laugh of a woman in company with the man she loves and has won from all other women—unlike anything else in nature. They marked the buoyancy of her tread, like the skim of a bird which has not quite alighted.

Her affection for him was now the breath and life of Tess's being; it enveloped her as a photosphere, irradiated her into forgetfulness of her past sorrows, keeping back the gloomy spectres that would persist in their attempts to touch her—doubt, fear, moodiness, care, shame. She knew that they were waiting like wolves just outside the circumscribing light, but she had long spells of power to keep them in hungry subjection there.

A spiritual forgetfulness co-existed with an intellectual remembrance. She walked in brightness, but she knew that in the background those shapes of darkness were always spread. They might be receding, or they might be approaching, one or the other, a little every day.

One evening Tess and Clare were obliged to sit indoors keeping house, all the other occupants of the domicile being away. As they talked she looked thoughtfully up at him, and met his two appreciative eyes.

'I am not worthy of you—no, I am not!' she burst out, jumping up from her low stool as though appalled at his homage, and the fulness of her own joy thereat.

Clare, deeming the whole basis of her excitement to be that which was only the smaller part of it, said—

'I won't have you speak like it, dear Tess! Distinction does not consist in the facile use of a contemptible set of conventions, but in being numbered among those who are true, and honest, and just, and pure, and lovely, and of good report[7]—as you are, my Tess.'

She struggled with the sob in her throat. How often had that string of excellences made her young heart ache in church of late years, and how strange that he should have cited them now.

'Why didn't you stay and love me when I—was sixteen; living with my little sisters and brothers, and you danced on the green? O, why didn't you, why didn't you!' she said, impetuously clasping her hands.

Angel began to comfort and reassure her, thinking to himself, truly enough, what a creature of moods she was, and how careful he would have to be of her when she depended for her happiness entirely on him.

'Ah—why didn't I stay!' he said. 'That is just what I feel. If I had only known! But you must not be so bitter in your regret—why should you be?'

With the woman's instinct to hide she diverged hastily—

'I should have had four years more of your heart than I can ever have now. Then I should not have wasted my time as I have done—I should have had so much longer happiness!'

It was no mature woman with a long dark vista of intrigue behind her who was tormented thus; but a girl of simple life, not yet one-and-twenty, who had been caught during her days of immaturity like a bird in a springe. To calm herself the more completely she rose from her little stool and left the room, overturning the stool with her skirts as she went.

He sat on by the cheerful firelight thrown from a bundle of green ash-sticks laid across the dogs; the sticks snapped pleasantly, and hissed out bubbles of sap from their ends. When she came back she was herself again.

'Do you not think you are just a wee bit capricious, fitful, Tess?' he said, good humouredly, as he spread a cushion for her on the

7. An echo of Philippians iv:8.

stool, and seated himself in the settle beside her. 'I wanted to ask you something, and just then you ran away.'

'Yes, perhaps I am capricious,' she murmured. She suddenly approached him, and put a hand upon each of his arms. 'No, Angel, I am not really so—by Nature, I mean!' The more particularly to assure him that she was not, she placed herself close to him in the settle, and allowed her head to find a resting-place against Clare's shoulder. 'What did you want to ask me—I am sure I will answer it,' she continued humbly.

'Well, you love me, and have agreed to marry me, and hence there follows a thirdly, "When shall the day be?"'

'I like living like this.'

'But I must think of starting in business on my own hook with the new year, or a little later. And before I get involved in the multifarious details of my new position, I should like to have secured my partner.'

'But,' she timidly answered, 'to talk quite practically, wouldn't it be best not to marry till after all that?—Though I can't bear the thought o' your going away and leaving me here!'

'Of course you cannot—and it is not best in this case. I want you to help me in many ways in making my start. When shall it be? Why not a fortnight from now?'

'No,' she said, becoming grave; 'I have so many things to think of first.'

'But——'

He drew her gently nearer to him.

The reality of marriage was startling when it loomed so near. Before discussion of the question had proceeded further there walked round the corner of the settle into the full firelight of the apartment Mr. Dairyman Crick, Mrs. Crick, and two of the milkmaids.

Tess sprang like an elastic ball from his side to her feet, while her face flushed and her eyes shone in the firelight.

'I knew how it would be if I sat so close to him!' she cried, with vexation. 'I said to myself, they are sure to come and catch us! But I wasn't really sitting on his knee, though it might ha' seemed as if I was almost!'

'Well—if so be you hadn't told us, I am sure we shouldn't ha' noticed that ye had been sitting anywhere at all in this light,' replied the dairyman. He continued to his wife, with the stolid mien of a man who understood nothing of the emotions relating to matrimony—'Now, Christianer, that shows that folks should never fancy other folks be supposing things when they bain't. O no, I should never ha' thought a word of where she was a sitting to, if she hadn't told me—not I.'

'We are going to be married soon,' said Clare, with improvised phlegm.

'Ah—and be ye! Well, I am truly glad to hear it, sir. I've thought you mid do such a thing for some time. She's too good for a dairymaid—I said so the very first day I zid her—and a prize for any man; and what's more, a wonderful woman for a gentleman-farmer's wife; he won't be at the mercy of his baily[8] wi' her at his side.'

Somehow Tess disappeared. She had been even more struck with the look of the girls who followed Crick than abashed by Crick's blunt praise.

After supper, when she reached her bedroom, they were all present. A light was burning, and each damsel was sitting up whitely in her bed, awaiting Tess, the whole like a row of avenging ghosts.

But she saw in a few moments that there was no malice in their mood. They could scarcely feel as a loss what they had never expected to have. Their condition was objective, contemplative.

'He's going to marry her!' murmured Retty, never taking eyes off Tess. 'How her face do show it!'

'You *be* going to marry him?' asked Marian.

'Yes,' said Tess.

'When?'

'Some day.'

They thought that this was evasiveness only.

'Yes—going to *marry* him—a gentleman!' repeated Izz Huett.

And by a sort of fascination the three girls, one after another, crept out of their beds, and came and stood barefooted round Tess. Retty put her hands upon Tess's shoulders, as if to realize her friend's corporeality after such a miracle, and the other two laid their arms round her waist, all looking into her face.

'How it do seem! Almost more than I can think of!' said Izz Huett.

Marian kissed Tess. 'Yes,' she murmured as she withdrew her lips.

'Was that because of love for her, or because other lips have touched there by now?' continued Izz drily to Marian.

'I wasn't thinking o' that,' said Marian simply. 'I was on'y feeling all the strangeness o't—that she is to be his wife, and nobody else. I don't say nay to it, nor either of us, because we did not think of it—only loved him. Still, nobody else is to marry'n in the world—no fine lady, nobody in silks and satins; but she who do live like we.'

8. Bailiff, a farm manager. [F]

'Are you sure you don't dislike me for it?' said Tess in a low voice.

They hung about her in their white nightgowns before replying, as if they considered their answer might lie in her look.

'I don't know—I don't know,' murmured Retty Priddle. 'I want to hate 'ee; but I cannot!'

'That's how I feel,' echoed Izz and Marian. 'I can't hate her. Somehow she hinders me!'

'He ought to marry one of you,' murmured Tess.

'Why?'

'You are all better than I.'

'We better than you?' said the girls in a low, slow whisper. 'No, no, dear Tess!'

'You are!' she contradicted impetuously. And suddenly tearing away from their clinging arms she burst into a hysterical fit of tears, bowing herself on the chest of drawers and repeating incessantly, 'O yes, yes, yes!'

Having once given way she could not stop her weeping.

'He ought to have had one of you!' she cried. 'I think I ought to make him even now! You would be better for him than—I don't know what I'm saying! O! O!'

They went up to her and clasped her round, but still her sobs tore her.

'Get some water,' said Marian. 'She's upset by us, poor thing, poor thing!'

They gently led her back to the side of her bed, where they kissed her warmly.

'You are best for'n,' said Marian. 'More ladylike, and a better scholar than we, especially since he has taught 'ee so much. But even you ought to be proud. You *be* proud, I'm sure!'

'Yes, I am,' she said; 'and I am ashamed at so breaking down!'

When they were all in bed, and the light was out, Marian whispered across to her—

'You will think of us when you be his wife, Tess, and of how we told 'ee that we loved him, and how we tried not to hate you, and did not hate you, and could not hate you, because you were his choice, and we never hoped to be chose by him.'

They were not aware that, at these words, salt, stinging tears trickled down upon Tess's pillow anew, and how she resolved, with a bursting heart, to tell all her history to Angel Clare, despite her mother's command—to let him for whom she lived and breathed despise her if he would, and her mother regard her as a fool, rather than preserve a silence which might be deemed a treachery to him, and which somehow seemed a wrong to these.

XXXII

This penitential mood kept her from naming the wedding-day. The beginning of November found its date still in abeyance, though he asked her at the most tempting times. But Tess's desire seemed to be for a perpetual betrothal in which everything should remain as it was then.

The meads were changing now; but it was still warm enough in early afternoons before milking to idle there awhile, and the state of dairy-work at this time of year allowed a spare hour for idling. Looking over the damp sod in the direction of the sun, a glistening ripple of gossamer webs was visible to their eyes under the luminary, like the track of moonlight on the sea. Gnats, knowing nothing of their brief glorification, wandered across the shimmer of this pathway, irradiated as if they bore fire within them, then passed out of its line, and were quite extinct. In the presence of these things he would remind her that the date was still the question.

Or he would ask her at night, when he accompanied her on some mission invented by Mrs. Crick to give him the opportunity. This was mostly a journey to the farmhouse on the slopes above the vale, to inquire how the advanced cows were getting on in the straw-barton to which they were relegated. For it was a time of the year that brought great changes to the world of kine. Batches of the animals were sent away daily to this lying-in hospital, where they lived on straw till their calves were born, after which event, and as soon as the calf could walk, mother and offspring were driven back to the dairy. In the interval which elasped before the calves were sold there was, of course, little milking to be done, but as soon as the calf had been taken away the milkmaids would have to set to work as usual.

Returning from one of these dark walks they reached a great gravel-cliff immediately over the levels, where they stood still and listened. The water was now high in the streams, squirting through the weirs, and tinkling under culverts; the smallest gullies were all full; there was no taking short cuts anywhere, and footpassengers were compelled to follow the permanent ways. From the whole extent of the invisible vale came a multitudinous intonation; it forced upon their fancy that a great city lay below them, and that the murmur was the vociferation of its populace.

'It seems like tens of thousands of them,' said Tess; 'holding public-meetings in their market-places, arguing, preaching, quarrelling, sobbing, groaning, praying, and cursing.'

Clare was not particularly heeding.

'Did Crick speak to you to-day, dear, about his not wanting much assistance during the winter months?'

'No.'

'The cows are going dry rapidly.'

'Yes. Six or seven went to the straw-barton yesterday, and three the day before, making nearly twenty in the straw already. Ah— is it that the farmer don't want my help for the calving? O, I am not wanted here any more! And I have tried so hard to——'

'Crick didn't exactly say that he would no longer require you. But, knowing what our relations were, he said in the most good-natured and respectful manner possible that he supposed on my leaving at Christmas I should take you with me, and on my asking what he would do without you he merely observed that, as a matter of fact, it was a time of year when he could do with a very little female help. I am afraid I was sinner enough to feel rather glad that he was in this way forcing your hand.'

'I don't think you ought to have felt glad, Angel. Because 'tis always mournful not to be wanted, even if at the same time 'tis convenient.'

'Well, it is convenient—you have admitted that.' He put his finger upon her cheek. 'Ah!' he said.

'What?'

'I feel the red rising up at her having been caught! But why should I trifle so! We will not trifle—life is too serious.'

'It is. Perhaps I saw that before you did.'

She was seeing it then. To decline to marry him after all— in obedience to her emotion of last night—and leave the dairy, meant to go to some strange place, not a dairy; for milkmaids were not in request now calving-time was coming on; to go to some arable farm where no divine being like Angel Clare was. She hated the thought, and she hated more the thought of going home.

'So that, seriously, dearest Tess,' he continued, 'since you will probably have to leave at Christmas, it is in every way desirable and convenient that I should carry you off then as my property. Besides, if you were not the most uncalculating girl in the world you would know that we could not go on like this for ever.'

'I wish we could. That it would always be summer and autumn, and you always courting me, and always thinking as much of me as you have done through the past summer-time!'

'I always shall.'

'O, I know you will!' she cried, with a sudden fervour of faith in him. 'Angel, I will fix the day when I will become yours for always!'

Thus at last it was arranged between them, during that dark

walk home, amid the myriads of liquid voices on the right and left.

When they reached the dairy Mr. and Mrs. Crick were promptly told—with injunctions to secrecy; for each of the lovers was desirous that the marriage should be kept as private as possible. The dairyman, though he had thought of dismissing her soon, now made a great concern about losing her. What should he do about his skimming? Who would make the ornamental butter-pats for the Anglebury and Sandbourne ladies? Mrs. Crick congratulated Tess on the shilly-shallying having at last come to an end, and said that directly she set eyes on Tess she divined that she was to be the chosen one of somebody who was no common outdoor man; Tess had looked so superior as she walked across the barton on that afternoon of her arrival; that she was of a good family she could have sworn. In point of fact Mrs. Crick did remember thinking that Tess was graceful and good-looking as she approached; but the superiority might have been a growth of the imagination aided by subsequent knowledge.

Tess was now carried along upon the wings of the hours, without the sense of a will. The word had been given; the number of the day written down. Her naturally bright intelligence had begun to admit the fatalistic convictions common to field-folk and those who associate more extensively with natural phenomena than with their fellow-creatures; and she accordingly drifted into that passive responsiveness to all things her lover suggested, characteristic of the frame of mind.

But she wrote anew to her mother, ostensibly to notify the wedding-day; really to again implore her advice. It was a gentleman who had chosen her, which perhaps her mother had not sufficiently considered. A post-nuptial explanation, which might be accepted with a light heart by a rougher man, might not be received with the same feeling by him. But this communication brought no reply from Mrs. Durbeyfield.

Despite Angel Clare's plausible representations to himself and to Tess of the practical need for their immediate marriage, there was in truth an element of precipitancy in the step, as became apparent at a later date. He loved her dearly, though perhaps rather ideally and fancifully than with the impassioned thoroughness of her feeling for him. He had entertained no notion, when doomed as he had thought to an unintellectual bucolic life, that such charms as he beheld in this idyllic creature would be found behind the scenes. Unsophistication was a thing to talk of; but he had not known how it really struck one until he came here. Yet he was very far from seeing his future track clearly, and it might be a year or two before he would be able to consider himself fairly started in life. The secret lay in the tinge of reck-lessness imparted to his career and character by the sense that he had been made to miss his true destiny through the prejudices of his family.

'Don't you think 'twould have been better for us to wait till you were quite settled in your midland farm?' she once asked timidly. (A midland farm was the idea just then.)

'To tell the truth, my Tess, I don't like you to be left anywhere away from my protection and sympathy.'

The reason was a good one, so far as it went. His influence over her had been so marked that she had caught his manner and habits, his speech and phrases, his likings and his aversions. And to leave her in farmland would be to let her slip back again out of accord with him. He wished to have her under his charge for another reason. His parents had naturally desired to see her once at least before he carried her off to a distant settle-ment, English or colonial; and as no opinion of theirs was to be allowed to change his intention, he judged that a couple of months' life with him in lodgings whilst seeking for an advanta-geous opening would be of some social assistance to her at what she might feel to be a trying ordeal—her presentation to his mother at the Vicarage.

Next, he wished to see a little of the working of a flour-mill, having an idea that he might combine the use of one with corn-growing. The proprietor of a large old water-mill at Wellbridge —once the mill of an Abbey—had offered him the inspection of his time-honoured mode of procedure, and a hand in the operations for a few days, whenever he should choose to come. Clare paid a visit to the place, some few miles distant, one day at this time, to inquire particulars, and returned to Talbothays in the evening. She found him determined to spend a short time at the Well-bridge flour-mills. And what had determined him? Less the oppor-tunity of an insight into grinding and bolting than the casual fact that lodgings were to be obtained in that very farmhouse which, be-fore its mutilation, had been the mansion of a branch of the d'Urber-ville family. This was always how Clare settled practical questions; by a sentiment which had nothing to do with them. They decided to go immediately after the wedding, and remain for a fortnight, in-stead of journeying to towns and inns.

'Then we will start off to examine some farms on the other side of London that I have heard of,' he said, 'and by March or April we will pay a visit to my father and mother.'

Questions of procedure such as these arose and passed, and the day, the incredible day, on which she was to become his, loomed large in the near future. The thirty-first of December, New Year's

Eve, was the date. His wife, she said to herself. Could it ever be? Their two selves together, nothing to divide them, every incident shared by them; why not? And yet why?

One Sunday morning Izz Huett returned from church, and spoke privately to Tess.

'You was not called home[9] this morning.'

'What?'

'It should ha' been the first time of asking to-day,' she answered, looking quietly at Tess. 'You meant to be married New Year's Eve, deary?'

The other returned a quick affirmative.

'And there must be three times of asking. And now there be only two Sundays left between.'

Tess felt her cheek paling; Izz was right; of course there must be three. Perhaps he had forgotten! If so, there must be a week's postponement, and that was unlucky. How could she remind her lover? She who had been so backward was suddenly fired with impatience and alarm lest she should lose her dear prize.

A natural incident relieved her anxiety. Izz mentioned the omission of the banns to Mrs. Crick, and Mrs. Crick assumed a matron's privilege of speaking to Angel on the point.

'Have ye forgot 'em, Mr. Clare? The banns, I mean.'

'No, I have not forgot 'em,' says Clare.

As soon as he caught Tess alone he assured her:

'Don't let them tease you about the banns. A license[10] will be quieter for us, and I have decided on a license without consulting you. So if you go to church on Sunday morning you will not hear your own name, if you wished to.'

'I didn't wish to hear it, dearest,' she said proudly.

But to know that things were in train was an immense relief to Tess notwithstanding, who had well-nigh feared that somebody would stand up and forbid the banns on the ground of her history. How events were favouring her!

'I don't quite feel easy,' she said to herself. 'All this good fortune may be scourged out of me afterwards by a lot of ill. That's how Heaven mostly does. I wish I could have had common banns!'

But everything went smoothly. She wondered whether he would like her to be married in her present best white frock, or if she ought to buy a new one. The question was set at rest by his forethought, disclosed by the arrival of some large packages addressed to her. Inside them she found a whole stock of clothing, from bonnet to shoes, including a perfect morning costume, such

9. "Local phrase for publication of banns" [*Hardy's note*].   10. A license from the bishop made the publication of banns unnecessary. [F]

as would well suit the simple wedding they planned. He entered the house shortly after the arrival of the packages, and heard her upstairs undoing them.

A minute later she came down with a flush on her face and tears in her eyes.

'How thoughtful you've been!' she murmured, her cheek upon his shoulder. 'Even to the gloves and handkerchief! My own love—how good, how kind!'

'No, no, Tess; just an order to a tradeswoman in London—nothing more.'

And to divert her from thinking too highly of him he told her to go upstairs, and take her time, and see if it all fitted; and, if not, to get the village sempstress to make a few alterations.

She did return upstairs, and put on the gown. Alone, she stood for a moment before the glass looking at the effect of her silk attire; and then there came into her head her mother's ballad of the mystic robe—

> That never would become that wife
> That had once done amiss,[1]

which Mrs. Durbeyfield had used to sing to her as a child, so blithely and so archly, her foot on the cradle, which she rocked to the tune. Suppose this robe should betray her by changing colour, as her robe had betrayed Queen Guénever. Since she had been at the dairy she had not once thought of the lines till now.

XXXIII

Angel felt that he would like to spend a day with her before the wedding, somewhere away from the dairy, as a last jaunt in her company while they were yet mere lover and mistress; a romantic day, in circumstances that would never be repeated; with that other and greater day beaming close ahead of them. During the preceding week, therefore, he suggested making a few purchases in the nearest town, and they started together.

Clare's life at the dairy had been that of a recluse in respect to the world of his own class. For months he had never gone near a town, and, requiring no vehicle, had never kept one, hiring the dairyman's cob or gig if he rode or drove. They went in the gig that day.

And then for the first time in their lives they shopped as partners in one concern. It was Christmas Eve, with its loads of holly and mistletoe, and the town was very full of strangers who had come in from all parts of the country on account of the day. Tess paid the penalty of walking about with happiness superadded

1. From "The Boy and the Mantle" (no. 29 in Child's *English and Scottish Popular Ballads*). [F]

to beauty on her countenance by being much stared at as she moved amid them on his arm.

In the evening they returned to the inn at which they had put up, and Tess waited in the entry while Angel went to see the horse and gig brought to the door. The general sitting-room was full of guests, who were continually going in and out. As the door opened and shut each time for the passage of these, the light within the parlour fell full upon Tess's face. Two men came out and passed by her among the rest. One of them had stared her up and down in surprise, and she fancied he was a Trantridge man, though that village lay so many miles off that Trantridge folk were rarities here.

'A comely maid that,' said the other.

'True, comely enough. But unless I make a great mistake——' And he negatived the remainder of the definition forthwith.

Clare had just returned from the stable-yard, and, confronting the man on the threshold, heard the words, and saw the shrinking of Tess. The insult to her stung him to the quick, and before he had considered anything at all he struck the man on the chin with the full force of his fist, sending him staggering backwards into the passage.

The man recovered himself, and seemed inclined to come on, and Clare, stepping outside the door, put himself in a posture of defense. But his opponent began to think better of the matter. He looked anew at Tess as he passed her, and said to Clare—

'I beg pardon, sir; 'twas a complete mistake. I thought she was another woman, forty miles from here.'

Clare, feeling then that he had been too hasty, and that he was, moreover, to blame for leaving her standing in an inn-passage, did what he usually did in such cases, gave the man five shillings to plaster the blow; and thus they parted, bidding each other a pacific good-night. As soon as Clare had taken the reins from the ostler, and the young couple had driven off, the two men went in the other direction.

'And was it a mistake?' said the second one.

'Not a bit of it. But I didn't want to hurt the gentleman's feelings—not I.'

In the meantime the lovers were driving onward.

'Could we put off our wedding till a little later?' Tess asked in a dry dull voice. 'I mean if we wished?'

'No, my love. Calm yourself. Do you mean that the fellow may have time to summon me for assault?' he asked good-humouredly.

'No—I only meant—if it should have to be put off.'

What she meant was not very clear, and he directed her to dismiss such fancies from her mind, which she obediently did as well as she could. But she was grave, very grave, all the way home; till she thought, 'We shall go away, a very long distance, hundreds of miles from these parts, and such as this can never happen again, and no ghost of the past reach there.'

They parted tenderly that night on the landing, and Clare ascended to his attic. Tess sat up getting on with some little requisites, lest the few remaining days should not afford sufficient time. While she sat she heard a noise in Angel's room overhead, a sound of thumping and struggling. Everybody else in the house was asleep, and in her anxiety lest Clare should be ill she ran up and knocked at his door, and asked him what was the matter.

'Oh, nothing, dear,' he said from within. 'I am so sorry I disturbed you! But the reason is rather an amusing one: I fell asleep and dreamt that I was fighting that fellow again who insulted you, and the noise you heard was my pummelling away with my fists at my portmanteau, which I pulled out to-day for packing. I am occasionally liable to these freaks in my sleep. Go to bed and think of it no more.'

This was the last drachm required to turn the scale of her indecision. Declare the past to him by word of mouth she could not; but there was another way. She sat down and wrote on the four pages of a note-sheet a succinct narrative of those events of three or four years ago, put it into an envelope, and directed it to Clare. Then, lest the flesh should again be weak, she crept upstairs without any shoes and slipped the note under his door.

Her night was a broken one, as it well might be, and she listened for the first faint noise overhead. It came, as usual; he descended, as usual. She descended. He met her at the bottom of the stairs and kissed her. Surely it was as warmly as ever!

He looked a little disturbed and worn, she thought. But he said not a word to her about her revelation, even when they were alone. Could he have had it? Unless he began the subject she felt that she could say nothing. So the day passed, and it was evident that whatever he thought he meant to keep to himself. Yet he was frank and affectionate as before. Could it be that her doubts were childish? that he forgave her; that he loved her for what she was, just as she was, and smiled at her disquiet as at a foolish nightmare? Had he really received her note? She glanced into his room, and could see nothing of it. It might be that he forgave her. But even if he had not received it she had a sudden enthusiastic trust that he surely would forgive her.

Every morning and night he was the same, and thus New Year's Eve broke—the wedding-day.

The lovers did not rise at milking-time, having through the whole of this last week of their sojourn at the dairy been accorded something of the position of guests, Tess being honoured with a

room of her own. When they arrived downstairs at breakfast-
time they were surprised to see what effects had been produced in
the large kitchen for their glory since they had last beheld it. At
some unnatural hour of the morning the dairyman had caused
the yawning chimney-corner to be whitened, and the brick hearth
reddened, and a blazing yellow damask blower[2] to be hung across
the arch in place of the old grimy blue cotton one with a black
sprig pattern which had formerly done duty here. This renovated
aspect of what was the focus indeed of the room on a dull winter
morning, threw a smiling demeanour over the whole apartment.

'I was determined to do summat in honour o't,' said the dairyman. 'And as you wouldn't hear of my gieing a rattling good
randy[3] wi' fiddles and bass-viols complete, as we should ha' done
in old times, this was all I could think o' as a noiseless
thing.'

Tess's friends lived so far off that none could conveniently have
been present at the ceremony, even had any been asked; but as a
fact nobody was invited from Marlott. As for Angel's family,
he had written and duly informed them of the time, and assured
them that he would be glad to see one at least of them there
for the day if he would like to come. His brothers had not replied
at all, seeming to be indignant with him; while his father and
mother had written a rather sad letter, deploring his precipitancy
in rushing into marriage, but making the best of the matter by
saying that, though a dairywoman was the last daughter-in-law
they could have expected, their son had arrived at an age at
which he might be supposed to be the best judge.

This coolness in his relations distressed Clare less than it would
have done had he been without the grand card with which he
meant to surprise them ere long. To produce Tess, fresh from the
dairy, as a d'Urberville and a lady, he had felt to be temerari-
ous and risky; hence he had concealed her lineage till such time
as, familiarized with worldly ways by a few months' travel and
reading with him, he could take her on a visit to his parents,
and impart the knowledge while triumphantly producing her as
worthy of such an ancient line. It was a pretty lover's dream, if
no more. Perhaps Tess's lineage had more value for himself than
for anybody in the world besides.

Her perception that Angel's bearing towards her still remained in no whit altered by her own communication rendered
Tess guiltily doubtful if he could have received it. She rose from
breakfast before he had finished, and hastened upstairs. It had
occurred to her to look once more into the queer gaunt room which

2. A curtain hung over the top part of
the opening of a fireplace to increase
the draft. [F]
3. Celebration.

had been Clare's den, or rather eyrie, for so long, and climbing the ladder she stood at the open door of the apartment, regarding and pondering. She stooped to the threshold of the doorway, where she had pushed in the note two or three days earlier in such excitement. The carpet reached close to the sill, and under the edge of the carpet she discerned the faint white margin of the envelope containing her letter to him, which he obviously had never seen, owing to her having in her haste thrust it beneath the carpet as well as beneath the door.

With a feeling of faintness she withdrew the letter. There it was—sealed up, just as it had left her hands. The mountain had not yet been removed. She could not let him read it now, the house being in full bustle of preparation; and descending to her own room she destroyed the letter there.

She was so pale when he saw her again that he felt quite anxious. The incident of the misplaced letter she had jumped at as if it prevented a confession; but she knew in her conscience that it need not; there was still time. Yet everything was in a stir; there was coming and going; all had to dress, the dairyman and Mrs. Crick having been asked to accompany them as witnesses; and reflection or deliberate talk was well-nigh impossible. The only minute Tess could get to be alone with Clare was when they met upon the landing.

'I am so anxious to talk to you—I want to confess all my faults and blunders!' she said with attempted lightness.

'No, no—we can't have faults talked of—you must be deemed perfect to-day at least, my Sweet!' he cried. 'We shall have plenty of time, hereafter, I hope, to talk over our failings. I will confess mine at the same time.'

'But it would be better for me to do it now, I think, so that you could not say——'

'Well, my quixotic one, you shall tell me anything—say, as soon as we are settled in our lodging; not now. I, too, will tell you my faults then. But do not let us spoil the day with them; they will be excellent matter for a dull time.'

'Then you don't wish me to, dearest?'

'I do not, Tessy, really.'

The hurry of dressing and starting left no time for more than this. Those words of his seemed to reassure her on further reflection. She was whirled onward through the next couple of critical hours by the mastering tide of her devotion to him, which closed up further meditation. Her one desire, so long resisted, to make herself his, to call him her lord, her own—then, if necessary, to die—had at last lifted her up from her plodding reflective pathway. In dressing, she moved about in a mental cloud of many-coloured idealities, which eclipsed all sinister contingencies by its brightness.

The church was a long way off, and they were obliged to drive, particularly as it was winter. A close carriage was ordered from a roadside inn, a vehicle which had been kept there ever since the old days of post-chaise travelling. It had stout wheel-spokes, and heavy felloes, a great curved bed, immense straps and springs, and a pole like a battering-ram. The postilion was a venerable 'boy' of sixty—a martyr to rheumatic gout, the result of excessive exposure in youth, counteracted by strong liquors—who had stood at inn-doors doing nothing for the whole five-and-twenty years that had elapsed since he had no longer been required to ride professionally, as if expecting the old times to come back again. He had a permanent running wound on the outside of his right leg, originated by the constant bruisings of aristocratic carriage-poles during the many years that he had been in regular employ at the King's Arms, Casterbridge.

Inside this cumbrous and creaking structure, and behind this decayed conductor, the *partie carrée*[4] took their seats—the bride and bridegroom and Mr. and Mrs. Crick. Angel would have liked one at least of his brothers to be present as groomsman, but their silence after his gentle hint to that effect by letter had signified that they did not care to come. They disapproved of the marriage, and could not be expected to countenance it. Perhaps it was as well that they could not be present. They were not worldly young fellows, but fraternizing with dairy-folk would have struck unpleasantly upon their biassed niceness, apart from their views of the match.

Upheld by the momentum of the time Tess knew nothing of this; did not see anything; did not know the road they were taking to the church. She knew that Angel was close to her; all the rest was a luminous mist. She was a sort of celestial person, who owed her being to poetry—one of those classical divinities Clare was accustomed to talk to her about when they took their walks together.

The marriage being by license there were only a dozen or so of people in the church; had there been a thousand they would have produced no more effect upon her. They were at stellar distances from her present world. In the ecstatic solemnity with which she swore her faith to him the ordinary sensibilities of sex seemed a flippancy. At a pause in the service, while they were kneeling together, she unconsciously inclined herself towards him, so that her shoulder touched his arm; she had been frightened by a passing thought, and the movement had been automatic, to assure her-

4. *I.e.*, two couples.

self that he was really there, and to fortify her belief that his fidelity would be proof against all things.

Clare knew that she loved him—every curve of her form showed that—but he did not know at that time the full depth of her devotion, its single-mindedness, its meekness; what long-suffering it guaranteed, what honesty, what endurance, what good faith.

As they came out of church the ringers swung the bells off their rests, and a modest peal of three notes broke forth—that limited amount of expression having been deemed sufficient by the church builders for the joys of such a small parish. Passing by the tower with her husband on the path to the gate she could feel the vibrant air humming round them from the louvred belfry in a circle of sound, and it matched the highly-charged mental atmosphere in which she was living.

This condition of mind, wherein she felt glorified by an irradiation not her own, like the angel whom St. John saw in the sun,[5] lasted till the sound of the church bells had died away, and the emotions of the wedding-service had calmed down. Her eyes could dwell upon details more clearly now, and Mr. and Mrs. Crick having directed their own gig to be sent for them, to leave the carriage to the young couple, she observed the build and character of that conveyance for the first time. Sitting in silence she regarded it long.

'I fancy you seem oppressed, Tessy,' said Clare.

'Yes,' she answered, putting her hand to her brow. 'I tremble at many things. It is all so serious, Angel. Among other things I seem to have seen this carriage before, to be very well acquainted with it. It is very odd—I must have seen it in a dream.'

'Oh—you have heard the legend of the d'Urberville Coach—that well-known superstition of this county about your family when they were very popular here; and this lumbering old thing reminds you of it.'

'I have never heard of it to my knowledge,' said she. 'What is the legend—may I know it?'

'Well—I would rather not tell it in detail just now. A certain d'Urberville of the sixteenth or seventeenth century committed a dreadful crime in his family coach; and since that time members of the family see or hear the old coach whenever——But I'll tell you another day—it is rather gloomy. Evidently some dim knowledge of it has been brought back to your mind by the sight of this venerable caravan.'

'I don't remember hearing it before,' she murmured. 'Is it when we are going to die, Angel, that members of my family see it, or is it when we have committed a crime?'

'Now, Tess!'

He silenced her by a kiss.

5. Revelation xix:17.

By the time they reached home she was contrite and spiritless. She was Mrs. Angel Clare, indeed, but had she any moral right to the name? Was she not more truly Mrs. Alexander d'Urberville? Could intensity of love justify what might be considered in upright souls as culpable reticence? She knew not what was expected of women in such cases; and she had no counsellor.

However, when she found herself alone in her room for a few minutes—the last day this on which she was ever to enter it— she knelt down and prayed. She tried to pray to God, but it was her husband who really had her supplication. Her idolatry of this man was such that she herself almost feared it to be ill-omened. She was conscious of the notion expressed by Friar Laurence: 'These violent delights have violent ends.'[6] It might be too desperate for human conditions—too rank, too wild, too deadly.

'O my love, my love, why do I love you so!' she whispered there alone; 'for she you love is not my real self, but one in my image; the one I might have been!'

Afternoon came, and with it the hour for departure. They had decided to fulfil the plan of going for a few days to the lodgings in the old farmhouse near Wellbridge Mill, at which he meant to reside during his investigation of flour processes. At two o'clock there was nothing left to do but to start. All the servantry of the dairy were standing in the red-brick entry to see them go out, the dairyman and his wife following to the door. Tess saw her three chamber-mates in a row against the wall, pensively inclining their heads. She had much questioned if they would appear at the parting moment; but there they were, stoical and staunch to the last. She knew why the delicate Retty looked so fragile, and Izz so tragically sorrowful, and Marian so blank; and she forgot her own dogging shadow for a moment in contemplating theirs.

She impulsively whispered to him—

'Will you kiss 'em all, once, poor things, for the first and last time?'

Clare had not the least objection to such a farewell formality —which was all that it was to him—and as he passed them he kissed them in succession where they stood, saying 'Good-bye' to each as he did so. When they reached the door Tess femininely glanced back to discern the effect of that kiss of charity; there was no triumph in her glance, as there might have been. If there had it would have disappeared when she saw how moved the girls all were. The kiss had obviously done harm by awakening feelings they were trying to subdue.

Of all this Clare was unconscious. Passing on to the wicket-

6. *Romeo and Juliet*, II.vi.9.

gate he shook hands with the dairyman and his wife, and expressed his last thanks to them for their attentions; after which there was a moment of silence before they had moved off. It was interrupted by the crowing of a cock. The white one with the rose comb had come and settled on the palings in front of the house, within a few yards of them, and his notes thrilled their ears through, dwindling away like echoes down a valley of rocks.

'Oh?' said Mrs. Crick. 'An afternoon crow!'

Two men were standing by the yard gate, holding it open.

'That's bad,' one murmured to the other, not thinking that the words could be heard by the group at the door-wicket.

The cock crew again—straight towards Clare.

'Well!' said the dairyman.

'I don't like to hear him!' said Tess to her husband. 'Tell the man to drive on. Good-bye, good-bye!'

The cock crew again.

'Hoosh! Just you be off, sir, or I'll twist your neck!' said the dairyman with some irritation, turning to the bird and driving him away. And to his wife as they went indoors: 'Now, to think o' that just to-day! I've not heard his crow of an afternoon all the year afore.'

'It only means a change in the weather,' said she; 'not what you think: 'tis impossible!'

XXXIV

They drove by the level road along the valley to a distance of a few miles, and, reaching Wellbridge, turned away from the village to the left, and over the great Elizabethan bridge which gives the place half its name. Immediately behind it stood the house wherein they had engaged lodgings, whose exterior features are so well known to all travellers through the Froom Valley; once portion of a fine manorial residence, and the property and seat of a d'Urberville, but since its partial demolition a farm-house.

'Welcome to one of your ancestral mansions!' said Clare as he handed her down. But he regretted the pleasantry; it was too near a satire.

On entering they found that, though they had only engaged a couple of rooms, the farmer had taken advantage of their proposed presence during the coming days to pay a New Year's visit to some friends, leaving a woman from a neighbouring cottage to minister to their few wants. The absoluteness of possession pleased them, and they realized it as the first moment of their experience under their own exclusive roof-tree.

But he found that the mouldy old habitation somewhat depressed his bride. When the carriage was gone they ascended the stairs to wash their hands, the charwoman showing the way. On the landing Tess stopped and started.

'What's the matter?' said he.

'Those horrid women!' she answered, with a smile. 'How they frightened me.'

He looked up, and perceived two life-size portraits on panels built into the masonry. As all visitors to the mansion are aware, these paintings represent women of middle age, of a date some two hundred years ago, whose lineaments once seen can never be forgotten. The long pointed features, narrow eye, and smirk of the one, so suggestive of merciless treachery; the bill-hook nose, large teeth, and bold eye of the other, suggesting arrogance to the point of ferocity, haunt the beholder afterwards in his dreams.

'Whose portraits are those?' asked Clare of the charwoman.

'I have been told by old folk that they were ladies of the d'Urberville family, the ancient lords of this manor,' she said. 'Owing to their being builded into the wall they can't be moved away.'

The unpleasantness of the matter was that, in addition to their effect upon Tess, her fine features were unquestionably traceable in these exaggerated forms. He said nothing of this, however, and, regretting that he had gone out of his way to choose the house for their bridal time, went on into the adjoining room. The place having been rather hastily prepared for them they washed their hands in one basin. Clare touched hers under the water.

'Which are my fingers and which are yours?' he said, looking up. 'They are very much mixed.'

'They are all yours,' said she, very prettily, and endeavoured to be gayer than she was. He had not been displeased with her thoughtfulness on such an occasion; it was what every sensible woman would show: but Tess knew that she had been thoughtful to excess, and struggled against it.

The sun was so low on that short last afternoon of the year that it shone in through a small opening and formed a golden staff which stretched across to her skirt, where it made a spot like a paint-mark set upon her. They went into the ancient parlour to tea, and here they shared their first common meal alone. Such was their childishness, or rather his, that he found it interesting to use the same bread-and-butter plate as herself, and to brush crumbs from her lips with his own. He wondered a little that she did not enter into these frivolities with his own zest.

Looking at her silently for a long time; 'She is a dear dear Tess,' he thought to himself, as one deciding on the true construction of a difficult passage. 'Do I realize solemnly enough how utterly and irretrievably this little womanly thing is the creature of my good or bad faith and fortune? I think not. I think I could not, unless I were a woman myself. What I am in worldly estate, she is. What I become, she must become. What I cannot be, she cannot be. And shall I ever neglect her, or hurt her, or even forget to consider her? God forbid such a crime!'

They sat on over the tea-table waiting for their luggage, which the dairyman had promised to send before it grew dark. But evening began to close in, and the luggage did not arrive, and they had brought nothing more than they stood in. With the departure of the sun the calm mood of the winter day changed. Out of doors there began noises as of silk smartly rubbed; the restful dead leaves of the preceding autumn were stirred to irritated resurrection, and whirled about unwillingly, and tapped against the shutters. It soon began to rain.

'That cock knew the weather was going to change,' said Clare.

The woman who had attended upon them had gone home for the night, but she had placed candles upon the table, and now they lit them. Each candle-flame drew towards the fireplace.

'These old houses are so draughty,' continued Angel, looking at the flames, and at the grease guttering down the sides. 'I wonder where that luggage is. We haven't even a brush and comb.'

'I don't know,' she answered, absent-minded.

'Tess, you are not a bit cheerful this evening—not at all as you used to be. Those harridans on the panels upstairs have unsettled you. I am sorry I brought you here. I wonder if you really love me, after all?'

He knew that she did, and the words had no serious intent; but she was surcharged with emotion, and winced like a wounded animal. Though she tried not to shed tears she could not help showing one or two.

'I did not mean it!' said he, sorry. 'You are worried at not having your things, I know. I cannot think why old Jonathan has not come with them. Why, it is seven o'clock? Ah, there he is!'

A knock had come to the door, and, there being nobody else to answer it Clare went out. He returned to the room with a small package in his hand.

'It is not Jonathan, after all,' he said.

'How vexing!' said Tess.

The packet had been brought by a special messenger, who had arrived at Talbothays from Emminster Vicarage immediately after the departure of the married couple, and had followed them hither, being under injunction to deliver it into nobody's hands but theirs. Clare brought it to the light. It was less than a foot long, sewed up in canvas, sealed in red wax with his father's seal, and directed in his father's hand to 'Mrs. Angel Clare.'

'It is a little wedding-present for you, Tess,' said he, handing it to her. 'How thoughtful they are!'

Tess looked a little flustered as she took it.

'I think I would rather have you open it, dearest,' said she, turning over the parcel. 'I don't like to break those great seals; they look so serious. Please open it for me!'

He undid the parcel. Inside was a case of morocco leather, on the top of which lay a note and a key.

The note was for Clare, in the following words:

My Dear Son,—Possibly you have forgotten that on the death of your godmother, Mrs. Pitney, when you were a lad, she—vain, kind woman that she was—left to me a portion of the contents of her jewel-case in trust for your wife, if you should ever have one, as a mark of her affection for you and whomsoever you should choose. This trust I have fulfilled, and the diamonds have been locked up at my banker's ever since. Though I feel it to be a somewhat incongruous act in the circumstances, I am, as you will see, bound to hand over the articles to the woman to whom the use of them for her lifetime will now rightly belong, and they are therefore promptly sent. They become, I believe, heirlooms, strictly speaking, according to the terms of your godmother's will. The precise words of the clause that refers to this matter are enclosed.

'I do remember,' said Clare; 'but I had quite forgotten.'

Unlocking the case, they found it to contain a necklace, with pendant, bracelets, and ear-rings; and also some other small ornaments.

Tess seemed afraid to touch them at first, but her eyes sparkled for a moment as much as the stones when Clare spread out the set.

'Are they mine?' she asked incredulously.

'They are, certainly,' said he.

He looked into the fire. He remembered how, when he was a lad of fifteen, his godmother, the Squire's wife—the only rich person with whom he had ever come in contact—had pinned her faith to his success; had prophesied a wondrous career for him. There had seemed nothing at all out of keeping with such a conjectured career in the storing up of these showy ornaments for his wife and the wives of her descendants. They gleamed somewhat ironically now. 'Yet why?' he asked himself. It was but a question of vanity throughout; and if that were admitted into one side of the equation it should be admitted into the other. His wife was a d'Urberville: whom could they become better than her?

Suddenly he said with enthusiasm—

'Tess, put them on—put them on!' And he turned from the fire to help her.

But as if by magic she had already donned them—necklace, ear-rings, bracelets, and all.

'But the gown isn't right, Tess,' said Clare. 'It ought to be a low one for a set of brilliants like that.'

'Ought it?' said Tess.

'Yes,' said he.

He suggested to her how to tuck in the upper edge of her bodice, so as to make it roughly approximate to the cut for evening wear; and when she had done this, and the pendant to the necklace hung isolated amid the whiteness of her throat, as it was designed to do, he stepped back to survey her.

'My heavens,' said Clare, 'how beautiful you are!'

As everybody knows, fine feathers make fine birds; a peasant girl but very moderately prepossessing to the casual observer in her simple condition and attire, will bloom as an amazing beauty if clothed as a woman of fashion with the aids that Art can render; while the beauty of the midnight crush would often cut but a sorry figure if placed inside the field-woman's wrapper upon a monotonous acreage of turnips on a dull day.[7] He had never till now estimated the artistic excellence of Tess's limbs and features.

'If you were only to appear in a ball-room!' he said. 'But no—no, dearest; I think I love you best in the wing-bonnet and cotton-frock —yes, better than in this, well as you support these dignities.'

Tess's sense of her striking appearance had given her a flush of excitement, which was yet not happiness.

'I'll take them off,' she said, 'in case Jonathan should see me. They are not fit for me, are they? They must be sold, I suppose?'

'Let them stay a few minutes longer. Sell them? Never. It would be a breach of faith.'

Influenced by a second thought she readily obeyed. She had something to tell, and there might be help in these. She sat down with the jewels upon her; and they again indulged in conjectures as to where Jonathan could possibly be with their baggage. The ale they had poured out for his consumption when he came had gone flat with long standing.

Shortly after this they began supper, which was already laid on a side-table. Ere they had finished there was a jerk in the fire-smoke, the rising skein of which bulged out into the room, as if some giant had laid his hand on the chimney-top for a moment. It had been caused by the opening of the outer door. A heavy step was now heard in the passage, and Angel went out.

'I couldn' make nobody hear at all by knocking,' apologized Jonathan Kail, for it was he at last; 'and as't was raining out I opened the door. I've brought the things, sir.'

'I am very glad to see them. But you are very late.'

'Well, yes, sir.'

There was something subdued in Jonathan Kail's tone which had not been there in the day, and lines of concern were ploughed upon his forehead in addition to the lines of years. He continued—

7. On March 15, 1890, Hardy made this entry in his notebook: "With E. [his wife] to a crush at the Jeunes'. Met Mrs. T. and her great eyes in a corner of the rooms, as if washed up by the surging crowd. The most beautiful woman present. * * * But these women! If put into rough wrappers in a turnip-field, where would their beauty be?" (*The Early Life.* P. 293.) [W]

'We've all been gallied[8] at the dairy at what might ha' been a most terrible affliction since you and your Mis'ess—so to name her now—left us this a'ternoon. Perhaps you ha'nt forgot the cock's afternoon crow?'

'Dear me;—what——'

'Well, some says it do mane one thing, and some another; but what's happened is that poor little Retty Priddle hev tried to drown herself.'

'No! Really! Why, she bade us good-bye with the rest——'

'Yes. Well, sir, when you and your Mis'ess—so to name what she lawful is—when you two drove away, as I say, Retty and Marian put on their bonnets and went out; and as there is not much doing now, being New Year's Eve, and folks mops and brooms[9] from what's inside 'em, nobody took much notice. They went on to Lew-Everard, where they had summut to drink, and then on they vamped to Dree-armed Cross,[1] and there they seemed to have parted, Retty striking across the water-meads as if for home, and Marian going on to the next village, where there's another public-house. Nothing more was zeed or heard o' Retty till the waterman,[2] on his way home, noticed something by the Great Pool; 'twas her bonnet and shawl packed up. In the water he found her. He and another man brought her home, thinking 'a was dead; but she fetched round by degrees.'

Angel, suddenly recollecting that Tess was overhearing this gloomy tale, went to shut the door between the passage and the ante-room to the inner parlour where she was; but his wife, flinging a shawl round her, had come to the outer room and was listening to the man's narrative, her eyes resting absently on the luggage and the drops of rain glistening upon it.

'And, more than this, there's Marian; she's been found dead drunk by the withy-bed[3]—a girl who hev never been known to touch anything before except shilling ale; though, to be sure, 'a was always a good trencher-woman, as her face showed. It seems as if the maids had all gone out o' their minds!'

'And Izz?' asked Tess.

'Izz is about house as usual; but 'a do say 'a can guess how it happened; and she seems to be very low in mind about it, poor maid, as well she mid be. And so you see, sir, as all this happened just when we was packing your few traps and your Mis'ess's night-rail[4] and dressing things into the cart, why, it belated me.'

'Yes. Well, Jonathan, will you get the trunks upstairs, and drink a cup of ale, and hasten back as soon as you can, in case you should be wanted?'

---

8. Upset, worried.
9. Are intoxicated.
1. A pub whose sign was probably a cross of Lorraine.

2. A man engaged in the irrigation of water-meadows. [*OED*]
3. A stand of willows.
4. Dressing-gown.

Tess had gone back to the inner parlour, and sat down by the fire, looking wistfully into it. She heard Jonathan Kail's heavy footsteps up and down the stairs till he had done placing the luggage, and heard him express his thanks for the ale her husband took out to him, and for the gratuity he received. Jonathan's footsteps then died from the door, and his cart creaked away.

Angel slid forward the massive oak bar which secured the door, and coming in to where she sat over the hearth, pressed her cheeks between his hands from behind. He expected her to jump up gaily and unpack the toilet-gear that she had been so anxious about, but as she did not rise he sat down with her in the firelight, the candles on the supper-table being too thin and glimmering to interfere with its glow.

'I am so sorry you should have heard this sad story about the girls,' he said. 'Still, don't let it depress you. Retty was naturally morbid, you know.'

'Without the least cause,' said Tess. 'While they who have cause to be, hide it, and pretend they are not.'

This incident had turned the scale for her. They were simple and innocent girls on whom the unhappiness of unrequited love had fallen; they had deserved better at the hands of Fate. She had deserved worse—yet she was the chosen one. It was wicked of her to take all without paying. She would pay to the uttermost farthing; she would tell, there and then. This final determination she came to when she looked into the fire, he holding her hand.

A steady glare from the now flameless embers painted the sides and back of the fireplace with its colour, and the well-polished andirons, and the old brass tongs that would not meet. The underside of the mantel-shelf was flushed with the high-colored light, and the legs of the table nearest the fire. Tess's face and neck reflected the same warmth, which each gem turned into an Aldebaran or a Sirius—a constellation of white, red, and green flashes, that interchanged their hues with her every pulsation.

'Do you remember what we said to each other this morning about telling our faults?' he asked abruptly, finding that she still remained immovable. 'We spoke lightly perhaps, and you may well have done so. But for me it was no light promise. I want to make a confession to you, Love.'

This, from him, so unexpectedly apposite, had the effect upon her of a Providential interposition.

'You have to confess something?' she said quickly, and even with gladness and relief.

'You did not expect it? Ah—you thought too highly of me. Now listen. Put your head there, because I want you to forgive me and not to be indignant with me for not telling you before, as perhaps I ought to have done.'

How strange it was! He seemed to be her double. She did not speak, and Clare went on—

'I did not mention it because I was afraid of endangering my chance of you, darling, the great prize of my life—my Fellowship I call you. My brother's Fellowship was won at his college, mine at Talbothays Dairy. Well, I would not risk it. I was going to tell you a month ago—at the time you agreed to be mine, but I could not; I thought it might frighten you away from me. I put it off; then I thought I would tell you yesterday, to give you a chance at least of escaping me. But I did not. And I did not this morning, when you proposed our confessing our faults on the landing—the sinner that I was! But I must, now I see you sitting there so solemnly. I wonder if you will forgive me?'

'O yes! I am sure that——'

'Well, I hope so. But wait a minute. You don't know. To begin at the beginning. Though I imagine my poor father fears that I am one of the eternally lost for my doctrines, I am of course, a believer in good morals, Tess, as much as you. I used to wish to be a teacher of men, and it was a great disappointment to me when I found I could not enter the Church. I admired spotlessness, even though I could lay no claim to it, and hated impurity, as I hope I do now. Whatever one may think of plenary inspiration,[5] one must heartily subscribe to these words of Paul: "Be thou an example—in word, in conversation, in charity, in spirit, in faith, in purity."[6] It is the only safeguard for us poor human beings. "Integer vitae,"[7] says a Roman poet, who is strange company for St. Paul—

> The man of upright life, from frailties free,
> Stands not in need of Moorish spear or bow.

Well, a certain place is paved with good intentions, and having felt all that so strongly, you will see what a terrible remorse it bred in me when, in the midst of my fine aims for other people, I myself fell.'

He then told her of that time of his life to which allusion has been made when, tossed about by doubts and difficulties in London, like a cork on the waves, he plunged into eight-and-forty hours' dissipation with a stranger.

'Happily I awoke almost immediately to a sense of my folly,' he continued. 'I would have no more to say to her, and I came

5. "According to which [theory] the in-spiration of the writers extends to all subjects treated of, so that all their statements are to be received as infallibly true." [*OED*]
6. I Timothy iv:12.
7. The first two words of a famous ode of Horace (i.22).

home. I have never repeated the offence. But I felt I should like to treat you with perfect frankness and honour, and I could not do so without telling this. Do you forgive me?'

She pressed his hand tightly for an answer.

'Then we will dismiss it at once and for ever!—too painful as it is for the occasion—and talk of something lighter.'

'O, Angel—I am almost glad—because now *you* can forgive *me*! I have not made my confession. I have a confession, too—remember, I said so.'

'Ah, to be sure! Now then for it, wicked little one.'

'Perhaps, although you smile, it is as serious as yours, or more so.'

'It can hardly be more serious, dearest.'

'It cannot—O no, it cannot!' She jumped up joyfully at the hope. 'No, it cannot be more serious, certainly,' she cried, 'because 'tis just the same! I will tell you now.'

She sat down again.

Their hands were still joined. The ashes under the grate were lit by the fire vertically, like a torrid waste. Imagination might have beheld a Last Day luridness in this red-coaled glow, which fell on his face and hand, and on hers, peering into the loose hair about her brow, and firing the delicate skin underneath. A large shadow of her shape rose upon the wall and ceiling. She bent forward, at which each diamond on her neck gave a sinister wink like a toad's; and pressing her forehead against his temple she entered on her story of her acquaintance with Alec d'Urberville and its results, murmuring the words without flinching, and with her eyelids drooping down.

END OF PHASE THE FOURTH

Phase the Fifth—The Woman Pays

XXXV

Her narrative ended; even its re-assertions and secondary explanations were done. Tess's voice throughout had hardly risen higher than its opening tone; there had been no exculpatory phrase of any kind, and she had not wept.

But the complexion even of external things seemed to suffer transmutation as her announcement progressed. The fire in the grate looked impish—demoniacally funny, as if it did not care in the least about her strait. The fender grinned idly, as if it too did not care. The light from the water-bottle was merely engaged in a chromatic problem. All material objects around announced their irresponsibility with terrible iteration. And yet nothing had changed since the moments when he had been kissing her; or rather, nothing in the substance of things. But the essence of things had changed.

When she ceased the auricular impressions from their previous endearments seemed to hustle away into the corners of their brains, repeating themselves as echoes from a time of supremely purblind foolishness.

Clare performed the irrelevant act of stirring the fire; the intelligence had not even yet got to the bottom of him. After stirring the embers he rose to his feet; all the force of her disclosure had imparted itself now. His face had withered. In the strenuousness of his concentration he treadled fitfully on the floor. He could not, by any contrivance, think closely enough; that was the meaning of his vague movement. When he spoke it was in the most inadequate, commonplace voice of the many varied tones she had heard from him.

'Tess!'

'Yes, dearest.'

'Am I to believe this? From your manner I am to take it as true. O you cannot be out of your mind! You ought to be! Yet you are not. . . . My wife, my Tess—nothing in you warrants such a supposition as that?'

'I am not out of my mind,' she said.

'And yet——' He looked vacantly at her, to resume with dazed senses: 'Why didn't you tell me before? Ah, yes, you would have told me, in a way—but I hindered you, I remember!'

These and other of his words were nothing but the perfunctory babble of the surface while the depths remained paralyzed. He turned away, and bent over a chair. Tess followed him to the middle of the room where he was, and stood there staring at him with eyes that did not weep. Presently she slid down upon her knees beside his foot, and from this position she crouched in a heap.

'In the name of our love, forgive me!' she whispered with a dry mouth. 'I have forgiven you for the same!'

And, as he did not answer, she said again—

'Forgive me as you are forgiven! *I* forgive *you*, Angel.'

'You—yes, you do.'

'But you do not forgive me?'

'O Tess, forgiveness does not apply to the case! You were one person; now you are another. My God—how can forgiveness meet such a grotesque—prestidigitation as that!'

He paused, contemplating this definition; then suddenly broke into horrible laughter—as unnatural and ghastly as a laugh in hell.

'Don't—don't! It kills me quite, that!' she shrieked. 'O have mercy upon me—have mercy!'

He did not answer; and, sickly white, she jumped up.

'Angel, Angel! what do you mean by that laugh?' she cried out. 'Do you know what this is to me?'

He shook his head.

'I have been hoping, longing, praying, to make you happy! I have thought what joy it will be to do it, what an unworthy wife I shall be if I do not! That's what I have felt, Angel!'

'I know that.'

'I thought, Angel, that you loved me—me, my very self! If it is I you do love, O how can it be that you look and speak so? It frightens me! Having begun to love you, I love you for ever—in all changes, in all disgraces, because you are yourself. I ask no more. Then how can you, O my own husband, stop loving me?'

'I repeat, the woman I. have been loving is not you.'

'But who?'

'Another woman in your shape.'

She perceived in his words the realization of her own apprehensive foreboding in former times. He looked upon her as a species of impostor; a guilty woman in the guise of an innocent one. Terror was upon her white face as she saw it; her cheek was flaccid, and her mouth had almost the aspect of a round little hole. The horrible sense of his view of her so deadened her that she staggered; and he stepped forward, thinking she was going to fall.

'Sit down, sit down,' he said gently. 'You are ill; and it is natural that you should be.'

She did sit down, without knowing where she was, that strained look still upon her face, and her eyes such as to make his flesh creep.

'I don't belong to you any more, then; do I, Angel?' she asked helplessly. 'It is not me, but another woman like me that he loved, he says.'

The image raised caused her to take pity upon herself as one who was ill-used. Her eyes filled as she regarded her position further; she turned round and burst into a flood of self-sympathetic tears.

Clare was relieved at this change, for the effect on her of what had happened was beginning to be a trouble to him only less than the woe of the disclosure itself. He waited patiently, apathetically, till the violence of her grief had worn itself out, and her rush of weeping had lessened to a catching gasp at intervals.

'Angel,' she said suddenly, in her natural tones, the insane, dry voice of terror having left her now. 'Angel, am I too wicked for you and me to live together?'

'I have not been able to think what we can do.'

'I shan't ask you to let me live with you, Angel, because I have no right to! I shall not write to mother and sisters to say we be married, as I said I would do; and I shan't finish the good-hussif'[8] I cut out and meant to make while we were in lodgings.'

'Shan't you?'

'No, I shan't do anything, unless you order me to; and if you go away from me I shall not follow 'ee; and if you never speak to me any more I shall not ask why, unless you tell me I may.'

'And if I do order you to do anything?'

'I will obey you like your wretched slave, even if it is to lie down and die.'

'You are very good. But it strikes me that there is a want of harmony between your present mood of self-sacrifice and your past mood of self-preservation.'

These were the first words of antagonism. To fling elaborate sarcasms at Tess, however, was much like flinging them at a dog or cat. The charms of their subtlety passed by her unappreciated, and she only received them as inimical sounds which meant that anger ruled. She remained mute, not knowing that he was smothering his affection for her. She hardly observed that a tear descended slowly upon his cheek, a tear so large that it magnified the pores of the skin over which it rolled, like the object lens of a microscope. Meanwhile reillumination as to the terrible and total change that her confession had wrought in his life, in his universe, returned to him, and he tried desperately to advance among the new conditions in which he stood. Some consequent action was necessary; yet what?

'Tess,' he said, as gently as he could speak, 'I cannot stay—in this room—just now. I will walk out a little way.'

He quietly left the room, and the two glasses of wine that he had poured out for their supper—one for her, one for him—remained on the table untasted. This was what their *Agape*[9] had come to. At tea, two or three hours earlier, they had, in the freakishness of affection, drunk from one cup.

The closing of the door behind him, gently as it had been pulled to, roused Tess from her stupor. He was gone; she could not stay. Hastily flinging her cloak around her she opened the door and followed, putting out the candles as if she were never coming back. The rain was over and the night was now clear.

She was soon close at his heels, for Clare walked slowly and without purpose. His form beside her light gray figure looked black, sinister, and forbidding, and she felt as sarcasm the touch of the jewels of which she had been momentarily so proud. Clare turned

8. A sewing kit.
9. A "love-feast" held by the early Christians in connection with the Lord's Supper.

at hearing her footsteps, but his recognition of her presence seemed to make no difference in him, and he went on over the five yawning arches of the great bridge in front of the house.

The cow and horse tracks in the road were full of water, the rain having been enough to charge them, but not enough to wash them away. Across these minute pools the reflected stars flitted in a quick transit as she passed; she would not have known they were shining overhead if she had not seen them there—the vastest things of the universe imaged in objects so mean.

The place to which they had travelled to-day was in the same valley as Talbothays, but some miles lower down the river; and the surroundings being open she kept easily in sight of him. Away from the house the road wound through the meads, and along these she followed Clare without any attempt to come up with him or to attract him, but with dumb and vacant fidelity.

At last, however, her listless walk brought her up alongside him, and still he said nothing. The cruelty of fooled honesty is often great after enlightenment, and it was mighty in Clare now. The outdoor air had apparently taken away from him all tendency to act on impulse; she knew that he saw her without irradiation—in all her bareness; that Time was chanting his satiric psalm at her then—

Behold, when thy face is made bare, he that loved thee shall hate;
Thy face shall be no more fair at the fall of thy fate.
For thy life shall fall as a leaf and be shed as the rain;
And the veil of thine head shall be grief, and the crown shall
    be pain.[1]

He was still intently thinking, and her companionship had now insufficient power to break or divert the strain of thought. What a weak thing her presence must have become to him! She could not help addressing Clare.

'What have I done—what *have* I done! I have not told of anything that interferes with or belies my love for you. You don't think I planned it, do you? It is in your own mind what you are angry at, Angel; it is not in me. O, it is not in me, and I am not that deceitful woman you think me!'

'H'm—well. Not deceitful, my wife; but not the same. No, not the same. But do not make me reproach you. I have sworn that I will not; and I will do everything to avoid it.'

But she went on pleading in her distraction; and perhaps said things that would have been better left to silence.

'Angel!—Angel! I was a child—a child when it happened! I knew nothing of men.'

'You were more sinned against than sinning,[2] that I admit.'

1. Conclusion of the lyric beginning "Not as with sundering of the earth," in   Swinburne's *Atalanta in Calydon*.
2. *King Lear*, III.ii.60.

'Then will you not forgive me?'

'I do forgive you, but forgiveness is not all.'

'And love me?'

To this question he did not answer.

'O Angel— my mother says that it sometimes happens so!—she knows several cases where they were worse than I, and the husband has not minded it much—has got over it at least. And yet the woman has not loved him as I do you!'

'Don't, Tess; don't argue. Different societies, different manners. You almost make me say you are an unapprehending peasant woman, who have never been initiated into the proportions of social things. You don't know what you say.'

'I am only a peasant by position, not by nature!'

She spoke with an impulse to anger, but it went as it came.

'So much the worse for you. I think that parson who unearthed your pedigree would have done better if he had held his tongue. I cannot help associating your decline as a family with this other fact—of your want of firmness. Decrepit families imply decrepit wills, decrepit conduct. Heaven, why did you give me a handle for despising you more by informing me of your descent! Here was I thinking you a new-sprung child of nature; there were you, the belated seedling of an effete aristocracy!'

'Lots of families are as bad as mine in that! Retty's family were once large landowners, and so were Dairyman Billett's. And the Debbyhouses, who now are carters, were once the De Bayeux family. You find such as I everywhere; 'tis a feature of our county, and I can't help it.'

'So much the worse for the county.'

She took these reproaches in their bulk simply, not in their particulars; he did not love her as he had loved her hitherto, and to all else she was indifferent.

They wandered on again in silence. It was said afterwards that a cottager of Wellbridge, who went out late that night for a doctor, met two lovers in the pastures, walking very slowly, without converse, one behind the other, as in a funeral procession, and the glimpse that he obtained of their faces seemed to denote that they were anxious and sad. Returning later, he passed them again in the same field, progressing just as slowly, and as regardless of the hour and of the cheerless night as before. It was only on account of his preoccupation with his own affairs, and the illness in his house, that he did not bear in mind the curious incident, which, however, he recalled a long while after.

During the interval of the cottager's going and coming, she had said to her husband—

'I don't see how I can help being the cause of much misery to you all your life. The river is down there. I can put an end to myself in it. I am not afraid.'

'I don't wish to add murder to my other follies,' he said.

'I will leave something to show that I did it myself—on account of my shame. They will not blame you then.'

'Don't speak so absurdly—I wish not to hear it. It is nonsense to have such thoughts in this kind of case, which is rather one for satirical laughter than for tragedy. You don't in the least understand the quality of the mishap. It would be viewed in the light of a joke by nine-tenths of the world if it were known. Please oblige me by returning to the house, and going to bed.'

'I will,' said she dutifully.

They had rambled round by a road which led to the well-known ruins of the Cistercian abbey behind the mill, the latter having, in centuries past, been attached to the monastic establishment. The mill still worked on, food being a perennial necessity; the abbey had perished, creeds being transient. One continually sees the ministration of the temporary outlasting the ministration of the eternal. Their walk having been circuitous they were still not far from the house, and in obeying his direction she only had to reach the large stone bridge across the main river, and follow the road for a few yards. When she got back everything remained as she had left it, the fire being still burning. She did not stay downstairs for more than a minute, but proceeded to her chamber, whither the luggage had been taken. Here she sat down on the edge of the bed, looking blankly around, and presently began to undress. In removing the light towards the bedstead its rays fell upon the tester of white dimity; something was hanging beneath it, and she lifted the candle to see what it was. A bough of mistletoe. Angel had put it there; she knew that in an instant. This was the explanation of that mysterious parcel which it had been so difficult to pack and bring; whose contents he would not explain to her, saying that time would soon show her the purpose thereof. In his zest and his gaiety he had hung it there. How foolish and inopportune that mistletoe looked now.

Having nothing more to fear, having scarce anything to hope, for that he would relent there seemed no promise whatever, she lay down dully. When sorrow ceases to be speculative sleep sees her opportunity. Among so many happier moods which forbid repose this was a mood which welcomed it, and in a few minutes the lonely Tess forgot existence, surrounded by the aromatic stillness of the chamber that had once, possibly, been the bride-chamber of her own ancestry.

Later on that night Clare also retraced his steps to the house. Entering softly to the sitting-room he obtained a light, and with the manner of one who had considered his course he spread his rugs upon the old horse-hair sofa which stood there, and roughly shaped it to a sleeping-couch. Before lying down he crept shoeless upstairs, and listened at the door of her apartment. Her measured breathing told that she was sleeping profoundly.

'Thank God!' murmured Clare; and yet he was conscious of a pang of bitterness at the thought—approximately true, though not wholly so—that having shifted the burden of her life to his shoulders she was now reposing without care.

He turned away to descend; then, irresolute, faced round to her door again. In the act he caught sight of one of the d'Urberville dames, whose portrait was immediately over the entrance to Tess's bedchamber. In the candlelight the painting was more than unpleasant. Sinister design lurked in the woman's features, a concentrated purpose of revenge on the other sex—so it seemed to him then. The Caroline bodice of the portrait was low—precisely as Tess's had been when he tucked it in to show the necklace; and again he experienced the distressing sensation of a resemblance between them.

The check was sufficient. He resumed his retreat and descended.

His air remained calm and cold, his small compressed mouth indexing his powers of self-control; his face wearing still that terribly sterile expression which had spread thereon since her disclosure. It was the face of a man who was no longer passion's slave,[3] yet who found no advantage in his enfranchisement. He was simply regarding the harrowing contingencies of human experience, the unexpectedness of things. Nothing so pure, so sweet, so virginal as Tess had seemed possible all the long while that he had adored her, up to an hour ago; but

> The little less, and what worlds away![4]

He argued erroneously when he said to himself that her heart was not indexed in the honest freshness of her face; but Tess had no advocate to set him right. Could it be possible, he continued, that eyes which as they gazed never expressed any divergence from what the tongue was telling, were yet ever seeing another world behind her ostensible one, discordant and contrasting.

He reclined on his couch in the sitting-room, and extinguished the light. The night came in, and took up its place there, unconcerned and indifferent; the night which had already swallowed up his happiness, and was now digesting it listlessly; and was ready to swallow up the happiness of a thousand other people with as little disturbance or change of mien.

XXXVI

Clare arose in the light of a dawn that was ashy and furtive, as though associated with crime. The fireplace confronted him with

3. Cf. *Hamlet* III.ii.71ff.   4. From Browning's "By the Fire-Side," xxxix.

its extinct embers; the spread supper-table, whereon stood the two full glasses of untasted wine, now flat and filmy; her vacated seat and his own; the other articles of furniture, with their eternal look of not being able to help it, their intolerable inquiry what was to be done? From above there was no sound; but in a few minutes there came a knock at the door. He remembered that it would be the neighbouring cottager's wife, who was to minister to their wants while they remained here.

The presence of a third person in the house would be extremely awkward just now, and, being already dressed, he opened the window and informed her that they could manage to shift for themselves that morning. She had a milk-can in her hand, which he told her to leave at the door. When the dame had gone away he searched in the back quarters of the house for fuel, and speedily lit a fire. There was plenty of eggs, butter, bread, and so on in the larder, and Clare soon had breakfast laid, his experiences at the dairy having rendered him facile in domestic preparations. The smoke of the kindled wood rose from the chimney without like a lotus-headed column; local people who were passing by saw it, and thought of the newly-married couple, and envied their happiness.

Angel cast a final glance round, and then going to the foot of the stairs, called in a conventional voice—

'Breakfast is ready!'

He opened the front door, and took a few steps in the morning air. When, after a short space, he came back she was already in the sitting-room, mechanically readjusting the breakfast things. As she was fully attired, and the interval since his calling her had been but two or three minutes, she must have been dressed or nearly so before he went to summon her. Her hair was twisted up in a large round mass at the back of her head, and she had put on one of the new frocks—a pale blue woollen garment with neck-frillings of white. Her hands and face appeared to be cold, and she had possibly been sitting dressed in the bedroom a long time without any fire. The marked civility of Clare's tone in calling her seemed to have inspired her, for the moment, with a new glimmer of hope. But it soon died when she looked at him.

The pair were, in truth, but the ashes of their former fires. To the hot sorrow of the previous night had succeeded heaviness; it seemed as if nothing could kindle either of them to fervour of sensation any more.

He spoke gently to her, and she replied with a like undemonstrativeness. At last she came up to him, looking in his sharply-defined face as one who had no consciousness that her own formed a visible object also.

'Angel!' she said, and paused, touching him with her fingers

lightly as a breeze, as though she could hardly believe to be there
in the flesh the man who was once her lover. Her eyes were bright,
her pale cheek still showed its wonted roundness, though half-dried
tears had left glistening traces thereon; and the usually ripe red
mouth was almost as pale as her cheek. Throbbingly alive as she
was still, under the stress of her mental grief the life beat so
brokenly, that a little further pull upon it would cause real illness,
dull her characteristic eyes, and make her mouth thin.

She looked absolutely pure. Nature, in her fantastic trickery, had
set such a seal of maidenhood upon Tess's countenance that he
gazed at her with a stupefied air.

'Tess! Say it is not true! No, it is not true!'

'It is true.'

'Every word?'

'Every word.'

He looked at her imploringly, as if he would willingly have taken
a lie from her lips, knowing it to be one, and have made of it,
by some sort of sophistry, a valid denial. However, she only repeated—

'It is true.'

'Is he living?' Angel then asked.

'The baby died.'

'But the man?'

'He is alive.'

A last despair passed over Clare's face.

'Is he in England?'

'Yes.'

He took a few vague steps.

'My position — is this,' he said abruptly. 'I thought — any man
would have thought—that by giving up all ambition to win a
wife with social standing, with fortune, with knowledge of the world,
I should secure rustic innocence as surely as I should secure pink
cheeks; but—— However, I am no man to reproach you, and I
will not.'

Tess felt his position so entirely that the remainder had not been
needed. Therein lay just the distress of it; she saw that he had lost
all round.

'Angel—I should not have let it go on to marriage with you if
I had not known that, after all, there was a last way out of it for
you; though I hoped you would never——'

Her voice grew husky.

'A last way?'

'I mean, to get rid of me. You *can* get rid of me.'

'How?'

'By divorcing me.'

'Good heavens—how can you be so simple! How can I divorce you?'

'Can't you—now I have told you? I thought my confession would give you grounds for that.'

'O Tess—you are too, too—childish—unformed—crude, I suppose! I don't know what you are. You don't understand the law—you don't understand!'

'What—you cannot?'

'Indeed I cannot.'

A quick shame mixed with the misery upon his listener's face.

'I thought—I thought,' she whispered. 'O, now I see how wicked I seem to you! Believe me—believe me, on my soul, I never thought but that you could! I hoped you would not; yet I believed, without a doubt, that you could cast me off if you were determined, and didn't love me at—at—all!'

'You were mistaken,' he said.

'O, then I ought to have done it, to have done it last night! But I hadn't the courage. That's just like me!'

'The courage to do what?'

As she did not answer he took her by the hand.

'What were you thinking of doing?' he inquired.

'Of putting an end to myself.'

'When?'

She writhed under this inquisitorial manner of his. 'Last night,' she answered.

'Where?'

'Under your mistletoe.'

'My good— ! How?' he asked sternly.

'I'll tell you, if you won't be angry with me!' she said, shrinking. 'It was with the cord of my box. But I could not—do the last thing! I was afraid that it might cause a scandal to your name.'

The unexpected quality of this confession, wrung from her, and not volunteered, shook him perceptibly. But he still held her, and, letting his glance fall from her face downwards, he said,

'Now, listen to this. You must not dare to think of such a horrible thing! How could you! You will promise me as your husband to attempt that no more.'

'I am ready to promise. I saw how wicked it was.'

'Wicked! The idea was unworthy of you beyond description.'

'But, Angel,' she pleaded, enlarging her eyes in calm unconcern upon him, 'it was thought of entirely on your account—to set you free without the scandal of the divorce that I thought you would have to get. I should never have dreamt of doing it on mine. However, to do it with my own hand is too good for me, after all. It is you, my ruined husband, who ought to strike the blow. I think I should love you more, if that were possible, if you could bring yourself to do it, since there's no other way of escape for 'ee. I feel I am so utterly worthless! So very greatly in the way!'

'Ssh!'

'Well, since you say no, I won't. I have no wish opposed to yours.'

He knew this to be true enough. Since the desperation of the night her activities had dropped to zero, and there was no further rashness to be feared.

Tess tried to busy herself again over the breakfast-table with more or less success, and they sat down both on the same side, so that their glances did not meet. There was at first something awkward in hearing each other eat and drink, but this could not be escaped; moreover, the amount of eating done was small on both sides. Breakfast over he rose, and telling her the hour at which he might be expected to dinner, went off to the miller's in a mechanical pursuance of the plan of studying that business, which had been his only practical reason for coming here.

When he was gone Tess stood at the window, and presently saw his form crossing the great stone bridge which conducted to the mill premises. He sank behind it, crossed the railway beyond, and disappeared. Then, without a sigh, she turned her attention to the room, and began clearing the table and setting it in order.

The charwoman soon came. Her presence was at first a strain upon Tess, but afterwards an alleviation. At half-past twelve she left her assistant alone in the kitchen, and, returning to the sitting-room, waited for the reappearance of Angel's form behind the bridge.

About one he showed himself. Her face flushed, although he was a quarter of a mile off. She ran to the kitchen to get the dinner served by the time he should enter. He went first to the room where they had washed their hands together the day before, and as he entered the sitting-room the dish-covers rose from the dishes as if by his own motion.

'How punctual!' he said.

'Yes. I saw you coming over the bridge,' said she.

The meal was passed in commonplace talk of what he had been doing during the morning at the Abbey Mill, of the methods of bolting and the old-fashioned machinery, which he feared would not enlighten him greatly on modern improved methods, some of it seeming to have been in use ever since the days it ground for the monks in the adjoining conventual buildings—now a heap of ruins. He left the house again in the course of an hour, coming home at dusk, and occupying himself through the evening with his papers. She feared she was in the way, and, when the old woman was gone, retired to the kitchen, where she made herself busy as well as she could for more than an hour.

Clare's shape appeared at the door.

'You must not work like this,' he said. 'You are not my servant; you are my wife.'

She raised her eyes, and brightened somewhat. 'I may think myself that—indeed?' she murmured, in piteous raillery. 'You mean in name! Well, I don't want to be anything more.'

'You *may* think so, Tess! You are. What do you mean?'

'I don't know,' she said hastily, with tears in her accents. 'I thought I—because I am not respectable, I mean. I told you I thought I was not respectable enough long ago—and on that account I didn't want to marry you, only—only you urged me!'

She broke into sobs, and turned her back to him. It would almost have won round any man but Angel Clare. Within the remote depths of his constitution, so gentle and affectionate as he was in general, there lay hidden a hard logical deposit, like a vein of metal in a soft loam, which turned the edge of everything that attempted to traverse it. It had blocked his acceptance of the Church; it blocked his acceptance of Tess. Moreover, his affection itself was less fire than radiance, and, with regard to the other sex, when he ceased to believe he ceased to follow: contrasting in this with many impressionable natures, who remain sensuously infatuated with what they intellectually despise. He waited till her sobbing ceased.

'I wish half the women in England were as respectable as you,' he said, in an ebullition of bitterness against womankind in general. 'It isn't a question of respectability, but one of principle!'

He spoke such things as these and more of a kindred sort to her, being still swayed by the antipathetic wave which warps direct souls with such persistence when once their vision finds itself mocked by appearances. There was, it is true, underneath, a back current of sympathy through which a woman of the world might have conquered him. But Tess did not think of this; she took everything as her deserts, and hardly opened her mouth. The firmness of her devotion to him was indeed almost pitiful; quick-tempered as she naturally was, nothing that he could say made her unseemly; she sought not her own; was not provoked;[5] thought no evil of his treatment of her. She might just now have been Apostolic Charity herself returned to a self-seeking modern world.

This evening, night, and morning were passed precisely as the preceding ones had been passed. On one, and only one, occasion did she—the formerly free and independent Tess—venture to make any advances. It was on the third occasion of his starting after a meal to go out to the flour-mill. As he was leaving the table he said 'Good-bye,' and she replied in the same words, at the same time inclining her mouth in the way of his. He did not avail himself of the invitation, saying, as he turned hastily aside—

'I shall be home punctually.'

Tess shrank into herself as if she had been struck. Often enough had he tried to reach those lips against her consent—often had he said gaily that her mouth and breath tasted of the butter and eggs and milk and honey on which she mainly lived, that he drew sustenance from them, and other follies of that sort. But he did not care for them now. He observed her sudden shrinking, and said gently—

'You know, I have to think of a course. It was imperative that we should stay together a little while, to avoid the scandal to you that would have resulted from our immediate parting. But you must see it is only for form's sake.'

'Yes,' said Tess absently.

He went out, and on his way to the mill stood still, and wished for a moment that he had responded yet more kindly, and kissed her once at least.

Thus they lived through this despairing day or two; in the same house, truly; but more widely apart than before they were lovers. It was evident to her that he was, as he had said, living with paralyzed activities, in his endeavour to think of a plan of procedure. She was awe-stricken to discover such determination under such apparent flexibility. His consistency was, indeed, too cruel. She no longer expected forgiveness now. More than once she thought of going away from him during his absence at the mill; but she feared that this, instead of benefiting him, might be the means of hampering and humiliating him yet more if it should become known.

Meanwhile Clare was meditating, verily. His thought had been unsuspended; he was becoming ill with thinking; eaten out with thinking, withered by thinking; scourged out of all his former pulsating flexuous domesticity. He walked about saying to himself, 'What's to be done—what's to be done?' and by chance she overheard him. It caused her to break the reserve about their future which had hitherto prevailed.

'I suppose—you are not going to live with me—long, are you, Angel?' she asked, the sunk corners of her mouth betraying how purely mechanical were the means by which she retained that expression of chastened calm upon her face.

'I cannot,' he said, 'without despising myself, and what is worse, perhaps, despising you. I mean, of course, cannot live with you in the ordinary sense. At present, whatever I feel, I do not despise you. And, let me speak plainly, or you may not see all my difficulties. How can we live together while that man lives?—he being your husband in

Nature, and not I. If he were dead it might be different. . . . Besides, that's not all the difficulty; it lies in another consideration—one bearing upon the future of other people than ourselves. Think of years to come, and children being born to us, and this past matter getting known—for it must get known. There is not an uttermost part of the earth but somebody comes from it or goes to it from elsewhere. Well, think of wretches of our flesh and blood growing up under a taunt which they will gradually get to feel the full force of with their expanding years. What an awakening for them! What a prospect! Can you honestly say Remain, after contemplating this contingency? Don't you think we had better endure the ills we have than fly to others?'[6]

Her eyelids, weighted with trouble, continued drooping as before.

'I cannot say Remain,' she answered. 'I cannot; I had not thought so far.'

Tess's feminine hope—shall we confess it—had been so obstinately recuperative as to revive in her surreptitious visions of a domiciliary intimacy continued long enough to break down his coldness even against his judgment. Though unsophisticated in the usual sense, she was not incomplete; and it would have denoted deficiency of womanhood if she had not instinctively known what an argument lies in propinquity. Nothing else would serve her, she knew, if this failed. It was wrong to hope in what was of the nature of strategy, she said to herself: yet that sort of hope she could not extinguish. His last representation had now been made, and it was, as she said, a new view. She had truly never thought so far as that, and his lucid picture of possible offspring who would scorn her was one that brought deadly conviction to an honest heart which was humanitarian to its centre. Sheer experience had already taught her that, in some circumstances, there was one thing better than to lead a good life, and that was to be saved from leading any life whatever. Like all who have been previsioned by suffering, she could, in the words of M. Sully-Prudhomme, hear a penal sentence in the fiat, 'You shall be born,' particularly if addressed to potential issue of hers.

Yet such is the vulpine slyness of Dame Nature, that, till now, Tess had been hoodwinked by her love for Clare into forgetting it might result in vitalizations that would inflict upon others what she had bewailed as a misfortune to herself.

She therefore could not withstand his argument. But with the self-combating proclivity of the supersensitive, an answer thereto arose in Clare's own mind, and he almost feared it. It was based on her exceptional physical nature; and she might have used it promisingly. She might have added besides: 'On an Australian upland or Texan plain, who is to know or care about my misfortunes, or to reproach

6. An echo of *Hamlet*, III.i.81-82.

me or you?' Yet, like the majority of women, she accepted the momentary presentment as if it were the inevitable. And she may have been right. The intuitive heart of woman knoweth not only its own bitterness, but its husband's, and even if these assumed reproaches were not likely to be addressed to him or to his by strangers, they might have reached his ears from his own fastidious brain.

It was the third day of the estrangement. Some might risk the odd paradox that with more animalism he would have been the nobler man. We do not say it. Yet Clare's love was doubtless ethereal to a fault, imaginative to impracticability. With these natures, corporeal presence is sometimes less appealing than corporeal absence; the latter creating an ideal presence that conveniently drops the defects of the real. She found that her personality did not plead her cause so forcibly as she had anticipated. The figurative phrase was true: she was another woman than the one who had excited his desire.

'I have thought over what you say,' she remarked to him, moving her forefinger over the tablecloth, her other hand, which bore the ring that mocked them both, supporting her forehead. 'It is quite true all of it; it must be. You must go away from me.'

'But what can you do?'

'I can go home.'

Clare had not thought of that.

'Are you sure?' he inquired.

'Quite sure. We ought to part, and we may as well get it past and done. You once said that I was apt to win men against their better judgment; and if I am constantly before your eyes I may cause you to change your plans in opposition to your reason and wish; and afterwards your repentance and my sorrow will be terrible.'

'And you would like to go home?' he asked.

'I want to leave you, and go home.'

'Then it shall be so.'

Though she did not look up at him, she started. There was a difference between the proposition and the covenant, which she had felt only too quickly.

'I feared it would come to this,' she murmured, her countenance meekly fixed. 'I don't complain, Angel. I—I think it best. What you said has quite convinced me. Yes, though nobody else should reproach me if we should stay together, yet somewhen, years hence, you might get angry with me for any ordinary matter, and knowing what you do of my bygones you yourself might be tempted to say words, and they might be overheard, perhaps by my own children. O, what only hurts me now would torture and kill me then! I will go—to-morrow.'

'And I shall not stay here. Though I didn't like to initiate it, I have seen that it was advisable we should part—at least for a while, till I can better see the shape that things have taken, and can write to you.'

Tess stole a glance at her husband. He was pale, even tremulous; but, as before, she was appalled by the determination revealed in the depths of this gentle being she had married—the will to subdue the grosser to the subtler emotion, the substance to the conception, the flesh to the spirit. Propensities, tendencies, habits, were as dead leaves upon the tyrannous wind of his imaginative ascendency.

He may have observed her look, for he explained—

'I think of people more kindly when I am away from them;' adding cynically, 'God knows; perhaps we shall shake down together some day, for weariness; thousands have done it!'

That day he began to pack up, and she went upstairs and began to pack also. Both knew that it was in their two minds that they might part the next morning for ever, despite the gloss of assuaging conjectures thrown over their proceeding because they were of the sort to whom any parting which has an air of finality is a torture. He knew, and she knew, that, though the fascination which each had exercised over the other—on her part independently of accomplishments— would probably in the first days of their separation be even more potent than ever, time must attenuate that effect; the practical arguments against accepting her as a housemate might pronounce themselves more strongly in the boreal light of a remoter view. Moreover, when two people are once parted—have abandoned a common domicile and a common environment—new growths insensibly bud upward to fill each vacated place; unforeseen accidents hinder intentions, and old plans are forgotten.

XXXVII

Midnight came and passed silently, for there was nothing to announce it in the Valley of the Froom.

Not long after one o'clock there was a slight creak in the darkened farmhouse once the mansion of the d'Urbervilles. Tess, who used the upper chamber, heard it and awoke. It had come from the corner step of the staircase, which, as usual, was loosely nailed. She saw the door of her bedroom open, and the figure of her husband crossed the stream of moonlight with a curiously careful tread. He was in his shirt and trousers only, and her first flush of joy died when she perceived that his eyes were fixed in an unnatural stare on vacancy. When he reached the middle of the room he stood still and murmured, in tones of indescribable sadness—

'Dead! dead! dead!'

Under the influence of any strongly-disturbing force Clare would occasionally walk in his sleep, and even perform strange feats, such as he had done on the night of their return from market just before their marriage, when he re-enacted in his bedroom his combat with the man who had insulted her. Tess saw that continued mental distress had wrought him into that somnambulistic state now.

Her loyal confidence in him lay so deep down in her heart that, awake or asleep, he inspired her with no sort of personal fear. If he had entered with a pistol in his hand he would scarcely have disturbed her trust in his protectiveness.

Clare came close, and bent over her. 'Dead, dead, dead!' he murmured.

After fixedly regarding her for some moments with the same gaze of unmeasurable woe he bent lower, enclosed her in his arms, and rolled her in the sheet as in a shroud. Then lifting her from the bed with as much respect as one would show to a dead body, he carried her across the room, murmuring—

'My poor, poor Tess—my dearest, darling Tess! So sweet, so good, so true!'

The words of endearment, withheld so severely in his waking hours, were inexpressibly sweet to her forlorn and hungry heart. If it had been to save her weary life she would not, by moving or struggling, have put an end to the position she found herself in. Thus she lay in absolute stillness, scarcely venturing to breathe, and, wondering what he was going to do with her, suffered herself to be borne out upon the landing.

'My wife—dead, dead!' he said.

He paused in his labours for a moment to lean with her against the banister. Was he going to throw her down? Self-solicitude was near extinction in her, and in the knowledge that he had planned to depart on the morrow, possibly for always, she lay in his arms in this precarious position with a sense rather of luxury than of terror. If they could only fall together, and both be dashed to pieces, how fit, how desirable.

However, he did not let her fall, but took advantage of the support of the handrail to imprint a kiss upon her lips—lips in the daytime scorned. Then he clasped her with a renewed firmness of hold, and descended the staircase. The creak of the loose stair did not awaken him, and they reached the ground-floor safely. Freeing one of his hands from his grasp of her for a moment, he slid back the door-bar and passed out, slightly striking his stockinged toe against the edge of the door. But this he seemed not to mind, and, having room for extension in the open air, he lifted her against his shoulder, so that he could carry her with ease, the absence of clothes taking much from his burden. Thus he bore her off the premises in the direction of the river a few yards distant.

His ultimate intention, if he had any, she had not yet divined; and she found herself conjecturing on the matter as a third person might have done. So easefully had she delivered her whole being up to him that it pleased her to think he was regarding her as his absolute possession, to dispose of as he should choose. It was consoling, under the hovering terror of tomorrow's separation, to feel that he really recognized her now as his wife Tess, and did not cast her off, even if in that recognition he went so far as to arrogate to himself the right of harming her.

Ah! now she knew what he was dreaming of—that Sunday morning when he had borne her along through the water with the other dairymaids, who had loved him nearly as much as she, if that were possible, which Tess could hardly admit. Clare did not cross the bridge with her, but proceeding several paces on the same side towards the adjoining mill, at length stood still on the brink of the river.

Its waters, in creeping down these miles of meadowland, frequently divided, serpentining in purposeless curves, looping themselves around little islands that had no name, returning and re-embodying themselves as a broad main stream further on. Opposite the spot to which he had brought her was such a general confluence, and the river was proportionately voluminous and deep. Across it was a narrow foot-bridge; but now the autumn flood had washed the handrail away, leaving the bare plank only, which, lying a few inches above the speeding current, formed a giddy pathway for even steady heads; and Tess had noticed from the window of the house in the daytime young men walking across upon it as a feat in balancing. Her husband had possibly observed the same performance; anyhow, he now mounted the plank, and, sliding one foot forward, advanced along it.

Was he going to drown her? Probably he was. The spot was lonely, the river deep and wide enough to make such a purpose easy of accomplishment. He might drown her if he would; it would be better than parting to-morrow to lead severed lives.

The swift stream raced and gyrated under them, tossing, distorting, and splitting the moon's reflected face. Spots of froth travelled past, and intercepted weeds waved behind the piles. If they could both fall together into the current now, their arms would be so tightly clasped together that they could not be saved; they would go out of the world almost painlessly, and there would be no more reproach to her, or to him for marrying her. His last half-hour with her would have been a loving one, while if they lived till he awoke his daytime aversion would return, and this hour would remain to be contemplated only as a transient dream.

The impulse stirred in her, yet she dared not indulge it, to make a movement that would have precipitated them both into the gulf. How she valued her own life had been proved; but his—she had no right to tamper with it. He reached the other side with her in safety.

Here they were within a plantation which formed the Abbey grounds, and taking a new hold of her he went onward a few steps till they reached the ruined choir of the Abbey-church. Against the north wall was the empty stone coffin of an abbot, in which every tourist with a turn for grim humour was accustomed to stretch himself. In this Clare carefully laid Tess. Having kissed her lips a second time he breathed deeply, as if a greatly desired end were attained. Clare then lay down on the ground alongside, when he immediately fell into the deep dead slumber of exhaustion, and remained motionless as a log. The spurt of mental excitement which had produced the effort was now over.

Tess sat up in the coffin. The night, though dry and mild for the season, was more than sufficiently cold to make it dangerous for him to remain here long, in his half-clothed state. If he were left to himself he would in all probability stay there till the morning, and be chilled to certain death. She had heard of such deaths after sleep-walking. But how could she dare to awaken him, and let him know what he had been doing, when it would mortify him to discover his folly in respect of her? Tess, however, stepping out of her stone confine, shook him slightly, but was unable to arouse him without being violent. It was indispensable to do something, for she was beginning to shiver, the sheet being but a poor protection. Her excitement had in a measure kept her warm during the few minutes' adventure; but that beatific interval was over.

It suddenly occurred to her to try persuasion; and accordingly she whispered in his ear, with as much firmness and decision as she could summon—

'Let us walk on, darling,' at the same time taking him suggestively by the arm. To her relief, he unresistingly acquiesced; her words had apparently thrown him back into his dream, which thenceforward seemed to enter on a new phase, wherein he fancied she had risen as a spirit, and was leading him to Heaven. Thus she conducted him by the arm to the stone bridge in front of their residence, crossing which they stood at the manor-house door. Tess's feet were quite bare, and the stones hurt her, and chilled her to the bone; but Clare was in his woollen stockings, and appeared to feel no discomfort.

There was no further difficulty. She induced him to lie down on his own sofa bed, and covered him up warmly, lighting a temporary fire of wood, to dry any dampness out of him. The noise of these attentions she thought might awaken him, and secretly wished that they might. But the exhaustion of his mind and body was such that he remained undisturbed.

As soon as they met the next morning Tess divined that Angel knew little or nothing of how far she had been concerned in the night's excursion, though, as regarded himself he may have been aware that he had not lain still. In truth, he had awakened that morning from a sleep deep as annihilation; and during those first few moments in which the brain, like a Samson shaking himself,[7] is trying its strength, he had some dim notion of an unusual nocturnal proceeding. But the realities of his situation soon displaced conjecture on the other subject.

He waited in expectancy to discern some mental pointing; he knew that if any intention of his, concluded over-night, did not vanish in the light of morning, it stood on a basis approximating to one of pure reason, even if initiated by impulse of feeling; that it was so far, therefore, to be trusted. He thus beheld in the pale morning light the resolve to separate from her; not as a hot and indignant instinct, but denuded of the passionateness which had made it scorch and burn; standing in its bones; nothing but a skeleton, but none the less there. Clare no longer hesitated.

At breakfast, and while they were packing the few remaining articles, he showed his weariness from the night's effort so unmistakably that Tess was on the point of revealing all that had happened; but the reflection that it would anger him, grieve him, stultify him, to know that he had instinctively manifested a fondness for her of which his common-sense did not approve; that his inclination had compromised his dignity when reason slept, again deterred her. It was too much like laughing at a man when sober for his erratic deeds during intoxication.

It just crossed her mind, too, that he might have a faint recollection of his tender vagary, and was disinclined to allude to it from a conviction that she would take amatory advantage of the opportunity it gave her of appealing to him anew not to go.

He had ordered by letter a vehicle from the nearest town, and soon after breakfast it arrived. She saw in it the beginning of the end— the temporary end, at least, for the revelation of his tenderness by the incident of the night raised dreams of a possible future with him. The luggage was put on the top, and the man drove them off, the miller and the old waiting-woman expressing some surprise at their precipitate departure, which Clare attributed to his discovery that the mill-work was not of the modern kind which he wished to investigate, a statement that was true so far as it went. Beyond this there was nothing in the manner of their leaving to suggest a *fiasco*, or that they were not going together to visit friends.

Their route lay near the dairy from which they had started with such solemn joy in each other a few days back, and, as Clare wished

7. Judges xvi:20: "And [Samson] awoke out of his sleep, and said, I will go out as at other times before, and shake myself."

to wind up his business with Mr. Crick, Tess could hardly avoid paying Mrs. Crick a call at the same time, unless she would excite suspicion of their unhappy state.

To make the call as unobtrusive as possible they left the carriage by the wicket leading down from the high road to the dairy-house, and descended the track on foot, side by side. The withy-bed had been cut, and they could see over the stumps the spot to which Clare had followed her when he pressed her to be his wife; to the left the enclosure in which she had been fascinated by his harp; and far away behind the cowstalls the mead which had been the scene of their first embrace. The gold of the summer picture was now gray, the colours mean, the rich soil mud, and the river cold.

Over the barton-gate the dairyman saw them, and came forward, throwing into his face the kind of jocularity deemed appropriate in Talbothays and its vicinity on the re-appearance of the newly-married. Then Mrs. Crick emerged from the house, and several others of their old acquaintance, though Marian and Retty did not seem to be there.

Tess valiantly bore their sly attacks and friendly humours, which affected her far otherwise than they supposed. In the tacit agreement of husband and wife to keep their estrangement a secret they behaved as would have been ordinary. And then, although she would rather there had been no word spoken on the subject, Tess had to hear in detail the story of Marian and Retty. The latter had gone home to her father's, and Marian had left to look for employment elsewhere. They feared she would come to no good.

To dissipate the sadness of this recital Tess went and bade all her favourite cows good-bye, touching each of them with her hand, and as she and Clare stood side by side at leaving, as if united body and soul, there would have been something peculiarly sorry in their aspect to one who should have seen it truly; two limbs of one life, as they outwardly were, his arm touching hers, her skirts touching him, facing one way, as against all the dairy facing the other, speaking in their adieux as 'we,' and yet sundered like the poles. Perhaps something unusually stiff and embarrassed in their attitude, some awkwardness in acting up to their profession of unity, different from the natural shyness of young couples, may have been apparent, for when they were gone Mrs. Crick said to her husband—

'How onnatural the brightness of her eyes did seem, and how they stood like waxen images and talked as if they were in a dream! Didn't it strike 'ee that 'twas so? Tess had always sommat strange in her, and she's not now quite like the proud young bride of a well-be-doing man.'

They re-entered the vehicle, and were driven along the roads towards Weatherbury and Stagfoot Lane, till they reached the Lane inn, where Clare dismissed the fly and man. They rested here a while, and entering the Vale were next driven onward towards her home by a stranger who did not know their relations. At a midway point, when Nuttlebury had been passed, and where there were cross-roads, Clare stopped the conveyance and said to Tess that if she meant to return to her mother's house it was here that he would leave her. As they could not talk with freedom in the driver's presence he asked her to accompany him for a few steps on foot along one of the branch roads; she assented, and directing the man to wait a few minutes they strolled away.

'Now, let us understand each other,' he said gently. 'There is no anger between us, though there is that which I cannot endure at present. I will try to bring myself to endure it. I will let you know where I go to as soon as I know myself. And if I can bring myself to bear it— if it is desirable, possible—I will come to you. But until I come to you it will be better that you should not try to come to me.'

The severity of the decree seemed deadly to Tess; she saw his view of her clearly enough; he could regard her in no other light than that of one who had practised gross deceit upon him. Yet could a woman who had done even what she had done deserve all this? But she could contest the point with him no further. She simply repeated after him his own words.

'Until you come to me I must not try to come to you?'

'Just so.'

'May I write to you?'

'O yes—if you are ill, or want anything at all. I hope that will not be the case; so that it may happen that I write first to you.'

'I agree to the conditions, Angel; because you know best what my punishment ought to be; only—only—don't make it more than I can bear!'

That was all she said on the matter. If Tess had been artful, had she made a scene, fainted, wept hysterically, in that lonely lane, notwithstanding the fury of fastidiousness with which he was possessed, he would probably not have withstood her. But her mood of long-suffering made his way easy for him, and she herself was his best advocate. Pride, too, entered into her submission—which perhaps was a symptom of that reckless acquiescence in chance too apparent in the whole d'Urberville family—and the many effective chords which she could have stirred by an appeal were left untouched.

The remainder of their discourse was on practical matters only. He now handed her a packet containing a fairly good sum of money, which he had obtained from his bankers for the purpose. The brilliants, the interest in which seemed to be Tess's for her life only (if he understood the wording of the will), he advised her to let him send to a bank for safety; and to this she readily agreed.

These things arranged he walked with Tess back to the carriage, and handed her in. The coachman was paid and told where to drive her. Taking next his own bag and umbrella—the sole articles he had brought with him hitherwards—he bade her good-bye; and they parted there and then.

The fly moved creepingly up a hill, and Clare watched it go with an unpremeditated hope that Tess would look out of the window for one moment. But that she never thought of doing, would not have ventured to do, lying in a half-dead faint inside. Thus he beheld her recede, and in the anguish of his heart quoted a line from a poet, with peculiar emendations of his own—

God's *not* in his heaven: all's *wrong* with the world![8]

When Tess had passed over the crest of the hill he turned to go his own way, and hardly knew that he loved her still.

XXXVIII

As she drove on through Blackmoor Vale, and the landscape of her youth began to open around her, Tess aroused herself from her stupor. Her first thought was how would she be able to face her parents?

She reached a turnpike-gate which stood upon the highway to the village. It was thrown open by a stranger, not by the old man who had kept it for many years, and to whom she had been known; he had probably left on New Year's Day, the date when such changes were made. Having received no intelligence lately from her home, she asked the turnpike-keeper for news.

'Oh—nothing, miss,' he answered. 'Marlott is Marlott still. Folks have died and that. John Durbeyfield, too, hev had a daughter married this week to a gentleman-farmer; not from John's own house, you know; they was married elsewhere; the gentleman being of that high standing that John's own folk was not considered well-be-doing enough to have any part in it, the bridegroom seeming not to know how't have been discovered that John is a old and ancient nobleman himself by blood, with family skillentons in their own vaults to this day, but done out of his property in the time o' the Romans. However, Sir John, as we call'n now, kept up the wedding-day as well as he could, and stood treat to everybody in the parish; and John's wife sung songs at The Pure Drop till past eleven o'clock.'

Hearing this, Tess felt so sick at heart that she could not decide to go home publicly in the fly with her luggage and belongings. She asked the turnpike-keeper if she might deposit her things at his house for a while, and, on his offering no objection, she dismissed her carriage, and went on to the village alone by a back lane.

At sight of her father's chimney she asked herself how she could

---

8. In Browning's *Pippa Passes*, lines 7 and 8 of the Morning Song are: "God's in his heaven—/All's right with the world."

possibly enter the house? Inside that cottage her relations were calmly supposing her far away on a wedding-tour with a comparatively rich man, who was to conduct her to bouncing prosperity; while here she was, friendless, creeping up to the old door quite by herself, with no better place to go in the world.

She did not reach the house unobserved. Just by the garden-hedge she was met by a girl who knew her—one of the two or three with whom she had been intimate at school. After making a few inquiries as to how Tess came there, her friend, unheeding her tragic look, interrupted with—

'But where's thy gentleman, Tess?'

Tess hastily explained that he had been called away on business, and, leaving her interlocutor, clambered over the garden-hedge, and thus made her way to the house.

As she went up the garden-path she heard her mother singing by the back door, coming in sight of which she perceived Mrs. Durbeyfield on the door step in the act of wringing a sheet. Having performed this without observing Tess, she went indoors, and her daughter followed her.

The washing-tub stood in the same old place on the same old quarter-hogshead, and her mother, having thrown the sheet aside, was about to plunge her arms in anew.

'Why—Tess!—my chil'—I thought you was married!—married really and truly this time—we sent the cider——'

'Yes, mother; so I am.'

'Going to be?'

'No—I am married.'

'Married! Then where's thy husband?'

'Oh, he's gone away for a time.'

'Gone away! When was you married, then? The day you said?'

'Yes, Tuesday, mother.'

'And now 'tis on'y Saturday, and he gone away?'

'Yes; he's gone.'

'What's the meaning o' that? 'Nation seize such husbands as you seem to get, say I!'

'Mother!' Tess went across to Joan Durbeyfield, laid her face upon the matron's bosom, and burst into sobs. 'I don't know how to tell 'ee, mother! You said to me, and wrote to me, that I was not to tell him. But I did tell him—I couldn't help it—and he went away!'

'O you little fool—you little fool!' burst out Mrs. Durbeyfield, splashing Tess and herself in her agitation. 'My good God! that ever I should ha' lived to say it, but I say it again, you little fool!'

Tess was convulsed with weeping, the tension of so many days having relaxed at last.

'I know it—I know—I know!' she gasped through her sobs. 'But,

O my mother, I could not help it! He was so good—and I felt the wickedness of trying to blind him as to what had happened! If—if—it were to be done again—I should do the same. I could not—I dared not—so sin—against him!'

'But you sinned enough to marry him first!'

'Yes, yes; that's where my misery do lie! But I thought he could get rid o' me by law if he were determined not to overlook it. And O, if you knew—if you could only half know how I loved him—how anxious I was to have him—and how wrung I was between caring so much for him and my wish to be fair to him!'

Tess was so shaken that she could get no further, and sank a helpless thing into a chair.

'Well, well; what's done can't be undone! I'm sure I don't know why children o' my bringing forth should all be bigger simpletons than other people's—not to know better than to blab such a thing as that, when he couldn't ha' found it out till too late!' Here Mrs. Durbeyfield began shedding tears on her own account as a mother to be pitied. 'What your father will say I don't know,' she continued; 'for he's been talking about the wedding up at Rolliver's and The Pure Drop every day since, and about his family getting back to their rightful position through you—poor silly man!—and now you've made this mess of it. The Lord-a-Lord!'

As if to bring matters to a focus, Tess's father was heard approaching at that moment. He did not, however, enter immediately, and Mrs. Durbeyfield said that she would break the bad news to him herself, Tess keeping out of sight for the present. After her first burst of disappointment Joan began to take the mishap as she had taken Tess's original trouble, as she would have taken a wet holiday or failure in the potato-crop; as a thing which had come upon them irrespective of desert or folly; a chance external impingement to be borne with; not a lesson.

Tess retreated upstairs, and beheld casually that the beds had been shifted, and new arrangements made. Her old bed had been adapted for two younger children. There was no place here for her now.

The room below being unceiled she could hear most of what went on there. Presently her father entered, apparently carrying a live hen. He was a foot-haggler now, having been obliged to sell his second horse, and he travelled with his basket on his arm. The hen had been carried about this morning as it was often carried, to show people that he was in his work, though it had lain, with its legs tied, under the table at Rolliver's for more than an hour.

'We've just had up a story about——' Durbeyfield began, and thereupon related in detail to his wife a discussion which had arisen at the inn about the clergy, originated by the fact of his daughter having married into a clerical family. 'They was formerly styled "sir," like my own ancestry,' he said, 'though nowadays their true style, strictly speaking, is "clerk" only.' As Tess had wished that no great publicity should be given to the event, he had mentioned no particulars. He hoped she would remove that prohibition soon. He proposed that the couple should take Tess's own name, d'Urberville, as uncorrupted. It was better than her husband's. He asked if any letter had come from her that day.

Then Mrs. Durbeyfield informed him that no letter had come, but Tess unfortunately had come herself.

When at length the collapse was explained to him a sullen mortification, not usual with Durbeyfield, overpowered the influence of the cheering glass. Yet the intrinsic quality of the event moved his touchy sensitiveness less than its conjectured effect upon the minds of others.

'To think, now, that this was to be the end o't!' said Sir John. 'And I with a family vault under that there church of Kingsbere as big as Squire Jollard's ale-cellar, and my folk lying there in sixes and sevens, as genuine county bones and marrow as any recorded in history. And now to be sure what they fellers at Rolliver's and The Pure Drop will say to me! How they'll squint and glane,[9] and say, "This is yer mighty match is it; this is yer getting back to the true level of yer forefathers in King Norman's time!" I feel this is too much, Joan; I shall put an end to myself, title and all—I can bear it no longer! . . . But she can make him keep her if he's married her?'

'Why, yes. But she won't think o' doing that.'

'D'ye think he really have married her?—or is it like the first——'

Poor Tess, who had heard as far as this, could not bear to hear more. The perception that her word could be doubted even here, in her own parental house, set her mind against the spot as nothing else could have done. How unexpected were the attacks of destiny! And if her father doubted her a little, would not neightbors and acquaintance doubt her much? O, she could not live long at home!

A few days, accordingly, were all that she allowed herself here, at the end of which time she received a short note from Clare, informing her that he had gone to the North of England to look at a farm. In her craving for the lustre of her true position as his wife, and to hide from her parents the vast extent of the division between them, she made use of this letter as her reason for again departing, leaving them under the impression that she was setting out to join him. Still further to screen her husband from any imputation of unkindness to her, she took twenty-five of the fifty pounds Clare had given her, and handed the sum over to her mother, as if the wife of a man like Angel Clare could well afford it, saying that it was a slight return for the trouble and humiliation she had brought upon them in years past. With this assertion of her dignity she bade them farewell; and after that there were lively doings in the Durbeyfield household for

9. Look askance, leer, jeer.

some time on the strength of Tess's bounty, her mother saying, and, indeed, believing, that the rupture which had arisen between the young husband and wife had adjusted itself under their strong feeling that they could not live apart from each other.

XXXIX

It was three weeks after the marriage that Clare found himself descending the hill which led to the well-known parsonage of his father. With his downward course the tower of the church rose into the evening sky in a manner of inquiry as to why he had come; and no living person in the twilighted town seemed to notice him, still less to expect him. He was arriving like a ghost, and the sound of his own footsteps was almost an encumbrance to be got rid of.

The picture of life had changed for him. Before this time he had known it but speculatively; now he thought he knew it as a practical man; though perhaps he did not, even yet. Nevertheless humanity stood before him no longer in the pensive sweetness of Italian art, but in the staring and ghastly attitudes of a Wiertz Museum, and with the leer of a study by Van Beers.[1]

His conduct during these first weeks had been desultory beyond description. After mechanically attempting to pursue his agricultural plans as though nothing unusual had happened, in the manner recommended by the great and wise men of all ages, he concluded that very few of those great and wise men had ever gone so far outside themselves as to test the feasibility of their counsel. 'This is the chief thing: be not perturbed,' said the Pagan moralist.[2] That was just Clare's own opinion. But he was perturbed. 'Let not your heart be troubled, neither let it be afraid,' said the Nazarene.[3] Clare chimed in cordially; but his heart was troubled all the same. How he would have liked to confront those two great thinkers, and earnestly appeal to them as fellow-man to fellow-men, and ask them to tell him their method!

His mood transmuted itself into a dogged indifference till at length he fancied he was looking on his own existence with the passive interest of an outsider.

He was embittered by the conviction that all this desolation had been brought about by the accident of her being a d'Urberville. When he found that Tess came of that exhausted ancient line, and was not of the new tribes from below, as he had fondly dreamed, why had

1. The Wiertz Museum, in Brussels, contains the work of Anton Wiertz (1806-65), whose characteristically large canvasses are full of figures such as Hardy describes. Jan Van Beers (b. 1852) was a minor Belgian painter. [W]
2. Under the date of December 31, 1885, Hardy had written in his note-book: "This is the chief thing: Be not perturbed; for all things are according to the nature of the universal." When this entry was published in *The Early Life*, Mrs. Hardy added "[Marcus Aurelius]". [W]
3. John xiv:27.

he not stoically abandoned her, in fidelity to his principles? This was what he had got by apostasy, and his punishment was deserved.

Then he became weary and anxious, and his anxiety increased. He wondered if he had treated her unfairly. He ate without knowing that he ate, and drank without tasting. As the hours dropped past, as the motive of each act in the long series of bygone days presented itself to his view, he perceived how intimately the notion of having Tess as a dear possession was mixed up with all his schemes and words and ways.

In going hither and thither he observed in the outskirts of a small town a red-and-blue placard setting forth the great advantages of the Empire of Brazil as a field for the emigrating agriculturist. Land was offered there on exceptionally advantageous terms. Brazil somewhat attracted him as a new idea. Tess could eventually join him there, and perhaps in that country of contrasting scenes and notions and habits the conventions would not be so operative which made life with her seem impracticable to him here. In brief he was strongly inclined to try Brazil, especially as the season for going thither was just at hand.

With this view he was returning to Emminster to disclose his plan to his parents, and to make the best explanation he could make of arriving without Tess, short of revealing what had actually separated them. As he reached the door the new moon shone upon his face, just as the old one had done in the small hours of that morning when he had carried his wife in his arms across the river to the graveyard of the monks; but his face was thinner now.

Clare had given his parents no warning of his visit, and his arrival stirred the atmosphere of the Vicarage as the dive of the kingfisher stirs a quiet pool. His father and mother were both in the drawing-room, but neither of his brothers was now at home. Angel entered, and closed the door quietly behind him.

'But—where's your wife, dear Angel?' cried his mother. 'How you surprise us!'

'She is at her mother's—temporarily. I have come home rather in a hurry because I've decided to go to Brazil.'

'Brazil! Why they are all Roman Catholics there surely!'

'Are they? I hadn't thought of that.'

But even the novelty and painfulness of his going to a Papistical land could not displace for long Mr. and Mrs. Clare's natural interest in their son's marriage.

'We had your brief note three weeks ago announcing that it had taken place,' said Mrs. Clare, 'and your father sent your godmother's gift to her, as you know. Of course it was best that none of us should be present, especially as you preferred to marry her from the dairy, and not at her home, wherever that may be. It would have embarrassed you, and given us no pleasure. Your brothers felt that very strongly. Now it is done we do not complain, particularly if she suits you for the business you have chosen to follow instead of the ministry of the Gospel. . . . Yet I wish I could have seen her first, Angel, or have known a little more about her. We sent her no present of our own, not knowing what would best give her pleasure, but you must suppose it only delayed. Angel, there is no irritation in my mind or your father's against you for this marriage; but we have thought it much better to reserve our liking for your wife till we could see her. And now you have not brought her. It seems strange. What has happened?'

He replied that it had been thought best by them that she should go to her parents' home for the present, whilst he came there.

'I don't mind telling you, dear mother,' he said, 'that I always meant to keep her away from this house till I should feel she could come with credit to you. But this idea of Brazil is quite a recent one. If I do go it will be unadvisable for me to take her on this my first journey. She will remain at her mother's till I come back.'

'And I shall not see her before you start?'

He was afraid they would not. His original plan had been, as he had said, to refrain from bringing her there for some little while—not to wound their prejudices—feelings—in any way; and for other reasons he had adhered to it. He would have to visit home in the course of a year, if he went out at once; and it would be possible for them to see her before he started a second time—with her.

A hastily prepared supper was brought in, and Clare made further exposition of his plans. His mother's disappointment at not seeing the bride still remained with her. Clare's late enthusiasm for Tess had infected her through her maternal sympathies, till she had almost fancied that a good thing could come out of Nazareth[4]—a charming woman out of Talbothays Dairy. She watched her son as he ate.

'Cannot you describe her? I am sure she is very pretty, Angel.'

'Of that there can be no question!' he said, with a zest which covered its bitterness.

'And that she is pure and virtuous goes without question?'

'Pure and virtuous, of course, she is.'

'I can see her quite distinctly. You said the other day that she was fine in figure; roundly built; had deep red lips like Cupid's bow; dark eyelashes and brows, an immense rope of hair like a ship's cable; and large eyes violety-bluey-blackish.'

'I did, mother.'

'I quite see her. And living in such seclusion she naturally had scarce ever seen any young man from the world without till she saw you.'

'Scarcely.'

4. John i:46: "Can there be any good thing come out of Nazareth?"

'You were her first love?'

'Of course.'

'There are worse wives than these simple, rosy-mouthed, robust girls of the farm. Certainly I could have wished—well, since my son is to be an agriculturist, it is perhaps but proper that his wife should have been accustomed to an outdoor life.'

His father was less inquisitive; but when the time came for the chapter from the Bible which was always read before evening prayers, the Vicar observed to Mrs. Clare —

'I think, since Angel has come, that it will be more appropriate to read the thirty-first of Proverbs than the chapter which we should have had in the usual course of our reading?'

'Yes, certainly,' said Mrs. Clare. 'The words of King Lemuel' (she could cite chapter and verse as well as her husband). 'My dear son, your father has decided to read us the chapter in Proverbs in praise of a virtuous wife. We shall not need to be reminded to apply the words to the absent one. May Heaven shield her in all her ways!'

A lump rose in Clare's throat. The portable lectern was taken out from the corner and set in the middle of the fireplace, the two old servants came in, and Angel's father began to read at the tenth verse of the aforesaid chapter—

' "Who can find a virtuous woman? for her price is far above rubies. She riseth while it is yet night, and giveth meat to her household. She girdeth her loins with strength and strengtheneth her arms. She perceiveth that her merchandise is good; her candle goeth not out by night. She looketh well to the ways of her household, and eateth not the bread of idleness. Her children arise up and call her blessed; her husband also, and he praiseth her. Many daughters have done virtuously, but thou excellest them all." '

When prayers were over, his mother said—

'I could not help thinking how very aptly that chapter your dear father read applied, in some of its particulars, to the woman you have chosen. The perfect woman, you see, was a working woman; not an idler; not a fine lady; but one who used her hands and her head and her heart for the good of others. "Her children arise up and call her blessed; her husband also, and he praiseth her. Many daughters have done virtuously, but she excelleth them all." Well, I wish I could have seen her, Angel. Since she is pure and chaste she would have been refined enough for me.'

Clare could bear this no longer. His eyes were full of tears, which seemed like drops of molten lead. He bade a quick good-night to these sincere and simple souls whom he loved so well; who knew neither the world, the flesh, nor the devil[5] in their own hearts; only as something vague and external to themselves. He went to his own chamber.

5. From the "Litany" in the Book of Common Prayer.

His mother followed him, and tapped at his door. Clare opened it to discover her standing without, with anxious eyes.

'Angel,' she asked, 'is there something wrong that you go away so soon? I am quite sure you are not yourself.'

'I am not, quite, mother,' said he.

'About her? Now, my son, I know it is that—I know it is about her! Have you quarrelled in these three weeks?'

'We have not exactly quarrelled,' he said. 'But we have had a difference——'

'Angel—is she a young woman whose history will bear investigation?'

With a mother's instinct Mrs. Clare had put her finger on the kind of trouble that would cause such a disquiet as seemed to agitate her son.

'She is spotless!' he replied; and felt that if it had sent him to eternal hell there and then he would have told that lie.

'Then never mind the rest. After all, there are few purer things in nature than an unsullied country maid. Any crudeness of manner which may offend your more educated sense at first, will, I am sure, disappear under the influence of your companionship and tuition.'

Such terrible sarcasm of blind magnanimity brought home to Clare the secondary perception that he had utterly wrecked his career by this marriage, which had not been among his early thoughts after the disclosure. True, on his own account he cared very little about his career; but he had wished to make it at least a respectable one on account of his parents and brothers. And now as he looked into the candle its flame dumbly expressed to him that it was made to shine on sensible people, and that it abhorred lighting the face of a dupe and a failure.

When his agitation had cooled he would be at moments incensed with his poor wife for causing a situation in which he was obliged to practise deception on his parents. He almost talked to her in his anger, as if she had been in the room. And then her cooing voice, plaintive in expostulation, disturbed the darkness, the velvet touch of her lips passed over his brow, and he could distinguish in the air the warmth of her breath.

This night the woman of his belittling deprecations was thinking how great and good her husband was. But over them both there hung a deeper shade than the shade which Angel Clare perceived, namely, the shade of his own limitations. With all his attempted independence of judgment this advanced and well-meaning young man, a sample product of the last five-and-twenty years, was yet the slave to custom and conventionality when surprised back into his early teachings. No prophet had told him, and he was not prophet enough to tell himself, that essentially this young wife of his was as deserving of the praise of King Lemuel as any other woman endowed with the same dislike of evil, her moral value having to be reckoned not by achievement but by tendency. Moreover, the figure near at hand suffers on such occasions, because it shows up its sorriness without shade; while vague figures afar off are honoured, in that their distance makes artistic virtues of their stains. In considering what Tess was not, he overlooked what she was, and forgot that the defective can be more than the entire.

XL

At breakfast Brazil was the topic, and all endeavoured to take a hopeful view of Clare's proposed experiment with that country's soil, notwithstanding the discouraging reports of some farm-labourers who had emigrated thither and returned home within the twelve months. After breakfast Clare went into the little town to wind up such trifling matters as he was concerned with there, and to get from the local bank all the money he possessed. On his way back he encountered Miss Mercy Chant by the church, from whose walls she seemed to be a sort of emanation. She was carrying an armful of Bibles for her class, and such was her view of life that events which produced heartache in others wrought beatific smiles upon her—an enviable result, although, in the opinion of Angel, it was obtained by a curiously unnatural sacrifice of humanity to mysticism.

She had learnt that he was about to leave England, and observed what an excellent and promising scheme it seemed to be.

'Yes; it is a likely scheme enough in a commercial sense, no doubt,' he replied. 'But, my dear Mercy, it snaps the continuity of existence. Perhaps a cloister would be preferable.'

'A cloister! O, Angel Clare!'

'Well?'

'Why, you wicked man, a cloister implies a monk, and a monk Roman Catholicism.'

'And Roman Catholicism sin, and sin damnation. Thou art in a parlous state, Angel Clare.' [6]

'*I* glory in my Protestantism!' she said severely.

Then Clare, thrown by sheer misery into one of the demoniacal moods in which a man does despite to his true principles, called her close to him, and fiendishly whispered in her ear the most heterodox ideas he could think of. His momentary laughter at the horror which appeared on her fair face ceased when it merged in pain and anxiety for his welfare.

'Dear Mercy,' he said, 'you must forgive me. I think I am going crazy!'

6. "Angel is parodying Touchstone's words in *As You Like It*, Act III, sc. ii: 'Why if thou never wast at court, thou never saw'st good manners; if thou never saw'st good manners, then thy manners must be wicked; and wickedness is sin, and sin is damnation. Thou art in a parlous state, shepherd.'" [F]

She thought that he was; and thus the interview ended, and Clare re-entered the Vicarage. With the local banker he deposited the jewels till happier days should arise. He also paid into the bank thirty pounds—to be sent to Tess in a few months, as she might require; and wrote to her at her parents' home in Blackmoor Vale to inform her of what he had done. This amount, with the sum he had already placed in her hands—about fifty pounds—he hoped would be amply sufficient for her wants just at present, particularly as in an emergency she had been directed to apply to his father.

He deemed it best not to put his parents into communication with her by informing them of her address; and, being unaware of what had really happened to estrange the two, neither his father nor his mother suggested that he should do so. During the day he left the parsonage, for what he had to complete he wished to get done quickly.

As the last duty before leaving this part of England it was necessary for him to call at the Wellbridge farmhouse, in which he had spent with Tess the first three days of their marriage, the trifle of rent having to be paid, the key given up of the rooms they had occupied, and two or three small articles fetched away that they had left behind. It was under this roof that the deepest shadow ever thrown upon his life had stretched its gloom over him. Yet when he had unlocked the door of the sitting-room and looked into it, the memory which returned first upon him was that of their happy arrival on a similar afternoon, the first fresh sense of sharing a habitation conjointly, the first meal together, the chatting by the fire with joined hands.

The farmer and his wife were in the fields at the moment of his visit, and Clare was in the rooms alone for some time. Inwardly swollen with a renewal of sentiments that he had not quite reckoned with, he went upstairs to her chamber, which had never been his. The bed was smooth as she had made it with her own hands on the morning of leaving. The mistletoe hung under the tester just as he had placed it. Having been there three or four weeks it was turning colour, and the leaves and berries were wrinkled. Angel took it down and crushed it into the grate. Standing there he for the first time doubted whether his course in this conjunction had been a wise, much less a generous, one. But had he not been cruelly blinded? In the incoherent multitude of his emotions he knelt down at the bedside wet-eyed. 'O Tess! If you had only told me sooner, I would have forgiven you!' he mourned.

Hearing a footstep below he rose and went to the top of the stairs. At the bottom of the flight he saw a woman standing, and on her turning up her face recognized the pale, dark-eyed Izz Huett.

'Mr. Clare,' she said, 'I've called to see you and Mrs. Clare, and to inquire if ye be well. I thought you might be back here again.'

This was a girl whose secret he had guessed, but who had not yet guessed his; an honest girl who loved him—one who would have made as good, or nearly as good, a practical farmer's wife as Tess.

'I am here alone,' he said; 'we are not living here now.' Explaining why he had come, he asked, 'Which way are you going home, Izz?'

'I have no home at Talbothays Dairy now, sir,' she said.

'Why is that?'

Izz looked down.

'It was so dismal there that I left! I am staying out this way.' She pointed in a contrary direction, the direction in which he was journeying.

'Well—are you going there now? I can take you if you wish for a lift.'

Her olive complexion grew richer in hue.

'Thank 'ee, Mr. Clare,' she said.

He soon found the farmer, and settled the account for his rent and the few other items which had to be considered by reason of the sudden abandonment of the lodgings. On Clare's return to his horse and gig Izz jumped up beside him.

'I am going to leave England, Izz,' he said, as they drove on. 'Going to Brazil.'

'And do Mrs. Clare like the notion of such a journey?' she asked.

'She is not going at present—say for a year or so. I am going out to reconnoitre—to see what life there is like.'

They sped along eastward for some considerable distance, Izz making no observation.

'How are the others?' he inquired. 'How is Retty?'

She was in a sort of nervous state when I zid[7] her last; and so thin and hollow-cheeked that 'a do seem in a decline. Nobody will ever fall in love wi' her any more,' said Izz absently.

'And Marian?'

Izz lowered her voice.

'Marian drinks.'

'Indeed!'

'Yes. The dairyman has got rid of her.'

'And you!'

'I don't drink, and I bain't in a decline. But—I am no great things at singing afore breakfast now!'

'How is that? Do you remember how neatly you used to turn " 'Twas down in Cupid's Gardens" and "The Tailor's Breeches" at morning milking?'

'Ah, yes! When you first came, sir, that was. Not when you had been there a bit.'

'Why was that falling-off?'

---

7. "Seed," *i.e.*, saw.

Her black eyes flashed up to his face for one moment by way of answer.

'Izz!—how weak of you—for such as I!' he said, and fell into reverie. 'Then—suppose I had asked *you* to marry me?'

'If you had I should have said "Yes," and you would have married a woman who loved 'ee!'

'Really!'

'Down to the ground!' she whispered vehemently. 'O my God! did you never guess it till now!'

By-and-by they reached a branch road to a village.

'I must get down. I live out there,' said Izz abruptly, never having spoken since her avowal.

Clare slowed the horse. He was incensed against his fate, bitterly disposed towards social ordinances; for they had cooped him up in a corner, out of which there was no legitimate pathway. Why not be revenged on society by shaping his future domesticities loosely, instead of kissing the pedagogic rod of convention in this ensnaring manner.

'I am going to Brazil alone, Izz,' said he. 'I have separated from my wife for personal, not voyaging, reasons. I may never live with her again. I may not be able to love you; but—will you go with me instead of her?'

'You truly wish me to go?'

'I do. I have been badly used enough to wish for relief. And you at least love me disinterestedly.'

'Yes—I will go,' said Izz, after a pause.

'You will? You know what it means, Izz?'

'It means that I shall live with you for the time you are over there —that's good enough for me.'

'Remember, you are not to trust me in morals now. But I ought to remind you that it will be wrong-doing in the eyes of civilization— Western civilization, that is to say.'

'I don't mind that; no woman do when it comes to agony-point, and there's no other way!'

'Then don't get down, but sit where you are.'

He drove past the cross-roads, one mile, two miles, without showing any signs of affection.

'You love me very, very much, Izz?' he suddenly asked.

'I do—I have said I do! I loved you all the time we was at the dairy together!'

'More than Tess?'

She shook her head.

'No,' she murmured, 'not more than she.'

'How's that?'

'Because nobody could love 'ee more than Tess did! . . . She would have laid down her life for 'ee. I could do no more.'

Like the prophet on the top of Peor[8] Izz Huett would fain have spoken perversely at such a moment, but the fascination exercised over her rougher nature by Tess's character compelled her to grace.

Clare was silent; his heart had risen at these straightforward words from such an unexpected, unimpeachable quarter. In his throat was something as if a sob had solidified there. His ears repeated, '*She would have laid down her life for 'ee. I could do no more!*'

'Forget our idle talk, Izz,' he said, turning the horse's head suddenly. 'I don't know what I've been saying! I will now drive you back to where your lane branches off.'

'So much for honesty towards 'ee! O—how can I bear it—how can I—how can I!'

Izz Huett burst into wild tears, and beat her forehead as she saw what she had done.

'Do you regret that poor little act of justice to an absent one? O, Izz, don't spoil it by regret!'

She stilled herself by degrees.

'Very well, sir. Perhaps I didn't know what I was saying, either, wh— when I agreed to go! I wish—what cannot be!'

'Because I have a loving wife already.'

'Yes, yes! You have.'

They reached the corner of the lane which they had passed half an hour earlier, and she hopped down.

'Izz—please, please forget my momentary levity!' he cried. 'It was so ill-considered, so ill-advised!'

'Forget it? Never, never! O, it was no levity to me!'

He felt how richly he deserved the reproach that the wounded cry conveyed, and, in a sorrow that was inexpressible, leapt down and took her hand.

'Well, but, Izz, we'll part friends, anyhow? You don't know what I've had to bear!'

She was a really generous girl, and allowed no further bitterness to mar their adieux.

'I forgive 'ee, sir!' she said.

'Now Izz,' he said, while she stood beside him there, forcing himself to the mentor's part he was far from feeling; 'I want you to tell Marian when you see her that she is to be a good woman, and not to give way to folly. Promise that, and tell Retty that there are more worthy men than I in the world, that for my sake she is to act wisely and well—remember the words—wisely and well—for my sake. I send this message to them as a dying man to the dying; for I shall never see them again. And you, Izzy, you have saved me by your honest words about my wife from an incredible impulse towards folly and

8. *I.e.*, Balaam, refusing to obey Balak's order to curse the Israelites, praised them instead. See Numbers xxiii and xxiv.

treachery. Women may be bad, but they are not so bad as men in these things! On that one account I can never forget you. Be always the good and sincere girl you have hitherto been; and think of me as a worthless lover, but a faithful friend. Promise.'

She gave the promise.

'Heaven bless and keep you, sir. Good-bye!'

He drove on; but no sooner had Izz turned into the lane, and Clare was out of sight, than she flung herself down on the bank in a fit of racking anguish; and it was with a strained unnatural face that she entered her mother's cottage late that night. Nobody ever was told how Izz spent the dark hours that intervened between Angel Clare's parting from her and her arrival home.

Clare, too, after bidding the girl farewell, was wrought to aching thoughts and quivering lips. But his sorrow was not for Izz. That evening he was within a feather-weight's turn of abandoning his road to the nearest station, and driving across that elevated dorsal line of South Wessex which divided him from his Tess's home. It was neither a contempt for her nature, nor the probable state of her heart, which deterred him.

No; it was a sense that, despite her love, as corroborated by Izz's admission, the facts had not changed. If he was right at first, he was right now. And the momentum of the course on which he had embarked tended to keep him going in it, unless diverted by a stronger, more sustained force than had played upon him this afternoon. He could soon come back to her. He took the train that night for London, and five days after shook hands in farewell of his brothers at the port of embarkation.

XLI

From the foregoing events of the winter-time let us press on to an October day, more than eight months subsequent to the parting of Clare and Tess. We discover the latter in changed conditions; instead of a bride with boxes and trunks which others bore, we see her a lonely woman with a basket and a bundle in her own porterage, as at an earlier time when she was no bride; instead of the ample means that were projected by her husband for her comfort through this probationary period, she can produce only a flattened purse.

After again leaving Marlott, her home, she had got through the spring and summer without any great stress upon her physical powers, the time being mainly spent in rendering light irregular service at dairy-work near Port-Bredy to the west of the Blackmoor Valley, equally remote from her native place and from Talbothays. She preferred this to living on his allowance. Mentally she remained in utter stagnation, a condition which the mechanical occupation rather fostered than checked. Her consciousness was at that other dairy, at that other season, in the presence of the tender lover who had confronted her there—he who, the moment she had grasped him to keep for her own, had disappeared like a shape in a vision.

The dairy-work lasted only till the milk began to lessen, for she had not met with a second regular engagement as at Talbothays, but had done duty as a supernumerary only. However, as harvest was now beginning, she had simply to remove from the pasture to the stubble to find plenty of further occupation, and this continued till harvest was done.

Of the five-and-twenty pounds which had remained to her of Clare's allowance, after deducting the other half of the fifty as a contribution to her parents for the trouble and expense to which she had put them, she had as yet spent but little. But there now followed an unfortunate interval of wet weather, during which she was obliged to fall back upon her sovereigns.

She could not bear to let them go. Angel had put them into her hand, had obtained them bright and new from his bank for her; his touch had consecrated them to souvenirs of himself—they appeared to have had as yet no other history than such as was created by his and her own experiences—and to disperse them was like giving away relics. But she had to do it, and one by one they left her hands.

She had been compelled to send her mother her address from time to time, but she concealed her circumstances. When her money had almost gone a letter from her mother reached her. Joan stated that they were in dreadful difficulty; the autumn rains had gone through the thatch of the house, which required entire renewal; but this could not be done because the previous thatching had never been paid for. New rafters and a new ceiling upstairs also were required, which, with the previous bill, would amount to a sum of twenty pounds. As her husband was a man of means, and had doubtless returned by this time, could she not send them the money?

Tess had thirty pounds coming to her almost immediately from Angel's bankers, and, the case being so deplorable, as soon as the sum was received she sent the twenty as requested. Part of the remainder she was obliged to expend in winter clothing, leaving only a nominal sum for the whole inclement season at hand. When the last pound had gone, a remark of Angel's that whenever she required further resources she was to apply to his father, remained to be considered.

But the more Tess thought of the step the more reluctant was she to take it. The same delicacy, pride, false shame, whatever it may be called, on Clare's account, which had led her to hide from her own parents the prolongation of the estrangement, hindered her in owning to his that she was in want after the fair allowance he had left her. They probably despised her already; how much more they would despise her in the character of a mendicant! The consequence was that by no effort could the parson's daughter-in-law bring herself to let him know her state.

Her reluctance to communicate with her husband's parents might, she thought, lessen with the lapse of time; but with her own the reverse obtained. On her leaving their house after the short visit subsequent to her marriage they were under the impression that she was ultimately going to join her husband; and from that time to the present she had done nothing to disturb their belief that she was awaiting his return in comfort, hoping against hope that his journey to Brazil would result in a short stay only, after which he would come to fetch her, or that he would write for her to join him; in any case that they would soon present a united front to their families and the world. This hope she still fostered. To let her parents know that she was a deserted wife, dependent, now that she had relieved their necessities, on her own hands for a living, after the *éclat* of a marriage which was to nullify the collapse of the first attempt, would be too much indeed.

The set of brilliants returned to her mind. Where Clare had deposited them she did not know, and it mattered little, if it were true that she could only use and not sell them. Even were they absolutely hers it would be passing mean to enrich herself by a legal title to them which was not essentially hers at all.

Meanwhile her husband's days had been by no means free from trial. At this moment he was lying ill of fever in the clay lands near Curitiba in Brazil, having been drenched with thunder-storms and persecuted by other hardships, in common with all the English farmers and farm-labourers who, just at this time, were deluded into going thither by the promises of the Brazilian Government, and by the baseless assumption that those frames which, ploughing and sowing on English uplands, had resisted all the weathers to whose moods they had been born, could resist equally well all the weathers by which they were surprised on Brazilian plains. [9]

To return. Thus it happened that when the last of Tess's sovereigns had been spent she was unprovided with others to take their place, while on account of the season she found it increasingly difficult to get employment. Not being aware of the rarity of intelligence, energy, health, and willingness in any sphere of life, she refrained from seeking an indoor occupation; fearing towns, large houses, people of means and social sophistication, and of manners other than rural. From that direction of gentility Black Care had come. Society might be better than she supposed from her slight experience of it. But she had no proof of this, and her instinct in the circumstances was to avoid its purlieus.

The small dairies to the west, beyond Port-Bredy, in which she had served as supernumerary milkmaid during the spring and summer

9. Hardy seems to have confused "the rainy clay lands of the Amazonian plain" with the "high and healthful plateau, 2,000 miles to the north," where is located Curitiba, to which in 1870 large numbers of Algerian French, and in 1880 about 2,000 Russians, emigrated in ventures that were both disastrous. [W and F]

required no further aid. Room would probably have been made for her at Talbothays, if only out of sheer compassion; but comfortable as her life had been there she could not go back. The anti-climax would be too intolerable; and her return might bring reproach upon her idolized husband. She could not have borne their pity, and their whispered remarks to one another upon her strange situation; though she would almost have faced a knowledge of her circumstances by every individual there, so long as her story had remained isolated in the mind of each. It was the interchange of ideas about her that made her sensitiveness wince. Tess could not account for this distinction; she simply knew that she felt it.

She was now on her way to an upland farm in the centre of the county, to which she had been recommended by a wandering letter which had reached her from Marian. Marian had somehow heard that Tess was separated from her husband—probably through Izz Huett—and the good-natured and now tippling girl, deeming Tess in trouble, had hastened to notify to her former friend that she herself had gone to this upland spot after leaving the dairy, and would like to see her there, where there was room for other hands, if it was really true that she worked again as of old.

With the shortening of the days all hope of obtaining her husband's forgiveness began to leave her; and there was something of the habitude of the wild animal in the unreflecting instinct with which she rambled on—disconnecting herself by littles from her eventful past at every step, obliterating her identity, giving no thought to accidents or contingencies which might make a quick discovery of her whereabouts by others of importance to her own happiness, if not to theirs.

Among the difficulties of her lonely position not the least was the attention she excited by her appearance, a certain bearing of distinction, which she had caught from Clare, being superadded to her natural attractiveness. Whilst the clothes lasted which had been prepared for her marriage, these casual glances of interest caused her no inconvenience, but as soon as she was compelled to don the wrapper of a fieldwoman, rude words were addressed to her more than once; but nothing occurred to cause her bodily fear till a particular November afternoon.

She had preferred the country west of the River Brit to the upland farm for which she was now bound, because, for one thing, it was nearer to the home of her husband's father; and to hover about that region unrecognized, with the notion that she might decide to call at the Vicarage some day, gave her pleasure. But having once decided to try the higher and drier levels, she pressed back eastward, marching afoot towards the village of Chalk-Newton, where she meant to pass the night.

The lane was long and unvaried, and, owing to the rapid shortening of the days, dusk came upon her before she was aware. She had reached the top of a hill down which the lane stretched its serpentine length in glimpses, when she heard footsteps behind her back, and in a few moments she was overtaken by a man. He stepped up along-side Tess and said—

'Good-night, my pretty maid:' to which she civilly replied.

The light still remaining in the sky lit up her face, though the landscape was nearly dark. The man turned and stared hard at her.

'Why, surely, it is the young wench who was at Trantridge awhile —young Squire d'Urberville's friend? I was there at that time, though I don't live there now.'

She recognized in him the well-to-do boor whom Angel had knock-ed down at the inn for addressing her coarsely. A spasm of anguish shot through her, and she returned him no answer.

'Be honest enough to own it, and that what I said in the town was true, though your fancy-man was so up about it—hey, my sly one? You ought to beg my pardon for that blow of his, considering.'

Still no answer came from Tess. There seemed only one escape for her hunted soul. She suddenly took to her heels with the speed of the wind, and, without looking behind her, ran along the road till she came to a gate which opened directly into a plantation. Into this she plunged, and did not pause till she was deep enough in its shade to be safe against any possibility of discovery.

Under foot the leaves were dry, and the foliage of some holly bushes which grew among the deciduous trees was dense enough to keep off draughts. She scraped together the dead leaves till she had formed them into a large heap, making a sort of nest in the middle. Into this Tess crept.

Such sleep as she got was naturally fitful; she fancied she heard strange noises, but persuaded herself that they were caused by the breeze. She thought of her husband in some vague warm clime on the other side of the globe, while she was here in the cold. Was there another such a wretched being as she in the world? Tess asked herself; and, thinking of her wasted life, said, 'All is vanity.'[1] She repeated the words mechanically, till she reflected that this was a most inade-quate thought for modern days. Solomon had thought as far as that more than two thousand years ago; she herself, though not in the van of thinkers, had got much further. If all were only vanity, who would mind it? All was, alas, worse than vanity—injustice, punishment, exaction, death. The wife of Angel Clare put her hand to her brow, and felt its curve, and the edges of her eye-sockets perceptible under the soft skin, and thought as she did so that a time would come

1. Ecclesiastes i:2: "Vanity of vanities, saith the preacher, vanity of vanities; all is vanity."

when that bone would be bare. 'I wish it were now,' she said.

In the midst of these whimsical fancies she heard a new strange sound among the leaves. It might be the wind; yet there was scarcely any wind. Sometimes it was a palpitation, sometimes a flutter; sometimes it was a sort of gasp or gurgle. Soon she was certain that the noises came from wild creatures of some kind, the more so when, originating in the boughs overhead, they were followed by the fall of a heavy body upon the ground. Had she been ensconced here under other and more pleasant conditions she would have become alarmed; but, outside humanity, she had at present no fear.

Day at length broke in the sky. When it had been day aloft for some little while it became day in the wood.

Directly the assuring and prosaic light of the world's active hours had grown strong she crept from under her hillock of leaves, and looked around boldly. Then she perceived what had been going on to disturb her. The plantation wherein she had taken shelter ran down at this spot into a peak, which ended it hitherward, outside the hedge being arable ground. Under the trees several pheasants lay about, their rich plumage dabbled with blood; some were dead, some feebly twitching a wing, some staring up at the sky, some pulsating quickly, some contorted, some stretched out—all of them writhing in agony, except the fortunate ones whose tortures had ended during the night by the inability of nature to bear more.

Tess guessed at once the meaning of this. The birds had been driven down into this corner the day before by some shooting-party; and while those that had dropped dead under the shot, or had died before nightfall, had been searched for and carried off, many badly wounded birds had escaped and hidden themselves away, or risen among the thick boughs, where they had maintained their position till they grew weaker with loss of blood in the night-time, when they had fallen one by one as she had heard them.

She had occasionally caught glimpses of these men in girlhood, looking over hedges, or peering through bushes, and pointing their guns, strangely accoutred, a bloodthirsty light in their eyes. She had been told that, rough and brutal as they seemed just then, they were not like this all the year round, but were, in fact, quite civil persons save during certain weeks of autumn and winter, when, like the inhabitants of the Malay Peninsula, they ran amuck, and made it their purpose to destroy life—in this case harmless feathered creatures, brought into being by artificial means solely to gratify these propensities—at once so unmannerly and so unchivalrous towards their weaker fellows in Nature's teeming family.

With the impulse of a soul who could feel for kindred sufferers as much as for herself, Tess's first thought was to put the still living birds out of their torture, and to this end with her own hands she broke the necks of as many as she could find, leaving them to lie where she had found them till the gamekeepers should come—as they probably would come to look for them a second time.

'Poor darlings—to suppose myself the most miserable being on earth in the sight o' such misery as yours!' she exclaimed, her tears running down as she killed the birds tenderly. 'And not a twinge of bodily pain about me! I be not mangled, and I be not bleeding, and I have two hands to feed and clothe me.' She was ashamed of herself for her gloom of the night, based on nothing more tangible than a sense of condemnation under an arbitrary law of society which had no foundation in Nature.

XLII

It was now broad day, and she started again, emerging cautiously upon the highway. But there was no need for caution; not a soul was at hand, and Tess went onward with fortitude, her recollection of the birds' silent endurance of their night of agony impressing upon her the relativity of sorrows and the tolerable nature of her own, if she could once rise high enough to despise opinion. But that she could not do so long as it was held by Clare.

She reached Chalk-Newton, and breakfasted at an inn, where several young men were troublesomely complimentary to her good looks. Somehow she felt hopeful, for was it not possible that her husband also might say these same things to her even yet? She was bound to take care of herself on the chance of it, and keep off these casual lovers. To this end Tess resolved to run no further risks from her appearance. As soon as she got out of the village she entered a thicket and took from her basket one of the oldest field-gowns, which she had never put on even at the dairy—never since she had worked among the stubble at Marlott. She also, by a felicitous thought, took a handkerchief from her bundle and tied it round her face under her bonnet, covering her chin and half her cheeks and temples, as if she were suffering from toothache. Then with her little scissors, by the aid of a pocket looking-glass, she mercilessly nipped her eyebrows off, and thus insured against aggressive admiration she went on her uneven way.

'What a mommet of a maid!' said the next man who met her to a companion.

Tears came into her eyes for very pity of herself as she heard him.

'But I don't care!' she said. 'O no—I don't care! I'll always be ugly now, because Angel is not here, and I have nobody to take care of me. My husband that was is gone away, and never will love me any more; but I love him just the same, and hate all other men, and like to make 'em think scornfully of me!'

Thus Tess walks on; a figure which is part of the landscape; a fieldwoman pure and simple, in winter guise; a gray serge cape, a red woollen cravat, a stuff skirt covered by a whitey-brown rough wrapper, and buff-leather gloves. Every thread of that old attire has become faded and thin under the stroke of raindrops, the burn of sunbeams, and the stress of winds. There is no sign of young passion in her now—

> The maiden's mouth is cold
>
> .   .   .   .   .
>
> Fold over simple fold
> Binding her head.[2]

Inside this exterior, over which the eye might have roved as over a thing scarcely percipient, almost inorganic, there was the record of a pulsing life which had learnt too well, for its years, of the dust and ashes of things, of the cruelty of lust and the fragility of love.

Next day the weather was bad, but she trudged on, the honesty, directness, and impartiality of elemental enmity disconcerting her but little. Her object being a winter's occupation and a winter's home, there was no time to lose. Her experience of short hirings had been such that she was determined to accept no more.

Thus she went forward from farm to farm in the direction of the place whence Marian had written to her, which she determined to make use of as a last shift only, its rumoured stringencies being the reverse of tempting. First she inquired for the lighter kinds of employment, and, as acceptance in any variety of these grew hopeless, applied next for the less light, till, beginning with the dairy and poultry tendance that she liked best, she ended with the heavy and coarse pursuits which she liked least—work on arable land: work of such roughness, indeed, as she would never have deliberately volunteered for.

Towards the second evening she reached the irregular chalk table-land or plateau, bosomed with semi-globular tumuli—as if Cybele the Many-breasted were supinely extended there—which stretched between the valley of her birth and the valley of her love.

Here the air was dry and cold, and the long cart-roads were blown white and dusty within a few hours after rain. There were few trees, or none, those that would have grown in the hedges being mercilessly plashed down with the quickset by the tenant-farmers, the natural enemies of tree, bush, and brake. In the middle distance ahead of her she could see the summits of Bulbarrow and of Nettlecombe Tout, and they seemed friendly. They had a low and unassuming aspect

---

2. From Swinburne's "Fragoletta," lines 41-45 (*Poem and Ballads*): "Ah sweet, the maiden's mouth is cold,/Her breast blossoms are simply red,/Her hair mere brown or gold,/Fold over simple fold/Binding her head."

from this upland, though as approached on the other side from Blackmoor in her childhood they were as lofty bastions against the sky. Southerly, at many miles' distance, and over the hills and ridges coastward, she could discern a surface like polished steel: it was the English Channel at a point far out towards France.

Before her, in a slight depression, were the remains of a village. She had, in fact, reached Flintcomb-Ash, the place of Marian's sojourn. There seemed to be no help for it; hither she was doomed to come. The stubborn soil around her showed plainly enough that the kind of labour in demand here was of the roughest kind; but it was time to rest from searching, and she resolved to stay, particularly as it began to rain. At the entrance to the village was a cottage whose gable jutted into the road, and before applying for a lodging she stood under its shelter, and watched the evening close in.

'Who would think I was Mrs. Angel Clare!' she said.

The wall felt warm to her back and shoulders, and she found that immediately within the gable was the cottage fireplace, the heat of which came through the bricks. She warmed her hands upon them, and also put her cheek—red and moist with the drizzle—against their comforting surface. The wall seemed to be the only friend she had. She had so little wish to leave it that she could have stayed there all night.

Tess could hear the occupants of the cottage—gathered together after their day's labour—talking to each other within, and the rattle of their supper-plates was also audible. But in the village-street she had seen no soul as yet. The solitude was at last broken by the approach of one feminine figure, who, though the evening was cold, wore the print gown and the tilt-bonnet of summer time. Tess instinctively thought it might be Marian, and when she came near enough to be distinguishable in the gloom surely enough it was she. Marian was even stouter and redder in the face than formerly, and decidedly shabbier in attire. At any previous period of her existence Tess would hardly have cared to renew the acquaintance in such conditions; but her loneliness was excessive, and she responded readily to Marian's greeting.

Marian was quite respectful in her inquiries, but seemed much moved by the fact that Tess should still continue in no better condition than at first; though she had dimly heard of the separation.

'Tess—Mrs. Clare—the dear wife of dear he! And is it really so bad as this, my child? Why is your cwomely face tied up in such a way? Anybody been beating 'ee? Not *he* ?'

'No, no, no! I merely did it not to be clipsed or colled, Marian.' She pulled off in disgust a bandage which could suggest such wild thoughts.

'And you've got no collar on' (Tess had been accustomed to wear a little white collar at the dairy).

'I know it, Marian.'

'You've lost it travelling.'

'I've not lost it. The truth is, I don't care anything about my looks; and so I didn't put it on.'

'And you don't wear your wedding-ring?'

'Yes, I do; but not in public. I wear it round my neck on a ribbon. I don't wish people to think who I am by marriage, or that I am married at all; it would be so awkward while I lead my present life.'

Marian paused.

'But you *be* a gentleman's wife; and it seems hardly fair that you should live like this!'

'O yes it is, quite fair; though I am very unhappy.'

'Well, well. *He* married you—and you can be unhappy!'

'Wives are unhappy sometimes; from no fault of their husbands—from their own.'

'You've no faults, deary; that I'm sure of. And he's none. So it must be something outside ye both.'

'Marian, dear Marian, will you do me a good turn without asking questions? My husband has gone abroad, and somehow I have over-run my allowance, so that I have to fall back upon my old work for a time. Do not call me Mrs. Clare, but Tess, as before. Do they want a hand here?'

'O yes; they'll take one always, because few care to come. 'Tis a starve-acre place. Corn and swedes are all they grow. Though I be here myself, I feel 'tis a pity for such as you to come.'

'But you used to be as good a dairywoman as I.'

'Yes; but I've got out o' that since I took to drink. Lord, that's the only comfort I've got now! If you engage, you'll be set swede-hacking. That's what I be doing; but you won't like it.'

'O—anything! Will you speak for me?'

'You will do better by speaking for yourself.'

'Very well. Now, Marian, remember—nothing about *him*, if I get the place. I don't wish to bring his name down to the dirt.'

Marian, who was really a trustworthy girl though of coarser grain than Tess, promised anything she asked.

'This is pay-night,' she said, 'and if you were to come with me you would know at once. I be real sorry that you are not happy; but 'tis because he's away, I know. You couldn't be unhappy if he were here, even if he gie'd ye no money—even if he used you like a drudge.'

'That's true; I could not!'

They walked on together, and soon reached the farmhouse, which was almost sublime in its dreariness. There was not a tree within sight; there was not, at this season, a green pasture—nothing but fallow and turnips everywhere; in large fields divided by hedges plashed to unrelieved levels.

Tess waited outside the door of the farmhouse till the group of workfolk had received their wages, and then Marian introduced her. The farmer himself, it appeared, was not at home, but his wife, who represented him this evening, made no objection to hiring Tess, on her agreeing to remain till Old Lady-Day.[3] Female field-labour was seldom offered now, and its cheapness made it profitable for tasks which women could perform as readily as men.

Having signed the agreement, there was nothing more for Tess to do at present than to get a lodging, and she found one in the house at whose gable-wall she had warmed herself. It was a poor subsistence that she had ensured, but it would afford a shelter for the winter at any rate.

That night she wrote to inform her parents of her new address, in case a letter should arrive at Marlott from her husband. But she did not tell them of the sorriness of her situation: it might have brought reproach upon him.

XLIII

There was no exaggeration in Marian's definition of Flintcomb-Ash farm as a starve-acre place. The single fat thing on the soil was Marian herself; and she was an importation. Of the three classes of village, the village cared for by its lord, the village cared for by itself, and the village uncared for either by itself or by its lord (in other words, the village of a resident squire's tenantry, the village of free or copy-holders, and the absentee-owner's village, farmed with the land) this place, Flintcomb-Ash, was the third.

But Tess set to work. Patience, that blending of moral courage with physical timidity, was now no longer a minor feature in Mrs. Angel Clare; and it sustained her.

The swede-field in which she and her companion were set hacking was a stretch of a hundred odd acres, in one patch, on the highest ground of the farm, rising above stony lanchets or lynchets[4]—the outcrop of siliceous veins in the chalk formation, composed of myriads of loose white flints in bulbous, cusped, and phallic shapes. The upper half of each turnip had been eaten off by the live-stock, and it was the business of the two women to grub up the lower or earthy half of the root with a hooked fork called a hacker, that it might be eaten also. Every leaf of the vegetable having already been consumed, the whole field was in colour a desolate drab; it was a complexion without features, as if a face, from chin to brow, should be only an expanse of skin. The sky wore, in another colour, the same likeness; a white vacuity of countenance with the lineaments gone. So these two upper and nether visages confronted each other all day long, the white face

3. Lady Day is a holiday, the Feast of the Annunciation, March 25th; "Old Lady-Day" was the day on which this holiday fell under the old-style calendar, *i.e.*, April 6 (the new calendar was established in 1752).
4. A lynchet is a slope or terrace along the face of a chalk down.

looking down on the brown face, and the brown face looking up at the white face, without anything standing between them but the two girls crawling over the surface of the former like flies.

Nobody came near them, and their movements showed a mechanical regularity; their forms standing enshrouded in Hessian 'wroppers' —sleeved brown pinafores, tied behind to the bottom, to keep their gowns from blowing about—scant skirts revealing boots that reached high up the ankles, and yellow sheepskin gloves with gauntlets. The pensive character which the curtained hood lent to their bent heads would have reminded the observer of some early Italian conception of the two Marys.

They worked on hour after hour, unconscious of the forlorn aspect they bore in the landscape, not thinking of the justice or injustice of their lot. Even in such a position as theirs it was possible to exist in a dream. In the afternoon the rain came on again, and Marian said that they need not work any more. But if they did not work they would not be paid; so they worked on. It was so high a situation, this field, that the rain had no occasion to fall, but raced along horizontally upon the yelling wind, sticking into them like glass splinters till they were wet through. Tess had not known till now what was really meant by that. There are degrees of dampness, and a very little is called being wet through in common talk. But to stand working slowly in a field, and feel the creep of rain-water, first in legs and shoulders, then on hips and head, then at back, front, and sides, and yet to work on till the leaden light diminishes and marks that the sun is down, demands a distinct modicum of stoicism, even of valour.

Yet they did not feel the wetness so much as might be supposed. They were both young, and they were talking of the time when they lived and loved together at Talbothays Dairy, that happy green tract of land where summer had been liberal in her gifts; in substance to all, emotionally to these. Tess would fain not have conversed with Marian of the man who was legally, if not actually, her husband; but the irresistible fascination of the subject betrayed her into reciprocating Marian's remarks. And thus, as has been said, though the damp curtains of their bonnets flapped smartly into their faces, and their wrappers clung about them to wearisomeness, they lived all this afternoon in memories of green, sunny, romantic Talbothays.

'You can see a gleam of a hill within a few miles o' Froom Valley from here when 'tis fine,' said Marian.

'Ah! Can you?' said Tess, awake to the new value of this locality.

So the two forces were at work here as everywhere, the inherent will to enjoy, and the circumstantial will against enjoyment. Marian's will had a method of assisting itself by taking from her pocket as the afternoon wore on a pint bottle corked with white rag, from which she invited Tess to drink. Tess's unassisted power of dreaming, however, being enough for her sublimation at present, she declined except the merest sip, and then Marian took a pull herself from the spirits.

'I've got used to it,' she said, 'and can't leave it off now. 'Tis my only comfort—— You see I lost him: you didn't; and you can do without it perhaps.'

Tess thought her loss as great as Marian's, but upheld by the dignity of being Angel's wife, in the letter at least, she accepted Marian's differentiation.

Amid this scene Tess slaved in the morning frosts and in the afternoon rains. When it was not swede-grubbing it was swede-trimming, in which process they sliced off the earth and the fibres with a bill-hook before storing the roots for future use. At this occupation they could shelter themselves by a thatched hurdle if it rained; but if it was frosty even their thick leather gloves could not prevent the frozen masses they handled from biting their fingers. Still Tess hoped. She had a conviction that sooner or later the magnanimity which she persisted in reckoning as a chief ingredient of Clare's character would lead him to rejoin her.

Marian, primed to a humorous mood, would discover the queer-shaped flints aforesaid, and shriek with laughter, Tess remaining severely obtuse. They often looked across the country to where the Var or Froom was known to stretch, even though they might not be able to see it; and, fixing their eyes on the cloaking gray mist, imagined the old times they had spent out there.

'Ah,' said Marian, 'how I should like another or two of our old set to come here! Then we could bring up Talbothays every day here afield, and talk of he, and of what nice times we had there, and o' the old things we used to know, and make it all come back again a'most, in seeming!' Marian's eyes softened, and her voice grew vague as the visions returned. 'I'll write to Izz Huett,' she said. 'She's biding at home doing nothing now, I know, and I'll tell her we be here, and ask her to come; and perhaps Retty is well enough now.'

Tess had nothing to say against the proposal, and the next she heard of this plan for importing old Talbothays' joys was two or three days later, when Marian informed her that Izz had replied to her inquiry, and had promised to come if she could.

There had not been such a winter for years. It came on in stealthy and measured glides, like the moves of a chess-player. One morning the few lonely trees and the thorns of the hedgerows appeared as if they had put off a vegetable for an animal integument. Every twig was covered with a white nap as of fur grown from the rind during the night, giving it four times its usual stoutness; the whole bush or tree forming a staring sketch in white lines on the mournful gray of the sky and horizon. Cobwebs revealed their presence on sheds and walls where none had ever been observed till brought out into visibility by the crystallizing atmosphere, hanging like loops of white worsted from salient points of the out-houses, posts, and gates.

After this season of congealed dampness came a spell of dry frost, when strange birds from behind the North Pole began to arrive silently on the upland of Flintcomb-Ash; gaunt spectral creatures with tragical eyes—eyes which had witnessed scenes of cataclysmal horror in inaccessible polar regions of a magnitude such as no human being had ever conceived, in curdling temperatures that no man could endure; which had beheld the crash of icebergs and the slide of snow-hills by the shooting light of the Aurora; been half blinded by the whirl of colossal storms and terraqueous distortions; and retained the expression of feature that such scenes had engendered. These nameless birds came quite near to Tess and Marian, but of all they had seen which humanity would never see, they brought no account. The traveller's ambition to tell was not theirs, and, with dumb impassivity, they dismissed experiences which they did not value for the immediate incidents of this homely upland—the trivial movements of the two girls in disturbing the clods with their hackers so as to uncover something or other that these visitants relished as food.

Then one day a peculiar quality invaded the air of this open country. There came a moisture which was not of rain, and a cold which was not of frost. It chilled the eyeballs of the twain, made their brows ache, penetrated to their skeletons, affecting the surface of the body less than its core. They knew that it meant snow, and in the night the snow came. Tess, who continued to live at the cottage with the warm gable that cheered any lonely pedestrian who paused beside it, awoke in the night, and heard above the thatch noises which seemed to signify that the roof had turned itself into a gymnasium of all the winds. When she lit her lamp to get up in the morning she found that the snow had blown through a chink in the casement, forming a white cone of the finest powder against the inside, and had also come down the chimney, so that it lay sole-deep upon the floor, on which her shoes left tracks when she moved about. Without, the storm drove so fast as to create a snow-mist in the kitchen; but as yet it was too dark out-of-doors to see anything.

Tess knew that it was impossible to go on with the swedes; and by the time she had finished breakfast beside the solitary little lamp, Marian arrived to tell her that they were to join the rest of the women at reed-drawing[5] in the barn till the weather changed. As soon, therefore, as the uniform cloak of darkness without began to turn to a disordered medley of grays, they blew out the lamp, wrapped themselves up in their thickest pinners, tied their woollen cravats round their necks and across their chests, and started for the barn.

5. The process of preparing straw for use in thatching.

The snow had followed the birds from the polar basin as a white pillar of a cloud, and individual flakes could not be seen. The blast smelt of icebergs, arctic seas, whales, and white bears, carrying the snow so that it licked the land but did not deepen on it. They trudged onwards with slanted bodies through the flossy fields, keeping as well as they could in the shelter of hedges, which, however, acted as strainers rather than screens. The air, afflicted to pallor with the hoary multitudes that infested it, twisted and spun them eccentrically, suggesting an achromatic chaos of things. But both the young women were fairly cheerful; such weather on a dry upland is not in itself dispiriting.

'Ha-ha! the cunning northern birds knew this was coming,' said Marian. 'Depend upon't, they keep just in front o't all the way from the North Star. Your husband, my dear, is, I make no doubt, having scorching weather all this time. Lord, if he could only see his pretty wife now! Not that this weather hurts your beauty at all—in fact, it rather does it good.'

'You mustn't talk about him to me, Marian,' said Tess severely.

'Well, but—surely you care for 'n! Do you?'

Instead of answering, Tess, with tears in her eyes, impulsively faced in the direction in which she imagined South America to lie, and, putting up her lips, blew out a passionate kiss upon the snowy wind.

'Well, well, I know you do. But 'pon my body, it is a rum life for a married couple! There—I won't say another word! Well, as for the weather, it won't hurt us in the wheat-barn; but reed-drawing is fearful hard work—worse than swede-hacking. I can stand it because I'm stout; but you be slimmer than I. I can't think why maister should have set 'ee at it.'

They reached the wheat-barn and entered it. One end of the long structure was full of corn; the middle was where the reed-drawing was carried on, and there had already been placed in the reed-press the evening before as many sheaves of wheat as would be sufficient for the women to draw from during the day.

'Why, here's Izz!' said Marian.

Izz it was, and she came forward. She had walked all the way from her mother's home on the previous afternoon, and, not deeming the distance so great, had been belated, arriving, however, just before the snow began, and sleeping at the ale-house. The farmer had agreed with her mother at market to take her on if she came to-day, and she had been afraid to disappoint him by delay.

In addition to Tess, Marian, and Izz, there were two women from a neighbouring village; two Amazonian sisters, whom Tess with a start remembered as Dark Car the Queen of Spades and her junior the Queen of Diamonds—those who had tried to fight with her in the midnight quarrel at Trantridge. They showed no recognition of her, and possibly had none, for they had been under the influence of liquor on that occasion, and were only temporary sojourners there as here. They did all kinds of men's work by preference, including well-sinking, hedging, ditching, and excavating, without any sense of fatigue. Noted reed-drawers were they too, and looked round upon the other three with some superciliousness.

Putting on their gloves all set to work in a row in front of the press, an erection formed of two posts connected by a cross-beam, under which the sheaves to be drawn from were laid ears outward, the beam being pegged down by pins in the uprights, and lowered as the sheaves diminished.

The day hardened in colour, the light coming in at the barn-doors upwards from the snow instead of downwards from the sky. The girls pulled handful after handful from the press; but by reason of the presence of the strange women, who were recounting scandals, Marian and Izz could not at first talk of old times as they wished to do. Presently they heard the muffled tread of a horse, and the farmer rode up to the barn-door. When he had dismounted he came close to Tess, and remained looking musingly at the side of her face. She had not turned at first, but his fixed attitude led her to look round, when she perceived that her employer was the native of Trantridge from whom she had taken flight on the high-road because of his allusion to her history.

He waited till she had carried the drawn bundles to the pile outside, when he said, 'So you be the young woman who took my civility in such ill part? Be drowned if I didn't think you might be as soon as I heard of your being hired! Well, you thought you had got the better of me the first time at the inn with your fancy-man, and the second time on the road, when you bolted; but now I think I've got the better of you.' He concluded with a hard laugh.

Tess, between the Amazons and the farmer like a bird caught in a clap-net, returned no answer, continuing to pull the straw. She could read character sufficiently well to know by this time that she had nothing to fear from her employer's gallantry; it was rather the tyranny induced by his mortification at Clare's treatment of him. Upon the whole she preferred that sentiment in man and felt brave enough to endure it.

'You thought I was in love with 'ee I suppose? Some women are such fools, to take every look as serious earnest. But there's nothing like a winter afield for taking that nonsense out o' young wenches' heads; and you've signed and agreed till Lady-Day. Now, are you going to beg my pardon?'

'I think you ought to beg mine.'

'Very well—as you like. But we'll see which is master here. Be they all the sheaves you've done to-day?'

'Yes, sir.'

"Tis a very poor show. Just see what they've done over there' (pointing to the two stalwart women). 'The rest, too, have done better than you.'

'They've all practised it before, and I have not. And I thought it made no difference to you as it is task work, and we are only paid for what we do.'

'Oh, but it does. I want the barn cleared.'

'I am going to work all the afternoon instead of leaving at two as the others will do.'

He looked sullenly at her and went away. Tess felt that she could not have come to a much worse place; but anything was better than gallantry. When two o'clock arrived the professional reed-drawers tossed off the last half-pint in their flagon, put down their hooks, tied their last sheaves, and went away. Marian and Izz would have done likewise, but on hearing that Tess meant to stay, to make up by longer hours for her lack of skill, they would not leave her. Looking out at the snow, which still fell, Marian exclaimed, 'Now, we've got it all to ourselves.' And so at last the conversation turned to their own experiences at the dairy; and, of course, the incidents of their affection for Angel Clare.

'Izz and Marian,' said Mrs. Angel Clare, with a dignity which was extremely touching, seeing how very little of a wife she was: 'I can't join in talk with you now, as I used to do, about Mr. Clare; you will see that I cannot; because, although he is gone away from me for the present, he is my husband.'

Izz was by nature the sauciest and most caustic of all the four girls who had loved Clare. 'He was a very splendid lover, no doubt,' she said; 'but I don't think he is a too fond husband to go away from you so soon.'

'He had to go—he was obliged to go, to see about the land over there!' pleaded Tess.

'He might have tided 'ee over the winter.'

'Ah—that's owing to an accident—a misunderstanding; and we won't argue it,' Tess answered, with tearfulness in her words. 'Perhaps there's a good deal to be said for him! He did not go away, like some husbands, without telling me; and I can always find out where he is.'

After this they continued for some long time in a reverie, as they went on seizing the ears of corn, drawing out the straw, gathering it under their arms, and cutting off the ears with their bill-hooks, nothing sounding in the barn but the swish of the straw and the crunch of the hook. Then Tess suddenly flagged, and sank down upon the heap of wheat-ears at her feet.

'I knew you wouldn't be able to stand it!' cried Marian. 'It wants harder flesh than yours for this work.'

Just then the farmer entered. 'Oh, that's how you get on when I am away,' he said to her.

'But it is my own loss,' she pleaded. 'Not yours.'

'I want it finished,' he said doggedly, as he crossed the barn and went out at the other door.

'Don't 'ee mind him, there's a dear,' said Marian. 'I've worked here before. Now you go and lie down there, and Izz and I will make up your number.'

'I don't like to let you do that. I'm taller than you, too.'

However, she was so overcome that she consented to lie down awhile, and reclined on a heap of pull–tails—the refuse after the straight straw had been drawn—thrown up at the further side of the barn. Her succumbing had been as largely owing to agitation at re-opening the subject of her separation from her husband as to the hard work. She lay in a state of percipience without volition, and the rustle of the straw and the cutting of the ears by the others had the weight of bodily touches.

She could hear from her corner, in addition to these noises, the murmur of their voices. She felt certain that they were continuing the subject already broached, but their voices were so low that she could not catch the words. At last Tess grew more and more anxious to know what they were saying, and, persuading herself that she felt better, she got up and resumed work.

Then Izz Huett broke down. She had walked more than a dozen miles the previous evening, had gone to bed at midnight, and had risen again at five o'clock. Marian alone, thanks to her bottle of liquor and her stoutness of build, stood the strain upon back and arms without suffering. Tess urged Izz to leave off, agreeing, as she felt better, to finish the day without her, and make equal division of the number of sheaves.

Izz accepted the offer gratefully, and disappeared through the great door into the snowy track to her lodging. Marian, as was the case every afternoon at this time on account of the bottle, began to feel in a romantic vein.

'I should not have thought it of him—never!' she said in a dreamy tone. 'And I loved him so! I didn't mind his having *you*. But this about Izz is too bad!'

Tess, in her start at the words, narrowly missed cutting off a finger with the bill-hook.

'Is it about my husband?' she stammered.

'Well, yes. Izz said, "Don't 'ee tell her;" but I am sure I can't help it! It was what he wanted Izz to do. He wanted her to go off to Brazil with him.'

Tess's face faded as white as the scene without, and its curves straightened. 'And did Izz refuse to go?' she asked.

'I don't know. Anyhow he changed his mind.'

'Pooh—then he didn't mean it! 'Twas just a man's jest!'

'Yes he did; for he drove her a good-ways towards the station.'

'He didn't take her!'

They pulled on in silence till Tess, without any premonitory symptoms, burst out crying.

'There!' said Marian. 'Now I wish I hadn't told 'ee!'

'No. It is a very good thing that you have done! I have been living on in a thirtover,[6] lackaday way, and have not seen what it may lead to! I ought to have sent him a letter oftener. He said I could not go to him, but he didn't say I was not to write as often as I liked. I won't dally like this any longer! I have been very wrong and neglectful in leaving everything to be done by him!'

The dim light in the barn grew dimmer, and they could see to work no longer. When Tess had reached home that evening, and had entered into the privacy of her little white-washed chamber, she began impetuously writing a letter to Clare. But falling into doubt she could not finish it. Afterwards she took the ring from the ribbon on which she wore it next her heart, and retained it on her finger all night, as if to fortify herself in the sensation that she was really the wife of this elusive lover of hers, who could propose that Izz should go with him abroad, so shortly after he had left her. Knowing that, how could she write entreaties to him, or show that she cared for him any more?

XLIV

By the disclosure in the barn her thoughts were led anew in the direction which they had taken more than once of late—to the distant Emminster Vicarage. It was through her husband's parents that she had been charged to send a letter to Clare if she desired; and to write to them direct if in difficulty. But that sense of her having morally no claim upon him had always led Tess to suspend her impulse to send these notes; and to the family at the Vicarage, therefore, as to her own parents since her marriage, she was virtually non-existent. This self-effacement in both directions had been quite in consonance with her independent character of desiring nothing by way of favour or pity to which she was not entitled on a fair consideration of her deserts. She had set herself to stand or fall by her qualities, and to waive such merely technical claims upon a strange family as had been established for her by the flimsy fact of a member of that family, in a season of impulse, writing his name in a church-book beside hers.

But now that she was stung to a fever by Izz's tale there was a

6. Morose.

limit to her powers of renunciation. Why had her husband not written to her? He had distinctly implied that he would at least let her know of the locality to which he had journeyed; but he had not sent a line to notify his address. Was he really indifferent? But was he ill? Was it for her to make some advance? Surely she might summon the courage of solicitude, call at the Vicarage for intelligence, and express her grief at his silence. If Angel's father were the good man she had heard him represented to be, he would be able to enter into her heart-starved situation. Her social hardships she could conceal.

To leave the farm on a week-day was not in her power; Sunday was the only possible opportunity. Flintcomb-Ash being in the middle of the cretaceous tableland over which no railway had climbed as yet, it would be necessary to walk. And the distance being fifteen miles each way she would have to allow herself a long day for the undertaking by rising early.

A fortnight later, when the snow had gone, and had been followed by a hard black frost, she took advantage of the state of the roads to try the experiment. At four o'clock that Sunday morning she came downstairs and stepped out into the starlight. The weather was still favourable, the ground ringing under her feet like an anvil.

Marian and Izz were much interested in her excursion, knowing that the journey concerned her husband. Their lodgings were in a cottage a little further along the lane, but they came and assisted Tess in her departure, and argued that she should dress up in her very prettiest guise to captivate the hearts of her parents-in-law; though she, knowing of the austere and Calvinistic tenets of old Mr. Clare, was indifferent, and even doubtful. A year had now elapsed since her sad marriage, but she had preserved sufficient draperies from the wreck of her then full wardrobe to clothe her very charmingly as a simple country girl with no pretensions to recent fashion; a soft gray woollen gown, with white crape quilling against the pink skin of her face and neck, and a black velvet jacket and hat.

' 'Tis a thousand pities your husband can't see 'ee now—you do look a real beauty!' said Izz Huett, regarding Tess as she stood on the threshold between the steely starlight without and the yellow candle-light within. Izz spoke with a magnanimous abandonment of herself to the situation; she could not be—no woman with a heart bigger than a hazel-nut could be—antagonistic to Tess in her presence, the influence which she exercised over those of her own sex being of a warmth and strength quite unusual, curiously overpowering the less worthy feminine feelings of spite and rivalry.

With a final tug and touch here, and a slight brush there, they let her go; and she was absorbed into the pearly air of the fore-dawn. They heard her footsteps tap along the hard road as she stepped out to her full pace. Even Izz hoped she would win, and, though without any particular respect for her own virtue, felt glad that she had been prevented wronging her friend when momentarily tempted by Clare.

It was a year ago, all but a day, that Clare had married Tess, and only a few days less than a year that he had been absent from her. Still, to start on a brisk walk, and on such an errand as hers, on a dry clear wintry morning, through the rarefied air of these chalky hogs'-backs, was not depressing; and there is no doubt that her dream at starting was to win the heart of her mother-in-law, tell her whole history to that lady, enlist her on her side, and so gain back the truant.

In time she reached the edge of the vast escarpment below which stretched the loamy Vale of Blackmoor, now lying misty and still in the dawn. Instead of the colourless air of the uplands the atmosphere down there was a deep blue. Instead of the great enclosures of a hundred acres in which she was now accustomed to toil there were little fields below her of less than half-a-dozen acres, so numerous that they looked from this height like the meshes of a net. Here the landscape was whitey-brown; down there, as in Froom Valley, it was always green. Yet it was in that vale that her sorrow had taken shape, and she did not love it as formerly. Beauty to her, as to all who have felt, lay not in the thing, but in what the thing symbolized.

Keeping the Vale on her right she steered steadily westward; passing above the Hintocks, crossing at right-angles the high-road from Sherton-Abbas to Casterbridge, and skirting Dogbury Hill and High-Stoy, with the dell between them called 'The Devil's Kitchen.' Still following the elevated way she reached Cross-in-Hand, where the stone pillar stands desolate and silent, to mark the site of a miracle, or murder, or both. Three miles further she cut across the straight and deserted Roman road called Long-Ash Lane; leaving which as soon as she reached it she dipped down a hill by a transverse lane into the small town or village of Evershead, being now about half-way over the distance. She made a halt here, and breakfasted a second time, heartily enough—not at the Sow-and-Acorn, for she avoided inns, but at a cottage by the church.

The second half of her journey was through a more gentle country, by way of Benvill Lane. But as the mileage lessened between her and the spot of her pilgrimage, so did Tess's confidence decrease, and her enterprise loom out more formidably. She saw her purpose in such staring lines, and the landscape so faintly, that she was sometimes in danger of losing her way. However, about noon she paused by a gate on the edge of the basin in which Emminster and its Vicarage lay.

The square tower, beneath which she knew that at that moment the Vicar and his congregation were gathered, had a severe look in her eyes. She wished that she had somehow contrived to come on a week-day. Such a good man might be prejudiced against a woman who had chosen Sunday, never realizing the necessities of her case. But it was incumbent upon her to go on now. She took off the thick boots in which she had walked thus far, put on her pretty thin ones of patent leather, and, stuffing the former into the hedge by the gate-post where she might readily find them again, descended the hill; the freshness of colour she had derived from the keen air thinning away in spite of her as she drew near the parsonage.

Tess hoped for some accident that might favour her, but nothing favoured her. The shrubs on the Vicarage lawn rustled uncomfortably in the frosty breeze; she could not feel by any stretch of imagination, dressed to her highest as she was, that the house was the residence of near relations; and yet nothing essential, in nature or emotion, divided her from them: in pains, pleasures, thoughts, birth, death, and after-death, they were the same.

She nerved herself by an effort, entered the swing-gate, and rang the door-bell. The thing was done; there could be no retreat. No; the thing was not done. Nobody answered to her ringing. The effort had to be risen to and made again. She rang a second time, and the agitation of the act, coupled with her weariness after the fifteen miles' walk, led her to support herself while she waited by resting her hand on her hip, and her elbow against the wall of the porch. The wind was so nipping that the ivy-leaves had become wizened and gray, each tapping incessantly upon its neighbour with a disquieting stir of her nerves. A piece of blood-stained paper, caught up from some meat-buyer's dust-heap, beat up and down the road without the gate; too flimsy to rest, too heavy to fly away; and a few straws kept it company.

The second peal had been louder, and still nobody came. Then she walked out of the porch, opened the gate, and passed through. And though she looked dubiously at the house-front as if inclined to return, it was with a breath of relief that she closed the gate. A feeling haunted her that she might have been recognized (though how she could not tell), and orders been given not to admit her.

Tess went as far as the corner. She had done all she could do; but determined not to escape present trepidation at the expense of future distress, she walked back again quite past the house, looking up at all the windows.

Ah—the explanation was that they were all at church, every one. She remembered her husband saying that his father always insisted upon the household, servants included, going to morning-service, and, as a consequence, eating cold food when they came home. It was, therefore, only necessary to wait till the service was over. She would not make herself conspicuous by waiting on the spot, and she started to get past the church into the lane. But as she reached the church-yard-gate the people began pouring out, and Tess found herself in the midst of them.

The Emminster congregation looked at her as only a congregation of small country-townsfolk walking home at its leisure can look at a woman out of the common whom it perceives to be a stranger. She quickened her pace, and ascended the road by which she had come, to find a retreat between its hedges till the Vicar's family should have lunched, and it might be convenient for them to receive her. She soon distanced the churchgoers, except two youngish men, who, linked arm-in-arm, were beating up behind her at a quick step.

As they drew nearer she could hear their voices engaged in earnest discourse, and, with the natural quickness of a woman in her situation, did not fail to recognize in those voices the quality of her husband's tones. The pedestrians were his two brothers. Forgetting all her plans, Tess's one dread was lest they should overtake her now, in her disorganized condition, before she was prepared to confront them; for though she felt that they could not identify her she instinctively dreaded their scrutiny. The more briskly they walked the more briskly walked she. They were plainly bent upon taking a short quick stroll before going indoors to lunch or dinner, to restore warmth to limbs chilled with sitting through a long service.

Only one person had preceded Tess up the hill—a ladylike young woman, somewhat interesting, though, perhaps, a trifle *guindée*[7] and prudish. Tess had nearly overtaken her when the speed of her brothers-in-law brought them so nearly behind her back that she could hear every word of their conversation. They said nothing, however, which particularly interested her till, observing the young lady still further in front, one of them remarked, 'There is Mercy Chant. Let us overtake her.'

Tess knew the name. It was the woman who had been destined for Angel's life-companion by his and her parents, and whom he probably would have married but for her intrusive self. She would have known as much without previous information if she had waited a moment, for one of the brothers proceeded to say: 'Ah! poor Angel, poor Angel! I never see that nice girl without more and more regretting his precipitancy in throwing himself away upon a dairymaid, or whatever she may be. It is a queer business, apparently. Whether she has joined him yet or not I don't know; but she had not done so some months ago when I heard from him.'

'I can't say. He never tells me anything nowadays. His ill-considered marriage seems to have completed that estrangement from me which was begun by his extraordinary opinions.'

Tess beat up the long hill still faster; but she could not outwalk them without exciting notice. At last they outsped her altogether, and passed her by. The young lady still further ahead heard their foot-

7. Stilted, stiff, unnatural.

steps and turned. Then there was a greeting and a shaking of hands, and the three went on together.

They soon reached the summit of the hill, and, evidently intending this point to be the limit of their promenade, slackened pace and turned all three aside to the gate whereat Tess had paused an hour before that time to reconnoitre the town before descending into it. During their discourse one of the clerical brothers probed the hedge carefully with his umbrella, and dragged something to light.

'Here's a pair of old boots,' he said. 'Thrown away, I suppose, by some tramp or other.'

'Some impostor who wished to come into the town barefoot, perhaps, and so excite our sympathies,' said Miss Chant, 'Yes, it must have been, for they are excellent walking-boots—by no means worn out. What a wicked thing to do! I'll carry them home for some poor person.'

Cuthbert Clare, who had been the one to find them, picked them up for her with the crook of his stick; and Tess's boots were appropriated.

She, who had heard this, walked past under the screen of her woollen veil, till, presently looking back, she perceived that the church partly had left the gate with her boots and retreated down the hill.

Thereupon our heroine resumed her walk. Tears, blinding tears, were running down her face. She knew that it was all sentiment, all baseless impressibility, which had caused her to read the scene as her own condemnation; nevertheless she could not get over it; she could not contravene in her own defenceless person all these untoward omens. It was impossible to think of returning to the Vicarage. Angel's wife felt almost as if she had been hounded up that hill like a scorned thing by those—to her—superfine clerics. Innocently as the slight had been inflicted, it was somewhat unfortunate that she had encountered the sons and not the father, who, despite his narrowness, was far less starched and ironed than they, and had to the full the gift of charity. As she again thought of her dusty boots she almost pitied those habiliments for the quizzing to which they had been subjected, and felt how hopeless life was for their owner.

'Ah!' she said, still sighing in pity of herself, '*they* didn't know that I wore those over the roughest part of the road to save these pretty ones *he* bought for me—no—they did not know it! And they didn't think that *he* chose the colour o' my pretty frock—no—how could they? If they had known perhaps they would not have cared, for they don't care much for him, poor thing!'

Then she grieved for the beloved man whose conventional standard of judgment had caused her all these latter sorrows; and she went her way without knowing that the greatest misfortune of her life was this feminine loss of courage at the last and critical moment through her estimating her father-in-law by his sons. Her present condition was precisely one which would have enlisted the sympathies of old Mr.

and Mrs. Clare. Their hearts went out of them at a bound towards extreme cases, when the subtle mental troubles of the less desperate among mankind failed to win their interest or regard. In jumping at Publicans and Sinners they would forget that a word might be said for the worries of Scribes and Pharisees;[8] and this defect or limitation might have recommended their own daughter-in-law to them at this moment as a fairly choice sort of lost person for their love.

Thereupon she began to plod back along the road by which she had come not altogether full of hope, but full of a conviction that a crisis in her life was approaching. No crisis, apparently, had supervened; and there was nothing left for her to do but to continue upon that starve-acre farm till she could again summon courage to face the vicarage. She did, indeed, take sufficient interest in herself to throw up her veil on this return journey, as if to let the world see that she could at least exhibit a face such as Mercy Chant could not show. But it was done with a sorry shake of the head. 'It is nothing—it is nothing!' she said. 'Nobody loves it; nobody sees it. Who cares about the looks of a castaway like me!'

Her journey back was rather a meander than a march. It had no sprightliness, no purpose; only a tendency. Along the tedious length of Benvill Lane she began to grow tired, and she leant upon gates and paused by milestones.

She did not enter any house till, at the seventh or eighth mile, she descended the steep long hill below which lay the village or townlet of Evershead, where in the morning she had breakfasted with such contrasting expectations. The cottage by the church, in which she again sat down, was almost the first at that end of the village, and while the woman fetched her some milk from the pantry, Tess, looking down the street, perceived that the place seemed quite deserted.

'The people are gone to afternoon service, I suppose?' she said.

'No, my dear,' said the old woman. ' 'Tis too soon for that; the bells hain't strook out yet. They be all gone to hear the preaching in yonder barn. A ranter[9] preaches there between the services—an excellent fiery, Christian man, they say. But, Lord, I don't go to hear'n! What comes in the regular way over the pulpit is hot enough for I.'

Tess soon went onward into the village, her footsteps echoing against the houses as though it were a place of the dead. Nearing the central part her echoes were intruded on by other sounds; and seeing

8. Mark ii:16: "And when the scribes and Pharisees saw him eat with publicans and sinners they said unto his disciples, How is it that he eateth and drinketh with publicans and sinners?" The scribes and Pharisees were strict observers of the law; the publicans and sinners made no pretensions about their righteousness.

9. "Fanatical noncomformist preacher —more particularly a member of the Primitive Methodists." [F]

the barn not far off the road, she guessed these to be the utterances of the preacher.

His voice became so distinct in the still clear air that she could soon catch his sentences, though she was on the closed side of the barn. The sermon, as might be expected, was of the extremest antinomian type; on justification by faith, as exponded in the theology of St. Paul. This fixed idea of the rhapsodist was delivered with animated enthusiasm, in a manner entirely declamatory, for he had plainly no skill as a dialectician. Although Tess had not heard the beginning of the address, she learnt what the text had been from its constant iteration—

'O foolish Galatians, who hath bewitched you, that ye should not obey the truth, before whose eyes Jesus Christ hath been evidently set forth, crucified among you?'[1]

Tess was all the more interested, as she stood listening behind, in finding that the preacher's doctrine was a vehement form of the views of Angel's father, and her interest intensified when the speaker began to detail his own spiritual experiences of how he had come by those views. He had, he said, been the greatest of sinners. He had scoffed; he had wantonly associated with the reckless and the lewd. But a day of awakening had come, and, in a human sense, it had been brought about mainly by the influence of a certain clergyman, whom he had at first grossly insulted; but whose parting words had sunk into his heart, and had remained there, till by the grace of Heaven they had worked this change in him, and made him what they saw him.

But more startling to Tess than the doctrine had been the voice, which, impossible as it seemed, was precisely that of Alec d'Urberville. Her face fixed in painful suspense she came round to the front of the barn, and passed before it. The low winter sun beamed directly upon the great double-doored entrance on this side; one of the doors being open, so that the rays stretched far in over the threshing-floor to the preacher and his audience, all snugly sheltered from the northern breeze. The listeners were entirely villagers, among them being the man whom she had seen carrying the red paint-pot on a former memorable occasion. But her attention was given to the central figure, who stood upon some sacks of corn, facing the people and the door. The three o'clock sun shone full upon him, and the strange enervating conviction that her seducer confronted her, which had been gaining ground in Tess ever since she had heard his words distinctly, was at last established as a fact indeed.

END OF PHASE THE FIFTH

1. Galatians iii:1.

Phase the Sixth—The Convert

XLV

Till this moment she had never seen or heard from d'Urberville since her departure from Trantridge.

The rencounter came at a heavy moment, one of all moments calculated to permit its impact with the least emotional shock. But such was unreasoning memory that, though he stood there openly and palpably a converted man, who was sorrowing for his past irregularities, a fear overcame her, paralyzing her movement so that she neither retreated nor advanced.

To think of what emanated from that countenance when she saw it last, and to behold it now! . . . There was the same handsome unpleasantness of mien, but now he wore neatly trimmed, old-fashioned whiskers, the sable moustache having disappeared; and his dress was half-clerical, a modification which had changed his expression sufficiently to abstract the dandyism from his features, and to hinder for a second her belief in his identity.

To Tess's sense there was, just at first, a ghastly *bizarrerie*, a grim incongruity, in the march of these solemn words of Scripture out of such a mouth. This too familiar intonation, less than four years earlier, had brought to her ears expressions of such divergent purpose that her heart became quite sick at the irony of the contrast.

It was less a reform than a transfiguration. The former curves of sensuousness were now modulated to lines of devotional passion. The lip-shapes that had meant seductiveness were now made to express supplication; the glow on the cheek that yesterday could be translated as riotousness was evangelized to-day into the splendour of pious rhetoric; animalism had become fanaticism; Paganism Paulinism,[2] the bold rolling eye that had flashed upon her form in the old time with such mastery now beamed with the rude energy of a theolatry that was almost ferocious. Those black angularities which his face had used to put on when his wishes were thwarted now did duty in picturing the incorrigible backslider who would insist upon turning again to his wallowing in the mire.

The lineaments, as such, seemed to complain. They had been diverted from their hereditary connotation to signify impressions for which nature did not intend them. Strange that their very elevation was a misapplication, that to raise seemed to falsify.

Yet could it be so? She would admit the ungenerous sentiment no longer. D'Urberville was not the first wicked man who had turned

2. Evangelical Christianity.

away from his wickedness to save his soul alive, and why should she deem it unnatural in him? It was but the usage of thought which had been jarred in her at hearing good new words in bad old notes. The greater the sinner the greater the saint; it was not necessary to dive far into Christian history to discover that.

Such impressions as these moved her vaguely, and without strict definiteness. As soon as the nerveless pause of her surprise would allow her to stir, her impulse was to pass on out of his sight. He had obviously not discerned her yet in her position against the sun.

But the moment that she moved again he recognized her. The effect upon her old lover was electric, far stronger than the effect of his presence upon her. His fire, the tumultuous ring of his eloquence, seemed to go out of him. His lip struggled and trembled under the words that lay upon it; but deliver them it could not as long as she faced him. His eyes, after their first glance upon her face, hung confusedly in every other direction but hers, but came back in a desperate leap every few seconds. This paralysis lasted, however, but a short time; for Tess's energies returned with the atrophy of his, and she walked as fast as she was able past the barn and onward.

As soon as she could reflect it appalled her, this change in their relative platforms. He who had wrought her undoing was now on the side of the Spirit, while she remained unregenerate. And, as in the legend, it had resulted that her Cyprian image had suddenly appeared upon his altar, whereby the fire of the priest had been wellnigh extinguished.

She went on without turning her head. Her back seemed to be endowed with a sensitiveness to ocular beams—even her clothing—so alive was she to a fancied gaze which might be resting upon her from the outside of that barn. All the way along to this point her heart had been heavy with an inactive sorrow; now there was a change in the quality of its trouble. That hunger for affection too long withheld was for the time displaced by an almost physical sense of an implacable past which still engirdled her. It intensified her consciousness of error to a practical despair; the break of continuity between her earlier and present existence, which she had hoped for, had not, after all, taken place. Bygones would never be complete bygones till she was a bygone herself.

Thus absorbed she recrossed the northern part of Long-Ash Lane at right angles, and presently saw before her the road ascending whitely to the upland along whose margin the remainder of her journey lay. Its dry pale surface stretched severely onward, unbroken by a single figure, vehicle, or mark, save some occasional brown horse-droppings which dotted its cold aridity here and there. While slowly breasting this ascent Tess became conscious of footsteps behind her, and turning she saw approaching that well-known form—so strangely accoutred as the Methodist—the one personage in all the world she wished not to encounter alone on this side of the grave.

There was not much time, however, for thought or elusion, and she yielded as calmly as she could to the necessity of letting him overtake her. She saw that he was excited, less by the speed of his walk than by the feelings within him.

'Tess!' he said.

She slackened speed without looking round.

'Tess!' he repeated. 'It is I—Alec d'Urberville.'

She then looked back at him, and he came up.

'I see it is,' she answered coldly.

'Well—is that all? Yet I deserve no more! Of course,' he added, with a slight laugh, 'there is something of the ridiculous to your eyes in seeing me like this. But—I must put up with that. . . . I heard you had gone away, nobody knew where. Tess, you wonder why I have followed you?'

'I do, rather; and I would that you had not, with all my heart!'

'Yes—you may well say it,' he returned grimly, as they moved onward together, she with unwilling tread. 'But don't mistake me; I beg this because you may have been led to do so in noticing—if you did notice it—how your sudden appearance unnerved me down there. It was but a momentary faltering; and considering what you had been to me, it was natural enough. But will helped me through it—though perhaps you think me a humbug for saying it—and immediately afterwards I felt that, of all persons in the world whom it was my duty and desire to save from the wrath to come[3]—sneer if you like—the woman whom I had so grievously wronged was that person. I have come with that sole purpose in view—nothing more.'

There was the smallest vein of scorn in her words of rejoinder: 'Have you saved yourself? Charity begins at home, they say.'

'I have done nothing!' said he indifferently. 'Heaven, as I have been telling my hearers, has done all. No amount of contempt that you can pour upon me, Tess, will equal what I have poured upon myself—the old Adam of my former years! Well, it is a strange story; believe it or not; but I can tell you the means by which my conversion was brought about, and I hope you will be interested enough at least to listen. Have you ever heard the name of the parson of Emminster—you must have done so?—old Mr. Clare; one of the most earnest of his school; one of the few intense men left in the Church; not so intense as the extreme wing of Christian believers with which I have thrown in my lot, but quite an exception among the Established clergy, the younger of whom are gradually attenuating the true doctrines by their sophistries, till they are but the shadow of what they were. I only differ from him

3. Matthew iii:7: "O generation of vipers, who hath warned you to flee from the wrath to come?"

on the question of Church and State—the interpretation of the text, "Come out from among them and be ye separate, saith the Lord"[4] —that's all. He is one who, I firmly believe, has been the humble means of saving more souls in this country than any other man you can name. You have heard of him?'

'I have,' she said.

'He came to Trantridge two or three years ago to preach on behalf of some missionary society; and I, wretched fellow that I was, insulted him when, in his disinterestedness, he tried to reason with me and show me the way. He did not resent my conduct, he simply said that some day I should receive the first-fruits of the Spirit—that those who came to scoff sometimes remained to pray. There was a strange magic in his words. They sank into my mind. But the loss of my mother hit me most; and by degrees I was brought to see daylight. Since then my one desire has been to hand on the true view to others, and that is what I was trying to do to-day; though it is only lately that I have preached hereabout. The first months of my ministry have been spent in the North of England among strangers, where I preferred to make my earliest clumsy attempts, so as to acquire courage before under-going that severest of all tests of one's sincerity, addressing those who have known one, and have been one's companions in the days of dark-ness. If you could only know, Tess, the pleasure of having a good slap at yourself, I am sure——'

'Don't go on with it!' she cried passionately, as she turned away from him to a stile by the wayside, on which she bent herself. 'I can't believe in such sudden things! I feel indignant with you for talking to me like this, when you know—when you know what harm you've done me! You, and those like you, take your fill of pleasure on earth by making the life of such as me bitter and black with sorrow; and then it is a fine thing, when you have had enough of that, to think of securing your pleasure in heaven by becoming converted! Out upon such—I don't believe in you—I hate it!'

'Tess,' he insisted; 'don't speak so! It came to me like a jolly new idea! And you don't believe me? What don't you believe?'

'Your conversion. Your scheme of religion.'

'Why?'

She dropped her voice. 'Because a better man than you does not be-lieve in such.'

'What a woman's reason! Who is this better man?'

'I cannot tell you.'

'Well,' he declared, a resentment beneath his words seeming ready to spring out at a moment's notice, 'God forbid that I should say I

---

4. II Corinthians vi:17—a text inter-preted by some evangelical sects as justification for "separation" from the Established Church.

am a good man—and you know I don't say any such thing. I am new to goodness, truly; but new comers see furthest sometimes.'

'Yes,' she replied sadly. 'But I cannot believe in your conversion to a new spirit. Such flashes as you feel, Alec, I fear don't last!'

Thus speaking she turned from the stile over which she had been leaning, and faced him; whereupon his eyes, falling casually upon the familiar countenance and form, remained contemplating her. The inferior man was quiet in him now; but it was surely not extracted, nor even entirely subdued.

'Don't look at me like that!' he said abruptly.

Tess, who had been quite unconscious of her action and mien, instantly withdrew the large dark gaze of her eyes, stammering with a flush, 'I beg your pardon!' And there was revived in her the wretched sentiment which had often come to her before, that in inhabiting the fleshly tabernacle with which nature had endowed her she was somehow doing wrong.

'No, no! Don't beg my pardon. But since you wear a veil to hide your good looks, why don't you keep it down?'

She pulled down the veil, saying hastily, 'It was mostly to keep off the wind.'

'It may seem harsh of me to dictate like this,' he went on; 'but it is better that I should not look too often on you. It might be dangerous.'

'Ssh!' said Tess.

'Well, women's faces have had too much power over me already for me not to fear them! An evangelist has nothing to do with such as they; and it reminds me of the old times that I would forget!'

After this their conversation dwindled to a casual remark now and then as they rambled onward, Tess inwardly wondering how far he was going with her, and not liking to send him back by positive mandate. Frequently when they came to a gate or stile they found painted thereon in red or blue letters some text of Scripture, and she asked him if he knew who had been at the pains to blazon these announcements. He told her that the man was employed by himself and others who were working with him in that district, to paint these reminders that no means might be left untried which might move the hearts of a wicked generation.

At length the road touched the spot called 'Cross-in-Hand.' Of all spots on the bleached and desolate upland this was the most forlorn. It was so far removed from the charm which is sought in landscape by artists and view-lovers as to reach a new kind of beauty, a negative beauty of tragic tone. The place took its name from a stone pillar which stood there, a strange rude monolith, from a stratum unknown in any local quarry, on which was roughly carved a human hand. Differing accounts were given of its history and purport. Some authorities stated that a devotional cross had once formed the complete erection thereon, of which the present relic was but the stump; others that the stone as it stood was entire, and that it had been fixed there to mark a boundary or place of meeting. Anyhow, whatever the origin of the relic, there was and is something sinister, or solemn, according to mood, in the scene amid which it stands; something tending to impress the most phlegmatic passer-by.

'I think I must leave you now,' he remarked, as they drew near to this spot. 'I have to preach at Abbot's-Cernel at six this evening, and my way lies across to the right from here. And you upset me somewhat too, Tessy—I cannot, will not, say why. I must go away and get strength. . . . How is it that you speak so fluently now? Who has taught you such good English?'

'I have learnt things in my troubles,' she said evasively.

'What troubles have you had?'

She told him of the first one—the only one that related to him.

D'Urberville was struck mute. 'I knew nothing of this till now!' he next murmured. 'Why didn't you write to me when you felt your trouble coming on?'

She did not reply; and he broke the silence by adding: 'Well—you will see me again.'

'No,' she answered. 'Do not again come near me!'

'I will think. But before we part come here.' He stepped up to the pillar. 'This was once a Holy Cross. Relics are not in my creed; but I fear you at moments—far more than you need fear me at present; and to lessen my fear, put your hand upon that stone hand, and swear that you will never tempt me—by your charms or ways.'

'Good God—how can you ask what is so unnecessary! All that is furthest from my thought!'

'Yes—but swear it.'

Tess, half frightened, gave way to his importunity; placed her hand upon the stone and swore.

'I am sorry you are not a believer,' he continued; 'that some unbeliever should have got hold of you and unsettled your mind. But no more now. At home at least I can pray for you; and I will; and who knows what may not happen? I'm off. Good-bye!'

He turned to a hunting-gate in the hedge, and without letting his eyes again rest upon her leapt over, and struck out across the down in the direction of Abbot's-Cernel. As he walked his pace showed perturbation, and by-and-by, as if instigated by a former thought, he drew from his pocket a small book, between the leaves of which was folded a letter, worn and soiled, as from much re-reading. D'Urberville opened the letter. It was dated several months before this time, and was signed by Parson Clare.

The letter began by expressing the writer's unfeigned joy at d'Urberville's conversion, and thanked him for his kindness in communicating with the parson on the subject. It expressed Mr. Clare's warm assurance of forgiveness for d'Urberville's former conduct, and his interest in the young man's plans for the future. He, Mr. Clare, would much have liked to see d'Urberville in the Church to whose ministry he had devoted so many years of his own life, and would have helped him to enter a theological college to that end; but since his correspondent had possibly not cared to do this on account of the delay it would have entailed, he was not the man to insist upon its paramount importance. Every man must work as he could best work, and in the method towards which he felt impelled by the Spirit.

D'Urberville read and re-read this letter, and seemed to quiz himself cynically. He also read some passages from memoranda as he walked till his face assumed a calm, and apparently the image of Tess no longer troubled his mind.

She meanwhile had kept along the edge of the hill by which lay her nearest way home. Within the distance of a mile she met a solitary shepherd.

'What is the meaning of that old stone I have passed?' she asked of him. 'Was it ever a Holy Cross?'

'Cross—no; 'twer not a cross! 'Tis a thing of ill-omen, Miss. It was put up in wuld times by the relations of a malefactor who was tortured there by nailing his hand to a post and afterwards hung. The bones lie underneath. They say he sold his soul to the devil, and that he walks at times.'

She felt the *petite mort*[5] at this unexpectedly gruesome information, and left the solitary man behind her. It was dusk when she drew near to Flintcomb-Ash, and in the lane at the entrance to the hamlet she approached a girl and her lover without their observing her. They were talking no secrets, and the clear unconcerned voice of the young woman, in response to the warmer accents of the man, spread into the chilly air as the one soothing thing within the dusky horizon, full of a stagnant obscurity upon which nothing else intruded. For a moment the voices cheered the heart of Tess, till she reasoned that this interview had its origin, on one side or the other, in the same attraction which had been the prelude to her own tribulation. When she came close the girl turned serenely and recognized her, the young man walking off in embarrassment. The woman was Izz Huett, whose interest in Tess's excursion immediately superseded her own proceedings. Tess did not explain very clearly its results, and Izz, who was a girl of tact, began to speak of her own little affair, a phase of which Tess had just witnessed.

'He is Amby Seedling, a chap who used to sometimes come and help at Talbothays,' she explained indifferently. 'He actually inquired

5. A shudder.

and found out that I had come here, and has followed me. He says he's been in love wi' me these two years. But I've hardly answered him.'

XLVI

Several days had passed since her futile journey, and Tess was afield. The dry winter wind still blew, but a screen of thatched hurdles erected in the eye of the blast kept its force away from her. On the sheltered side was a turnip-slicing machine, whose bright blue hue of new paint seemed almost vocal in the otherwise subdued scene. Opposite its front was a long mound or 'grave,' in which the roots had been preserved since early winter. Tess was standing at the un-covered end, chopping off with a bill-hook the fibres and earth from each root, and throwing it after the operation into the slicer. A man was turning the handle of the machine, and from its trough came the newly-cut swedes, the fresh smell of whose yellow chips was accom-panied by the sounds of the snuffling wind, the smart swish of the slicing-blades, and the choppings of the hook in Tess's leather-gloved hand.

The wide acreage of blank agricultural brownness, apparent where the swedes had been pulled, was beginning to be striped in wales of darker brown, gradually broadening to ribands. Along the edge of each of these something crept upon ten legs, moving without haste and without rest up and down the whole length of the field; it was two horses and a man, the plough going between them, turning up the cleared ground for a spring sowing.

For hours nothing relieved the joyless monotony of things. Then, far beyond the ploughing-teams, a black speck was seen. It had come from the corner of a fence, where there was a gap, and its tendency was up the incline, towards the swede-cutters. From the proportions of a mere point it advanced to the shape of a ninepin, and was soon perceived to be a man in black, arriving from the direction of Flint-comb-Ash. The man at the slicer, having nothing else to do with his eyes, continually observed the comer, but Tess, who was occupied, did not perceive him till her companion directed her attention to his approach.

It was not her hard taskmaster, Farmer Groby; it was one in a semi-clerical costume, who now represented what had once been the free-and-easy Alec d'Urberville. Not being hot at his preaching there was less enthusiasm about him now, and the presence of the grinder seemed to embarrass him. A pale distress was already on Tess's face, and she pulled her curtained hood further over it.

D'Urberville came up and said quietly—

'I want to speak to you, Tess.'

'You have refused my last request, not to come near me!' said she.

'Yes, but I have a good reason.'

'Well, tell it.'

'It is more serious than you may think.'

He glanced round to see if he were overheard. They were at some distance from the man who turned the slicer, and the movement of the machine, too, sufficiently prevented Alec's words reaching other ears. D'Urberville placed himself so as to screen Tess from the labourer, turning his back to the latter.

'It is this,' he continued, with capricious compunction. 'In thinking of your soul and mine when we last met, I neglected to inquire as to your worldly condition. You were well dressed, and I did not think of it. But I see now that it is hard—harder than it used to be when I—knew you—harder than you deserve. Perhaps a good deal of it is owing to me!'

She did not answer, and he watched her inquiringly, as, with bent head, her face completely screened by the hood, she resumed her trimming of the swedes. By going on with her work she felt better able to keep him outside her emotions.

'Tess,' he added, with a sigh of discontent,—'yours was the very worst case I ever was concerned in! I had no idea of what had resulted till you told me. Scamp that I was to foul that innocent life! The whole blame was mine—the whole unconventional business of our time at Trantridge. You, too, the real blood of which I am but the base imitation, what a blind young thing you were as to possibilities! I say in all earnestness that it is a shame for parents to bring up their girls in such dangerous ignorance of the gins and nets that the wicked may set for them, whether their motive be a good one or the result of simple indifference.'

Tess still did no more than listen, throwing down one globular root and taking up another with automatic regularity, the pensive contour of the mere fieldwoman alone marking her.

'But it is not that I came to say,' d'Urberville went on. 'My circumstances are these. I have lost my mother since you were at Trantridge, and the place is my own. But I intend to sell it, and devote myself to missionary work in Africa. A devil of a poor hand I shall make at the trade, no doubt. However, what I want to ask you is, will you put it in my power to do my duty—to make the only reparation I can make for the trick played you: that is, will you be my wife, and go with me? . . . I have already obtained this precious document. It was my old mother's dying wish.'

He drew a piece of parchment from his pocket, with a slight fumbling of embarrassment.

'What is it?' said she.

'A marriage licence.'

'O no, sir—no!' she said quickly, starting back.

'You will not? Why is that?'

And as he asked the question a disappointment which was not entirely the disappointment of thwarted duty crossed d'Urberville's face. It was unmistakably a symptom that something of his old passion for her had been revived; duty and desire ran hand-in-hand.

'Surely,' he began again, in more impetuous tones, and then looked round at the labourer who turned the slicer.

Tess, too, felt that the argument could not be ended there. Informing the man that a gentleman had come to see her, with whom she wished to walk a little way, she moved off with d'Urberville across the zebra-striped field. When they reached the first newly-ploughed section he held out his hand to help her over it; but she stepped forward on the summits of the earth-rolls as if she did not see him.

'You will not marry me, Tess, and make me a self-respecting man?' he repeated, as soon as they were over the furrows.

'I cannot.'

'But why?'

'You know I have no affection for you.'

'But you would get to feel that in time, perhaps—as soon as you really could forgive me?'

'Never!'

'Why so positive?'

'I love somebody else.'

The words seemed to astonish him.

'You do?' he cried. 'Somebody else? But has not a sense of what is morally right and proper any weight with you?'

'No, no, no—don't say that!'

'Anyhow, then, your love for this other man may be only a passing feeling which you will overcome——'

'No—no.'

'Yes, yes! Why not?'

'I cannot tell you.'

'You must in honour!'

'Well then . . . I have married him.'

'Ah!' he exclaimed; and he stopped dead and gazed at her.

'I did not wish to tell—I did not mean to!' she pleaded. 'It is a secret here, or at any rate but dimly known. So will you, *please* will you, keep from questioning me? You must remember that we are now strangers.'

'Strangers—are we? Strangers!'

For a moment a flash of his old irony marked his face; but he determinedly chastened it down.

'Is that man your husband?' he asked mechanically, denoting by a sign the labourer who turned the machine.

'That man!' she said proudly. 'I should think not!'

'Who, then?'

'Do not ask what I do not wish to tell!' she begged, and flashed her appeal to him from her upturned face and lash-shadowed eyes.

D'Urberville was disturbed.

'But I only asked for your sake!' he retorted hotly. 'Angels of heaven!—God forgive me for such an expression—I came here, I swear, as I thought for your good. Tess—don't look at me so—I cannot stand your looks! There never were such eyes, surely, before Christianity or since! There—I won't lose my head; I dare not. I own that the sight of you has waked up my love for you, which, I believed, was extinguished with all such feelings. But I thought that our marriage might be a sanctification for us both. "The unbelieving husband is sanctified by the wife, and the unbelieving wife is sanctified by the husband,"[6] I said to myself. But my plan is dashed from me; and I must bear the disappointment!'

He moodily reflected with his eyes on the ground.

'Married. Married! . . . Well, that being so,' he added, quite calmly, tearing the licence slowly into halves and putting them in his pocket; 'that being prevented, I should like to do some good to you and your husband, whoever he may be. There are many questions that I am tempted to ask, but I will not do so, of course, in opposition to your wishes. Though, if I could know your husband, I might more easily benefit him and you. Is he on this farm?'

'No,' she murmured. 'He is far away.'

'Far away? From *you*? What sort of husband can he be?'

'O, do not speak against him! It was through you! He found out——'

'Ah, is it so! . . . That's sad, Tess!'

'Yes.'

'But to stay away from you—to leave you to work like this!'

'He does not leave me to work!' she cried, springing to the defence of the absent one with all her fervour. 'He don't know it! It is by my own arrangement.'

'Then, does he write?'

'I—I cannot tell you. There are things which are private to ourselves.'

'Of course that means that he does not. You are a deserted wife, my fair Tess!'

In an impulse he turned suddenly to take her hand; the buff-glove was on it, and he seized only the rough leather fingers which did not express the life or shape of those within.

'You must not—you must not!' she cried fearfully, slipping her hand from the glove as from a pocket, and leaving it in his grasp. 'O, will you go away—for the sake of me and my husband—go, in the name of your own Christianity!'

6. I Corinthians vii:14.

'Yes, yes; I will,' he said abruptly, and thrusting the glove back to her turned to leave. Facing round, however, he said, 'Tess, as God is my judge, I meant no humbug in taking your hand!'

A pattering of hoofs on the soil of the field, which they had not noticed in their pre-occupation, ceased close behind them; and a voice reached her ear:

'What the devil are you doing away from your work at this time o' day?'

Farmer Groby had espied the two figures from the distance, and had inquisitively ridden across, to learn what was their business in his field.

'Don't speak like that to her!' said d'Urberville, his face blackening with something that was not Christianity.

'Indeed, Mister! And what mid Methodist pa'sons have to do with she?'

'Who is the fellow?' asked d'Urberville, turning to Tess.

She went close up to him.

'Go—I do beg you!' she said.

'What! And leave you to that tyrant? I can see in his face what a churl he is.'

'He won't hurt me. *He's* not in love with me. I can leave at Lady-Day.'

'Well, I have no right but to obey, I suppose. But—well, good-bye!'

Her defender, whom she dreaded more than her assailant, having reluctantly disappeared, the farmer continued his reprimand, which Tess took with the greatest coolness, that sort of attack being independent of sex. To have as a master this man of stone, who would have cuffed her if he had dared, was almost a relief after her former experiences. She silently walked back towards the summit of the field that was the scene of her labour, so absorbed in the interview which had just taken place that she was hardly aware that the nose of Groby's horse almost touched her shoulders.

'If so be you make an agreement to work for me till Lady-Day, I'll see that you carry it out,' he growled. ' 'Od rot the women—now 'tis one thing, and then 'tis another. But I'll put up with it no longer!'

Knowing very well that he did not harass the other women of the farm as he harassed her out of spite for the flooring he had once received, she did for one moment picture what might have been the result if she had been free to accept the offer just made her of being the monied Alec's wife. It would have lifted her completely out of subjection, not only to her present oppressive employer, but to a whole world who seemed to despise her. 'But no, no!' she said breathlessly; 'I could not have married him now! He is so unpleasant to me.'

That very night she began an appealing letter to Clare, concealing from him her hardships, and assuring him of her undying affection.

Any one who had been in a position to read between the lines would have seen that at the back of her great love was some monstrous fear —almost a desperation—as to some secret contingencies which were not disclosed. But again she did not finish her effusion; he had asked Izz to go with him, and perhaps he did not care for her at all. She put the letter in her box, and wondered if it would ever reach Angel's hands.

After this her daily tasks were gone through heavily enough, and brought on the day which was of great import to agriculturists—the day of the Candlemas Fair. It was at this fair that new engagements were entered into for the twelve months following the ensuing Lady-Day, and those of the farming population who thought of changing their places duly attended at the county-town where the fair was held. Nearly all the labourers on Flintcomb-Ash Farm intended flight, and early in the morning there was a general exodus in the direction of the town, which lay at a distance of from ten to a dozen miles over hilly country. Though Tess also meant to leave at the quarter-day she was one of the few who did not go to the fair, having a vaguely-shaped hope that something would happen to render another outdoor engagement unnecessary.

It was a peaceful February day, of wonderful softness for the time, and one would almost have thought that winter was over. She had hardly finished her dinner when d'Urberville's figure darkened the window of the cottage wherein she was a lodger, which she had all to herself to-day.

Tess jumped up, but her visitor had knocked at the door, and she could hardly in reason run away. D'Urberville's knock, his walk up to the door, had some indescribable quality of difference from his air when she last saw him. They seemed to be acts of which the doer was ashamed. She thought that she would not open the door; but, as there was no sense in that either, she arose, and having lifted the latch stepped back quickly. He came in, saw her, and flung himself down into a chair before speaking.

'Tess—I couldn't help it!' he began desperately, as he wiped his heated face, which had also a superimposed flush of excitement. 'I felt that I must call at least to ask how you are. I assure you I had not been thinking of you at all till I saw you that Sunday; now I cannot get rid of your image, try how I may! It is hard that a good woman should do harm to a bad man; yet so it is. If you would only pray for me, Tess!'

The suppressed discontent of his manner was almost pitiable, and yet Tess did not pity him.

'How can I pray for you,' she said, 'when I am forbidden to believe that the great Power who moves the world would alter His plans on my account?'

'You really think that?'

'Yes. I have been cured of the presumption of thinking otherwise.'

'Cured? By whom?'

'By my husband, if I must tell.'

'Ah—your husband—your husband! How strange it seems! I remember you hinted something of the sort the other day. What do you really believe in these matters, Tess?' he asked. 'You seem to have no religion—perhaps owing to me.'

'But I have. Though I don't believe in anything supernatural.'

D'Urberville looked at her with misgiving.

'Then do you think that the line I take is all wrong?'

'A good deal of it.'

'H'm—and yet I've felt so sure about it,' he said uneasily.

'I believe in the *spirit* of the Sermon on the Mount,[7] and so did my dear husband. . . . But I don't believe——'

Here she gave her negations.

'The fact is,' said d'Urberville drily, 'whatever your dear husband believed you accept, and whatever he rejected you reject, without the least inquiry or reasoning on your own part. That's just like you women. Your mind is enslaved to his.'

'Ah, because he knew everything!' said she, with a triumphant simplicity of faith in Angel Clare that the most perfect man could hardly have deserved, much less her husband.

'Yes, but you should not take negative opinions wholesale from another person like that. A pretty fellow he must be to teach you such scepticism!'

'He never forced my judgment! He would never argue on the subject with me! But I looked at it in this way; what he believed, after inquiring deep into doctrines, was much more likely to be right than what I might believe, who hadn't looked into doctrines at all.'

'What used he to say? He must have said something?'

She reflected; and with her acute memory for the letter of Angel Clare's remarks, even when she did not comprehend their spirit, she recalled a merciless polemical syllogism that she had heard him use when, as it occasionally happened, he indulged in a species of thinking aloud with her at his side. In delivering it she gave also Clare's accent and manner with reverential faithfulness.

'Say that again,' asked d'Urberville, who had listened with the greatest attention.

She repeated the argument, and d'Urberville thoughtfully murmured the words after her.

'Anything else?' he presently asked.

7. Matthew v-vii.

'He said at another time something like this;' and she gave another, which might possibly have been paralleled in many a work of the pedigree ranging from the *Dictionnaire Philosophique* to Huxley's *Essays*.[8]

'Ah—ha! How do you remember them?'

'I wanted to believe what he believed, though he didn't wish me to; and I managed to coax him to tell me a few of his thoughts. I can't say I quite understand that one; but I know it is right.'

'H'm. Fancy your being able to teach me what you don't know yourself!'

He fell into thought.

'And so I threw in my spiritual lot with his,' she resumed. 'I didn't wish it to be different. What's good enough for him is good enough for me.'

'Does he know that you are as big an infidel as he?'

'No—I never told him—if I am an infidel.'

'Well—you are better off to-day than I am, Tess, after all! You don't believe that you ought to preach my doctrine, and, therefore, do no despite to your conscience in abstaining. I do believe I ought to preach it, but like the devils I believe and tremble,[9] for I suddenly leave off preaching it, and give way to my passion for you.'

'How?'

'Why,' he said aridly; 'I have come all the way here to see you to-day! But I started from home to go to Casterbridge Fair, where I have undertaken to preach the Word from a waggon at half-past two this afternoon, and where all the brethren are expecting me this minute. Here's the announcement.'

He drew from his breast-pocket a poster whereon was printed the day, hour, and place of meeting, at which he, d'Urberville, would preach the Gospel as aforesaid.

'But how can you get there?' said Tess, looking at the clock.

'I cannot get there! I have come here.'

'What, you have really arranged to preach, and——'

'I have arranged to preach, and I shall not be there—by reason of my burning desire to see a woman whom I once despised!—No, by my word and truth, I never despised you; if I had I should not love you now! Why I did not despise you was on account of your being un-smirched in spite of all; you withdrew yourself from me so quickly and resolutely when you saw the situation; you did not remain at my pleasure; so there was one petticoat in the world for whom I had no contempt, and you are she. But you may well despise me now! I

8. The *Dictionnaire* is composed of essays by Voltaire, who attacked many aspects of Christianity. The reference to *Essays upon Some Controverted Questions* (1892) was added in 1895, after the death of Thomas Huxley, the scientist and popularizer of Darwin's theory of evolution.

9. Cf. James ii:19: "the devils also believe, and tremble." [F]

thought I worshipped on the mountains, but I find I still serve in the groves![1] Ha! ha!'

'O Alec d'Urberville! what does this mean? What have I done!'

'Done?' he said, with a soulless sneer in the word. 'Nothing intentionally. But you have been the means—the innocent means—of my backsliding, as they call it. I ask myself, am I, indeed, one of those "servants of corruption" who, "after they have escaped the pollutions of the world, are again entangled therein and overcome"—whose latter end is worse than their beginning?'[2] He laid his hand on her shoulder. 'Tess, my girl, I was on the way to, at least, social salvation till I saw you again!' he said freakishly shaking her, as if she were á child. 'And why then have you tempted me? I was firm as a man could be till I saw those eyes and that mouth again—surely there never was such a maddening mouth since Eve's!' His voice sank, and a hot archness shot from his own black eyes. 'You temptress, Tess; you dear damned witch of Babylon[3]—I could not resist you as soon as I met you again!'

'I couldn't help your seeing me again!' said Tess, recoiling.

'I know it—I repeat that I do not blame you. But the fact remains. When I saw you ill-used on the farm that day I was nearly mad to think that I had no legal right to protect you—that I could not have it; whilst he who has it seems to neglect you utterly!'

'Don't speak against him—he is absent!' she cried in much excitement. 'Treat him honourably—he has never wronged you! O leave his wife before any scandal spreads that may do harm to his honest name!'

'I will—I will,' he said, like a man awakening from a luring dream. 'I have broken my engagement to preach to those poor drunken boobies at the fair—it is the first time I have played such a practical joke. A month ago I should have been horrified at such a possibility. I'll go away—to swear—and—ah, can I! to keep away.' Then, suddenly: 'One clasp, Tessy—one! Only for old friendship——'

'I am without defence, Alec! A good man's honour is in my keeping —think—be ashamed!'

'Pooh! Well yes—yes!'

He clenched his lips, mortified with himself for his weakness. His eyes were equally barren of worldly and religious faith. The corpses of those old fitful passions which had lain inanimate amid the lines of his face ever since his reformation seemed to wake and come together as in a resurrection. He went out indeterminately.

Though d'Urberville had declared that this breach of his engage-

---

1. "The worship of Jehova was associated with high places, but the worship of Baal with groves." [F]

2. Peter ii:19, 20.

3. The Whore of Babylon is referred to several times in Revelation xvii.

ment to-day was the simple backsliding of a believer, Tess's words, as echoed from Angel Clare, had made a deep impression upon him, and continued to do so after he had left her. He moved on in silence, as if his energies were benumbed by the hitherto undreamt-of possibility that his position was untenable. Reason had had nothing to do with his whimsical conversion, which was perhaps the mere freak of a careless man in search of a new sensation, and temporarily impressed by his mother's death.

The drops of logic Tess had let fall into the sea of his enthusiasm served to chill its effervescence to stagnation. He said to himself, as he pondered again and again over the crystallized phrases that she had handed on to him, 'That clever fellow little thought that, by telling her those things, he might be paving my way back to her!'

XLVII

It is the threshing of the last wheat-rick at Flintcomb-Ash Farm. The dawn of the March morning is singularly inexpressive, and there is nothing to show where the eastern horizon lies. Against the twilight rises the trapezoidal top of the stack, which has stood forlornly here through the washing and bleaching of the wintry weather.

When Izz Huett and Tess arrived at the scene of operations only a rustling denoted that others had preceded them; to which, as the light increased, there were presently added the silhouettes of two men on the summit. They were busily 'unhaling' the rick, that is, stripping off the thatch before beginning to throw down the sheaves; and while this was in progress Izz and Tess, with the other women-workers, in their whitey-brown pinners, stood waiting and shivering, Farmer Groby having insisted upon their being on the spot thus early to get the job over if possible by the end of the day. Close under the eaves of the stack, and as yet barely visible, was the red tyrant that the women had come to serve—a timber-framed construction, with straps and wheels appertaining—the threshing-machine which, whilst it was going, kept up a despotic demand upon the endurance of their muscles and nerves.

A little way off there was another indistinct figure; this one black, with a sustained hiss that spoke of strength very much in reserve. The long chimney running up beside an ash-tree, and the warmth which radiated from the spot, explained without the necessity of much daylight that here was the engine which was to act as the *primum mobile* of this little world. By the engine stood a dark motionless being, a sooty and grimy embodiment of tallness, in a sort of trance, with a heap of coals by his side: it was the engineman. The isolation of his manner and colour lent him the appearance of a creature from Tophet, who had strayed into the pellucid smokelessness of this region of yellow grain and pale soil, with which he had nothing in common, to amaze and to discompose its aborigines.

What he looked he felt. He was in the agricultural world, but not of it. He served fire and smoke; these denizens of the fields served vegetation, weather, frost, and sun. He travelled with his engine from farm to farm, from county to county, for as yet the steam threshing-machine was itinerant in this part of Wessex. He spoke in a strange northern accent; his thoughts being turned inwards upon himself, his eye on his iron charge, hardly perceiving the scenes around him, and caring for them not at all: holding only strictly necessary intercourse with the natives, as if some ancient doom compelled him to wander here against his will in the service of his Plutonic master. The long strap which ran from the driving-wheel of his engine to the red thresher under the rick was the sole tie-line between agriculture and him.

While they uncovered the sheaves he stood apathetic beside his portable repository of force, round whose hot blackness the morning air quivered. He had nothing to do with preparatory labour. His fire was waiting incandescent, his steam was at high pressure, in a few seconds he could make the long strap move at an invisible velocity. Beyond its extent the environment might be corn, straw, or chaos; it was all the same to him. If any of the autochthonous idlers asked him what he called himself, he replied shortly, 'an engineer.'

The rick was unhaled by full daylight; the men then took their places, the women mounted, and the work began. Farmer Groby—or, as they called him, 'he'—had arrived ere this, and by his orders Tess was placed on the platform of the machine, close to the man who fed it, her business being to untie every sheaf of corn handed on to her by Izz Huett, who stood next, but on the rick; so that the feeder could seize it and spread it over the revolving drum, which whisked out every grain in one moment.

They were soon in full progress, after a preparatory hitch or two, which rejoiced the hearts of those who hated machinery. The work sped on till breakfast-time, when the thresher was stopped for half an hour; and on starting again after the meal the whole supplementary strength of the farm was thrown into the labour of constructing the straw-rick, which began to grow beside the stack of corn. A hasty lunch was eaten as they stood, without leaving their positions, and then another couple of hours brought them near to dinner-time; the inexorable wheels continuing to spin, and the penetrating hum of the thresher to thrill to the very marrow all who were near the revolving wire-cage.

The old men on the rising straw-rick talked of the past days when they had been accustomed to thresh with flails on the oaken barn-floor; when everything, even to winnowing, was effected by hand-labour, which, to their thinking, though slow, produced better results. Those, too, on the corn-rick talked a little; but the perspiring ones at the machine, including Tess, could not lighten their duties by the exchange of many words. It was the ceaselessness of the work which tried her so severely, and began to make her wish that she had never come to Flintcomb-Ash. The women on the corn-rick—Marian, who was one of them, in particular—could stop to drink ale or cold tea from the flagon now and then, or to exchange a few gossiping remarks while they wiped their faces or cleared the fragments of straw and husk from their clothing; but for Tess there was no respite; for, as the drum never stopped, the man who fed it could not stop, and she, who had to supply the man with untied sheaves, could not stop either, unless Marian changed places with her, which she sometimes did for half an hour in spite of Groby's objection that she was too slow-handed for a feeder.

For some probably economical reason it was usually a woman who was chosen for this particular duty, and Groby gave as his motive in selecting Tess that she was one of those who best combined strength with quickness in untying, and both with staying power, and this may have been true. The hum of the thresher, which prevented speech, increased to a raving whenever the supply of corn fell short of the regular quantity. As Tess and the man who fed could never turn their heads she did not know that just before the dinner-hour a person had come silently into the field by the gate, and had been standing under a second rick watching the scene, and Tess in particular. He was dressed in a tweed suit of fashionable pattern, and he twirled a gay walking-cane.

'Who is that?' said Izz Huett to Marian. She had at first addressed the inquiry to Tess, but the latter could not hear it.

'Somebody's fancy-man, I s'pose,' said Marian laconically.

'I'll lay a guinea he's after Tess.'

'O no. 'Tis a ranter pa'son who's been sniffing after her lately; not a dandy like this.'

'Well—this is the same man.'

'The same man as the preacher? But he's quite different!'

'He hev left off his black coat and white neckercher, and hev cut off his whiskers; but he's the same man for all that.'

'D'ye really think so? Then I'll tell her,' said Marian.

'Don't. She'll see him soon enough, good-now.'

'Well, I don't think it at all right for him to join his preaching to courting a married woman, even though her husband mid be abroad, and she, in a sense, a widow.'

'Oh—he can do her no harm,' said Izz drily. 'Her mind can no more be heaved from that one place where it do bide than a stooded waggon from the hole he's in. Lord love 'ee, neither court-paying, nor preaching, nor the seven thunders[4] themselves, can wean a woman when 'twould be better for her that she should be weaned.'

Dinner-time came, and the whirling ceased; whereupon Tess left her post, her knees trembling so wretchedly with the shaking of the machine that she could scarcely walk.

'You ought to het a quart o' drink into 'ee, as I've done,' said Marian. 'You wouldn't look so white then. Why, souls above us, your face is as if you'd been hagrode!'

It occurred to the good-natured Marian that, as Tess was so tired, her discovery of her visitor's presence might have the bad effect of taking away her appetite; and Marian was thinking of inducing Tess to descend by a ladder on the further side of the stack when the gentleman came forward and looked up.

Tess uttered a short little 'Oh!' And a moment after she said, quickly, 'I shall eat my dinner here—right on the rick.'

Sometimes, when they were so far from their cottages, they all did this; but as there was rather a keen wind going to-day, Marian and the rest descended, and sat under the straw-stack.

The new-comer was, indeed, Alec d'Urberville, the late Evangelist, despite his changed attire and aspect. It was obvious at a glance that the original *Weltlust*[5] had come back; that he had restored himself, as nearly as a man could do who had grown three or four years older, to the old jaunty, slap-dash guise under which Tess had first known her admirer, and cousin so-called. Having decided to remain where she was, Tess sat down among the bundles, out of sight of the ground, and began her meal; till, by-and-by, she heard footsteps on the ladder, and immediately after Alec appeared upon the stack—now an oblong and level platform of sheaves. He strode across them, and sat down opposite to her without a word.

Tess continued to eat her modest dinner, a slice of thick pancake which she had brought with her. The other workfolk were by this time all gathered under the rick, where the loose straw formed a comfortable retreat.

'I am here again, as you see,' said d'Urberville.

'Why do you trouble me so!' she cried, reproach flashing from her very finger-ends.

'I trouble *you*? I think I may ask, why do you trouble me?'

'Sure, I don't trouble you any-when!'

'You say you don't? But you do! You haunt me. Those very eyes that you turned upon me with such a bitter flash a moment ago, they come to me just as you showed them then, in the night and in the day! Tess, ever since you told me of that child of ours, it is just as

4. Revelation x:3: "And cried with a loud voice, as when a lion roareth; and when he had cried, seven thunders uttered their voices."
5. Worldly pleasure.

if my feelings, which have been flowing in a strong puritanical stream, had suddenly found a way open in the direction of you, and had all at once gushed through. The religious channel is left dry forthwith; and it is you who have done it!'

She gazed in silence.

'What—you have given up your preaching entirely?' she asked.

She had gathered from Angel sufficient of the incredulity of modern thought to despise flash enthusiasms; but, as a woman, she was somewhat appalled.

In affected severity d'Urberville continued—

'Entirely. I have broken every engagement since that afternoon I was to address the drunkards at Casterbridge Fair. The deuce only knows what I am thought of by the brethren. Ah-ha! The brethren! No doubt they pray for me—weep for me; for they are kind people in their way. But what do I care? How could I go on with the thing when I had lost my faith in it?—it would have been hypocrisy of the basest kind! Among them I should have stood like Hymenaeus and Alexander,[6] who were delivered over to Satan that they might learn not to blaspheme. What a grand revenge you have taken! I saw you innocent, and I deceived you. Four years after, you find me a Christian enthusiast; you then work upon me, perhaps to my complete perdition! But Tess, my coz, as I used to call you, this is only my way of talking, and you must not look so horribly concerned. Of course you have done nothing except retain your pretty face and shapely figure. I saw it on the rick before you saw me—that tight pinafore-thing sets it off, and that wing-bonnet—you field-girls should never wear those bonnets if you wish to keep out of danger.' He regarded her silently for a few moments, and with a short cynical laugh resumed: 'I believe that if the bachelor-apostle, whose deputy I thought I was, had been tempted by such a pretty face, he would have let go the plough for her sake as I do!'[7]

Tess attempted to expostulate, but at this juncture all her fluency failed her, and without heeding he added:

'Well, this paradise that you supply is perhaps as good as any other, after all. But to speak seriously, Tess.' D'Urberville rose and came nearer, reclining sideways amid the sheaves, and resting upon his elbow. 'Since I last saw you, I have been thinking of what you said that *he* said. I have come to the conclusion that there does seem rather a want of common-sense in these threadbare old propositions; how I could have been so fired by poor Parson Clare's enthusiasm, and have

6. In I Timothy i:19, Paul is telling Timothy of his ministry: "Holding faith, and a good conscience; which some having put away concerning faith have made shipwreck: Of whom is Hymenaeus and Alexander; whom I have delivered unto Satan, that they may learn not to blaspheme."

7. St. Paul was a bachelor. Luke ix:62: "No man having put his hand to the plough, and looking back, is fit for the kingdom of God."

gone so madly to work, transcending even him, I cannot make out! As for what you said last time, on the strength of your wonderful husband's intelligence—whose name you have never told me—about having what they call an ethical system without any dogma, I don't see my way to that at all.'

'Why, you can have the religion of loving-kindness and purity at least, if you can't have—what do you call it—dogma.'

'O no! I'm a different sort of fellow from that! If there's nobody to say, "Do this, and it will be a good thing for you after you are dead; do that, and it will be a bad thing for you," I can't warm up. Hang it, I am not going to feel responsible for my deeds and passions if there's nobody to be responsible to; and if I were you, my dear, I wouldn't either!'

She tried to argue, and tell him that he had mixed in his dull brain two matters, theology and morals, which in the primitive days of mankind had been quite distinct. But owing to Angel Clare's reticence, to her absolute want of training, and to her being a vessel of emotions rather than reasons, she could not get on.

'Well, never mind,' he resumed. 'Here I am, my love, as in the old times!'

'Not as then—never as then—'tis different!' she entreated. 'And there was never warmth with me! O why didn't you keep your faith, if the loss of it has brought you to speak to me like this!'

'Because you've knocked it out of me; so the evil be upon your sweet head! Your husband little thought how his teaching would recoil upon him! Ha-ha—I'm awfully glad you have made an apostate of me all the same! Tess, I am more taken with you than ever, and I pity you too. For all your closeness, I see you are in a bad way—neglected by one who ought to cherish you.'

She could not get her morsels of food down her throat; her lips were dry, and she was ready to choke. The voices and laughs of the workfolk eating and drinking under the rick came to her as if they were a quarter of a mile off.

'It is cruelty to me!' she said. 'How—how can you treat me to this talk, if you care ever so little for me?'

'True, true,' he said, wincing a little. 'I did not come to reproach you for my deeds. I came, Tess, to say that I don't like you to be working like this, and I have come on purpose for you. You say you have a husband who is not I. Well, perhaps you have; but I've never seen him, and you've not told me his name; and altogether he seems rather a mythological personage. However, even if you have one, I think I am nearer to you than he is. I, at any rate, try to help you out of trouble, but he does not, bless his invisible face! The words of the stern prophet Hosea that I used to read come back to me. Don't you know them, Tess?—"And she shall follow after her lover, but she shall not overtake him; and she shall seek him, but shall not find him; then shall she say, I will go and return to my first husband; for then was it better with me than now!"[8] . . . Tess, my trap is waiting just under the hill, and—darling mine, not his!—you know the rest.'

Her face had been rising to a dull crimson fire while he spoke; but she did not answer.

'You have been the cause of my backsliding,' he continued, stretching his arm towards her waist; 'you should be willing to share it, and leave that mule you call husband for ever.'

One of her leather gloves, which she had taken off to eat her skimmer-cake,[9] lay in her lap, and without the slightest warning she passionately swung the glove by the gauntlet directly in his face. It was heavy and thick as a warrior's, and it struck him flat on the mouth. Fancy might have regarded the act as the recrudescence of a trick in which her armed progenitors were not unpractised. Alec fiercely started up from his reclining position. A scarlet oozing appeared where her blow had alighted, and in a moment the blood began dropping from his mouth upon the straw. But he soon controlled himself, calmly drew his handkerchief from his pocket, and mopped his bleeding lips.

She too had sprung up, but she sank down again.

'Now, punish me!' she said, turning up her eyes to him with the hopeless defiance of the sparrow's gaze before its captor twists its neck. 'Whip me, crush me; you need not mind those people under the rick! I shall not cry out. Once victim, always victim—that's the law!'

'O no, no, Tess,' he said blandly. 'I can make full allowance for this. Yet you most unjustly forget one thing, that I would have married you if you had not put it out of my power to do so. Did I not ask you flatly to be my wife—hey? Answer me.'

'You did.'

'And you cannot be. But remember one thing!' His voice hardened as his temper got the better of him with the recollection of his sincerity in asking her and her present ingratitude, and he stepped across to her side and held her by the shoulders, so that she shook under his grasp. 'Remember, my lady, I was your master once! I will be your master again. If you are any man's wife you are mine!'

The threshers now began to stir below.

'So much for our quarrel,' he said, letting her go. 'Now I shall leave you, and shall come again for your answer during the afternoon. You don't know me yet! But I know you.'

She had not spoken again, remaining as if stunned. D'Urberville retreated over the sheaves, and descended the ladder, while the workers

8. Hosea ii:7.
9. A cake cooked . . . in a dish with which milk is skimmed. [*EDD*]

below rose and stretched their arms, and shook down the beer they had drunk. Then the threshing-machine started afresh; and amid the renewed rustle of the straw Tess resumed her position by the buzzing drum as one in a dream, untying sheaf after sheaf in endless succession.

XLVIII

In the afternoon the farmer made it known that the rick was to be finished that night, since there was a moon by which they could see to work, and the man with the engine was engaged for another farm on the morrow. Hence the twanging and humming and rustling proceeded with even less intermission than usual.

It was not till 'nammet'[1]-time, about three o'clock, that Tess raised her eyes and gave a momentary glance round. She felt but little surprise at seeing that Alec d'Urberville had come back, and was standing under the hedge by the gate. He had seen her lift her eyes, and waved his hand urbanely to her, while he blew her a kiss. It meant that their quarrel was over. Tess looked down again, and carefully abstained from gazing in that direction.

Thus the afternoon dragged on. The wheat-rick shrank lower, and the straw-rick grew higher, and the corn-sacks were carted way. At six o'clock the wheat-rick was about shoulder-high from the ground. But the unthreshed sheaves remaining untouched seemed countless still, notwithstanding the enormous numbers that had been gulped down by the insatiable swallower, fed by the man and Tess, through whose two young hands the greater part of them had passed. And the immense stack of straw where in the morning there had been nothing, appeared as the *faeces* of the same buzzing red glutton. From the west sky a wrathful shine—all that wild March could afford in the way of sunset—had burst forth after the cloudy day, flooding the tired and sticky faces of the threshers, and dyeing them with a coppery light, as also the flapping garments of the women, which clung to them like dull flames.

A panting ache ran through the rick. The man who fed was weary, and Tess could see that the red nape of his neck was encrusted with dirt and husks. She still stood at her post, her flushed and perspiring face coated with the corn-dust, and her white bonnet embrowned by it. She was the only woman whose place was upon the machine so as to be shaken bodily by its spinning, and the decrease of the stack now separated her from Marian and Izz, and prevented their changing duties with her as they had done. The incessant quivering, in which every fibre of her frame participated, had thrown her into a stupefied reverie in which her arms worked on independently of her consciousness. She hardly knew where she was, and did not hear Izz Huett tell her from below that her hair was tumbling down.

By degrees the freshest among them began to grow cadaverous and

1. A mid-morning or mid-afternoon snack.

saucer-eyed. Whenever Tess lifted her head she beheld always the great upgrown straw-stack, with the men in shirt-sleeves upon it, against the gray north sky; in front of it the long red elevator like a Jacob's ladder,[2] on which a perpetual stream of threshed straw ascended, a yellow river running up-hill, and spouting out on the top of the rick.

She knew that Alec d'Urberville was still on the scene, observing her from some point or other, though she could not say where. There was an excuse for his remaining, for when the threshed rick drew near its final sheaves a little ratting was always done, and men unconnected with the threshing sometimes dropped in for that performance—sporting characters of all descriptions, gents with terriers and facetious pipes, roughs with sticks and stones.

But there was another hour's work before the layer of live rats at the base of the stack would be reached; and as the evening light in the direction of the Giant's Hill by Abbot's-Cernel dissolved away, the white-faced moon of the season arose from the horizon that lay towards Middleton Abbey and Shottsford on the other side. For the last hour or two Marian had felt uneasy about Tess, whom she could not get near enough to speak to, the other women having kept up their strength by drinking ale, and Tess having done without it through traditionary dread, owing to its results at her home in childhood. But Tess still kept going: if she could not fill her part she would have to leave; and this contingency, which she would have regarded with equanimity and even with relief a month or two earlier, had become a terror since d'Urberville had begun to hover round her.

The sheaf-pitchers and feeders had now worked the rick so low that people on the ground could talk to them. To Tess's surprise Farmer Groby came up on the machine to her, and said that if she desired to join her friend he did not wish her to keep on any longer, and would send somebody else to take her place. The 'friend' was d'Urberville, she knew, and also that this concession had been granted in obedience to the request of that friend, or enemy. She shook her head and toiled on.

The time for the rat-catching arrived at last, and the hunt began. The creatures had crept downwards with the subsidence of the rick till they were all together at the bottom, and being now uncovered from their last refuge they ran across the open ground in all directions, a loud shriek from the by-this-time half-tipsy Marian informing her companions that one of the rats had invaded her person—a terror which the rest of the women had guarded against by various schemes of skirt-tucking and self-elevation. The rat was at last dislodged, and,

2. Genesis xxviii:12: "And he dreamed, and behold a ladder set up on the earth, and the top of it reached to heaven: and behold the angels of God ascending and descending on it."

amid the barking of dogs, masculine shouts, feminine screams, oaths, stampings, and confusion as of Pandemonium, Tess untied her last sheaf; the drum slowed, the whizzing ceased, and she stepped from the machine to the ground.

Her lover, who had only looked on at the rat-catching, was promptly at her side.

'What—after all—my insulting slap, too!' said she in an underbreath. She was so utterly exhausted that she had not strength to speak louder.

'I should indeed be foolish to feel offended at anything you say or do,' he answered, in the seductive voice of the Trantridge time. 'How the little limbs tremble! You are as weak as a bled calf, you know you are; and yet you need have done nothing since I arrived. How could you be so obstinate? However, I have told the farmer that he has no right to employ women at steam-threshing. It is not proper work for them; and on all the better class of farms it has been given up, as he knows very well. I will walk with you as far as your home.'

'O yes,' she answered with a jaded gait. 'Walk wi' me if you will! I do bear in mind that you came to marry me before you knew o' my state. Perhaps—perhaps you are a little better and kinder than I have been thinking you were. Whatever is meant as kindness I am grateful for; whatever is meant in any other way I am angered at. I cannot sense your meaning sometimes.'

'If I cannot legitimize our former relations at least I can assist you. And I will do it with much more regard for your feelings than I formerly showed. My religious mania, or whatever it was, is over. But I retain a little good nature; I hope I do. Now Tess, by all that's tender and strong between man and woman, trust me! I have enough and more than enough to put you out of anxiety, both for yourself and your parents and sisters. I can make them all comfortable if you will only show confidence in me.'

'Have you seen 'em lately?' she quickly inquired.

'Yes. They didn't know where you were. It was only by chance that I found you here.'

The cold moon looked aslant upon Tess's fagged face between the twigs of the garden-hedge as she paused outside the cottage which was her temporary home, d'Urberville pausing beside her.

'Don't mention my little brothers and sisters—don't make me break down quite!' she said. 'If you want to help them—God knows they need it—do it without telling me. But no, no!' she cried. 'I will take nothing from you, either for them or for me!'

He did not accompany her further, since, as she lived with the household, all was public indoors. No sooner had she herself entered, laved herself in a washing-tub, and shared supper with the family than she fell into thought, and withdrawing to the table under the wall, by the light of her own little lamp wrote in a passionate mood—

MY OWN HUSBAND,—Let me call you so—I must—even if it makes you angry to think of such an unworthy wife as I. I must cry to you in my trouble—I have no one else! I am so exposed to temptation, Angel. I fear to say who it is, and I do not like to write about it at all. But I cling to you in a way you cannot think! Can you not come to me now, at once, before anything terrible happens? O, I know you cannot, because you are so far away! I think I must die if you do not come soon, or tell me to come to you. The punishment you have measured out to me is deserved—I do know that—well deserved—and you are right and just to be angry with me. But, Angel, please, please, not to be just—only a little kind to me, even if I do not deserve it, and come to me! If you would come, I could die in your arms! I would be well content to do that if so be you had forgiven me!

Angel, I live entirely for you. I love you too much to blame you for going away, and I know it was necessary you should find a farm. Do not think I shall say a word of sting or bitterness. Only come back to me. I am desolate without you, my darling, O, so desolate! I do not mind having to work: but if you will send me one little line, and say, '*I am coming soon*,' I will bide on, Angel—O, so cheerfully!

It has been so much my religion ever since we were married to be faithful to you in every thought and look, that even when a man speaks a compliment to me before I am aware, it seems wronging you. Have you never felt one little bit of what you used to feel when we were at the dairy? If you have, how can you keep away from me? I am the same woman, Angel, as you fell in love with; yes, the very same!—not the one you disliked but never saw. What was the past to me as soon as I met you? It was a dead thing altogether. I became another woman, filled full of new life from you. How could I be the early one? Why do you not see this? Dear, if you would only be a little more conceited, and believe in yourself so far as to see that you were strong enough to work this change in me, you would perhaps be in a mind to come to me, your poor wife.

How silly I was in my happiness when I thought I could trust you always to love me! I ought to have known that such as that was not for poor me. But I am sick at heart, not only for old times, but for the present. Think—think how it do hurt my heart not to see you ever—ever! Ah, if I could only make your dear heart ache one little minute of each day as mine does every day and all day long, it might lead you to show pity to your poor lonely one.

People still say that I am rather pretty, Angel (handsome is the word they use, since I wish to be truthful). Perhaps I am what they say. But I do not value my good looks; I only like to have them because they belong to you, my dear, and that there may be at least one thing about me worth your having. So much have I felt this, that when I met with annoyance on account of the same I tied up my face in a bandage as long as people would believe in it. O Angel,

I tell you all this not from vanity—you will certainly know I do not—but only that you may come to me!

If you really cannot come to me will you let me come to you! I am, as I say, worried, pressed to do what I will not do. It cannot be that I shall yield one inch, yet I am in terror as to what an accident might lead to, and I so defenceless on account of my first error. I cannot say more about this—it makes me too miserable. But if I break down by falling into some fearful snare, my last state will be worse than my first. O God, I cannot think of it! Let me come at once, or at once come to me!

I would be content, ay, glad, to live with you as your servant, if I may not as your wife; so that I could only be near you, and get glimpses of you, and think of you as mine.

The daylight has nothing to show me, since you are not here, and I don't like to see the rooks and starlings in the fields, because I grieve and grieve to miss you who used to see them with me. I long for only one thing in heaven or earth or under the earth, to meet you, my own dear! Come to me—come to me, and save me from what threatens me!—Your faithful heartbroken

Tess.

XLIX

The appeal duly found its way to the breakfast-table of the quiet Vicarage to the westward, in that valley where the air is so soft and the soil so rich that the effort of growth requires but superficial aid by comparison with the tillage at Flintcomb-Ash, and where to Tess the human world seemed so different (though it was much the same). It was purely for security that she had been requested by Angel to send her communications through his father, whom he kept pretty well informed of his changing addresses in the country he had gone to exploit for himself with a heavy heart.

'Now,' said old Mr. Clare to his wife, when he had read the envelope, 'if Angel proposes leaving Rio for a visit home at the end of next month, as he told us that he hoped to do, I think this may hasten his plans; for I believe it to be from his wife.' He breathed deeply at the thought of her; and the letter was redirected to be promptly sent on to Angel.

'Dear fellow, I hope he will get home safely,' murmured Mrs. Clare. 'To my dying day I shall feel that he has been ill-used. You should have sent him to Cambridge in spite of his want of faith, and given him the same chance as the other boys had. He would have grown out of it under proper influence, and perhaps would have taken Orders after all. Church or no Church, it would have been fairer to him.'

This was the only wail with which Mrs. Clare ever disturbed her husband's peace in respect of their sons. And she did not vent this often; for she was as considerate as she was devout, and knew that his mind too was troubled by doubts as to his justice in this matter. Only too often had she heard him lying awake at night, stifling sighs for Angel with prayers. But the uncompromising Evangelical did not even now hold that he would have been justified in giving his son, an unbeliever, the same academic advantages that he had given to the two others, when it was possible, if not probable, that those very advantages might have been used to decry the doctrines which he had made it his life's mission and desire to propagate, and the mission of his ordained sons likewise. To put with one hand a pedestal under the feet of the two faithful ones, and with the other to exalt the unfaithful by the same artificial means, he deemed to be alike inconsistent with his convictions, his position, and his hopes. Nevertheless, he loved his misnamed Angel, and in secret mourned over this treatment of him as Abraham might have mourned over the doomed Isaac while they went up the hill together.[3] His silent self-generated regrets were far bitterer than the reproaches which his wife rendered audible.

They blamed themselves for this unlucky marriage. If Angel had never been destined for a farmer he would never have been thrown with agricultural girls. They did not distinctly know what had separated him and his wife, nor the date on which the separation had taken place. At first they had supposed it must be something of the nature of a serious aversion. But in his later letters he occasionally alluded to the intention of coming home to fetch her; from which expressions they hoped the division might not owe its origin to anything so hopelessly permanent as that. He had told them that she was with her relatives, and in their doubts they had decided not to intrude into a situation which they knew no way of bettering.

The eyes for which Tess's letter was intended were gazing at this time on a limitless expanse of country from the back of a mule which was bearing him from the interior of the South-American Continent towards the coast. His experiences of this strange land had been sad. The severe illness from which he had suffered shortly after his arrival had never wholly left him, and he had by degrees almost decided to relinquish his hope of farming here, though, as long as the bare possibility existed of his remaining, he kept this change of view a secret from his parents.

The crowds of agricultural labourers who had come out to the country in his wake, dazzled by representations of easy independence, had suffered, died, and wasted away. He would see mothers from English farms trudging along with their infants in their arms, when the child would be stricken with fever and would die; the mother would pause to dig a hole in the loose earth with her bare hands, would bury the babe there in with the same natural grave-tools, shed one tear, and again trudge on.

3. Genesis xxii:1-13.

Angel's original intention had not been emigration to Brazil, but a northern or eastern farm in his own country. He had come to this place in a fit of desperation, the Brazil movement among the English agriculturists having by chance coincided with his desire to escape from his past existence.

During this time of absence he had mentally aged a dozen years. What arrested him now as of value in life was less its beauty than its pathos. Having long discredited the old systems of mysticism, he now began to discredit the old appraisements of morality. He thought they wanted readjusting. Who was the moral man? Still more pertinently, who was the moral woman? The beauty or ugliness of a character lay not only in its achievements, but in its aims and impulses; its true history lay, not among things done, but among things willed.

How, then, about Tess?

Viewing her in these lights, a regret for his hasty judgment began to oppress him. Did he reject her eternally, or did he not? He could no longer say that he would always reject her, and not to say that was in spirit to accept her now.

This growing fondness for her memory coincided in point of time with her residence at Flintcomb-Ash, but it was before she had felt herself at liberty to trouble him with a word about her circumstances or her feelings. He was greatly perplexed; and in his perplexity as to her motives in withholding intelligence he did not inquire. Thus her silence of docility was misinterpreted. How much it really said if he had understood!—that she adhered with literal exactness to orders which he had given and forgotten; that despite her natural fearlessness she asserted no rights, admitted his judgment to be in every respect the true one, and bent her head dumbly thereto.

In the before-mentioned journey by mules through the interior of the country, another man rode beside him. Angel's companion was also an Englishman, bent on the same errand, though he came from another part of the island. They were both in a state of mental depression, and they spoke of home affairs. Confidence begat confidence. With that curious tendency evinced by men, more especially when in distant lands, to entrust to strangers details of their lives which they would on no account mention to friends, Angel admitted to this man as they rode along the sorrowful facts of his marriage.

The stranger had sojourned in many more lands and among many more peoples than Angel; to his cosmopolitan mind such deviations from the social norm, so immense to domesticity, were no more than are the irregularities of vale and mountain-chain to the whole terrestrial curve. He viewed the matter in quite a different light from Angel; thought that what Tess had been was of no importance beside what she would be, and plainly told Clare that he was wrong in coming away from her.

The next day they were drenched in a thunderstorm. Angel's companion was struck down with fever, and died by the week's end. Clare waited a few hours to bury him, and then went on his way.

The cursory remarks of the large-minded stranger, of whom he knew absolutedly nothing beyond a commonplace name, were sublimed by his death, and influenced Clare more than all the reasoned ethics of the philosophers. His own parochialism made him ashamed by its contrast. His inconsistencies rushed upon him in a flood. He had persistently elevated Hellenic Paganism at the expense of Christianity; yet in that civilization an illegal surrender was not certain disesteem. Surely then he might have regarded that abhorrence of the un-intact state, which he had inherited with the creed of mysticism, as at least open to correction when the result was due to treachery. A remorse struck into him. The words of Izz Huett, never quite stilled in his memory, came back to him. He had asked Izz if she loved him, and she had replied in the affirmative. Did she love him more than Tess did? No, she had replied; Tess would lay down her life for him, and she herself could do no more.

He thought of Tess as she had appeared on the day of the wedding. How her eyes had lingered upon him; how she had hung upon his words as if they were a god's! And during the terrible evening over the hearth, when her simple soul uncovered itself to his, how pitiful her face had looked by the rays of the fire, in her inability to realize that his love and protection could possibly be withdrawn.

Thus from being her critic he grew to be her advocate. Cynical things he had uttered to himself about her; but no man can be always a cynic and live; and he withdrew them. The mistake of expressing them had arisen from his allowing himself to be influenced by general principles to the disregard of the particular instance.

But the reasoning is somewhat musty;[4] lovers and husbands have gone over the ground before to-day. Clare had been harsh towards her; there is no doubt of it. Men are too often harsh with women they love or have loved; women with men. And yet these harshnesses are tenderness itself when compared with the universal harshness out of which they grow; the harshness of the position towards the temperament, of the means towards the aims, of to-day towards yesterday, of hereafter towards to-day.

The historic interest of her family—that masterful line of d'Urbervilles—whom he had despised as a spent force, touched his sentiments now. Why had he not known the difference between the political value and the imaginative value of these things? In the latter aspect her d'Urberville descent was a fact of great dimensions; worthless to economics, it was a most useful ingredient to the dreamer, to the moralizer on declines and falls. It was a fact that would soon be forgotten—that bit of distinction in poor Tess's blood and name, and

4. "Cf. Hamlet III.ii.343: 'Ay, sir, but "While the grass grows"—the proverb is something musty.'" [F]

oblivion would fall upon her hereditary link with the marble monuments and leaded skeletons at Kingsbere. So does Time ruthlessly destroy his own romances. In recalling her face again and again, he thought now that he could see therein a flash of the dignity which must have graced her grand-dames; and the vision sent that *aura* through his veins which he had formerly felt, and which left behind it a sense of sickness.

Despite her not inviolate past, what still abode in such a woman as Tess outvalued the freshness of her fellows. Was not the gleaning of the grapes of Ephraim better than the vintage of Abi-ezer?[5]

So spoke love renascent, preparing the way for Tess's devoted outpouring, which was then just being forwarded to him by his father; though owing to his distance inland it was to be a long time in reaching him.

Meanwhile the writer's expectation that Angel would come in response to the entreaty was alternately great and small. What lessened it was that the facts of her life which had led to the parting had not changed—could never change; and that, if her presence had not attenuated them, her absence could not. Nevertheless she addressed her mind to the tender question of what she could do to please him best if he should arrive. Sighs were expended on the wish that she had taken more notice of the tunes he played on his harp, that she had inquired more curiously of him which were his favourite ballads among those the country-girls sang. She indirectly inquired of Amby Seedling, who had followed Izz from Talbothays, and by chance Amby remembered that, amongst the snatches of melody in which they had indulged at the dairyman's, to induce the cows to let down their milk, Clare had seemed to like 'Cupid's Gardens,' 'I have parks, I have hounds,' and 'The break o' the day;' and had seemed not to care for 'The Tailor's Breeches,' and 'Such a beauty I did grow,' excellent ditties as they were.

To perfect the ballads was now her whimsical desire. She practised them privately at odd moments, especially 'The break o' the day:'

> Arise, arise, arise!
> And pick your love a posy,
> All o' the sweetest flowers
> That in the garden grow.
> The turtle doves and sma' birds
> In every bough a-building,
> So early in the May-time
> At the break o' the day!

It would have melted the heart of a stone to hear her singing these ditties, whenever she worked apart from the rest of the girls in this cold dry time; the tears running down her cheeks all the while at the

5. Judges viii:2.

thought that perhaps he would not, after all, come to hear her, and the simple silly words of the songs resounding in painful mockery of the aching heart of the singer.

Tess was so wrapt up in this fanciful dream that she seemed not to know how the season was advancing; that the days had lengthened, that Lady-Day was at hand, and would soon be followed by Old Lady-Day, the end of her term here.

But before the quarter-day had quite come something happened which made Tess think of far different matters. She was at her lodging as usual one evening, sitting in the downstairs room with the rest of the family, when somebody knocked at the door and inquired for Tess. Through the doorway she saw against the declining light a figure with the height of a woman and the breadth of a child, a tall, thin, girlish creature whom she did not recognize in the twilight till the girl said 'Tess!'

'What—is it 'Liza-Lu?' asked Tess, in startled accents. Her sister, whom a little over a year ago she had left at home as a child, had sprung up by a sudden shoot to a form of this presentation, of which as yet Lu seemed herself scarce able to understand the meaning. Her thin legs, visible below her once long frock, now short by her growing, and her uncomfortable hands and arms, revealed her youth and inexperience.

'Yes, I have been traipsing about all day, Tess,' said Lu, with unemotional gravity, 'a-trying to find 'ee; and I'm very tired.'

'What is the matter at home?'

'Mother is took very bad, and the doctor says she's dying, and as father is not very well neither, and says 'tis wrong for a man of such a high family as his to slave and drave at common labouring work, we don't know what to do.'

Tess stood in reverie a long time before she thought of asking 'Liza-Lu to come in and sit down. When she had done so, and 'Liza-Lu was having some tea, she came to a decision. It was imperative that she should go home. Her agreement did not end till Old Lady-Day, the sixth of April, but as the interval thereto was not a long one she resolved to run the risk of starting at once.

To go that night would be a gain of twelve hours; but her sister was too tired to undertake such a distance till the morrow. Tess ran down to where Marian and Izz lived, informed them of what had happened, and begged them to make the best of her case to the farmer. Returning, she got Lu a supper, and after that, having tucked the younger into her own bed, packed up as many of her belongings as would go into a withy basket, and started, directing Lu to follow her next morning.

L

She plunged into the chilly equinoctial darkness as the clock struck ten, for her fifteen miles' walk under the steely stars. In lonely districts night is a protection rather than a danger to a noiseless pedestrian, and knowing this Tess pursued the nearest course along by-lanes that she would almost have feared in the day time; but marauders were wanting now, and spectral fears were driven out of her mind by thoughts of her mother. Thus she proceeded mile after mile, ascending and descending till she came to Bulbarrow, and about midnight looked from that height into the abyss of chaotic shade which was all that revealed itself of the vale on whose further side she was born. Having already traversed about five miles on the upland she had now some ten or eleven in the lowland before her journey would be finished. The winding road downwards became just visible to her under the wan starlight as she followed it, and soon she paced a soil so contrasting with that above it that the difference was perceptible to the tread and to the smell. It was the heavy clay land of Blackmoor Vale, and a part of the Vale to which turnpike-roads had never penetrated. Superstitions linger longest on these heavy soils. Having once been forest, at this shadowy time it seemed to assert something of its old character, the far and the near being blended, and every tree and tall hedge making the most of its presence. The harts that had been hunted here, the witches that had been pricked and ducked,[6] the green-spangled fairies that 'whickered'[7] at you as you passed;—the place teemed with beliefs in them still, and they formed an impish multitude now.

At Nuttlebury she passed the village inn, whose sign creaked in response to the greeting of her footsteps, which not a human soul heard but herself. Under the thatched roofs her mind's eye beheld relaxed tendons and flaccid muscles, spread out in the darkness beneath coverlets made of little purple patchwork squares, and undergoing a bracing process at the hands of sleep for renewed labour on the morrow, as soon as a hint of pink nebulosity appeared on Hambledon Hill.

At three she turned the last corner of the maze of lanes she had threaded, and entered Marlott, passing the field in which, as a club-girl, she had first seen Angel Clare, when he had not danced with her; the sense of disappointment remained with her yet. In the direction of her mother's house she saw a light. It came from the bedroom window, and a branch waved in front of it and made it wink at her. As soon as she could discern the outline of the house—newly thatched with her money—it had all its old effect upon Tess's imagination.

---

6. "One of the ordeals imposed on witches in the seventeenth-century was the pricking of any excrescence on their body, in the belief that, if it proved insensitive, it was likely to be an extra pap for the sucking of imps. Another was ducking: a witch, having rejected baptism, would be in turn rejected by water—i.e. would float." [F]

7. Snickered.

Part of her body and life it ever seemed to be; the slope of its dormers, the finish of its gables, the broken courses of brick which topped the chimney, all had something in common with her personal character. A stupefaction had come into these features, to her regard; it meant the illness of her mother.

She opened the door so softly as to disturb nobody; the lower room was vacant, but the neighbour who was sitting up with her mother came to the top of the stairs, and whispered that Mrs. Durbeyfield was no better, though she was sleeping just then. Tess prepared herself a breakfast, and then took her place as nurse in her mother's chamber.

In the morning, when she contemplated the children, they had all a curiously elongated look; although she had been away little more than a year their growth was astounding; and the necessity of applying herself heart and soul to their needs took her out of her own cares.

Her father's ill-health was of the same indefinite kind, and he sat in his chair as usual. But the day after her arrival he was unusually bright. He had a rational scheme for living, and Tess asked him what it was.

'I'm thinking of sending round to all the old antiqueerians in this part of England,' he said, 'asking them to subscribe to a fund to maintain me. I'm sure they'd see it as a romantical, artistical, and proper thing to do. They spend lots o' money in keeping up old ruins, and finding the bones o' things, and such like; and living remains must be more interesting to 'em still, if they only knowed of me. Would that somebody would go round and tell 'em what there is living among 'em, and they thinking nothing of him! If Pa'son Tringham, who discovered me, had lived, he'd ha' done it, I'm sure.'

Tess postponed her arguments on this high project till she had grappled with pressing matters in hand, which seemed little improved by her remittances. When indoor necessities had been eased she turned her attention to external things. It was now the season for planting and sowing; many gardens and allotments of the villagers had already received their spring tillage; but the garden and the allotment of the Durbeyfields were behindhand. She found, to her dismay, that this was owing to their having eaten all the seed potatoes,—that last lapse of the improvident. At the earliest moment she obtained what others she could procure, and in a few days her father was well enough to see to the garden, under Tess's persuasive efforts: while she herself undertook the allotment-plot which they rented in a field a couple of hundred yards out of the village.

She liked doing it after the confinement of the sick chamber, where she was not now required by reason of her mother's improvement. Violent motion relieved thought. The plot of ground was in a high, dry, open enclosure, where there were forty or fifty such pieces, and where labour was at its briskest when the hired labour of the day had ended. Digging began usually at six o'clock, and extended indefinitely into the dusk or moonlight. Just now heaps of dead weeds and refuse were burning on many of the plots, the dry weather favouring their combustion.

One fine day Tess and 'Liza-Lu worked on here with their neighbours till the last rays of the sun smote flat upon the white pegs that divided the plots. As soon as twilight succeeded to sunset the flare of the couch-grass and cabbage-stalk fires began to light up the allotments fitfully, their outlines appearing and disappearing under the dense smoke as wafted by the wind. When a fire glowed, banks of smoke, blown level along the ground, would themselves become illuminated to an opaque lustre, screening the workpeople from one another; and the meaning of the 'pillar of a cloud,' which was a wall by day and a light by night, could be understood.[8]

As evening thickened some of the gardening men and women gave over for the night, but the greater number remained to get their planting done, Tess being among them, though she sent her sister home. It was on one of the couch-burning plots that she laboured with her fork, its four shining prongs resounding against the stones and dry clods in little clicks. Sometimes she was completely involved in the smoke of her fire; then it would leave her figure free, irradiated by the brassy glare from the heap. She was oddly dressed to-night, and presented a somewhat staring aspect, her attire being a gown bleached by many washings, with a short black jacket over it, the effect of the whole being that of a wedding and funeral guest in one. The women further back wore white aprons, which, with their pale faces, were all that could be seen of them in the gloom, except when at moments they caught a flash from the flames.

Westward, the wiry boughs of the bare thorn hedge which formed the boundary of the field rose against the pale opalescence of the lower sky. Above, Jupiter hung like a full-blown jonquil, so bright as almost to throw a shade. A few small nondescript stars were appearing elsewhere. In the distance a dog barked, and wheels occasionally rattled along the dry road.

Still the prongs continued to click assiduously, for it was not late; and though the air was fresh and keen there was a whisper of spring in it that cheered the workers on. Something in the place, the hour, the crackling fires, the fantastic mysteries of light and shade, made others as well as Tess enjoy being there. Nightfall, which in the frost of winter comes as a fiend and in the warmth of summer as a lover, came as a tranquillizer on this March day.

8. Exodus xiii:21: "And the Lord went before them by day in a pillar of a cloud, to lead them the way; and by night in a pillar of fire, to give them light."

Nobody looked at his or her companions. The eyes of all were on the soil as its turned surface was revealed by the fires. Hence as Tess stirred the clods, and sang her foolish little songs with scarce now a hope that Clare would ever hear them, she did not for a long time notice the person who worked nearest to her—a man in a long smock-frock who, she found, was forking the same plot as herself, and whom she supposed her father had sent there to advance the work. She became more conscious of him when the direction of his digging brought him closer. Sometimes the smoke divided them; then it swerved, and the two were visible to each other but divided from all the rest.

Tess did not speak to her fellow-worker, nor did he speak to her. Nor did she think of him further than to recollect that he had not been there when it was broad daylight, and that she did not know him as any one of the Marlott labourers, which was no wonder, her absences having been so long and frequent of late years. By-and-by he dug so close to her that the fire-beams were reflected as distinctly from the steel prongs of his fork as from her own. On going up to the fire to throw a pitch of dead weeds upon it, she found that he did the same on the other side. The fire flared up, and she beheld the face of d'Urberville.

The unexpectedness of his presence, the grotesqueness of his appearance in a gathered smockfrock, such as was now worn only by the most old-fashioned of the labourers, had a ghastly comicality that chilled her as to its bearing. D'Urberville emitted a low long laugh.

'If I were inclined to joke I should say, How much this seems like Paradise!' he remarked whimsically, looking at her with an inclined head.

'What do you say?' she weakly asked.

'A jester might say this is just like Paradise. You are Eve, and I am the old Other One come to tempt you in the disguise of an inferior animal. I used to be quite up in that scene of Milton's when I was theological. Some of it goes —

> "Empress, the way is ready, and not long,
> Beyond a row of myrtles. . . .
> . . . If thou accept
> My conduct, I can bring thee thither soon."
> "Lead then," said Eve.[9]

And so on. My dear, dear Tess, I am only putting this to you as a thing that you might have supposed or said quite untruly, because you think so badly of me.'

'I never said you were Satan, or thought it. I don't think of you in that way at all. My thoughts of you are quite cold, except when you affront me. What, did you come digging here entirely because of me?'

9. *Paradise Lost*, IX.626-31.

'Entirely. To see you; nothing more. The smockfrock, which I saw hanging for sale as I came along, was an after-thought, that I mightn't be noticed. I come to protest against your working like this.'

'But I like doing it—it is for my father.'

'Your engagement at the other place is ended?'

'Yes.'

'Where are you going to next? To join your dear husband?'

She could not bear the humiliating reminder.

'O—I don't know!' she said bitterly. 'I have no husband!'

'It is quite true—in the sense you mean. But you have a friend, and I have determined that you shall be comfortable in spite of yourself. When you get down to your house you will see what I have sent there for you.'

'O, Alec, I wish you wouldn't give me anything at all! I cannot take it from you! I don't like—it is not right!'

'It *is* right!' he cried lightly. 'I am not going to see a woman whom I feel so tenderly for as I do for you, in trouble without trying to help her.'

'But I am very well off! I am only in trouble about—about—not about living at all!'

She turned, and desperately resumed her digging, tears dripping upon the fork-handle and upon the clods.

'About the children—your brothers and sisters,' he resumed. 'I've been thinking of them.'

Tess's heart quivered—he was touching her in a weak place. He had divined her chief anxiety. Since returning home her soul had gone out to those children with an affection that was passionate.

'If your mother does not recover, somebody ought to do something for them; since your father will not be able to do much, I suppose?'

'He can with my assistance. He must!'

'And with mine.'

'No, sir!'

'How damned foolish this is!' burst out d'Urberville. 'Why, he thinks we are the same family; and will be quite satisfied!'

'He don't. I've undeceived him.'

'The more fool you!'

D'Urberville in anger retreated from her to the hedge, where he pulled off the long smockfrock which had disguised him; and rolling it up and pushing it into the couch-fire, went away.

Tess could not get on with her digging after this; she felt restless; she wondered if he had gone back to her father's house; and taking the fork in her hand proceeded homewards.

Some twenty yards from the house she was met by one of her sisters.

'O, Tessy—what do you think! 'Liza-Lu is a-crying, and there's a lot of folk in the house, and mother is a good deal better, but they think father is dead!'

The child realized the grandeur of the news; but not as yet its sadness; and stood looking at Tess with round-eyed importance, till, beholding the effect produced upon her, she said —

'What, Tess, shan't we talk to father never no more?'

'But father was only a little bit ill!' exclaimed Tess distractedly.

'Liza-Lu came up.

'He dropped down just now, and the doctor who was there for mother said there was no chance for him, because his heart was growed in.'

Yes; the Durbeyfield couple had changed places; the dying one was out of danger, and the indisposed one was dead. The news meant even more than it sounded. Her father's life had a value apart from his personal achievements, or perhaps it would not have had much. It was the last of the three lives for whose duration the house and premises were held under a lease; and it had long been coveted by the tenant-farmer for his regular labourers, who were stinted in cottage accommodation. Moreover, 'liviers' were disapproved of in villages almost as much as little freeholders, because of their independence of manner, and when a lease determined it was never renewed.[1]

Thus the Durbeyfields, once d'Urbervilles, saw descending upon them the destiny which, no doubt, when they were among the Olympians of the county, they had caused to descend many a time, and severely enough, upon the heads of such landless ones as they themselves were now. So do flux and reflux—the rhythm of change—alternate and persist in everything under the sky.

LI

At length it was the eve of Old Lady-Day, and the agricultural world was in a fever of mobility such as only occurs at that particular date of the year. It is a day of fulfilment; agreements for outdoor service during the ensuing year, entered into at Candlemas, are to be now carried out. The labourers—or 'workfolk,' as they used to call themselves immemorially till the other word was introduced from without—who wish to remain no longer in old places are removing to the new farms.

These annual migrations from farm to farm were on the increase here. When Tess's mother was a child the majority of the field-folk about Marlott had remained all their lives on one farm, which had been the home also of their fathers and grandfathers; but latterly the desire for yearly removal had risen to a high pitch. With the younger families it was a pleasant excitement which might possibly be an ad-

1. A livier was a tenant whose lease was good for a term of one or more lives, or lifetimes; a freeholder's lease could be passed on to his heirs forever.

vantage. The Egypt of one family was the Land of Promise to the family who saw it from a distance, till by residence there it became in turn their Egypt also;[2] and so they changed and changed.

However, all the mutations so increasingly discernible in village life did not originate entirely in the agricultural unrest. A depopulation was also going on. The village had formerly contained, side by side with the agricultural labourers, an interesting and better-informed class, ranking distinctly above the former—the class to which Tess's father and mother had belonged—and including the carpenter, the smith, the shoemaker, the huckster, together with nondescript workers other than farm-labourers; a set of people who owed a certain stability of aim and conduct to the fact of their being life-holders like Tess's father, or copyholders, or, occasionally, small freeholders. But as the long holdings fell in they were seldom again let to similar tenants, and were mostly pulled down, if not absolutely required by the farmer for his hands. Cottagers who were not directly employed on the land were looked upon with disfavour, and the banishment of some starved the trade of others, who were thus obliged to follow. These families, who had formed the backbone of the village life in the past, who were the depositaries of the village traditions, had to seek refuge in the large centres; the process, humorously designated by statisticians as 'the tendency of the rural population towards the large towns,' being really the tendency of water to flow uphill when forced by machinery.

The cottage accommodation at Marlott having been in this manner considerably curtailed by demolitions, every house which remained standing was required by the agriculturist for his work-people. Ever since the occurrence of the event which had cast such a shadow over Tess's life, the Durbeyfield family (whose descent was not credited) had been tacitly looked on as one which would have to go when their lease ended, if only in the interests of morality. It was, indeed, quite true that the household had not been shining examples either of temperance, soberness, or chastity. The father, and even the mother, had got drunk at times, the younger children seldom had gone to church, and the eldest daughter had made queer unions. By some means the village had to be kept pure. So on this, the first Lady-Day on which the Durbeyfields were expellable, the house, being roomy, was required for a carter with a large family; and Widow Joan, her daughters Tess and 'Liza-Lu, the boy Abraham and the younger children, had to go elsewhere.

On the evening preceding their removal it was getting dark betimes by reason of a drizzling rain which blurred the sky. As it was the last night they would spend in the village which had been their home and

2. The Israelites suffered in bondage in Egypt; they looked forward to returning to their homes in the Promised Land. The story is told in Exodus.

birthplace, Mrs. Durbeyfield, 'Liza-Lu, and Abraham had gone out to bid some friends good-bye, and Tess was keeping house till they should return.

She was kneeling in the window-bench, her face close to the casement, where an outer pane of rain-water was sliding down the inner pane of glass. Her eyes rested on the web of a spider, probably starved long ago, which had been mistakenly placed in a corner where no flies ever came, and shivered in the slight draught through the casement. Tess was reflecting on the position of the household, in which she perceived her own evil influence. Had she not come home her mother and the children might probably have been allowed to stay on as weekly tenants. But she had been observed almost immediately on her return by some people of scrupulous character and great influence: they had seen her idling in the churchyard, restoring as well as she could with a little trowel a baby's obliterated grave. By this means they had found that she was living here again; her mother was scolded for 'harbouring' her; sharp retorts had ensued from Joan, who had independently offered to leave at once; she had been taken at her word; and here was the result.

'I ought never to have come home,' said Tess to herself, bitterly.

She was so intent upon these thoughts that she hardly at first took note of a man in a white mackintosh whom she saw riding down the street. Possibly it was owing to her face being near to the pane that he saw her so quickly, and directed his horse so close to the cottage-front that his hoofs were almost upon the narrow border for plants growing under the wall. It was not till he touched the window with his riding-crop that she observed him. The rain had nearly ceased, and she opened the casement in obedience to his gesture.

'Didn't you see me?' asked d'Urberville.

'I was not attending,' she said. 'I heard you, I believe, though I fancied it was a carriage and horses. I was in a sort of dream.'

'Ah! you heard the d'Urberville Coach, perhaps. You know the legend, I suppose?'

'No. My—somebody was going to tell it me once, but didn't.'

'If you are a genuine d'Urberville I ought not to tell you either, I suppose. As for me, I'm a sham one, so it doesn't matter. It is rather dismal. It is that this sound of a non-existent coach can only be heard by one of d'Urberville blood, and it is held to be of ill-omen to the one who hears it. It has to do with a murder, committed by one of the family, centuries ago.'

'Now you have begun it, finish it.'

'Very well. One of the family is said to have abducted some beautiful woman, who tried to escape from the coach in which he was carrying her off, and in the struggle he killed her—or she killed him—I forget which. Such is one version of the tale. . . . I see that your tubs and buckets are packed. Going away, aren't you?'

'Yes, to-morrow—Old Lady-Day.'

'I heard you were, but could hardly believe it; it seems so sudden. Why is it?'

'Father's was the last life on the property, and when that dropped we had no further right to stay. Though we might, perhaps, have stayed as weekly tenants—if it had not been for me.'

'What about you?'

'I am not a—proper woman.'

D'Urberville's face flushed.

'What a blasted shame! Miserable snobs! May their dirty souls be burnt to cinders!' he exclaimed in tones of ironic resentment. 'That's why you are going, is it? Turned out?'

'We are not turned out exactly; but as they said we should have to go soon, it was best to go now everybody was moving, because there are better chances.'

'Where are you going to?'

'Kingsbere. We have taken rooms there. Mother is so foolish about father's people that she will go there.'

'But your mother's family are not fit for lodgings, and in a little hole of a town like that. Now why not come to my garden-house at Trantridge? There are hardly any poultry now, since my mother's death; but there's the house, as you know it, and the garden. It can be whitewashed in a day, and your mother can live there quite comfortably; and I will put the children to a good school. Really I ought to do something for you!'

'But we have already taken the rooms at Kingsbere!' she declared. 'And we can wait there——'

'Wait—what for? For that nice husband, no doubt. Now look here, Tess, I know what men are, and, bearing in mind the *grounds* of your separation, I am quite positive he will never make it up with you. Now, though I have been your enemy, I am your friend, even if you won't believe it. Come to this cottage of mine. We'll get up a regular colony of fowls, and your mother can attend to them excellently; and the children can go to school.'

Tess breathed more and more quickly, and at length she said—

'How do I know that you would do all this? Your views may change—and then—we should be—my mother would be—homeless again.'

'O no—no. I would guarantee you against such as that in writing, if necessary. Think it over.'

Tess shook her head. But d'Urberville persisted; she had seldom seen him so determined; he would not take a negative.

'Please just tell your mother,' he said, in emphatic tones. 'It is her business to judge—not yours. I shall get the house swept out and whitened to-morrow morning, and fires lit; and it will be dry by the evening, so that you can come straight there. Now mind, I shall expect you.'

Tess again shook her head; her throat swelling with complicated emotion. She could not look up at d'Urberville.

'I owe you something for the past, you know,' he resumed. 'And you cured me, too, of that craze; so I am glad——'

'I would rather you had kept the craze, so that you had kept the practice which went with it!'

'I am glad of this opportunity of repaying you a little. To-morrow I shall expect to hear your mother's goods unloading. . . . Give me your hand on it now—dear, beautiful Tess!'

With the last sentence he had dropped his voice to a murmur, and put his hand in at the half-open casement. With stormy eyes she pulled the stay-bar quickly, and, in doing so, caught his arm between the casement and the stone mullion.

'Damnation—you are very cruel!' he said, snatching out his arm. 'No, no!—I know you didn't do it on purpose. Well, I shall expect you, or your mother and the children at least.'

'I shall not come—I have plenty of money!' she cried.

'Where?'

'At my father-in-law's, if I ask for it.'

'*If* you ask for it. But you won't, Tess; I know you; you'll never ask for it—you'll starve first!'

With these words he rode off. Just at the corner of the street he met the man with the paint-pot, who asked him if he had deserted the brethren.

'You go to the devil!' said d'Urberville.

Tess remained where she was a long while, till a sudden rebellious sense of injustice caused the region of her eyes to swell with the rush of hot tears thither. Her husband, Angel Clare himself, had, like others, dealt out hard measure to her, surely he had! She had never before admitted such a thought; but he had surely! Never in her life—she could swear it from the bottom of her soul—had she ever intended to do wrong; yet these hard judgments had come. Whatever her sins, they were not sins of intention, but of inadvertence, and why should she have been punished so persistently?

She passionately seized the first piece of paper that came to hand, and scribbled the following lines:

O why have you treated me so monstrously, Angel! I do not deserve it. I have thought it all over carefully, and I can never, never forgive you! You know that I did not intend to wrong you—why have you so wronged me? You are cruel, cruel indeed! I will try to forget you. It is all injustice I have received at your hands! T.

She watched till the postman passed by, ran out to him with her epistle, and then again took her listless place inside the window-panes.

It was just as well to write like that as to write tenderly. How could he give way to entreaty? The facts had not changed: there was no new event to alter his opinion.

It grew darker, the fire-light shining over the room. The two biggest of the younger children had gone out with their mother; the four smallest, their ages ranging from three-and-a-half years to eleven, all in black frocks, were gathered round the hearth babbling their own little subjects. Tess at length joined them, without lighting a candle.

'This is the last night that we shall sleep here, dears, in the house where we were born,' she said quickly. 'We ought to think of it, oughtn't we?'

They all became silent; with the impressibility of their age they were ready to burst into tears at the picture of finality she had conjured up, though all the day hitherto they had been rejoicing in the idea of a new place. Tess changed the subject.

'Sing to me, dears,' she said.

'What shall we sing?'

'Anything you know; I don't mind.'

There was a momentary pause; it was broken, first, by one little tentative note; then a second voice strengthened it, and a third and a fourth chimed in in unison, with words they had learnt at the Sunday-school—

> Here we suffer grief and pain,
> Here we meet to part again;
> In Heaven we part no more.[3]

The four sang on with the phlegmatic passivity of persons who had long ago settled the question, and there being no mistake about it, felt that further thought was not required. With features strained hard to enunciate the syllables they continued to regard the centre of the flickering fire, the notes of the youngest straying over into the pauses of the rest.

Tess turned from them, and went to the window again. Darkness had now fallen without, but she put her face to the pane as though to peer into the gloom. It was really to hide her tears. If she could only believe what the children were singing; if she were only sure, how different all would now be; how confidently she would leave them to Providence and their future kingdom! But, in default of that, it behoved her to do something; to be their Providence; for to Tess, as to not a few millions of others, there was ghastly satire in the poet's lines—

> Not in utter nakedness
> But trailing clouds of glory do we come.[4]

3. This hymn, entitled *Joyful*, was first published in "The Infant School Teachers' Assistant" in 1832. [W]

4. Wordsworth, "Ode. Intimations of Immortality," lines 63-64.

To her and her like, birth itself was an ordeal of degrading personal compulsion, whose gratuitousness nothing in the result seemed to justify, and at best could only palliate.

In the shades of the wet road she soon discerned her mother with tall 'Liza-Lu and Abraham. Mrs. Durbeyfield's pattens clicked up to the door, and Tess opened it.

'I see the tracks of a horse outside the window,' said Joan. 'Hev somebody called?'

'No,' said Tess.

The children by the fire looked gravely at her, and one murmured—

'Why, Tess, the gentleman a-horseback!'

'He didn't call,' said Tess. 'He spoke to me in passing.'

'Who was the gentleman?' asked her mother. 'Your husband?'

'No. He'll never, never come,' answered Tess in stony hopelessness.

'Then who was it?'

'Oh, you needn't ask. You've seen him before, and so have I.'

'Ah! What did he say?' said Joan curiously.

'I will tell you when we are settled in our lodgings at Kingsbere to-morrow—every word.'

It was not her husband, she had said. Yet a consciousness that in a physical sense this man alone was her husband seemed to weigh on her more and more.

LII

During the small hours of the next morning, while it was still dark, dwellers near the highways were conscious of a disturbance of their night's rest by rumbling noises, intermittently continuing till daylight —noises as certain to recur in this particular first week of the month as the voice of the cuckoo in the third week of the same. They were the preliminaries of the general removal, the passing of the empty waggons and teams to fetch the goods of the migrating families; for it was always by the vehicle of the farmer who required his services that the hired man was conveyed to his destination. That this might be accomplished within the day was the explanation of the reverberation occurring so soon after midnight, the aim of the carters being to reach the door of the outgoing households by six o'clock, when the loading of their movables at once began.

But to Tess and her mother's household no such anxious farmer sent his team. They were only women; they were not regular labourers; they were not particularly required anywhere; hence they had to hire a waggon at their own expense, and got nothing sent gratuitously.

It was a relief to Tess, when she looked out of the window that morning, to find that though the weather was windy and louring, it did not rain, and that the waggon had come. A wet Lady-Day was a spectre which removing families never forgot; damp furniture, damp bedding, damp clothing accompanied it, and left a train of ills.

Her mother, 'Liza-Lu, and Abraham were also awake, but the younger children were let sleep on. The four breakfasted by the thin light, and the 'house-ridding' was taken in hand.

It proceeded with some cheerfulness, a friendly neighbour or two assisting. When the large articles of furniture had been packed in position a circular nest was made of the beds and bedding, in which Joan Durbeyfield and the young children were to sit through the journey. After loading there was a long delay before the horses were brought, these having been unharnessed during the ridding; but at length, about two o'clock, the whole was under way, the cooking-pot swinging from the axle of the waggon, Mrs. Durbeyfield and family at the top, the matron having in her lap, to prevent injury to its works, the head of the clock, which, at any exceptional lurch of the waggon, struck one, or one-and-a-half, in hurt tones. Tess and the next eldest girl walked alongside till they were out of the village.

They had called on a few neighbours that morning and the previous evening, and some came to see them off, all wishing them well, though, in their secret hearts, hardly expecting welfare possible to such a family, harmless as the Durbeyfields were to all except themselves. Soon the equipage began to ascend to higher ground, and the wind grew keener with the change of level and soil.

The day being the sixth of April, the Durbeyfield waggon met many other waggons with families on the summit of the load, which was built on a wellnigh unvarying principle, as peculiar, probably, to the rural labourer as the hexagon to the bee. The groundwork of the arrangement was the family dresser, which, with its shining handles, and finger-marks, and domestic evidences thick upon it, stood importantly in front, over the tails of the shaft-horses, in its erect and natural position, like some Ark of the Covenant[5] that they were bound to carry reverently.

Some of the households were lively, some mournful; some were stopping at the doors of wayside inns; where, in due time, the Durbeyfield menagerie also drew up to bait horses and refresh the travellers.

During the halt Tess's eyes fell upon a three-pint blue mug, which was ascending and descending through the air to and from the feminine section of a household, sitting on the summit of a load that had also drawn up at a little distance from the same inn. She followed one of the mug's journeys upward, and perceived it to be clasped by hands whose owner she well knew. Tess went towards the waggon.

'Marian and Izz!' she cried to the girls, for it was they, sitting with the moving family at whose house they had lodged. 'Are you house-ridding to-day, like everybody else?'

They were, they said. It had been too rough a life for them at Flintcomb-Ash, and they had come away, almost without notice, leaving Groby to prosecute them if he chose. They told Tess their destination, and Tess told them hers.

Marian leant over the load, and lowered her voice. 'Do you know that the gentleman who follows 'ee—you'll guess who I mean—came to ask for 'ee at Flintcomb after you had gone? We didn't tell'n where you was, knowing you wouldn't wish to see him.'

'Ah—but I did see him!' Tess murmured. 'He found me.'

'And do he know where you be going?'

'I think so.'

'Husband come back?'

'No.'

She bade her acquaintance good-bye—for the respective carters had now come out from the inn—and the two waggons resumed their journey in opposite directions; the vehicle whereon sat Marian, Izz, and the ploughman's family with whom they had thrown in their lot, being brightly painted, and drawn by three powerful horses with shining brass ornaments on their harness; while the waggon on which Mrs. Durbeyfield and her family rode was a creaking erection that would scarcely bear the weight of the superincumbent load; one which had known no paint since it was made, and drawn by two horses only. The contrast well marked the difference between being fetched by a thriving farmer and conveying oneself whither no hirer waited one's coming.

The distance was great—too great for a day's journey—and it was with the utmost difficulty that the horses performed it. Though they had started so early it was quite late in the afternoon when they turned the flank of an eminence which formed part of the upland called Greenhill. While the horses stood to stale and breathe themselves Tess looked around. Under the hill, and just ahead of them, was the half-dead townlet of their pilgrimage, Kingsbere, where lay those ancestors of whom her father had spoken and sung to painfulness: Kingsbere, the spot of all spots in the world which could be considered the d'Urbervilles' home, since they had resided there for full five hundred years.

A man could be seen advancing from the outskirts towards them, and when he beheld the nature of their waggon-load he quickened his steps.

'You be the woman they call Mrs. Durbeyfield, I reckon?' he said to Tess's mother, who had descended to walk the remainder of the way.

She nodded. 'Though widow of the late Sir John d'Urberville, poor nobleman, if I cared for my rights; and returning to the domain of his forefathers.'

'Oh? Well, I know nothing about that; but if you be Mrs. Durbeyfield, I am sent to tell 'ee that the rooms you wanted be let. We didn't know you was coming till we got your letter this morning—when 'twas too late. But no doubt you can get other lodgings somewhere.'

The man had noticed the face of Tess, which had become ash-pale at his intelligence. Her mother looked hopelessly at fault. 'What shall we do now, Tess?' she said bitterly. 'Here's a welcome to your ancestors' lands! However, let's try further.'

They moved on into the town, and tried with all their might, Tess remaining with the waggon to take care of the children whilst her mother and 'Liza-Lu made inquiries. At the last return of Joan to the vehicle, an hour later, when her search for accommodation had still been fruitless, the driver of the waggon said the goods must be unloaded, as the horses were half-dead, and he was bound to return part of the way at least that night.

'Very well—unload it here,' said Joan recklessly. 'I'll get shelter somewhere.'

The waggon had drawn up under the churchyard wall, in a spot screened from view, and the driver, nothing loth, soon hauled down the poor heap of household goods. This done she paid him, reducing herself to almost her last shilling thereby, and he moved off and left them, only too glad to get out of further dealings with such a family. It was a dry night, and he guessed that they would come to no harm.

Tess gazed desperately at the pile of furniture. The cold sunlight of this spring evening peered invidiously upon the crocks and kettles, upon the bunches of dried herbs shivering in the breeze, upon the brass handles of the dresser, upon the wicker-cradle they had all been rocked in, and upon the well-rubbed clock-case, all of which gave out the reproachful gleam of indoor articles abandoned to the vicissitudes of a roofless exposure for which they were never made. Round about were deparked[6] hills and slopes—now cut up into little paddocks—and the green foundations that showed where the d'Urberville mansion once had stood; also an outlying stretch of Egdon Heath that had always belonged to the estate. Hard by, the aisle of the church called the d'Urberville Aisle looked on imperturbably.

'Isn't your family vault your own freehold?' said Tess's mother, as she returned from a reconnoitre of the church and graveyard. 'Why of course 'tis, and that's where we will camp, girls, till the place of your ancestors finds us a roof! Now Tess and 'Liza and Abraham, you help me. We'll make a nest for these children, and then we'll have another look round.'

6. A park was "an enclosed tract of land held by royal grant or prescription for keeping beasts of the chase." [*OED*]

Tess listlessly lent a hand, and in a quarter of an hour the old four-post bedstead was dissociated from the heap of goods, and erected under the south wall of the church, the part of the building known as the d'Urberville Aisle, beneath which the huge vaults lay. Over the tester of the bedstead was a beautifully traceried window, of many lights, its date being the fifteenth century. It was called the d'Uberville Window, and in the upper part could be discerned heraldic emblems like those on Durbeyfield's old seal and spoon.

Joan drew the curtains round the bed so as to make an excellent tent of it, and put the smaller children inside. 'If it comes to the worst we can sleep there too, for one night,' she said. 'But let us try further on, and get something for the dears to eat! O, Tess, what's the use of your playing at marrying gentlemen, if it leaves us like this!'

Accompanied by 'Liza-Lu and the boy she again ascended the little lane which secluded the church from the townlet. As soon as they got into the street they beheld a man on horseback gazing up and down. 'Ah—I'm looking for you!' he said, riding up to them. 'This is indeed a family gathering on the historic spot!'

It was Alec d'Urberville. 'Where is Tess?' he asked.

Personally Joan had no liking for Alec. She cursorily signified the direction of the church, and went on, d'Urberville saying that he would see them again, in case they should be still unsuccessful in their search for shelter, of which he had just heard. When they had gone d'Urberville rode to the inn, and shortly after came out on foot.

In the interim Tess, left with the children inside the bedstead, remained talking with them awhile, till, seeing that no more could be done to make them comfortable just then, she walked about the churchyard, now beginning to be embrowned by the shades of nightfall. The door of the church was unfastened, and she entered it for the first time in her life.

Within the window under which the bedstead stood were the tombs of the family, covering in their dates several centuries. They were canopied, altar-shaped, and plain; their carvings being defaced and broken; their brasses torn from the matrices, the rivet-holes remaining like martin-holes in a sand-cliff. Of all the reminders that she had ever received that her people were socially extinct there was none so forcible as this spoliation.

She drew near to a dark stone on which was inscribed:

Ostium sepulchri antiquae familiae d'Urberville.[7]

Tess did not read Church-Latin like a Cardinal, but she knew that this was the door of her ancestral sepulchre, and that the tall knights of whom her father had chanted in his cups lay inside.

She musingly turned to withdraw, passing near an altar-tomb, the

7. Door of the tomb of the ancient family of d'Urberville.

oldest of them all, on which was a recumbent figure. In the dusk she had not noticed it before, and would hardly have noticed it now but for an odd fancy that the effigy moved. As soon as she drew close to it she discovered all in a moment that the figure was a living person; and the shock to her sense of not having been alone was so violent that she was quite overcome, and sank down nigh to fainting, not however till she had recognized Alec d'Urberville in the form.

He leapt off the slab and supported her.

'I saw you come in,' he said smiling, 'and got up there not to interrupt your meditations. A family gathering, is it not, with these old fellows under us here? Listen.'

He stamped with his heel heavily on the floor; whereupon there arose a hollow echo from below.

'That shook them a bit, I'll warrant!' he continued. 'And you thought I was the mere stone reproduction of one of them. But no. The old order changeth.[8] The little finger of the sham d'Urberville can do more for you than the whole dynasty of the real underneath. . . . Now command me. What shall I do?'

'Go away!' she murmured.

'I will—I'll look for your mother,' said he blandly. But in passing her he whispered: 'Mind this; you'll be civil yet!'

When he was gone she bent down upon the entrance to the vaults, and said—

'Why am I on the wrong side of this door!'

In the meantime Marian and Izz Huett had journeyed onward with the chattels of the ploughman in the direction of their land of Canaan —the Egypt of some other family who had left it only that morning. But the girls did not for a long time think of where they were going. Their talk was of Angel Clare and Tess, and Tess's persistent lover, whose connection with her previous history they had partly heard and partly guessed ere this.

' 'Tisn't as though she had never known him before,' said Marian. 'His having won her once makes all the difference in the world. 'Twould be a thousand pities if he were to tole[9] her away again. Mr. Clare can never be anything to us, Izz; and why should we grudge him to her, and not try to mend this quarrel? If he could on'y know what straits she's put to, and what's hovering round, he might come to take care of his own.'

'Could we let him know?'

They thought of this all the way to their destination; but the bustle of re-establishment in their new place took up all their attention then. But when they were settled, a month later, they heard of Clare's approaching return, though they had learnt nothing more of Tess. Upon

8. Tennyson's *Morte d'Arthur*, line 240.

9. To entice, allure, beguile.

that, agitated anew by their attachment to him, yet honourably disposed to her, Marian uncorked the penny ink-bottle they shared, and a few lines were concocted between the two girls.

> HONOUR'D SIR—Look to your Wife if you do love her as much as she do love you. For she is sore put to by an Enemy in the shape of a Friend. Sir, there is one near her who ought to be Away. A woman should not be try'd beyond her Strength, and continual dropping will wear away a Stone—ay, more—a Diamond.
>
> FROM TWO WELL-WISHERS.

This they addressed to Angel Clare at the only place they had ever heard him to be connected with, Emminster Vicarage; after which they continued in a mood of emotional exaltation at their own generosity, which made them sing in hysterical snatches and weep at the same time.

END OF PHASE THE SIXTH

Phase the Seventh—Fulfilment

LIII

It was evening at Emminster Vicarage. The two customary candles were burning under their green shades in the Vicar's study, but he had not been sitting there. Occasionally he came in, stirred the small fire which sufficed for the increasing mildness of the spring, and went out again; sometimes pausing at the front door, going on to the drawing-room, then returning again to the front door.

It faced westward, and though gloom prevailed inside, there was still light enough without to see with distinctness. Mrs. Clare, who had been sitting in the drawing-room, followed him hither.

'Plenty of time yet,' said the Vicar. 'He doesn't reach Chalk-Newton till six, even if the train should be punctual, and ten miles of country-road, five of them in Crimmercrock Lane, are not jogged over in a hurry by our old horse.'

'But he has done it in an hour with us, my dear.'

'Years ago.'

Thus they passed the minutes, each well knowing that this was only waste of breath, the one essential being simply to wait.

At length there was a slight noise in the lane, and the old pony-chaise appeared indeed outside the railings. They saw alight therefrom a form which they affected to recognize, but would actually have passed by in the street without identifying had he not got out of their carriage at the particular moment when a particular person was due.

Mrs. Clare rushed through the dark passage to the door, and her husband came more slowly after her.

The new arrival, who was just about to enter, saw their anxious faces in the doorway and the gleam of the west in their spectacles because they confronted the last rays of day; but they could only see his shape against the light.

'O, my boy, my boy—home again at last!' cried Mrs. Clare, who cared no more at that moment for the stains of heterodoxy which had caused all this separation than for the dust upon his clothes. What woman, indeed, among the most faithful adherents of the truth, believes the promises and threats of the Word in the sense in which she believes in her own children, or would not throw her theology to the wind if weighed against their happiness? As soon as they reached the room where the candles were lighted she looked at his face.

'O, it is not Angel—not my son—the Angel who went away!' she cried in all the irony of sorrow, as she turned herself aside.

His father, too, was shocked to see him, so reduced was that figure from its former contours by worry and the bad season that Clare had experienced, in the climate to which he had so rashly hurried in his first aversion to the mockery of events at·home. You could see the skeleton behind the man, and almost the ghost behind the skeleton. He matched Crivelli's dead *Christus*.[1] His sunken eye-pits were of morbid hue, and the light in his eyes had waned. The angular hollows and lines of his aged ancestors had succeeded to their reign in his face twenty years before their time.

'I was ill over there, you know,' he said. 'I am all right now.'

As if, however, to falsify this assertion, his legs seemed to give way, and he suddenly sat down to save himself from falling. It was only a slight attack of faintness, resulting from the tedious day's journey, and the excitement of arrival.

'Has any letter come for me lately?' he asked. 'I received the last you sent on by the merest chance, and after considerable delay through being inland; or I might have come sooner.'

'It was from your wife, we supposed?'

'It was.'

Only one other had recently come. They had not sent it on to him, knowing he would start for home so soon.

He hastily opened the letter produced, and was much disturbed to read in Tess's handwriting the sentiments expressed in her last hurried scrawl to him.

O why have you treated me so monstrously, Angel! I do not deserve it. I have thought it all over carefully, and I can never, never forgive you! You know that I did not intend to wrong you—why

---

1. A "Pieta" by the fifteenth century Venetian painter Carlo Crivelli is in the National Gallery in London.

have you so wronged me? You are cruel, cruel indeed! I will try to forget you. It is all injustice I have received at your hands.   T.

'It is quite true!' said Angel, throwing down the letter. 'Perhaps she will never be reconciled to me!'

'Don't, Angel, be so anxious about a mere child of the soil!' said his mother.

'Child of the soil! Well, we all are children of the soil. I wish she were so in the sense you mean; but let me now explain to you what I have never explained before, that her father is a descendant in the male line of one of the oldest Norman houses, like a good many others who lead obscure agricultural lives in our villages, and are dubbed "sons of the soil." '

He soon retired to bed; and the next morning, feeling exceedingly unwell, he remained in his room pondering. The circumstances amid which he had left Tess were such that though, while on the south of the Equator and just in receipt of her loving epistle, it had seemed the easiest thing in the world to rush back into her arms the moment he chose to forgive her, now that he had arrived it was not so easy as it had seemed. She was passionate, and her present letter, showing that her estimate of him had changed under his delay—too justly changed, he sadly owned,—made him ask himself if it would be wise to confront her unannounced in the presence of her parents. Supposing that her love had indeed turned to dislike during the last weeks of separation, a sudden meeting might lead to bitter words.

Clare therefore thought it would be best to prepare Tess and her family by sending a line to Marlott announcing his return, and his hope that she was still living with them there, as he had arranged for her to do when he left England. He despatched the inquiry that very day, and before the week was out there came a short reply from Mrs. Durbeyfield which did not remove his embarrassment, for it bore no address, though to his surprise it was not written from Marlott.

Sɪʀ—J write these few lines to say that my Daughter is away from me at present, and J am not sure when she will return, but J will let you know as Soon as she do. J do not feel at liberty to tell you Where she is temperly biding. J should say that me and my Family have left Marlott for some Time.—Yours,

J. Durbeyfield.

It was such a relief to Clare to learn that Tess was at least apparently well that her mother's stiff reticence as to her whereabouts did not long distress him. They were all angry with him, evidently. He would wait till Mrs. Durbeyfield could inform him of Tess's return, which her letter implied to be soon. He deserved no more. His had been a love 'which alters when it alteration finds.'[2] He had

2. Shakespeare, Sonnet 116.

undergone some strange experiences in his absence; he had seen the virtual Faustina in the literal Cornelia, a spiritual Lucretia in a corporeal Phryne;[3] he had thought of the woman taken and set in the midst as one deserving to be stoned, and of the wife of Uriah being made a queen;[4] and he had asked himself why he had not judged Tess constructively rather than biographically, by the will rather than by the deed?

A day or two passed while he waited at his father's house for the promised second note from Joan Durbeyfield, and indirectly to recover a little more strength. The strength showed signs of coming back, but there was no sign of Joan's letter. Then he hunted up the old letter sent on to him in Brazil, which Tess had written from Flintcomb-Ash, and re-read it. The sentences touched him now as much as when he had first perused them.

> I must cry to you in my trouble—I have no one else. . . . I think I must die if you do not come soon, or tell me to come to you. . . . Please, please not to be just; only a little kind to me! . . . If you would come I could die in your arms! I would be well content to do that if so be you had forgiven me! . . . If you will send me one little line and say, *I am coming soon,* I will bide on, Angel, O so cheerfully! . . . Think how it do hurt my heart not to see you ever, ever! Ah, if I could only make your dear heart ache one little minute of each day as mine does every day and all day long, it might lead you to show pity to your poor lonely one. . . . I would be content, ay, glad, to live with you as your servant, if I may not as your wife; so that I could only be near you, and get glimpses of you, and think of you as mine. . . . I long for only one thing in heaven, or earth, or under the earth, to meet you, my own dear! Come to me, come to me, and save me from what threatens me.

Clare determined that he would no longer believe in her more recent and severer regard of him; but would go and find her immediately. He asked his father if she had applied for any money during his absence. His father returned a negative, and then for the first time it occurred to Angel that her pride had stood in her way, and that she had suffered privation. From his remarks his parents now gathered the real reason of the separation; and their Christianity was such that, reprobates being their especial care, the tenderness

3. Faustina, wife of Roman emperor Antonius, was famous for her debaucheries, and her beautiful, witty daughter, of the same name, wife of Marcus Aurelius, was "the most abandoned of her sex." Cornelia, wife of Pompey, was the Roman ideal of motherhood. Lucretia (Lucrece), famous for her chastity, killed herself after she was raped. Phryne was a celebrated Athen-ian prostitute and artists' (Praxiteles' and Apelles') model.
4. John viii:3-7: "And the scribes and Pharisees brought unto him a woman taken in adultery. * * * [Christ] said unto them, He that is without sin among you, let him first cast a stone at her." "The wife of Uriah": Bathsheba, whom King David made his wife after arranging Uriah's death.

towards Tess which her blood, her simplicity, even her poverty, had not engendered, was instantly excited by her sin.

Whilst he was hastily packing together a few articles for his journey he glanced over a poor plain missive also lately come to hand—the one from Marian and Izz Huett, beginning—

'HONOUR'D SIR—Look to your wife if you do love her as much as she do you,' and signed, 'FROM TWO WELL-WISHERS.'

LIV

In a quarter of an hour Clare was leaving the house, whence his mother watched his thin figure as it disappeared into the street. He had declined to borrow his father's old mare, well knowing of its necessity to the household. He went to the inn, where he hired a trap, and could hardly wait during the harnessing. In a very few minutes after he was driving up the hill out of the town which, three or four months earlier in the year, Tess had descended with such hopes and ascended with such shattered purposes.

Benvill Lane soon stretched before him, its hedges and trees purple with buds; but he was looking at other things, and only recalled himself to the scene sufficiently to enable him to keep the way. In something less than an hour-and-a-half he had skirted the south of the King's Hintock estates and ascended to the untoward solitude of Cross-in-Hand, the unholy stone whereon Tess had been compelled by Alec d'Urberville, in his whim of reformation, to swear the strange oath that she would never wilfully tempt him again. The pale and blasted nettle-stems of the preceding year even now lingered nakedly in the banks, young green nettles of the present spring growing from their roots.

Thence he went along the verge of the upland overhanging the other Hintocks, and, turning to the right, plunged into the bracing calcareous region of Flintcomb-Ash, the address from which she had written to him in one of the letters, and which he supposed to be the place of sojourn referred to by her mother. Here, of course, he did not find her; and what added to his depression was the discovery that no 'Mrs. Clare' had ever been heard of by the cottagers or by the farmer himself, though Tess was remembered well enough by her Christian name. His name she had obviously never used during their separation, and her dignified sense of their total severance was shown not much less by this abstention than by the hardships she had chosen to undergo (of which he now learnt for the first time) rather than apply to his father for more funds.

From this place they told him Tess Durbeyfield had gone, without due notice, to the home of her parents on the other side of Black-moor, and it therefore became necessary to find Mrs. Durbeyfield. She had told him she was not now at Marlott, but had been curiously reticent as to her actual address, and the only course was to go to Marlott and inquire for it. The farmer who had been so churlish with Tess was quite smooth-tongued to Clare, and lent him a horse and man to drive him towards Marlott, the gig he had arrived in being sent back to Emminster; for the limit of a day's journey with that horse was reached.

Clare would not accept the loan of the farmer's vehicle for a further distance than to the outskirts of the Vale, and, sending it back with the man who had driven him, he put up at an inn, and next day entered on foot the region wherein was the spot of his dear Tess's birth. It was as yet too early in the year for much colour to appear in the gardens and foliage; the so-called spring was but winter overlaid with a thin coat of greenness, and it was of a parcel with his expectations.

The house in which Tess had passed the years of her childhood was now inhabited by another family who had never known her. The new residents were in the garden, taking as much interest in their own doings as if the homestead had never passed its primal time in con-junction with the histories of others, beside which the histories of these were but as a tale told by an idiot.[5] They walked about the garden paths with thoughts of their own concerns entirely uppermost, bringing their actions at every moment into jarring collision with the dim ghosts behind them, talking as though the time when Tess lived there were not one whit intenser in story than now. Even the spring birds sang over their heads as if they thought there was nobody miss-ing in particular.

On inquiry of these precious innocents, to whom even the name of their predecessors was a failing memory, Clare learned that John Dur-beyfield was dead; that his widow and children had left Marlott, de-claring that they were going to live at Kingsbere, but instead of doing so had gone on to another place they mentioned. By this time Clare abhorred the house for ceasing to contain Tess, and hastened away from its hated presence without once looking back.

His way was by the field in which he had first beheld her at the dance. It was as bad as the house—even worse. He passed on through the churchyard, where, amongst the new headstones, he saw one of a somewhat superior design to the rest. The inscription ran thus:

> In memory of John Durbeyfield, rightly d'Urberville, of the once powerful family of that Name, and Direct Descendant through an

Illustrious Line from Sir Pagan d'Urberville, one of the Knights of the Conqueror. Died March 10th, 18——

HOW ARE THE MIGHTY FALLEN.[6]

Some man, apparently the sexton, had observed Clare standing there, and drew nigh. 'Ah, sir, now that's a man who didn't want to lie here, but wished to be carried to Kingsbere, where his ancestors be.'

'And why didn't they respect his wish?'

'Oh—no money. Bless your soul, sir, why—there, I wouldn't wish to say it everywhere, but—even this headstone, for all the flourish wrote upon en, is not paid for.'

'Ah, who put it up?'

The man told the name of a mason in the village, and, on leaving the churchyard, Clare called at the mason's house. He found that the statement was true, and paid the bill. This done he turned in the direction of the migrants.

The distance was too long for a walk, but Clare felt such a strong desire for isolation that at first he would neither hire a conveyance nor go to a circuitous line of railway by which he might eventually reach the place. At Shaston, however, he found he must hire; but the way was such that he did not enter Joan's place till about seven o'clock in the evening, having traversed a distance of over twenty miles since leaving Marlott.

The village being small he had little difficulty in finding Mrs. Durbeyfield's tenement, which was a house in a walled garden, remote from the main road, where she had stowed away her clumsy old furniture as best she could. It was plain that for some reason or other she had not wished him to visit her, and he felt his call to be somewhat of an intrusion. She came to the door herself, and the light from the evening sky fell upon her face.

This was the first time that Clare had ever met her, but he was too preoccupied to observe more than that she was still a handsome woman, in the garb of a respectable widow. He was obliged to explain that he was Tess's husband, and his object in coming there, and he did it awkwardly enough. 'I want to see her at once,' he added. 'You said you would write to me again, but you have not done so.'

'Because she've not come home,' said Joan.

'Do you know if she is well?'

'I don't. But you ought to, sir,' said she.

'I admit it. Where is she staying?'

From the beginning of the interview Joan had disclosed her embarrassment by keeping her hand to the side of her cheek.

'I—don't know exactly where she is staying,' she answered. 'She was—but——'

6. II Samuel i:19.

'Where was she?'

'Well, she is not there now.'

In her evasiveness she paused again, and the younger children had by this time crept to the door, where, pulling at his mother's skirts, the youngest murmured—

'Is this the gentleman who is going to marry Tess?'

'He has married her,' Joan whispered. 'Go inside.'

Clare saw her efforts for reticence, and asked—

'Do you think Tess would wish me to try and find her? If not, of course——'

'I don't think she would.'

'Are you sure?'

'I am sure she wouldn't.'

He was turning away; and then he thought of Tess's tender letter.

'I am sure she would!' he retorted passionately. 'I know her better than you do.'

'That's very likely, sir; for I have never really known her.'

'Please tell me her address, Mrs. Durbeyfield, in kindness to a lonely wretched man!'

Tess's mother again restlessly swept her cheek with her vertical hand, and seeing that he suffered, she at last said, in a low voice—

'She is at Sandbourne.'

'Ah—where there? Sandbourne has become a large place, they say.'

'I don't know more particularly than I have said—Sandbourne. For myself, I was never there.'

It was apparent that Joan spoke the truth in this, and he pressed her no further.

'Are you in want of anything?' he said gently.

'No, sir,' she replied. 'We are fairly well provided for.'

Without entering the house Clare turned away. There was a station three miles ahead, and paying off his coachman, he walked thither. The last train to Sandbourne left shortly after, and it bore Clare on its wheels.

LV

At eleven o'clock that night, having secured a bed at one of the hotels and telegraphed his address to his father immediately on his arrival, he walked out into the streets of Sandbourne. It was too late to call on or inquire for any one, and he reluctantly postponed his purpose till the morning. But he could not retire to rest just yet.

This fashionable watering-place, with its eastern and its western stations, its piers, its groves of pines, its promenades, and its covered gardens, was, to Angel Clare, like a fairy place suddenly created by the stroke of a wand, and allowed to get a little dusty.

An outlying eastern tract of the enormous Egdon Waste was close
at hand, yet on the very verge of that tawny piece of antiquity such
a glittering novelty as this pleasure city had chosen to spring up.
Within the space of a mile from its outskirts every irregularity of the
soil was prehistoric, every channel an undisturbed British trackway;
not a sod having been turned there since the days of the Caesars.
Yet the exotic had grown here, suddenly as the prophet's gourd;[7] and
had drawn hither Tess.

By the midnight lamps he went up and down the winding ways
of this new world in an old one, and could discern between the
trees and against the stars the lofty roofs, chimneys, gazebos, and
towers of the numerous fanciful residences of which the place was
composed. It was a city of detached mansions; a Mediterranean
lounging-place on the English Channel; and as seen now by night
it seemed even more imposing than it was.

The sea was near at hand, but not intrusive: it murmured, and he
thought it was the pines; the pines murmured in precisely the same
tones, and he thought they were the sea.

Where could Tess possibly be, a cottage-girl, his young wife,
amidst all this wealth and fashion? The more he pondered the
more was he puzzled. Were there any cows to milk here? There
certainly were no fields to till. She was most probably engaged to
do something in one of these large houses; and he sauntered
along, looking at the chamber-windows and their lights going out
one by one; and wondered which of them might be hers.

Conjecture was useless, and just after twelve o'clock he entered
and went to bed. Before putting out his light he re-read Tess's impassioned letter. Sleep, however, he could not,—so near her, yet so
far from her—and he continually lifted the window-blind and regarded the backs of the opposite houses, and wondered behind
which of the sashes she reposed at that moment.

He might almost as well have sat up all night. In the morning
he arose at seven, and shortly after went out, taking the direction
of the chief post-office. At the door he met an intelligent postman
coming out with letters for the morning delivery.

'Do you know the address of a Mrs. Clare?' asked Angel.

The postman shook his head.

Then, remembering that she would have been likely to continue
the use of her maiden name, Clare said—

'Or a Miss Durbeyfield?'

'Durbeyfield?'

This also was strange to the postman addressed.

7. Jonah iv:6: "And the Lord God prepared a gourd, and made it to come up
over Jonah, that it might be a shadow
over his head, to deliver him from his
grief."

'There's visitors coming and going every day, as you know, sir,' he said; 'and without the name of the house 'tis impossible to find 'em.'

One of his comrades hastening out at that moment, the name was repeated to him.

'I know no name of Durbeyfield; but there is the name of d'Urberville at The Herons,' said the second.

'That's it!' cried Clare, pleased to think that she had reverted to the real pronunciation. 'What place is The Herons?'

'A stylish lodging-house. 'Tis all lodging-houses here, bless 'ee.'

Clare received directions how to find the house, and hastened thither, arriving with the milkman. The Herons, though an ordinary villa, stood in its own grounds, and was certainly the last place in which one would have expected to find lodgings, so private was its appearance. If poor Tess was a servant here, as he feared, she would go to the back-door to that milkman, and he was inclined to go thither also. However, in his doubts he turned to the front, and rang.

The hour being early the landlady herself opened the door. Clare inquired for Teresa d'Urberville or Durbeyfield.

'Mrs. d'Urberville?'

'Yes.'

Tess, then, passed as a married woman, and he felt glad, even though she had not adopted his name.

'Will you kindly tell her that a relative is anxious to see her?'

'It is rather early. What name shall I give, sir?'

'Angel.'

'Mr. Angel?'

'No; Angel. It is my Christian name. She'll understand.'

'I'll see if she is awake.'

He was shown into the front room—the dining-room—and looked out through the spring curtains at the little lawn, and the rhododendrons and other shrubs upon it. Obviously her position was by no means so bad as he had feared, and it crossed his mind that she must somehow have claimed and sold the jewels to attain it. He did not blame her for one moment. Soon his sharpened ear detected footsteps upon the stairs, at which his heart thumped so painfully that he could hardly stand firm. 'Dear me! what will she think of me, so altered as I am!' he said to himself; and the door opened.

Tess appeared on the threshold—not at all as he had expected to see her—bewilderingly otherwise, indeed. Her great natural beauty was, if not heightened, rendered more obvious by her attire. She was loosely wrapped in a cashmere dressing-gown of gray-white, embroidered in half-mourning tints, and she wore slippers of the same hue. Her neck rose out of a frill of down, and her well-remembered cable of dark-brown hair was partially coiled up in a mass at the back of her head and partly hanging on her shoulder—the evident result of haste.

He had held out his arms, but they had fallen again to his side; for she had not come forward, remaining still in the opening of the doorway. Mere yellow skeleton that he was now he felt the contrast between them, and thought his appearance distasteful to her.

'Tess!' he said huskily, 'can you forgive me for going away? Can't you—come to me? How do you get to be—like this?'

'It is too late,' said she, her voice sounding hard through the room, her eyes shining unnaturally.

'I did not think rightly of you—I did not see you as you were!' he continued to plead. 'I have learnt to since, dearest Tessy mine!'

'Too late, too late!' she said, waving her hand in the impatience of a person whose tortures cause every instant to seem an hour. 'Don't come close to me, Angel! No—you must not. Keep away.'

'But don't you love me, my dear wife, because I have been so pulled down by illness? You are not so fickle—I am come on purpose for you—my mother and father will welcome you now!'

'Yes—O, yes, yes! But I say, I say it is too late.'

She seemed to feel like a fugitive in a dream, who tries to move away, but cannot. 'Don't you know all—don't you know it? Yet how do you come here if you do not know?'

'I inquired here and there, and I found the way.'

'I waited and waited for you,' she went on, her tones suddenly resuming their old fluty pathos. 'But you did not come! And I wrote to you, and you did not come! He kept on saying you would never come any more, and that I was a foolish woman. He was very kind to me, and to mother, and to all of us after father's death. He——'[8]

'I don't understand.'

'He has won me back to him.'

Clare looked at her keenly, then, gathering her meaning, flagged like one plague-stricken, and his glance sank; it fell on her hands, which, once rosy, were now white and more delicate.

She continued—

'He is upstairs. I hate him now, because he told me a lie—that you would not come again; and you *have* come! These clothes are what he's put upon me: I didn't care what he did wi' me! But—will you go away, Angel, please, and never come any more?'

8. In the edition of 1892 this read, "He bought me." [W]

They stood fixed, their baffled hearts looking out of their eyes with a joylessness pitful to see. Both seemed to implore something to shelter them from reality.

'Ah—it is my fault!' said Clare.

But he could not get on. Speech was as inexpressive as silence. But he had a vague consciousness of one thing, though it was not clear to him till later; that his original Tess had spiritually ceased to recognize the body before him as hers—allowing it to drift, like a corpse upon the current, in a direction dissociated from its living will.

A few instants passed, and he found that Tess was gone. His face grew colder and more shrunken as he stood concentrated on the moment, and a minute or two after he found himself in the street, walking along he did not know whither.

LVI

Mrs. Brooks, the lady who was the householder at The Herons, and owner of all the handsome furniture, was not a person of an unusually curious turn of mind. She was too deeply materialized, poor woman, by her long and enforced bondage to that arithmetical demon Profit-and-Loss, to retain much curiosity for its own sake, and apart from possible lodgers' pockets. Nevertheless, the visit of Angel Clare to her well-paying tenants, Mr. and Mrs. d'Urberville, as she deemed them, was sufficiently exceptional in point of time and manner to reinvigorate the feminine proclivity which had been stifled down as useless save in its bearings on the letting trade.

Tess had spoken to her husband from the doorway, without entering the dining-room, and Mrs. Brooks, who stood within the partly-closed door of her own sitting-room at the back of the passage, could hear fragments of the conversation—if conversation it could be called—between those two wretched souls. She heard Tess re-ascend the stairs to the first floor, and the departure of Clare, and the closing of the front door behind him. Then the door of the room above was shut, and Mrs. Brooks knew that Tess had re-entered her apartment. As the young lady was not fully dressed Mrs. Brooks knew that she would not emerge again for some time.

She accordingly ascended the stairs softly, and stood at the door of the front room—a drawing-room, connected with the room immediately behind it (which was a bedroom) by folding-doors in the common manner. This first floor, containing Mrs. Brooks's best apartments, had been taken by the week by the d'Urbervilles. The back room was now in silence; but from the drawing-room there came sounds.

All that she could at first distinguish of them was one syllable, continually repeated in a low note of moaning, as if it came from a soul bound to some Ixionian wheel—

'O—O—O!'

Then a silence, then a heavy sigh, and again—

'O—O—O!'

The landlady looked through the keyhole. Only a small space of the room inside was visible, but within that space came a corner of the breakfast table, which was already spread for the meal, and also a chair beside. Over the seat of the chair Tess's face was bowed, her posture being a kneeling one in front of it; her hands were clasped over her head, the skirts of her dressing-gown and the embroidery of her night-gown flowed upon the floor behind her, and her stockingless feet, from which the slippers had fallen, protruded upon the carpet. It was from her lips that came the murmur of unspeakable despair.

Then a man's voice from the adjoining bedroom—

'What's the matter?'

She did not answer, but went on, in a tone which was a soliloquy rather than an exclamation, and a dirge rather than a soliloquy. Mrs. Brooks could only catch a portion:

'And then my dear, dear husband came home to me . . . and I did not know it! . . . And you had used your cruel persuasion upon me . . . you did not stop using it—no—you did not stop! My little sisters and brothers and my mother's needs—they were the things you moved me by . . . and you said my husband would never come back—never; and you taunted me, and said what a simpleton I was to expect him!. . . And at last I believed you and gave way! . . . And then he came back! Now he is gone. Gone a second time, and I have lost him now for ever . . . and he will not love me the littlest bit ever any more— only hate me! . . . O yes, I have lost him now—again because of—you!'

In writhing, with her head on the chair, she turned her face towards the door, and Mrs. Brooks could see the pain upon it; and that her lips were bleeding from the clench of her teeth upon them, and that the long lashes of her closed eyes stuck in wet tags to her cheeks. She continued: 'And he is dying—he looks as if he is dying! . . . And my sin will kill him and not kill me! . . . O, you have torn my life all to pieces . . . made me be what I prayed you in pity not to make me be again! . . . My own true husband will never, never—O God—I can't bear this! —I cannot!'

There were more and sharper words from the man; then a sudden rustle; she had sprung to her feet. Mrs. Brooks, thinking that the speaker was coming to rush out of the door, hastily retreated down the stairs.

She need not have done so, however, for the door of the sitting-room was not opened. But Mrs. Brooks felt it unsafe to watch on the landing again, and entered her own parlour below.

She could hear nothing through the floor, although she listened intently, and thereupon went to the kitchen to finish her interrupted breakfast. Coming up presently to the front room on the ground floor she took up some sewing, waiting for her lodgers to ring that she might take away the breakfast, which she meant to do herself, to discover what was the matter if possible. Overhead, as she sat, she could now hear the floor-boards slightly creak, as if some one were walking about, and presently the movement was explained by the rustle of garments against the banisters, the opening and the closing of the front door, and the form of Tess passing to the gate on her way in to the street. She was fully dressed now in the walking costume of a well-to-do young lady in which she had arrived, with the sole addition that over her hat and black feathers a veil was drawn.

Mrs. Brooks had not been able to catch any word of farewell, temporary or otherwise, between her tenants at the door above. They might have quarrelled, or Mr. d'Urberville might still be asleep, for he was not an early riser.

She went into the back room which was more especially her own apartment, and continued her sewing there. The lady lodger did not return, nor did the gentleman ring his bell. Mrs. Brooks pondered on the delay, and on what probable relation the visitor who had called so early bore to the couple upstairs. In reflecting she leant back in her chair.

As she did so her eyes glanced casually over the ceiling till they were arrested by a spot in the middle of its white surface which she had never noticed there before. It was about the size of a wafer when she first observed it, but it speedily grew as large as the palm of her hand, and then she could perceive that it was red. The oblong white ceiling, with this scarlet blot in the midst, had the appearance of a gigantic ace of hearts.

Mrs. Brooks had strange qualms of misgiving. She got upon the table, and touched the spot in the ceiling with her fingers. It was damp, and she fancied that it was a blood stain.

Descending from the table, she left the parlour, and went upstairs, intending to enter the room overhead, which was the bedchamber at the back of the drawing-room. But, nerveless woman as she had now become, she could not bring herself to attempt the handle. She listened. The dead silence within was broken only by a regular beat.

Drip, drip, drip.

Mrs. Brooks hastened downstairs, opened the front door, and ran into the street. A man she knew, one of the workmen employed at an adjoining villa, was passing by, and she begged him to come in and go upstairs with her; she feared something had happened to one of her lodgers. The workman assented, and followed her to the landing.

She opened the door of the drawing-room, and stood back for him to pass in, entering herself behind him. The room was empty; the breakfast—a substantial repast of coffee, eggs, and a cold ham—lay spread upon the table untouched, as when she had taken it up, excepting that the carving knife was missing. She asked the man to go through the folding-doors into the adjoining room.

He opened the doors, entered a step or two, and came back almost instantly with a rigid face. 'My good God, the gentleman in bed is dead! I think he has been hurt with a knife—a lot of blood has run down upon the floor!'

The alarm was soon given, and the house which had lately been so quiet resounded with the tramp of many footsteps, a surgeon among the rest. The wound was small, but the point of the blade had touched the heart of the victim, who lay on his back, pale, fixed, dead, as if he had scarcely moved after the infliction of the blow. In a quarter of an hour the news that a gentleman who was a temporary visitor to the town had been stabbed in his bed, spread through every street and villa of the popular watering-place.

LVII

Meanwhile Angel Clare had walked automatically along the way by which he had come, and, entering his hotel, sat down over the breakfast, staring at nothingness. He went on eating and drinking unconsciously till on a sudden he demanded his bill; having paid which he took his dressing-bag in his hand, the only luggage he had brought with him, and went out.

At the moment of his departure a telegram was handed to him—a few words from his mother, stating that they were glad to know his address, and informing him that his brother Cuthbert had proposed to and been accepted by Mercy Chant.

Clare crumpled up the paper, and followed the route to the station; reaching it, he found that there would be no train leaving for an hour and more. He sat down to wait, and having waited a quarter of an hour felt that he could wait there no longer. Broken in heart and numbed, he had nothing to hurry for; but he wished to get out of a town which had been the scene of such an experience, and turned to walk to the first station onward, and let the train pick him up there.

The highway that he followed was open, and at a little distance dipped into a valley, across which it could be seen running from edge to edge. He had traversed the greater part of this depression, and was climbing the western acclivity, when, pausing for breath, he unconsciously looked back. Why he did so he could not say, but something seemed to impel him to the act. The tape-like surface of the road diminished in his rear as far as he could see, and as he gazed a moving spot intruded on the white vacuity of its perspective.

It was a human figure running. Clare waited, with a dim sense that somebody was trying to overtake him.

The form descending the incline was a woman's, yet so entirely was his mind blinded to the idea of his wife's following him that even when she came nearer he did not recognize her under the totally changed attire in which he now beheld her. It was not till she was quite close that he could believe her to be Tess.

'I saw you—turn away from the station—just before I got there—and I have been following you all this way!'

She was so pale, so breathless, so quivering in every muscle, that he did not ask her a single question, but seizing her hand, and pulling it within his arm, he led her along. To avoid meeting any possible wayfarers he left the high road, and took a footpath under some fir-trees. When they were deep among the moaning boughs he stopped and looked at her inquiringly.

'Angel,' she said, as if waiting for this, 'do you know what I have been running after you for? To tell you that I have killed him!' A pitiful white smile lit her face as she spoke.

'What!' said he, thinking from the strangeness of her manner that she was in some delirium.

'I have done it—I don't know how,' she continued. 'Still, I owed it to you, and to myself, Angel. I feared long ago, when I struck him on the mouth with my glove, that I might do it some day for the trap he set for me in my simple youth, and his wrong to you through me. He has come between us and ruined us, and now he can never do it any more. I never loved him at all, Angel, as I loved you. You know it, don't you? You believe it? You didn't come back to me, and I was obliged to go back to him. Why did you go away—why did you—when I loved you so? I can't think why you did it. But I don't blame you; only, Angel, will you forgive me my sin against you, now I have killed him? I thought as I ran along that you would be sure to forgive me now I have done that. It came to me as a shining light that I should get you back that way. I could not bear the loss of you any longer—you don't know how entirely I was unable to bear your not loving me! Say you do now, dear, dear husband; say you do, now I have killed him!'

'I do love you, Tess—O, I do—it is all come back!' he said, tightening his arms round her with fervid pressure. 'But how do you mean—you have killed him?'

'I mean that I have,' she murmured in a reverie.

'What, bodily? Is he dead?'

'Yes. He heard me crying about you, and he bitterly taunted me; and called you by a foul name; and then I did it. My heart could not bear it. He had nagged me about you before. And then I dressed myself and came away to find you.'

By degrees he was inclined to believe that she had faintly attempted, at least, what she said she had done; and his horror at her impulse was mixed with amazement at the strength of her affection for himself, and at the strangeness of its quality, which had apparently extinguished her moral sense altogether. Unable to realize the gravity of her conduct she seemed at last content; and he looked at her as she lay upon his shoulder, weeping with happiness, and wondered what obscure strain in the d'Urberville blood had led to this aberration—if it were an aberration. There momentarily flashed through his mind that the family tradition of the coach and murder might have arisen because the d'Urbervilles had been known to do these things. As well as his confused and excited ideas could reason, he supposed that in the moment of mad grief of which she spoke her mind had lost its balance, and plunged her into this abyss.

It was very terrible if true; if a temporary hallucination, sad. But, anyhow, here was this deserted wife of his, this passionately-fond woman, clinging to him without a suspicion that he would be anything to her but a protector. He saw that for him to be otherwise was not, in her mind, within the region of the possible. Tenderness was absolutely dominant in Clare at last. He kissed her endlessly with his white lips, and held her hand, and said—

'I will not desert you! I will protect you by every means in my power, dearest love, whatever you may have done or not have done!'

They then walked on under the trees, Tess turning her head every now and then to look at him. Worn and unhandsome as he had become, it was plain that she did not discern the least fault in his appearance. To her he was, as of old, all that was perfection, personally and mentally. He was still her Antinous,[9] her Apollo even; his sickly face was beautiful as the morning to her affectionate regard on this day no less than when she first beheld him; for was it not the face of the one man on earth who had loved her purely, and who had believed in her as pure.

With an instinct as to possibilities he did not now, as he had

9. One of Emperor Hadrian's slaves, famous for his beauty.

intended, make for the first station beyond the town, but plunged still farther under the firs, which here abounded for miles. Each clasping the other round the waist they promenaded over the dry bed of fir-needles, thrown into a vague intoxicating atmosphere at the consciousness of being together at last, with no living soul between them; ignoring that there was a corpse. Thus they proceeded for several miles till Tess, arousing herself, looked about her, and said, timidly—

'Are we going anywhere in particular?'

'I don't know, dearest. Why?'

'I don't know.'

'Well, we might walk a few miles further, and when it is evening find lodgings somewhere or other—in a lonely cottage, perhaps. Can you walk well, Tessy?'

'O yes! I could walk for ever and ever with your arm round me!'

Upon the whole it seemed a good thing to do. Thereupon they quickened their pace, avoiding high roads, and following obscure paths tending more or less northward. But there was an unpractical vagueness in their movements throughout the day; neither one of them seemed to consider any question of effectual escape, disguise, or long concealment. Their every idea was temporary and unforefending, like the plans of two children.

At mid-day they drew near to a roadside inn, and Tess would have entered it with him to get something to eat, but he persuaded her to remain among the trees and bushes of this half-woodland, half-moorland part of the country, till he should come back. Her clothes were of recent fashion; even the ivory-handled parasol that she carried was of a shape unknown in the retired spot to which they had now wandered; and the cut of such articles would have attracted attention in the settle of a tavern. He soon returned, with food enough for half-a-dozen people and two bottles of wine —enough to last them for a day or more, should any emergency arise.

They sat down upon some dead boughs and shared their meal. Between one and two o'clock they packed up the remainder and went on again.

'I feel strong enough to walk any distance,' said she.

'I think we may as well steer in a general way towards the interior of the country, where we can hide for a time, and are less likely to be looked for than anywhere near the coast,' Clare remarked. 'Later on, when they have forgotten us, we can make for some port.'

She made no reply to this beyond that of grasping him more tightly, and straight inland they went. Though the season was an English May the weather was serenely bright, and during the afternoon it was quite warm. Through the latter miles of their walk their footpath had taken them into the depths of the New Forest, and towards evening, turning the corner of a lane, they perceived behind a brook and bridge a large board on which was painted in white letters, 'This desirable Mansion to be Let Furnished;' particulars following, with directions to apply to some London agents. Passing through the gate they could see the house, an old brick building of regular design and large accommodation.

'I know it,' said Clare. 'It is Bramshurst Court. You can see that it is shut up, and grass is growing on the drive.'

'Some of the windows are open,' said Tess.

'Just to air the rooms, I suppose.'

'All these rooms empty, and we without a roof to our heads!'

'You are getting tired, my Tess!' he said. 'We'll stop soon.' And kissing her sad mouth he again led her onwards.

He was growing weary likewise, for they had wandered a dozen or fifteen miles, and it became necessary to consider what they should do for rest. They looked from afar at isolated cottages and little inns, and were inclined to approach one of the latter, when their hearts failed them, and they sheered off. At length their gait dragged, and they stood still.

'Could we sleep under the trees?' she asked.

He thought the season insufficiently advanced.

'I have been thinking of that empty mansion we passed,' he said. 'Let us go back towards it again.'

They retraced their steps, but it was half an hour before they stood without the entrance-gate as earlier. He then requested her to stay where she was, whilst he went to see who was within.

She sat down among the bushes within the gate, and Clare crept towards the house. His absence lasted some considerable time, and when he returned Tess was wildly anxious, not for herself, but for him. He had found out from a boy that there was only an old woman in charge as caretaker, and she only came there on fine days, from the hamlet near, to open and shut the windows. She would come to shut them at sunset. 'Now, we can get in through one of the lower windows, and rest there,' said he.

Under his escort she went tardily forward to the main front, whose shuttered windows, like sightless eyeballs, excluded the possibility of watchers. The door was reached a few steps further, and one of the windows beside it was open. Clare clambered in, and pulled Tess in after him.

Except the hall the rooms were all in darkness, and they ascended the staircase. Up here also the shutters were tightly closed, the ventilation being perfunctorily done, for this day at least, by opening the hall-window in front and an upper window behind. Clare unlatched the door of a large chamber, felt his way across it, and parted the shutters to the width of two or three inches. A shaft of dazzling sunlight glanced into the room, revealing heavy, old-fashioned furniture, crimson damask hangings, and an enormous four-post bedstead, along the head of which were carved running figures, apparently Atalanta's race.[1]

'Rest at last!' said he, setting down his bag and the parcel of viands.

They remained in great quietness till the caretaker should have come to shut the windows: as a precaution, putting themselves in total darkness by barring the shutters as before, lest the woman should open the door of their chamber for any casual reason. Between six and seven o'clock she came, but did not approach the wing they were in. They heard her close the windows, fasten them, lock the door, and go away. Then Clare again stole a chink of light from the window, and they shared another meal, till by-and-by they were enveloped in the shades of night which they had no candle to disperse.

LVIII

The night was strangely solemn and still. In the small hours she whispered to him the whole story of how he had walked in his sleep with her in his arms acoss the Froom stream, at the imminent risk of both their lives, and laid her down in the stone coffin at the ruined abbey. He had never known of that till now.

'Why didn't you tell me next day?' he said. 'It might have prevented much misunderstanding and woe.'

'Don't think of what's past!' said she. 'I am not going to think outside of now. Why should we! Who knows what to-morrow has in store?'

But it apparently had no sorrow. The morning was wet and foggy, and Clare, rightly informed that the caretaker only opened the windows on fine days, ventured to creep out of their chamber, and explore the house, leaving Tess asleep. There was no food on the premises, but there was water, and he took advantage of the fog to emerge from the mansion, and fetch tea, bread, and butter from a shop in a little place two miles beyond, as also a small tin kettle and spirit-lamp, that they might get fire without smoke. His re-entry awoke her; and they breakfasted on what he had brought.

They were indisposed to stir abroad, and the day passed, and the night following, and the next, and next; till, almost without their being aware, five days had slipped by in absolute seclusion,

1. Having been warned that marriage would bring her unhappiness, Atalanta announced that she would marry only the man who could beat her in a race.

not a sight or sound of a human being disturbing their peaceful-
ness, such as it was. The changes of the weather were their only
events, the birds of the New Forest their only company. By tacit
consent they hardly once spoke of any incident of the past subsequent to their wedding-day. The gloomy intervening time seemed
to sink into chaos, over which the present and prior times closed as
if it never had been. Whenever he suggested that they should leave
their shelter, and go forwards towards Southampton or London,
she showed a strange unwillingness to move.

'Why should we put an end to all that's sweet and lovely!' she
deprecated. 'What must come will come.' And, looking through
the shutter-chink: 'All is trouble outside there; inside here
content.'

He peeped out also. It was quite true; within was affection,
union, error forgiven: outside was the inexorable.

'And—and,' she said, pressing her cheek against his; 'I fear
that what you think of me now may not last. I do not wish to
outlive your present feeling for me. I would rather not. I would
rather be dead and buried when the time comes for you to despise
me, so that it may never be known to me that you despised me.'

'I cannot ever despise you.'

'I also hope that. But considering what my life has been I cannot see why any man should, sooner or later, be able to help
despising me. . . . How wickedly mad I was! Yet formerly I never
could bear to hurt a fly or a worm, and the sight of a bird in
a cage used often to make me cry.'

They remained yet another day. In the night the dull sky
cleared, and the result was that the old caretaker at the cottage
awoke early. The brilliant sunrise made her unusually brisk; she
decided to open the contiguous mansion immediately, and to air
it thoroughly on such a day. Thus it occurred that, having arrived
and opened the lower rooms before six o'clock, she ascended to the
bedchambers, and was about to turn the handle of the one
wherein they lay. At that moment she fancied she could hear the
breathing of persons within. Her slippers and her antiquity had
rendered her progress a noiseless one so far, and she made for
instant retreat; then, deeming that her hearing might have
deceived her, she turned anew to the door and softly tried the handle. The lock was out of order, but a piece of furniture had been
moved forward on the inside, which prevented her opening the door
more than inch or two. A stream of morning light through the
shutter-chink fell upon the faces of the pair, wrapped in profound
slumber, Tess's lips being parted like a half-opened flower near
his cheek. The caretaker was so struck with their innocent appearance, and with the elegance of Tess's gown hanging across a

chair, her silk stockings beside it, the pretty parasol, and the other habits in which she had arrived because she had none else, that her first indignation at the effrontery of tramps and vagabonds gave way to a momentary sentimentality over this genteel elopement, as it seemed. She closed the door, and withdrew as softly as she had come, to go and consult with her neighbours on the odd discovery.

Not more than a minute had elapsed after her withdrawal when Tess woke, and then Clare. Both had a sense that something had disturbed them, though they could not say what; and the uneasy feeling which it engendered grew stronger. As soon as he was dressed he narrowly scanned the lawn through the two or three inches of shutter-chink.

'I think we will leave at once,' said he. 'It is a fine day. And I cannot help fancying somebody is about the house. At any rate, the woman will be sure to come to-day.'

She passively assented, and putting the room in order they took up the few articles that belonged to them, and departed noiselessly. When they had got into the Forest she turned to take a last look at the house.

'Ah, happy house—good-bye!' she said. 'My life can only be a question of a few weeks. Why should we not have stayed there?'

'Don't say it, Tess! We shall soon get out of this district altogether. We'll continue our course as we've begun it, and keep straight north. Nobody will think of looking for us there. We shall be looked for at the Wessex ports if we are sought at all. When we are in the north we will get to a port and away.'

Having thus persuaded her the plan was pursued, and they kept a bee line northward. Their long repose at the manor-house lent them walking power now; and towards mid-day they found that they were approaching the steepled city of Melchester, which lay directly in their way. He decided to rest her in a clump of trees during the afternoon, and push onward under cover of darkness. At dusk Clare purchased food as usual, and their night march began, the boundary between Upper and Mid-Wessex being crossed about eight o'clock.

To walk across country without much regard to roads was not new to Tess, and she showed her old agility in the performance. The intercepting city, ancient Melchester, they were obliged to pass through in order to take advantage of the town bridge for crossing a large river that obstructed them. It was about midnight when they went along the deserted streets, lighted fitfully by the few lamps, keeping off the pavement that it might not echo their footsteps. The graceful pile of cathedral architecture rose dimly on their left hand, but it was lost upon them now. Once out of the town they followed the turnpike-road, which after a few miles plunged across an open plain.

Though the sky was dense with cloud a diffused light from some fragment of a moon had hitherto helped them a little. But the moon had now sunk, the clouds seemed to settle almost on their heads, and the night grew as dark as a cave. However, they found their way along, keeping as much on the turf as possible that their tread might not resound, which it was easy to do, there being no hedge or fence of any kind. All around was open loneliness and black solitude, over which a stiff breeze blew.

They had proceeded thus gropingly two or three miles further when on a sudden Clare became conscious of some vast erection close in his front, rising sheer from the grass. They had almost struck themselves against it.

'What monstrous place is this?' said Angel.

'It hums,' said she. 'Hearken!'

He listened. The wind, playing upon the edifice, produced a booming tune, like the note of some gigantic one-stringed harp. No other sound came from it, and lifting his hand and advancing a step or two, Clare felt the vertical surface of the structure. It seemed to be of solid stone, without joint or moulding. Carrying his fingers onward he found that what he had come in contact with was a colossal rectangular pillar; by stretching out his left hand he could feel a similar one adjoining. At an indefinite height overhead something made the black sky blacker, which had the semblance of a vast architrave uniting the pillars horizontally. They carefully entered beneath and between; the surfaces echoed their soft rustle; but they seemed to be still out of doors. The place was roofless. Tess drew her breath fearfully, and Angel, perplexed, said—

'What can it be?'

Feeling sideways they encountered another tower-like pillar, square and uncompromsing as the first; beyond it another and another. The place was all doors and pillars, some connected above by continuous architraves.

'A very Temple of the Winds,' he said.

The next pillar was isolated; others composed a trilithon;[2] others were prostrate, their flanks forming a causeway wide enough for a carriage; and it was soon obvious that they made up a forest of monoliths grouped upon the grassy expanse of the plain. The couple advanced further into this pavilion of the night till they stood in its midst.

2. "A prehistoric structure or monument consisting of three large stones, two upright and one resting upon them as a lintel." [*OED*]

'It is Stonehenge!' said Clare.

'The heathen temple, you mean?'

'Yes. Older than the centuries; older than the d'Urbervilles! Well, what shall we do, darling? We may find shelter further on.'

But Tess, really tired by this time, flung herself upon an oblong slab that lay close at hand, and was sheltered from the wind by a pillar. Owing to the action of the sun during the preceding day the stone was warm and dry, in comforting contrast to the rough and chill grass around, which had damped her skirts and shoes.

'I don't want to go any further, Angel,' she said stretching out her hand for his. 'Can't we bide here?'

'I fear not. This spot is visible for miles by day, although it does not seem so now.'

'One of my mother's people was a shepherd here-abouts, now I think of it. And you used to say at Talbothays that I was a heathen. So now I am at home.'

He knelt down beside her outstretched form, and put his lips upon hers.

'Sleepy are you, dear? I think you are lying on an altar.'

'I like very much to be here,' she murmured. 'It is so solemn and lonely—after my great happiness—with nothing but the sky above my face. It seems as if there were no folk in the world but we two; and I wish there were not—except 'Liza-Lu.'

Clare thought she might as well rest here till it should get a little lighter, and he flung his overcoat upon her, and sat down by her side.

'Angel, if anything happens to me, will you watch over 'Liza-Lu for my sake?' she asked when they had listened a long time to the wind among the pillars.

'I will.'

'She is so good and simple and pure. O, Angel—I wish you would marry her if you lose me, as you will do shortly. O, if you would!'

'If I lose you I lose all! And she is my sister-in-law.'

'That's nothing, dearest. People marry sister-laws continually about Marlott; and 'Liza-Lu is so gentle and sweet, and she is growing so beautiful. O I could share you with her willingly when we are spirits! If you would train her and teach her, Angel, and bring her up for your own self! . . . She has all the best of me without the bad of me; and if she were to become yours it would almost seem as if death had not divided us. . . . Well, I have said it. I won't mention it again.'

She ceased, and he fell into thought. In the far north-east sky he could see between the pillars a level streak of light. The uniform concavity of black cloud was lifting bodily like the lid of a pot, letting in at the earth's edge the coming day, against which the towering monoliths and trilithons began to be blackly defined.

'Did they sacrifice to God here?' asked she.

'No,' said he.

'Who to?'

'I believe to the sun. That lofty stone set away by itself is in the direction of the sun, which will presently rise behind it.'

'This reminds me, dear,' she said. 'You remember you never would interfere with any belief of mine before we were married? But I knew your mind all the same, and I thought as you thought —not from any reasons of my own, but because you thought so. Tell me now, Angel, do you think we shall meet again after we are dead? I want to know.'

He kissed her to avoid a reply at such a time.

'O, Angel—I fear that means no!' said she, with a suppressed sob. 'And I wanted so to see you again—so much, so much! What —not even you and I, Angel, who love each other so well?'

Like a greater than himself, to the critical question at the critical time he did not answer;[3] and they were again silent. In a minute or two her breathing became more regular, her clasp of his hand relaxed, and she fell asleep. The band of silver paleness along the east horizon made even the distant parts of the Great Plain appear dark and near; and the whole enormous landscape bore that impress of reserve, taciturnity, and hesitation which is usual just before day. The eastward pillars and their architraves stood up blackly against the light, and the great flame-shaped Sun-stone beyond them; and the Stone of Sacrifice midway. Presently the night wind died out, and the quivering little pools in the cup-like hollows of the stones lay still. At the same time something seemed to move on the verge of the dip eastward—a mere dot. It was the head of a man approaching them from the hollow beyond the Sun-stone. Clare wished they had gone onward, but in the circumstances decided to remain quiet. The figure came straight towards the circle of pillars in which they were.

He heard something behind him, the brush of feet. Turning, he saw over the prostrate columns another figure; then before he was aware, another was at hand on the right, under a trilithon, and another on the left. The dawn shone full on the front of the man westward, and Clare could discern from this that he was tall, and walked as if trained. They all closed in with evident purpose. Her story then was true! Springing to his feet, he looked around for a weapon, loose stone, means of escape, anything. By this time the nearest man was upon him.

'It is no use, sir,' he said. 'There are sixteen of us on the Plain, and the whole country is reared.'

3. Matthew xxvi: 62-63: "And the high priest arose, and said unto him, Answerest thou nothing? What is it which these witness against thee? But Jesus held his peace."

'Let her finish her sleep!' he implored in a whisper of the men as they gathered round.

When they saw where she lay, which they had not done till then, they showed no objection, and stood watching her, as still as the pillars around. He went to the stone and bent over her, holding one poor little hand; her breathing now was quick and small, like that of a lesser creature than a woman. All waited in the growing light, their faces and hands as if they were silvered, the remainder of their figures dark, the stones glistening green-gray, the Plain still a mass of shade. Soon the light was strong, and a ray shone upon her unconscious form, peering under her eyelids and waking her.

'What is it, Angel?' she said, starting up. 'Have they come for me?'

'Yes, dearest,' he said. 'They have come.'

'It is as it should be,' she murmured. 'Angel, I am almost glad —yes, glad! This happiness could not have lasted. It was too much. I have had enough; and now I shall not.live for you to despise me!'

She stood up, shook herself, and went forward, neither of the men having moved.

'I am ready,' she said quietly.

LIX

The city of Wintoncester, that fine old city, aforetime capital of Wessex, lay amidst its convex and concave downlands in all the brightness and warmth of a July morning. The gabled brick, tile, and freestone houses had almost dried off for the season their integument of lichen, the streams in the meadows were low, and in the sloping High Street, from the West Gateway to the mediaeval cross, and from the mediaeval cross to the bridge, that leisurely dusting and sweeping was in progress which usually ushers in an old-fashioned market-day.

From the western gate aforesaid the highway, as every Wintoncestrian knows, ascends a long and regular incline of the exact length of a measured mile, leaving the houses gradually behind. Up this road from the precincts of the city two persons were walking rapidly, as if unconscious of the trying ascent—unconscious through preoccupation and not through buoyancy. They had emerged upon this road through a narrow barred wicket in a high wall a little lower down. They seemed anxious to get out of the sight of the houses and of their kind, and this road appeared to offer the quickest means of doing so. Though they were young they walked with bowed heads, which gait of grief the sun's rays smiled on pitilessly.

One of the pair was Angel Clare, the other a tall budding

creature—half girl, half woman—a spiritualized image of Tess, slighter than she, but with the same beautiful eyes—Clare's sister-in-law, 'Liza-Lu. Their pale faces seemed to have shrunk to half their natural size. They moved on hand in hand, and never spoke a word, the drooping of their heads being that of Giotto's 'Two Apostles.'[4]

When they had nearly reached the top of the great West Hill the clocks in the town struck eight. Each gave a start at the notes, and, walking onward yet a few steps, they reached the first milestone, standing whitely on the green margin of the grass, and backed by the down, which here was open to the road. They entered upon the turf, and, impelled by a force that seemed to overrule their will, suddenly stood still, turned, and waited in paralyzed suspense beside the stone.

The prospect from this summit was almost unlimited. In the valley beneath lay the city they had just left, its more prominent buildings showing as in an isometric drawing—among them the broad cathedral tower, with its Norman windows and immense length of aisle and nave, the spires of St. Thomas's, the pinnacled tower of the College, and, more to the right, the tower and gables of the ancient hospice, where to this day the pilgrim may receive his dole of bread and ale. Behind the city swept the rotund upland of St. Catherine's Hill; further off, landscape beyond landscape, till the horizon was lost in the radiance of the sun hanging above it.

Against these far stretches of country rose, in front of the other city edifices, a large red-brick building, with level gray roofs, and rows of short barred windows bespeaking captivity, the whole contrasting greatly by its formalism with the quaint irregularities of the Gothic erections. It was somewhat disguised from the road in passing it by yews and evergreen oaks, but it was visible enough up here. The wicket from which the pair had lately emerged was in the wall of this structure. From the middle of the building an ugly flat-topped octagonal tower ascended against the east horizon, and viewed from this spot, on its shady side and against the light, it seemed the one blot on the city's beauty. Yet it was with this blot, and not with the beauty, that the two gazers were concerned.

Upon the cornice of the tower a tall staff was fixed. Their eyes were riveted on it. A few minutes after the hour had struck something moved slowly up the staff, and extended itself upon the breeze. It was a black flag.

4. "This is the fresco 'Two Haloed Mourners' in the National Gallery, now attributed to Spinello Aretino." [F]

'Justice' was done, and the President of the Immortals, in Aeschylean phrase,[5] had ended his sport with Tess. And the d'Urberville knights and dames slept on in their tombs unknowing. The two speechless gazers bent themselves down to the earth, as if in prayer, and remained thus a long time, absolutely motionless: the flag continued to wave silently. As soon as they had strength they arose, joined hands again, and went on.

5. "President of the Immortals" is a literal translation of two words in line 169 of *Prometheus Bound*.

Hardy and
the Novel

Background: Hardy's Poems[†]

"Poetry. Perhaps I can express more fully in verse ideas and emotions which run counter to the inert crystallized opinion—hard as a rock—which the vast body of men have vested interests in supporting. To cry out in a passionate poem that (for instance) the Supreme Mover or Movers, the Prime Force or Forces, must be either limited in power, unknowing, or cruel—which is obvious enough, and has been for centuries—will cause them merely a shake of the head; but to put it in argumentative prose will make them sneer, or foam, and set all the literary contortionists jumping upon me, a harmless agnostic, as if I were a clamorous atheist, which in their crass illiteracy they seem to think is the same thing. . . . If Galileo had said in verse that the world moved, the Inquisition might have let him alone."

—HARDY'S NOTEBOOKS, in *The Later Years*, pp. 57-58.

Hap

If but some vengeful god would call to me
From up the sky, and laugh: "Thou suffering thing,
Know that thy sorrow is my ecstasy,
That thy love's loss is my hate's profiting!"

Then would I bear it, clench myself, and die,   5
Steeled by the sense of ire unmerited;
Half-eased in that a Powerfuller than I
Had willed and meted me the tears I shed.

But not so. How arrives it joy lies slain,
And why unblooms the best hope ever sown?   10
—Crass Casualty obstructs the sun and rain,
And dicing Time for gladness casts a moan. . . .
These purblind Doomsters had as readily strown
Blisses about my pilgrimage as pain.

† From *Collected Poems of Thomas Hardy* (1919).

The Sleep-Worker

When wilt thou wake, O Mother, wake and see—
As one who, held in trance, has laboured long
By vacant rote and prepossession strong—
The coils that thou hast wrought unwittingly;

Wherein have place, unrealized by thee,   5
Fair growths, foul cankers, right enmeshed with wrong,
Strange orchestras of victim-shriek and song,
And curious blends of ache and ecstasy?—

Should that morn come, and show thy opened eyes
All that Life's palpitating tissues feel,   10
How wilt thou bear thyself in thy surprise?—

Wilt thou destroy, in one wild shock of shame,
Thy whole high heaving firmamental frame,
Or patiently adjust, amend, and heal?

New Year's Eve

"I have finished another year," said God,
    "In grey, green, white, and brown;
I have strewn the leaf upon the sod,
Sealed up the worm within the clod,
    And let the last sun down."   5

"And what's the good of it?" I said,
    "What reasons made you call
From formless void this earth we tread,
When nine-and-ninety can be read
    Why nought should be at all?   10

"Yea, Sire; why shaped you us, 'who in
    This tabernacle groan'—
If ever a joy be found herein,
Such joy no man had wished to win
    If he had never known!"   15

Then he: "My labours—logicless—
    You may explain; not I:
Sense-sealed I have wrought, without a guess
That I evolved a Consciousness
    To ask for reasons why.   20

"Strange that ephemeral creatures who
　　By my own ordering are,
Should see the shortness of my view,
Use ethic tests I never knew,
　　Or made provision for!"　　　　　　　25

He sank to raptness as of yore,
　　And opening New Year's Day
Wove it by rote as theretofore,
And went on working evermore
　　In his unweeting way.　　　　　　　30

"Speaking generally, there is more autobiography in a hundred
lines of Mr. Hardy's poetry than in all the novels."

　　　　—FLORENCE EMILY HARDY, in *The Later Years*, p. 196.

At An Inn

When we as strangers sought
　　Their catering care,
Veiled smiles bespoke their thought
　　Of what we were.
They warmed as they opined　　　　　　5
　　Us more than friends—
That we had all resigned
　　For love's dear ends.

And that swift sympathy
　　With living love　　　　　　　　10
Which quicks the world—maybe
　　The spheres above,
Made them our ministers,
　　Moved them to say,
"Ah, God, that bliss like theirs　　　　15
　　Would flush our day!"

And we were left alone
　　As Love's own pair;
Yet never the love-light shone
　　Between us there!　　　　　　　20
But that which chilled the breath
　　Of afternoon,
And palsied unto death
　　The pane-fly's tune.

The kiss their zeal foretold,
 And now deemed come,
Came not: within his hold
 Love lingered numb.
Why cast he on our port
 A bloom not ours?
Why shaped us for his sport
 In after-hours?

As we seemed we were not
 That day afar,
And now we seem not what
 We aching are.
O severing sea and land,
 O laws of men,
Ere death, once let us stand
 As we stood then!

———————

"[In March, 1897] a revised form of a novel of [Hardy's] which had been published serially in 1892 as *The Pursuit of the Well-Beloved: A Sketch of a Temperament*, was issued in volume form as *The Well-Beloved*. The theory on which this fantastic tale of a subjective idea was constructed is explained in the preface to the novel, and again exemplified in a poem bearing the same name, written about this time and published with *Poems of the Past and the Present* in 1901—the theory of the transmigration of the ideal beloved one, who only exists in the lover, from material woman to material woman—as exemplified also by Proust many years later. Certain critics affected to find unmentionable moral atrocities in its pages, but Hardy did not answer any of the charges further than by defining in a letter to a literary periodical the scheme of the story somewhat more fully than he had done in the preface:

"Not only was it published serially five years ago but it was sketched many years before that date, when I was comparatively a young man, and interested in the Platonic Idea, which, considering its charm and its poetry, one could well wish to be interested in always. . . . There is, of course, underlying the fantasy followed by the visionary artist the truth that all men are pursuing a shadow, the Unattainable, and I venture to hope that this may redeem the tragicomedy from the charge of frivolity."

—HARDY in *The Later Years*, p. 59.

The Well-Beloved

I went by star and planet shine
 Towards the dear one's home
At Kingsbere, there to make her mine
 When the next sun upclomb.

I edged the ancient hill and wood
 Beside the Ikling Way,
Nigh where the Pagan temple stood
 In the world's earlier day.

And as I quick and quicker walked
    On gravel and on green,   10
I sang to sky, and tree, or talked
    Of her I called my queen.

—"O faultless is her dainty form,
    And luminous her mind;
She is the God-created norm   15
    Of perfect womankind!"

A shape whereon one star-blink gleamed
    Slid softly by my side,
A woman's; and her motion seemed
    The motion of my bride.   20

And yet methought she'd drawn erstwhile
    Out from the ancient leaze,
Where once were pile and peristyle
    For men's idolatries.

—"O maiden lithe and lone, what may   25
    Thy name and lineage be
Who so resemblest by this ray
    My darling?—Art thou she?"

The Shape: "Thy bride remains within
    Her father's grange and grove."   30
—"Thou speakest rightly," I broke in,
    "Thou art not she I love."

—"Nay: though thy bride remains inside
    Her father's walls," said she,
"The one most dear is with thee here,   35
    For thou dost love but me."

Then I: "But she, my only choice,
    Is now at Kingsbere Grove?"
Again her soft mysterious voice:
    "I am thy only Love."   40

Thus still she vouched, and still I said,
    "O sprite, that cannot be!" . . .
It was as if my bosom bled,
    So much she troubled me.

The sprite resumed: "Thou has transferred   45
    To her dull form awhile
My beauty, fame, and deed, and word,
    My gestures and my smile.

"O fatuous man, this truth infer,
    Brides are not what they seem;   50
Thou lovest what thou dreamest her;
    I am thy very dream!"

—"O then," I answered miserably,
    Speaking as scarce I knew,
"My loved one, I must wed with thee   55
    If what thou sayest be true!"

She, proudly, thinning in the gloom:
    "Though, since troth-plight began,
I have ever stood as bride to groom,
    I wed no mortal man!"   60

Thereat she vanished by the lane
    Adjoining Kingsbere town,
Near where, men say, once stood the Fane
    To Venus, on the Down.

—When I arrived and met my bride   65
    Her look was pinched and thin,
As if her soul had shrunk and died,
    And left a waste within.

"A story must be exceptional enough to justify its telling. We tale-tellers are all Ancient Mariners, and none of us is warranted in stopping Wedding Guests (in other words, the hurrying public) unless he has something more unusual to relate than the ordinary experience of every average man and woman.

"The whole secret of fiction and the drama—in the constructional part—lies in the adjustment of things unusual to things eternal and universal. The writer who knows exactly how exceptional, and how non-exceptional, his events should be made, possesses the key to the art."

—HARDY'S NOTEBOOKS, in *The Later Years*, pp. 15-16.

The Supplanter

A TALE

He bends his travel-tarnished feet
    To where she wastes in clay:
From day-dawn until eve he fares
    Along the wintry way;
From day-dawn until eve he bears   5
    A wreath of blooms and bay.

"Are these the gravestone shapes that meet
    My forward-straining view?
Or forms that cross a window-blind
    In circle, knot, and queue: 10
Gay forms, that cross and whirl and wind
    To music throbbing through?"—

"The Keeper of the Field of Tombs
    Dwells by its gateway-pier;
He celebrates with feast and dance   15
    His daughter's twentieth year:
He celebrates with wine of France
    The birthday of his dear."—

"The gates are shut when evening glooms:
    Lay down your wreath, sad wight;   20
To-morrow is a time more fit
    For placing flowers aright:
The morning is the time for it;
    Come, wake with us to-night!"—

He drops his wreath, and enters in,   25
    And sits, and shares their cheer.—
"I fain would foot with you, young man,
    Before all others here;
I fain would foot it for a span
    With such a cavalier!"   30

She coaxes, clasps, nor fails to win
    His first-unwilling hand:
The merry music strikes its staves,
    The dancers quickly band;
And with the Damsel of the Graves   35
    He duly takes his stand.

"You dance divinely, stranger swain,
    Such grace I've never known.
O longer stay! Breathe not adieu
    And leave me here alone!   40
O longer stay: to her be true
    Whose heart is all your own!"—

"I mark a phantom through the pane,
    That beckons in despair,
Its mouth all drawn with heavy moan—   45
    Her to whom once I sware!"—
"Nay; 'tis the lately carven stone
    Of some strange girl laid there!"—

"I see white flowers upon the floor
    Betrodden to a clot; 50
My wreath were they?"—"Nay; love me much,
    Swear you'll forget me not!
'Twas but a wreath! Full many such
    Are brought here and forgot."

The watches of the night grow hoar, 55
    He wakens with the sun;
"Now could I kill thee here!" he says,
    "For winning me from one
Who ever in her living days
    Was pure as cloistered nun!" 60

She cowers; and, rising, roves he then
    Afar for many a mile,
For evermore to be apart
    From her who could beguile
His senses by her burning heart, 65
    And win his love awhile.

A year beholds him wend again
    To her who wastes in clay;
From day-dawn until eve he fares
    Along the wintry way, 70
From day-dawn until eve repairs
    Towards her mound to pray.

And there he sets him to fulfil
    His frustrate first intent:
And lay upon her bed, at last, 75
    The offering earlier meant:
When, on his stooping figure, ghast
    And haggard eyes are bent.

"O surely for a little while
    You can be kind to me. 80
For do you love her, do you hate,
    She knows not—cares not she:
Only the living feel the weight
    Of loveless misery!

"I own my sin; I've paid its cost, 85
    Being outcast, shamed, and bare:
I give you daily my whole heart,
    Your child my tender care,
I pour you prayers; this life apart
    Is more than I can bear!" 90

He turns—unpitying, passion-tossed;
    "I know you not!" he cries,
"Nor know your child. I knew this maid,
    But she's in Paradise!"
And he has vanished in the shade   95
    From her beseeching eyes.

Growth in May[1]

I enter a daisy-and-buttercup land,
    And thence thread a jungle of grass:
Hurdles and stiles scarce visible stand
    Above the lush stems as I pass.

Hedges peer over, and try to be seen,   5
    And seem to reveal a dim sense
That amid such ambitious and elbow-high green
    They make a mean show as a fence.

Elsewhere the mead is possessed of the neats,
    That range not greatly above   10
The rich rank thicket which brushes their teats,
    And *her* gown, as she waits for her Love.

We Field-Women

    How it rained
When we worked at Flintcomb-Ash,
And could not stand upon the hill
Trimming swedes for the slicing-mill.
The wet washed through us—plash, plash, plash: 5
    How it rained!

    How it snowed
When we crossed from Flintcomb-Ash
To the Great Barn for drawing reed,
Since we could nowise chop a swede.—   10
Flakes in each doorway and casement-sash:
    How it snowed!

    How it shone
When we went from Flintcomb-Ash
To start at dairywork once more   15
In the laughing meads, with cows three-score,
And pails, and songs, and love—too rash:
    How it shone!

1. Other poems that echo characters or scenes in *Tess of the d'Urbervilles* are: "The Slow Nature," "Tess's Lament," "At Middle-Field Gate in February."

Beyond the Last Lamp
(Near Tooting Common)

While rain, with eve in partnership,
Descended darkly, drip, drip, drip,
Beyond the last lone lamp I passed
    Walking slowly, whispering sadly,
    Two linked loiterers, wan, downcast: 5
Some heavy thought constrained each face,
And blinded them to time and place.

The pair seemed lovers, yet absorbed
In mental scenes no longer orbed
By love's young rays. Each countenance   10
    As it slowly, as it sadly
    Caught the lamplight's yellow glance,
Held in suspense a misery
At things which had been or might be.

When I retrod that watery way   15
Some hours beyond the droop of day,
Still I found pacing there the twain
    Just as slowly, just as sadly,
    Heedless of the night and rain.
One could but wonder who they were,   20
And what wild woe detained them there.

Though thirty years of blur and blot
Have slid since I beheld that spot,
And saw in curious converse there
    Moving slowly, moving sadly   25
    That mysterious tragic pair,
Its olden look may linger on—
All but the couple; they have gone.

Whither? Who knows, indeed. . . . And yet
To me, when nights are weird and wet,   30
Without those comrades there at tryst
    Creeping slowly, creeping sadly,
    That lone lane does not exist.
There they seem brooding on their pain,
And will, while such a lane remain.   35

"*The Athenaeum* says 'The glass-stainer maintains his existence at the sacrifice of everything the painter holds dear. In place of the freedom and sweet abandonment which is Nature's own charm and which the painter can achieve, the glass-stainer gives us splendour as luminous as that of the rainbow . . . in patches, and stripes, and bars.' The above canons are interesting in their conveyance of a half truth. All art is only approximative—not exact, as the reviewer thinks; and hence the methods of all art differ from that of the glass-stainer but in degree."

—HARDY'S NOTEBOOKS, in *The Early Life*, p. 213.

The Young Glass-Stainer

"These Gothic windows, how they wear me out
With cusp and foil, and nothing straight or square,
Crude colours, leaden borders roundabout,
And fitting in Peter here, and Matthew there!

"What a vocation! Here do I draw now
The abnormal, loving the Hellenic norm;
Martha I paint, and dream of Hera's brow,
Mary, and think of Aphrodite's form."

Background:
Hardy's Autobiography[†]

The family, on Hardy's paternal side, like all the Hardys of the south-west, derived from the Jersey le Hardys who sailed across to Dorset for centuries—the coasts being just opposite. Hardy often thought he would like to restore the "le" to his name, and call himself "Thomas le Hardy"; but he never did so. The Dorset Hardys were traditionally said to descend in particular from a Clement le Hardy, Baily of Jersey, whose son John settled hereabouts in the fifteenth century, having probably landed at Wareham, then a port. They all had the characteristics of an old family of spent social energies, that were revealed even in the Thomas Hardy of this memoir (as in his father and grandfather), who never cared to take advantage of the many worldly opportunities that his popularity and esteem as an author afforded him. They had dwelt for many generations in or near the valley of the River Froom or Frome, which extends inland from Wareham, occupying various properties whose sites lay scattered about from Woolcombe, Toller-Welme, and Up-Sydling, (near the higher course of the river), down the stream to Dorchester, Weymouth, and onward to Wareham, where the Froom flows into Poole Harbour. * * *

But at the birth of the subject of this biography [on June 2, 1840,] the family had declined, so far as its Dorset representatives were concerned, from whatever importance it once might have been able to claim there; and at his father's death the latter was, it is believed, the only landowner of the name in the county, his property being, besides the acre-and-half lifehold at Bockhamp-

† *The Early Life of Thomas Hardy, 1840–1891* (New York, 1928) and *The Later Years of Thomas Hardy, 1892-1928* (New York, 1930).

Both "by Florence Emily Hardy," the novelist's second wife, the books are "in reality an autobiography"; Mrs. Hardy's "work was confined to a few edi-torial touches, and the writing is throughout Hardy's own" (Richard Purdy, *Thomas Hardy: A Bibliographical Study*, New York, 1954, pp. 265, 272-73). The work was, as the title page of the first volume indicates, "compiled largely from contemporary notes, letters, diaries, and biographical memorandas."

ton, a small freehold farm at Talbothays, with some houses there, and about a dozen freehold cottages and a brick-yard-and-kiln elsewhere. The Talbothays farm was a small outlying property standing detached in a ring fence, its possessors in the reign of Henry VIII. having been Talbots. * * *

Though healthy he was fragile, and precocious to a degree, being able to read almost before he could walk, and to tune a violin when of quite tender years. He was of ecstatic temperament, extraordinarily sensitive to music, and among the endless jigs, hornpipes, reels, waltzes, and country-dances that his father played of an evening in his early married years, and to which the boy danced a *pas seul*[1] in the middle of the room, there were three or four that always moved the child to tears, though he strenuously tried to hide them. Among the airs (though he did not know their names at that time) were, by the way, "Enrico" (popular in the Regency), "The Fairy Dance", "Miss Macleod of Ayr" (an old Scotch tune to which Burns may have danced), and a melody named "My Fancy-Lad" or, "Johnny's gone to sea".

* * *

[*When he was about ten "Tommy" went to a harvest-home supper at a nearby farm.*]

It may be worthy of note that this harvest-home was among the last at which the old traditional ballads were sung, the railway having been extended to Dorchester just then, and the orally transmitted ditties of centuries being slain at a stroke by the London comic songs that were introduced. The particular ballad which he remembered hearing that night from the lips of the farm-women was that one variously called "The Outlandish Knight", "May Colvine", "The Western Tragedy", etc. He could recall to old age the scene of the young women in their light gowns sitting on a bench against the wall in the barn, and leaning against each other as they warbled the Dorset version of the ballad, which differed a little from the northern:

> "Lie there, lie there, thou false-hearted man,
>   Lie there instead o' me;
> For six pretty maidens thou hast a-drown'd here,
>   But the seventh hath drown-ed thee!"

> "O tell no more, my pretty par-rot,
>   Lay not the blame on me;
> And your cage shall be made o' the glittering gold,
>   Wi' a door o' the white ivo-rie!"

1. A solo dance [*Editor*].

And it was about this date [1855] that he formed one of a trio of youths (the vicar's sons being the other two) who taught in the Sunday School of the parish, where as a pupil in his class he had a dairymaid four years older than himself, who afterwards appeared in *Tess of the d'Urbervilles* as Marian—one of the few portraits from life in his works. This pink and plump damsel had a marvellous power of memorizing whole chapters in the Bible, and would repeat to him by heart in class, to his boredom, the long gospels before Easter without missing a word, and with evident delight in her facility; though she was by no means a model of virtue in her love-affairs.

Somewhat later, though it may as well be mentioned here among other such trivialities, he lost his heart for a few days to a young girl who had come from Windsor just after he had been reading Ainsworth's *Windsor Castle*.[2] But she disappointed him on his finding that she took no interest in Herne the Hunter or Anne Boleyn. In this kind there was another young girl, a gamekeeper's pretty daughter, who won Hardy's boyish admiration because of her beautiful bay-red hair. But she despised him, as being two or three years her junior, and married early. He celebrated her later on as "Lizbie Browne". Yet another attachment, somewhat later, which went deeper, was to a farmer's daughter named Louisa. There were more probably. They all appear, however, to have been quite fugitive, except perhaps the one for Louisa.

He believed that his attachment to this damsel was reciprocated, for on one occasion when he was walking home from Dorchester he beheld her sauntering down the lane as if to meet him. He longed to speak to her, but bashfulness overcame him, and he passed on with a murmured "Good evening", while poor Louisa had no word to say.

Later he heard that she had gone to Weymouth to a boarding school for young ladies, and thither he went, Sunday after Sunday, until he discovered the church which the maiden of his affections attended with her fellow scholars. But, alas, all that resulted from these efforts was a shy smile from Louisa.

* * *

[*From 1856, when he was 16, till 1862, Hardy studied architecture in the office of John Hicks in Dorchester.*]

An unusual incident occurred during his pupillage at Hick's which, though it had nothing to do with his own life, was dramatic enough to have mention. One summer morning at Bockhampton, just before he sat down to breakfast, he remembered that a man

2. This "pseudo-historical romance," published in 1843, was a kind of Gothic thriller [*Editor*].

was to be hanged at eight o'clock at Dorchester. He took up the big brass telescope that had been handed on in the family, and hastened to a hill on the heath a quarter of a mile from the house, whence he looked towards the town. The sun behind his back shone straight on the white stone façade of the gaol, the gallows upon it, and the form of the murderer in white fustian, the executioner and officials in dark clothing and the crowd below being invisible at this distance of nearly three miles. At the moment of his placing the glass to his eye the white figure dropped downwards, and the faint note of the town clock struck eight.

The whole thing had been so sudden that the glass nearly fell from Hardy's hands. He seemed alone on the heath with the hanged man, and crept homeward wishing he had not been so curious. It was the second and last execution he witnessed, the first having been that of a woman two or three years earlier, when he stood close to the gallows.

* * *

His immaturity, above alluded to, was greater than is common for his years, and it may be mentioned here that a clue to much of his character and action throughout his life is afforded by his lateness of development in virility, while mentally precocious. He himself said humorously in later times that he was a child till he was sixteen, a youth till he was five-and-twenty, and a young man till he was nearly fifty. Whether this was intrinsic, or owed anything to his having lived in a remote spot in early life, is an open question.

During the years of architectural pupillage Hardy had two other literary friends in Dorchester. * * * [One] was Horace Moule of Queens' College, Cambridge, just then beginning practice as author and reviewer. Walks in the fields with each of these friends biassed Thomas Hardy still further in the direction of books, two works among those he met with impressing him much—the newly published *Essays and Reviews* by "The Seven against Christ", as the authors were nicknamed; and Walter Bagehot's *Estimates* (afterwards called *Literary Studies*).[3] He began writing verses, and also a few prose articles, which do not appear to have been printed anywhere. * * *

It seems he had also set to work on the *Agamemnon* or the *Oedipus*; but on his inquiring of Moule—who was a fine Greek scholar and was always ready to act the tutor in any classical

3. The seven contributors to *Essays and Reviews*, 1860, expressed the Broad Church doctrine that the discoveries of science did not threaten but would, in fact, strengthen religion. Bagehot's collection of essays on such poets as Shakespeare, Wordsworth, Browning, and Tennyson was not published until 1879 [*Editor*].

difficulty—if he ought not to go on reading some Greek plays, Moule's reluctant opinion was that if Hardy really had (as his father had insisted, and as indeed was reasonable, since he never as yet had earned a farthing in his life) to make an income in some way by architecture in 1862, it would be hardly worth while for him to read Aeschylus or Sophocles in 1859-61. He had secretly wished that Moule would advise him to go on with Greek plays, in spite of the serious damage it might do his architecture; but he felt bound to listen to reason and prudence. So, as much Greek as he had got he had to be content with, the language being almost dropped from that date; for though he did take up one or two of the dramatists again some years later, it was in a fragmentary way only. Nevertheless his substantial knowledge of them was not small.

It may be permissible to ponder whether Hardy's career might not have been altogether different if Moule's opinion had been the contrary one, and he had advised going on with Greek plays. The younger man would hardly have resisted the suggestion, and might have risked the consequences, so strong was his bias that way. The upshot might have been his abandonment of architecture for a University career, his father never absolutely refusing to advance him money in a good cause. Having every instinct of a scholar he might have ended his life as a Don of whom it could be said that

> He settled *Hoti's* business,
> Properly based *Oun*.[4]

But this was not to be, and it was possibly better so.

* * *

[*In a letter to his sister May, from London, in 1863, Hardy wrote:*]

About Thackeray. You must read something of his. He is considered to be the greatest novelist of the day—looking at novel writing of the highest kind as a perfect and truthful representation of actual life—which is no doubt the proper view to take. Hence, because his novels stand so high as works of Art or Truth, they often have anything but an elevating tendency, and on that account are particularly unfitted for young people—from their very truthfulness. People say that it is beyond Mr. Thackeray to paint a perfect man or woman—a great fault if novels are intended to instruct, but just the opposite if they are to be considered merely as Pictures. *Vanity Fair* is considered one of his best.

* * *

4. From Browning's "A Grammarian's Funeral" [*Editor*].

[Having settled in London and] feeling that architectural drawing in which the actual designing had no great part was monotonous and mechanical; having besides little inclination for pushing his way into influential sets which would help him to start a practice of his own, Hardy's tastes reverted to the literary pursuits that he had been compelled to abandon in 1861, and had not resumed except to write the Prize Architectural Essay beforementioned. By as early as the end of 1863 he had recommenced to read a great deal, with a growing tendency towards poetry. But he was forced to consider ways and means, and it was suggested to him that he might combine literature with architecture by becoming an art-critic for the press, particularly in the province of architectural art. It is probable that he might easily have carried this out, reviewers with a speciality being then, and possibly now, in demand. His preparations for such a course were, however, quickly abandoned, and by 1865 he had begun to write verses, and by 1866 to send his productions to magazines. That these were rejected by editors, and that he paid such respect to their judgment as scarcely ever to send out a MS. twice, was in one feature fortunate for him, since in years long after he was able to examine those poems of which he kept copies, and by the mere change of a few words or the rewriting of a line or two to make them quite worthy of publication. Such of them as are dated in these years were all written in his lodgings at 16 Westbourne Park Villas. He also began turning the Book of Ecclesiastes into Spenserian stanzas, but finding the original unmatchable abandoned the task.

* * *

However, as yet he did not by any means abandon verse, which he wrote constantly, but kept private, through the years 1866 and most of 1867, resolving to send no more to magazines whose editors probably did not know good poetry from bad, and forming meanwhile the quixotic opinion that, as in verse was concentrated the essence of all imaginative and emotional literature, to read verse and nothing else was the shortest way to the fountain-head of such, for one who had not a great deal of spare time. And in fact for nearly or quite two years he did not read a word of prose except such as came under his eye in the daily newspapers and weekly reviews. Thus his reading naturally covered a fairly large tract of English poetry, and it may be mentioned, as showing that he had some views of his own, that he preferred Scott the poet to Scott the novelist, and never ceased to regret that the author of "the most Homeric poem in the English langauage—*Marmion*"—should later have declined on prose fiction.

* * *

About this time Hardy nourished a scheme of a highly visionary character. He perceived from the impossibility of getting his verses accepted by magazines that he could not live by poetry, and (rather strangely) thought that architecture and poetry—particularly architecture in London—would not work well together. So he formed the idea of combining poetry and the Church—towards which he had long had a leaning—and wrote to a friend in Cambridge for particulars as to matriculation at that University, which with his late classical reading would have been easy for him. He knew that what money he could not muster himself for keeping terms his father would lend him for a few years, his idea being that of a curacy in a country village. This fell through less because of its difficulty than from a conscientious feeling, after some theological study, that he could hardly take the step with honour while holding the views which on examination he found himself to hold. And so he allowed the curious scheme to drift out of sight, though not till after he had begun to practice orthodoxy.

* * *

[*After an illness in London during the summer of 1867 Hardy returned home to "regain vigour."*]

An effect among others of his return to the country was to take him out of the fitful yet mechanical and monotonous existence that befalls many a young man in London lodgings. Almost suddenly he became more practical, and queried of himself definitely how to achieve some tangible result from his desultory yet strenuous labours at literature during the previous four years. He considered that he knew fairly well both West-country life in its less explored recesses and the life of an isolated student cast upon the billows of London with no protection but his brains—the young man of whom it may be said more truly than perhaps of any, that "save his own soul he hath no star". The two contrasting experiences seemed to afford him abundant materials out of which to evolve a striking socialistic novel—not that he mentally defined it as such, for the word had probably never, or scarcely ever, been heard of at that date.

So down he sat in one of the intervals of his attendances at Mr. Hicks's drawing-office (which were not regular), and, abandoning verse as a waste of labour—though he had resumed it awhile on arriving in the country—he began the novel the title of which is here written as it was at first intended to be:

THE POOR MAN AND THE LADY
A Story with no Plot
Containing some original verses

This, however, he plainly did not like, for it was ultimately abridged to

THE POOR MAN AND THE LADY
BY THE POOR MAN

And the narrative was proceeded with till, in October of this year (1867), he paid a flying visit to London to fetch his books and other impedimenta.

Thus it happened that under the stress of necessity he had set about a kind of literature in which he had hitherto taken but little interest—prose fiction.

* * *

He went in March [1869], by appointment as to the day and hour, it is believed, not knowing that the "gentleman" was George Meredith.[5] He was shown into a back room of the publishing offices (opposite Sackville Street, and where Prince's Restaurant now stands); and before him, in the dusty and untidy apartment, piled with books and papers, was a handsome man in a frock coat—"buttoned at the waist, but loose above"—no other than Meredith in person, his ample dark-brown beard, wavy locks, and somewhat dramatic manner lending him a striking appearance to the younger man's eye, who even then did not know his name.

Meredith had the manuscript [of *The Poor man and the Lady*] in his hand, and began lecturing Hardy upon it in a sonorous voice. No record was kept by the latter of their conversation, but the gist of it he remembered very well. It was that the firm were willing to publish the novel as agreed, but that he, the speaker, strongly advised its author not to "nail his colours to the mast" so definitely in a first book, if he wished to do anything practical in literature; for if he printed so pronounced a thing he would be attacked on all sides by the conventional reviewers, and his future injured. The story was, in fact, a sweeping dramatic satire of the squirearchy and nobility, London society, the vulgarity of the middle class, modern Christianity, church restoration, and political and domestic morals in general, the author's views, in fact, being obviously those of a young man with a passion for reforming the world—those of many a young man before and after him; the tendency of the writing being socialistic, not to say revolutionary; yet not argumentatively so, the style having the affected simplicity of Defoe's (which had long attracted Hardy, as it did Stevenson, years later, to imitiation of it). This naive realism in circumstantial details that were pure inventions was so well assumed that

5. This episode took place ten years after George Meredith had published *The Ordeal of Richard Feverel*, and ten years before *The Egoist* [*Editor*].

both Macmillan and Morley[6] had been perhaps a little, or more than a little, deceived by its seeming actuality; to Hardy's surprise, when he thought the matter over in later years, that his inexperienced imagination should have created figments that could win credence from such experienced heads.

The satire was obviously pushed too far—as sometimes in Swift and Defoe themselves—and portions of the book, apparently taken in earnest by both his readers, had no foundation either in Hardy's beliefs or his experience. One instance he could remember was a chapter in which, with every circumstantial detail, he described in the first person his introduction to the kept mistress of an architect who "took in washing" (as it was called in the profession)—that is, worked at his own office for other architects—the said mistress adding to her lover's income by designing for him the pulpits, altars, reredoses, texts, holy vessels, crucifixes, and other ecclesiastical furniture which were handed on to him by the nominal architects who employed her protector—the lady herself being a dancer at a music-hall when not engaged in designing Christian emblems—all told so plausibly as to seem actual proof of the degeneracy of the age.

Whatever might have been the case with the other two, Meredith was not taken in by the affected simplicity of the narrative, and that was obviously why he warned his young acquaintance that the press would be about his ears like hornets if he published his manuscript. For though the novel might have been accepted calmly enough by the reviewers and public in these days, in genteel mid-Victorian 1869 it would no doubt have incurred, as Meredith judged, severe strictures which might have handicapped a young writer for a long time. * * *

The upshot of this interview was that Hardy took away the MS. with him to decide on a course.

Meredith had added that Hardy could rewrite the story, softening it down considerably; or what would be much better, put it away altogether for the present, and attempt a novel with a purely artistic purpose, giving it a more complicated "plot" than was attempted with *The Poor Man and the Lady*.

* * *

In the first week of January 1874 the story [*Far from the Madding Crowd*] was noticed in a marked degree by the *Spectator*, and a guess hazarded that it might be from the pen of George Eliot—why, the author could never understand, since, so far as he

6. Alexander Macmillan, the publisher to whom Hardy had first sent the MS, and John Morley, to whom Macmillan had shown the MS. Both thought Hardy's social satire grounded on truth, but "excessive" [*Editor*].

had read that great thinker—one of the greatest living, he thought, though not a born storyteller by any means—she had never touched the life of the fields: her country-people having seemed to him, too, more like small townsfolk than rustics; and as evidencing a woman's wit cast in country dialogue rather than real country humour, which he regarded as rather of the Shakespeare and Fielding sort. However, he conjectured, as a possible reason for the flattering guess, that he had latterly been reading Comte's *Positive Philosophy*,[7] and writings of that school, some of whose expressions had thus passed into his vocabulary, expressions which were also common to George Eliot. * * *

One reflection about himself at this date [1874] sometimes made Hardy uneasy. He perceived that he was "up against" the position of having to carry on his life not as an emotion, but as a scientific game; that he was committed by circumstances to novel-writing as a regular trade, as much as he had formerly been to architecture; and that hence he would, he deemed, have to look for material in manners—in ordinary social and fashionable life as other novelists did. Yet he took no interest in manners, but in the substance of life only. So far what he had written had not been novels at all, as usually understood—that is pictures of modern customs and observances—and might not long sustain the interest of the circulating library subscriber who cared mainly for those things. On the other hand, to go about to dinners and club and crushes as a business was not much to his mind. Yet that was necessary meat and drink to the popular author. Not that he was unsociable, but events and long habit had accustomed him to solitary living. So it was also with his wife, of whom he wrote later, in the poem entitled "A Dream or No":

> Lonely I found her,
> The sea-birds around her,
> And other than nigh things uncaring to know.

* * *

Another incident which added to his dubiety was the arrival of a letter from Coventry Patmore,[8] a total stranger to him, expressing the view that A *Pair of Blue Eyes* was in its nature not a conception for prose, and that he "regretted at almost every page that such unequalled beauty and power should not have assured themselves the immortality which would have been impressed upon them by the form of verse". Hardy was much struck by this opinion from Patmore. However, finding himself committed to

7. Auguste Comte (1798-1857) founded a school of philosophy based on experi- ence and science [*Editor*].
8. A then-well-known poet [*Editor*].

prose, he renewed his consideration of a prose style, as it is evident from the following note:

"Read again Addison, Macaulay, Newman, Sterne, Defoe, Lamb, Gibbon, Burke, Times Leaders,[9] etc., in a study of style. Am more and more confirmed in an idea I have long held, as a matter of commonsense, long before I thought of any old aphorism bearing on the subject: 'Ars est celare artem'.[1] The whole secret of a living style and the difference between it and a dead style, lies in not having too much style—being—in fact, a little careless, or rather seeming to be, here and there. It brings wonderful life into the writing:

> "A sweet disorder in the dress . . .
>   A careless shoe-string, in whose tie
>   I see a wild civility,
>   Do more bewitch me than when art
>   Is too precise in every part.[2]

"Otherwise your style is like worn half-pence—all the fresh images rounded off by rubbing, and no crispness or movement at all.

"It is, of course, simply a carrying into prose the knowledge I have acquired in poetry—that inexact rhymes and rhythms now and then are far more pleasing than correct ones."

* * *

[*Passages from Hardy's notebooks are scattered throughout the two volumes of the biography. They are set in quotation marks, as follows:*]

"There is enough poetry in what is left [in life], after all the false romance has been abstracted, to make a sweet pattern: *e.g.*, the poem by H. Coleridge:

> She is not fair to outward view.

"So, then, if Nature's defects must be looked in the face and transcribed, whence arises the *art* in poetry and novel-writing? which must certainly show art, or it becomes merely mechanical reporting. I think the art lies in making these defects the basis of a hitherto unperceived beauty, by irradiating them with 'the light that never was'[3] on their surface, but is seen to be latent in them by the spiritual eye."

9. *I.e.*, editorials or leading articles in the London *Times* [*Editor*].
1. "Art is to conceal art," or "True art conceals art" [*Editor*].
2. From Robert Herrick's "Delight in Disorder" (1648) [*Editor*].
3. Ah! then, if mine had been the Painter's hand,

To express what then I saw; and add the gleam,
The light that never was, on sea or land,
The consecration, and the Poet's dream . . . .
Wordsworth, "Elegiac Stanzas," lines 13-16 [*Editor*].

"*June* 28 [1876]. Being Coronation Day there are games and dancing on the green at Sturminster Newton. The stewards with white rosettes. One is very anxious, fearing that while he is attending to the runners the leg of mutton on the pole will go wrong; hence he walks hither and thither with a compressed countenance and eyes far ahead.

"The pretty girls, just before a dance, stand in inviting positions on the grass. As the couples in each figure pass near where their immediate friends loiter, each girl-partner gives a laughing glance at such friends, and whirls on."

* * *

"Note. A Plot, or Tragedy, should arise from the gradual closing in of a situation that comes of ordinary human passions, prejudices, and ambitions, by reason of the characters taking no trouble to ward off the disastrous events produced by the said passions, prejudices, and ambitions."

* * *

"*April* 22 [1878]. The method of Boldini, the painter of 'The Morning Walk' in the French Gallery two or three years ago (a young lady beside an ugly blank wall on an ugly highway)—of Hobbema, in his view of a road with formal lopped trees and flat tame scenery—is of that infusing emotion into the baldest external objects either by the presence of a human figure among them, or by mark of some human connection with them."

* * *

He wrote to Messrs Smith and Elder [the publishers]:

"I enclose a sketch-map of the supposed scene in which *The Return of the Native* is laid, copied from the one I used in writing the story; and my suggestion is that we place an engraving of it as frontispiece to the first volume. Unity of place is so seldom preserved in novels that a map of the scene of action is as a rule quite impracticable. But since the present story affords an opportunity of doing so I am of opinion that it would be a desirable novelty." The publishers fell in with the idea and the map was made.

* * *

Since coming into contact with Leslie Stephen about 1873, as has been shown, Hardy had been much influenced by his philosophy, and also by his criticism. He quotes the following sentence from Stephen in his notebook under the date of July 1, 1879:

"The ultimate aim of the poet should be to touch our hearts by showing his own, and not to exhibit his learning, or his fine taste, or his skill in mimicking the notes of his predecessors." That Hardy adhered pretty closely to this principle when he resumed the writing of poetry can hardly be denied.

* * *

"*January* 1881. My third month in bed. Driving snow: fine, and so fast that individual flakes cannot be seen. In sheltered places they occasionally stop, and balance themselves in the air like hawks. . . . It creeps into the house, the window-plants being covered as if out-of-doors. Our passage (downstairs) is sole-deep, Em says, and feet leave tracks on it."

(Same month.) "Style—Consider the Wordsworthian dictum (the more perfectly the natural object is reproduced, the more truly poetic the picture). This reproduction is achieved by seeing into the *heart of a thing* (as rain, wind, for instance), and is realism, in fact, though through being pursued by means of the imagination it is confounded with invention, which is pursued by the same means. It is, in short, reached by what M. Arnold calls 'the imaginative reason.' "

* *² *

In July he jots down some notes on fiction, possibly for an article that was never written:

"The real, if unavowed, purpose of fiction is to give pleasure by gratifying the love of the uncommon in human experience, mental or corporeal.

"This is done all the more perfectly in proportion as the reader is illuded to believe the personages true and real like himself.

"Solely to this latter end a work of fiction should be a precise transcript of ordinary life: but,

"The uncommon would be absent and the interest lost. Hence,

"The writer's problem is, how to strike the balance between the uncommon and the ordinary so as on the one hand to give interest, on the other to give reality.

"In working out this problem, human nature must never be made abnormal, which is introducing incredibility. The uncommonness must be in the events, not in the characters; and the writer's art lies in shaping that uncommonness while disguising its unlikelihood, if it be unlikely."

* * *

"*January* 26 [1882]. Coleridge says, aim at *illusion* in audience or readers—*i.e.*, the mental state when dreaming, intermediate between complete *delusion* (which the French mistakenly aim at) and a clear perception of falsity."

* * *

"*August*. An ample theme: the intense interests, passions, and strategy that throb through the commonest lives.

"This month blackbirds and thrushes creep about under fruit-bushes and in other shady places in gardens rather like four-legged animals than birds. . . . I notice that a blackbird has eaten nearly a whole pear lying in the garden-path in the course of the day."

* * *

"*October* 20 [1884]. Query: Is not the present quasi-scientific system of writing history mere charlatanism? Events and tendencies are traced as if they were rivers of voluntary activity, and courses reasoned out from the circumstances in which natures, religions, or what-not, have found themselves. But are they not in the main the outcome of *passivity*—acted upon by unconscious propensity?"

* * *

"Evidences of art in Bible narratives. They are written with a watchful attention (though disguised) as to their effect on their reader. Their so-called simplicity is, in fact, the simplicity of the highest cunning. And one is led to inquire, when even in these latter days artistic development and arrangement are the qualities least appreciated by readers, who was there likely to appreciate the art in these chronicles at that day?

"Looking round on a well-selected shelf of fiction or history, how few stories of any length does one recognize as well told from beginning to end! The first half of this story, the last half of that, the middle of another. . . . The modern art of narration is yet in its infancy.

"But in these Bible lives and adventures there is the spherical completeness of perfect art. And our first, and second, feeling that they must be true because they are so impressive, becomes, as a third feeling, modified to, 'Are they so very true, after all?' Is not the fact of their being so convincing an argument, not for their actuality, but for the actuality of a consummate artist who was no more content with what Nature offered than Sophocles and Pheidias were content?"

* * *

"*April* 19 [1885]. The business of the poet and novelist is to show the sorriness underlying the grandest things, and the grandeur underlying the sorriest things."

* * *

"*March* 4 [1886]. Novel-writing as an art cannot go backward. Having reached the analytic stage it must transcend it by going still further in the same direction. Why not by rendering as visible essences, spectres, etc., the abstract thoughts of the analytic school?"

* * *

"[*January*, 1887]. After looking at the landscape ascribed to Bonington in our drawing-room I feel that Nature is played out as a Beauty, but not as a Mystery. I don't want to see landscapes, *i.e.*, scenic paintings of them, because I don't want to see the original realities—as optical effects, that is. I want to see the deeper reality underlying the scenic, the expression of what are sometimes called abstract imaginings.

"The 'simply natural' is interesting no longer. The much decried, mad, late-Turner rendering is now necessary to create my interest. The exact truth as to material fact ceases to be of importance in art—it is a student's style—the style of a period when the mind is serene and unawakened to the tragical mysteries of life; when it does not bring anything to the object that coalesces with and translates the qualities that are already there,—half hidden, it may be—and the two united are depicted as the All."

* * *

"[*December* 31, 1887.] Books read or pieces looked at this year: Milton, Dante, Calderon, Goethe. Homer, Virgil, Moliere, Scott. The Cid, Nibelungen, Crusoe, Don Quixote. Aristophanes, Theocritus, Boccaccio. Canterbury Tales, Shakespeare's Sonnets, Lycidas. Malory, Vicar of Wakefield, Ode to the West Wind, Ode to Grecian Urn. Christabel, Wye above Tintern. Chapman's Iliad, Lord Derby's ditto, Worsley's Odyssey."

* * *

"I was thinking a night or two ago that people are somnambulists—that the material is not the real—only the visible, the real being invisible optically. That it is because we are in a somnambulistic hallucination that we think the real to be what we see as real."

* * *

In the latter part of this month [February, 1888] there arrived the following:

"The Rev. Dr. A. B. Grosart ventures to address Mr. Hardy on a problem that is of life and death; personally, and in relation to young eager intellects for whom he is responsible. . . . Dr. Grosart finds abundant evidence that the facts and mysteries of nature and human nature have come urgently before Mr. Hardy's penetrative brain."

He enumerated some of the horrors of human and animal life, particularly parasitic, and added:

"The problem is how to reconcile these with the absolute goodness and non-limitation of God."

Hardy replied: "Mr. Hardy regrets that he is unable to suggest any hypothesis which would reconcile the existence of such evils as Dr. Grosart describes with the idea of omnipotent goodness. Perhaps Dr. Grosart might be helped to a provisional view of the universe by the recently published Life of Darwin, and the works of Herbert Spencer and other agnostics."

He met Leslie Stephen shortly after, and Stephen told him that he too had received a similar letter from Grosart; to which he had replied that as the reverend doctor was a professor of theology, and he himself only a layman, he should have thought it was the doctor's business to explain the difficulty to his correspondent, and not his to explain it to the doctor.

* * *

"[*July* 9.] Reading H. James's *Reverberator*. After this kind of work one feels inclined to be purposely careless in detail. The great novels of the future will certainly not concern themselves with the minutiae of manners. . . . James's subjects are those one could be interested in at moments when there is nothing larger to think of."

* * *

"*September* 30. 'The Valley of the Great Dairies'.—Froom.

" 'The Valley of the Little Dairies'.—Blackmoor.

"In the afternoon by train to Evershot. Walked to Woolcombe, a property once owned by a—I think the senior—branch of the Hardys. Woolcombe House was to the left of where the dairy now is. On by the lane and path to Bubb-Down. Looking east you see High Stoy and the escarpment below it. The Vale of Blackmoor is almost entirely green, every hedge being studded with trees. On the left you see to an immense distance, including Shaftesbury.

"The decline and fall of the Hardys much in evidence hereabout. An instance: Becky S.'s mother's sister married one of the Hardys of this branch, who was considered to have bemeaned himself by the marriage. 'All Woolcombe and Froom Quintin belonged to them at one time,' Becky used to say proudly. She might have added Up-Sydling and Toller Welme. This particular couple had an enormous lot of children. I remember when young seeing the man—tall and thin—walking beside a horse and common spring trap, and my mother pointing him out to me and saying he represented what was once the leading branch of the family. So we go down, down, down."

"*October* 7. The besetting sin of modern literature is its insincerity. Half its utterances are qualified, even contradicted, by an aside, and this particularly in morals and religion. When dogma has to be balanced on its feet by such hair-splitting as the late Mr. M. Arnold's it must be in a very bad way."

* * *

"*February* 26 [1889]. In time one might get to regard every object, and every action, as composed, not of this or that material, this or that movement, but of the qualities pleasure and pain in varying proportions."

* * *

At the end of [July, 1889] they gave up their rooms in Bayswater and returned to Dorchester; where during August Hardy settled down daily to writing the new story he had conceived, which was *Tess of the d'Urbervilles*, though it had not as yet been christened. During the month he jots down as a casual thought:

"When a married woman who has a lover kills her husband, she does not really wish to kill the husband; she wishes to kill the situation. Of course in Clytaemnestra's case it was not exactly so, since there was the added grievance of Iphigenia, which half-justified her."[4]

* * *

However, the business immediately in hand was the new story *Tess of the d'Urbervilles*, for the serial use of which Hardy had three requests, if not more, on his list; and in October [1889] as much of it as was written was offered to the first who had asked for it, the editor of *Murray's Magazine*. It was declined and returned to him in the middle of November virtually on the score of its improper explicitness. It was at once sent on to the second, the editor of *Macmillan's Magazine*, and on the 25th was declined by him for practically the same reason. Hardy would now have much preferred to finish the story and bring it out in volume form only, but there were reasons why he could not afford to do this; and he adopted a plan till then, it is believed, unprecedented in the annals of fiction. This was not to offer the novel intact to the third editor on his list (his experience with the first two editors having taught him that it would be useless to send it to the third as it stood), but to send it up with some chapters or parts of chapters cut out, and instead of destroying these to publish them, or much of them, elsewhere, if practicable, as episodic adventures of anonymous personages (which in fact was done, with the omission of a few paragraphs); till they could be put back in their places at the printing of the whole in volume form. In addition several passages were modified. Hardy carried out this unceremonious concession to

4. Agamemnon, Clytemnestra's husband, had sacrificed his daughter Iphigenia to the goddess Artemis [*Editor*].

conventionality with cynical amusement, knowing the novel was moral enough and to spare. But the work was sheer drudgery, the modified passages having to be written in coloured ink, that the originals might be easily restored, and he frequently asserted that it would have been almost easier for him to write a new story altogether. Hence the labour brought no profit. He resolved to get away from the supply of family fiction to magazines as soon as he conveniently could do so.

However, the treatment was a complete success, and the mutilated novel was accepted by the editor of the *Graphic*, the third editor on Hardy's list, and an arrangement come to for beginning it in the pages of that paper in July 1891. It may be mentioned that no complaint of impropriety in its cut-down form was made by readers, except by one gentleman with a family of daughters, who thought the blood-stain on the ceiling indecent—Hardy could never understand why.

* * *

"*March-April* [1890]. * * * Art consists in so depicting the common events of life as to bring out the features which illustrate the author's idiosyncratic mode of regard; making old incidents and things seem as new."

* * *

"*October* 28 [1891]. It is the incompleteness that is loved, when love is sterling and true. This is what differentiates the real one from the imaginary, the practicable from the impossible, the Love who returns the kiss from the Vision that melts away. A man sees the Diana or the Venus in his Beloved, but what he loves is the difference."

* * *

"*October* 30. Howells and those of his school forget that a story *must* be striking enough to be worth telling. Therein lies the problem—to reconcile the average with that uncommonness which alone makes it natural that a tale or experience would dwell in the memory and induce repetition."

* * *

As the year drew to a close an incident that took place during the publication of *Tess of the d'Urbervilles* as a serial in the *Graphic* might have prepared him for certain events that were to follow. The editor objected to the description of Angel Clare carrying in his arms, across a flooded lane, Tess and her three dairy-maid companions. He suggested that it would be more decorous and suitable for the pages of a periodical intended for family reading if the damsels were wheeled across the lane in a wheelbarrow. This was accordingly done.

Also the *Graphic* refused to print the chapter describing the christening of the infant child of Tess. This appeared in Henley's *Scots Observer*, and was afterwards restored to the novel, where it was considered one of the finest passages.

Tess of the d'Urbervilles; a Pure Woman Faithfully Presented was published complete about the last day of November, with what results Hardy could scarcely have foreseen, since the book, notwithstanding its exceptional popularity, was the beginning of the end of his career as a novelist.

* * *

As *Tess of the d'Urbervilles* got into general circulation it attracted an attention that Hardy had apparently not foreseen, for at the time of its publication he was planning something of quite a different kind, according to an entry he made:

"Title:—'Songs of Five-and-Twenty Years'. Arrangement of the songs: Lyric Ecstasy inspired by music to have precedence."

However, reviews, letters, and other intelligence speedily called him from these casual thoughts back to the novel, which the tediousness of the alterations and restorations had made him weary of. From the prefaces to later editions can be gathered more or less clearly what happened to the book as, passing into great popularity, an endeavour was made by some critics to change it to scandalous notoriety—the latter kind of clamour, raised by a certain small section of the public and the press, being quite inexplicable to the writer himself.

* * *

"[*April*] 15. *Good Friday* [1892]. Read review of *Tess* in *The Quarterly*.[5] A smart and amusing article; but it is easy to be smart and amusing if a man will forgo veracity and sincerity. . . . How strange that one may write a book without knowing what one puts into it—or rather, the reader reads into it. Well, if this sort of thing continues no more novel-writing for me. A man must be a fool to deliberately stand up to be shot at."

* * *

"16. Dr. Walter Lock, Warden of Keble, Oxford, called. '*Tess*', he said, 'is the Agamemnon without the remainder of the Oresteian trilogy.' This is inexact, but suggestive as to how people think."

* * *

He had received many requests for a dramatic version of the novel, but he found that nothing could be done with it among London actor-managers, all of them in their notorious timidity

5. See p. 382 [*Editor*].

being afraid of the censure from conventional critics that had resisted Ibsen; and he abandoned all idea of producing it, one prominent actor telling him frankly that he could not play such a dubious character as Angel Clare (which would have suited him precisely) "because I have my name to make, and it would risk my reputation with the public if I played anything but a heroic character without spot". Hardy thought of the limited artistic sense of even a leading English actor. Yet before and after this time Hardy received letters or oral messages from almost every actress of note in Europe asking for an opportunity of appearing in the part of "Tess"—among them being Mrs. Patrick Campbell, Ellen Terry, Sarah Bernhardt, and Eleanora Duse.

* * *

During this year 1895, and before and after, *Tess of the d'Urbervilles* went through Europe in translations, German, French, Russian, Dutch, Italian, and other tongues, Hardy as a rule stipulating that the translation should be complete and unabridged, on a guarantee of which he would make no charge. Some of the renderings, however, were much hacked about in spite of him. The Russian translation appears to have been read and approved by Tolstoi during its twelve-month's career in a Moscow monthly periodical.

At the beginning of March [1897,] a dramatization of *Tess of the d'Urbervilles* was produced in America with much success by Mr. Fiske. * * *

The misrepresentations of the last two or three years affected by little, if at all, the informed appreciation of Hardy's writings, being heeded almost entirely by those who had not read him; and turned out ultimately to be the best thing that could have happened; for they wellnigh compelled him, in his own judgement at any rate, if he wished to retain any shadow of self-respect, to abandon at once a form of literary art he had long intended to abandon at some indefinite time, and resume openly that form of it which had always been more instinctive with him, and which he had just been able to keep alive from his early years, half in secrecy, under the pressure of magazine writing. He abandoned it with all the less reluctance in that the novel was, in his own words, "gradually losing artistic form, with a beginning, middle, and end, and becoming a spasmodic inventory of items, which has nothing to do with art."

The change, after all, was not so great as it seemed. It was not as if he had been a writer of novels proper, and as more specifically understood, that is, stories of modern artificial life and manners showing a certain smartness of treatment. He had mostly aimed at keeping his narratives close to natural life and as near to poetry in their subject as the conditions would allow, and had often regretted that those conditions would not let him keep them nearer still.

* * *

For several years some of the members of the Dorchester Debating and Dramatic Society had wished to perform a dramatization of *Tess of the d'Urbervilles*. After much hesitation Hardy handed over [in 1924] his own dramatization, although, as he notes in his diary, he had come to the conclusion that to dramatize a novel was a mistake in art; moreover, that the play ruined the novel and the novel the play. However, the result was that the company, self-styled "The Hardy Players," produced *Tess* with such unexpected success at Dorchester and Weymouth that it was asked for in London, and the following year produced there by professional actors for over a hundred nights, Miss Gwen Ffrangçon-Davies taking the part of "Tess."

* * *

On December 6 [1925] the company of players from the Garrick Theatre arrived at Max Gate⁶ in the evening for the purpose of giving a performance of *Tess* in the drawing-room. The following description of this incident is taken from a letter written by one of the company to a correspondent in America who had particularly desired her impression of the visit: * * *

"We played the scenes of Tess's home with chairs and a tiny drawing-room table to represent farm furniture—tea-cups for drinking mugs—when the chairs and tables were removed the corner of the drawing-room became Stonehenge, and yet in some strange way those present said the play gained from the simplicity.

"It had seemed as if it would be a paralysingly difficult thing to do, to get the atmosphere at all within a few feet of the author himself and without any of the usual theatrical illusion, but speaking for myself, after the first few seconds it was perfectly easy, and Miss Ffrangçon-Davies's beautiful voice and exquisite playing of the Stonehenge scene in the shadows thrown by the firelight was a thing that I shall never forget. It was beautiful.

"Mr. Hardy insisted on talking to us until the last minute. He talked of Tess as if she was someone real whom he had known and liked tremendously." * * *

[*Hardy died January 11, 1928, at the age of 87.*]

6. The house Hardy had built in Dorchester forty years before and had lived in ever since [*Editor*].

Composition and Publication

RICHARD PURDY
[*Tess* as a Serial]†

Tess of the d'Urbervilles was written at Max Gate and seems to have been started as early as the autumn of 1888. It was designed from the first for Tillotson & Son of Bolton [1] and their newspaper syndicate, for which Hardy had already provided three short stories. From letters of February 1889 it is apparent the novel was well under way and that serial publication was to begin before the end of the year, under the title 'Too Late Beloved' (or 'Too Late, Beloved!').[2] On 23 August 1889 Hardy sent Tillotson's 'a list of some scenes from the story, that your artist may choose which he prefers', and promised an instalment of the MS. would be sent shortly, and on 9 September he forwarded 'a portion of the MS. of "Too Late Beloved"—equal to about one-half, I think. . . . The remainder to follow as per agreement.' This MS., which included the daring and controversial seduction and midnight baptism scenes, was at once given to the printers, and it was not until proofs were in their hands that Tillotson's realized the nature of the story they had agreed to publish, no prospectus of a forthcoming work being required in their contracts. They were distinctly taken aback. W. F. Tillotson had been a leading Congregationalist and Sunday School worker and held strong views as to the tone of all material in his own papers and the family newspapers that were his clients. Though he had died six months before this time, his firm and particularly his colleague and editor, William Brimelow, faithfully reflected his policies. They at once suggested that the story should be recast and certain scenes and incidents deleted entirely. Hardy would not agree to this, and after a further exchange Tillotson's

† From Richard Purdy, *Thomas Hardy: A Bibliographical Study* (New York, 1954), pp. 69, 71–73. Some of the author's footnotes have been omitted.
1. Who had offered Hardy one thousand guineas for serial rights in England and America. See J. T. Laird, *The Shaping of "Tess of the D'Urbervilles"* (Oxford, 1975), p. 3 [*Editor*].
2. This original title is echoed in Tess's desperate words to Angel Clare at Sandbourne, towards the close of Ch. 55.

announced that they could not issue the story although they would pay for it as arranged. On this Hardy suggested that their agreement should be cancelled, and so the matter was settled, with no ill feeling on either side. * * *

The whole business must have been distasteful to Hardy, especially in view of his continuing difficulties with the novel, and in the *Early Life* there is no mention of *Tess* before August 1889, when 'Hardy settled down daily to writing the new story he had conceived, which was *Tess of the d'Urbervilles*, though it had not as yet been christened.' The novel, not yet finished, was offered to *Murray's Magazine* in October but refused by Edward Arnold on 15 November, 'virtually on the score of its improper explicitness.' It was next offered to *Macmillan's Magazine*, but Mowbray Morris likewise rejected it ten days later. Hardy then undertook 'with cynical amusement' the dismemberment and modification of the text which made it acceptable to Arthur Locker and the *Graphic*. * * *

This work was not completed until the latter part of 1890, and it was 4 July 1891 before serial publication commenced, though Hardy had accepted Harper's terms for the serial publication of *Tess* in America as far back as 7 March 1890.

* * *

Two episodes, 'more especially addressed to adult readers' as Hardy described them, proved unacceptable to the editor of the *Graphic* and were first printed elsewhere. In each case new material was added to meet the demands of an independent sketch and indications of the real origin of the episode, particularly the name 'Tess', removed. Chaps. 10 and 11, the seduction of Tess by Alec d'Urberville, were printed under the title 'Saturday Night in Arcady' in a Special Literary Supplement of the *National Observer* (Edinburgh), 14 November 1891; Chap. 14, the baptism and death of Tess's baby, was printed under the title 'The Midnight Baptism, A Study in Christianity' in the *Fortnightly Review*, May 1891 (two months, it will be noticed, before serial publication of the novel began).

This temporary dismemberment of the novel necessitated changes in plot, such as the introduction of a mock marriage and the omission of the encounter with the painter of texts (in Chap. 12), and there were numerous scattered bowdlerizations and omissions. When the novel was published in book form the original text was, of course, restored, and Hardy was able 'to piece the trunk and limbs of the novel together, and print it complete, as originally written . . .' though with further revisions in detail.

IAN GREGOR and BRIAN NICHOLAS
[Hardy's Concessions] †

By a pleasant stroke of irony [Hardy] had been invited to contribute at the beginning of [1890] to the *New Review* an article on 'Candour in English Fiction'. Hardy certainly had reason for thinking that he was an authority on the subject, and, as letters of rejection [concerning his manuscript of *Tess*] were arriving virtually while he was composing the article, it must have been an overwhelming temptation to point his argument with particular illustrations. He resisted, however, and the argument is a general one. Beginning with the observation, which his recent editorial encounters made heavily ironical, that 'even imagination is the slave of stolid circumstance', he goes on to consider how a novelist's sincerity is constantly being compromised by the machinery of the publishing world, by which he means the magazine and the circulating library, and also by the expectations of the novel-reading public itself. The latter,

> acting under the censorship of prudery rigorously exclude from the pages they regulate subjects that have been made, by general approval of the best judges, the bases of the finest imaginative compositions, since literature rose to the dignity of an art. The crash of broken commandments is as necessary an accompaniment to the catastrophe of a tragedy, as the noise of drum and cymbals to a triumphal march. But the crash of broken commandments shall not be heard. . . . More precisely, an arbitrary proclamation has gone forth that certain picked commandments of the ten shall be preserved intact—to wit, the first, third, and seventh; that the ninth shall be infringed but gingerly; the sixth only as much as necessary; and the remainder alone as much as you please, in a genteel manner. . . . The writer may print the '*not*' of his broken commandment in letters of flame; and it makes no difference. A question which should be wholly a question of treatment is confusedly regarded as a question of subject.

The interest of Hardy's article is chiefly autobiographical, coming just when it did, and when he turns to offer solutions to solve the novelist's dilemma they are sketchy and half-hearted. Encouragement should be given to the purchase, rather than the borrowing of novels; indiscriminate family reading in newspapers and magazines should be broken down by the publication of special magazines aimed exclusively at an adult audience, and supplements, similarly aimed,

† From Ian Gregor and Brian Nicholas,   pp. 132-35.
The Moral and the Story (London,1962),

should be issued with newspapers. But these recommendations are hurried into a final paragraph, and Hardy's main interest is to state as forcibly as he can the *crise de conscience* that faces the serious contemporary novelist. It is certainly a situation which exposes the kind of grip that serial publication and the circulating library had on a writer's work, even at this comparatively late date.

Having had an unexpected opportunity to express his views on public taste directly, Hardy now returned to consider the ways in which *Tess* could overcome the 'stolid circumstance' of continuous editorial rejections. Two incidents, in particular, were causing the trouble—the seduction scene, which was obliquely presented, and the baptism of Tess's child. Hardy decided to replace the first by a mock-marriage with Alec, so Tess's story to her mother appeared in this form to serial readers:

> 'He made love to me, as you said he would do; and he asked me to marry him, also just as you declared he would. I never have liked him; but at last I agreed, knowing you'd be angry, if I didn't. He said, it must be private even from you, on account of his mother; and by special licence; and foolish I agreed to that likewise, to get rid of his pestering. I drove with him to Melchester, and there in a private room I went through the form of marriage with him as before a registrar. A few weeks after, I found out that it was not the registrar's house we had gone to, as I had supposed, but the houes of a friend of his, who had played the part of the registrar. I then came away from Trantridge instantly, though he wished me to stay; and here I am.'

The letter of the law is preserved; Tess's seduction is made socially acceptable by the fact that she thought she was marrying Alec. In fact, Tess is morally obtuse here in a way she is not in the book, committing herself to marrying a man she despises, because she is afraid of her mother's anger and his pestering. And on these inadequate and rather shoddy moral and dramatic motives the serial version is built.

In this version there is no child, and consequently the second troublesome incident, the baptism, is by-passed. After these major changes, the rest of the 'moral' adaptations are small; perhaps the most interesting occurs in the final section. In the serial, we are made to realize, by various touches, that Tess is not living in Sandbourne as Alec's wife. This time defence of the letter leads actually to the creation of a morally perverse situation. If Tess is simply living in Sandbourne, as the serial says, 'to be friends with him', there can be no dramatic catastrophe when Angel Clare arrives. Further, Tess's killing of Alec then becomes gratuitous in a way that *is* morally shocking. Now that the novel had been made by the strict observance of conventional relationships both morally dubious and dramatically false, the way was clear to acceptance for serial publication.

Accordingly, Hardy sent it to the illustrated weekly newspaper, the *Graphic*, and there, flanked by pictures of the Kaiser's visit to London and the building of the Manchester Ship Canal, it appeared in twenty-four illustrated weekly instalments from 4th July to 26th December 1891. Once publication had started everything went smoothly, except for one of the August numbers. The editor objected to the scene where Clare carries the three girls over the flooded lane. He suggested a wheelbarrow would be more fitting. Hardy, obedient to the last, complied, and accordingly readers of the serial read: ' "I'll wheel you through the pool—all of you—with pleasure, if you'll wait till I get a barrow. . . . There's a barrow in the shed yonder." ' Even in questions of transport 'imagination had been made the slave of stolid circumstance'.

* * *

While the serial was running its course in the *Graphic*, Hardy was getting ready for the publication of the book by reassembling the original structure and making certain small stylistic revisions. Hardy's last act before returning the final proofs to the publishers was to redraft the title page, and add the sub-title 'A Pure Woman', together with the quotation from *Two Gentlemen of Verona*:

'Poor wounded name! My bosom as a bed/Shall lodge thee.' In his preface to the 1912 edition Hardy wrote: 'Respecting the sub-title . . . it was appended at the last moment . . . as being the estimate left in a candid mind of the heroine's character—an estimate that nobody would be likely to dispute. It was disputed more than anything else in the book.' During the last week of November—a month before the serial ended in the *Graphic*—*Tess of the D'Urbervilles* was finally published in volume form.

Such was the tortuous course into print of the first novel to allow a seduced woman to appear as an unqualified heroine. It was now given over to the reading public at large—and to the critics.

RICHARD PURDY
[Later Editions]†

Tess of the d'Urbervilles was published at 31s. 6d. in an edition of 1,000 copies some time in the week of 29 November 1891. * * *

† From Richard Purdy, *Thomas Hardy: A Bibliographical Study* (New York, 1954), pp. 73–77, 285.

Hardy wrote to Edmund Gosse 20 January 1892 to thank him for a generous letter about *Tess* and added, 'The same post brings one from the publishers, from which I find that since Saturday the orders have been in larger numbers: so that the review[1] has done no harm. They are reprinting frantically, but unfortunately they will have to keep people waiting a few days I fear.' The publishers advertised on 30 January, 'The large Edition of Thomas Hardy's New Novel, Tess of the D'Urbervilles, having been exhausted, a Second Edition is in rapid preparation, and will be ready immediately', and this second impression of 500 copies was published shortly after (the British Museum copy bears the accession date '8 Fe 92'). * * *

The first one-volume edition of *Tess*, called the 'Fifth Edition', uniform with *A Group of Noble Dames* and containing a portrait of Hardy as frontispiece, was published at 6s. in an edition of 5,000 copies, 30 September 1892. In this form there were five impressions totalling 17,000 copies before the end of the year. For this edition Hardy prepared an important Preface dated July 1892, and he inscribed copies of the book to many friends. * * *

The novel was further revised for Osgood, McIlvaine's edition of the Wessex Novels and an additional Preface, dated January 1895, prepared. For Macmillan's definitive Wessex Edition Hardy added a note to his previous Prefaces in March 1912, calling attention in particular to the fact that a few pages in Chap. 10, overlooked 'when the detached episodes were collected as stated in the preface of 1891, . . . though they were in the original manuscript', were now printed in the novel for the first time. These pages (76-79) contain the episode of the dance at the hay-trusser's as it had appeared in 'Saturday Night in Arcady'. * * *

The Wessex Edition is in every sense the definitive edition of Hardy's work and the last authority in questions of text.[2]

1. *The Saturday Review*, 16 January 1892: ". . . Mr. Hardy, it must be conceded, tells an unpleasant story in a very unpleasant way."

2. According to J. T. Laird, *The Shaping of "Tess of the d'Urbervilles"* (Oxford, 1975), p. 3, f.n. 1: "The Macmillan Wessex Edition of *Tess*, published in 1912, is the last edition to have been thoroughly revised by Hardy and to embody textual changes of sufficient substance to be of interest to the literary critic. It is not, however, the definitive text of the novel. This title must be reserved for the 1920 reprint of the Wessex Edition, which incorporates in addition to its own small group of trifling revisions a few equally trifling amendments which had first appeared during 1919 in the sumptuous Mellstock Edition. The trivial nature of Hardy's amendments in the Mellstock Edition of *Tess* may be illustrated by the following (italicized) insertion in chapter 18: 'The conventional farm-folk of his imagination—personified *in the newspaper-press* by the pitiable dummy known as Hodge—were obliterated after a few days' residence' (vol. I, p. 157). Moreover, as his letters to Macmillan during 1919 show, Hardy did not check the proofs of *Tess* in the Mellstock Edition (*M139*, pp. 114, 122). The nine pages of 'corrections' submitted for the Mellstock Edition and the 1920 reprint of the Wessex Edition are still extant and are held at DCM [the Dorset County Museum, Dorchester, England—*Editor*].

J. T. LAIRD

Developments in the Printed Versions†

* * *

One of the more surprising features of the First Edition is its occasional bowdlerization of both manuscript and *Graphic* material. It is, of course, well known that, in general terms, the First Edition offers an infinitely more honest and satisfying account of the story than does the *Graphic*: what is not widely appreciated is the fact that some of the manuscript passages, modified or omitted on moralistic grounds in the *Graphic*, were not fully restored when the First Edition appeared. This discrepancy is especially noticeable in passages relating to events of the night of the seduction. Nor is it realized by most students of the novel that the First Edition is sometimes less frank than the *Graphic* in describing the feelings and behaviour of Tess and Angel during the courtship period at Talbothays.

Although the account of the actual seduction is incomplete in the B.M. MS.,[1] owing to the fact that ff. 100–1 are no longer extant, the beginning of the scene on f. 99 is described with a certain amount of realistic detail, as the following extract shows:

> *obscurity*
> There was no answer. & The ~~blackness~~ was now so intense that he
> *The red rug, & the white muslin figure he had*
> could see absolutely nothing. ∧
> *left upon it, were now all——blackness alike.* ~~Hawnferne~~ [?]
> He   stooped, & heard a
>
> *She was sleeping soundly.*
> gentle regular breathing. ∧   He knelt, & bent lower, & her breath
> *warmed*   & *with her hair,*
> ~~touched~~ his face, & in a moment his cheek was in contact with hers ∧
>
> & *her eyes. A damp wetness accompanied the touch——of her eye*
> ~~Sue was sleeping soundly, & there was damp about her lashes~~
> *upon his face,*
> ∧   as if she had wept.
>
> (f. 99)

In the First Edition, which was the next text to contain an account of this episode, much of the realistic detail has disappeared, the paragraph now ending with the sentence 'She was sleeping soundly': 'There was no answer. The obscurity was now so great that he could see absolutely nothing but a pale nebulousness at his feet, which represented the white muslin figure he had left upon the dead leaves. Everything else was blackness alike. D'Urberville stooped; and heard a gentle regular breathing. She was sleeping soundly' (I. 140).

* * *

† From J. T. Laird, "Developments in the Printed Versions," in *The Shaping of "Tess of the d'Urbervilles,"* (Oxford, 1975), pp. 158–60, 162–63, 165–66, 169–71, 175–77; and from "Conclusion," pp. 190–92. Some of the author's notes have been omitted.
1. The manuscript of *Tess* in the British Museum (note that in this manuscript the character later called "Tess" is named "Sue") [*Editor*].

Somewhat earlier in the story, the manuscript contains an account of the Chaseborough dance (ff. 81–5), which, although omitted from the *Graphic*, was to appear in an abridged form in the sketch, 'Saturday Night in Arcady'. When Hardy came to prepare the text of the First Edition, for some reason this episode was not included, although it was to be reinserted in the novel when the 'Wessex' version was published in 1912. In the preface to that edition Hardy claimed that the relevant manuscript leaves had been 'overlooked' at the First Edition stage. As has earlier been noted, the omission of the Chaseborough dance could not have been accidental, and the evidence for this deduction is given in the next chapter. What is most pertinent, at this juncture, is that we should remember that the Chaseborough dance episode contains several patterns of rich erotic imagery: it is thus conceivable that one of Hardy's motives for omitting the episode was the desire to avoid drawing upon himself criticism occasioned by its erotic tone.

* * *

There is also present in the First Edition a group of bowdlerizations for which magazine editors cannot in any way be held responsible. In the three examples cited immediately below, the amendments represent a toning down of the language describing the heroine's emotional responsiveness to Angel's advances during the courtship scenes at Talbothays, and would seem to have been influenced mainly by Hardy's desire to continue the trend, apparent in the later manuscript layers, of placing increased emphasis on the modesty of Tess. Thus, after Angel has embraced her and asked her to be his wife, the manuscript and the *Graphic* read, 'She turned quite pale. She had *yielded* to the inevitable result of *contact* . . . ' (G. 329); but in the First Edition this becomes, 'She turned quite pale. She had *bowed* to the inevitable result of *proximity* . . . ' (II. 82). Later in the story, when she is standing on the staircase early one morning, the manuscript describes how, after Angel has impulsively kissed her cheek, 'She *warmed as she had done when they were at the whey-tub and* passed downstairs breathing quickly . . . ' (f. 261), which is also the reading in the *Graphic*, except for the alteration of 'breathing quickly' to 'very quickly' (G. 358). In the First Edition, however, all that remains of the sentence is 'She passed downstairs very quickly . . . ' (II. 107). Eventually, the heroine accepts Angel's proposal of marriage, and when he asks her to prove that she loves him, the manuscript and *Graphic* describe how she kisses him passionately on the lips, continuing, ' "There—now do you believe?" she asked, wiping her eyes' (G. 359). In the First Edition, however, the final sentence is amended to read: ' "There—now do you believe?" she asked, *flushed, and* wiping her eyes' (II. 123).

Two amendments, also uninfluenced by magazine editors, show

a corresponding toning down of language describing Angel's em-
bracings of the heroine, and these changes would seem to be continuing trends already noted in the later manuscript layers relating
to both Angel and the heroine.

* * *

Thematically, the First Edition is important for the increased
emphasis it gives to the two related ideas of social intolerance and
religious obscurantism, both of which have their origin in the older
theme of Nature as norm. The first of these themes, which stresses
the wrong-headedness of conventional nineteenth-century bourgeois
attitudes towards the seduced woman occurs by implication in the
manuscript in the scenes displaying Angel's incredulous horror at
the news that his bride is not the virgin he had fondly believed her
to be. But it was not until the printed versions—or so it would
seem from the evidence still available—that Hardy employed any
of the passages of explicit comment with which the reader of the
definitive version is familiar.

One such passage, first found in the *Graphic* (the relevant manuscript leaf being no longer extant), stresses that the heroine ought
to dismiss all feelings of guilt relating to her seduction, because her
situation is 'in accord' with the natural order of things:

> Walking among the sleeping birds in the hedges, watching the
> skipping rabbits on a moonlit warren, or standing under a
> pheasant-laden bough, she looked upon herself as a figure of Guilt
> intruding into the haunts of Innocence. But all the while she was
> making a distinction where there was no difference. Feeling her-
> self in antagonism she was quite in accord. She might have been
> a party to the tampering with a social law, but with no law known
> to the environment in which she fancied herself such an anomaly.
> (G. 161)

The *Graphic* also includes Hardy's comment that Society is less
than honest in claiming that the seduced woman has little to live
for or look forward to:

> Let the truth be told—women do as a rule live through such
> humiliations, and regain their spirits, and again look about them
> with an interested eye. While there's life there's hope is a convic-
> tion not so entirely unknown to the 'deceived' as some amiable
> sentimentalists would have us believe.
>
> Tess Durbeyfield, in good heart, and full of zest for life, de-
> scended the Egdon slopes lower and lower towards the dairy of
> her pilgrimage. (G. 162)

In the First Edition Hardy alters the final sentence of the first of
these two *Graphic* passages, so that, instead of 'She might have
been a party to the tampering with a social law . . . ', it reads, 'She

had been made to break a necessary social law . . . ' (I. 167). Here, although it is conceded that the law is 'necessary', the emphasis is falling on compulsion, on the use of force (*'made* to break'); and later, in the 1892 edition Hardy was to alter the wording even more significantly when he wrote, 'She had been made to break an *accepted* social law . . . ' (X. 108). The First Edition also inserts into that part of the text transmitted from 'The Midnight Baptism' a number of other passages of social comment, such as the following italicized sentence: '*But now that her moral sorrows were passing away a fresh one arose on the natural side of her which knew no social law.* When she reached home it was to learn to her grief that the baby had been suddenly taken ill since the afternoon' (I. 180–1).

* * *

One of the results of the bowdlerization process and the emphasis on social and religious themes in the First Edition is a stressing of certain key elements in the characterization of the two main personages—namely the modesty and purity of Tess, and the combination of idealistic ethical standards, advanced religious views, but essentially conservative social attitudes in Angel Clare. In addition, we may note two other kinds of amendments affecting Tess—one imparting to her more gracefulness and gentleness, the other accentuating her fidelity towards her absent husband—together with a series of amendments which emphasize Angel's blind idealizing of the physical fact of virginity.

The most revealing change concerned with the heroine's increased gracefulness and gentleness is to be found during the section of the novel devoted to her ride through the Chase with the villain on the night of the seduction. The manuscript describes how she is being driven in the villain's gig when she almost falls asleep from fatigue, to find herself quickly supported by his arm around her waist. The original (L1)[2] text on f. 93 continues thus: 'This put her on the alert immediately. She started, and pushed him from her, with such unexpected force that he lost his balance, and, to her horror, rolled over the off-wheel into the road.' The manuscript shows the beginning of the process of refining, with the insertion of additional words immediately before 'pushed', which read, 'with one of those sudden impulses of reprisal to which she was liable'. But it is not until we come to the First Edition (where the two characters are now on horseback) that we find the more graceful and gentle action of the heroine that the reader of the definitive text is familiar with: 'This immediately put her on the defensive, and with one of those sudden impulses of reprisal to which she was liable she gave him a

2. The "first layer" of a revised manuscript [*Editor*].

*little push from her. In his ticklish position he nearly lost his bal-
ance and only just avoided rolling over into the road, the horse,
though a powerful one, being fortunately the quietest he rode'*
(I. 133).

Tess's faithfulness to Angel, despite his unjust treatment of her,
is made especially clear through the First Edition insertions which
show her reacting violently to insulting remarks about him.

* * *

Angel's idealizing of virginity receives especial emphasis both in
the First Edition and in the edition of 1892. Typical of such amendments is the following, in which the word 'truthful', as used in
both the manuscript and the *Graphic* (G. 450), has given way to
'virginal' in the First Edition:

> Nothing so pure, so sweet, so *virginal* as Tess had seemed possible
> all the long while that he had adored her, up to an hour ago; but
>   The little less, and what worlds away!
>
> (II. 215)

Similar changes involve the replacement of 'girlishness' (G. 450)
by 'maidenhood' (II. 220), and 'perfect' (G. 483) by 'spotless'
(II. 276); together with the subsequent changes of the First Edition
'genuine' (I. 240) to 'fresh and virginal' (X. 155) and 'unsophistication' (II. 221) to 'innocence' (X. 308).

* * *

The vigorous tone of this defence[3] helps us to understand the
reasons for some of the changes we find in the novel itself, when it
finally appeared in its revised form on 30 September 1892, as the
'Fifth Edition'.

The relative frankness of the 1892 edition has already been noted
in relation to the description of the actions of the villain at the
beginning of the seduction scene, which was considerably bowdler-
ized in the First Edition. For it is the 1892 edition which publishes
for the first time the details italicized in the following extract: '*He
knelt and bent lower, till her breath warmed his face, and in a
moment his cheek was in contact with hers.* She was sleeping
soundly, *and upon her eyelashes there lingered tears'* (X. 89–90).
* * * Similarly, in the following descriptive passage the simile, 'as if
Cybele the Many-breasted were supinely extended there', was not
included in any version before that of 1892: 'Towards the second
evening she reached the irregular chalk table-land or plateau,
bosomed with semi-globular tumuli—*as if Cybele the Many-
breasted were supinely extended thore* [sic]—which stretched between the valley of her birth and the valley of her love' (X. 363).

3. Hardy's defense, in the original version of his "Preface to the Fifth Edition" (1892), against the critics who
had objected to both the matter and
the manner of the novel [*Editor*].

The fact that the heroine had stayed on at 'The Slopes' as Alec's mistress for some time after her seduction is also brought out more specifically in the 1892 edition. This is seen in the following italicized insertion, in which the author explains that Tess had been 'temporarily blinded by his flash manners' and 'stirred to confused surrender awhile', before suddenly despising and disliking him and running away:

> She had never wholly cared for him, she did not at all care for him now. She had dreaded him, winced before him, succumbed to *a cruel advantage he took of her helplessness; then, temporarily blinded by his flash manners, had been stirred to confused surrender awhile: had suddenly despised and disliked him, and had run away.* That was all. Hate him she did not quite; but he was dust and ashes to her, and even for her name's sake she scarcely wished to marry him. (X. 102)

In the earlier part of this insertion the words 'cruel advantage he took of her helplessness' refer to the seduction itself. The words 'cruel advantage', in particular, suggest the harshness of Alec's nature and behaviour and reinforce the implications of force and compulsion conveyed by an earlier-noted amendment in the First Edition—'She had been *made to break* a . . . social law.'

The implications of force are conveyed most strongly in a passage which constitutes the most significant single amendment in the 1892 edition. This is the interpolation in chapter 14, during which the field woman comments to a companion, as she watches Tess moodily kissing her baby in the cornfield near Marlott, that 'A little more than persuading had to do wi' the coming o't, I reckon':

> 'A little more than persuading had to do wi' the coming o't, I reckon. There were they that heard a sobbing one night last year in The Chase; and it mid ha' gone hard wi' a certain party if folks had come along.'
> 'Well, a little more, or a little less . . .'
>
> (X. 114)

It is this passage, more than any other in the novel, which conveys to the reader the notion that the defloration of Tess should be termed an act of rape rather than a seduction. Its introduction, without doubt, serves to win for the heroine additional sympathy and respect, and, in so doing, underlines the concept of her essential purity, which, as we have seen, is already vigorously propounded in the Preface.

* * *

The heroine's character received most of its final shaping during the last three layers of the manuscript, and the concept of Tess as 'a pure woman' continued to engage Hardy's attention during the revisions which attended the publication of the *Graphic*, the First Edition, and the edition of 1892. It was not until these printed texts, indeed, that Hardy first included the comments which emphasized Tess's innocence in the eyes of Nature, stressed that her original surrender had been a matter of compulsion rather than will, and suggested that 'with more animalism' Angel would have been the nobler man'. The transformation of Alec d'Urberville from a mere figure of melodrama into a character possessing considerable symbolic significance was also effected during the later layers of the manuscript, as were the expansion of John Durbeyfield's role and his transmutation into a symbol of rural decadence. Similarly, such important symbolic images as the hunted animal, the altar victim, and the willing scapegoat, date mainly from the later stage of manuscript development, as do the cosmic, agricultural, and heredity themes; while the themes of social intolerance and religious obscurantism were not to receive their main emphasis until the First Edition.

The extreme reticence which marks the treatment of some of the key scenes in the novel—such as the actual seduction, the heroine's conversation with her mother on her return home from her stay at 'The Slopes', and her confession to Angel on her wedding-night— would seem to reflect not only editorial pressures but also Hardy's growing determination after November 1889 to defend Tess as a pure and modest woman, this intention being even more clearly illustrated by the First Edition bowdlerizations of some of the courtship scenes at Talbothays. The same attitude of moral commitment to his heroine would seem to have been responsible, at least in part, for the note of sentimentality which Hardy allowed to creep into Tess's renunciation of Angel in favour of 'Liza-Lu in the First Edition, for the anomalies and inconsistencies in the character-study of Angel Clare, in both the manuscript and the printed texts, and for the artistic crudity which mars some of the First Edition passages of ironic comment relating to the painter of texts and the vicar of Marlott.

For the element of thematic confusion in *Tess*, the whole curious history of the novel's development must clearly bear much of the blame; while for the presence of melodrama in scenes involving Alec d'Urberville during the last two 'Phases' of the novel some of the responsibility must be borne by the editors of the family magazines and newspapers of the day, of whose standards of taste and morality Hardy had been made only to well aware by the time that he came to write the final layers of his manuscript.

There remains the controversial critical problem of Hardy's 'authorial intrusions' in *Tess*. These, as has earlier been noted. have incurred the wrath of critics as diverse as Lionel Johnson and Dorothy Van Ghent, both of whom have condemned the intrusions as inartistic and philosophically confused. On this vexed question I shall offer three comments.

First, it should be noted that the increased bitterness of the philosophic comments from L3[4] onwards indicates that they represent an angry, and understandable, reaction by Hardy to the prevailing ethos of his time, as made clear to him through the hostile comments of editors such as Edward Arnold, Mowbray Morris, Arthur Locker, and, later, of reviewers such as Andrew Lang.[5]

Secondly, it is a perfectly tenable proposition that the presence of the narrator's personality in *Tess* should be accepted as an integral part of Hardy's narrative method, which, in turn, constitutes 'the appropriate form' (to use Barbara Hardy's well-known phrase)[6] for Hardy's special fictional requirements.

Finally, it may be argued, with some justification, that the distinctive narrative voice, which is heard in varying degree in all Hardy novels, is not that of Hardy the man, but is the voice of an anonymous narrator, representing a dramatized version of Hardy. It is this kind of view which is put forward by J. Hillis Miller, who asserts that 'The narrative voice of Hardy's novels is as much a fictional invention as any other aspect of the story', and, thus, a device for achieving a degree of objectivity. Miller continues:

> His goal seems to have been to escape from the dangers of direct involvement in life and to imagine himself in a position where he could safely see life as it is without being seen and could report on that seeing. To protect himself and to play the role of someone who would have unique access to the truth—these motives lie behind Hardy's creation of the narrative voice and point of view which are characteristic of his fiction.[7]

Whether or not we accept Miller's thesis completely, one conclusion is clear: that we should no longer meekly accept the older critical notion that the philosophic comments in *Tess* are mere excrescences. They constitute, in fact, an inalienable element in the narrative, without which the novel would necessarily have been an entirely different kind of book, with an entirely different kind of impact.

---

4. The third "layer" or stage in the development of the novel—the second revision [*Editor*].
5. See the *New Review* of February 1892.
6. Barbara Hardy, *The Appropriate Form*, London, 1964.
7. *Thomas Hardy: Distance and Desire*, Cambridge, Mass., 1970, pp. 41, 43.

Contemporary Critical Reception

From *The Athenaeum* (January 9, 1892)

* * * Mr. Hardy has written a novel that is not only good, but great. Tess herself stands, a credible, sympathetic creature in the very forefront of his women. * * * It is impossible not to feel for her as we feel for the most lovable of Mr. Meredith's women.

But was it needful that Mr. Hardy should challenge criticism upon what is after all a side issue? His business was rather to fashion (as he has done) a being of flesh and blood than to propose the suffering woman's view of a controversy which only the dabbler in sexual ethics can enjoy. Why should a novelist embroil himself in moral technicalities? As it is, one half suspects Mr. Hardy of a desire to argue out the justice of the comparative punishments meted to man and to woman for sexual aberrations. To have fashioned a faultless piece of art built upon the great tragic model were surely sufficient. And, as a matter of fact, the "argumentation" is confined to the preface and sub-title, which are, to our thinking, needless and a diversion from the main interest, which lies not in Tess, the sinner or sinned against, but in Tess the woman. Mr. Hardy's style is here, as always, suave and supple, although his use of scientific and ecclesiastical terminology grows excessive. Nor is it quite befitting that a novelist should sneer at a character with the word "antinomianism," and employ "determinism" for his own purposes a page or two later. And a writer who aims so evidently at impartiality had been well advised in restraining a slight animosity (subtly expressed though it be) against certain conventions which some people even yet respect. However, all things taken into account, 'Tess of the D'Urbervilles' is well in front of Mr. Hardy's previous work, and is destined, there can be no doubt, to rank high among the achievements of Victorian novelists.

From The London *Times* (January 13, 1892)

* * * Mr. Hardy's latest novel is his greatest. Amid his beloved Wessex valleys and uplands and among the unsophisticated folk in whose lives and labours we have learned from him to find unsuspected dignity and romance, he has founded a story, daring in its treatment of conventional ideas, pathetic in its sadness, and profoundly stirring in its tragic power * * * It is well that an idealist like Mr. Hardy should remind us how terribly defective are our means of judging others.

* * *

From *The Saturday Review* (January 16, 1892)

* * * Let it at once be said that there is not one single touch of nature either in John Durbeyfield or in any other character in the book. All are stagey, and some are farcical. Tess herself comes the nearest to possibility, and is an attractive figure; but even she is suggestive of the carefully-studied simplicity of the theatre, and not at all of the carelessness of the fields. * * * The story gains nothing by the reader being let into the secret of the physical attributes which especially fascinated [Alec D'Urberville] in Tess. Most people can fill in blanks for themselves, without its being necessary to put the dots on the i's so very plainly; but Mr. Hardy leaves little unsaid. "She had an attribute which amounted to a disadvantage just now; and it was this that caused Alec D'Urberville's eyes to rivet themselves upon her. It was a luxuriance of aspect; a fulness of growth, which made her appear more of a woman than she really was. She had inherited the feature from her mother without the quality it denoted" (vol. i. p. 75). It is these side suggestions that render Mr. Hardy's story so very disagreeable, and *Tess* is full of them. * * * It matters much less what a story is about than how that story is told, and Mr. Hardy, it must be conceded, tells an unpleasant story in a very unpleasant way. He says that it "represents, on the whole, a true sequence of events"; but does it? The impression of most readers will be that Tess, never having cared for D'Urberville even in her early days, hating him as the cause of her ruin, and, more so, as the cause of her separation from Clare, whom she madly loved, would have died by the roadside sooner than go back and live with him and be decked out with fine clothes. Still, Mr. Hardy did well to let her pay the full penalty, and not die among the monoliths of Stonehenge, as many writers would have done. * * *

From *The New Review* (February, 1892)[1]

Mr. Hardy's new novel, *Tess of the D'Urbervilles* (Osgood and McIlvaine), demands more space than, in a crowd of hustling books, it is likely to receive. Indeed, the story is an excellent text for a sermon or subtly Spectatorial[2] article on old times and new, on modern misery, on the presence among us of the spirit of Augustus Moddle.[3] That we should be depressed is very natural, all things considered; and, indeed, I suppose we shall be no better till we have got the Revolution over, sunk to the nadir of humanity, and reached the middle barbarism again. Then, *sursum corda!*[4] Mr. Hardy's story, though probably he does not know it, is a rural tragedy of the last century—reversed. In a little book on *The Quantocks*, by Mr. W. L. Nichols (Sampson Low), may be read the history of "Poor Jack Walford." Wordsworth wrote a poem on it in the Spenserian measure, but he felt that his work was a failure, and it remains unpublished.[5] Reverse the *rôles* of the man and woman in this old and true tale, add a good deal of fantastic though not impossible matters about the D'Urbervilles, and you have the elements of *Tess*. The conclusion of *Tess* is rather improbable in this age of halfpenny newspapers and appeals to the British public. The black flag would never have been hoisted, as in the final page. But one is afraid of revealing the story to people who have not yet read it. The persistent melancholy they perhaps like, or perhaps can make up their minds to endure. The rustic heroine, in the very opening of the book, explains to her little brothers that our planet is "a blighted star." Her mother possesses "the mind of a happy child," yet coolly sends her into conspicuous danger, remarking, "If he don't marry her afore, he will after." Poor Tess is set between the lusts of one Alec D'Urberville and the love, such as it was, of one Angel Claire. "Now Alec was a Bounder," to quote Mr. Besant; and Angel was a prig, whereas Tess was a human being, of human passions. Here are all the ingredients of the blackest misery, and the misery darkens till "The President of the Immortals has finished his sport with Tess." I cannot say how much this phrase jars on one. If there be a God, who can seriously think of Him as a malicious fiend? And if there be none, the expression is meaningless. I have lately been reading the works of an old novelist, who

1. By Andrew Lang [*Editor*].
2. *I.e.*, in the manner of the *Spectator*, a "liberal" weekly journal of news, politics, literature, and science [*Editor*].
3. The man in Dickens' *Martin Chuzzlewit* who deserted Charity Pecksniff [*Editor*].
4. "Lift up your hearts," from the Mass [*Editor*].
5. The MS of the poem was destroyed by Gordon Wordsworth because he thought the poet "had no desire for its preservation," and because "it was in no way calculated to add to his reputation" [*Editor*].

was very active between 1814 and 1831.[6] He is not a terse, nor an accurate, nor a philosophic, nor even a very grammatical writer, but how different, and, to my poor thinking, how much wiser, kinder, happier, and more human is his mood. It is pity, one knows, that causes this bitterness in Mr. Hardy's mood. But Homer is not less pitiful of mortal fortunes and man "the most forlorn of all creatures that walk on earth," and Homer's faith cannot be called consolation: yet there is no bitterness in him; and probably bitterness is never a mark of the greatest art and noblest thought.[7]

* * *

From *The Academy* (February 6, 1892)[8]

Perhaps the most subtly drawn, as it is in some ways the most perplexing and difficult character, is that of Angel Clare, with his half-ethereal passion for Tess—'an emotion which could jealously guard the loved one against his very self.' But one of the problems of the book, for the reader, is involved in the question how far Mr. Hardy's own moral sympathies go with Clare in the supreme crisis of his and Tess's fate. Her seducer, the spurious D'Urberville, is entirely detestable, but it often happens that one's fiercest indignation demands a nobler object than such a sorry animal as that; and there are probably many readers who, after Tess's marriage with Clare, her spontaneous disclosure to him of her soiled though guiltless past, and his consequent alienation and cruelty, will be conscious of a worse anger against this intellectual, virtuous, and unfortunate man than they could spare for the heartless and worthless libertine who had wrecked these two lives. It is at this very point, however, that the masterliness of the conception, and its imaginative validity, are most conclusively manifest, for it is here that we perceive Clare's nature to be consistently inconsistent throughout. As his delineator himself says of him: 'With all his attempted independence of judgment, this advanced man was yet the slave to custom and conventionality when surprised back into his early teachings.' He had carefully schooled himself into a democratic aversion from everything connected with the pride of aristocratic lineage; but when he is suddenly made aware that Tess is the daughter of five centuries of knightly D'Urbervilles, he unfeignedly exults in her splendid ancestry. He had become a rationalist in morals no less than an agnostic in religion; yet no sooner does this emancipated man learn from his wife's own most loving lips the story of her sinless fall,

6. Presumably, Sir Walter Scott [*Editor*].
7. Hardy replied to this criticism in the

Preface to the fifth edition; see p. 1 [*Editor*].
8. By William Watson [*Editor*].

than his affection appears to wither at the roots. 'But for the world's opinion,' says Mr. Hardy, somewhat boldly, her experiences 'would have been simply a liberal education.' Yet it is these experiences which place her for a time outside the human sympathy of her husband, with all his fancied superiority to conventionalisms and independence of tradition. The reader pities Clare profoundly, yet cannot but feel a certain contempt for the shallowness of his casuistry, and a keen resentment of his harsh judgment upon the helpless woman— all the more so since it is her own meek and uncomplaining submission that aids him in his cruel punishment of her. 'Her mood of long-suffering made his way easy for him, and she herself was his best advocate.' Considering the proud ancestry whose blood was in her veins, and the high spirit and even fierce temper she exhibits on occasion, one almost wonders at her absolute passivity under such treatment as he subjects her to; but the explanation obviously lies in her own unquestioning conviction of the justice of his procedure.

* * *

From *The Quarterly Review* (April, 1892) †

Mr. Hardy assures us that 'The story is sent out in all sincerity of purpose, as representing on the whole a true sequence of things.' We have no wish to doubt him, but we could wish that he had made his qualifying phrase clearer by explaining where the sequence of things was not true; without this knowledge his purpose must necessarily remain somewhat doubtful. Is it in the episodic sketches, and the passages that his first editor requested him to modify, that the sequence departs from the straight road of truth? This doubt, we say, throws none on Mr. Hardy's sincerity, yet it cannot but throw some on his purpose. When Tess removes the obstacle with a carving-knife, the sincerity of her purpose is unquestionable; but that unfortunately in the existing state of the law only makes matters worse for her. For the first half of his story the reader may indeed conceive it to have been Mr. Hardy's design to show how a woman essentially honest and pure at heart will, through the adverse shocks of fate, eventually rise to higher things. But if this were his original purpose he must have forgotten it before his tale was told, or perhaps the 'true sequence of things' was too strong for him. For what are the higher things to which this poor creature eventually rises? She rises through seduction to adultery, murder, and the gallows.* * *

Considering the book then, with our necessarily imperfect knowledge, it seems only that Mr. Hardy has told an extremely disagreeable

† By Mowbray Morris, who "as editor of *Macmillan's Magazine* had rejected the manuscript of Tess" (J. T. Laird, *The Shaping of "Tess of the d'Urbervilles,"* p. 174).

story in an extremely disagreeable manner, which is not rendered less so by his affectation of expounding a great moral law, or by the ridiculous character of some of the scenes into which this affectation plunges the reader. No one who remembers how Mr. Hardy used to write in his earlier and happier moods, can accuse him of having been born without the sense of humour. But his assumption of the garb of the moral teacher would appear to have destroyed his relish for this salt of life. * * *

Not long since Mr. Hardy published in one of the magazines his recipe for renewing the youth of fiction,[9] which he conceived, and not without justice, to have grown, like Doll Tearsheet, 'sick of a calm.'[1] The national taste and the national genius have returned, he said, to the great tragic motives so greatly handled by the dramatists of the Periclean and Elizabethan ages. But the national genius perceives also that these tragic motives 'Demand enrichment by further truths—in other words, original treatment; treatment which seeks to show Nature's unconsciousness, not of essential laws, but those laws framed merely as social expedients by humanity, without a basis in the heart of things.' Here, it will be observed, Mr. Hardy speaks only, and prudently, for himself as representing the national genius, being evidently conscious that the national taste might decline his interpretation. But was there ever such foolish talking? Mr. Hardy must have read the dramatists of the Periclean and Elizabethan ages very carelessly, or have strangely forgotten them, if he conceives that there is any analogy between their great handling of great tragic motives and this clumsy sordid tale of boorish brutality and lust. Has the common feeling of humanity against seduction, adultery, and murder no basis in the heart of things? It is the very foundation of human society. In the explanatory note from which we have already quoted, a sentence of St. Jerome's is offered as a sop to 'Any too genteel reader who cannot endure to have it said what everybody thinks and feels.' Does everybody then think and feel that seduction, adultery, and murder have their basis in the heart of things, that they are the essential laws of Nature? If Mr. Hardy's apology is, in truth, as much beside the mark as the sentence from St. Jerome with which he thinks to enforce it: 'If an offence come out of the truth, better is it that the offence come than that the truth be concealed.' Now this,—and here we must be excused for plain speaking—this is pure cant, and the worst form of cant which takes its stand on a mischievous reading of the old aphorism, 'To the pure all things are pure.' St. Jerome's argument would be a good one enough to salve the conscience of a delicate-minded

9. "Candour in English Fiction" first appeared in *The New Review* (January, 1890), 15-21. It is reprinted in *Life and Art by Thomas Hardy*, ed. Ernest Brennecke, Jr., New York, 1965, along with Hardy's two other essays on fiction [*Editor*].
1. In 2 *Henry IV*, II. iv. 38; she meant *qualm* [*Editor*].

witness in a court of law, who in the interests of truth might be required to speak of inconvenient things. It is absolutely no argument for a novelist who, in his own interests, has gratuitously chosen to tell a coarse and disagreeable story in a coarse and disagreeable manner.

As we have found fault with Mr. Hardy's manner, equally with his subject, we must spare a few words to that. Coarse it is not, in the sense of employing coarse words; indeed he is too apt to affect a certain preciosity of phrase which has a somewhat incongruous effect in a tale of rustic life; he is too fond,—and the practice has been growing on him through all his later books—of writing like a man 'who has been at a great feast of languages and stolen the scraps,' or, in plain English, of making experiments in a form of language which he does not seem clearly to understand, and in a style for which he was assuredly not born. * * * To borrow a familiar phrase, Mr. Hardy never fails to put the dots on all his i's, he never leaves you in doubt as to his meaning. Poor Tess's sensual qualifications for the part of heroine are paraded over and over again with a persistence like that of a horse-dealer egging on some wavering customer to a deal, or a slave-dealer appraising his wares to some full-blooded pasha. We shall not illustrate our meaning; there are more than enough chapters in the three volumes to make it only too clear. The shadow of the goddess Aselgeia[2] broods over the whole book. It darkens the sunny landscape of the Froom valley equally with the poultry-farm and gardens of the Slopes, the silent glades of the Chase with the seaside villa at Sandbourne; for Angel Clare is as much a prey to its influence as Alec d'Urberville, and the three dairy-maids as much as Tess. From first to last his book recalls the terrible sentence passed by Wordsworth on 'Wilhelm Meister': 'It is like the crossing of flies in the air.'

From *Longman's Magazine* (November, 1892)[3]

As to *Tess* and my own comparative distaste for that lady and her melancholy adventures, let me be unchristian for half-an-hour and give my reasons. But, first, let me confess that I am in an insignificant minority. On all sides—not only from the essays of reviewers, but from the spoken opinions of the most various kinds of readers—one learns that *Tess* is a masterpiece. * * * There is no absolute standard of taste in literature, but such a consensus of opinion comes as near

2. The Greek word for licentiousness [*Editor*].
3. Andrew Lang's reply to Hardy's criticism of Lang's review of *Tess* in *The New Review*; see pp. 1, 2 and 380. [*Editor*].

being a standard as one generation can supply. So I confess myself in the wrong, as far as an exterior test can make me in the wrong; and yet a reviewer can only give his own impression, and state his reasons, as far as he knows them, for that impression. In the *Illustrated London News* of October 1 there is not only the beginning of a new tale by Mr. Hardy, but an eloquent estimate of Mr. Hardy's genius by Mr. Frederick Greenwood. * * * Mr. Greenwood, greatly admiring, as every one must admire, the talent of Mr. Hardy, says that one of his tales (*The Hand of Ethelberta*) is 'forbidding in conception.' Now, to my private taste —and *on n'a que soi*,[4] even when one is a reviewer—*Tess* is also 'forbidding in conception.'

* * *

I find a similar 'forbidding' quality in *Tess*, as I do, and have always done, in *Clarissa Harlowe*. Poor Tess, a most poetical, if not a very credible character, is a rural Clarissa Harlowe. She is very unlike most rural maids, but then she comes of a noble lineage. She is not avenged by the sword of Colonel Morden, but by that lodging-house carving-knife, which seems anything but a trusty stiletto. She does not die, like Clarissa, as the ermine martin dies of the stain on its snowy fur, but she goes back to the atrocious cad who betrayed her, and wears—not caring what she wears—the parasol of pomp and the pretty slippers of iniquity. To say that all this is out of character and out of keeping is only to set my theory of human nature against Mr. Hardy's knowledge of it. I never knew a Tess, as Mr. Thackeray was never personally acquainted with a convict. Her behaviour does not invariably seem to me that of 'a pure woman,' but perhaps I am no judge of purity, at all events in such extraordinarily disadvantageous circumstances. As to purity, people are generally about to talk nastily when they dwell on the word. The kind of 'catastrophe' spoken of by Mr. Hardy has been adequately treated of by St. Augustine, in his *De Civitate Dei*. To my own gentility it is no stumbling-block. Other girls in fiction have been seduced with more blame, and have not lost our sympathy, or ceased to be what Mr. Hardy calls 'protagonists.' The case of Effie Deans[5] will occur to the studious reader. It is not the question of 'purity' that offends me, but that of credibility in character and language. The villain Alec and the prig Angel Clare seem to me equally unnatural, incredible, and out of the course of experience. But that may only prove one's experience to be fortunately limited. When all these persons, whose conduct and conversation are so far from plausible, combine in a tale of which the whole management is, to one's own taste, unnatural and 'forbidding,' how

4. One has only oneself [*Editor*].
5. In Sir Walter Scott's novel, *The Heart of Midlothian* [*Editor*].

can one pretend to believe or to admire without reserve? Of course it may be no fault in a book that it is 'forbidding;' many people even think it a merit. *Le Père Goriot* is 'forbidding;' *Madame Bovary* is 'forbidding,'[6] yet nobody in his senses denies their merit. But then, to myself, those tales are credible and real. *Tess* is not real nor credible, judged by the same personal standard. To be sure, *Tess*, unlike *Madame Bovary*, is at all events and undeniably a romance. When Angel Clare, walking in his sleep, carries the portly Tess, with all her opulent charms and 'ethereal beauty' to a very considerable distance, he does what Porthos, or Guy Livingstone,[7] could hardly have done when wide awake. It is a romantic incident, but if an otherwise romantic writer had introduced it, the critics, one fears, would have laughed. At all events, when any reader finds that a book is beyond his belief, in character, in language, and in event, the book must, for him, lose much of its interest. Again, if he be struck by such a defect of style as the use of semi-scientific phraseology out of place, he must say so; he must point out the neighbourhood of the reef on which George Eliot was wrecking her English. An example of a fault so manifest, and of such easy remedy (for nobody need write jargon), I selected and reproduce. A rustic wife is sitting in a tavern, taking her ease at her inn. 'A sort of halo, an occidental glow, came over life then. Troubles and other realities took on themselves a metaphysical impalpability, sinking to mere cerebral phenomena for serene contemplation, and no longer stood as pressing concretions which chafed body and soul.' 'Men and hangels igsplain this,' cried Jeames, on less provocation. First, one does not know whether this description of Mrs. Durbeyfield's tavern content is to be understood as her way of 'envisaging' it, or as Mr. Hardy's. It can hardly be Mrs. Durbeyfield's, because the words 'cerebral' and 'metaphysical' were probably not in her West Saxon vocabulary. So the statement must be Mr. Hardy's manner of making clear and lucid to us the mood of Mrs. Durbeyfield. It is, apparently, a mood which the philosopher may experimentally reproduce by eating as good a dinner as he can get, and drinking a fair quantity of liquor, such as his soul loves, when he is troubled and anxious. Now, if I may venture to imagine Mr. Herbert Spencer in these conditions, and analysing his own state of mind, after dinner, for *Typical Developments*, he probably would, and he legitimately might, put his results into technical language. But where a novelist, or a poet, deals with a very unscientific character, like Mrs. Durbeyfield or Sir John Falstaff, then the use of psy-

---

6. *Le Père Goriot* (1834), by Balzac, and *Madame Bovary* (1857), by Flaubert, are famous French realistic novels [*Editor*].

7. Porthos was one of the *Three Musketeers*, and Guy Livingstone was the hero of a popular nineteenth-century adventure story [*Editor*].

chological terminology seems to my sense out of place. How can a trouble, say want of pence, become a metaphysical impalpability? How can it sink to a cerebral phenomenon, and how is it lightened by so sinking? Everything, all experience, is a cerebral phenomenon. How a trouble, not being a 'gathering,' can be a 'pressing concretion,' or wherefore a 'concretion' at all, are questions which baffle one. Intelligible or not (and I confess to being no metaphysician), the phraseology seems inappropriate. Inappropriateness, as far as I am able to judge, often marks the language of Mr. Hardy's characters. To take a specimen at random. Alec, who has been 'converted' for a moment from his profession as a rural Don Juan, meets Tess again, and says, 'Ever since you told me of that babe of ours, it is just as if my emotions, which have been flowing in a strong stream heavenward, had suddenly found a sluice open in the direction of you through which they have at once gushed.' Now 'babe' is good, is part of the patois of Zion, but the rest of the statement is so expressed as to increase one's feeling of unreality, as if one were reading a morally squalid fairy tale. And this sense of unreality is exactly what I complain of in *Tess*.

Well, for all these reasons—for its forbidding conception, for its apparent unreality, for its defects of style, so provokingly superfluous —*Tess* failed to captivate me, in spite of the poetry and beauty and economic value of its rural descriptions, in spite of the genius which is obvious and undeniable in many charming scenes. To be more sensitive to certain faults than to great merits, to let the faults spoil for you the whole, is a critical misfortune, if not a critical crime. Here, too, all is subjective and personal; all depends on the critic's taste, and how it reacts against a particular kind of error.

* * * Arguing about it proves nothing, especially in the face of a consensus of praise from almost everybody who is not 'genteel.' I might say that *Tess* is not only a romance, but a *tendenz*[8] story, a story with a moral, that moral, or part of it, being, apparently, the malignant topsy-turviness of things, the malevolent constitution of the world, the misfortunes of virtue, the conspiracy of circumstances against the good and 'pure.' A lurking vein of optimism may make one distrust this conclusion (if this indeed be the conclusion), and one may be comforted by one's very powerlessness to believe; may say, like the unconsciously heterodox old woman, 'After all, perhaps it is not true.' And that is a consolation for oneself, but not good for the novel. So I have ventured to say my say, though I had not intended at any time to speak again about any work of Mr. Hardy's. * * *

8. *Ein tendenz-roman* is a novel written to prove a thesis [*Editor*].

[RLS and James on *Tess*]†

[Robert Louis Stevenson wrote Henry James, on December 5, 1892, as follows:]

Hurry up with another book of stories. I am now reduced to two of my contemporaries, you and Barrie—O and Kipling! I did like Haggard's Nada the Lily;[9] it isn't great but it's big. As for Hardy—you remember the old gag?—Are you wownded, my lord?—Wownded, Ardy.—Mortually, my lord?—Mortually, Ardy.—Well, I was mortually wownded by Tess of the Durberfields [*sic*]. I do not know that I am exaggerative in criticism; but I will say that Tess is one of the worst, weakest, least sane, most *voulu*[1] books I have yet read. Bar the style, it seems to be about as bad as Reynolds[2]—I maintain it—Reynolds: or to be more plain, to have no earthly connection with human life or human nature; and to be merely the ungracious portrait of a weakish man under a vow to appear clever, as a ricketty schoolchild setting up to be naughty and not knowing how. I should tell you in fairness I could never finish it; there may be the treasures of the Indies further on; but so far as I read, James, it was (in one word) damnable. *Not alive, not true,* was my continual comment as I read; and at last—*not even honest!* was the verdict with which I spewed it from my mouth. I write in anger? I almost think I do; I was betrayed in a friend's house—and I was pained to hear that other friends delighted in that barmicide feast. I cannot read a page of Hardy for many a long day, my confidence [in him] is gone. So that you and Barrie and Kipling are now my Muses Three.

[In his reply, Henry James wrote, on February 17, 1893:]

I grant you Hardy with all my heart and even with a certain quantity of my boot-toe. I am meek and ashamed where the public clatter is deafening—so I bowed my head and let "Tess of the D's" pass. But oh yes, dear Louis, she is vile. The pretence of "sexuality" is only equalled by the absence of it, and the abomination of the language by the author's reputation for style. There are indeed some pretty smells and sights and sounds. But you have better ones in Polynesia.

† From Dan H. Laurence, "Henry James and Stevenson Discuss 'Vile' *Tess*," in *Colby Library Quarterly*, Series III (May, 1953), 164-68. Reprinted by permission of the editor, *Colby Library Quarterly*.
9. James Barrie, the author of *Peter Pan*, had written two popular novels by this time, *The Little Minister* (1891) and *A Window in Thrums* (1889).

Rudyard Kipling's *Plain Tales from the Hills* had appeared in 1888 and *The Light that Failed* in 1890. Rider Haggard's novels were popular for their exotic settings. *Nada the Lily* appeared in 1892 [*Editor*].
1. Forced [*Editor*].
2. G. W. M. Reynolds (1814-79) whose sensational novels were popular.

Essays in Criticism

LIONEL JOHNSON

[The Argument]†

I have read *Tess*, some eight or ten times: at first, with that ravishment and enthusiasm which great art, art great in spite of imperfection, must always cause. Still the grandeur of the book, its human tragedy, holds and masters me: 'how largely it is all planned!' as Goethe said of Marlowe's *Faustus*. But gradually, difficulties, unfelt under the first spell of enchauntment, begin to appear: it were unjust to Mr. Hardy to ignore them. Doubtless, there is something prosaic in scrutinizing, with unmoved tranquillity, the argument of so piteous a story: why not accept its simple beauty and its simple pity, the moving passion of it; without curiously considering those places, where the writer's personal convictions have expressed themselves in irony and in anger? That is impossible: because *Tess* is more than the history of a woman's life and death; it is also an indictment of 'Justice,' human and divine, as the *Oresteia*[1] is its vindication. Either the story should bear its own burden of spiritual sorrow, each calamity and woe crushing out of us all hope, by its own resistless weight: or the bitter sentences of comment should be lucid and cogent. But had Mr. Hardy denied himself all commentary, and left the story to carry its own moral into our hearts; I doubt, whether we should all have received quite the same moral: to prevent any such 'perverse' resistance to his intended moral, Mr. Hardy has not denied himself the luxury, or perhaps the superfluity, of comments at once inartistic and obscure. The sincerity of the book is indubitable: but the passion of revolt has led the writer to renounce his impassive temper; and to encounter grave difficulties, in that departure from his wonted attitude towards art.

In art, nothing is more difficult than to turn theories of ethics, or of metaphysics, into living motives: than the expression of them through the treatment of human characters and of human actions:

† From Lionel Johnson, *The Art of Thomas Hardy* (London, 1895), pp. 245-56, 262-64, 267-76. Rev. ed. 1928. Reprinted, New York, 1968.

1. The trilogy of Aeschylus, consisting of the *Agamemnon*, the *Choephori*, and the *Eumenides* [Editor].

the genius of Browning could not always overcome that difficulty. For a false step here is irrecoverable: a false thought may vitiate the whole book. It is not so with the treatment of facts, for their own sake, as great things to see or hear: a mistake is deplorable, but not fatal. Hugo may give us impossible science, grotesque history, confused learning: but it is not that, which can condemn him, just as it is not absurdities of detail, which can condemn Euripides: it is bad logic, bad inference, misrepresentation of a mind. Various artists have various ways: Lucretius, whose argument is much that of Mr. Hardy, has no hesitation in stating his plain reasons in unadorned language, one by one, orderly and simply: that done, the spirit of poetry leaps from its restraint, and chaunts the dirge of worlds and men. Shakespeare goes delicately, suffusing all his work with the spirit of his thought. But it is useless to attempt a combination of methods: when the reader is following the fortunes of Tess, he hates to fall into some track of thought, which leads him to the debateable land, where he must listen to Aristotle and Rousseau, Aquinas and Hegel, Hobbes and Mill, Sir Henry Maine and Mr. Herbert Spencer.[2] It is a question of manner: things, intolerable in one manner, are delightful in another. If I wish to study certain aspects of English melancholy, at various times, I can turn to Burton's *Anatomy*, to Cheyne's *English Malady*, to Thomson's *City of Dreadful Night*:[3] if French melancholy be my study, there are Pascal, Rousseau, Baudelaire, ready at hand: all these tell their tale with greater or with less felicity: their spirit and their form, are well consorted. But Mr. Hardy is not content to frame his indictment, by the stern narration of sad facts: he inserts fragments of that reasoning, which has brought him to his dark conclusion. They are too many, too bitter, too passionate, to be but an overflow, as it were, from his narration: they are too sparse, too ironical, too declamatory, to be quite intelligible. After enjoying their grimness, I want definitions of *nature*, *law*, *society*, and *justice*: the want is coarse, doubtless, and unimaginative; but I cannot suppress it. It is the fashion of to-day to mock at those scholastic disputations, which enlivened the scholars of old time: logical quibblings, we say, useless and trivial, a vain logomachy! But we greatly need something of their discipline now: for there will presently remain few words of philosophic language, unburdened with several meanings in several mouths. To one man the phrase, *physical realism*, suggests a question in the metaphysics: to another, a question in the arts. Many misty persons, who exercise 'the right of the individual to general haziness,' would feel most unhappy, confronted with the

2. Among these philosophers, John Stuart Mill (1806-73), Sir Henry Maine (1822-88), and Herbert Spencer (1820-1903) were English contemporaries of Hardy and Johnson [*Editor*].

3. Robert Burton's *Anatomy of Melancholy* appeared in 1621; Dr. George Cheyne's work on hypochondria, in 1733; and James Thomson's poem, in 1874 [*Editor*].

great Doctors, the Subtile, the Irrefragable, the Special, the Admirable, the Solid, and the Profound.[4] Without doubt, Mr. Hardy is a man of his mind, with careful conclusions upon perplexing points: but his thought is something elusive, in such passages, as I have quoted.

Nature's plan is not 'holy,' as Wordsworth taught, because children come unconsulted into a world, where endless miseries may await them.[5] Nature has no respect for the civil law, and none for the conventions of society about sexual commerce. Nature's law is cruel: exciting sensations, which cannot be gratified; and desires, which civilization cannot justify. Tess felt herself condemned by an 'arbitrary' social law, with no foundation in Nature: yet the law, which she was made to break, was a 'necessary' social law. She rebuked herself for her self-pity, because she was suffering no physical pain, in a world full of animal pains: and she was wrong in feeling a consciousness of guilt, among the scenes and creatures of the woods, because, like any other animal, she had but fulfilled a physical function of nature. Not her 'innate sensations,' but the conventions of society, caused most of her misery at the thought of her unmarried motherhood: upon a desert island, she would have taken pleasure in it: but for public opinion, her seduction and her motherhood would have been but 'a liberal education.' After all, organic nature is full of recuperative power: does not that power extend to lost maidenhood? After all, men and women are helpless before that 'appetite for joy,' which rules all creation, and is far too strong to be controlled by disquisitions about social rites and customs: its full force cannot be checked by creeds, but only paltered with and winked at by wisdom: it leads, at worst, in Lovelace'[6] phrase, to 'a transitory evil, an evil which a mere church-form makes none.' And the world is only a psychological phenomenon: and the First Cause is unsympathetic: nay, is fiendish, because the children suffer for the fathers; and sportive, because the fate of Tess was a prolonged caricature of justice, ending in the supreme jest of her violent death.

I know not, who can lie under a stronger necessity to realize the sorrow of the world, than a Catholic: but he lies under no obligation to abnegate his reason: and I cannot, with all the will in the world, to understand Mr. Hardy's indictment, understand one word of it. Making all allowance for mere sentiment, and all deductions for mere passion, I can see in it but a tangle of inconsistencies. What is this 'Nature,' of which or of whom, Mr. Hardy speaks? Is it a *Natura natu-*

---

4. The great Scholastic philosophers were given such titles: e.g., Duns Scotus was called Doctor Subtilis, and Alexander of Hales, Doctor Irrefragabilis [*Editor*].
5. See p. 19. In the rest of this para-

graph Johnson paraphrases some of Hardy's interpretative comments scattered throughout the novel [*Editor*].
6. The rake who seduces the heroine in Samuel Richardson's novel *Clarissa,* 1747-48 [*Editor*].

rata, or a *Natura naturans*?[7] Is it a conscious Power? or a convenient name for the whole mass of physical facts? * * *

Let us take Nature to be no more than a personification of physical facts: neither moral nor immoral: 'power is in nature,' says Emerson, 'the essential measure of right'; that is a calm statement, preferable to Mr. Hardy's 'cruelty': and M. Renan may give us a graceful statement of nature's productive desire, in place of Mr. Hardy's 'tremendous force.' 'Si la nature était méchante, elle serait laide. . . . La nature a du gout: seulement elle ne va pas à la morale; elle ne va pas au delà de l'armour.'[8] All this is but the doctrine of modern science about the physical conditions of life: conflict and survival, both caused by strong forces of impulse. But Mr. Hardy juggles with 'Nature': now she is cruel, which is a reproach to divine justice; now she is kindly, whereas society is harsh. 'To remove and cast off a heap of rubbish that has been gathering upon the soul from our very infancy requires great courage and great strength of faculties. Our philosophers, therefore, do well deserve the name of *espirits forts, men of strong heads, free-thinkers,* and such like appellations, betokening great force and liberty of mind. It is very possible the heroic labours of these men may be represented (for what is not capable of misrepresentation?) as a piratical plundering, and stripping the mind of its wealth and ornaments, when it is in truth divesting it only of its prejudices, and reducing it to its untainted original state of nature. Oh nature! the genuine beauty of pure nature!' Thus Alciphron, in the manner of Mr. Squeers upon the same theme: and thus Euphorion, in answer.[9] 'You seem very much taken with the beauty of nature. Be pleased to tell me, Alciphron, what those things are which you esteem *natural,* or by what mark I may know them.' Whereat Alciphron falls into the prettiest confusion possible. And Mr. Hardy's praise of nature is in the very dialect of the eighteenth century: the suggestion, that on a desert island, away from censorious eyes, Tess would have felt innocent and unashamed, is worthy of Rousseau. Nature alone has essential laws: society has but expedient laws; 'arbitrary,' in the sense that they are *only* expedient. Such seems to be Mr. Hardy's position. Now, the misfortune of Tess, her seduction, was in conformity with Nature, as a simple, physical occurrence: it was out of conformity with Society, because it broke a social law, necessary, if arbitrary: but a state of Nature precedes a state of Society, and has therefore deeper, wider, larger laws: Society, then, was

---

7. Is it creation (created things) or is it God? [*Editor*].

8. Ernest Renan (1823–92), French historian of religion who denied the divinity of Christ. "If nature were malicious, it would be ugly . . . . Nature has taste: only it is not a taste for morality; it does not go beyond love" [*Editor*].

9. Squeers is a character in Dickens' *Nicholas Nickleby;* Alciphron and Euphranor (Johnson misremembers) are characters in a philosophical dialogue by Bishop Berkeley called *Alciphron: or the Minute Philosopher* (1732) [*Editor*].

but prejudiced in favour of its own well-being, when it condemned Tess: therefore Society was unjust, preferring its necessary laws of expediency to the great fundamental laws of Nature. Tess, from fulfilling against her will her natural function, was driven on by iron forces, till at last she committed murder: she could not help herself: why was she hanged, unless to amuse God? True, she was at first haunted by a sense of guilt: but conscience is a conventional thing, the utilitarian product of racial experience: it merely meant, that her misfortune, though nothing in the sight of Nature, belonged to a class of acts prejudicial to Society: true, she yielded at the last to her old seducer; but that was in despair, and to help her family; she was but *vulning*[1] herself, as heralds say of the pelican in her piety; and, once more, since the rabbits and the pheasants would have seen no harm in it, why should she, merely an animal, higher in the scale of physical development?

It is perplexing: some one, some thing, must be to blame. It cannot be Nature, because you cannot blame an abstraction: it cannot be Society, unless you would have it commit suicide: it must be God.

> 'Like flies to wanton boys, are we to the gods:
> They kill us for their sport.'[2]

There is almost a delicious irony in the thought: no need for reverence remains: if this be true, no *gaminerie*[3] can be too bitter an insult to the God of Israel and of the Christians. One can but stand up in righteous wrath, and repeat the severe rebukes of Mill, against so monstrous a divinity. It might be thought, even so, that dignity counselled silence and endurance: *Gloria in terra Homini*, beyond question: but perhaps it were only respectful to add, with Lucretius, *et in caelo pax deis nullius voluntatis*: to assume, that the gods are at rest in an impassive peace; and to revile some blind Will, or superior Fate, instead. But that were to forego much occasion of rhetoric: *Victrix causa deis placuit, sed victa Catoni*:[4] 'morality good enough for divinities, but scorned by average human nature': ' "Justice" was done, and the President of the Immortals (in Aeschylean phrase) had ended his sport with Tess.'

It is characteristic of Mr. Hardy to quote the *Prometheus*: that one play of Aeschylus, which may be thought to show a malevolence of God to man.

> 'Do you not see, dear friend, that thus
> You leave Saint Paul for Aeschylus?'[5]

1. Wounding [*Editor*].
2. This chapter was written before, and has not been altered since, the publication of Mr. Hardy's new preface to *Tess*.
3. Roguery, or thoughtless pranks [*Editor*].
4. Lucan, *Pharsalia*, I, 128: "For, if the victor had the gods on his side, the vanquished had Cato." Trans. J. D. Duff, in the Loeb Classical Library, Cambridge, Mass., 1962 [*Editor*].
5. Browning's "Easter Day," xii [*Editor*].

asks Browning: but Mr. Hardy has left even Aeschylus, for 'nursery children'; the babes and sucklings of our disillusioned day, to whom 'the grimness of the general situation' is revealed, and out of whose mouths pessimism perfected. But I am content with Aeschylus.

> 'O prima infelix fingenti terra Prometheo!
> Ille parum cauti pectoris egit opus:
> Corpora disponens mentem non vidit in arte.
> Recta animi primum debuit esse via.'[6]

If Propertius were right in so criticising the labours of Prometheus, Zeus were also right in refusing to bless them: but it is no true criticism. Nor have we a right to infer the faith of Aeschylus, from but one part of a mutilated trilogy: as well might we reason about the faith of Dante, with sole reference to the *Inferno*. In the *Oresteia*, those three poems beyond all human praise, Aeschylus has declared the grounds of his faith in a just ordering of the world. I believe, speaking in reverence and under correction, that a simple, full, literal exposition of Aeschylus' moral system would be found to correspond, without any forcing of phrases, with the catholic doctrine of sin, punishment, free-will, and fate. That no man is compelled to sin; that sin is the act of a bad will; that punishment is the correlative of sin; that suffering is discipline; that no inherited tendency to sin is too strong for a good will; that with God is no caprice nor tyranny: all this is the faith of millions to-day. There is no literature more melancholy, from end to end, than the Greek; but it is often with a gracious wistfulness: and there is no literature more full of faith in a divine justice. With Plato in his *Gorgias*, the great spirits of men have constantly upheld the teaching, that to do evil is worse than to suffer it: and that to go unpunished is an injustice to the evil-doer. *Nulla poena, quanta poena!*[7] As Herbert[8] said, the 'divine regiment,' the government of God, is 'clad in simpleness and sad events': and elsewhere he wrote a word of spiritual cunning:

> 'life's poore span
> Make not an ell, by trifling in thy woe.'

It is Mr. Hardy's apparent denial of anything like conscience in men, that makes his impressive argument so sterile: granted, that there is no sign of conscious morality in the world, apart from man; and it is a vast concession; yet, to place man upon the level of other animals

---

6. Propertius, *Elegies*, III, v, 7-10: "Ah! primeval earth so unkind to Prometheus' fashioning hand! With too little care he moulded the human heart. He ordered men's bodies, but forgot the mind as he plied his art; straight before all else should have been the path of the soul." Trans. H. E. Butler, in the Loeb Classical Library, Cambridge, Mass., 1962 [*Editor*].

7. What great punishment is no punishment! [*Editor*].

8. George Herbert (1593-1633): "Frailtie" and "The Church-Porch," stanza 77 [*Editor*].

is to ignore the whole weight of evidence from the history of mankind in general, and of single men in particular; and also to ignore difficulties connected with the nature of the mind, which no man of commanding science has even professed to explain. When Amiel asked M. Renan, what he made of sin? M. Renan, with a sweet unreasonableness, replied: 'Je crois bien qu'en effet je le supprime.'[9] That is practically Mr. Hardy's answer: and his view of conscience is scarce more convincing, than that of Swedenborg's men of medicine: who defined it to be 'an uneasy pain, which seizes both the head and the *parenchyma* of the heart, and thence the *epigastric* and *hypogastric* regions beneath.'[1] The unhappy sentiments of Tess are attributed to a vague sense of social misdemeanor, to a wandering drift of superstitious ideas, to a childish misconception of her experience, that 'liberal education': not to any deep cry from the heart and soul, bearing true witness to the wrong, that she had suffered. It is a pity, that she was ignorant of Hume's doctrine upon the nature of chastity:[2] it might have established her in a rational content, and in 'a cool self-love.' As it was, she did but illustrate, in her darkling conscience, a great sentence of Leo XIII.: *Ita magnam in animis coelesti doctrina carentibus vim habuit natura rerum, memoria originum, conscientia generis humani!*[3]

* * *

Doubtless, from the days of Ezekiel and of Aeschylus, men's minds have been occupied by the thought of transmitted tendencies and of vicarious sufferings: but only in our day has the creed of 'determinism' taken body and form: and that, with a somewhat premature decision. Considering the great conflicts of opinion upon the matter of heredity, among leading men of science, we can only assume the truth of it, in any one form, at some risk of reputation to come. But Mr. Hardy keeps ever in our view the inherited impulses of Tess: by hints and fanciful suggestions, he turns our minds towards the knightly D'Urbervilles, men of violence and of blood, lawless, passionate, rude. Whether she throw her glove in Alec's face, or stab him with a knife, we are led to look upon her, as an inheritor of ancestral passions: society demands her punishment, in reparation and in self-defence: but, since she was at the mercy of her inherited nature, she claims

9. Henri Amiel (1821-80) was a Swiss philosopher. Renan's reply: "I believe, indeed, that I have abolished it" [*Editor*].
1. Emanuel Swedenborg (1688-1772) was a Swedish scientist and philosopher interested in, among many other things, the relationship between the physiological and psychological processes in man. In later life he became a mystic and his followers founded a religion on his teachings [*Editor*].
2. In his *Treatise of Human Nature* (1739-40), III, ii, 12, Hume says that it is in the interest of civil society that women's obligation to chastity should be greater than men's because the integrity of the family depends upon woman's chastity more than upon the man's [*Editor*].
3. Perhaps from the encyclical *Humanum Genus* (1884): "So the nature of things has great force in the hearts of those who lack heavenly wisdom, memories of their origin, and a consciousness of the human kind" [*Editor*].

our pity and our pardon. Certainly, no one can read her story, and be unmoved:

> 'Io son fatta da Dio, sua mercè, tale,
> Che la vostra miseria non mi tange,
> Nè fiamma d' esto incendio non m'assale.'[4]

So she seems to say, all through her troubled life: and to take for epitaph:

> 'Weep only o'er my dust, and say, Here lies
> To Love and Fate an equal sacrifice.'

Not indeed, 'so made by the compassion of God' as to pass unscathed among the flames of this world: but so made by the indifference of Nature, as to be forced among them, to suffer them, yet to be at heart, innocent and pure.

But, winning and appealing as she seems, there remains in the background that haunting and disenchaunting thought, that upon the determinist principle, she could not help herself: she fulfilled a mechanical destiny. There is nothing tragic in that, except by an illusion: like any other machine, she 'did her work,' and that is all. Those, who held the automatic theory of the lower animals, were yet compelled to speak of them in the common, illogical language, as capable of cognition: just so, Tess is pitiable, because we retain the illusion of freedom. Tragedy, said Chaucer, versifying the old view of it,

> 'Tragedie is to sayn a certain storie,
> As olde bookes maken us memorie,
> Of him that stood in gret prosperitee,
> And is yfallen out of high degree,
> In to miserie, and endeth wretchedly.'[5]

The tragedy of Tess does indeed rouse in us 'pity and fear': it does indeed purge us of 'pity and fear': but with what a parody of Aristotle! For, as Butler[6] has it, 'Things are what they are, and the consequences of them will be what they will be; why, then, should we desire to be deceived?' Upon Mr. Hardy's principles, there was no real struggle of the will with adverse circumstance, no conflict of emotions, nor battle of passions: all was fated and determined: the apparent energies of will, regrets of soul, in Tess, were but as the muscular movements of a dead body: 'Simulars' of freedom and of life. Our pity and our fear are not purified merely: they are destroyed, and no room is left for them: in Cudworth's phrase, we have but 'Belluine Liberty and

4. Dante, *Inferno*, ii: "I am made such by God, in his grace, that your misery does not touch me; nor the flame of this burning assail me." Trans. John Aitkin Carlyle, in the Modern Library edition, New York, 1932 [*Editor*].

5. In the Prologue of the "Monk's Tale" [*Editor*].

6. Joseph Butler (1692-1752), the English bishop who wrote *Analogy of Religion, Natural and Revealed, to the Constitution and Course of Nature* (1736), a defense of orthodoxy against deism [*Editor*].

Brutish Force.'[7] It may be urged, that in the very illusion lies the tragedy: 'All this passion, sorrow, and death, inevitable and sure, to come upon one poor girl, whose struggles were ordained by the same force, that ordained their vanity! Is there no tragedy in that?' I can find none: I can find in it nothing, but a reason for keeping unbroken silence. Least of all, do I find in it an excuse for setting up a scarecrow God, upon whom to vent our spleen.

* * *

It was no blindness to the facts of life, that made it impossible, for Pascal and for Newman, to draw such conclusions from the world, as logic is forced to draw from *Tess*, upon a scrutiny of each word and sentence. But without changing a single incident of the story, it is possible to reject Mr. Hardy's moral: read it apart from his commentary, and it loses nothing of its strength: rather, it gains much. Tess is no longer presented to us, as predestined to her fate: she once more takes the tragic place. Beginning in 'great prosperitee,' as a girl of generous thought and sentiment, rich in beauty, rich in the natural joys of life, she is brought into collision with the harshness of life: she may have inherited impulses, vehement abettors of her temptations: circumstances may be against her always: the conflict will be an agony between the world and the will. Like Marty South,[8] she might have been austerely strong, with a bitter maceration of her desires: like Teresa of the Carmelites,[9] she might have learned to long for suffering or for death, *aut pati aut mori*, as a more joyous denial of joy, than any 'appetite for joy': with Miss Rossetti, she might have said, 'Bitterness that may turn to sweetness is better than sweetness that must turn to bitterness.' Since she was so 'Hellenic,' she might have realized with the Greeks, that happiness is lower than beatitude, and prosperity than blessedness. She did none of those things: the world was very strong; her conscience was blinded and bewildered; she did some things nobly, and some despairingly: but there is nothing, not even in studies of criminal anthropology or of morbid pathology, to suggest that she was wholly an irresponsible victim of her own temperament, and of adverse circumstances. *Oportet te transire per ignem et aquam, antequam veneris in refrigerium*:[1] like Maggie Tulliver,[2] Tess might have gone to Thomas à Kempis: one of the very few writers, whom experience does not prove untrue. She went through fire and water, and made no true use of them: she is pitiable, but not admirable.

7. In the Preface to *The True Intellectual System of the Universe, wherein . . . Atheism is Confuted* (1678), by Ralph Cudworth [*Editor*].
8. A character in Hardy's *The Woodlanders* [*Editor*].
9. Theresa of Avila (1515-82), a Spanish saint [*Editor*].

1. Thomas à Kempis, *Imitation of Christ*, I, xxii, 60-61: "You must go through fire and water before you reach the place of refreshing." Trans. Edgar Daplyn, New York, 1950 [*Editor*].
2. The heroine of George Eliot's *Mill on the Floss* [*Editor*].

Mr. Hardy's last book, then, contains much that may be disliked, much that may seem untrue, and much that may seem inartistic: but it is among the books of most ardent sincerity, that I have yet read. There is nothing in it capable of producing even a 'labefactation of principles': or, at the least, nothing directed to that end. Mr. Hardy's art is not of the sort described by Bishop Blougram:

> 'Our interest's on the dangerous edge of things.
> The honest thief, the tender murderer,
> The superstitious atheist, demirep
> That loves and saves her soul in new French books—
> We watch while these in equilibrium keep
> The giddy line midway: one step aside,
> They're classed and done with.'[3]

Tess is 'good, but not religious-good,' as a rustic casuist of Wessex puts it. Much hostile criticism comes of the eternal separation between man and man: that isolation, alone with his thoughts, in which each man lives, and which no intimacy can abolish. For, as Newman said in one of his Dublin lectures upon literature, all literature and style are personal, the expression of a personality: with the greatest pains, no reader can perfectly pass into the writer's mind: nor can the writer draw him in thither. And so, if I see in this or that passage of Mr. Hardy, what he has called 'an odd mixture of scientific earnestness and melancholy distrust of all things human,' my own temperament may disqualify me for a criticism of that mixture. I will but say, that in the new battle between the philosophy of faith, and a philosophy of the senses, Mr. Hardy seems to take the vehement part of a Luther, Calvin, Knox, rather than the serene part of an Erasmus, Colet, More. Yet he belongs to a nobler company of artists, than they who are simply clamouring for some new thing, and his works witness to his sincerity: *nemo enim illic vitia ridet, nec corrumpere et corrumpi saeculum vocatur.*[4] He has never condoned corruption, as *saeculum*, the spirit of the age: or, as the silly dialect of the day has it, as *fin de siècle*.

* * *

Time has shown, that there is little writing by modern men, which is more wanted, more acceptable, than the writing of Mr. Hardy. Think what we may of his implicit philosophy, of its rationality and truth, we can hardly refuse our praise to a writer of so much power. Like Crabbe's ideal poet:

3. Browning's "Bishop Blougram's Apology," lines 395-401 [*Editor*].
4. For no one in that place scoffs at vice, nor is the age incited to corrupt or to be corrupted [*Editor*].

'He loves the Mind, in all its modes, to trace,
And all the Manners of the changing Race;
Silent he walks the Road of Life along,
And views the aims of its tumultuous throng:
He finds what shapes the Proteus-Passions take,
And what strange waste of Life and Joy they make';

and that, because

' 'Tis good to know, 'tis pleasant to impart,
These turns and movements of the human Heart.'[5]

Good to know, and pleasant to impart: no phrases of a more perfect precision could be found. There is nothing so dreadful and so dark, that art cannot take pleasure in moulding it into fine form, nor the mind be bettered by the knowledge thus won. In Mr. Hardy's fifteen books, there is a wealth of fine form, enclosing a wealth of good knowledge.

'If thou hast in thee any Country-Quicksilver,' come and watch the lives of country 'souls': find tragedy and comedy in poor men trudging to their work, along the lanes of Wessex: understand, in spite of Sappho, how even 'a peasant girl,' with no acquired courtliness, can 'charm the heart.' The country folk of Mr. Hardy, with their Wessex homes and labours, are the material of his great achievements: of these he is a master, and his work in this kind will surely stand the test of time. It is the work of long thought about familiar things: the two conditions of the best writing. There is much, that may grow dim with time, though to us it have a living brilliance: it is not within our province to discuss that. But we have the right, looking back over the history of literature, and assaying by that test the books of Mr. Hardy, to pronounce, that if posterity care nothing for him, posterity will have come to care nothing for many a name, which generations of men have venerated. Not even in art, is it 'in mortals to command success': but there is no sphere of human action, in which they, who deserve success, more commonly achieve it. Much, again, of Mr. Hardy's work is an austere descant upon 'the dust and ashes of things, the cruelty of lust, and the fragility of love': unwelcome truths; and not all the truths, there are. But they are very old and very grave truths: and Mr. Hardy presents them with a consciousness of their greatness. By the severity of thought and of style, which he rarely deserts, he takes his place among those writers, who from the early ages of literature have expressed in art a reasonable sadness. That deep solemnity of the earth in its woods, and fields, and lonely places, has passed into his work: and when he takes it in hand, to deal with the passions of men, that spirit directs and guides

5. George Crabbe's *The Borough* (1810), "Letter XXIV" [*Editor*].

him. I do not find his books quite free of all offence, of anything that can hurt and distress; but I never find them merely painful: their occasional offences are light enough, and unessential; the pain, they sometimes give, is often salutary, even for those who still hold, with Aeschylus, to the truth of that ancient doctrine, which makes the sorrow of the world, a discipline: *The Gods are upon their holy thrones: the grace of the Gods constraineth us.*[6]

VIRGINIA WOOLF

[Hardy's Moments of Vision]†

Some writers are born conscious of everything; others are unconscious of many things. Some, like Henry James and Flaubert, are able not merely to make the best use of the spoil their gifts bring in, but control their genius in the act of creation; they are aware of all the possibilities of every situation, and are never taken by surprise. The unconscious writers, on the other hand, like Dickens and Scott, seem suddenly and without their own consent to be lifted up and swept onwards. The wave sinks and they cannot say what has happened or why. Among them—it is the source of his strength and of his weakness—we must place Hardy. His own word, "moments of vision", exactly describes those passages of astonishing beauty and force which are to be found in every book that he wrote. With a sudden quickening of power which we cannot foretell, nor he, it seems, control, a single scene breaks off from the rest. We see, as if it existed alone and for all time, the wagon with Fanny's dead body inside travelling along the road under the dripping trees; we see the bloated sheep struggling among the clover; we see Troy flashing his sword round Bathsheba where she stands motionless, cutting the lock off her head and spitting the caterpillar on her breast.[1] Vivid to the eye, but not to the eye alone, for every sense participates, such scenes dawn upon us and their splendour remains. But the power goes as it comes. The moment of vision is succeeded by long stretches of plain daylight, nor can we believe that any craft or skill could have caught the wild power and turned it to a better use. The novels therefore are full of inequalities; they are lumpish and dull and inexpressive; but they are never arid;

6. *Agamemnon*, lines 192-93 [*Editor*].
† From Virginia Woolf, "The Novels of Thomas Hardy," in *The Second Common Reader* (New York, 1932), pp. 266-80. First published in the *Times*

Literary Supplement (January 19, 1928) on the occasion of Hardy's death.
1. Characters in *Far from the Madding Crowd* [*Editor*].

there is always about them a little blur of unconsciousness, that halo of freshness and margin of the unexpressed which often produce the most profound sense of satisfaction. It is as if Hardy himself were not quite aware of what he did, as if his consciousness held more than he could produce, and he left it for his readers to make out his full meaning and to supplement it from their own experience.

For these reasons Hardy's genius was uncertain in development, uneven in accomplishment, but, when the moment came, magnificent in achievement. The moment came, completely and fully, in *Far from the Madding Crowd*. The subject was right; the method was right; the poet and the countryman, the sensual man, the sombre reflective man, the man of learning, all enlisted to produce a book which, however fashions may chop and change, must hold its place among the great English novels. There is, in the first place, that sense of the physical world which Hardy more than any novelist can bring before us; the sense that the little prospect of man's existence is ringed by a landscape which, while it exists apart, yet confers a deep and solemn beauty upon his drama. The dark downland, marked by the barrows of the dead and the huts of shepherds, rises against the sky, smooth as a wave of the sea, but solid and eternal; rolling away to the infinite distance, but sheltering in its folds quiet villages whose smoke rises in frail columns by day, whose lamps burn in the immense darkness by night. Gabriel Oak tending his sheep up there on the back of the world is the eternal shepherd; the stars are ancient beacons; and for ages he has watched beside his sheep.

But down in the valley the earth is full of warmth and life; the farms are busy, the barns stored, the fields loud with the lowing of cattle and the bleating of sheep. Nature is prolific, splendid, and lustful; not yet malignant and still the Great Mother of labouring men. And now for the first time Hardy gives full play to his humour, where it is freest and most rich, upon the lips of country men. Jan Coggan and Henry Fray and Joseph Poorgrass gather in the malthouse when the day's work is over and give vent to that half-shrewd, half-poetic humour which has been brewing in their brains and finding expression over their beer since the pilgrims tramped the Pilgrims' Way; which Shakespeare and Scott and George Eliot all loved to overhear, but none loved better or heard with greater understanding than Hardy. But it is not the part of the peasants in the Wessex novels to stand out as individuals. They compose a pool of common wisdom, of common humour, a fund of perpetual life. They comment upon the actions of the hero and heroine, but while Troy or Oak or Fanny or Bathsheba come in and out and pass away, Jan Coggan and Henry Fray and Joseph Poorgrass remain. They drink by night and they plough the fields by day. They are eternal. We meet them over and over again in the novels, and they always have something typical about them, more of the character that marks a race than of the features which belong to an individual. The peasants are the great sanctuary of sanity, the country the last stronghold of happiness. When they disappear, there is no hope for the race.

With Oak and Troy and Bathsheba and Fanny Robin we come to the men and women of the novels at their full stature. In every book three or four figures predominate, and stand up like lightning conductors to attract the force of the elements. Oak and Troy and Bathsheba; Eustacia, Wildeve, and Venn; Henchard, Lucetta, and Farfrae; Jude, Sue Bridehead, and Phillotson.[2] There is even a certain likeness between the different groups. They live as individuals and they differ as individuals; but they also live as types and have a likeness as types. Bathsheba is Bathsheba, but she is woman and sister to Eustacia and Lucetta and Sue; Gabriel Oak is Gabriel Oak, but he is man and brother to Henchard, Venn, and Jude. However lovable and charming Bathsheba may be, still she is weak; however stubborn and ill-guided Henchard may be, still he is strong. This is a fundamental part of Hardy's vision; the staple of many of his books. The woman is the weaker and the fleshlier, and she clings to the stronger and obscures his vision. How freely, nevertheless, in his greater books life is poured over the unalterable frame-work! When Bathsheba sits in the wagon among her plants, smiling at her own loveliness in the little looking-glass, we may know, and it is proof of Hardy's power that we do know, how severely she will suffer and cause others to suffer before the end. But the moment has all the bloom and beauty of life. And so it is, time and time again. His characters, both men and women, were creatures to him of an infinite attraction. For the women he shows a more tender solicitude than for the men, and in them, perhaps, he takes a keener interest. Vain might their beauty be and terrible their fate, but while the glow of life is in them their step is free, their laughter sweet, and theirs is the power to sink into the breast of Nature and become part of her silence and solemnity, or to rise and put on them the movement of the clouds and the wildness of the flowering woodlands. The men who suffer, not like the women through dependence upon other human beings, but through conflict with fate, enlist our sterner sympathies. For such a man as Gabriel Oak we need have no passing fears. Honour him we must, though it is not granted us to love him quite so freely. He is firmly set upon his feet and can give as shrewd a blow, to men at least, as any he is likely to receive. He has a prevision of what is to be expected that springs from character rather than from educa-

2. Characters in *Far from the Madding Crowd; The Return of the Native; The Mayor of Casterbridge; Jude the Obscure* [Editor].

tion. He is stable in his temperament, steadfast in his affections, and capable of open-eyed endurance without flinching. But he, too, is no puppet. He is a homely, humdrum fellow on ordinary occasions. He can walk the street without making people turn to stare at him. In short, nobody can deny Hardy's power—the true novelist's power—to make us believe that his characters are fellow-beings driven by their own passions and idiosyncrasies, while they have—and this is the poet's gift—something symbolical about them which is common to us all.

And it is when we are considering Hardy's power of creating men and women that we become most conscious of the profound differences that distinguish him from his peers. We look back at a number of these characters and ask ourselves what it is that we remember them for. We recall their passions. We remember how deeply they have loved each other and often with what tragic results. We remember the faithful love of Oak for Bathsheba; the tumultuous but fleeting passions of men like Wildeve, Troy, and Fitzpiers; we remember the filial love of Clym for his mother, the jealous paternal passion of Henchard for Elizabeth Jane. But we do not remember how they have loved. We do not remember how they talked and changed and got to know each other, finely, gradually, from step to step and from stage to stage. Their relationship is not composed of those intellectual apprehensions and subtleties of perception which seem so slight yet are so profound. In all the books love is one of the great facts that mould human life. But it is a catastrophe; it happens suddenly and overwhelmingly, and there is little to be said about it. The talk between the lovers when it is not passionate is practical or philosophic, as though the discharge of their daily duties left them with more desire to question life and its purpose than to investigate each other's sensibilities. Even if it were in their power to analyse their emotions, life is too stirring to give them time. They need all their strength to deal with the downright blows, the freakish ingenuity, the gradually increasing malignity of fate. They have none to spend upon the subtleties and delicacies of the human comedy.

Thus there comes a time when we can say with certainty that we shall not find in Hardy some of the qualities that have given us most delight in the works of other novelists. He has not the perfection of Jane Austen, or the wit of Meredith, or the range of Thackeray, or Tolstoy's amazing intellectual power. There is in the work of the great classical writers a finality of effect which places certain of their scenes, apart from the story, beyond the reach of change. We do not ask what bearing they have upon the narrative, nor do we make use of them to interpret problems which lie on the outskirts of the scene. A laugh, a blush, half a dozen words of dialogue, and it is enough; the source of our delight is perennial. But Hardy has none of this concentration and completeness. His light does not fall directly upon the human heart. It passes over it and out on to the darkness of the heath and upon the trees swaying in the storm. When we look back into the room the group by the fireside is dispersed. Each man or woman is battling with the storm, alone, revealing himself most when he is least under the observation of other human beings. We do not know them as we know Pierre or Natasha or Becky Sharp.[3] We do not know them in and out and all round as they are revealed to the casual caller, to the Government official, to the great lady, to the general on the battlefield. We do not know the complication and involvement and turmoil of their thoughts. Geographically, too, they remain fixed to the same stretch of the English country-side. It is seldom, and always with unhappy results, that Hardy leaves the yeoman or farmer to describe the class above theirs in the social scale. In the drawing-room and clubroom and ballroom, where people of leisure and education come together, where comedy is bred and shades of character revealed, he is awkward and ill at ease. But the opposite is equally true. If we do not know his men and women in their relations to each other, we know them in their relations to time, death, and fate. If we do not see them in quick agitation against the lights and crowds of cities, we see them against the earth, the storm, and the seasons. We know their attitude towards some of the most tremendous problems that can confront mankind. They take on a more than mortal size in memory. We see them, not in detail but enlarged and dignified. We see Tess reading the baptismal service in her nightgown "with an impress of dignity that was almost regal". We see Marty South,[4] "like a being who had rejected with indifference the attribute of sex for the loftier quality of abstract humanism", laying the flowers on Winterbourne's grave. Their speech has a Biblical dignity and poetry. They have a force in them which cannot be defined, a force of love or of hate, a force which in the men is the cause of rebellion against life, and in the women implies an illimitable capacity for suffering, and it is this which dominates the character and makes it unnecessary that we should see the finer features that lie hid. This is the tragic power; and, if we are to place Hardy among his fellows, we must call him the greatest tragic writer among English novelists.

* * *

Before such power as this we are made to feel that the ordinary tests which we apply to fiction are futile enough. Do we insist that a great novelist shall be a master of melodious prose? Hardy was no

3. Characters in Tolstoy's *War and Peace* and Thackeray's *Vanity Fair* [*Editor*].

4. Character in *The Woodlanders* [*Editor*].

such thing. He feels his way by dint of sagacity and uncompromising sincerity to the phrase he wants, and it is often of unforgettable pungency. Failing it, he will make do with any homely or clumsy or old-fashioned turn of speech, now of the utmost angularity, now of a bookish elaboration. No style in literature, save Scott's, is so difficult to analyse; it is on the face of it so bad, yet it achieves its aim so unmistakably. As well might one attempt to rationalise the charm of a muddy country road, or of a plain field of roots in winter. And then like Dorsetshire itself out of these very elements of stiffness and angularity his prose will put on greatness; will roll with a Latin sonority; will shape itself in a massive and monumental symmetry like that of his own bare downs. Then again, do we require that a novelist shall observe the probabilities, and keep close to reality? To find anything approaching the violence and convolution of Hardy's plots one must go back to the Elizabethan drama. Yet we accept his story completely as we read it; more than that, it becomes obvious that his violence and his melodrama, when they are not due to a curious peasant-like love of the monstrous for its own sake, are part of that wild spirit of poetry which saw with intense irony and grimness that no reading of life can possibly outdo the strangeness of life itself, no symbol of caprice and unreason be too extreme to represent the astonishing circumstances of our existence.

But as we consider the great structure of the Wessex novels it seems irrelevant to fasten on little points—this character, that scene, this phrase of deep and poetic beauty. It is something larger that Hardy has bequeathed to us. The Wessex novels are not one book, but many. They cover an immense stretch; inevitably they are full of imperfections—some are failures, and others exhibit only the wrong side of their maker's genius. But undoubtedly, when we have submitted ourselves fully to them, when we come to take stock of our impression of the whole, the effect is commanding and satisfactory. We have been freed from the cramp and pettiness imposed by life. Our imaginations have been stretched and heightened; our humour has been made to laugh out; we have drunk deep of the beauty of the earth. Also we have been made to enter the shade of a sorrowful and brooding spirit which, even in its saddest mood, bore itself with a grave uprightness and never, even when most moved to anger, lost its deep compassion for the sufferings of men and women. Thus it is no mere transcript of life at a certain time and place that Hardy has given us. It is a vision of the world and of man's lot as they revealed themselves to a powerful imagination, a profound and poetic genius, a gentle and humane soul.

D. H. LAWRENCE

[The Male and Female Principles in
Tess of the d'Urbervilles]†

Tess sets out, not as any positive thing, containing all purpose, but as the acquiescent complement to the male. The female in her has become inert. Then Alec d'Urberville comes along, and possesses her. From the man who takes her Tess expects her own consummation, the singling out of herself, the addition of the male complement. She is of an old line, and has the aristocratic quality of respect for the other being. She does not see the other person as an extension of herself, existing in a universe of which she is the centre and pivot. She knows that other people are outside her. Therein she is an aristocrat. And out of this attitude to the other person came her passivity. It is not the same as the passive quality in the other little heroines, such as the girl in *The Woodlanders*, who is passive because she is small.

Tess is passive out of self-acceptance, a true aristocratic quality, amounting almost to self-indifference. She knows she is herself incontrovertibly, and she knows that other people are not herself. This is a very rare quality, even in a woman. And in a civilization so unequal, it is almost a weakness.

Tess never tries to alter or to change anybody, neither to alter nor to change nor to divert. What another person decides, that is his decision. She respects utterly the other's right to be. She is herself always.

But the others do not respect her right to be. Alec d'Urberville sees her as the embodied fulfilment of his own desire: something, that is, belonging to him. She cannot, in his conception, exist apart from him nor have any being apart from his being. For she is the embodiment of his desire.

This is very natural and common in men, this attitude to the world. But in Alec d'Urberville it applies only to the woman of his desire. He cares only for her. Such a man adheres to the female like a parasite.

It is a male quality to resolve a purpose to its fulfilment. It is the male quality, to seek the motive power in the female, and to convey this to a fulfilment; to receive some impulse into his senses, and to transmit it into expression.

Alec d'Urberville does not do this. He is male enough, in his way; but only physically male. He is constitutionally an enemy of the prin-

† From "A Study of Thomas Hardy," in *Phoenix: The Posthumous Papers of* *D. H. Lawrence*, ed. Edward D. Mc-Donald (New York, 1936), pp. 483–88.

ciple of self-subordination, which principle is inherent in every man. It is this principle which makes a man, a true male, see his job through, at no matter what cost. A man is strictly only himself when he is fulfilling some purpose he has conceived: so that the principle is not of self-subordination, but of continuity, of development. Only when insisted on, as in Christianity, does it become self-sacrifice. And this resistance to self-sacrifice on Alec d'Urberville's part does not make him an individualist, an egoist, but rather a non-individual, an incomplete, almost a fragmentary thing.

There seems to be in d'Urberville an inherent antagonism to any progression in himself. Yet he seeks with all his power for the source of stimulus in woman. He takes the deep impulse from the female. In this he is exceptional. No ordinary man could really have betrayed Tess. Even if she had had an illegitimate child to another man, to Angel Clare, for example, it would not have shattered her as did her connexion with Alec d'Urberville. For Alec d'Urberville could reach some of the real sources of the female in a woman, and draw from them. And, as a woman instinctively knows, such men are rare. Therefore they have a power over a woman. They draw from the depth of her being.

And what they draw, they betray. With a natural male, what he draws from the source of the female, the impulse he receives from the source he transmits through his own being into utterance, motion, action, expression. But [Alec d'Urberville,] what [he] received [he] knew only as gratification in the senses; some perverse will prevented [him] from submitting to it, from becoming instrumental to it.

Which was why Tess was shattered by Alec d'Urberville, and why she murdered him in the end. The murder is badly done, altogether the book is botched, owing to the way of thinking in the author, owing to the weak yet obstinate theory of being. Nevertheless, the murder is true, the whole book is true, in its conception.

Angel Clare has the very opposite qualities to those of Alec d'Urberville. To the latter, the female in himself is the only part of himself he will acknowledge; the body, the senses, that which he shares with the female, which the female shares with him. To Angel Clare, the female in himself is detestable, the body, the senses, that which he will share with a woman, is held degraded. What he wants really is to receive the female impulse other than through the body. But his thinking has made him criticize Christianity, his deeper instinct has forbidden him to deny his body any further, a deadlock in his own being, which denies him any purpose, so that he must take to hand, labour out of sheer impotence to resolve himself, drives him unwillingly to woman. But he must see her only as the Female Principle, he cannot bear to see her as the Woman in the Body. Her he thinks degraded. To marry her, to have a physical marriage with her, he must overcome all his ascetic revulsion, he must, in his own mind, put off his own divinity, his pure maleness, his singleness, his pure completeness, and descend to the heated welter of the flesh. It is objectionable to him. Yet his body, his life, is too strong for him.

Who is he, that he shall be pure male, and deny the existence of the female? This is the question the Creator asks of him. Is then the male the exclusive whole of life?—is he even the higher or supreme part of life? Angel Clare thinks so: as Christ thought.

Yet it is not so, as even Angel Clare must find out. Life, that is Two-in-One, Male and Female. Nor is either part greater than the other.

It is not Angel Clare's fault that he cannot come to Tess when he finds that she has, in his words, been defiled. It is the result of generations of ultra-Christian training, which had left in him an inherent aversion to the female, and to all in himself which pertained to the female. What he, in his Christian sense, conceived of as Woman, was only the servant and attendant and administering spirit to the male. He had no idea that there was such a thing as positive Woman, as the Female, another great living Principle counterbalancing his own male principle. He conceived of the world as consisting of the One, the Male Principle.

Which conception was already gendered in Botticelli, whence the melancholy of the Virgin. Which conception reached its fullest in Turner's pictures, which were utterly bodiless; and also in the great scientists or thinkers of the last generation, even Darwin and Spencer and Huxley. For these last conceived of evolution, of one spirit or principle starting at the far end of time, and lonelily traversing Time. But there is not one principle, there are two, travelling always to meet, each step of each one lessening the distance between the two of them. And Space, which so frightened Herbert Spencer, is as a Bride to us. And the cry of Man does not ring out into the Void. It rings out to Woman, whom we know not.

This Tess knew, unconsciously. An aristocrat she was, developed through generations to the belief in her own self-establishment. She could help, but she could not be helped. She could give, but she could not receive. She could attend to the wants of the other person, but no other person, save another aristocrat—and there is scarcely such a thing as another aristocrat—could attend to her wants, her deepest wants.

So it is the aristocrat alone who has any real and vital sense of "the neighbour," of the other person; who has the habit of submerging himself, putting himself entirely away before the other person: because he expects to receive nothing from the other person. So that now he has lost much of his initiative force, and exists almost isolated detached, and without the surging ego of the ordinary man, because he has controlled his nature according to the other man, to exclude him.

And Tess, despising herself in the flesh, despising the deep Female she was, because Alec d'Urberville had betrayed her very source, loved Angel Clare, who also despised and hated the flesh. She did not hate d'Urberville. What a man did, he did, and if he did it to her, it was her look-out. She did not conceive of him as having any human duty towards her.

The same with Angel Clare as with Alec d'Urberville. She was very grateful to him for saving her from her despair of contamination, and from her bewildered isolation. But when he accused her, she could not plead or answer. For she had no right to his goodness. She stood alone.

The female was strong in her. She was herself. But she was out of place, utterly out of her element and her times. Hence her utter bewilderment. This is the reason why she was so overcome. She was outwearied from the start, in her spirit. For it is only by receiving from all our fellows that we are kept fresh and vital. Tess was herself, female, intrinsically a woman.

The female in her was indomitable, unchangeable, she was utterly constant to herself. But she was, by long breeding, intact from mankind. Though Alec d'Urberville was of no kin to her, yet, in the book, he has always a quality of kinship. It was as if only a kinsman, an aristocrat, could approach her. And this to her undoing. Angel Clare would never have reached her. She would have abandoned herself to him, but he would never have reached her. It needed a physical aristocrat. She would have lived with her husband, Clare, in a state of abandon to him, like a coma. Alec d'Urberville forced her to realize him, and to realize herself. He came close to her, as Clare could never have done. So she murdered him. For she was herself.

And just as the aristocratic principle had isolated Tess, it had isolated Alec d'Urberville. For though Hardy consciously made the young betrayer a plebeian and an imposter, unconsciously, with the supreme justice of the artist, he made him a true aristocrat. He did not give him the tiredness, the touch of exhaustion necessary, in Hardy's mind, to an aristocrat. But he gave him the intrinsic qualities.

With the men as with the women of old descent: they have nothing to do with mankind in general, they are exceedingly personal. For many generations they have been accustomed to regard their own desires as their own supreme laws. They have not been bound by the conventional morality: this they have transcended, being a code unto themselves. The other person has been always present to their imagination, in the spectacular sense. He has always existed to them. But he has always existed as something other than themselves.

* * *

It may be, also, that in the aristocrat a certain weariness makes him purposeless, vicious, like a form of death. But that is not necessary. One feels that in Alec d'Urbervil' , there is good stuff gone wrong. Just as in Angel Clare, there is g od stuff gone wrong in the other direction.

There can never be one extreme of wrong, without the other extreme. If there had never been the extravagant Puritan idea, that the Female Principle was to be denied, cast out by man from his soul, that only the Male Principle, of Abstraction, of Good, of Public Good, of the Community, embodied in "Thou shalt love thy neighbour as thyself," really existed, there would never have been produced the extreme Cavalier type, which says that only the Female Principle endures in man, that all the Abstraction, the Good, the Public Elevation, the Community, was a grovelling cowardice, and that man lived by enjoyment, through his senses, enjoyment which ended in his senses. Or perhaps better, if the extreme Cavalier type had never been produced, we should not have had the Puritan, the extreme correction.

The one extreme produces the other. It is inevitable for Angel Clare and for Alec d'Urberville mutually to destroy the woman they both loved. Each does her the extreme of wrong, so she is destroyed.

The book is handled with very uncertain skill, botched and bungled. But it contains the elements of the greatest tragedy: Alec d'Urberville, who has killed the male in himself, as Clytemnestra symbolically for Orestes killed Agamemnon; Angel Clare, who has killed the female in himself, as Orestes killed Clytemnestra: and Tess, the Woman, the Life, destroyed by a mechanical fate, in the communal law.

There is no reconciliation. Tess, Angel Clare, Alec d'Urberville, they are all as good as dead. For Angel Clare, though still apparently alive, is in reality no more than a mouth, a piece of paper. * * *

There is no reconciliation, only death. And so Hardy really states his case, which is not his consciously stated metaphysic, by any means, but a statement how man has gone wrong and brought death on himself: how man has violated the Law, how he has supererogated himself, gone so far in his male conceit as to supersede the Creator, and win death as a reward. Indeed, the works of supererogation of our male assiduity help us to a better salvation.

DONALD DAVIDSON

The Traditional Basis of Thomas Hardy's Fiction†

Hardy wrote, or tried to write, more or less as a modern—modern, for him, being late nineteenth century. But he thought, or artistically conceived, like a man of another century—indeed, of a century that we should be hard put to name. It might be better to say that he wrote like a creator of tales and poems who is a little embarrassed at having to adapt the creation of tales and poems to the conditions of a written, or printed, literature, and yet tries to do his faithful best under the regrettable circumstances. He is not in any sense a "folk author," and yet he does approach his tale-telling and poem-making as if three centuries of Renaissance effort had worked only upon the outward form of tale and poem without changing its essential character. He wrote as a ballad-maker would write if a ballad-maker were to have to write novels; or as a bardic or epic poet would write if faced with the necessity of performing in the quasi-lyrical but non-singable strains of the nineteenth century and later.

* * *

Hardy was born early enough—and far enough away from looming Arnoldian or Marxian influences—to receive a conception of art as something homely, natural, functional, and in short traditional. He grew up in a Dorset where fiction was a tale told or sung; and where the art of music, always important to him, was primarily for worship or merriment. * * * At one notable harvest-home he heard the maids sing ballads. Among these Hardy remembered particularly "The Outlandish Knight"—a Dorset version of the ballad recorded by Child as "Lady Isabel and the Elf Knight."

And of course he must have heard, in time, many another ballad, if we may make a justifiable inference from the snatches of balladry in the novels and tales, and if Dorset was the kind of countryside we are led to think it to be. * * *

For what it may be worth I note that Hardy first conceived *The Dynasts* as a ballad, or group of ballads. In May, 1875, he wrote in his journal:

> Mem: A Ballad of the Hundred Days. Then another of Moscow. Others of earlier campaigns—forming altogether an Iliad of Europe from 1789 to 1815.

† From Donald Davidson, *Still Rebels, Still Yankees* (Baton Rouge, 1957), pp. 43-61. First published in *The* *Southern Review* VI (Summer, 1940), 164-78.

This, Mrs. Hardy says, is the first mention in Hardy's memoranda of the conception later to take shape in the epic drama. Again, on March 27, 1881, Hardy referred to his scheme: "A Homeric Ballad in which Napoleon is a sort of Achilles, to be written."

To evidence of this kind I should naturally add the following facts: that Hardy wrote a number of ballads, like "The Bride-Night Fire," and ballad-like poems; that his poems like his novels are full of references to old singers, tunes, and dances, and that many of the poems proceed from the same sources as his novels; that he is fond of inserting in his journals, among philosophizings and other memoranda, summaries of anecdotes or stories he had heard. * * *

* * *

My thesis is that the characteristic Hardy novel is conceived as a *told* (or *sung*) story, or at least not as a literary story; that it is an extension, in the form of a modern prose fiction, of a traditional ballad or an oral tale—a tale of the kind which Hardy reproduces with great skill in *A Few Crusted Characters* and less successfully in *A Group of Noble Dames*; but, furthermore, that this habit of mind is a rather unconscious element in Hardy's art. The conscious side of his art manifests itself in two ways: first, he "works up" his core of traditional, or nonliterary narrative into a literary form; but, second, at the same time he labors to establish, in his "Wessex," the kind of artistic climate and environment which will enable him to handle his traditional story with conviction—a world in which typical ballad heroes and heroines can flourish with a thoroughly rationalized "mythology" to sustain them. The novels that support this thesis are the great Hardy novels: *Under the Greenwood Tree, Far from the Madding Crowd, The Mayor of Casterbridge, The Return of the Native, The Woodlanders,* and *Tess of the D'Urbervilles*—in other words, the Wessex novels proper. *Jude the Obscure* and *The Trumpet Major* can be included, with some reservations, in the same list. * * *

The fictions that result from Hardy's habit of mind resemble traditional, or nonliterary, types of narrative in many ways. They are always conceived of as stories primarily, with the narrative always of foremost interest. They have the rounded, often intricate plot and the balance and antithesis of characters associated with traditional fiction from ancient times. It is natural, of course, that they should in such respects resemble classic drama. But that does not mean that Hardy thought in terms of dramatic composition. His studies in Greek (like his experience in architecture) simply reinforced an original tendency. The interspersed descriptive elements—always important, but not overwhelmingly important, in a Hardy novel—do not encumber the narrative, as they invariably do in the works of novelists who conceive their task in wholly literary terms; but they blend rather quickly into the narrative. Action, not description, is always foremost; the event dominates, rather than motive, or psychology, or comment. There is no loose episodic structure. Hardy does not write the chronicle novel or the biographical novel. Nor does he build up circumstantial detail like a Zola or a Flaubert.

* * *

Tess of the D'Urbervilles, whatever else she may be, is once more the deserted maiden who finally murders her seducer with a knife in the effective ballad way. And she, with the love-stricken trio—Marian, Retty, and Izz—is a milkmaid; and milkmaids, in balladry, folk song, and folk tale, are somehow peculiarly subject to seduction.

The high degree of coincidence in the typical Hardy narrative has been noted by all observers, often unfavorably. Mr. Samuel Chew explains it as partly a result of the influence of the "sensation novelists," and partly as a deliberate emphasis on "the persistence of the unforeseen"—hence a grim, if exaggerated, evidence of the sardonic humor of the purblind Doomsters. Let us pay this view all respect, and still remember that such conscious and artful emphasis may be only a rationalization of unconscious habit. The logic of the traditional story is not the logic of modern literary fiction. The traditional story admits, and even cherishes, the improbable and unpredictable. The miraculous, or nearly miraculous, is what makes a story a story, in the old way. Unless a story has some strange and unusual features it will hardly be told and will not be remembered. Most of the anecdotes that Hardy records in his journal savor of the odd and unusual.

* * *

Thus coincidence in Hardy's narratives represents a conviction about the nature of story as such. Hardy's world is of course not the world of the most antique ballads and folk tales—where devils, demons, fairies, and mermaids intervene in human affairs, and ghosts, witches, and revenants are commonplace. It is a world like that of later balladry and folk tale, from which old beliefs have receded, leaving a residue of the merely strange. Improbability and accident have replaced the miraculous. The process is illustrated in the ballad "Mollie Vaughn" (sometimes Van, Bond, or Baun), in which the speaker, warning young men not to go shooting after sundown, tells how Mollie was shot by her lover. I quote from an American version recorded by Louise Pond:

> Jim Random was out hunting, a-hunting in the dark;
> He shot at his true love and missed not his mark.
> With a white apron pinned around her he took her for a swan,
> He shot her and killed her, and it was Mollie Bond.

In many versions, even the American ones, Mollie's ghost appears in court and testifies, in her lover's behalf, that the shooting was indeed accidental. But the ballad very likely preserves echoes, misunderstood by a later generation, of an actual swan maiden and her lover. This particular ballad is certainly unusual in admitting the presence of a ghost in a court of law. But at least the apparition is a ghost, not a swan maiden, and so we get the event rationalized in terms of an unlikely but not impossible accident: he saw the apron and "took her for a swan."

Hardy's coincidences may be explained as a similar kind of substitution. He felt that the unlikely (or quasi-miraculous) element belonged in any proper story—especially a Wessex story; but he would go only so far as the late ballads and country tales went, in substituting improbabilities for supernaturalisms. Never does he concoct a pseudo-folk tale like Stephen V. Benét's "The Devil and Daniel Webster." Superstitions are used in the background of his narrative; coincidence, in the actual mechanics. Tess hears the legend of the D'Urberville phantom coach, but does not actually see it, though the moment is appropriate for its appearance. * * *

If we use a similar approach to the problem of Hardy's pessimism, it is easy to see why he was irritated by insensitive and obtuse critics. Are the ballad stories of "Edward," "Little Musgrave," and "Johnnie Armstrong" pessimistic? Were their unknown authors convinced of the fatal indifference of the Universe toward human beings? Should we, reading such stories, take the next step in the context of modern critical realism and advocate psychoanalysis for Edward's mother and social security for Johnnie Armstrong? In formal doctrine Hardy professed himself to be an "evolutionary meliorist," or almost a conventional modern. But that had nothing to do with the stories that started up in his head. The charge of pessimism has about the same relevance as the charge of indelicacy which Hardy encountered when he first began to publish. An age of polite literature, which had lost touch with the oral arts—except so far as they might survive in chit-chat, gossip, and risqué stories—could not believe that an author who embodied in his serious stories the typical seductions, rapes, murders, and lusty lovemakings of the old tradition intended anything but a breach of decorum. Even today, I suppose, a group gathered for tea might be a little astonished if a respectable old gentleman in spats suddenly began to warble the outrageous ballad of Little Musgrave. But Hardy did not know he was being rough, and had no more notion than a ballad-maker of turning out a story to be either pessimistic or optimistic.

To be sure, Hardy is a little to blame, since he does moralize at times. But the passage about the President of the Immortals in *Tess* and about the persistence of the unforeseen in *The Mayor of Casterbridge* probably came to him like such ballad tags as "Better they'd never beeen born" or "Young men, take warning from me." * * *

The most striking feature of Hardy's habit of mind, as traditional narrator, is in his creation of characters. The characters of the Wessex novels, with certain important exceptions, are fixed, or "non-developing" characters. Their fortunes may change, but they do not change with their fortunes. Once fully established as characters, they move unchanged through the narrative and at the end are what they were at the beginning. They have the changelessness of the figures of traditional narrative from epic, saga, and romance to broadside balladry and its prose parallels. In this respect they differ fundamentally from the typical characters of modern literary fiction. Our story-writers have learned how to exploit the possibilities of the changing, or changeful, or "developing" character. The theory of progress has seemed to influence them to apply an analogical generalization to the heroes of their stories: to wit, the only good hero in a serious novel is one that *changes* in some important respect during the course of the narrative; and the essence of the story is the change. This has become almost an aesthetic axiom. It is assumed that a story has no merit unless it is based on a changing character. If the modern author uses the changeless character, it is only in a minor rôle, or as a foil; or he may appear as a caricature.

But we have forgotten a truth that Hardy must have known from the time when, as a child, he heard at the harvest home the ballad of the outlandish knight. The changeless character has as much aesthetic richness as the changeful character. Traditional narrative of every sort is built upon the changeless character. It is a defect in modern fiction that the value of the changeless character is apparently not even suspected. But since the human desire for the changeless character is after all insatiable, we do have our changeless characters—in the comic strips, the movies, the detective story. Perhaps all is not well with a literary art that leaves the rôle of Achilles to be filled by Pop-Eye.

* * *

LORD DAVID CECIL

[The Elizabethan Tradition and Hardy's Talent]†

* * *

Hardy's imaginative range, then, covers the struggle of mankind with Destiny as exemplified by life in the humbler ranks of a rural society, now specifically the society of early nineteenth-century Wessex. Compared with that of some great novelists, this is a limited range. The theatre of Hardy's drama is built on the grandest scale,

† From Lord David Cecil, *Hardy, the Novelist* (London, 1943), pp. 34–39, 147–53.

but it is sparsely furnished. His range does not allow him to present the vast, varied panorama of human life that we find in "War and Peace" or "L'Education Sentimentale."[1] His scene is too narrow. Many people in the world are not Wessex countrymen, and many of the most important types of people; statesmen, for example, or artists, or philosophers, or men of the world. You will not find these people in Hardy's books. Nor do you find any account of the sort of worlds in which they live. The subtleties of intellectual life, the complexities of public life, the sophistications of social life, these do not kindle Hardy's imagination to work. In fact, it is no good going to him for a picture of the finer shades of civilised life or of the diversity of the human scene as a whole. The life he portrays is life reduced to its basic elements. People in Hardy's books are born, work hard for their living, fall in love and die: they do not do anything else. Such a life limits in its turn the range of their emotions. There is comedy in Hardy's books, and poetry and tragedy; but his comedy is limited to the humours of rustic life, his poetry is the poetry of the folk-song, his tragedy is the stark and simple tragedy of the poor.

The limits imposed by his scenes are increased by those of the perspective in which he sees them. After all, only a very few situations illustrate man's relation to the universal plan. There are many other facets of human nature besides those which appear in the conflict of mankind with Fate. Let us imagine a typical figure of man, let us call him John Brown. In addition to Hardy's John Brown—a soul facing the universe—there is also John Brown the citizen, John Brown the Englishman, Jack the family man, John the friend, Brown the member of a profession and Mr. Brown the snob.

Hardy's appreciation of the basic human character enables him to give some account of Jack the family man, his sense of the past reveals to him something of John Brown the Englishman; though even these aspects of John Brown's nature he portrays only in summary outline. But of the others—the citizen, the professional man, the snob—he gives us nothing at all. For, seen in the terrific perspective in which Hardy surveys the human being, man's struggles as a political and social character seem too insignificant to fire his creative spark. Compared with his relation to the nature of the universe, his relation to government and social systems dwindles to such infinitesimal proportions as to be invisible. And the working of the individual consciousness seems equally insignificant. How can we bother, when we are watching mankind's life-and-death struggle with Fate, to examine the process of the individual's private thought and feeling with the elaborate introspectiveness of Henry James or Proust?

Indeed, Hardy—and here he is very different from almost every

1. By Gustave Flaubert, published in 1869 [*Editor*].

other great novelist—does not put his chief stress on individual qualities. As I have said, he writes about man, not about men. Though his great characters are distinguished one from another clearly enough, their individual qualities are made subsidiary to their typical human qualities. And as their stories increase in tension, so do his characters tend to shed individual differences and to assume the impersonal majesty of a representative of all mankind. Giles stands for all faithful lovers, Tess for all betrayed women, Eustacia for all passionate imprisoned spirits.[2]

Hardy's characters linger in our imagination as grand typical figures silhouetted against the huge horizon of the universe. Here they resemble characters of epic and tragedy. Indeed, alike in his themes and his treatment of them, Hardy has less in common with the typical novelist than with the typical author of tragedy and epic. And we must adjust our mental eye to envisage life in the tragic and epic focus if we are to see his vision in the right perspective.

We are assisted to do this by the convention he adopts. For our preparations for judging him are not complete when we have realised his range. We must also acquaint ourselves with the conventions within which he elected to compose his pictures. * * *

Hardy's convention was that of an earlier age, the convention invented by Fielding. The novel is a new form, as forms go, and it was some time before it discovered the convention most appropriate to its matter. It aimed at giving a realistic picture of actual life. How was this to be given a shapely form? Various writers experimented to solve the problem in various ways. Defoe put his tales in the form of autobiography, Richardson in the form of a correspondence. Fielding, who had begun his career as a dramatist, turned to the drama for help. The English novel, as created by Fielding, descends directly from the English drama. Now, that drama was unrealistic. In Shakespeare's day it did not even try to be realistic. It aimed at entertaining its audiences by showing them a world as little like their own as possible: a world in which heroic and dramatic personages took part in picturesque, sensational adventures. The writers of Restoration comedy modified this convention a little. They set their scene in contemporary England and made their characters talk in something approaching the language of real conversation. But essentially their plays remained unrealistic; their plots were highly artificial, their dialogue stiff with ornament and their characters stylised.

Bred to this tradition, Fielding and his followers took for granted that a mere accurate chronicle of ordinary life would be intolerably dull to the reader. So they evolved a working compromise. The setting and characters of their stories were carefully realistic, but they were

2. Giles Winterborne, in Hardy's *Woodlanders*, and Eustacia Vye, in *The Return of the Native* [*Editor*].

fitted into a framework of non-realistic plot derived from the drama, consisting of an intrigue enlivened by all sorts of sensational events—conspiracies, children changed at birth, mistakes of identity—centring round a handsome ideal hero and heroine and a sinister villain, and solved neatly in the last chapter. As in the drama, the characters revealed themselves mainly through speech and action—there is not much analysis of them by the author—and the serious tension is relieved by a number of specifically comic characters drawn in a convention of slight caricature.

* * *

This convention was a loose makeshift affair. But it proved less clumsy and more effective than any other hitherto proposed. And, though it gradually discarded its more artificial devices, some elements at least of it were accepted by most English novelists until the time of George Eliot. She was a revolutionary in her sober way. In her books we are presented for the first time with a form of fiction freed from the last vestiges of the dramatic tradition—novels without romantic heroes and villains, with lengthy analysis of motive and character, and in which action is determined by no conventions of plot, but solely by the logical demands of character and situation. In addition, George Eliot, extremely intellectual and uncompromisingly serious, employed her books to expound her most considered reflections on human conduct.

The next generation of novelists carried this change still further. With Henry James, Meredith and George Moore, the novel showed itself as fully entered on a new phase.

Now, Hardy has been looked on usually as part of this new phase. It is natural. For one thing, he was the contemporary of the new novelists; and for another, his books do have some elements in common with theirs. Intellectually, Hardy was a man of the new age—a so-called advanced thinker, in open rebellion against traditional orthodox views about religion, sex and so on—and he used his novels to preach these heretical opinions. Drawing his inspiration largely, as we have seen, from his vision of man's relation to ultimate Fate, he welcomed the movement to deepen and elevate the subject-matter of the novel. Since he wanted to write about tragic and epic subjects, he was pleased that the novel should be regarded as a form capable of achieving tragic and epic dignity. Enthusiastically he discarded the happy ending and made his stories the mouthpieces of his most serious views.

But although intellectually Hardy was a man of the future, aesthetically, he was a man of the past. His broad conception of the novel form was much more like that of Fielding than it was like that of Henry James.

* * *

The peculiar nature of Hardy's inspiration would have been hampered by a more realistic mode of expression. A poetic talent is most at home in a stylised form. It is noteworthy that in so far as Hardy did modify the convention he inherited, it was in a different direction to his contemporaries. Like them, he aspired to add intellectual and emotional weight to the novel, to raise it to the status of great poetry and great drama. But he sought to further this end by making it less, rather than more, realistic. To achieve tragic intensity he turned to tragedy for a model; and to find true tragedy in English letters he had to go back to writers who lived before the novel was invented. Tess differs from a Dickens heroine. She is not more like Anna Karenina, however. She is more like the Duchess of Malfi.³ * * *

Indeed, it is with the creators of these characters that Hardy's essential affinity lay. Here at last we come to the central significance of the truth about his genius, the key to his riddle, the figure in his carpet. This is the fact that strikes us, now that his figure has receded far enough into the past for its true place in the perspective of English literature to be visible. Hardy was a man born after his time—the last lonely representative of an ancient race, strayed, by some accident of Destiny, into the alien world of the later nineteenth century. His circumstances were peculiar. The society in which he was brought up was that in which the ancient mode of life lingered longest. Rural Wessex was still feudal pre-industrial Wessex, with its villages clustering round the great houses and church, with its long-established families and time-hallowed customs, its whole habit of mind moulded by the tradition of the past. Further, this life found in Hardy a subject especially susceptible to its influence. He was the typical child of such a society—simple, unselfconscious, passionate, instinctively turning for his imaginative nourishment to the fundamental drama and comedy of human life, responsive to the basic joys and sorrows of mankind, to the love of home, to the beauty of spring and sunshine, the charm of innocence; to fun and conviviality and the grandeur of heroism; to the horror of death and the terrors of superstition. His talent was of a piece with the rest of him—naïve and epic, massive and careless, quaint and majestic, ignorant of the niceties of craft, delighting shamelessly in a sensational tale, but able to rise to the boldest flights of imagination. So far from being the first of the modern school of novelists, Hardy is the last representative of the tradition and spirit of the Elizabethan drama.

The last—but with a difference; for the age in which he lived made it impossible for him to perceive in that human life which is his subject, the same significance as the Elizabethans did. They saw man

3. The heroine of John Webster's tragedy, first published in 1623.

against a religious background, as a Lord of Creation, a Child of God, a soul born to immortality. The scientific and rationalist view of the universe which Hardy found himself reluctantly forced to accept made him unable to take such a view. To him, man was the late and transient product of some automatic principle of life which had cast him into a universe of which he knew nothing, and to whom—as far as he could see—his hopes and fears were of no significance whatever. The consequence of this is that Hardy's picture differs profoundly from that of his ancestors. The old world seems very changed when we look at it in the sunless light of the new science. Hardy's England may have the same features as the old England; but, surveyed against the new cosmic background, it has shrunk to a tiny ephemeral fragment of matter, lost in a measureless universe and dissolving swiftly to extinction. Hardy's characters may be the Elizabethan characters; but how different they look when we realise that the fierce passions animating them are ineffectual to influence their destiny, that their ideal beliefs and fantasies fleet but for a moment across a background of nothingness. A profound irony shadows Hardy's figures. Though we enter with heartfelt sympathy into their hopes and joys and fears and agonies, yet always we are aware that soon they will be gone for ever, and that behind them stands the indifferent universe, working out its inscrutable purpose, careless whether they live or die. It is still the Elizabethan world, but the Elizabethan world with the lights going down; and gathering round it the dusk that heralds its final oblivion.

Such a view entails a loss; dusk is darker and colder than noonday. And, obscured by its encroaching shadow, Clym and Henchard loom somehow dimmer than Othello. Bereft of their power to control their fates, the Elizabethan figures dwindle in vitality. And not only in vitality: Hardy's characters retain the Elizabethan grandeur, but not the Elizabethan glory. For that glory was the reflected radiance of their spiritual significance. Immortal souls, they towered over mortal matter, proud of their stature. How they dominate circumstance! how their spirit rises to resist the challenge of catastrophe! Even the moment of their death is irradiated by a terrible spendour. Is not death the culmination of their lives, the assertion of the victory of their spirit over mortality? For Hardy's characters, on the other hand, death is only the same meaningless and haphazard extinction as must in the end overtake alike the greatest hero and the meanest insect. They confront it with outward fortitude or outward resignation, they may even welcome it as a release from the intolerable agony of living, but always they meet it with despair in their hearts. Shakespeare's tragic emotion is a blazing flame; Hardy's broods like a thundercloud.

* * *

Over and above all this, Hardy's vision of life gains immensely in power from the fact that his talent was of the old calibre. Dwelling though he did in this setting part of the time, he was yet gifted with that sheer intensity of creative imagination which seems, alas, to dwindle with every advance of self-consciousness and sophistication. The spectacle of the universe, as conceived by rationalist science, is presented to us for once through the eyes of an intense poetic vision. Hardy's sad, latter-day wisdom incarnates itself in tales that have the breadth, the soaring fancy, the zestful, crowding fecundity of invention, which is generally found only in the morning of literature. He may be the latest of his race, but he is not the least. We take our farewell gaze at the England of Shakespeare through the eyes of one who, in spite of all his imperfections, is the last English writer to be built on the grand Shakespearean scale.

ALBERT J. GUERARD

[Hardy and the Modern Reader: A Revaluation]†

* * *

There is another reason why Hardy asks for revaluation. Most of Hardy's critics, from Lionel Johnson (1895) to Lord David Cecil (1946), belong to a "generation," and this generation is not ours.[1] That earlier generation, which I shall call post-Victorian, looked upon its everyday experience as placid, plausible, and reasonably decent; it assumed that the novel should provide an accurate reflection of this sane everyday experience and perhaps a consolation for its rare shortcomings. It assumed that realism was the proper medium of fiction— and that to see a preponderance of evil and brute chance in life was to be unrealistic. In 1871 the *Spectator* thought Hardy absurd for supposing it "possible that an unmarried lady owning an estate could have an illegitimate child";[2] in 1890 Walter Besant asserted that though there are "closed chapters" in the lives of some British men, no British woman "above a certain level" ever commits an indiscretion;[3] in 1938 William Rutland described Arabella and Sue Bride-

---

† From Albert J. Guerard, *Thomas Hardy: The Novels and Stories* (Cambridge, Mass., 1949), pp. 2–6, 82–85.
1. Needless to say, intellectual generations defy chronology. Joyce and Gide, for instance, belong to a later generation than Samuel Chew, William Rutland, Carl Weber, and Lord David Cecil; that is, Joyce and Gide long ago abandoned attitudes still held by these much younger men.

2. Florence Emily Hardy, *The Early Life of Thomas Hardy* (London, 1928), p. 110.
3. "Candour in English Fiction," *The New Review*, II (1890), 8. In the same issue and on the same subject Hardy wrote that the "crash of broken commandments is as necessary to the catastrophe of a tragedy as the noise of drums and cymbals to a triumphal march" (p. 18).

head as "two such women as are not often found in real life."[4] Does not the same innocence shine through these three opinions; or, perhaps, the same determination to look on the sweeter side of things?

Much as they liked him, Hardy's post-Victorian critics were made uneasy by his use of melodrama, by his occasional later "nastiness," by his grotesque and macabre deviations from the placid reality they saw. They were drawn to his novels in spite of these things by his exciting Pamela plots and his "Franciscan tenderness in regard to children, animals, laborers, the poor, the mad, the insulted and injured."[5] The gulf between two generations becomes most apparent in the attitude of readers toward this tenderness. To the poet Howard Baker the chief virtue of Hardy's "system" was that "it stiffened and consolidated a mind that otherwise would have been extremely tender and diffuse."[6] Samuel Chew regretted on the other hand that Hardy's novels, though "tender" and "sympathetic," were not "sweet."[7] Mr. Chew's generation, whether it found the sweetness or not, saw Hardy's deliberate anti-realism[8] (his juxtaposition of implausible incident and plausible human character) as a perverse continuation of the Victorian sensation novel. But we now accept Hardy's extreme conjunctions, in the best novels at least, as highly convincing foreshortenings of the actual and absurd world.

We should look on Mr. Chew's generation with envy rather than with disrespect, and perhaps we shall have to win our way back to that sweet and gentlemanly confidence. But we have been to a different school. We have rediscovered, to our sorrow, the demonic in human nature as well as in political process; our everyday experience has been both intolerable and improbable, but even more improbable than intolerable. Significantly, Hardy's critics long refused to see that Hardy introduced an at least metaphorical Devil into three of his stories, for the Devil belonged to the improbable middle ages. But today the Devil appears in fiction (from the Devil of Gide to the Devil of Thomas Mann) with increasing frequency, and we can now admit his presence in Hardy. Between the two wars the most vital literary movements, following widely separated paths through reality, arrived at the same conclusions concerning it: that a cosmic absurdity pervades all appearance, that evil has an aggressively real existence,

4. William R. Rutland, *Thomas Hardy: A Study of His Writings and Their Background* (Oxford, 1938), p. 187.
5. Katherine Anne Porter, "Notes on a Criticism of Thomas Hardy," Thomas Hardy Centennial Issue, *The Southern Review*, VI (Summer, 1940), p. 156.
6. Howard Baker, "Hardy's Poetic Certitude," *ibid.*, p. 54.
7. Samuel C. Chew, *Thomas Hardy:*

Poet and Novelist (New York, 1928), p. 134. *The Mayor of Casterbridge* lacks "charm, sweetness, poetry" (p. 49).
8. Thomas Hardy, "The Profitable Reading of Fiction," *The Forum*, V (1888), 58, 65. See also *The Early Life of Thomas Hardy*, pp. 193, 194, 231, 232, 242, 299, and Florence Emily Hardy, *The Later Years of Thomas Hardy* (New York, 1930), p. 16.

that experience is more often macabre than not. Symbolism, expressionism, and surrealism explored the Freudian labyrinth while naturalism explored the violence latent in society, investigated *bas-fonds* which Zola and Gissing and Bennett never knew. But what both surrealism and naturalism discovered was a more than Gothic horror. This *littérature noire* may give a false picture of our world, but it does help us to suspend disbelief in Hardy's most startling excursions. The famous midnight scene in *Desperate Remedies*, in which Anne Seaway watches Miss Aldclyffe watch a detective watch Manston bury the corpse of his first wife, caused Hardy's genteel and realistically minded critics more distress than any other chapter in his writings. But this extreme foreshortening of reality would seem "probable" enough to the readers of *Les Caves du Vatican*, *The Castle*, *The Wild Goose Chase*, *Au Château d'Argol*—and *Intruder in the Dust*. William Faulkner has consistently used the distortions of popular storytelling—exaggeration, grotesque horror, macabre coincidence—to achieve his darker truth; they are part of his reading of life. Just so Hardy made something visionary out of Victorian coincidence by juxtaposing the fantastic and the everyday.

There are several reasons for the increasing sensationalism of serious modern fiction. Perhaps the most alarming one is that we are victims of a law of diminishing returns. We are preoccupied with defining guilt and evil, but the disappearance of social convention makes a definition of evil through behavior exceedingly difficult. The fictional heroine or villainess who in 1870 permitted a premarital kiss must in 1915 commit adultery if she wishes to provoke the same horror in her readers; by 1945 she must be a pervert or a murderess. (Similarly, an Anne Seaway can no longer dispose of and hide a poisoned drink by pouring it into the bosom of her dress, an Elfride can no longer summon enough underclothing to fashion a lifesaving rope, and a Captain De Stancy is no longer likely to be inflamed by the spectacle of a young lady in a pink flannel gymnasium suit.) The modern novelist is often more concerned with the problem of good and evil than his Victorian predecessor was, though less concerned with the problem of social conformity. But he no longer has at hand accepted symbols with which to dramatize that problem conveniently. And he must convince a reader who has seen a good deal of horror himself. A great artist—but only a great artist, an Elizabeth Bowen, for instance—can still create a quiet fictional world and provoke the reader's moral judgment by showing minute deviations from that quiet norm. Hardy limited himself in this fashion once, in *Under the Greenwood Tree*, with notable success. This deliberately slight early work is not Hardy's greatest novel, but it strikes me as his most perfect work of art.

More legitimately, the contemporary novelist wants to express a vision of the world rather than to give an accurate picture of Main Street or the Five Towns. Even the naturalistic novel is in full reaction against a realism which reduced art to photography and which bored two generations of readers. If the more respectable of the best sellers are still in bondage to the hard stubborn facts and massive probabilities of Galsworthy and Bennett, the best contemporary novelists are trying to recover Stendhal's daring economy, Melville's freedom to indulge fantasy and speculation, Dickens' sheer and abundant creativity. When the sombre metaphysical interpreters have had their say, we may come to admire Kafka and Faulkner above all for their great inventiveness and Graham Greene for his ability to tell a story. And we are now willing to go back to Hardy for the qualities which in 1920 seemed so old-fashioned: the absurd coincidences, the grotesque heightenings of reality, the sense of mystery inhabiting hostile circumstance and nature itself. We go back too for the tales themselves—as stark and tragic and traditional as any ballads.[9] We are no longer willing to dismiss some of Hardy's finest inventions, as does Mr. Chew—Sergeant Troy's sword exercise, Henchard's sale of his wife, Knight suspended on the face of the cliff, the gambling on the heath in The Return of the Native, the death of Jude's children—merely because they are "sensational" and "too remote from ordinary experience." We are in fact attracted by much that made the post-Victorian realist uneasy: the inventiveness and improbability, the symbolic use of reappearance and coincidence, the wanderings of a macabre imagination, the suggestions of supernatural agency; the frank acknowledgement that love is basically sexual and marriage usually unhappy; the demons of plot, irony, and myth. And we are repelled or left indifferent by what charmed that earlier generation: the regionalist's ear for dialect, the botanist's eye for the

9. See Donald Davidson's excellent "The Traditional Basis of Thomas Hardy's Fiction," The Southern Review, VI (Summer, 1940), 162-178. Ruth A. Firor's Folkways in Thomas Hardy (Philadelphia, 1931) is an exhaustive and learned but highly readable treatise not only on Hardy's use of folk material but on this folk material itself.
1. We do not have to agree with George Moore (who singled out this famous flight at the beginning of The Return of the Native) that Thomas Hardy wrote the worst prose of the nineteenth century (Conversations in Ebury Street [New York, 1924], pp. 118, 140-143). Temperament generally gets into and compensates for the doggedness of Hardy's prose structure and the heaviness with which he plans a major effect. The judgment of Katherine Anne Porter seems to me a fair one: "Who does not remember it? And in actual re-reading, what could be duller? What could be more labored than his introduction of the widow Yeobright at the heath fire among the dancers, or more unconvincing than the fears of the timid boy that the assembly are literally raising the Devil? Except for this: in my memory of that episode, as in dozens of others in many of Hardy's novels, I have seen it, I was there. When I read it, it almost disappears from view, and afterward comes back, phraseless, living in its sombre clearness, as Hardy meant it to do, I feel certain" (The Southern Review, VI [Summer, 1940], 161). As Havelock Ellis said, Hardy was without training as a literary artist: "It is genius that carries him through" (Introduction to Pierre d'Exideuil, The Human Pair in the Work of Thomas Hardy [London, n.d.], p. xv).

minutiae of field and tree, the architect's eye for ancient mansions, and the farmer's eye for sheepshearings; the pretentious meditation on Egdon Heath;[1] the discernible architecture of the novels and the paraphrasable metaphysic; the Franciscan tenderness and sympathy —and, I'm afraid, the finally unqualified faith in the goodness of a humanity more sinned against than sinning. We can say this without re-creating Hardy in the image of our own difficulties and intentions. Hardy was in many ways a Victorian and may well have been, as Lord David Cecil says, the last of the Elizabethans.[2] I merely mean that we are less likely to be disturbed by Hardy's Victorian or Elizabethan oddities than was the reader of Arnold Bennett; and, possibly, we are more willing to be entertained.

* * *

It is not merely in terms of our present taste that Hardy seems something very different from a realist. He himself was explicit enough about his intentions, though many of his critics refused to take him at his word. In 1881 he noted that the "real, if unavowed, purpose of fiction is to give pleasure by gratifying the love of the uncommon in human experience, mental or corporeal,"[3] and he went on to argue that the uncommonness must be in the events rather than the characters. In 1890 he took more definite stand:

> Art is a disproportioning—(i.e. distorting, throwing out of proportion)—of realities, to show more clearly the features that matter in those realities, which, if merely copied or reported inventorially, might possibly be observed, but would more probably be overlooked. Hence "realism is not Art."[4]

The disproportioning, he had already explained in 1882, depended on the artist's temperament: "so in life the seer should watch that pattern among general things which his idiosyncrasy moves him to observe, and describe that alone."[5] Hardy was drawn by a strong natural piety to the everyday material world. But his "idiosyncrasy" led him to see and describe much beyond it: macabre ironies, visible absurdities, and unseen hostilities; witches, demons, ghosts.

Some of the greatest writers of the later nineteenth century saw demons and ghosts, but seldom the same demons and ghosts. *Anti-realist* is an embarrassingly comprehensive term, which may serve Huysmanns and Péladan as well as Melville; the term *symbolist* is scarcely more satisfactory and has the added disadvantage of referring also to particular literary groups. The anti-realists had this much in common: they found that the prevailing positivist complacency and bondage to hard fact threatened art or ethics or both. Beyond this

2. Lord David Cecil, *Hardy the Novelist: An Essay in Criticism* (New York, 1946), p. 218.
3. *The Early Life of Thomas Hardy*, p. 193.
4. *Ibid.*, p. 299.
5. *Ibid.*, p. 198.

it is very difficult to assimilate them under a single banner and intention. The complacency of Mrs. Grundy concerning the niceties of the British Sunday and the British home provoked one kind of reaction; the complacency of Taine, who systematically drove the occult into a corner, provoked a quite different one. How then can we group together Aubrey Beardsley's erotic reveries and Baudelaire's anguished Catholic efforts to prove the existence of evil? Flaubert was the greatest realist of the century; yet even he, hedged in by drabness, invoked madness some years before madness really threatened. Dostoevsky, who sought the devil in the subconscious, was an anti-realist. But so too was Melville, who tried to justify his inherited sense that the outer universe was divine or diabolic and in any event meaningful; and Poe, drunk with rhythms and words; and Dickens and Hardy in their different ways. And so too at the end of the century were Conrad and the young André Gide. Some anti-realists wanted to revitalize art, wanted to add something to the mirror in a country lane. Others wanted to revitalize ethics by finding a missing link of freedom in the inexorable chain of determined cause and effect. Not a few merely wanted to shock their betters. There is little in common between the anti-realism of Conrad and that of Wilde; nor could Hardy's anti-realism be farther removed from the anti-realism of the decadents.

Hardy's anti-realism was more popular and less metaphysical than that of his greatest contemporaries; he is one of the few anti-realists to whom the term *romantic* may at times be applied in other than a pejorative sense. Obviously he wanted to avoid the sterility of mere observation and Gradgrind common sense; he was an anti-realist on aesthetic grounds. But also he was a pure romantic, like Scott, appealing to the surprised child who lingers in us all; he was a popular teller of tales. The appearance of the Devil in the poetry and fiction of the last hundred years often signifies a skeptic's search for God. But Hardy, though he used the preternatural now and then, was very rarely concerned with damnation, with crime and guilt and remorse. His rare preternatural beings are there to puzzle and excite us, and because they have a time-honored place in the traditional ballad and tale. Significantly, Conrad departs farthest from realism, in *The Secret Sharer*, to create a ghostly image of the divided and damning ego. Hardy departs farthest from realism, in *The Romantic Adventures of a Milkmaid*, to tell us a fairy story. Nearly all the anti-realists were intensely subjective writers and were often markedly neurotic; Hardy as a novelist was neither. He was less serious than many of them, but also in some sense purer.

This is of course a relative judgment. For Hardy was also at times a genuine symbolist. His anti-realism added up to a distinct vision of things, however accidental or deliberate. Thus the extraordinary amount of lying and concealment in his books responds to the human fact that everyone has something to conceal. The large part given to chance and ironic mischance similarly responds to an actual absurdity in things: the discrépancy between the human longing for order and the disorder of daily circumstance. And to imagine macabre situations—that a secret lover should die in one's bedroom, for instance, and have to be dragged out secretly[6] is to acknowledge that life frequently makes demands of us quite disproportionate to our strength. Finally, to suppose active hostilities—intruding preternatural hostilities, hostilities of physical nature, hostilities within the psyche—is to recognize the obvious fact that the world was not tailored to human measure. Hardy did not always think as explicitly as this and as a rule was commonplace when he did so. His anti-realism was more often the natural expression of a particular temperament (the "idiosyncrasy") and a great dramatic gift. A grotesque chapter may thus exhibit simultaneously the pessimist's disgust with the absurdity of things and the dramatist's delight in presenting that absurdity. A ferocious sense of fun may accompany a wholly genuine horror, in Hardy as in Dostoevsky or Kafka or Faulkner. The difference is that Hardy, unlike the others, seldom went "underground." He was startled rather than obsessed.

* * *

DOROTHY VAN GHENT

On *Tess of the d'Urbervilles* [†]

It was Hardy who said of Meredith that "he would not, or could not—at any rate did not—when aiming to represent the 'Comic Spirit,' let himself discover the tragedy that always underlies comedy if you only scratch deeply enough." Hardy's statement does not really suggest that comedy is somehow tragedy *manqué*, that writers of comedy would write tragedies if they only "scratched deeply enough." What he says is what Socrates said to Aristophanes and Agathon at the end of the *Symposium*—that the genius of tragedy is the same as that of comedy. It is what Cervantes knew, whose great comic hero, Quixote, walks in the same shades with Orestes and Oedipus, Hamlet and Lear. It is what Molière knew. Even Jane Austen knew it. The precariousness of moral consciousness in its brute instinctual and physical circumstances, its fragility as an instrument for the regeneration of the will: this generic disproportion

6. "The Marchioness of Stonehenge," *A Group of Noble Dames.*
† From Dorothy Van Ghent, *The Eng-lish Novel: Form and Function* (New York, 1953), pp. 195–209.

in the human condition comedy develops by grotesque enlargement
of one or another aberrated faculty; tragedy, by grotesque enlargement of the imbalance between human motive and the effect of
action. The special point to our purpose is, however, another:
neither tragic figure nor comic figure is merely phenomenal and
spectacular if it truly serves the function common to both genres—
the catharsis; acting as scapegoats for the absurdity of the human
dilemma, they are humanity's thoughtful or intuitive comment on
itself. We return, thus, deviously by way of the kinship of tragedy
and comedy, to the matter of "internal relations." The human condition, whether in the "drawing-room of civilized men and women"
or on a wild heath in ancient Britain, shows, if scratched deeply
enough, the binding ironies that bind the spectacular destiny of the
hero with the unspectacular common destiny; and it is in the internal relations of the art form, the aesthetic structure, that these
bonds have symbolic representation. * * *

*   *   *

To turn to one of Hardy's great tragic novels is to put "internal
relations" in the novel to peculiar test, for there is perhaps no other
novelist, of a stature equal to Hardy's, who so stubbornly and flag-
rantly foisted upon the novel elements resistant to aesthetic co-
hesion. We shall want to speak of these elements first, simply to
clear away and free ourselves from the temptation to appraise Hardy
by his "philosophy"—that is, the temptation to mistake bits of
philosophic adhesive tape, rather dampened and rumpled by time,
for the deeply animated vision of experience which our novel, *Tess*,
holds. We can quickly summon examples, for they crop out obviously enough. Before one has got beyond twenty pages one finds
this paragraph on the ignominy and helplessness of the human estate: * * *[1] Whenever, in this book, Hardy finds either a butt or
a sanction in a poet, one can expect the inevitable intrusion of a
form of discourse that infers proofs and opinions and competition in
"truth" that belongs to an intellectual battlefield alien from the
novel's imaginative concretions. On the eve of the Durbeyfield family's forced deracination and migration, we are told that

> to Tess, as to some few millions of others, there was ghastly satire
> in the poet's lines:
> > *Not in utter nakedness*
> > *But trailing clouds of glory do we come.*
> To her and her like, birth itself was an ordeal of degrading per-
> sonal compulsion, whose gratuitousness nothing in the result
> seemed to justify, and at best could only palliate.

1. See above, p. 19, paragraph beginning "All these young souls . . ."
[*Editor*].

Aside from the fact that no circumstances have been suggested in which Tess could have had time or opportunity or the requisite development of critical aptitudes to brood so formidably on Wordsworth's lines, who are those "few millions" who are the "like" of Tess? as, who are the "some people" in the previous quotation? and in what way do these statistical generalizations add to the already sufficient meaning of Tess's situation? At the end of the book, with the "Aeschylean phrase" on the sport of the gods, we feel again that intrusion of a commentary which belongs to another order of discourse. The gibbet is enough. The vision is deep and clear and can only be marred by any exploitation of it as a datum in support of abstraction. We could even do without the note of "ameliorism" in the joined hands of Clare and Tess's younger sister at the end: the philosophy of an evolutionary hope has nothing essential to do with Tess's fate and her common meaning; she is too humanly adequate for evolutionary ethics to comment upon, and furthermore we do not believe that young girls make ameliorated lives out of witness of a sister's hanging.

What philosophical vision honestly inheres in a novel inheres as the signifying form of a certain concrete body of experience; it is what the experience "means" because it is what, structurally, the experience *is*. When it can be loosened away from the novel to compete in the general field of abstract truth—as frequently in Hardy— it has the weakness of any abstraction that statistics and history and science may be allowed to criticize; whether true or false for one generation or another, or for one reader or another, or even for one personal mood or another, its status as truth is relative to conditions of evidence and belief existing outside the novel and existing there quite irrelevant to whatever body of particularized life the novel itself might contain. But as a structural principle active within the particulars of the novel, local and inherent there through a maximum of organic dependencies, the philosophical vision has the unassailable truth of living form.

We wish to press this difference a bit further by considering— deliberately in a few minor instances, for in the minor notation is the furthest reach of form—the internality and essentiality of Hardy's vision, just as we have previously considered instances of its externalization and devitalization. Significantly, his "ideas" remain the same in either case. They are abruptly articulated in incident, early in the book, with the death of Prince, appearing here with almost ideographical simplicity. * * *[2] With this accident are concatenated in fatal union Tess's going to "claim kin" of the D'Urbervilles and all the other links in her tragedy down to the murder of

2. See fourth line from bottom of p. 26, above, to middle of p. 27 [*Editor*].

Alec. The symbolism of the detail is naïve and forthright to the point of temerity: the accident occurs in darkness and Tess has fallen asleep—just as the whole system of mischances and cross-purposes in the novel is a function of psychic and cosmic blindness; she "put her hand upon the hole"—and the gesture is as absurdly ineffectual as all her effort will be; the only result is that she becomes splashed with blood—as she will be at the end; the shaft pierces Prince's breast "like a sword"—Alec is stabbed in the heart with a knife; with the arousal and twittering of the birds we are aware of the oblivious manifold of nature stretching infinite and detached beyond the isolated human figure; the iridescence of the coagulating blood is, in its incongruity with the dark human trouble, a note of the same indifferent cosmic chemistry that has brought about the accident; and the smallness of the hole in Prince's chest, that looked "scarcely large enough to have let out all that had animated him," is the minor remark of that irony by which Tess's great cruel trial appears as a vanishing incidental in the blind waste of time and space and biological repetition. Nevertheless, there is nothing in this event that has not the natural "grain" of concrete fact; and what it signifies—of the complicity of doom with the most random occurrence, of the cross-purposing of purpose in a multiple world, of cosmic indifference and of moral desolation—is a local truth of a particular experience and irrefutable as the experience itself.

In the second chapter of *Tess* the gathering for the May-day "club-walking" is described, a debased "local Cerealia" that has lost its ancient motive as fertility rite and that subsists as a social habit among the village young people. Here Clare sees Tess for the first time, in white dress, with peeled willow wand and bunch of white flowers. But it is too late for him to stop, the clock has struck, he must be on his way to join his companions. Later, when he wants to marry Tess, he will tell his parents of the "pure and virtuous" bride he has chosen, when her robe is no longer the white robe of the May-walking but the chameleon robe of Queen Guinevere,

> *That never would become that wife*
> *That had once done amiss.*

In the scene of the May-walking, the lovers are "star-crossed" not by obscure celestial intent but by ordinary multiplicity of purposes and suitabilities; but in the submerged and debased fertility ritual—ironically doubled here with the symbolism of the white dress (a symbolism which Clare himself will later debase by his prudish perversity)—is shadowed a more savage doom brought about by a more violent potency, that of sexual instinct, by which Tess will be victimized. Owing its form entirely to the vision that shapes the whole of Tess's tragedy, the minor incident of the May-walking has the assurance of particularized reality and the truth of the naturally given.

Nothing could be more brutally factual than the description of the swede field at Flintcomb-Ash, nor convey more ecnomically and transparently Hardy's vision of human abandonment in the dis-severing earth. * * *3 The visitation of the winter birds has the same grain of local reality, and yet all the signifying and representa-tive disaster of Tess's situation—its loneliness, its bleak triviality, its irrelevance in the dumb digestion of earth—is focused in the mir-roring eyes of the birds. * * *4 There is the same sensitive honesty to the detail and expression of fact, the same inherence of vision in the particulars of experience, in the description of the weeds where Tess hears Clare thrumming his harp. * * *5 The weeds, circum-stantial as they are, have an astonishingly cunning and bold meta-phorical function. They grow at Talbothays, in that healing pro-creative idyl of milk and mist and passive biology, and they too are bountiful with life, but they stain and slime and blight; and it is in this part of Paradise (an "outskirt of the garden"—there are even apple trees here) that the minister's son is hidden, who, in his con-ceited impotence, will violate Tess more nastily than her sensual seducer: who but Hardy would have dared to give him the name Angel, and a harp too? It is Hardy's incorruptible feeling for the actual that allows his symbolism its amazingly blunt privileges and that at the same time subdues it to and absorbs it into the concrete circumstance of experience, real as touch.

The dilemma of Tess is the dilemma of morally individualizing consciousness in its earthy mixture. The subject is mythological, for it places the human protagonist in dramatic relationship with the nonhuman and orients his destiny among preternatural powers. The most primitive antagonist of consciousness is, on the simplest prem-ise, the earth itself. It acts so in *Tess*, clogging action and defy-ing conscious motive; or, in the long dream of Talbothays, conspir-ing with its ancient sensuality to provoke instinct; or, on the farm at Flintcomb-Ash, demoralizing consciousness by its mere geological flintiness. But the earth is "natural," while, dramatically visualized as antagonist, it transcends the natural. The integrity of the myth thus depends, paradoxically, upon naturalism; and it is because of that intimate dependence between the natural and the mytholog-ical, a dependence that is organic to the subject, that Hardy's vision

3. See last ten lines on p. 237, above [*Editor*].
4. See p. 240, above, paragraph be-ginning "After ahis . . ." [*Editor*].
5. See p. 104, above, paragraph be-ginning "The outskirt . . ." [*Editor*].

is able to impregnate so deeply and shape so unobtrusively the naturalistic particulars of the story.

In *Tess*, of all his novels, the earth is most actual as a dramatic factor—that is, as a factor of causation; and by this we refer simply to the long stretches of earth that have to be trudged in order that a person may get from one place to another, the slowness of the business, the irreducible reality of it (for one has only one's feet), its grimness of soul-wearying fatigue and shelterlessness and doubtful issue at the other end of the journey where nobody may be at home. * * * In *Tess* the earth is *primarily not a metaphor but a real thing* that one has to move on in order to get anywhere or do anything, and it constantly acts in its own motivating, causational substantiality by being there in the way of human purposes to encounter, to harass them, detour them, seduce them, defeat them.

In the accident of Prince's death, the road itself is, in a manner of speaking, responsible, merely by being the same road that the mail cart travels. The seduction of Tess is as closely related, causally, to the distance between Trantridge and Chaseborough as it is to Tess's naïveté and to Alec's egoism; the physical distance itself causes Tess's fatigue and provides Alec's opportunity. The insidiously demoralizing effect of Tess's desolate journeys on foot as she seeks dairy work and field work here and there after the collapse of her marriage, brutal months that are foreshortened to the plodding trip over the chalk uplands to Flintcomb-Ash, is, again, as directly as anything, an effect of the irreducible *thereness of* the territory she has to cover. There are other fatal elements in her ineffectual trip from the farm to Emminster to see Clare's parents, but fatal above all is the distance she must walk to see people who can have no foreknowledge of her coming and who are not at home when she gets there. Finally, with the uprooting and migration of the Durbeyfield family on Old Lady Day, the simple fatality of the earth as earth, in its measurelessness and anonymousness, with people having to move over it with no place to go, is decisive in the final event of Tess's tragedy—her return to Alec, for Alec provides at least a place to go.

The dramatic motivation provided by natural earth is central to every aspect of the book. It controls the style: page by page *Tess* has a wrought density of texture that is fairly unique in Hardy; symbolic depth is communicated by the physical surface of things with unhampered transparency while the homeliest conviction of fact is preserved ("The upper half of each turnip had been eaten off by the live-stock"); and one is aware of style not as a specifically verbal quality but as a quality of observation and intuition that are here— very often—wonderfully identical with each other, a quality of lucidity. Again, it is because of the *actual* motivational impact of the earth that Hardy is able to use setting and atmosphere for a symbolism that, considered in itself, is so astonishingly blunt and rudimentary. The green vale of Blackmoor, fertile, small, enclosed by hills, lying under a blue haze—the vale of birth, the cradle of innocence. The wide misty setting of Talbothays dairy, "oozing fatness and warm ferments," where the "rush of juices could almost be heard below the hiss of fertilization"—the sensual dream, the lost Paradise. The starved uplands of Flintcomb-Ash, with their ironic mimicry of the organs of generation, "myriads of loose white flints in bulbous, cusped, and phallic shapes," and the dun consuming ruin of the swede field—the mockery of impotence, the exile. Finally, that immensely courageous use of setting, Stonehenge and the stone of sacrifice. Obvious as these symbolisms are, their deep stress is maintained by Hardy's naturalistic premise. The earth exists here as Final Cause, and its omnipresence affords constantly to Hardy the textures that excited his eye and care, but affords them wholly charged with dramatic, causational necessity; and the symbolic values of setting are constituted, in large part, by the responses required of the characters themselves in their relationship with the earth.

Generally, the narrative system of the book—that is, the system of episodes—is a series of accidents and coincidences (although it is important to note that the really great crises are psychologically motivated: Alec's seduction of Tess, Clare's rejection of her, and the murder). It is accident that Clare does not meet Tess at the May-walking, when she was "pure" and when he might have begun to court her; coincidence that the mail cart rams Tess's wagon and kills Prince; coincidence that Tess and Clare meet at Talbothays, *after* her "trouble" rather than before; accident that the letter slips under the rug; coincidence that Clare's parents are not at home when she comes to the vicarage; and so on. Superficially it would seem that this type of event, the accidental and coincidental, is the very least credible of fictional devices, particularly when there is an accumulation of them; and we have all read or heard criticism of Hardy for his excessive reliance upon coincidence in the management of his narratives; if his invention of probabilities and inevitabilities of action does not seem simply poverty-stricken, he appears to be too much the puppeteer working wires or strings to make events conform to his "pessimistic" and "fatalistic" ideas. It is not enough to say that there is a certain justification for his large use of the accidental in the fact that "life is like that"—chance, mishap, accident, events that affect our lives while they remain far beyond our control, are a very large part of experience; but art differs from life precisely by making order out of this disorder, by finding causation in it. In the accidentalism of Hardy's universe we can recognize the profound truth of the darkness in which life is cast, darkness both within the soul and without, only insofar as his accidentalism *is not itself accidental* nor yet an ideology-obsessed puppeteer's manipulation of character and event; which is to say, only insofar as the universe he creates has aesthetic integrity, the flesh and bones and organic development of a concrete world. This is not true always of even the best of Hardy's novels; but it is so generally true of the construction of *Tess*—a novel in which the accidental is perhaps more preponderant than in any other Hardy—that we do not care to finick about incidental lapses. The naturalistic premise of the book—the condition of earth in which life is placed—is the most obvious, fundamental, and inexorable of facts; but because it is the physically "given," into which and beyond which there can be no penetration, it exists as mystery; it is thus, even as the basis of all natural manifestation, itself of the quality of the supernatural. On the earth, so conceived, coincidence and accident constitute order, the prime terrestrial order, for they too are "the given," impenetrable by human *ratio*, accountable only as mystery. By constructing the *Tess*-universe on the solid ground (one might say even literally on the "ground") of the earth as Final Cause, mysterious cause of causes, Hardy does not allow us to forget that what is most concrete in experience is also what is most inscrutable, that an overturned clod in a field or the posture of herons standing in a water mead or the shadows of cows thrown against a wall by evening sunlight are as essentially fathomless as the procreative yearning, and this in turn as fathomless as the sheerest accident in event. The accidentalism and coincidentalism in the narrative pattern of the book stand, thus, in perfectly orderly correlation with the grounding mystery of the physically concrete and the natural.

But Hardy has, with very great cunning, reinforced the *necessity* of this particular kind of narrative pattern by giving to it the background of the folk instinctivism, folk fatalism, and folk magic. If the narrative is conducted largely by coincidence, the broad folk background rationalizes coincidence by constant recognition of the mysteriously "given" as what "was to be"—the folk's humble presumption of order in a rule of mishap. The folk are the earth's pseudopodia, another fauna; and because they are so deeply rooted in the elemental life of the earth—like a sensitive animal extension of the earth itself—they share the authority of the natural. (Whether Hardy's "folk," in all the attributes he gives them, ever existed historically or not is scarcely pertinent; they exist here.) Their philosophy and their skills in living, even their gestures of tragic violence, are instinctive adaptations to "the given"; and because they are indestructible, their attitudes toward events authoritatively urge a similar fatalism upon the reader, impelling him to an imaginative acceptance of the doom-wrought series of accidents in the foreground of the action.

We have said that the dilemma of Tess is the dilemma of moral consciousness in its intractable earthy mixture; schematically simplified, the signifying form of the *Tess*-universe is the tragic heroism and tragic ineffectuality of such consciousness in an antagonistic earth where events shape themselves by accident rather than by moral design; and the *mythological* dimension of this form lies precisely in the earth's antagonism—for what is persistently antagonistic appears to have its own intentions, in this case mysterious, supernatural, for it is only thus that the earth can seem to have "intentions." The folk are the bridge between mere earth and moral individuality; of the earth as they are, separable conscious ego does not arise among them to weaken animal instinct and confuse response— it is the sports, the deracinated ones, like Tess and Clare and Alec, who are morally individualized and who are therefore able to suffer isolation, alienation, and abandonment, or to make others so suffer; the folk, while they remain folk, cannot be individually isolated, alienated, or lost, for they are amoral and their existence is colonial rather than personal. (There is no finer note of this matter—fine in factual and symbolic precision, and in its very inconspicuousness— than the paragraph describing the loaded wagons of the migrating families: * * *[6] Even in the event of mass uprooting, the folk character that is preserved is that of the tenacious, the colonial, the instinctive, for which Hardy finds the simile of the hexagon of the bee, converting it then, with Miltonic boldness, to its humanly tribal significance with the simile of the Ark of the Covenant.) Their fatalism is communal and ritual, an instinctive adaptation as accommodating to bad as to good weather, to misfortune as to luck, to birth as to death, a subjective economy by which emotion is subdued to the falling out of event and the destructiveness of resistance is avoided. In their fatalism lies their survival wisdom, as against the death direction of all moral deliberation. There is this wisdom in the cheerful compassion of the fieldwomen for Tess in her time of trouble: the trouble "was to be." It is in Joan Durbeyfield's Elizabethan ditties of lullaby:

> *I saw her lie do-own in yon-der green gro—ve;*
> *Come, love, and I'll tell you where.*

—the kind of ditty by which women of the folk induce maturity in the child by lulling him to sleep with visions of seduction, adultery, and despair. It is in the folk code of secrecy—as in Dairyman Crick's story of the widow who married Jack Dollop, or in Joan's letter of advice to her daughter, summoning the witness of ladies the highest in the land who had had their "trouble" too but who had not told.

6. See p. 298, above, paragraph beginning "The day . . . " [*Editor*].

Tess's tragedy turns on a secret revealed, that is, on the substitution in Tess of an individualizing morality for the folk instinct of concealment and anonymity.

While their fatalism is a passive adaptation to the earthy doom, the folk magic is an active luxury: the human being, having a mind, however incongruous with his animal condition, has to do something with it—and if the butter will not come and someone is in love in the house, the coexistence of the two facts offers a mental exercise in causation (though this is not really the "rights o't," about the butter, as Dairyman Crick himself observes; magical lore is not so dainty); yet the magic is no less a survival wisdom than the fatalism, inasmuch as it does offer mental exercise in causation, for man cannot live without a sense of cause. The magic is a knowledgeable mode of dealing with the unknowledgeable, and it is adaptive to the dooms of existence where moral reason is not adaptive, for moral reason seeks congruence between human intention and effect and is therefore always inapropos (in Hardy's universe, tragically inapropos), whereas magic seeks only likenesses, correspondences, analogies, and these are everywhere. Moral reason is in complete incommunication with the "given," for it cannot accept the "given" as such, cannot accept accident, cannot accept the obscure activities of instinct, cannot accept doom; but magic can not only accept but rationalize all these, for the correspondences that determine its strategies are themselves "given"—like is like, and that is the end of the matter. As the folk fatalism imbues the foreground accidents with the suggestion of necessity, the folk magic imbues them with the suggestion of the supernaturally motivated; and motivation of whatever kind makes an event seem "necessary," suitable, fitting. The intricate interknitting of all these motifs gives to Hardy's actually magical view of the universe and of human destiny a backing of concrete life, as his evocation of the earth as Cause gives to his vision the grounding of the naturalistic.

The folk magic is, after all, in its strategy of analogy, only a specialization and formalization of the novelist's use of the symbolism of natural detail, a symbolism of which we are constantly aware from beginning to end. Magical interpretation and prediction of events consist in seeing one event or thing as a "mimicry" of another—a present happening, for instance, as a mimicry of some future happening; that is, magic makes a system out of analogies, the correlative forms of things. Poets and novelists do likewise with their symbols. Burns's lines: "And my fause luver staw my rose, / But ah! he left the thorn wi' me," use this kind of mimicry, common to poetry and magic. When a thorn of Alec's roses pricks Tess's chin, the occurrence is read as an omen—and omens properly belong to the field of magic; but the difference between this symbol which is an omen, and the very similar symbol in Burns's lines, which acts only reminiscently, is a difference merely of timing—the one "mimics" a seduction which occurs later, the other "mimics" a seduction and its consequences which have already occurred. And there is very little difference, functionally, between Hardy's use of this popular symbol as an *omen* and his symbolic use of natural particulars—the chattering of the birds at dawn after the death of Prince and the iridescence of the coagulated blood, the swollen udders of the cows at Talbothays and the heavy fertilizing mists of the late summer mornings and evenings, the ravaged turnip field on Flintcomb-Ash and the visitation of the polar birds. All of these natural details are either predictive or interpretive or both, and prediction and interpretation of events through analogies are the profession of magic. When a piece of blood-stained butcher paper flies up in the road as Tess enters the gate of the vicarage at Emminster, the occurrence is natural while it is ominous; it is realistically observed, as part of the "given," while it inculcates the magical point of view. Novelistic symbolism *is* magical strategy. In *Tess*, which is through and through symbolic, magic is not only an adaptive specialization of the "folk," but it also determines the reader's response to the most naturalistic detail. Thus, though the story is grounded deeply in a naturalistic premise, Hardy's use of one of the commonest tools of novelists—symbolism—enforces a magical view of life.

Logically accommodated by this view of life is the presentation of supernatural characters. Alec D'Urberville does not appear in his full otherworldly character until late in the book, in the episode of the planting fires, where we see him with pitchfork among flames—and even then the local realism of the planting fires is such as almost to absorb the ghostliness of the apparition. The usual form of his appearance is as a stage villain, complete with curled mustache, checked suit, and cane; and actually it seems a bit easier for the reader to accept him as the Evil Spirit itself, even with a pitchfork, than in his secular accouterments of the villain of melodrama. But Hardy's logic faces its conclusions with superb boldness, as it does in giving Angel Clare his name and his harp and making him a minister's son; if Alec is the Evil One, there will be something queer about his ordinary tastes, and the queerness is shown in his stagy clothes (actually, this melodramatic stereotype is just as valid for a certain period of manners and dress as our own stereotype of the gunman leaning against a lamppost and striking a match against his thumbnail). Alec is the smart aleck of the Book of Job, the one who goes to and fro in the earth and walks up and down in it, the perfectly deracinated one, with his flash and new money and faked name and aggressive ego. If he becomes a religious convert even temporarily it is because he is not really so very much different from Angel (the smart aleck of the Book of Job was also an angel), for extreme implies extreme, and both Angel and Alec are foundered in egoism, the one in idealistic egoism, the other in sensual egoism, and Angel himself is diabolic enough in his prudery. When Alec plays his last frivolous trick on Tess, lying down on one of the slabs in the D'Urberville vaults and springing up at her like an animated corpse, his neuroticism finally wears, not the stagy traditional externals of the Evil Spirit, but the deeply convincing character of insanity—of that human evil which is identifiable with madness. Both Angel and Alec are metaphors of extremes of human behavior, when the human has been cut off from community and has been individualized by intellectual education or by material wealth and traditionless independence.

Between the stridencies of Angel's egoism and Alec's egoism is Tess—with her Sixth Standard training and some anachronistic D'Urberville current in her blood that makes for spiritual exacerbation just as it makes her cheeks paler, "the teeth more regular, the red lips thinner than is usual in a country-bred girl": incapacitated for life by her moral idealism, capacious of life through her sensualism. When, after Alec's evilly absurd trick, she bends down to whisper at the opening of the vaults, "Why am I on the wrong side of this door?" her words construct all the hopelessness of her cultural impasse. But her stabbing of Alec is her heroic return through the "door" into the folk fold, the fold of nature and instinct, the anonymous community. If both Alec and Angel are spiritually impotent in their separate ways, Tess is finally creative by the only measure of creativeness that this particular novelistic universe holds, the measure of the instinctive and the natural. Her gesture is the traditional gesture of the revenge of instinct, by which she joins an innumerable company of folk heroines who stabbed and were hanged—the spectacular but still anonymous and common gesture of common circumstances and common responses, which we, as habitual readers of newspaper crime headlines, find, unthinkingly, so shocking to our delicate notions of what is "natural." That she goes, in her wandering at the end, to Stonehenge, is an inevitable symbolic going—as all going and doing are symbolic—for it is here that the earthiness of her state is best recognized, by the monoliths of Stonehenge, and that the human dignity of her last gesture has the most austere recognition, by the ritual sacrifices that have been made on these stones.

IRVING HOWE

[*Tess of the d'Urbervilles*—At the Center of Hardy's Achievement]†

As a writer of novels Thomas Hardy was endowed with a precious gift: he liked women. There are not, when one comes to think of it, quite so many other nineteenth century novelists about whom as much can be said. With some, the need to keep returning in their fiction to the disheveled quarters of domesticity causes a sigh of weariness, even at times a suppressed snarl of discontent; for, by a certain measure, it must seem incongruous that writers intent on a fundamental criticism of human existence should be sentenced to indefinite commerce with sex, courtship, adultery and family quarrels. Hardy, by contrast, felt no such impatience with the usual materials of the novel. Though quite capable of releasing animus toward his women characters and casting them as figures of destruction, he could not imagine a universe without an active, even an intruding, feminine principle. The sexual exclusiveness of nineteenth century American writing would have been beyond his comprehension, though probably not beyond his sympathy.

Throughout his years as a novelist Hardy found steadily interesting the conceits and playfulness of women, the elaborate complex of stratagems in which the sexual relationship appears both as struggle and game. He liked the changefulness, sometimes even the caprice, of feminine personality; he marveled at the seemingly innate capacity of young girls to glide into easy adaptations and tactical charms. And he had a strong appreciation of the manipulative and malicious powers that might be gathered beneath a surface of delight. Except perhaps with Sue Bridehead,[1] he was seldom inclined to plunge into the analytic depths which mark the treatment of feminine character in George Eliot's later novels; but if he did not look as deeply as she did into the motivations of feminine character, he was remarkably keen at apprehending feminine behavior. He had observed and had watched, with uneasy alertness. The range of virtuosity which other writers had believed possible only in a stylized high society or sophisticated court, Hardy, in his plain and homely way, found among the country girls of southwest England.

Throughout Hardy's fiction, even in his lesser novels, there is a curious power of sexual insinuation, almost as if he were not locked into the limits of masculine perception but could shuttle between,

† From Irving Howe, "Let the Day Perish," in *Thomas Hardy* (New York, 1967), pp. 108–32.
1. In *Jude the Obscure* [*Editor*].

or for moments yoke together, the responses of the two sexes. This gift for creeping intuitively into the emotional life of women Hardy shared with a contemporary, George Gissing, though he was quite free of that bitter egocentrism which marred Gissing's work. And at the deepest level of his imagination, Hardy held to a vision of the feminine that was thoroughly traditional in celebrating the maternal, the protective, the fecund, the tender, the life-giving. It was Hardy's openness to the feminine principle that drew D. H. Lawrence to his work and led him to see there, with some justice, a kinship with his own. One may speculate that precisely those psychological elements which led Hardy to be so indulgent toward male passivity also enabled him to be so receptive to feminine devices. He understood and could portray aggression; but at least as a writer, he did not allow it to dominate or corrode his feelings about the other sex—and that, incidentally, is one reason he does not care to pass judgment on his characters. The feminine admixture is very strong in his work, a source both of his sly humor and his profound sympathy.

It is in *Tess of the D'Urbervilles* that this side of Hardy comes through with the most striking vitality. The book stands at the center of Hardy's achievement, if not as his greatest then certainly his most characteristic, and those readers or critics who cannot accept its emotional ripeness must admit that for them Hardy is not a significant novelist. For in *Tess* he stakes everything on his sensuous apprehension of a young woman's life, a girl who is at once a simple milkmaid and an archetype of feminine strength. Nothing finally matters in the novel nearly so much as Tess herself: not the other characters, not the philosophic underlay, not the social setting. In her violation, neglect and endurance, Tess comes to seem Hardy's most radical claim for the redemptive power of suffering; she stands, both in the economy of the book and as a figure rising beyond its pages and into common memory, for the unconditional authority of feeling.

Tess is one of the greatest examples we have in English literature of how a writer can take hold of a cultural stereotype and, through the sheer intensity of his affection, pare and purify it into something that is morally ennobling. Tess derives from Hardy's involvement with and reaction against the Victorian cult of chastity, which from the beginning of his career he had known to be corrupted by meanness and hysteria. She falls. She violates the standards and conventions of her day. And yet, in her incomparable vibrancy and lovingness, she comes to represent a spiritualized transcendence of chastity. She dies three times, to live again:—first with Alec D'Urberville, then with Angel Clare, and lastly with Alec again. Absolute victim of her wretched circumstances, she is ultimately beyond their stain. She embodies a feeling for the inviolability of the person, as it brings the absolute of chastity nearer to the warming Christian virtue of charity. Through a dialectic of negation, Tess reaches purity of spirit even as she fails to satisfy the standards of the world.

Perhaps because she fails to satisfy them? Not quite. What we have here is not the spiritual sensationalism of the Dostoevsky who now and again indulges himself in the notion that a surrender to licentiousness is a necessary condition for spiritual rebirth. Hardy's view is a more innocent one, both purer and less worldly. He does not seek the abyss nor glory in finding it. He is not a phenomenologist of the perverse. But as a man deeply schooled in the sheer difficulty of life, he does recognize that there is a morality of being as well as of doing, an imperative to compassion which weakens the grip of judgment. Once educated to humility, we do not care to judge Tess at all: we no longer feel ourselves qualified. And that, I think, is a triumph of the moral imagination.

In staking out these claims for *Tess of the D'Urbervilles* I recognize that Hardy's vision of Tess can hardly satisfy the rigorous morality of Protestantism which was a part of his heritage. Other forces are at work, both pre- and post-Christian: the stoicism of the folk ballad, from whose wronged heroines Tess descends, and the moral experiment of romanticism. Hardy could no more avoid the conditioning influence of romanticism than a serious writer can now avoid that of modernism; it was part of the air he breathed. His romanticism enabled Hardy to break past the repressions of the Protestant ethic and move into a kindlier climate shared by Christian charity and pagan acceptance; but it was also romanticism, with its problematic and perverse innovations, which threatened his wish for a return to a simple, primitive Christianity. In *Tess of the D'Urbervilles* the romantic element appears most valuably as an insistence upon the right of the individual person to create the terms of his being, despite the pressures and constraints of the external world. Yet, because Tess is a warmhearted and unpretentious country girl barely troubled by intellectual ambition, Hardy's stress is upon the right of the person and not, as it will be in *Jude the Obscure,* upon the subjective demands of personality. Sue Bridehead anticipates the modern cult of personality in all its urgency and clamor; Tes Durbeyfield represents something more deeply rooted in the substance of instinctual life.

There are, to be sure, instances of self-indulgent writing in this novel which can be described as late-romantic, even decadent, but the controlling perception of Tess is restrained and, if one cares to use such terms, "healthy." Tess demands nothing that can be regarded as the consequence of deracination or an overwrought will;

she is not gratuitously restless or neurotically bored; she is spontaneously committed to the most fundamental needs of human existence. Indeed, she provides a standard of what is right and essential for human beings to demand from life. And because we respond to her radiant wholeness, Tess stands somewhat apart from, nor can she be seriously damaged by, the romantic excesses into which Hardy's writing can lapse. Tess is finally one of the great images of human possibility, conceived in the chaste, and chastening, spirit of the New Testament. Very few proclaimed believers have written with so complete a Christian sentiment as the agnostic Thomas Hardy.

Simply as a work of fiction, *Tess of the D'Urbervilles* is singularly direct in its demands. It contains few of the elements we have come to know and expect in nineteenth century novels. There is little interplay of character as registered through nuances of social manners or the frictions of social class. None of the secondary figures has much interest in his own right, apart from his capacity to illuminate and enlarge the experience of Tess; all of them seem, by Hardy's evident choice, to be dwarfed beside her. The passages of philosophic comment, about which I will say more on a later page, surely do not provide a center of concern for the serious modern reader. And while the social setting—a setting that, in its several parts, forms a history of rural England leveled in space—comes to be quite essential for the development of the action, finally it is not to the world in which Tess moves, nor even the world Tess may symbolize, that we yield our deepest assent.

As for the plot, it seems in isolation a paltry thing, a mere scraping together of bits and pieces from popular melodrama: a pure girl betrayed, a woman's secret to be told or hidden, a piling on of woes that must strain the resources of ordinary credence. Whether Hardy was deliberately employing the threadbare stuff of melodrama in order to transcend it, or whether he shared in the emotional premises of such fiction but through his peculiar genius unconsciously raised it to the level of abiding art (as Dickens repeatedly did), is very hard to say. Perhaps, in the case of a writer like Hardy, it is a distinction without much difference.[2]

2. "There is no absolute divorce," writes Joseph Warren Beach in a keen paragraph, "between 'literature' proper and the literature of the dime novel. Themes which receive their crudely sentimental and melodramatic treatment in the one are sure to appear above the surface, somewhat refined, it may be, but recognizable. Meredith, when he put forth *Rhoda Fleming*, showed in his chapter headings a consciousness that he was writing somewhat in the manner of *East Lynne*. . . . *Tess of the d'Urbervilles* came at a time when, in serious literature, especially in plays, a great deal of attention was being paid to the subject of the *déclassée*—the woman who would come back, the woman who lives under 'the shadow of a sin,' the woman who has to pay for 'one false step.' *The Second Mrs. Tanqueray* will suffice to suggest the cur-

There is just enough plot loosely to thread together the several episodes that comprise the book, yet surely it is not here that one looks for Hardy's achievement. *Tess of the D'Urbervilles* can, in fact, profitably be regarded as a fiction in the line of *Pilgrim's Progress* rather than in the line of Jane Austen's and George Eliot's novels, for its structure is that of a journey in which each place of rest becomes a test for the soul and the function of plot is largely to serve as an agency for transporting the central figure from one point to another. *Tess* is clearly not an allegory and no one in his senses would wish that it were, but its pattern of narrative has something in common with, even if it does not directly draw upon, Bunyan's fiction. There are four sections or panels of representation: Tess at home and with Alec; Tess at Talbothays and with Angel; Tess at Flintcomb-Ash and again with Alec; Tess briefly happy with Angel and then in her concluding apotheosis at Stonehenge. None of these panels is quite self-sufficient, since narrative tension accumulates from part to part; but each has a distinctiveness of place, action and tone which makes it profitable to think of the novel as episodic. One is reminded of a medieval painting divided into panels, each telling part of a story and forming a progress in martyrdom. The martyrdom is that of Tess, upon whom everything rests and all value depends.

The novel opens with several compact vignettes. The first chapter, in which John Durbeyfield is told that he comes from an ancient but decayed aristocratic family, presents through comedy the dislocation which is to serve as pressure for Tess's odyssey. The second chapter, in which Tess, a healthy farm girl but "not handsomer than the others," is seen at the rite of "club-walking," has a double value: it quickly introduces the village of Marlott in the gentle Vale of Blackmoor, where something still remains of an independent yeomanry, small land holdings and traditional rural ways, yet where the old rituals have been shorn of their significance and reduced to pleasant customs. Tess, "a mere vessel of emotion untinctured by experience," has passed the Sixth Standard in a National School, but this should not be taken to suggest that she has been cut off from the life of Marlott. Indeed, the Sixth Standard is rapidly becoming part of that life. Hardy provides this piece of information about Tess's schooling in order to make more plausible her role as a country girl, not a mere dumb victim of incomprehensible social

rency of a theme which is treated by such other notable hands as Oscar Wilde and Henry Arthur Jones. So that Hardy's subject was timely from the point of view of the 'high brow' as well as popular in the original sense of the word. And that one of his novels which is most satisfying to the critic for the beauty and seriousness of its art is at the same time the one to make, from the time of its first appearance, an appeal to the widest circle of readers."

forces (as are her three young friends in the later portions of the book), but a figure with some articulateness and awareness. Her education underscores her representativeness, for there is just enough of it to endow her with consciousness while not enough to make her estranged.

A few pages later, for the first time, Tess takes the center of the stage: she is driving the family wagon in the dark of night, because her shiftless father has gotten drunk and the family's beehives must be delivered to Casterbridge. Dozing off, Tess fails to hear the mail-cart "with its two noiseless wheels, speeding along these lanes like an arrow," and in the ensuing accident the Durbeyfield horse, the family's main economic asset, is killed. Out of remorse and guilt, Tess then agrees to her mother's scheme that she visit the rich Trantridge D'Urbervilles who will make her fortune. That these cousins are not authentic offshoots of the aristocratic line, but *arriviste* bourgeois who have bought their way into the gentry and appropriated the name as a decoration, is a fine stroke.

The trap has been sprung for Tess, be it a trap of fatality, social pressure, family sloth or all at once. Throughout the remainder of the book, Hardy will employ a pattern of hunting images, as John Holloway has nicely observed.[3] Tess will be "harried from place to place at what seems like gradually increasing speed." Finally, "when the hunt is over, Tess is captured on the sacrificial stone at Stonehenge, the stone where once, like the hart at bay, the victim's throat was slit with the knife. With these things in mind, Hardy's much abused quotation from Aeschylus ('in Aeschylean phrase, the President of the Immortals had finished his sport with Tess') takes on a new meaning and aptness."

Thus far, in the first few chapters, Tess has not been cast in a strongly individual mold, except possibly during the poignant, if overburdened, conversation with her little brother Abraham as to whether "we be on a blighted star." She is shown in the ease of her natural surroundings, a long-cultivated and soft-featured rural landscape, but also in the discomfort of her social place, an idle crumbling family and a growing poverty that forces her to surrender her independence and appeal to her rich "cousins." As it happens— and Hardy is clearly starting to weave a social fable here—the rich cousin is Alec D'Urberville, shown at the outset as a stagy villain who greets Tess with the standard melodramatic gambit: "Well, my Beauty, what can I do for you?" The theatricality is deliberate. In this novel Hardy will achieve something that is rare in fiction: a fusion of theater and truth.

To prepare for the monstrousness of Alec's betrayal as well as to set off Tess from the subordinate figures that will surround her,

3. In *The Chartered Mirror* (London, 1960), pp. 104–7 [*Editor*].

Hardy starts to fill in the portrait of his heroine. We are still far from the depth that will characterize the later Tess, but we do now see her in characteristic health and country bloom. There is the marvelous passage in which Alec, during their first meeting, plies her with strawberries, insisting that he himself pop them in her mouth and meanwhile adding rose blossoms "to put in her bosom." One of those symbolic miniatures at which Hardy is so masterful, the passage radiates with suggestions of dominance, patronage, sexuality. Tess, stirred and bewildered, "obeyed like one in a dream."

The texture darkens a little, but only a little, when Alec drives Tess from her cottage to his mansion and begins to make advances to her. For if there is something ominous in the air, there is also fun and youthful zest in their sparring—Hardy's gift for evoking the play of flirtation seldom fails him. And the writing itself is notably delicate and vivacious. Forced to kiss Alec, Tess "unconsciously" wipes "the spot on her cheek that had been touched by his lips" and then, to prevent another embrace, tricks him into stopping the wagon so that she can jump off: * * *4

By the close of the incident Tess is still huffily refusing all pleas to remount. But, adds Hardy with a touch of slyness, "she did not object to his keeping his gig alongside her; and in this manner, at a slow pace, they advanced toward the village of Trantridge." It is a clash of pride and purpose, and its suggestion that Tess is not quite indifferent to Alec's commonplace charms adds a humanizing note: Tess is to be more than a stiff bundle of virtue. An equally affectionate feeling for the changeability of human response is shown in another passage between Tess and Alec, in which he is teaching her to whistle: * * *5

At this point Tess has a touch of Pamela, and later she will have still more of Clarissa.6

Hardy manages the seduction scene with a tact not always characteristic of his novels. With so much tact, indeed, that readers have often supposed Tess to be a victim of rape—though the sequel is surely no rape, Hardy declaring that Tess "had been stirred to confused surrender awhile . . ." The concluding passage of mournful reflection—"But, some might say, where was Tess's guardian angel? where was the providence of her simple faith?"—serves in this novel an over-all purpose to which I shall return, as well as the local purpose of what is called in film-making a "dissolve." We are led back, away from the event, so that we may regard it with the brooding helplessness which for Hardy is the ultimate register of trouble.

In any case, the overture is now done.

4. See p. 46, above, lines 13–26 [*Editor*].
5. See p. 50, above, lines 26–36 [*Editor*].

6. Heroines of two eighteenth-century novels by Samuel Richardson, which trace the progress of long seductions [*Editor*].

The Tess we next meet is a transformed young woman, "a person who did not find her especial burden in material things." There has been a fall from innocence, and in some ways—Hardy is by no means the first to notice this irony—it has been a fortunate fall. Tess's eye is now keener, her tongue sharper, her mind quicker. Innocence lost, she takes upon herself the weight of awareness. Her freedom will be steadily diminished, as she steps along the markings of fate; yet it is only now that she gains another freedom, since only now can she grasp the significance of choice. The book begins to mobilze and direct large masses of tension which, until the last page, will make the reading of it an experience slow and grueling, a drain upon emotion.

As Tess leaves Alec, she breaks into lucid and passionate speech such as could, in the earlier chapters, only have been anticipated: * * *[7]

The situation is trite enough, as are most of the central crises of of human experience, but the force of speech, and the intensity of represnted life which it conveys, is remarkable. Still more so is another passage on the following page: * * *[8]

The writing is rich with compressed significance. Tess bowing slightly to Alec, perhaps with ironic contempt, perhaps with recognition that, in some detested way, he has established a hold over her—it is from detail of this kind that a novel is made. Alec going through the motions of his dominance, half-languid but still appreciative of the prize he has had—this too is very fine. And then the comparison of Tess's cheeks with the skin of mushrooms closes the passage with a reverberating simile: as if her cheeks now had something of the inert sponginess, the yielding lifelessness of the plant.

Tess once more alone, there quickly follows another of those telling brief incidents which in Hardy's work gather together the symbolic purport of the narrative. Tess encounters the slightly crazed preacher who paints his signs of loveless theology "placing a comma after each word, as if to give pause while that word was driven well home to the reader's heart—

THY, DAMNATION, SLUMBERETH, NOT . . ."

The words do drive "well home" into Tess's heart, but she answers with an unexpected resilience of mind: "Pooh—I don't believe God said such things." It thereby becomes clear that Tess is not at all a broken woman; she has suffered, but as she "throbbingly resume[s] her walk," she cannot, if she would, suppress the life-force that surges through her. Returning to her mother, she cries out: "Why didn't you tell me there was danger in men-folks?" and

7. See dialogue beginning at bottom of p. 64, up to "some women may feel?" (line 19, p. 65) [*Editor*].
8. See passage beginning "She said that she did not wish . . . " at bottom of p. 65, up to line 19, p. 66 [*Editor*].

is answered with a cool mixture of sluttishness and peasant fatalism: "Well, we must make the best of it . . . 'Tis nater, after all, and what do please God." Tess will find no help here, as she will find little anywhere. On this ironic downbeat Chapter XII concludes, a triumph of Hardy's mature art.

The narrative voice now draws sharply away from Tess the individual, and for an interval we see her mainly from a distance, in the rhythms of sickness and recovery, which as Hardy describes them seem almost impersonal, since so often repeated in the experience of the race. These abrupt transitions from intimacy to distance and then back again to intimacy are used by Hardy to reinforce Tess's representative nature: * * *9

To renew herself through work, Tess goes to the Talbothays dairy, and in the pages that follow there can be found some of the most remarkable writing in Hardy's—for that matter, in all of English—fiction. At Talbothays both the natural world and Tess, who is part of that world yet distinct from it, come into ripe bloom. An ease of rhythm, a summer drowse, overtakes everything. Unexpended youth brings with it hope "and the invincible instinct toward self-delight." Tess, "warmed as a sunned cat," heals and opens. Working quietly on the farm; finding comfort in dairyman Crick's generosity and his wife's steadiness; immersing herself in the green life of the place; enjoying the cameraderie of her fellow-workers and the tales they tell; falling in love with Angel Clare, who seems all seriousness and refinement, to be worshipped in his purity where Alec had been despised for his designs—Tess reaches a radiant fullness. She and the land come together, in a metaphoric boldness * * *1

All of Tess's sexuality comes into readiness, but it is a sexuality superbly at ease with itself; she is the only one of Hardy's heroines who does not use it to manipulate or crush men. In her unaffectedly sexual charms, she is quite without self-consciousness: * * *2

In this eden of sensuousness Tess and Angel enact the rites of courtship, but with the faintest foreshadowing of disaster: * * *3

The metaphor of "pollen" weaves through the courtship scenes, linking natural fecundity and human desire: * * *4

Idyllic as they are, these scenes are never allowed to become mere idylls, for the courtship is being conducted within a community that registers and approves: * * *5

Surely it was passages like these which prompted D. H. Lawrence to say about Hardy that "his feeling, his instinct, his sensuous un-

---

9. See p. 77, lines 16–24 [*Editor*].
1. See p. 125, first paragraph of chapter XXIV [*Editor*].
2. See p. 104, paragraphs 2 and 3 [*Editor*].
3. See p. 111, paragraph beginning

"At these non-human hours . . . " and two paragraphs following [*Editor*].
4. See p. 163, lines 4–15 [*Editor*].
5. See p. 164, paragraph beginning "They walked later . . . " [*Editor*].

derstanding is . . . apart from his metaphysic, very great and deep, deeper than that, perhaps, of any other English novelist. Putting aside his metaphysic, which must always obtrude when he thinks of people, and turning to the earth, to landscape, then he is true to himself." To which it needs only be added: a passionate woman is the blessing of literature.

What keeps the Talbothays section from sliding into pantheist sentimentalism is the firmness with which Hardy grounds it in the commonplace world of human labor. The action is set within a recognizable milieu, and Tess is a woman who works with her hands. Benign as the atmosphere of Talbothays may be, personal as the relationship between dairyman Crick and his workers remains, there can be no doubt that in coming to Talbothays Tess has taken another step in her social descent: she is a hired hand and the work itself is seasonal. In a few months, the workers will scatter and their community dissolve. (It is notable, by the way, that in contrast to Tess neither Alec nor Angel does meaningful work: Alec is a wastrel, Angel a dilettante. Neither lives under the lash of necessity, neither defines himself through craft or occupation.)

There are moments when Tess and Angel go off into the woods, apart from the places of settlement, but most of the time they are shown within the bounds of structured society. Nothing about Talbothays is "primitive," and nothing "wild" or asocial in the manner of *Wuthering Heights*. The Talbothays farm is not a place of fantasy pitted against a decadent or corrupt civilization; it is itself representative of a phase in civilized existence. Centuries of effort have had to pass before the civilization of Talbothays could be achieved, though only a few decades of technological change would be required to destroy it. Rhapsodic and lyrical this section of *Tess of the D'Urbervilles* is meant to be, but the rhapsody celebrates a love of earthly creatures and the lyricism has nothing to do with primitivist negations. For a few months, Tess reaches an ecstasy resting upon commonplace human experience—and that is precisely what makes the ecstasy so remarkable.

Hardy's conception of Angel Clare is not, by itself, to be faulted: a timid convert to modernist thought who possesses neither the firmness of the old nor the boldness of the new. Scene by scene, as the action works itself out, Angel comes to seem the complement of Alec; indeed, the parallels might be trying, if they were not so strictly subordinated to the presentation of Tess herself. Alec assaults Tess physically, Angel violates her spiritually. Alec is a stage villain, Angel is an intellectual wretch. Alec has a certain charm, in his amiable slothful way; Angel bears an aura of tensed moralism. What they share is an incapacity to value the splendor of feeling which radiates from Tess. Each represents a deformation of masculinity, one high and the other low; they cannot appreciate, they cannot even *see* the richness of life that Tess embodies. Yet there are important differences. At least Alec does not pontificate, or wrap himself in a cloak of principles. He may not be admirable but he can be likable, simply because commonplace vice is easier to bear than elevated righteousness, And as Lawrence has shrewdly noticed, Alec "seeks with all his power for the source of stimulus in women. He takes the deep impulse from the female . . . he could reach some of the real sources of the female in a woman, and draw from them . . . [But Angel, as] the result of generations of ultra-Christian training, [has] an inherent aversion to the female . . ." Together the two men represent everything in Hardy's world, and not his alone, which betrays spontaneous feeling and the flow of instinctual life.

Angel's priggishness is not only hard to take, it is sometimes hard to credit. That he should condemn Tess for her sins directly after confessing his own, may not—in light of what we know about his character and his culture—be entirely implausible. But when seen in the context of the whole book, this seems another of those instances where Hardy abuses his plot in order to make clear what is already quite evident. Nor can one be certain that Hardy sees Angel for the insufferable prig he is—not because Hardy feels anything but dislike toward everything Angel stands for, but because at this point in the narrative Hardy is so caught up with Tess and her ordeal, he seems almost ready to share in her refusal to judge her adored lover.

Where Hardy's art can be brought into more serious question is in the famous sleepwalking scene. It is a set-piece that bears a relation to Hardy's work somewhat like the death of Little Joe[6] to Dickens's. The incident is affecting, it is bold, it is brilliant in conception. Angel, having learned about Tess's past, refuses to go to bed with her on their wedding night; but during a moment of sleepwalking, when his inhibitions are somewhat at rest, he carries her to a stone coffin and places her there lovingly. This piece of action can be seen as a forceful projection of Angel's psychology, in which love and death are sadly compounded. That Tess should submit to such a ghastly dumb show, and submit with all the trustfulness which marks her character, is also telling. That Tess should then lead the stricken Angel back to the house and that Hardy, plunging deeper and deeper into risk, should remark that Tess walks barefoot in the chill night while Angel is in his woolen socks (he would be!)—all this can be accepted as an expressionist strategy for acting out inner states of feeling.

Yet even if we accept this strategy as a way of coping with those

6. In *Bleak House* [*Editor*].

incidents in Hardy's fiction which are as improbable as they are crucial, there remain serious difficulties. Hardy is frequently lacking in tact. Almost obsessively, he needs to pile gratuitous excess on top of initial improbability. The idea of the sleepwalking, as it turns out, is not quite enough for him, and to add still another *frisson*—though, if we respond at all, our nerves are by now sufficiently strained—Angel must be shown carrying Tess across a narrow footbridge threatened by autumnal flood, "a giddy pathway for even steady heads." The detail itself hardly matters, but it may be just enough to break the current of conviction. In the large, then, the sleepwalking incident strikes one as a perilous touch of genius; it also suggests that genius can be quite compatible with bad taste.

About the sequence at Flintcomb-Ash, however, there is almost no disagreement. Even those critics and readers who question Hardy's place as a novelist are likely to acknowledge the disciplined power of this section. The writing is harsh and compact, absolutely without self-indulgence; there is frequent metaphoric intensification; every word is directed toward a fierce rendering of the sterility of place and the brutality of labor. Nothing in Zola or Dreiser surpasses these pages for a portrayal of human degradation—a portrayal compassionate through its severe objectivity.

The land is barren and flinty, the very opposite of Talbothays. The atmosphere is hushed, death-like. The weather is cruel, apocalyptic. And Tess has been reduced to an agricultural proletarian, working not for a benevolent dairyman but for an unseen landowner, under the nervous prodding of a foreman and the shock of the new farm machines. Mechanization, impersonality, alienation, the cash nexus, dehumanization—all these tags of modern thought, so worn and all too often true, are brought to quickened reality in Tess's ordeal at Flintcomb-Ash. What Marx wrote about the working day and the outrage of female labor becomes tangible and immediate. Tess as a woman, Tess as a distinctive person hardly exists; she has become a factor in the process of production.

The engineman who works the new threshing machine (that "red tyrant . . . the woman had come to serve") is presented with a Dickensian vividness. Hardy describes him not as a person but as a threatening force, a function: * * *[7]

Flintcomb-Ash is like a vision of hell, for Hardy what London was for Dickens: * * *[8]

These ghastly evocations are heightened by the swede-grubbing, by the "myriads of loose white flints in budbous, cusped and phallic shapes" which are dug up in the ground, and by the fields which

7. See last paragraph on p. 269 and first paragraph on p. 270 [*Editor*].
8. See p. 240, first paragraph and first two sentences of second paragraph [*Editor*].

have "a complexion without features, as if a face, from chin to brow, should be only an expanse of skin. The sky wore, in another colour, the same likeness; a white vacuity of countenance with the lineaments gone." It is Hardy's wasteland. And Tess, broken with fatigue, assumes the largeness of martyrdom: * * *[9]

Weaving through the Flintcomb-Ash sequence is a line of symbolic action—though to call it "symbolic" is to risk minimizing its strong immediacy—in which Alec d'Urberville, shed of religion and gone back to his calling of tempter, keeps appearing and reappearing at the swede-field, prepared to rescue Tess if only she will forget the husband who had left her. At this point Alec appears in a double guise: he is both kinder and crueler to Tess than is anyone else, both more humane and sinister. The tribute he pays Tess is that he always finds her interesting and wishes steadily to be near her—one glimpse of her eyes, he tells her during his phase as preacher, and he is undone! Only he among the figures surrounding her offers Tess and the disabled Durbeyfields any help. Yet it is also he who comes to seem a kind of devil, embodying the amiable sloth, the slackness of will and value, which is the devil's word. Tess succumbs to him and, succumbing, hates him; there is a frightful intimacy in their conversation, the intimacy of sinners. That Tess finally murders Alec does not, as one yields oneself to the momentum of the book, seem nearly so implausible or disconcerting as any number of earlier and less violent incidents. The murder is an act of desperate assertion which places Tess in the line of folk heroines who kill because they can no longer bear outrage, but it is also an act toward which our responses have been trained by Hardy to move past easy approval or easy rejection, indeed past any judgment. Given all that has happened, we accept the killing of Alec with a feeling that approaches relief, if only because we know that it signifies an end to Tess's journey. The murder of Alec is, I think, easier to credit than the sleepwalking scene with Angel, for the sleepwalking is eccentric, a stroke quite special to Hardy's imagination, while the killing is traditional, part of the accepted heritage that has come down to us through popular and literary channels.

There remains the interval in which Tess and Angel briefly come together as husband and wife, living, as it were, suspended from time, and then the climax at Stonehenge, staged by Hardy with a sharp eye for chiaroscuro effects. At once joyful and anxious, the reunion of Tess and Angel provides a rest in the accumulating tension of the novel: it reminds one, on a small scale, of the scene in Siberia where Zhivago and Lara have a short time of happiness be-

9. See p. 276, paragraph beginning "A panting ache . . . " and next paragraph [*Editor*].

fore their enforced separation.[1] After this interval, we are ready for the climax. Stonehenge is a place emanating inexplicable grandeurs and horrors: the scene is blunt in its demands, enormously ambitious in its grasp. Hardy's writing it very quiet, almost mere notation, as Tess fades from life. It is a scene that can best be understood and accepted in the terms proposed by John Holloway when he writes that Hardy's novels require "a special mode of reading. The incidents in them which strike us as improbable or strained or grotesque invite (this is not to say that they always deserve) the kind of response that we are accustomed to give, say, to the Dover Cliff scene in Lear. Admittedly, Hardy has local failures; but incidents like the one at Stonehenge are at some distance from the probable and the realistic. Almost, it is necessary for them to be unrealistic, in order that their other dimension of meaning, their relevance to the larger rhythms of the work, shall transpire."[2]

I have gone into such considerable detail of analysis and excerpt primarily because, of all Hardy's novels, Tess has the richest narrative texture and depends most upon that texture for its cumulative effects. It is the kind of novel in which the commanding design is relatively simple and the artistic realization is mostly a consequence of the depth and intensity with which the design has been worked out.

Where, then, is the center of interest in this book? There have appeared in recent years the thoughtful studies of Tess by English critics Douglas Brown and Arnold Kettle,[3] which see Tess as victim of a social disintegration that has been caused by the coming of industrialism to the countryside. Brown's stress is traditionalist and Kettle's Marxist, but both critics, while warning against the dangers of allegorical dryness, tend to read the book as a social fable—that is, a narrative in which attention is steadily being directed to a scheme of social relations behind the foreground events.

Tess, writes Brown, "is the agricultural predicament in metaphor, engaging Hardy's deepest impulses of sympathy and allegiance." In so reading the novel, Brown stresses the care with which Hardy fixes the action in the context of country ritual, even if a ritual fallen into neglect, half-forgotten and decadent; the novel is bounded by an early scene that describes the May-walking and a late scene that describes the uprooting of the Durbeyfields—but also of large numbers of other farm people—on Old Lady Day. Kettle writes that Tess has "the quality of a social document. It has even, for all its high-pitched emotional quality, the kind of impersonality

1. In Boris Pasternak's Doctor Zhivago [Editor].
2. Loc. cit. [Editor].
3. See Selected Bibliography [Editor].

that the expression suggests. Its subject is all-pervasive, affecting and determining the nature of every part. It is a novel with a thesis . . . and the thesis is true. The thesis is that in the latter half of the last century the disintegration of the peasantry—a process which had its roots deep in the past—had reached its final and tragic stage."

Now it would be foolish and ungenerous to deny that both critics are saying something valuable about *Tess*. Both are pointing, Brown with more subtlety than Kettle, to the superbly rendered social frame which makes Tess what she is and in which she acts out her ordeal. Though, like the greatest characters in literature, she lives beyond the final pages of the book as a permanent citizen of the imagination, Tess is inconceivable except as a Wessex girl rooted in Wessex particulars—and these particulars form part of the social substance which concerns Brown and Kettle. Whenever Hardy ventures upon his expressionist set-pieces and pictorial stylizations in trying to magnify the stature of Tess, the effort depends, first of all, on having grounded the story in commonplace social reality. And not only Tess as a country girl but the other figures—Alec as a sleazy *arriviste*, Angel as a neurotic moralist, Joan Durbeyfield as a good-natured slattern—gain their initial credence through their representativeness. That, to begin with, is how fictive individuals are created.

Yet I feel that, no matter how helpful and enriching this critical approach to *Tess* may be, it does not bring us to the vital heart of the book. The case is somewhat as with Kettle's reading of *Wuthering Heights*, in which he persuasively demonstrates that the action takes place not in a mythic cloud but in nineteenth century England, that Heathcliff is not merely a figure of satanism but a man determined to revenge social snobbery, and that throughout the book issues of class power and relationships are significant. All true; yet what is missing is precisely that which makes *Wuthering Heights* so remarkable a work. What is missing is the ravenous and deathly love between Heathcliff and Catherine, set in the very foreground, dominating everything near it, and certain to be regarded by a reader unburdened by theses as the center of the book.

Similar judgments hold for *Tess of the D'Urbervilles*. When the book is fully alive, forming a self-sufficient area of the imagination, I cannot for a moment believe that Tess is "the agricultural predicament in metaphor" or that she represents "the disintegration of the peasantry." These may well be elements contributing to her reality as a character in a novel, but they are not quite the reality itself. For when the book is indeed fully alive, we have no wish to look beyond her or to think of her as representing anything whatever; we are fully engaged with the motion and meaning of her behavior. Closer than Brown or Kettle to the heart of the book is the analysis offered by Dorothy Van Ghent: "The dilemma of Tess is the dilemma of morally individualizing consciousness in its earthy mixture. The subject is mythological, for it places the human protagonist in dramatic relationship with the nonhuman and orients his destiny among preternatural powers. The most primitive antagonist of consciousness is, on the simplest premise, the earth itself. It acts so in *Tess*, clogging action and defying conscious motive. . . ." This is fine; except that here too one suspects a thematic overload. Does the novel itself, as distinct from certain trends in contemporary criticism, enforce the mythological reference? If placing a human protagonist in dramatic relationship to the nonhuman makes a novel "mythological," is there a significant work of Western literature which is not "mythological"? And if as I suspect, there is not, where then can one locate the usable boundary of the description?

What matters in *Tess of the D'Urbervilles*, what pulses most strongly and gains our deepest imaginative complicity, is the figure of Tess herself. Tess as she is, a woman made real through the craft of art, and not Tess as she represents an idea. Marvelously high-spirited and resilient, Tess embodies a moral poise beyond the reach of most morality. Tess is that rare creature in literature: goodness made interesting. She is human life stretched and racked, yet forever springing back to renewal. And what must never be forgotten in thinking about her, as in reading the book it never can be: she is a woman. For Hardy she embodies the qualities of affection and trust, the powers of survival and suffering, which a woman can bring to the human enterprise. The novel may have a strong element of the pessimistic and the painful, but Tess herself is energy and joy, a life neither foolishly primitive nor feebly sophisticated. Though subjected to endless indignities, assaults and defeats, Tess remains a figure of harmony—between her self and her role, between her nature and her culture. Hardy presents her neither from the outside nor the inside exclusively, neither through event nor analysis alone; she is apprehended in her organic completeness, so that her objectivity and subjectivity become inseparable. A victim of civilization, she is also a gift of civilization. She comes to seem for us the potential of what life could be, just as what happens to her signifies what life too often becomes. She is Hardy's greatest tribute to the possibilities of human existence, for Tess is one of the greatest triumphs of civilization: a natural girl.

Simply as a fictional character, she is endlessly various. She can flirt, she can listen, she can sympathize, she can work with her hands. Except when it is mocked or thwarted, she is superbly at ease with her sexuality. In no way an intellectual, she has a clear sense of how to reject whatever fanatic or pious nonsense comes her way. After pleading with the vicar to give a Christian burial to her illegitimate child, she answers his refusal with the cry: "Then I don't like you! and I'll never come to your church no more!" A mere instance of feminine illogic? Not at all; for what Tess is saying is that a man so seemingly heartless deserves neither human affection nor religious respect. And she is right. Her womanly softness does not keep her from clear judgments, and even toward her beloved Angel she can sometimes be blunt. "It is in you, what you are angry at, Angel, it is not in me," she pointedly tells him when he announces that he cannot accept her. The letter she sends Angel during the Flintcomb-Ash ordeal is a marvelous expression of human need: "The daylight has nothing to show me, since you are not here . . ." At least twice in the book Tess seems to Hardy and the surrounding characters larger than life, but in all such instances it is not to make her a goddess or a metaphor, it is to underscore her embattled womanliness.

The secondary figures in the book have useful parts to play, but finally they are little more than accessories, whose task is not so much to draw attention in their own right as to heighten the reality of Tess. Only one "character" is almost as important as Tess, and that is Hardy himself. Through his musing voice, he makes his presence steadily felt. He hovers and watches over Tess, like a stricken father. He is as tender to Tess as Tess is to the world. Tender; and helpless. That the imagined place of Wessex, like the real places we inhabit, proves to be inadequate to a woman like Tess—this, if message there must be, is the message of the book. The clash between sterile denial and vital existence occurs repeatedly, in a wide range of episodes, yet through none of them can Hardy protect his heroine. And that, I think, is the full force of his darkness of vision: how little can be done for Tess.

If we see Hardy's relation to Tess in this way, we can be a good deal more patient with the passages of intermittent philosophizing that dot the book. These passages are not merely inert bits of intellectual flotsam marring a powerful narrative. They are evidence of Hardy's concern, tokens of his bafflement before the agony of the world. At best, if not always, the characters in *Tess* are not illustrations or symbols of a philosophic system; at best, if not always, the philosophic reflections comprise a gesture in response to the experience of the characters. It is Hardy ruminating upon the destruction of youth and hope—and if we thus see Hardy's role in his narrative, we can grasp fully the overwhelming force of the lines from Shakespeare with which he prefaces the book: ". . . *Poor wounded name! My bosom as a bed / Shall lodge thee.*" It is her only rest.

J. HILLIS MILLER

Howe on Hardy's Art†

It should be said at once that this is a good book, one of the best ever written on the ensemble of Hardy's work.[1] After providing a good opening chapter on Hardy's early life and background, Mr. Howe proceeds more or less chronologically through Hardy's career, discussing the novels one by one, with longer sections on the major novels, separate discussions of the short stories, *The Dynasts*, the lyric poetry, and then a final brief chapter on Hardy in old age. The student will find almost everything of importance in Hardy's work discussed in compact, separate sections. * * *

Mr. Howe's book has many virtues. A steady eloquence runs through it and allows the critic the advantages of concentration and of an exact notation of those more or less evanescent matters of tone and attitude which are so important in the interpretation of Hardy's work. In fact one of the best things in Howe's book is his definition of the attitudes and qualities of "the ruminative mind, at once tender and aloof," which persists through all Hardy's prose and verse. Many fine phrases here and there add nuances to this insight into the Hardyan tone. Of the lyric poems, for example, Mr. Howe remarks the "profound democracy of the feelings, an incomparable courtesy to all he sees and touches," Hardy's power "to bring his encompassing sympathy to bear upon a chosen situation and to examine it from both a minute closeness and the distance of timelessness," the "subdued glow of humaneness which brightens his pages," his "vision both hard and fraternal." "Hardy's major poetry," says Howe, "is marked by a splendid patience, a tender caring for and affinity with his subjects. If sometimes detached, he is never indifferent. He watches and waits, but in waiting, does not draw apart from the suffering of others and himself."

This delicacy (and accuracy) of definition is related to another admirable quality of Mr. Howe's book, his strong love for his man, his unwillingness to condescend to Hardy. Though his is a study in discriminations, though many works are dismissed as flawed or unsuccessful, nevertheless the negative criticism is always clearly performed as a strategy for rescuing what seem to Mr. Howe Hardy's unequivocal successes. For these he has unqualified affection and

† From J. Hillis Miller, "Howe on Hardy's Art," a review essay in *Novel*, II (1969), 272–77.
1. Irving Howe, *Thomas Hardy*, Masters of World Literature Series, ed. Louis Kronenberger (New York: The Macmillan Company; London: Collier-Macmillan Limited, 1967), pp. xiv + 206, $4.95.

respect. This is especially apparent in his sharp eye for details in Hardy's work which mark him as a great novelist or poet, a writer who can convey a great "intensity of represented life." Howe notes, for example, the scene in *Tess* in which Tess, taking leave of Trantridge, bows slightly to Alec, her seducer, "perhaps with ironic contempt, perhaps with recognition that, in some detested way, he has established a hold over her—it is from detail of this kind that a novel is made." Nothing is more important as a prerequisite to good criticism than this sympathy, this willingness to read an author on his own rather than the critic's terms. Mr. Howe has commitments, it is true, but his friendly closeness to his author is one source of his many insights into meanings and qualities in Hardy's work. For this all-too-rare gift of sympathetic understanding the reader can only be thankful.

The Hardy who emerges from Mr. Howe's pages has something in common with the Hardy identified by such previous good critics as John Holloway and Albert Guerard, but there are new emphases and refinements. Like Holloway, Howe puts great stress on Hardy's ties to a traditional rural culture, a culture rooted in ways of thinking and doing which have persisted almost unchanged for generations. Howe notes the way Christian patterns of thinking and feeling remained fixed in Hardy's imagination long after his loss of belief in Christian dogma. Hardy was, as he said of himself, "churchy; not in any intellectual sense, but insofar as instincts and emotions ruled." This insight is used to admirable effect in Howe's discussion of *Tess of the D'Urbervilles*, and it is used to good effect against T. S. Eliot's description[2] of Hardy as a man uprooted from tradition.

Howe also follows previous critics in seeing Hardy's fiction and poetry as enacting itself against a general nineteenth-century background of the slow destruction of the organic culture of Wessex. As a consequence, "deracination" is a central theme in Hardy's work, most explicitly in *Jude the Obscure*, but also peripherally in the other work. Nevertheless, Howe sees that deracination is not merely imposed on Hardy's characters from without. In his best novels the central figures are conscious rebels, characters who choose estrangement from the immemorial rhythms of Wessex life. Following Guerard, for example, Howe sees *The Mayor of Casterbridge* as a novel about the "potential for self-destruction" in a man who strives to "impose significance upon his life through a dramatic overreaching of the will." "Hardy believes," says Howe, "in the virtues of passivity, but somewhat as with Hawthorne, his strongest creative energies are stirred by the assertiveness of men defining themselves apart from and in opposition to the natural order. . . . There is a repeated conflict between the principle of submission and the temp-

2. In *After Strange Gods* (London, 1934), pp. 49–51 [*Editor*].

tation of the promethean; and from this conflict derives a large part of the drama and vitality in his novels."

Such themes, in Howe's view, are more important than the overt "philosophy" compounded out of Hardy's reading in Huxley, Mill, Spencer, von Hartmann, and Schopenhauer, which has seemed so important to some critics. Howe does not deny the existence of such philosophical motifs in Hardy's work, but he finds them often in conflict with the true direction of Hardy's imagination. * * * Howe's discussion of *Tess of the D'Urbervilles* is, in my view, the best section of this book. Like the book as a whole, it constitutes a reading of Hardy which emphasizes his power to represent in words a certain vision of the immediate quality of human existence. For Hardy, according to Howe, human life is rooted in a particular natural environment and yet subject to the universal sufferings of mankind, as well as to particular historical pains.

There is so much that is strong and right in Howe's book that it may seem ungracious to express some reservations. Nevertheless, my reading of Hardy overlaps with his rather than coinciding with it exactly, and it may be worth specifying the differences briefly. Partly these are a matter of a different perspective on what Howe sees, partly a matter of what he leaves out or minimizes.

Howe follows Guerard, again, in justifying deviations in Hardy's work from the conventions of nineteenth-century realism by a somewhat hesitant reference to "such terms as expressionist, stylized, grotesque, symbolic distortion." This opposition between realistic representation and grotesque stylization seems to me based on a somewhat naive view of the novel, a view bewitched by the fallacies of realism, or of imitative form—the notion that a novel somehow ought to be or could be a photographic representation of reality. Novels, as much recent criticism both American and Continental has argued, are, in spite of their derivation from a particular historical or social reality, self-referential works, like any other kind of literature. Their meaning is generated by means of highly elaborate linguistic conventions, conventions of tense or point of view, for example. Even the most "realistic" novel is highly stylized. In the light of this current interest in the complexities of novelistic form there is something a bit old-fashioned (perhaps to some attractively so), in Howe's tendency to assume, for example, that the narrator of Hardy's novels need not ever be distinguished from Hardy himself, or in his giving such high marks to Tess because of her "reality": "And what must never be forgotten in thinking about her, as in reading the book it never can be: she is a woman." One might wish that a novel could be identical with life, or an exact mirroring of it, but literature constitutes a realm apart. Tess can be met nowhere but in the novel, and no strategy can close the gap between literature and life.

Though I admire as does Howe the incomparable specificity with which the Wessex countryside and life are presented in Hardy's work, nevertheless it seems to me that Howe exaggerates, perhaps sentimentalizes a little, the degree of his closeness to it even in his most pastoral works. There is always, in my view, some irony, some distance, some sense of dissatisfaction or narrowness even in Hardy's most straightforward celebrations of Wessex country life. Howe, for example, reads *Under the Greenwood Tree* more or less without nuance as "a pastoral or prose idyll of English country life in the 1830s, before the intrusion of industrialism and modern sentiments." One would hesitate to fly in the face of the warning that *Under the Greenwood Tree* "is a book to savor, not dissect." Even so, it is perhaps important to note that Fancy Day's momentary betrayal of Dick Dewy when she briefly agrees to marry Mr. Maybold will remain an unrevealed secret between them, so that their marriage, in however mild a way, will be an early example of that theme of deception or of crossed fidelities so important throughout Hardy's work. *The Woodlanders*, to take another example, seems to me a far more serious and problematical work than Howe takes it to be, and a work with many more ties to Hardy's more famous novels. A final example is Howe's reading of the group of stories called "A Few Crusted Characters" as "an utterly winning survey of Wessex conduct and idiosyncrasy, free from the darkness of spirit that hovers over Hardy's novels and buoyant with the delight of coming back to a familiar world of youth." This may be true of the stories themselves, but the frame story tells of a man (significantly named Mr. Lackland), who returns to his native village after a long absence, intending to settle there for good. He hears the stories which make up the collection, realizes that the people he hears of and once knew in his youth are now moldering in the churchyard, and recognizes that it is no longer possible for him to live where he was born. The work as a whole, far from expressing the buoyant delight of coming back to a familiar world of youth, is a somber confrontation of the fact that you can't go home again: "Far from finding his heart ready-supplied with roots and tendrils here, he perceived that in returning to this spot it would be incumbent upon him to re-establish himself from the beginning, precisely as though he had never known the place, nor it him. Time had not condescended to wait his pleasure, nor local life his greeting."

This overemphasis, as it seems to me, on the pastoral quality of Hardy's work is related to another limitation in Howe's book. No one would deny that Hardy's work, both the fiction and the poetry, is uneven, and that a small group of novels represents his best work in fiction. * * * Uneven as a writer Hardy may be. Nevertheless, I think Howe dismisses the lesser novels too quickly as flawed or downright bad. At the very least, *Two on a Tower, The Well-*

Beloved, or *The Trumpet-Major*, even *Desperate Remedies* or (believe it or not) *The Hand of Ethelberta*, are continuous with the greater novels in theme and attitude. Even if they are bad, a judgment which would call for persuasive demonstration, no one but Hardy could have written them, and they are often invaluable in determining the weight or emphasis which should be given in interpreting aspects of Hardy's greater work. Hardy's writing, I am suggesting, is all of a piece. It must be read whole to be understood completely, and one of the limitations of Howe's book is a tendency to read even the greater novels more or less in isolation from one another, ignoring the continuities or repetitions with variation which run through Hardy's work and make it one.

This failure to read each work in the light of all the others is related to a final limitation. Howe never quite brings out into the open what is, in my reading of Hardy, the central theme of his work. Hardy, like most great writers, has an abiding concern which, it may be, will emerge clearly only through comparison of one work with another; this is as important an operation of criticism as seeing the individual work as it really is. The full identification of this central structuring principle in Hardy's work would be a complex matter, requiring more detailed discussion of the novels and poems than space will permit here. The central theme has, nevertheless, something to do with the unsuccessful attempt to make a god of another person in a world without God. Love is Hardy's obsessive theme both in his fiction and in his verse. Here one may agree with Howe that Hardy's sense of the quality of human existence is more important than his ideas. Hardy renders in novel after novel the dynamics of desire, and this rendering forms the impulse generating dramatic form in these novels. "Love," for Hardy, "lives on propinquity, but dies of contact."[3] It begins in a "fascination" by which the infatuated lover imputes to the beloved a divine power to radiate energy and order on the world. As soon as the lover possesses his lady, however, she loses her radiance, as does the world around her. He then finds himself back in a world without order or meaning. Soon he betrays her or is betrayed by her. This pattern is repeated with many variations throughout Hardy's work and forms its imaginative center. Howe's failure to see clearly this theme in Hardy weakens many of his otherwise fine readings, even those of the major novels.

* * *

3. Florence Emily Hardy, *The Life of Thomas Hardy 1840–1928* (New York, 1962), p. 220 [*Editor*].

HUGH KENNER

J. Hillis Miller, *Thomas Hardy: Distance and Desire*†

* * *

"There is no innocent reading," J. Hillis Miller remarks in his preface, "no reading which leaves the work exactly as it is." We may add at once that the work has not even an ideal state, "exactly as it is," for critical intrusion to dislodge it from. A thoroughly innocuous critique—a freshman theme—might leave the work exactly as it *was*, i.e., exactly as we understood it before the Immanent Will required us to read that theme, but that is not because literary works have a tendency to Platonic immutability. It is because we find the theme too uninteresting to let it come near our understanding of the work, which exists as we understand it, and in no other way. The critic in changing our understanding changes *it*. Miller's *Thomas Hardy: Distance and Desire* (Harvard, Belknap Press: $6.95) succeeds in changing Hardy radically. By the time Miller has finished, the collector of Life's Little Ironies has turned into a proto-Proust, connoisseur of Time and Memory and Wistful Desire.

A resemblance between Hardy and Proust is no willful novelty of Miller's. Proust himself detected an affinity, and Hardy in extreme old age had the interesting experience of being able to read a discussion of the novels he had written long before, embedded in a posthumous volume of *A la recherche du temps perdu*. Reflecting from his own side on their similarities, he quoted in 1926 (age 86) a phrase from *A l'ombre des jeunes filles en fleurs*: "le désir s'élève, se satisfait, disparaît—et c'est tout. Ainsi, la jeune fille qu'on épouse n'est pas celle dont on est tombé amoureux."[1] This appears in the *Life* which was signed by Mrs. Hardy though we understand it to have been written by Thomas, and moreover with a page reference that turns out to be wrong. All Miller's diligence has not located these sentences anywhere in Proust, and while we wait for a Proustian to turn them up we may find it amusing to speculate that Hardy, in the act of forging his biography, amused himself also with forging a detail for the Proustian canon.

Such a sly tampering with a reality he gives the appearance of invoking would accord with the character of his literary performance as Miller presents it. *Distance and Desire* postulates that Hardy was doing just one kind of thing all his life, a kind of thing that started with an act of evasion but then obeyed so ritualized a process that

† From *Nineteenth-Century Fiction*, vol. 26, no. 2, pp. 230–34.
1. "Desire arises, is satisfied, disap-pears—that's all. Thus, the girl one marries is not the girl one has fallen in love with " [*Editor*].

almost any work at all, in prose or verse, can be adduced to illustrate any stage of it. There are eight stages, with a chapter for each.

(1) Thomas Hardy declines to get involved with a universe into which he never asked to be born. (2) In covert fascination with the world he shrinks from, he tiptoes to his desk and writes novels that flirt with its realities, replacing them with a new reality of words. In these novels, always set somewhere in the past, a persona of Hardy's invisible to the characters—handbooks call him the third person narrator—advances and withdraws, spying at his ease. (3) The persona perceives a world bound by tradition and by nature, structured by custom and linguistic inheritance, in which all that is familiar is always changing—Mellstock Quire being superseded by the organist—and in which exceptional people are driven by a desire they cannot specify, a desire once called religious. (4) "Hardy's fiction has a single theme, 'fascination,'" for these exceptional people always hope that some other person will appease their yearning. Feeling is discharged toward someone barely glimpsed, and more and longer and closer glimpses are sought. This is "falling in love," and leads to episodes of covert watching, watched in turn by the narrator who himself assists Hardy and ourselves to watch. During this covert watching, one of the most Proustian of Hardy's motifs, "the beloved is by the strength of the lover's emotions identified inextricably with a characteristic scene, so that the two are ever afterward associated in his mind." Thus, for a while, the places that they know are "charged with the tensions between the characters": hence Hardy's brooding preoccupation with place. (5) Moving toward the object of desire with "the slowness, the reticence, the surreptitious indirection" that characterizes Hardy's protagonists, the people execute an intricate dance among obstacles, human and circumstantial, which the plot throws in their way, and their effort to circumvent which *is* the plot. (6) "With contact love dies," the world "becomes flat and dull once again," the void within reasserts itself.

And what happens here, Hillis Miller tells us, is Hardy's kind of oblique self-vindication. The characters, fallen out of love, "become what the narrator of their stories has been all along: onlookers, watchers from a distance. Abandoning all hope of achieving what they have sought in life, they separate themselves resolutely and look from the outside at everything, even at themselves." They arrive at the state Hardy was at when Miller's book began, convinced that it's better to live in disinvolvement. In successive novels the coincidence of the characters' ultimate viewpoint with the narrator's became closer and closer, and Miller thinks it was this, rather than the outcry over *Jude*, that led Hardy to abandon fiction.

It seems as if the cycle of novels undertaken to seek vicariously for a happy love comes to an end when the characters reach the same understanding of the futility of the search which the narrator possesses. The earlier heroes, even Jude, never understood their situations quite as well as the narrator. When the convergence is complete, as it seems to be in the second version of *The Well-Beloved*, then Hardy's kind of fiction, in which there always remains a distance between narrator and protagonist, becomes impossible. (215–16)

To resume: the characters, (7), in their last withering insight, perceive, too late, a pattern in their own lives. "Pattern," of course, is a space-word, and "space fatalizes," since to see everything at once, like a journey on the map, is to see that what once seemed the open future was all the while lying fully formed ahead. Hence the tight fit of detail, for "the Immanent Will works in its unconscious fabrications as though it were a good craftsman in that profession of architecture which was once Hardy's own." Hence, too, the tight plots, absurd, from one point of view, in their look of artifice. But that's the wrong point of view, for a pattern recognized in retrospect is always an artifice and always in balance. Hence their desire to be dead, to be forgotten, to be free. And yet, bitterly, not free; for the dead who speak in poem after poem of Hardy's are free only to perceive that there is no freedom, only an irremediable persistence, now, clearly seen, of every happening however dreadful; caught, like the people in the jars in Beckett's *Play*, in a chill eternal indifference of reenactment. And Hardy, (8), safeguarding the dead a little from such a fate, offers the Immanent Will his pen to write with, and writes for as many people as he can a kindlier eternity in which they can reenact their sad stories as long as the books are read, but reenact them in a cosmos where at least the novelist's and the novel-reader's compassionate comprehension may warm them a little.

We have, in short, neatly set forth, J. Hillis Miller's familiar morality play, the Disappearance of God[2] and His Supersession by the Artist. Thomas Hardy, in the last chapter, is "in his function as artist-preserver . . . the closest thing to a deity his universe has. He is an imaginary deity nevertheless, a God who exists only in the distance from reality maintained in literature by the fact that it is made of mediate words rather than of immediate facts. He saves things from that horrible parody of remembrance which is their continuation in the obscure surgings of eternity. He saves them by

2. J. Hillis Miller, *The Disappearance of God*, Cambridge, Mass., 1963 [*Editor*].

giving them clarity, pattern and meaning. . . . His writing, to give it a final definition, is a resurrection and safeguarding of the dead, a safeguarding within the fictive language of literature."

This Proustian Hardy is a character in a sort of abstract novel by J. Hillis Miller: a curious fate for a novelist. Yet the strategy seems just. If we get no "reading" of any particular Hardy novel, it isn't "readings" that are needed. One by one, they are easily read. Yet there seems to be more to them—most readers will probably agree —than any one of them succeeds in expressing; hence the frequent supposition that they express a subtle "philosophy," which paraphrase, however, can always reduce to two or three gloomy sentences. What Miller implies, though he doesn't contend, is that Hardy turns out to be rather a case than an artist—very nearly what Philip Young found himself, nearly against his will, to be implying about Hemingway,[3] to Hemingway's intense disapproval. If you don't want to think of Hemingway as a case, you can divert attention to his prose. Hardy's prose won't attract, or endure, that order of scrutiny: solid journeyman carpentry merely, sufficient to make his fictive structures substantial. And his situations? Melodrama. And his people? Phases in the sociology of fiction. Miller's Hardy, writing as it were that one novel which Miller has in fact written for him by patching together citations from all the novels and a good many poems too, may be the only Hardy it's possible any more to find very interesing. It's engagingly evasive of Miller not to come right out and say that.

3. Philip Young, *Ernest Hemingway*, New York, 1952 [*Editor*].

Selected Bibliography

Articles reprinted in this edition, and books from which excerpts have been reprinted, are not included in this bibliography.

BIBLIOGRAPHIES

Gerber, Helmut E., and W. Eugene Davis. *Thomas Hardy: An Annotated Bibliography of Writings About Him.* De Kalb., Ill., 1973
Weber, Carl J. *The First Hundred Years of Thomas Hardy, 1840–1940: A Centenary Bibliography of Hardiana.* Waterville, Me.: Colby College Library, 1942. Reprinted, New York, 1965.

THOMAS HARDY

Abercrombie, Lascelles. *Thomas Hardy: A Critical Study.* London, 1919.
Anderson, Carol R. "Time, Space, and Perspective in Thomas Hardy." *Nineteenth-Century Fiction,* IX (1954), 192–208.
Bailey, J. O. "Hardy's Visions of the Self." *Studies in Philology,* LVI (1959), 74–101.
Barber, D. F., ed. *Concerning Thomas Hardy: A Composite Portrait from Memory.* London, 1968.
Beach, Joseph Warren. *The Technique of Thomas Hardy.* Chicago, 1922.
Beckman, Richard. "A Character Typology for Hardy's Novels." *Journal of English Literary History,* XXX (1963), 70–87.
Bjork, Lennart A. *The Literary Notes of Thomas Hardy,* vol. I. Goteborg, 1974.
Blunden, Edmund C. *Thomas Hardy.* London, 1942. Reprinted, New York, 1958.
Brennecke, Ernest, Jr. *Thomas Hardy's Universe.* London, 1924. Reprinted, New York, 1966.
Brown, Douglas. *Thomas Hardy.* London and New York, 1954. Revised edition, London, 1961.
Carpenter, Richard. *Thomas Hardy.* New York, 1964.
Chase, Mary Ellen. *Thomas Hardy from Serial to Novel.* Minneapolis, 1927.
Chew, Samuel C. *Thomas Hardy, Poet and Novelist.* New York, 1928.
Cox, Reginald G., ed. *Thomas Hardy: The Critical Heritage.* New York, 1970.
Deacon, Lois. *Tryphena and Thomas Hardy.* Beaminster, Dorset, 1962.
Drabble, Margaret, ed. *The Genius of Thomas Hardy.* New York, 1976.
Duffin, Henry Charles. *Thomas Hardy: A Study of the Wessex Novels.* Manchester, England, 1916. Second edition, revised and enlarged, 1921; third edition, with further revisions and additions, 1937; reprinted, 1962.
Eliot, T. S. *After Strange Gods.* New York, 1934. Pp. 59–61.
Ellis, Havelock. "Hardy." In *From Marlowe to Shaw,* ed. John Gawsworth, pp. 203–90. London, 1950. (Three essays, which appeared in 1883, 1896, and 1930.)
d'Exideuil, Pierre. *The Human Pair in the Works of Thomas Hardy.* Trans. Felix W. Crosse, introduction by Havelock Ellis. London, 1930.
Firor, Ruth. *Folkways in Thomas Hardy.* Philadelphia, 1931. Reprinted, New York, 1962.
Friedman, Alan. "Thomas Hardy: 'Weddings Be Funerals.'" In *The Turn of the Novel,* pp. 38–65. New York, 1966.
Garwood, Helen. *Thomas Hardy: An Illustration of the Philosophy of Schopenhauer.* Philadelphia, 1911.
Gittings, Robert. *Young Thomas Hardy.* Boston, 1975.
Goldberg, M. A. "Hardy's Double-Visioned Universe." *Essays in Criticism,* VII (1957), 374–82.

Gregor, Ian. "What Kind of Fiction Did Hardy Write?" *Essays in Criticism*, XVI (1966), 290–308.
Guerard, Albert J., ed. *Hardy: A Collection of Critical Essays*. Englewood Cliffs. N.J., 1973.
Halliday, F. E. *Thomas Hardy: His Life and Work*. Bath, England, 1972.
Hardy, Evelyn. *Thomas Hardy: A Critical Biography*. London, 1954. Reprinted, New York, 1970.
Hardy, Thomas. *Life and Art . . . Essays, Notes and Letters*, ed. Ernest Brennecke, Jr. New York, 1925.
Hawkins, Desmond. *Thomas Hardy*. London, 1950.
Holloway, John. *The Victorian Sage*. London, 1953; New York, 1964.
Holloway, John. "Hardy's Major Fiction." In *The Charted Mirror: Literary and Critical Essays*, pp. 94–107. London, 1960.
Hynes, Samuel. "Hardy in His Time and Place." *Modern Language Quarterly*, XXXIV (1973), 325–30.
Johnson, H. A. T. *Thomas Hardy. London*, 1968.
McDowall, Arthur. *Thomas Hardy: A Critical Study*. London, 1931.
Meisel, Perry. *Thomas Hardy: The Return of the Repressed; A Study of the Major Fiction*. New Haven, 1972.
Miller, J. Hillis. *Thomas Hardy: Distance and Desire*. Cambridge, Mass., 1970.
Millgate, Michael. "Hardy's Fiction: Some Comments on the Present State of Criticism." *English Literature in Transition*, XIV (1970), 230–38.
Millgate, Michael. *Thomas Hardy: His Career as a Novelist*. New York, 1971.
Muller, Herbert. "Thomas Hardy," *Modern Fiction*. New York, 1937.
Pinion, F. B. *A Hardy Companion: A Guide to the Works of Thomas Hardy and Their Background*. New York, 1968.
Pinion, F. B., ed. *Thomas Hardy and the Modern World*. Dorchester, England, 1974.
Schwarz, Daniel R. "The Narrator as Character in Hardy's Major Fiction." *Modern Fiction Studies*, XVIII (1972), 155–72.
Southerington, F. R. *Hardy's Vision of Man*. New York, 1971.
The Southern Review, Thomas Hardy Centennial Issue, VI (Summer 1940).
Spivey, Ted R. "Thomas Hardy's Tragic Hero." *Nineteenth-Century Fiction*, IX (1954), 179–91.
Stewart, J. I. M. "Hardy." In *Eight Modern Writers*, pp. 19–71. Oxford, 1963.
Symons, Arthur. *A Study of Thomas Hardy*. London, 1927.
Weber, Carl Jefferson. *Hardy of Wessex, His Life and Literary Career*. Revised edition, New York, 1965.
Williams, Merryn. *Thomas Hardy and Rural England*. New York, 1972.
Wing, George. *Thomas Hardy*. New York, 1963.
Zabel, Morton Dauwen. "Hardy in Defense of His Art: The Aesthetic of Incongruity." In *Craft and Characters: Texts, Methods, and Vocation in Modern Fiction*, pp. 70–96. New York, 1957.

TESS OF THE D'URBERVILLES

Benzing, Rosemary. "In Defence of 'Tess'." *Contemporary Review*, 218 (1971), 202–4.
Brick, Allen. "Paradise and Consciousness in Hardy's *Tess*." *Nineteenth-Century Fiction*, XVII (1962), 115–34.
Brooks, Jean R. "*Tess of the d'Urbervilles:* A Novel of Assertion." In *Thomas Hardy: The Poetic Structure*, pp. 233–53. Ithaca, 1971.
Brooks, Jean R. "*Tess of the d'Urbervilles:* The Move towards Existentialism." In *Thomas Hardy and the Modern World*, ed. F. B. Pinion, pp. 48–59. Dorchester, England, 1974.
Burns, Wayne. "The Panzaic Principle in Hardy's *Tess of the d'Urbervilles*." *Recovering Literature*, vol. I, no. 1 (1972), 26–41. (See also Arthur Efron, "Just What and Where Is the Panzaic Principle in *Tess of the d'Urbervilles?* A Rebuttal to Wayne Burns," and Gerald Butler, "Against Responsibility: An Answer to Arthur Efron's Critique of 'The Panzaic Principle in Hardy's *Tess of the d'Urbervilles*' by Wayne Burns," both in *Recovering Literature*, vol. I, no. 2 (1972), 59–75.)
Davis, W. E., "*Tess of the d'Urbervilles:* Some Ambiguities about a Pure Woman." *Nineteenth-Century Fiction*, XXII (1968), 397–401.
De Laura, David J. " 'The Ache of Modernism' in Hardy's Later Novels." *Journal of English Literary History*, XXXIV (1967), 380–99.
Elsbree, Langdon. "Tess and the Local Cerelia." *Philological Quarterly*, XLV (1961), 606–8.
Furbank, P. N. Introduction to his edition of *Tess of the d'Urbervilles* (The New Wessex Edition). London, 1974.

Gordon, Jan B. "Origins, History, and the Reconstitution of Family: Tess' Journey." *Journal of English Literary History*, XLIII (1976), 366–88.

Gose, Elliott B., Jr. "Psychic Evolution: Darwinism and Initiation in *Tess of the d'Urbervilles*." *Nineteenth-Century Fiction*, XVIII (1963), 261–72.

Gregor, Ian. "The Novel as Moral Protest: *Tess of the d'Urbervilles*." In *The Moral and the Story*, by Ian Gregor and Brian Nicholas, pp. 135–50. London, 1962.

Gregor, Ian. " 'Poor Wounded Name': *Tess of the d'Urbervilles*." In *The Great Web: The Form of Hardy's Major Fiction*, pp. 173–204. Totowa, N. J., 1974.

Hamilton, Horace E. "A Reading of *Tess of the d'Urbervilles*." In *Essays in Literary History*, ed. Rudolf Kirk and C. F. Main, pp. 197–216. New Brunswick, N.J., 1960.

Hazen, James. "The Tragedy of Tess Durbeyfield." *Texas Studies in Literature and Language*, XI (1969), 779–94.

Herbert, Lucille. "Hardy's Views in *Tess of the d'Urbervilles*." *Journal of English Literary History*, XXXVII (1970), 77–94.

Herman, William R. "Hardy's *Tess of the d'Urbervilles*." *The Explicator*, XVIII (December 1959), item no. 16.

Hornback, Bert G. "Tess of the d'Urbervilles." In *The Metaphor of Chance: Vision and Technique in the Works of Thomas Hardy*, pp. 109–125. Athens, Ohio, 1971.

Horne, Lewis B. "The Darkening Sun of Tess Durbeyfield." *Texas Studies in Literature and Language*, XIII (1970), 299–311.

Jacobus, Mary. "Tess's Purity." *Essays in Criticism*, XXVI (1976), 318–38.

Kettle, Arnold. "Thomas Hardy: *Tess of the d'Urbervilles* (1891)." In *An Introduction to the English Novel*, vol. II, pp. 49–62. London, 1951, and New York, 1960.

Kozicki, Henry. "Myths of Redemption in Hardy's *Tess of the d'Urbervilles*." *Papers on Language and Literature*, X (1974), 150–58.

Kramer, Dale, "*Tess of the d'Urbervilles*: Pure Tragedy of Consciousness." In *Thomas Hardy: The Forms of Tragedy*, pp. 111–35. Detroit, 1975.

Laird, John, "The Manuscript of Hardy's *Tess of the d'Urbervilles* and What It Tells Us." *Journal of the Australasian Universities Language and Literature Association*, XXV (1966), 68–82.

La Valley, Albert J., ed. *Twentieth-Century Interpretations of "Tess of the d'Urbervilles*." Englewood Cliffs, N.J., 1969.

Lee, Vernon (pseud. for Violet Paget). "Hardy." In *The Handling of Words and Other Studies in Literary Psychology*, pp. 222–41. New York, 1923. (A study of Hardy's prose style in a critique of a passage from *Tess*.)

Lodge, David. "Tess, Nature, and the Voices of Hardy." In *The Language of Fiction*, pp. 164–88. New York, 1967.

Miller, J. Hillis. "Fiction and Repetition: *Tess of the d'Urbervilles*." In *Forms of Modern British Fiction*, ed. Alan Warren Friedman, pp. 43–71. Austin, 1975.

Morrell, Roy. "A Note on 'The President of the Immortals.' " In *Thomas Hardy: The Will and the Way*, pp. 35–41. Kuala Lumpur, 1965.

Morton, Peter. "*Tess of the d'Urbervilles*: A Neo-Darwinian Reading." *Southern Review: An Australian Journal of Literary Studies* (University of Adelaide), VII (1974), 38–50. (See also J. R. Ebbatson, "The Darwinian View of Tess: A Reply," and Morton's reply to Ebbatson, "*Tess* and August Weisman: Unholy Alliance?" in the same journal, vol. VIII (1975), 247–53 and 254–56.)

Paris, Bernard. " 'A Confusion of Many Standards.' " *Nineteenth-Century Fiction*, XXIV (1969), 57–79.

Roberts, Marquerite. *Tess in the Theatre: Two Dramatizations of "Tess of the d'Urbervilles" by Thomas Hardy, One by Lorimer Stoddard.* Toronto, 1950.

Simmonds, James C. "Ambiguities of Tess as a 'Pure' Woman." *American Notes & Queries*, X (1972), 86–88.

Stewart, J. I. M. "Tess of the d'Urbervilles." In *Thomas Hardy: A Critical Biography*, pp. 162–83. London, 1971.

Tanner, Tony. "Colour and Movement in Hardy's *Tess of the d'Urbervilles*." *The Critical Quarterly*, X (Autumn 1968), 219–39.

Tomlinson, T. B. "Hardy's Universe: *Tess of the d'Urbervilles*." *The Critical Review* (Melbourne; Sydney), XVI (1973), 19–38.

Vigar, Penelope. "*Tess of the d'Urbervilles*." In *The Novels of Thomas Hardy: Illusion and Reality*, pp. 169–88. London, 1974.

Webster, Harvey Curtis. "*Tess of the d'Urbervilles*." In *On a Darkling Plain: The Art and Thought of Thomas Hardy*, pp. 173–80. Chicago, 1947.

Wright, Terence. "Rhetorical and Lyrical Imagery in *Tess of the d'Urbervilles*." *Durham University Journal*, XXXIV (1973), 79–85.